The Princess Maura Tales
The Complete Five Book Series

Abigail Keam

Worker Bee Press

The Princess Maura Tales Complete 5-Book Series
Copyright © Abigail Keam 2018

ALL RIGHTS RESERVED

No part of this book may be reproduced or transmitted in any form without written permission from the author. All characters are fictional, and any similarity to any person, place, or thing is just a coincidence unless stated otherwise.

978 0 6921240 1 7

5 23 2018

Worker Bee Press
P.O. Box 485
Nicholasville, KY 40340

Table of Contents

Wall of Doom 1

Wall of Peril 185

Wall of Glory 323

Wall of Conquest 407

Wall of Victory 569

About The Author 721

Also by Abigail Keam 723

Also by Abigail Keam

The Josiah Reynolds Mystery Series
Death By A HoneyBee I
Death By Drowning II
Death By Bridle III
Death By Bourbon IV
Death By Lotto V
Death By Chocolate VI
Death By Haunting VII
Death By Derby VIII
Death By Design IX
Death By Malice X

The Princess Maura Fantasy Tales
Wall Of Doom I
Wall Of Peril II
Wall Of Glory III
Wall Of Conquest IV
Wall Of Victory V

Last Chance For Love Series
Last Chance Motel I
Gasping For Air II
The Siren's Call III
Hard Landing IV
The Mermaid's Carol V

The Princess Maura Series Glossary

Abisola de Magela (character) – ninth queen of Hasan Daeg and mother of Princess Maura

Aga (character) – term for king of the Bhuttanians

Akela (character) – homeless Bhuttanian waif who serves KiKu and Timon

Alexanee (character) – top Bhuttanian general, illegitimate older brother of Dorak

Anqara (place) – ancient cultural and banking city located in country of Kaysia

Atetelco (place) – former capital of the Dinii located in the Forbidden Zone

Beca (character) – Princess Maura's pony

Benzar (character) – gray male hawk from secret society that protects Maura

Bes Amon Ptah (character) – Moab prince hiding under the name of Timon Ben Ibin Moab

Bhutta (character) – female deity of Bhuttanians, wife of Bhuttu

Bhuttan (place) – country ruled by Zoar and his son, Dorak

Bhuttani (place) – capital of Bhuttan

Bhuttanians (characters) – nomadic people who rose to world domination under the leadership of Zoar

Bhuttu (character) – male deity of Bhuttanians whose worship calls for the sacrifice of one's life

Bilboa (characters) – race of people with red eyes who see in the dark

Bird People (characters) – the Dinii who were Overlords of Kaseri

Black Cacodemon (character) – evil wizard of Bhuttu

Blue and gold – royal colors of the Hasan Daegians

Blue Queen (character) – nickname for Maura

Boaeps – small domesticated hopping animals

Borax (both plural and singular) – bison-like animals with sharp blades down their spines

Camaroon (place) – borders Hasan Daeg, absorbed by Bhuttanian Empire
Cappet (character) – petty thief, controls eastern part of Bhuttani
Caromate plant – provides hypnotic mist when leaves are pressed
Chaun Maaun (character) – prince of the Dinii and son of the Dinii Empress Gitar
City of the Peaks (place) – city on top of highest peak in Hasan Daeg where the Dinii live
Colla – nuts from the colla tree, brewed for teas

de Magela (characters) – name of ruling family in Hasan Daeg
Dini (character) – singular of Dinii
Dinii (characters) – ancient rulers of Kaseri, formerly called Overlords, human-like beings covered with feathers who fly
Divigi (character) – spiritual leader of the Dinii and uncle to Empress Gitar
Dorak (character) – son of Zoar, aga of the Bhuttanians
Duchy of Enos (place) – estate passed down through the family of Iasos, husband of Queen Abisola
Duke Enos (character) – father of Iasos
Dyanna (character) – princess born to Maura and Dorak

Everlynd (character) – duchess of Enos and sister of Prince Consort Iasos

Forbidden Zone (place) – former home of the Dinii, cursed by both the Dinii and Hasan Daegians

Gitar (character) – empress of the Dinii and Hasan Daegians
Gootee – duck-like animal
Great Death – name given to the practice of Hasan Daegian queens willing themselves to die
Great Mother – title of respect for older women or those in power, including queens of Hasan Daeg

Hasan Daeg (place) – peaceful agricultural country ruled by the Dinii and the de Magela family
Hasan Daegian betrothal (custom) – woman asks man permission to court by kissing man's hand; if man wishes to engage, he returns the kiss; woman gives man flowers
Hasan Daegians (characters) – peaceful agricultural people who were former slaves of the Dinii
Hetmaan (character) – Bhuttanian term for Spymaster KiKu

Hittal (place) – country conquered by Zoar, land of KiKu the Hetmaan

House of Magi (place) – ancient residence of scholars in Anqara

Iasos (character) – consort of Queen Abisola and father of Princess Maura

Iegani (character) – uncle to Empress Gitar, spiritual advisor to the Dinii, and founder of secret society that protects Princess Maura

Jezra (character) – first wife to Dorak, mother of his first child

Jon (character) – minister to Governor Petenptope of the northern Hasan Daegian state of Kinton

Kaseri (place) – name of the planet

Kaysia (place) – land in which Anqara was located

KiKu (character) – Zoar's Hetmaan, former prince of Hittal who becomes a double spy

KiKusan (character) – daughter of Kiku and concubine of Zoar

Kimtimee (character) – Queen Abisola's highest-ranking general

Kinton (place) – northern region of Hasan Daeg

Kittum (place) – country to the east of Hasan Daeg which has a treaty with Bhuttan

Knoxel (character) – magician who was mentor to Zedek

Land of the Setting Sun (place) – romantic name given to Hasan Daeg by the Bhuttanians

Lahor (place) – former island home of the Lahorians

Lahorians (characters) – originally from Lahor and ancient enemies of the Dinii

Madric (character) – KiKu's first wife

Mamora (character) – first wife of Zoar and sister of KiKu

Maura (character) – tenth ruler of Hasan Daeg, daughter of Queen Abisola and Consort Iasos

Meagan of Skujpor (character) – healer to the royal house of de Magela and member of the House of Magi

Mehmet (character) – high priestess of the House of Magi

Mekonia (character) – nature goddess of the Hasan Daegians

MeNe (character) – Yesemek's first lieutenant

Mikkotto (character) – Hasan Daegian baroness who becomes a traitor and joins with Zoar

Mingo tree – tree with large, flat limbs that is treasured for its endurance, beauty, and strength

Mother Bogazkoy/Royal Bogazkoy – intelligent, self-aware plants that have a special relationship with Hasan Daegian rulers

Nani (character) – adopted granddaughter of Lady Sari

Noabini (character) – Mehmet's assistant who becomes high priestess of the House of Magi

O Konya (place) – capital of Hasan Daeg

Onxor (character) – priest of Bhuttu

Pearl (character) – second wife of KiKu and a healer

Petenptope (character) – governor of the northern Hasan Daegian province of Kinton

Plain of Moab (place) – traditional home of nomadic people

Prosperot (character) – one of two top Bhuttanian generals, along with Alexanee

Qatou (place) – Hasan Daegian city

Rakel (character) – Lahorian woman who helps Princess Maura

Red – royal color of the Bhuttanians

Renna (character) – daughter of Riza

Riza (character) – scion from oldest noble family in Hasan Daeg

Rooshars – rare marsh flower

Rosalind (character) – first queen of Hasan Daeg

Royal Bogazkoy – plant offspring of the Mother Bogazkoy

Rubank (character) – consul to Queen Abisola and then to Queen Maura

Sari (character) – Hasan Daegian nurse to Queen Maura/Queen Abisola and grandmother of Mikkotto and Nani

Shaybar – Bhuttanian drink of boiled water or milk mixed with an equal portion of borax blood

Siddig (character) – Bhuttanian healer who helped Timon

Sinjo – rare berry made into wine that stimulates feelings of pleasure

Siva (place) – desert country south of Hasan Daeg

Sivans (characters) – merchant desert people

Sumsumitoyo (character) – family name of Mikkotto and Sari

Tarsus (character) – gray male hawk Dini who belongs to secret society that protects Maura

Tippa/Tippu (characters) – third and fourth twin wives of KiKu

Tnpothar (character) – Zoar's father

Toppo (character) – red female hawk Dini, belongs to the secret society that protects Maura

Tsnsuni – ritualistic national prayer for the Hasan Daegian queen

Uultepes – mythical animals that are the symbol of Hasan Daegian royalty

Water Orbs – Lahorian mechanical devices constructed for transportation

Wise Ones (character) – title for the Lahorians

Yagomba tree – largest hardwood tree on Kaseri, has mystical powers

Yappor (place) – sacred lake of the Hasan Daegians and thought to be home of their goddess, Mekonia; home to the Lahorians

Yesemek (character) – commander-in-chief of the Dinii and wife to Iegani

Yeti (character) – red female hawk Dini, belongs to secret society that protects Maura

Yubuto (character) – sacrificed son of Mikkotto

Zedek (character) – Black Cacodemon's given name

Zoar (character) – aga (king) of the Bhuttanians

The Princess Maura Tales
The Complete Five Book Series

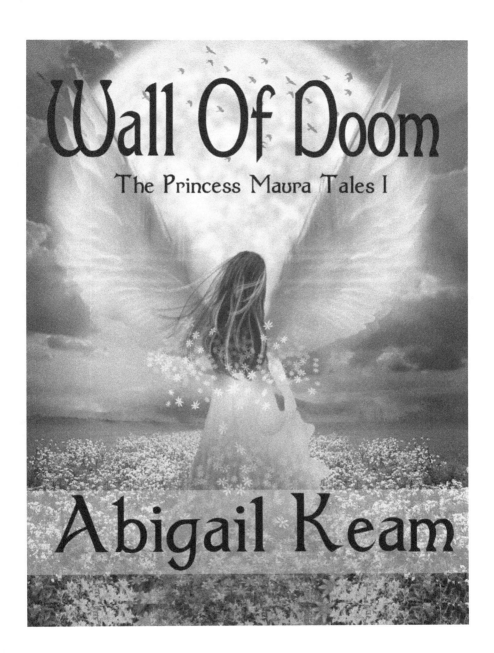

Wall Of Doom

The Princess Maura Tales
Saga of the de Magela Family

Book One

Abigail Keam

Worker Bee Press

Wall Of Doom
The Princess Maura Tales
Copyright © Abigail Keam 2018

ALL RIGHTS RESERVED

No part of this book may be reproduced or transmitted in any form without written permission of the author.

All characters, locations, and things are fictional and similarity to any living person, place, or thing is just coincidence unless stated otherwise.

If you are seeing the Dinii and wizards, you should really see a doctor.

Worker Bee Press
P.O. Box 485
Nicholasville, KY 40340

Acknowledgements

Thanks to my editors,
Patti DeYoung and Layla Darnell

Artwork by Karin Claesson
www.karinclaessonart.com

Special thanks to
Peter Keam, Sarah Moore, Deborah Struve,
Phil Criswell, and Betsy Meredith

Book Jacket by Peter Keam
Author's photograph by Peter Keam

Prologue

Queen Abisola sat numbly by the fire.

The shadow of the flames danced on Abisola's troubled face, eerily reflecting in her worried eyes. She was dressed in a foot soldier's battle attire, her long dark hair braided and tucked down the back of her tunic. The queen wore no insignias of any kind to note her rank. She waited deep in thought and wondered how her life could have come to such a pass. She waited and waited, this being the fourth day and night of waiting.

Iasos, her consort, gently rocked the baby he held, cooing if the child stirred. This was the child he had sired with his queen—Princess Maura. As Iasos gazed at his child, he did not wonder at the events he knew were to come, but his luck of having been chosen the Royal Consort. It was more than luck. The stars had decreed it to be his fate, for he truly loved his lady and had since the day he first met her.

Iasos had been sent by his father, Duke Enos, to further his education at the university in O Konya, the royal city. As he was of noble blood and his older sister was soon to inherit the Duchy of Enos, the boy was entitled to live at court during his stay in the city.

Duke Enos wanted his only son to make a grand impression at the royal court. Knowing the queen was fond of beautiful clothes, he gave Iasos shimmering cloth made by the nimble hands of the desert men from Siva as a gift to the monarch.

A nervous Iasos presented bolts of turquoise and iridescent white with river pearls for fringe. They had cost his father a year's profit from the duchy, so rare were they.

"These are from my father, Duke Enos," boasted young Iasos, waving his hand over the expensive bolts, "but this is from me." The handsome boy took a slim volume from his breast pocket.

The queen's personal guards quickly surrounded him.

"Oh, dear," he piped as he handed Rubank, the Royal Consul, his book.

After inspecting the volume, the Royal Consul placed it on a gold platter and handed it to the amused but wary Queen Abisola.

"I composed these poems myself in honor of our most beautiful and illustrious queen."

"You honor me," responded Queen Abisola. "I will certainly entertain your poems before I retire tonight. I hope I do them justice."

"You are most kind, Your Majesty," answered Iasos, blushing. He bowed very low, and the royal consul waved him back into the court audience.

Queen Abisola spent the rest of the afternoon meeting with impatient ambassadors, fawning nobility, wealthy merchants seeking charters, anxious artists needing a patron, and weary messengers from the far-off corners of her vast country. As she listened to the speeches and announcements drone on, she occasionally glanced at Iasos who stared sheepishly up at her. Something about him pleased her very much.

She gestured to Rubank. "I want Duke Enos and his family investigated. Find out everything there is to know, but do it discreetly."

Rubank nodded in reply, such was the custom as he could not speak. His tongue had been cut out voluntarily when he became consul to the queen.

The queen stood and left the throne room without glancing back, but she was smiling. She was still smiling when she entered her private quarters. Handing her crown, jewelry, and official robes to her maids, she quickly stripped and lay down on a table for her massage.

A woman in her late autumn years entered the room with a basket of herbs and oils. After selecting perfumed oil, she heated it by rubbing it between her hands and began massaging Abisola's shoulders. "You seem pleased tonight, Your Majesty. The cats seem almost at rest."

The masseuse was referring to the two tattooed jungle cats facing each other on either side of the queen's back, starting at her shoulders and extending down the back to the buttocks. They looked as though they were springing in mid-flight with their extended paws crisscrossing each other. Inside the figures of the cats were ancient symbols and words.

The cats, called uultepes, were the personal mascots of the Hasan Daegian royalty. However, by modern times, the majestic cats had been hunted to extinction. Many believed the cats existed in myth only, but the images of two springing uultepes were tattooed on every Hasan Daegian queen or king as dictated by tradition, the meaning of which no one could fathom any longer.

Abisola murmured, "Sari, do you believe in love at first sight?"

"No, Great Mother, can't say that I do."

"Then do you believe in lust at first sight?"

"Aye, that I can attest to. I fell under the spell of a fat cook with a nightmare of a wife and three grubby babes. But, oh, how that man could cook and make love after stuffing me with roasted eggs in a spinach base and hackleberry wine. No man has fed me so well since." Sari paused massaging, remembering.

"What happened to him?"

Sari poured more oil into her hands and stood thoughtfully. "His wife found out about us and kept whacking him on the head, so he told me I had to go."

"Hmm, by the Goddess, that feels good. Lower. Are you talking about Grebbe, the cook who died about forty years ago? He was found face down in a yoko root pudding."

"The very one."

"Sari, you didn't kill him?" gasped the queen, hiding her mirth.

"It was his heart. All that weight."

Abisola patted Sari's arm. "I'm just teasing, Sari."

"Oh."

"You're right. He was a wonderful cook. Too bad he died. Hmm, that feels wonderful," murmured Abisola, drifting off. "Sari, you are such a liar. What would a relative of mine be doing with a mere cook?" she mumbled sleepily.

"Your Majesty, has someone caught your eye?"

Queen Abisola didn't respond, for she was fast asleep.

Sari smiled to herself. "I will answer you now that you cannot hear me. He loved me truly even though I was royalty. Such is a rare commodity in life."

IT WAS ANOTHER three weeks before Abisola sent for Iasos. In her small private audience chamber, she told Iasos that she desired him and asked permission to court him if he so wished.

Iasos sighed with relief, for now he knew why he was being watched all the time. He stammered, "Ah, yes."

Abisola reached over and kissed his hand.

Iasos returned the hand kiss.

The queen handed him a flower, and the courtship officially began. He was a lad of twenty, and she had been the ruling monarch for over three hundred years.

THAT HAD BEEN three years ago. Now, Iasos looked down at his child. She was the color of a dark blue sea from the top of her royal crown to the bottom of her chubby royal heels. A dark indigo baby! She even cried blue tears. All royal Hasan Daegian babies were born blue and lightened to a bluish-white cast as they grew older.

As old as Abisola was, she still retained a bluish cast to her nails, the outlines of her eyes, and her sex. Their blue blood was a sign of the royal family's predestination to rule Hasan Daeg.

Iasos nuzzled the baby's cheek. The tension of waiting was beginning to strain his nerves. He was alone with his queen, having dismissed the servants. The guards were positioned down the mountain and ordered not to intrude no matter what they heard until the queen descended. The royal couple realized if anything went wrong, there would be no one to help them.

"Do you think she will come tonight?" asked Iasos impatiently.

There was no reply from his downcast wife.

"Abisola," he insisted.

Abisola jerked her head up. "Shh, listen!" She jumped up and strained to hear sounds in the night.

Iasos strained too, turning his head. There was a faint whooshing sound coming from the west. He dreaded the moment that would soon be at hand.

"She comes!" cried Abisola, jumping in front of Iasos and her child.

Their tent quivered in the loud and fearsome wake. Sticks and twigs, as well as their food and gear, scattered about the ground. A great cloud of dust flooded the air, making it hard for the royal couple to see.

A sharp cry pierced the sky. It was the cry of the great eagle as she snares her prey.

Both mother and father of the babe stood rooted, seemingly unable to move.

"Queen Abisola and Consort Iasos, come forth!" cried a loud and unnatural voice. A series of loud clicks followed.

Abisola looked questioningly at Iasos.

He nodded.

She tucked a dagger inside her tunic. Looking about, Abisola motioned for her husband to join her.

On a small knob not far from their camp, three figures stood silhouetted against the starry sky with their wings occasionally fluttering. Large these creatures were, just as the old stories stated.

Iasos shuddered to think he was going to hand his daughter over to the Dinii, Overlords of Kaseri, a race which had become a myth to his people.

The largest of the figures beckoned impatiently. "Hurry, there's not much time!"

Abisola and Iasos trudged silently to the hill, grateful that the baby had been given a mild sedative so she would not cry during the transfer. Abisola wished she had taken some of it herself.

Iasos could not feel his limbs move as he followed Abisola. He wondered how his wife could be so calm. Thinking he would explode at any moment, Iasos wished he had learned how to fight, but it was too late.

They stood before the mighty avian emissaries.

"Empress Gitar," addressed Abisola as she bowed.

Iasos bowed as low as he could with the baby.

"Queen Abisola and Consort Iasos," replied Empress Gitar, her wings expanding in acknowledgment and honor. "I wish we could meet on a more joyful occasion." She pointed to her two companions. "This is my Commander, Yesemek."

Yesemek pulled off her plumed leather helmet and made obeisance to Queen Abisola.

Queen Abisola nodded.

"And this is my uncle, Divigi Iegani," announced Empress Gitar.

Iegani stepped away from his empress and the commander, expanding his wings to their full breadth and bowed as low as his old bones would allow.

Queen Abisola heard him in her mind, "Salutations, Queen Abisola, Great Mother and Protector of Hasan Daeg."

The Hasan Daegian queen glanced at Iasos. She could tell from his wide-eyed expression that his mind had heard the Divigi too. She nodded to Iegani and turned her attention to Empress Gitar.

Gitar was an astounding presence. She stood over eight feet tall with a wingspan of fifteen. She was taller than her subjects by a head. Downy black feathers covered her body, which resembled a Hasan

Daegian's. The feathers on her head were white with the tips dyed purple while the rest of her black feathers sparkled with diamond dust. Her nails were purple too, and this same shade was used on her lips as well. She wore no clothes except for a V-shaped crown studded with multi-colored gems.

Abisola could see six nipples protruding from the feathers on her torso. She realized that Gitar must have recently given birth herself. That's why the Overlords had kept them waiting four days.

Iasos must have realized this too. "Empress," he said, stepping forward with the baby.

Abisola pulled him back and turned angrily to Gitar. "How do we know what you say is true?" she hissed.

Gitar held out her hands in supplication, understanding Abisola's indecision and anxiety.

Iegani spoke aloud. "My good queen, our spies tell us the same as yours. The enemy to the east makes ready to move on us. Not today, not tomorrow, not next year even, but they will come as sure as it rains upon the land. They will come before our deaths, before yours. Unless we move now and plan for the future, we will never be able to defeat them. Their armies will become too powerful, their magic makers too knowledgeable. You know this to be true. You've been getting reports for years."

Abisola blinked in confusion.

Yesemek clicked a message with her teeth to her ruler.

Gitar nodded.

Dropping her weapons on the ground, Yesemek bowed and stepped closer to Queen Abisola. "Your Majesty, if this were not true, why have you been sending out parties searching for the Mother Bogazkoy? It is because the Royal Bogazkoy, her offspring, is dying. It will cease to exist within forty years. Even now, you grow old as it can no longer sustain the Hasan Daegian queens as it once did."

Rattled, Abisola asked, "You know about the Royal Bogazkoy?"

"We gave the offshoot of the Mother Bogazkoy to the first queen of Hasan Daeg to bind our pact," replied Iegani.

"Do you know where the Mother resides?" asked Abisola.

Iegani shook his head. "That secret was not handed down. I'm sorry."

It was true that the Royal Bogazkoy was slowly dying, almost imperceptibly, but dying still. Abisola's grandmother had first discovered the awful truth when she plucked out her first gray hair at the age of two hundred. No ruler of Hasan Daeg had ever aged until released from ruling and from the Bogazkoy's powers.

"What can my child do about an unnamed enemy or the death of the Royal Bogazkoy? She's only a babe. Not even weaned," cried the desperate queen.

Empress Gitar spoke to her. "She will not be a babe always. We plan to teach her the way of the warrior. Our military is more modern. Your countrymen have not fought a battle in over six hundred years. We need her to fight and motivate others to pick up the sword, or we shall all perish!

"Over two thousand years ago, our ancestors allowed your people to settle in our kingdom. We needed beings to manage the land so it would attract the game needed to sustain us. In return, you would recognize our sovereignty. We are creatures of the air, not of terra firma. We are warriors, not farmers. As we hunt at night, your people rarely see us. Most do not even believe we exist." Gitar sighed. She wanted to sit down as she was fatigued. She clicked at Yesemek who spoke for her.

Yesemek affirmed, "We fly outside these borders and have seen first hand the destruction of the enemy. Their leader moves at random with no other purpose but to plunder and burn, terrorizing the population into submission. He is gathering a confederation of states controlled by his men that has become the bulwark for an empire. He is unstoppable, a great military mind who rarely shows mercy."

"This enemy which plagues us, what does he want?" asked Iasos.

"He is from the country of Bhuttan, thousands of miles to the east. He is called the aga and his name is Zoar. His followers believe him to have a religious destiny to rule. They worship him as the incarnation of Bhuttu, their god of destruction.

"We have only the basic facts about him and his people's beliefs. We do know they believe in a myth in which Bhuttu destroys the present world and joins with his wife Bhutta, giving birth to a new Kaseri. Zoar's people believe that he is the physical reincarnation of Bhuttu."

"What has this Bhuttu to do with us?" inquired Iasos.

Iegani straightened his shoulders, tired from the weight of his ponderous wings. "The Hasan Daegian culture has all the qualities of the Bhuttanian's goddess, Bhutta, who is the Great Mother who rejuvenates and restores the world. Like Bhutta, your culture stresses rejuvenation and health with the plants you cultivate. You rarely eat meat. There is little death, except from extreme age. Your bloodlines are through the female. Hasan Daegian queens are long-lived. They have the power to restore and heal. They are referred to as Great Mother and Protector. Even though the Royal Bogazkoy is dying, it is still potent. You are the living proof as you have lived many years. You have a secret the aga will want one day . . . longevity. Zoar will seek to possess the tree."

Iegani looked at Princess Maura. "And he will come for her, because through the princess, Zoar will aim to control the Royal Bogazkoy. I have just enough years left to teach her the way of the mystic. She will need many mental disciplines to accomplish what she has to do."

Iasos shuddered and clutched his baby closer.

"What *is* she to do?" asked Queen Abisola, quaking with dread.

Iegani looked into the queen's tearful eyes. "She must destroy the aga."

"Oh, Great Divigi, tell me. Can you foresee whether she succeeds?"

"She may and then she may not."

Iasos asked, "If she succeeds, will she know peace then?"

The owl-like man shrugged. "Upheaval is what she will know." He paused. "I'm sorry, but I do not write the future. I merely interpret it."

Iasos sobbed.

Abisola, able to stand it no more, took the baby from Iasos, gently kissed the baby's forehead, and gave her to Yesemek.

Both Yesemek and Iegani placed the baby securely in a pouch wrapped around Empress Gitar's neck and torso.

Without saying adieu, the empress of the Dinii and her companions spread their mighty wings and sped upward into the night sky, each crying its particular totem cry—those of the eagle, the hawk, and the owl.

Queen Abisola fell into her consort's arms and collapsed upon the ground from the great rush of wind pushing them down. As Abisola cried, she knew it was the end of peace for Hasan Daeg.

1

Aga Zoar awoke with a terrible thirst.

He rolled over onto his current wife, who was nursing their latest child. She cursed him for his clumsiness as she pushed him away. Looking about for some wine or even water and finding none, he rolled back to his wife, took her free breast in his mouth and began to suckle.

His wife slapped his face and kicked him, ranting at Zoar in a language he had never bothered to learn. She made gestures usually not demonstrated by a highborn woman before leaving in a huff with the baby.

Zoar rubbed his stinging face, wondering what she said to him. He did not doubt for one moment that it was not polite. Still, it would be nice to know what she uttered occasionally. He was just too lazy to learn her language, and she hated him enough not to learn his.

After killing his wife's family and torching her small mountain village, he gathered her upon his horse while she kicked and screamed as they rode away . . . and she hadn't stopped screaming at him since.

Zoar thought perhaps he should be kinder to her.

His wife had given him three children, including his heir, Prince Dorak, who was beautiful like his mother and intelligent.

Zoar was pleased with his first-born, legitimate son. He pondered on his pretty young wife again. He was sorry that her family had been killed, but that was the way of war. It was nothing personal. It was business.

He climbed off the bed and pulled on his pants and woven tunic. At the clapping of his hands, a servant girl entered with a tray that held a bowl of warm water and hand towels. He washed his face and hands before sitting back in a high leather chair for a young girl to braid his black hair, trim his beard, and clean his nails. Her hands trembled a bit.

Other servants entered carrying food and drink. After placing the trays near Zoar, they went off to the side, kowtowing and awaiting further instructions.

Standing silently behind the leather chair was KiKu, Zoar's advisor and spymaster. He was a tall, dark man with black eyes that missed nothing. KiKu waited patiently.

Zoar was suspicious that KiKu thought himself to be better than Zoar as his country had a more advanced culture. This irritated Zoar more than just a little.

Tired of waiting, KiKu coughed softly.

"What is it?" asked Zoar, gruffly.

"Great Aga, I bring reports of a fog barrier to the west of us." KiKu's eyes gleamed with excitement.

"And?"

"I believe there is land beyond this gray mist. It is not the end of the world as we thought. The fog is not a natural phenomenon. I believe it to be a defensive screen."

Zoar pulled at his beard. "How is it made? With magic?"

"We're not sure. Information is still coming in." KiKu stepped forward. His bald head gleamed in the smoking torchlight. "Great Aga, I have studied various reports over several months now, and I find them to be of great interest." KiKu shifted his weight. He wondered how to make this barbaric king understand there may be something astonishing to be discovered beyond the mist. How did one give another the gift of imagination?

"Do they concern gold?"

KiKu's heart sank. "Eh, no, Great Aga."

"Humph," groused Zoar before sucking on a peach.

KiKu quickly added, "Something better than gold. I've had all the ancient records and maps studied. Prior to six hundred years ago, there are records of a country called Hasan Daeg at war with the Cameroons. They lost the war and receded within their borders for good. After that, this fog appeared, and no one has seen anyone from Hasan Daeg again. The country was just forgotten and became the stuff of myths."

"How can you forget about a country's existence?"

"This fog or mist produces a hypnotic effect as one tries to penetrate it. It makes one forget why he wanted to go into the fog. I have gathered many reports of travelers, vagabonds, and merchants entering the fog only to wake up several days later with a terrible headache, but they have food and water beside them. For whatever reason, they never try to enter the fog again. They are not afraid. They simply don't want to."

Zoar thought hard. A fog which makes one lose heart. "I can see you are excited. There must be more, and I love a good story. You will make this a good story, won't you, KiKu?" purred Zoar. He watched KiKu blink.

KiKu blinked only when he was nervous. Otherwise, his eyes never closed but remained large black pupils, forever watching. Even when he killed, he never blinked.

Zoar had once watched him rip out a man's throat with two fingers. It had only taken a second. That's because Kiku had liked the man. If KiKu didn't like someone, he could make that person suffer a long time—very long time.

"Aga, Hasan Daeg is a culture older than two thousand years, according to the oldest records."

"What of it? I've conquered countries older than that."

KiKu's guts twitched. How very well he knew. His country had been one of them. "But this is a two-thousand-year-old state rumored to still exist, and it has had only seven queens and two kings."

"You mean they have lived in anarchy much of the time?"

"No, Great Aga."

"The place is run by priests?" Zoar loved baiting KiKu. He enjoyed the spylord's humiliation. It tasted sweet.

"No, Great Aga."

"I grow weary with your impudence," growled Zoar, throwing his peach pit at KiKu. "Be quick with your tongue or I'll feed it to a borax!"

KiKu sighed inwardly. "The people of this land have been ruled by the same family for over two thousand years, each ruler succeeding by right of ascendance from the last in an orderly and calm fashion. From my accounts, which are from both written and oral sources, the rulers of Hasan Daeg live to be an average of 370 years old, ascending the throne when they are about forty. They abdicate around the age of 330, and then they travel to the woods to meditate and wait for their impending death." KiKu stopped. He wanted his words to leave a strong impression.

Zoar stared at him for a long time. Finally, he murmured, "Let me understand. You are telling me there is a country to the west of us, which no one has seen in the last six hundred years, where the rulers live to be almost four hundred years old, and in two thousand years, they have had only nine rulers."

"Yes, Aga, it is a great mystery."

"If it is a mystery, how do you know your sources to be true?"

"Because one of my men penetrated the mist barrier."

The Aga leaned forward. KiKu now held his interest. "How did he manage that?"

"A year ago, I sent twelve men to explore this region. Eleven returned with strange tales, but none of them had been inside Hasan Daeg. Only one man returned, having been in this land several weeks ago. He had traveled the outskirts of the mist, always going southwest. At the southernmost region of the country, there is a corridor in the mist where one can enter freely as long as one is a Sivan. My man dressed as a Sivan merchant. He brought back not only wondrous tales but plant specimens and water samples."

"What is so important about plants and the water?"

"The plants sing. I know it sounds impossible, but I've heard them myself."

"Bring me such a plant. I wish to hear such a plant sing."

KiKu dropped his head. "Alas, Great Aga, I cannot. We did not know the proper way to care for the plants and they died."

"How unfortunate for the plants and perhaps for you," rasped Zoar. He grabbed a knife off a tray and began peeling a fruit. "What else?"

"The Hasan Daegians do not venture outside their borders. Their economy is an agricultural one. They make items such as hemp ropes, perfumes, oils, salt, and teas, but they are most famous for their herbal medicines, especially those used by women. They even make medicine from a fungus that stops infections within the body."

Zoar carefully cut the pear-like fruit into even slices. "I have never heard of this Hasan Daeg, even as a myth."

KiKu looked defeated as he now regretted mentioning this report. He could have escaped and made his way to Hasan Daeg, and Zoar would have never been able to find him. KiKu now realized how foolish he was to reveal these treasured secrets.

Only a great mind could fathom Hasan Daeg and what it could mean to the world. A great mind like his own and not this buffoon lounging before him, but KiKu plunged on.

"Aga, the desert men of Siva front for Hasan Daeg. For six hundred years, the Sivans have acted as middlemen for them, taking their goods at the southern border and trading in the Sivan name."

KiKu could see Zoar's face was starting to turn red. This was not a good sign.

"You said there had been seven queens and only two kings."

"Their society is a matriarchal one. The bloodline runs through the women."

Zoar looked truly baffled. "But that goes against nature. Who has heard of such a thing?"

KiKu did not remind Zoar that his own society had been matriarchal before Zoar had scattered the Hittal nobility to the four corners of Kaseri. KiKu shrugged.

"How do you explain the rulers' longevity?"

"My spies cannot answer this question, but there is an ancient tale that the first of the Hasan Daegian queens made a pact with a plant that needed a host in which to live." KiKu felt strained.

Couldn't Zoar see that he was handing him something more important than metal or land for conquest? KiKu was talking about life extremely long-lived. If they could get their hands on the secret, they could live four hundred years or more. Perhaps forever! This was information worth granting a slave his freedom. His heart raced at the thought of being free.

Zoar was enraged. KiKu was feeding him horse dung. A plant singing indeed! "I need to pay my soldiers. I need land to give my governors. A populace to govern. Slaves, minerals, grain. I don't need a bunch of old ladies growing pretty flowers. Does this country have anything else to offer?"

"No, Great Aga, nothing but health and long life." KiKu would not get his freedom now. He realized belatedly that a sneer was in his voice.

Zoar jumped up, grabbing KiKu's embroidered silver robe and pulling KiKu effortlessly toward him. "Take care. You try my patience. I've got a world to conquer, and I don't need silly fools like you daydreaming about singing plants and old hags who rule an imaginary kingdom."

KiKu knew it would be futile to attempt killing Zoar. He would be dead before he could raise his arm. Zoar's guards stood attentively around them, and since they regarded KiKu and the rest of his spies as not worthy of spit, they would have been only too glad to put a spear through KiKu's neck.

"I need facts," Zoar spat. "Hard facts. Just the plain truth like how many troops, the nature of the terrain, the climate, important details like that." He pushed KiKu to the floor. "What do you give me?" Zoar roared. "Fairy tales. Nothing but little children's bedtime stories!"

KiKu kowtowed. "Master, Master, forgive me. I thought you would be interested. All of your subjects adore you. We want you to live forever!"

Zoar gave him a vicious kick. "All of my subjects fear and hate me, you piece of borax feces. I am the Great Aga. I am a god-king. I have subjugated many peoples to do my bidding. And with all those millions, I have an addled-brained ninny like you in charge of my spy network. Get out of here! Go before I cut your liver out myself!" screamed Zoar, kicking KiKu.

KiKu, a once-proud prince now a slave, crawled out of the tent while grunting with each blow.

Zoar, working himself into a lather, paced his tent. He pounded his chest. "Idiots! Idiots! I am surrounded by fools." He flopped on a stool. "All my subjects fear and hate me," he muttered. The Aga winced at the enormity of his statement. Fear and hate were all he had ever known, even from his mother, and he barely remembered her.

It was all he would ever know. That's what power did to a man. So, why did he lust for it? Had he ever loved? Yes, he loved his son Dorak, and he loved his first wife for a brief time. They had been young but not careful. She died during a hunt when a borax charged, and her horse went down. He couldn't get to her in time.

Zoar saddened at the memory. He cried at his wife's funeral while placing zuni petals on her pyre. It had been her favorite flower. He stood until the fire burned itself out, and with it, a part of him died too. But, oddly, he felt relieved. He was free from the cares of love and would never have to give of himself again. Zoar had walked away from the smoldering pyre never to look back.

Now, he loved only power. A great empire was being born under his leadership. He scoffed at the notion of Hasan Daeg. Two thousand years be damned. He was building for ten thousand years and more!

Even after his death, his son Dorak would honor his father by constructing grand temples and monuments to the legend that was Zoar. He may never live to see the completion of his dream, but Dorak would. The Great Aga! Ruler of Kaseri!

2

This was a mistake!

Not only did Empress Gitar have her own chicks to nurture, but now she had a screaming Hasan Daegian baby to contend with and an ugly Hasan Daegian baby at that. She covered her ears with her taloned hands and spread her wings around her torso, covering her face. Gitar didn't think she could bear it much longer, worried she might be moved to throw the child over the precipice.

Iegani entered her room and asked permission to come forward.

The weary empress peeked out through her sparkly wings and nodded. There was no need for strict protocol. She didn't feel like a monarch, just a weary mother who was overwhelmed at the moment.

"Have you found out what is wrong?"

"Yes, the child is colicky. She will cry until the colic runs its course, and then she will stop of her own accord."

"It is nothing we have done?"

"No, Empress, sometimes Hasan Daegian babies get it for no reason. Queen Abisola said she had been the same way, crying for six weeks and then just stopped. The royal healer has prepared some herbs."

"For the princess?"

"Err, no, they are for you. Herbs to relax and soothe until the crying is over."

Empress Gitar did not look happy.

Iegani continued, "Also, I have brought a wet nurse for Princess Maura. Maybe your milk is too rich for her."

Gitar sat up straighter, looking brighter. "This means no more nightly feeding."

Iegani smiled. "Yes. You can now rest peacefully."

"Why didn't we think of a wet nurse before?"

Iegani smiled weakly. "We've never been in this situation before."

The Dinii did not have wet nurses in their culture as they breast-fed only in the early weeks following their chick's birth. Later, they regurgitated food into the chick's mouth until it was old enough to eat on its own.

Nodding, Gitar stretched and came down from her nest. "I can hunt again. Oh, how I've missed it."

"Your nights will be your own now."

Gitar looked thoughtful. "Do you think we can do this? I mean," she faltered for a moment, "the consequences are so far-reaching if we fail. Everything will be different. Everything will be changed. We will have no place to go if we fail."

"We have done all that we were instructed to do by the Lahorians," replied Iegani softly. "Even I do not understand the ultimate goals of what we are attempting. There have always been kings and queens who want total dominance over others." Iegani spread open his hands. "But this is the first time the Wise Ones of Lahor have interfered in my lifetime or many lifetimes. Zoar must be terrible indeed."

Gitar lowered her voice. She did not want anyone to overhear of the secret meeting with the Lahorians months ago. She did not even like thinking about the Wise Ones of Lahor. "I thought they were just the stuff of legends until I saw them." Gitar shuddered. "Abisola must never know."

"Yes, I agree. We have told too much already," Iegani asserted, leaning his head closer to his niece's.

Gitar looked away from her uncle. "We are sacrificing this child for a purpose we don't even understand." Guilt shone from Gitar's eyes.

Iegani took Gitar's hands in his. "We don't know if she will be sacrificed. We don't know the end, but we cannot defy the Wise Ones in this. They are too powerful."

Feeling tears spring to her eyes, Gitar lowered her head. "Why during my rule? Why do I have to bear this?"

Iegani put his arms around his niece. "Because they were waiting for you and Abisola. You two are the right ones. In what way, I don't know, but your fates are intertwined. You were both born to prepare the way for Princess Maura. You both will be the key to her success."

"Or failure."

"Perhaps there will be success in failure."

Gitar looked at him in disbelief. "Don't talk to me in riddles. No, no, you are wrong. She must succeed or the world will live in darkness." She pulled away from him. "Yes, yes, this is what I believe with all my heart."

Quivering with fear, Gitar would not be consoled.

3

Iegani seared Gitar's words in his mind.

He left to meditate at the top of the highest peak overlooking the valley. Perched on a craggy rock, he could see only clouds drifting below in the sky. Not even the sister vulture flew this high.

The cold felt good to him and helped him drift into the *seeing state*. After a lifetime of practice, it took him only minutes to reach an ultra-aware level. He tapped into his memory and relived the day the Wise Ones of Lahor materialized before him.

Empress Gitar and Iegani had been hunting when shimmering beings appeared suddenly on either side of Gitar.

Iegani flew to Gitar's defense but could not penetrate the transparent shield erected around his niece. Then, another being appeared beside Iegani and told him he could follow or not. It did not matter, but it was conveyed that Gitar had no choice. She would not be allowed to resist. Iegani followed Gitar and her captors, trying desperately to keep up.

Gitar's eyes were wide with panic. He saw her struggling in vain to change her course but to no avail. They were trapped by the legendary Wise Ones, their ancient enemies.

When Iegani thought he could fly no further, Gitar began descending. Slowly. Cautiously.

Even though Gitar was not the most courageous of rulers, she would still die well. She was an empress from one of the oldest ruling families still in existence and a Dinii. Iegani was determined that Gitar would die with honor and readied himself to die too.

Gitar finally came to rest on the bank of the Sacred Lake of Yappor.

Iegani settled on a tree branch behind her.

Exhausted, they both panted a long time while swiveling their heads, looking for the Lahorians. The Wise Ones were not to be seen.

When Gitar had rested, she edged toward the lake. Carefully, she scooped up water in her hand and sniffed. It looked clean. In fact, it was the clearest lake water Gitar had ever seen. She could see to the very bottom, which was made of fine sand, and see fish darting in and out of vegetation. She tasted the water. The water had a refreshing quality to it. She drank cautiously at first and then more until her thirst was quenched. Feeling dizzy, Gitar thought she had made a terrible mistake until her head suddenly cleared, and she experienced a serenity that she had never felt before.

Anxious, Iegani called out, "Niece, are you all right?"

She laughed, waving to him. "I've never felt better! Come join me."

Iegani shook his head and moved higher up in the tree.

Gitar stood up with her hands on her hips, surveying the sacred lake. "What do we do now, uncle?"

"I guess we wait unless you can leave."

Gitar bowed her head and thought for a moment. "No, I don't think I can, but you can go. They want only me."

Iegani bristled at the suggestion.

"I have no fear now. I don't think they will hurt me. They want to parley."

"Humph," snorted Iegani. "If the Wise Ones wanted to talk to you, why didn't they ask for an audience at court?"

Gitar shrugged. "I don't think they do things in such a fashion. We must wait, that's all." Not one to be idle, Gitar gathered reeds and made a bed, being too tired to perch. She was spent after her long flight. Her uncle would stand watch until she awakened, and then she would guard while he slept. She closed her wings over her face, wondering if search parties were looking for her. Gitar pushed such thoughts from her mind and fell into a deep sleep.

It was nearly dusk when she awoke. Gitar had slept the entire night and most of the next day. Looking for Iegani, she could not find him and became alarmed. Stumbling to the lake's edge, she took a drink of the pristine water and immediately became calm. She began thinking of ways to escape and look for her uncle but soon gave up.

Gitar knew intuitively that she would not be allowed to leave until the Wise Ones of Lahor spoke to her. Still, she was not angry, just thirsty. She drank more water, feeling very relaxed. Gitar stood her full eight feet, flapping her wings. With long talons, she preened her delicate feathers and washed her face. Her face felt tingly at the touch of the water just as her hands had felt each time she dipped them into the water.

"Empress."

Gitar heard Iegani speak to her mind. "Where are you?" called out Gitar, spinning around.

"Turn again. I'm in the yagomba tree."

Squinting, Gitar found her uncle. "Where did you go?"

"I was thirsty, so I went to find water."

"What? With all this water here?"

"I do not trust that water. I've watched you when you drink it. You seem as though under a spell," Iegani answered telepathically.

"You can leave at any time. I must stay."

"What do they want of you? We have not had contact with them for thousands of years. Our kind didn't even know they still existed," said Iegani, raising his voice in her mind.

Gitar shook her head, flapping her wings. "Quit yelling," she commanded.

Ignoring her order, Iegani continued. "You act as though kidnapping the ruler of the Dinii happens every day. This is madness. Fly off, I tell you! Fly off!"

"I cannot. Something keeps me here, and here I will stay until they are finished with me."

The old owl-man shook cumbersome branches in frustration.

Gitar called to him, "The Wise Ones will speak when they are ready. They are just waiting for something."

"What, what, what?" shouted Iegani at the heavens.

Without warning, a deafening clap of thunder sounded, although there were no clouds in the darkening night sky.

Iegani immediately flew down to Gitar and extended his talons, pushing her behind him. In his younger days, he had been a fierce warrior, and now with his special powers, he hoped he could stall the Lahorians long enough for Gitar to get away. She was the future of their people. He was the past.

Gitar clasped her hands over her ears at the continuing roar of thunder, and then remembering who she was, she extended her talons. If she was going to die, she was going to die as a Dini warrior. She would not dishonor her people. Gitar was ready for battle.

The sky turned an eerie black. The light from the stars and moons died from view.

Gitar could see nothing, even with her excellent vision.

An unearthly light shone from beneath the lake, rising and spreading from shore to shore.

Iegani strained his eyes, but he could not make out the source of the light.

Gitar glanced at Iegani. "Do you know of such power?"

"No, Empress," answered Iegani with his mind.

"Not even from our legends?"

He shook his head.

Gitar gaped at the lake as it filled with a yellow glow of shining light from beneath its surface.

Without warning, the thunder stopped. All was quiet for several minutes until the water in the middle of the lake began to roil as if boiling.

Huge bubbles popped up to the surface. Some floated into the sky and drifted off. Some dissipated. Other orbs rolled toward them as if with purpose.

Suddenly, one of the orbs burst, and there stood a woman who proceeded to walk calmly on the water toward them. She was clothed only by her long, dark hair. When she was ten feet from them, she stopped. Slowly lifting her hair, the woman turned, showing she carried no weapons.

Though the woman was seemingly middle-aged, her skin exhibited no signs of wrinkles, but was translucent, faintly showing her innards and blood rushing through her veins.

The woman held up her hands. In each palm was an open eye which blinked at them.

"May I approach?" she asked. Her voice echoed off the lakeshore.

Gitar nodded but stood with her talons extending.

The woman came to the lake's edge but did not leave the water. "We are called the Wise Ones of Lahor." She gestured to other beings appearing suddenly on the water. "We wish to speak with Empress Gitar."

"Just you," replied Gitar, pointing.

"We speak as one. We cannot separate ourselves from the other. We speak as one. We will come no closer."

"What do you want with me?" demanded Gitar.

"We have a mission."

"What mission?"

"Queen Abisola this night has borne a child. A female child. We want you to raise her as one of your own."

"For what purpose?"

The Lahorian woman closed her eyes for a moment. She reopened them. "We see no need to tell you. You are to do as you are told."

Iegani gasped at the strange woman's rudeness.

"I give orders, not accept them," barked Gitar. "Who are you to tell me what to do?"

"We are guardians. We watch and are disturbed by what we see. We have gazed into the future and saw Zoar. If we do not stop him, there will be no tomorrow. You must help."

"What's he to do with us?" roared Iegani.

"For centuries, the rulers of Hasan Daeg have depended upon the Royal Bogazkoy to be long-lived. We've allowed this, for the royal family has ruled wisely, and the secret was kept hidden from the rest of the world. Now, the secret is in jeopardy. It is only a matter of time before Aga Zoar discovers the secret, and this cannot be. The aga is the descendant of the god Bhuttu mating with mortal woman. He will covet long life if he discovers the Royal Bogazkoy. He must not have it."

"How do they know of the Bogazkoy?" demanded Gitar, glaring at Iegani.

Iegani shook his head.

The woman of the lake took no notice of Iegani, though he was sure she was scanning his thoughts. She continued speaking to Gitar.

"The kindred of the aga is of immortal and mortal blood. They tend to grow more immoral with each passing generation, so their evil grows. Now, Zoar seeks to become ruler of the known world. He is extremely talented, ambitious, and ruthless. He must be stopped before he discovers the Royal Bogazkoy."

"If you want him stopped, then kill him," retorted Gitar. "You seem to have great power."

The woman jerked. Both the eyes on her face and hands closed tightly as she stood quivering. After composing herself, all the eyes opened again slowly.

"We cannot kill, even for a just cause. Death of any kind is against our nature. To kill would destroy us."

"My good lady," sputtered Iegani, "we all must kill in order to survive. It is the way of nature."

"We do not. For one of us to commit an evil deed would condemn all of us. We are interconnected. We are one."

"So you want us to do your dirty work for you!" spat Gitar angrily.

"There is only one person in the foreseeable future who will be able to stop Zoar, and that is the daughter of Queen Abisola, but she will need training and guidance. You cannot refuse us. If you do not help, you will be condemning your race."

Gitar hissed, "You lie."

The woman seemed unperturbed. "We cannot lie."

Gitar turned to Iegani. "Discern if she is telling the truth."

"Permit me," said Iegani. He closed his eyes and searched the heart and mind of the Wise One. To his surprise, it was as she alleged. There were many hearts and minds intertwined with hers and there was no deception. He bowed his head before the Wise Woman of Lahor.

The Wise Woman extended her hand. "Look and see the future."

Both Gitar and Iegani stared at the hand with the open eye in its palm until they felt themselves being engulfed in the center of an unyielding force. In their minds, they saw scenes of great destruction. Foreign cities across the sea razed. Peoples they did not know existed were chained and sold into slavery. They witnessed mass starvation as the agricultural cycles were disturbed by war and mayhem. All freedoms were systematically stripped away. Places of worship were destroyed as holy leaders and their followers were hunted down.

Gitar gasped when she saw herself much older, fleeing with only a few of her race. A male she knew to be her son was wounded and dropped out of the sky onto the burning ground. She felt the emotions of the older Gitar, and she knew how despair felt. Gitar heard herself cry out, "No more, no more! Please!"

The visions stopped immediately.

Empress Gitar fell to her knees, sobbing. Feeling Iegani's arms around her, she realized he was weeping as well.

"We are sorry for the pain," said the Wise Woman, "but how else could we reach your hearts and minds? What you have witnessed are events that are to be in the future if the daughter of Queen Abisola does not succeed in her quest, but they are events that can be changed. You must help!"

"What must we do?" asked Empress Gitar.

"The princess must be raised as a warrior. She must train to kill, hunt, track, and live in the forest without benefit of civilization. That is the first step. For the rest of her training, we have others in mind. They will be contacted when the time is right."

"What makes you think Queen Abisola will hand over her only child to me?"

"Because you are her sovereign, and she is living on your land in accordance with ancient treaties and tradition. To defy you means war. This she will not abide.

"She is an intelligent and caring monarch. Queen Abisola will put personal feelings aside and do what is best for her people, regardless of her distaste for the task or you for that matter."

Empress Gitar looked at Iegani. He nodded and spoke to her telepathically. "It seems we have no choice if our way of life is to continue."

"That is correct," spoke the Wise Woman to Gitar.

Iegani realized the Wise Ones had been monitoring their thoughts throughout the entire interview. They must know Gitar was pregnant.

The Wise One continued, "You will communicate with Queen Abisola through special messenger according to protocol arranged by your ancestors. Since Queen Abisola has never been contacted by you, much less seen a Dini, she will probably ignore the initial message, but you must persist. Sooner or later, she will make the connection. Then you will take the child."

"How will I know what to do once I have the child?"

"We will send messages. You will know."

"What if I fail?" asked Empress Gitar, feeling overwhelmed.

"You will not as we will guide you," said the Wise Woman as a radiant orb began to envelope her, slowly sinking into the illuminated water. "We will always be with you. You will never be alone." And with that, she and the others were gone. The lake dimmed until it was as dark as the surrounding night.

Iegani looked up and noticed the stars. "It is over," he announced.

Empress Gitar stroked her belly while scanning the sky. "I feel strong. Let's fly home now. We could be there by morning."

"Yes, by morning," agreed Iegani, unfurling his wings to follow his empress into the night sky.

4

P rincess Maura was a sickly baby.
It was discovered she did not have the colic but was allergic to feathers . . . all kinds of feathers! Chicken feathers, hawk feathers, eagle feathers, pigeon feathers, finch feathers, duck feathers . . . the list went on and on. Of course, this information sent both Queen Abisola and Empress Gitar into a tailspin.

Queen Abisola and Consort Iasos came to stay with their child until the danger passed. Since there was no way to the City of the Peaks but through the air, a special litter was devised for the royal couple. Queen Abisola insisted that she and Iasos be flown up separately in case their litter was dropped, allowing at least one ruler to survive until Princess Maura became of age.

Empress Gitar ignored the implied insult and cheerfully bade her warriors to do as requested. She understood Abisola's anxiety. She was anxious herself, for she did not want a royal princess of another civilization to die in her care. She had bonded, albeit reluctantly, with the squalling, indigo-faced infant.

Gitar would coo to the female non-Dini as affectionately as she cooed to her chicks now molting their baby down.

This strange baby had bonded with her and her nursery mates as well. She would look at Gitar with wondering eyes and hold her mouth open as the other chicks did when it was feeding time.

There had been four chicks at birth. Now there were only three since a chick had died. Of Empress Gitar's hatchlings, there were two females and one male left. Still grieving for her dead baby, Gitar accepted the Hasan Daegian newborn with her blue-black hair, blue eyes, and even blue toes taking the place of her beloved blonde chick.

If she felt pain over one chick with three still living, how could she ignore the sufferings of one woman with one child. She understood completely. Pain from a mother's heart was universal.

Once Queen Abisola settled into the nursery, she clasped her hands and stood over the nest. "Oh my goodness, look how big she is!" she exclaimed.

Iegani stood silently by the door, appreciating the enchanting sight of a mother claiming her child. He watched intently for a few minutes, and then his thoughts drifted.

Sitting on a stool, Queen Abisola picked up her daughter and held her tight, kissing her face and hands.

Prince Iasos stood by beaming.

Queen Abisola counted her daughter's toes and fingers. The baby happily gurgled while Abisola removed the baby's clothing, inspecting for rashes or bruises.

Iegani straightened up.

On the baby's back was a tattoo of two large cats with all sorts of symbols and numbers. Since he had never been around when the baby was changed or bathed, he had not seen the tattoo. He sensed the tattoo was something significant. A piece of the riddle. Knowing he could not approach the queen now, he would wait until the dinner honoring her presence in the City of the Peaks.

Tables and chairs were available for the Hasan Daegians to dine on. The Bird People liked to perch while eating raw meat but sat at the tables while Queen Abisola and her husband stayed with them. Cooked boaeps with fresh greens were brought in on a large ceremonial platter. Queen Abisola eyed it gratefully. She was glad she was not expected to eat bloody meat. Her people seldom ate meat, but at least it was thoroughly cooked when they did.

Iegani sat uncomfortably on his chair while noticing the younger Dinii had no trouble at all sitting. "Old bones," he muttered.

"What's that?" asked Queen Abisola.

"Your Majesty, I was wondering about the tattoo on the back of Princess Maura," he asked innocently. "I did not know your people tattooed their young."

"We do not as a rule, just the monarchs. We prefer jewelry and flowers as adornment," Queen Abisola answered graciously.

"I might add you look stunning tonight. We are not accustomed to bright stones in necklaces such as you are wearing, but as you can see we like to color our feathers."

"Yes, such intricate and unusual designs," she answered, glancing around the room.

"Only our empress wears the bright stones. Our empress likes to grind stones such as you are wearing and sprinkle the dust on her. It gives her such a glittering effect, don't you think?"

"She looks lovely."

Iegani bowed his head to hide his smile. He knew the compliment had cost the Hasan Daegian queen.

"You say that only the queens have this tattoo?" he asked while pouring Sivan wine for Queen Abisola.

"Only the ruling monarch. The uultepes are the mascot of the Hasan Daegian royalty."

"And all of the Hasan Daegian rulers have had these same markings?"

"Yes, why do you ask?"

"As you know, our people do not read or write but commit our knowledge to memory. I find it very interesting that your rulers have a tattoo with very ancient-looking symbols. Can you tell me the meaning of the tattoo, that is, if I am not impertinent?"

"I don't know the meaning. I've always considered it just a mark of our station. As for the symbols, many of them are in our old way of writing from before we accepted the Sivan script for everyday use."

"And the other symbols?"

"I don't know to what they refer."

"Do you think there is anyone who can translate it?"

Abisola looked thoughtful. "I would guess the priestesses from the House of Magi could translate the symbols as they still read from texts in old languages, but I know of no one else. Why? Do you think it really means something?" She laughed. "Oh, believe me, it was some old crone who wanted to create some mystique for the royalty. I wouldn't think it would go beyond that."

Iegani lifted his goblet. "To your health and continued prosperity, Your Majesty."

Queen Abisola nodded and studied the old owl when he looked away. She would have to look into the matter of her tattoo. If this wise owl-man was asking questions, there was a reason beyond idle curiosity on his part. She turned and smiled at her husband. This would be a good project for him when they got home.

AFTER FIVE DAYS of negotiation, it was decided that Princess Maura would spend winter and spring under the loving protection of her parents and summer and fall with the Dinii who would train the princess as a huntress and warrior, but only in the presence of a Hasan Daegian nurse, nanny, and guard selected by Queen Abisola.

Consort Iasos taught Empress Gitar how to write her name. The empress practiced writing with a stick in the dirt for hours as she was excited to write her name on the written agreement concerning Princess Maura.

Finally, the Hasan Daegian queen with her consort and entourage, went back to O Konya, much to the relief of the Dinii.

The nurse, nanny, and guard did their best to fit in as best they could around seven-foot-tall birds that left the city every night to go hunting. The Dinii, not accustomed to the smells, sounds, and customs of Hasan Daegians in their midst, did their best to ignore and then gradually accept these beings who had no feathers. The three Hasan Daegians, in return, hid their alarm when the bird warriors would take Princess Maura high into the sky and then drop her hundreds of feet into the arms of a waiting hawk.

"It teaches our chicks not to fear heights," Empress Gitar explained patiently to the sweating and furious Hasan Daegian guard. She was perplexed. "Doesn't everyone do this?" It went without saying that no one reported this to the overprotective and quick-tempered Queen Abisola.

It was a struggle for everyone to get along, except for the princess, who thought all the attention was lovely, especially the rides in the sky. The baby laughed and grabbed the nose of her hawk rescuer who shed feathers at the thought she might miss catching the future ruler of Hasan Daeg.

Maura was a child who wanted to eat, sleep, and, most of all, be loved. What could she know of the harsh wind of evil preparing to blow into her country and destroy everything she would grow to cherish? She was just a babe, after all.

5

Iegani was anxious.

He left the City of the Peaks early one morning with several warriors.

They flew in a V formation with Iegani at the head. His mission was of the utmost importance. Only Iegani knew where they were going, and he was not telling. "Just follow me," he ordered.

Iegani wouldn't even tell Gitar where they were going or why. She didn't pursue the matter with Iegani, for she knew he acted for the good of their people. She also knew from her secret spies that Iegani had sent teams to search Hasan Daeg's cities for ancient scrolls. Gitar even knew that Iegani studied the tattoo on Princess Maura intensely.

He had burned wood for charcoal to copy the tattoo onto bark and hidden the copy in his nest house. But she didn't know why.

It wasn't that Gitar didn't trust her uncle. She did, but not so completely that she wouldn't embed a spy among one of the warriors accompanying him. She didn't trust anyone that much.

After Iegani flew away, Empress Gitar went to the nursery and picked up Princess Maura to study the tattoo. She held the baby upright and then dangled her by her foot, inspecting the tattoo. "I can't make heads nor tails of it," she sighed, handing the gurgling baby back to a distraught nanny. Bored, Gitar made her way back to the audience room. Bad times were coming soon enough. She did not need to go looking for trouble.

That was Iegani's department.

For now, she just wanted to hunt, raise her chicks, and make love with whom she desired . . . and they were many.

6

They flew all day.

After the initial day, Iegani and his bird warriors changed their routine. They traveled only at night, sleeping by day in mountain peaks or deep within forest treetops. They were careful not to be seen and left no trace of their presence. All debris and food carcasses were buried, as was any bodily waste.

While the Hasan Daegians were peaceful, the Dinii were not and often fought those who encroached on their hunting territory outside Hasan Daeg. They were skilled killers.

Iegani chose his warriors from the Hawk clan with care—two female and two male warriors who were not related to each other by marriage or kinship and possessed different skills, having shown valor in military operations.

The female red hawks, Yeti and Toppo, were larger than the male hawks, possessing endurance and strength. The male hawks, Benzar and Tarsus, were better at stealth and had more patience than their female counterparts.

Iegani paired them male and female. The females were in charge of hunting food and water while the males covered up their trail and conducted reconnaissance work. Since they ate their food raw, they did not worry about fires. If the night was chilly, they perched together to keep warm while one remained on watch.

For many nights they flew.

Iegani kept quiet with his thoughts. The others noticed that he carried a pouch from which he would pull a piece of bark covered with writing from time to time.

When they gathered close to see the writing, he would cluck a warning at them. After that, they kept their distance but secretly speculated on what their mission was and where they were going. They wondered if Iegani could read.

Each night before they began their flight, Iegani would scan their thoughts. As the hawks were young, they were eager to try their mettle, wishing for something thrilling to happen. He often chuckled to himself after reading their minds. *Was I ever this full of hubris?* Iegani thought. He was surprised to find that they were in awe and a little frightened of him. It gave him pause.

Soon they reached the eastern border of Hasan Daeg. The wall of mist caused no harm as they flew high above it. For two of the hawks, it was their first time they had gone beyond the borders of Hasan Daeg. They shivered with excitement.

For several more nights, they traveled toward a destination that only Iegani knew. One night they began to smell smoke in the air. They could see refugees clogging the main roads below. If the refugees kept traveling west, they would hit the mist wall but would be unable to penetrate it. They would have to travel north and finally come to the ocean or go south where they would be greeted by unsympathetic Sivan merchants and their hired mercenaries. To keep their whereabouts unnoticed, the Dinii turned northward and flew over less populated areas.

Everywhere they flew, they saw signs of war. And not the kind of skirmishes they were used to, but a new kind of warfare that not only killed large portions of the population but devastated the land as well. Food became increasingly scarce for the Bird People. They resorted to hunting and eating berries and nuts as did refugees fleeing from war-torn areas.

Due to their seclusion, the Dinii had enjoyed a mostly prosperous history. Not many peoples knew of their existence and the ones who did respected them as god-like creatures that swooped in deadly silence from the sky. They could slice the throat of a victim in a split second just as the poor wretch heard only a slight whoosh of wings. The Dinii didn't make a habit of killing people, especially Hasan Daegians. However, poachers were fair game, and their flesh was tasty indeed.

Iegani loved the taste of raw, bloody meat, although several times he had tried to become a vegetarian as he believed it was a higher step on the moral ladder. Each time he had failed, only to consume his fellow creatures with a relish topped with guilt, until one day he decided that each creature must be what she or he was. Nothing more.

Nothing less. Who was he to fight the inexplicable web of nature? Only nature herself understood the great workings and interconnections of Kaseri. He may not have believed in a supreme being, but he did believe in harmony. And to step out of one's nature was disharmony. This philosophy set his mind at ease.

But Iegani did not wish to eat the suffering refugees roaming below him. Still, they might suffice in a pinch as berries were becoming monotonous.

Iegani shook these thoughts out of his head. He realized that if he was thinking unclean thoughts with the little privation he suffered, what were the refugees themselves enduring? He would not add to their misery. He prayed that the mist would withstand the onslaught of these poor wanderers. If not, Hasan Daeg would be overrun in a matter of weeks. Their peaceful society could not cope with the demands of these angry, hateful outsiders who would, through sheer madness looking for food, trample the fields and destroy the crops. They would drink from the sacred black streams and cause harm through the insanity that would follow.

Yes. Yes, thought Iegani. *The world is being turned upside down because of an ambitious fool.*

Iegani felt rage at all the suffering. Righteous anger radiated from his being. He called his warriors to him. Perching on the limbs of a tall mingo tree, they looked at him with expectation.

"Warriors from the City of the Peaks, have you seen the suffering?"

The hawks nodded. They too were sickened by the evil they saw. They knew death. They were pledged to it. It was expected. But the destruction they saw had no honor. It seemed to be without purpose. Total destruction did not make sense. To them, war was simple. You had an enemy. You struck this enemy. You either lost or won. That was the end of it. You did not set the world on fire. What did the field mice, borax calves, or trees have to do with one's enemy? Why destroy their homes? What sense was there in making all creatures and plants feel one's hate?

"Never before have the Dinii seen such destruction."

They murmured in agreement with him.

Iegani continued, "I have a great tale to tell you. Listen carefully, my children, for what I tell you is true. We were once like the nomads of Bhuttan. Angry. Greedy. We were the Overlords of Kaseri, lords of the entire planet, but we were without code or honor. We took because it was in our power to do so. We enslaved smaller and weaker beings to do our bidding. We killed without discretion. We were lords of the most high. Very little could stop us until we encountered the Wise Ones of Lahor. They are no fable, my young ones. I have seen them with my own eyes."

The warriors gasped, staring at Iegani in astonishment.

"We all know the mythical story of Lahor, a great island of learning across the water, known for its art and science, immense libraries, and institutions of knowledge. Architecture such as the world has never seen before or since.

"But a great storm arose after a blazing star fell from the sky and engulfed the island. What you don't know is that many survived the great flood that ensued and crossed the water in quickly constructed rafts and makeshift boats. Many died at sea, but some landed near our old homeland, which extended to the sea, now in the Forbidden Zone.

"Our ancestors found these creatures and tried to enslave them as was our custom with inferior beings. But this ancient people resisted slavery, causing us great harm by their thoughts. These thoughts caused immense pain as if we were exploding from within.

"We had never encountered such an enemy. We were enraged and sought their destruction. We hunted them relentlessly. We knew their powers were limited and thought we would just wear them down by our sheer numbers. We did not. We did not understand their desire to be free was dearer than their fear of death. We killed hundreds of them, ripping their hearts out and eating the sometimes still-beating heart. Female, male, babe . . . it made no difference to us.

"But something started to happen. We began to think differently. We did not understand that eating the Lahorians' flesh would evoke subtle emotional changes within us. As we absorbed their flesh, their blood, we were absorbing their thoughts and values. Many of our ancestors committed suicide because they could not stand the internal conflict. Those who survived lost the taste for hunting the Wise Ones of Lahor.

"Because we were so ashamed of our barbarism, we resisted everything the Lahorians stood for and wished to erase them from our memory. We destroyed our centers for learning. We tossed our scrolls into the ocean, eventually forgetting how to read and write. No longer able to be humbled by our defeat, we fled our ancient homeland by the sea. We transported our remaining slaves over the mountains into Hasan Daeg, a land which had been used primarily for hunting. We set them free to work the land.

"Our ancestors cultivated the wall of mist to protect our freed slaves from raiders out of the east. With time, we gradually forgot about the danger of the Lahorians. We were convinced they were a people tied to the water and would remain near the sea if any of them were still alive. We had met our superiors, and they left us scarred. We withdrew to the City of the Peaks, letting the world do as it wished.

"Our former slaves grew into an intelligent and industrious people. Their specialty was plants. They had an understanding of nature that we did not foresee. We found that their agricultural methods and husbandry increased the animal population from which we fed. In return, we protected them but generally left them to their own devices.

"Once they established their own royalty, we made a formal treaty. They could live in our territory as long as they kept the land in good condition. Our former slaves grew fat and prosperous. We noticed that they had taken many of our customs and adopted them as their own.

"Time passed and they forgot about us as we were rarely seen, clinging to myths that they had been created by winged gods. The Wise Ones of Lahor became clouded in time for us too, until our empress and I discovered their existence again in the middle of the Sacred Lake of Yappor."

"How long have they been here?" asked Yeti, the largest of the red hawks.

"It seems for many centuries. They have established a colony. Their mental powers have increased to such an extent that it would be folly for us to resist," said Iegani.

Yeti gasped, "Do they mean to enslave us?"

Iegani shook his head. "It is hard to discern their true purpose. But I do not think they wish to harm us. It is not in their culture to enslave."

"Then they can stop Zoar," said Tarsus.

"They will not. The Wise Ones claim they cannot kill. They will help us destroy Zoar but will not directly cause his downfall," affirmed Iegani. "From what I can discern, they can only leave the water for short periods of time, and that's why they need our help to implement their plan."

"How is that?" asked Yeti.

"They are going to stop Zoar through Princess Maura."

Yeti laughed out loud while the others twittered. She quickly covered her mouth when Iegani sternly glared at her.

"You must understand," Iegani explained. "The Wise Ones of Lahor have mental powers of which we only can dream. They can look into the future and thus plan for the outcome they wish. Don't you think that a rather opportune skill, Yeti?"

"Oh, Great Divigi, I meant no disrespect," she replied awkwardly. "It's just that Princess Maura is a mere babe."

Iegani spread his wings for effect. "Babies sometimes have the bad manners to grow up."

The hawks were suitably impressed. Their eyes gleamed with excitement. While Princess Maura was still a riddle, their mission had now become clearer to them. They were attempting to solve the mystery of the Hasan Daegian baby.

Iegani pulled the bark scroll from his pouch and unrolled it.

The hawks moved closer to peer at it. He held it up for them. "On this scroll is an exact copy of the tattoo on Princess Maura. Even its dimensions are comparable."

"Yes, yes, this looks very much like it!" exclaimed Benzar, who had been assigned to take Princess Maura on flying assignments to accustom her to great heights.

"Did you never wonder about this tattoo?" asked Iegani, peering over the scroll.

"Yes, Great Divigi, but it is not my place to question."

"Good enough. Still, tell me what you think."

Benzar paused.

"Come, come now, don't be shy," encouraged Iegani.

"Well, I think," ventured Benzar, "that the tattoo is not merely for decoration."

"Why is that?" asked Iegani.

Benzar cast a glance at his comrades. He was afraid of making a fool out of himself.

Yeti nodded, giving him confidence.

"Well, Great Divigi, if the tattoo was for decoration or even for announcing the status of the wearer, it would not be placed on the back. It would be on the face or hands where it could be seen at all times, and there are numbers in a specific order. This tattoo is a message or code."

"Go on," encouraged Iegani.

"Also, the symbols seem to be in a pattern," blurted out Yeti, "like other writings we have seen. Oh, I'm sorry," she said, realizing she had spoken without waiting to be called.

Iegani was pleased with her reply, although he did not show it. He made a mental note to himself that he would have to curb Yeti's impulsive nature. Iegani pressed, "Why on the back?"

Benzar continued. "It makes perfect sense. If it's a message, it would be placed on an area that would be less vulnerable to scarring or damage, not on hands, feet, or even a face. As the wearer matures into adulthood, the writing on the back becomes larger, more discernible to the viewer."

Toppo looked questioningly at Iegani.

He nodded.

She gingerly reached out and touched the scroll, then jerked her hand back.

Iegani looked at her, waiting for a reply. Since the Dinii had forgotten reading and writing, they still needed a way to communicate with written symbols—those who had the ability developed powers for interpreting messages. They could not decipher the writing, but could read the intent and emotions from the vibrations in the message left by the writer.

"What do you feel, my young fledgling?" Iegani asked.

"Great Divigi, I feel nothing from the messenger, but strong vibrations from the scroll. No, that's not right. From the tattoo. It feels very powerful, like it has a beat to it."

"Like a heartbeat."

"Yes, you can say that. It feels very unnatural."

"I wrote that scroll myself, but only after I had emptied my mind of all thoughts and emotions. And still, it is as you say . . . strong." Iegani stared at the sky. "But not anything as powerful as when I touched the princess myself with both hands."

"What did you feel?" questioned Yeti.

Benzar nudged her.

"Was it evil?" asked Toppo, a wave of empathy spreading over her.

"I've never felt anything evil when touching her," said Yeti.

Toppo snapped back. "Some hawks do not possess the power to feel."

Iegani carefully rolled up the scroll and placed it in the pouch. "That's why you are here, my children. We must solve this riddle."

He slowly related the events at the Sacred Lake of Yappor when the Lahorians had captured Empress Gitar. Iegani spoke of the trust regarding Princess Maura and her future as seen by the Lahorians.

No one spoke when he finished.

He waited until Yeti asked, "What is our mission?"

Iegani knew they had accepted the facts and were willing to do as he requested. "I chose the four of you because each of you possesses a specific skill which will be needed in the future. Toppo, you are a seeress. Be my protégé, and I will teach you secrets that you cannot even suspect exist yet."

Toppo looked astonished. "I have only a little talent," she whispered.

"For now, that is true," replied Iegani, "but you have much potential."

Looking very pleased, Toppo bowed. "Thank you. Thank you, Great Divigi." She reached for his hand and kissed it.

Iegani patted her on the head. "My child, I don't think you will be thanking me in the dark days to come. I will ask of you sacrifices that will make you want to tear your heart out."

Each of the warriors looked alarmed.

"I see no other way," Iegani continued. He sighed. "You will form with me a secret society pledged to protect Princess Maura until she can finish her mission. In return, I will teach each of you the magical path that you may pass down to your children. I will give you power unknown to you."

He paused, closed his eyes, and whispered, "Are you with me?"

The warriors felt Iegani in their minds, moving among their secret thoughts. It was unnerving. They knew they could not hide their fears from him, the Great Divigi. There was no place to run, to hide. "Yes, we will follow you," their minds echoed back to him.

"Then you each pledge your heart, soul, and mind to me. Bind them with mine. Let us do what we must to save our land, our freedom, our people's existence. Let us not be tempted by the darkness that pervades Kaseri. Let us be strong, seeking to remove the hand of evil that attempts to strangle us."

"Yes, yes," answered the warriors, swaying with the hypnotic rhythm of Iegani's voice.

"Do you swear to me?" Iegani cried, stretching out his iridescent, white wings to their impressive size.

"Yes, we swear with our hearts and minds . . . our very souls." They shuddered upon speaking the vow. They knew their lives would never again be their own.

Iegani held out his hand. "Pledge your honor to me."

Each warrior placed her or his hand on Iegani's opened palm. "We pledge with our honor, Great Divigi!"

Iegani placed his other hand on top of theirs.

Each warrior shook with currents of power emanating from Iegani.

Iegani's eyes flew open and rolled back into his sockets. "It is done," he croaked. "It is done."

The warriors murmured in unison, "It is done."

Iegani broke his hands from theirs.

The hawks stumbled away.

Toppo wept.

Benzar held Toppo's hand, too dazed to do much else.

Yeti and Tarsus looked at each other with pride. They felt they had been given a great honor.

"Why are you crying?" snapped Tarsus, surprised at his vehemence since he seldom spoke.

"Because we came very close to death," answered Toppo. She stole a look at Iegani.

He nodded.

"If even one of us had not accepted the vow, Iegani would have slain us all," she asserted.

The rest of the warriors snapped their eyes to Iegani.

"It is true," Iegani confirmed. "I must have loyalty from all four, otherwise my plans would be at risk. I would have simply destroyed each of you and started over again."

The hawks exchanged stunned looks.

"I told you this would require sacrifices that might tear your hearts out." Iegani spread his wings to fly. "Next time, pay more attention to exactly what I say. I'm not one to speak in riddles." He looked about him. "It looks like it's going to be a beautiful evening. A good night for flying." He took off without looking behind him.

The others followed without a word.

7

The city of Anqara stank.

Its odor could be detected long before it came into view. Raw sewage was dumped into the river. Everyone knew not to eat fish unless it was imported. Only the rich could afford indoor plumbing. The poor threw their bodily waste, along with the kitchen scraps, into the streets.

Anqara, besides smelling like an old boot, was not pretty. It had no expansive boulevards. No grand fountains. It never entered anyone's mind to plant public gardens. Smoke from cooking fires blotted out the sky. People went for days without ever seeing the sun.

Crime was a constant nuisance. At least, everyone thought it was a nuisance rather than a problem. The criminals of Anqara were a good-natured lot and, although they threatened one's life with dull, rusty daggers, no one was ever injured. The well-to-do employed bodyguards, not because they feared for their safety, but because they disliked muggers pulling their hats over their heads, hiding their house keys, or tugging their whiskers.

Women especially disliked being held up for a token of their private undergarments only to see their garters worn on the sleeve of some ruffian weeks later in the bazaar. It seemed people were more concerned with their dignity rather than their purses.

Narrow streets meandered without rhyme or reason. During the summer, people lived on the roofs of their houses as the first floors were unbearable with the heat and fleas, which were always hopping on one's legs or in food.

Though Anqara was a smelly, rather unattractive city with swarms of common pickpockets and "kissing" bandits, it could boast of being one of the most populated and exciting cities.

It was the largest cultural center on Kaseri. Anqara was a city of more mildewed volumes of wisdom and drunken scholars than anywhere else. Hundreds of spectacled, hunched over, gnarled sages took to the streets every dawn, hurrying to their small cubicles where they pondered, reflected, and speculated on the wonders of the universe. And if not that, they drank a nice cup of hot tea with a little extra something added from their hip flasks. These old women were the guardians of the world's knowledge.

But none of this interested Zoar. It was the banking district of Anqara with its hundreds of secret deposits hidden in catacombs underground that took his fancy. He couldn't risk taking the city and allowing the banking houses to destroy or hide their entrusted wealth. Zoar knew that the scions of the banking world would never divulge their treasures' location even if the aga began cutting off their children's heads. They would just spit on Zoar's shoes in defiance. No, he would have to bide his time, trusting that his spies would find the hidden treasures before he entered the city.

This gave Anqara a respite and the bankers time to fund resistance groups throughout the country.

Iegani was not interested in any of this, although he was aware of Zoar's army surrounding Anqara. The divigi and his warriors hid in the woods outside Anqara and rested for several days.

At night, Benzar stole inside the city, scouting its convoluted passages.

Yeti would visit local butcher shops, taking provisions after leaving coins on the counter. Once she encountered an angry butcher working late. Yeti had to knock him in the head. She then threw distilled spirits on the unconscious merchant so no one would believe his story about a person of great height covered in feathers taking his best roast.

Iegani was unconcerned with the tales of encounters that Yeti and Benzar brought back. He only concentrated on a lighted window at the top of the highest tower in the city—the House of Magi!

The House of Magi was considered by the rest of the world to be a law unto itself. Remote, majestic, and cloaked in mystery, it stood as the tallest building in Anqara. Crumbling stairways, a block wide, stood below the marble-columned portico.

Only one magnificent doorway granted entrance with its doors that never shut. On either side of the portal stood colossal braziers in which yellow flames continually burned. No one ever saw a servant tending to them, nor was one tempted to cross the threshold—not even the most desperate thief. At night, windows threw misshapen shadows of priestesses as they paced back and forth in their studies in front of oil lamps.

It was said that every twenty years, the High Priestess of the House of Magi would consent to entertain application—those who sought the solitude of the House of Magi to contemplate and study. Once granted admission, they could pursue any project that would be funded for any length of time.

Scientists, scholars, and philosophers would go before the grand door, calling into the darkness their proposal of study. Most applicants waited years, sometimes decades, before a response was given. No matter where they were or what they were doing, an acceptance or rejection letter with the seal of the House of Magi appeared silently on their doorway or tent flap.

No one knew the origin of the House of Magi or the source of its wealth. The oldest city records mention the House of Magi standing quiet and forbidding by the river inside the first city walls with its open door and the huge fire sentinels guarding, guarding, guarding.

It was to the House of Magi that Iegani flew one smoke-filled night. To the highest window he flew. With beating wings, he hovered outside the window and tried the sash. The window was shut fast. Seeing no other way, he burst through the glass with great clamor and fury.

On the far side of the room behind a massive desk sat an old woman peering over some manuscripts. She looked up in surprise and gasped. Blinking hard, she waved her hand in front of her as if to ward Iegani away.

Iegani quickly folded his wings. "High Priestess of the House of Magi. I come in peace on a quest. I seek no lies, only truth to which you may possess the key!" He bowed very low in abject supplication, peering up at her from under his massive feather eyebrows.

"What damnation is this?" the priestess sputtered. "What foul evil is this that has a giant bird speaking?" She peered hard at Iegani. "A male bird, at that. Good gracious man, cover yourself. Who wants to look at your withering male tool?"

"Madam, you cannot see anything. My splendid feathers cover all."

The old woman laughed. "You are wrong. Breaking windows must excite you."

"Great Priestess, I did not come all this way to talk about my male anatomy."

"Have you come to kill me?" asked the old woman, eying Iegani with curiosity.

"Absolutely not."

"You're not some foul thing Zoar has conjured up to do away with the High Priestess of Magi?"

"I assure you that I have never met the aga and do not wish to."

"Mmm." The woman wet her lips with her tongue. "I need a drink. A little spirit to clear my head and steady my heart." She poured ale out of a pitcher and into a glass. "Did you not worry that you would cause me heart failure with your dramatic entrance?"

Iegani was disturbed. "To tell the truth, I never thought of it. My species does not suffer from the heart."

"Health of the heart or having one?" The woman got up and walked from around the desk toward him.

Iegani noticed she limped slightly.

She touched the feathers on Iegani's torso. "Are these glued on?"

"No, High Priestess, they are real. Go on. Feel them down to the quill. See how they grow out of my skin."

"Amazing." The woman stroked the feathers and pried them apart to investigate. "Come over here by the light so I can see better." She pulled at Iegani's feathers.

He obliged and followed her over to a lamp.

"They seem iridescent, almost glowing. Is that to reflect light? I have a hundred questions. Now, let's see, I must get paper and pen to write down your answers. Let me call for a scribe."

Iegani stopped her as she reached for the bell. He gently pushed her down into a soft chair near her desk. "There must be no witness to my visit. I'm sorry."

"Why is one of the Dinii here?"

Iegani looked surprised. "You know our name?"

"Yes, I thought I would never see an Overlord." The High Priestess stretched out her bad leg. "I know all about Hasan Daeg and its secret wall of mist."

Iegani felt truly humbled. "High Priestess, you are wise."

"Pshaw," she snorted, "One should gather some information when reading for over forty years, and quit calling me High Priestess. We worship no god here. We are devoted to the study of knowledge. I don't know why everyone keeps thinking we are some kind of a cult." She fussed with the pillows in her chair.

"What shall I call you?"

"Madam if you're the formal kind or Mehmet since that is my name." Mehmet beamed a smile at him. It was a lovely, dimpled smile.

"Mehmet suits you. I am Iegani, Great Divigi to the Empress Gitar."

"And why have you crashed into my chamber, Iegani, Great Divigi to Empress Gitar?"

Iegani gathered a stool and sat beside Mehmet. "I am here seeking information, Great Lady." He turned his head and whistled.

Toppo glided into the room with the leather pouch. She landed lightly on her feet, dodging the glass on the floor. Toppo smiled weakly at Mehmet and bowed. Handing the pouch to Iegani, she retreated to a far corner of the room and tried to look inconspicuous.

Mehmet seemed delighted with the arrival of Toppo and craned her neck to get a good look at the other Dini. "A female of your species!" Mehmet exclaimed. "Tell me, dear, all about your kind. I want to know about your mating rituals, how you raise your young?"

Toppo spread her wings about her, hiding her face and torso.

"Oh, goodness," pouted Mehmet, staring at Iegani. "She's awfully shy."

Iegani pulled the bark scroll out of the pouch and waited for Mehmet's attention.

Mehmet's eyes finally landed on the scroll. Curious, she reached for it.

The Great Divigi gently presented it to her.

The scholar studied the writing on the bark for a very long time.

Iegani watched her expression, but whatever Mehmet thought, she kept to herself.

"Where did you get this?" she asked, still holding the scroll tightly.

"I'm sorry, but I cannot tell you."

"Why do you want to know what it means?"

"I believe my kind are in danger, and this writing may help save us."

"The whole world is in danger. Did you not see the troops outside Anqara's walls?"

"True, but I am only concerned with my people," said Iegani. "It is selfish, I admit."

"But honest," declared Mehmet. "In this day and age, I appreciate your words." Mehmet raised her glass and swallowed. She rested the empty glass on the desk. "So, you are not noble."

"I care nothing about Zoar and his minions, except that they stop at my doorstep. He can tear the rest of the world apart as long as he leaves my homeland alone."

Mehmet clapped her hands. "Spoken like a true cynic, or so you try to appear. I will take your words at face value." She smiled. "For now, at least." Mehmet changed the subject. "Where did you get this?"

"The place where I found this writing is strange in itself. It is the same message handed down from one generation to the next."

"Yes, but where?"

"I cannot tell you."

Mehmet studied Iegani for a time. "It could just be gibberish," said Mehmet.

"I think not. I think this writing is a code," answered Iegani, pointing to the bark.

"Maybe so, but why bring it to me?"

"I could think of no place else to find someone who would be able to tell me what it means."

Mehmet sighed loudly. "Many of the world's intellectuals are either dead or in prison. But why do you think I will tell you the truth of what it is?"

"The House of Magi is honorable."

Mehmet looked pleased. "We do try," she said vainly. "But I cannot tell you what it means. It does seem to be a code, but its symbols are so ancient no one remains who would know what they mean. I know of no language that looks similar. It almost looks not of this world. See here," she said, pointing to a star symbol divided into four sections with a cross. "This symbol looks like ancient Lahorian writing when they were still using pictographs. It refers to long life."

"Lahorian!" exclaimed Iegani. "They are just the stuff of old wives' tales."

Mehmet gave Iegani a grave look. "Stop lying. You and I both know that the Lahorians exist. Being disingenuous with me will not make me help you." She turned her attention to the bark. "Oh, yes, I'd say about twelve thousand years old. But the rest of it, I don't know."

"Can you decipher it?"

"I think so. It will take time, of course. We have a very good linguist here."

Iegani held up his hand. "No one else may know of this."

"You expect me to decipher this alone? To drop all of my projects just because you want to know what this bit of wood says?" Mehmet drew herself up. "You must be mad."

Iegani nodded. "I think this bit of bark is so important that the High Priestess herself must decode it. I think the world depends on it."

"You said you didn't care about the world."

"Yes, Great Lady, but you do."

Mehmet laughed. "What a flatterer you are. Great Lady, indeed. So important it needs only my attention," she mimicked. "I suppose if I refuse, you will kill me."

Iegani said nothing.

Mehmet shrugged. "I guess I'm bored with studying the habits of the Kawanda giant beetle."

He handed her the pouch.

"I don't suppose you have a copy in case I lose this?"

Iegani pointed to his head. "It's up here."

"Birdman, you intrigue me. If I were younger, I might be interested in you."

The Great Divigi grinned. "I don't see what your age has to do with it. I like a bit of mature meat myself."

"Well, this venture may prove to be most interesting. Most interesting indeed."

Iegani plucked one of the beautiful white feathers from above his heart and presented it to Mehmet.

Mehmet eagerly took it. Looking at it closely, she murmured, "I've never seen anything like this. It changes color in the light like a prism."

Hearing a sudden whooshing sound, Mehmet looked up.

The Dinii were gone.

Alone in the room, she sat composing her erratic thoughts. Finally, Mehmet walked over to a portrait of herself and took it off the wall. A hidden door in the wall slid open, exposing a small antechamber. She quickly placed the scroll and pouch in the room and then replaced the portrait. The door to the room closed. Then she went to bed, holding the feather as she fell asleep.

Across from the House of Magi in a dark alley, a beggar made note of the exact time he saw two large birds fly out of the room of the High Priestess.

I have certainly earned my pay tonight, he chuckled to himself. Still playing the part of a beggar, the spy shuffled off into the darkness. He had much to report. He would make sure that he would report this to Zoar himself.

There might be a reward.

8

Zoar rested comfortably.

He lay on soft pillows and carpets as he watched a dance troop. Zoar had seen many dancing girls, but this group was particularly good. They combined acrobatics with dancing. Zoar loved acrobatics, and he especially liked watching well-toned and muscular girls dancing in skimpy attire. *Simple pleasures of life*, he thought to himself. He looked toward his son lying beside him quietly eating some fruit. Zoar tousled his hair.

The boy looked up at him questioningly.

Why doesn't he smile at me? thought Zoar. *It must be his mother's influence. I'll soon take care of that.* Zoar reached over and picked some other delicious tidbits and offered them to his son.

Shaking his head, his son continued to eat his fruit.

This refusal angered Zoar, but he didn't show it. He wanted his son to love him. Zoar would do anything for him. Reaching over, he stroked Dorak's cheek while watching the dancing girls, his heart a little wearier.

Out of the corner of his eye, he saw several of his commanders talking amongst themselves. *There is news, but they are deciding who will tell me. It must be bad. And whom shall I punish if it is bad?*

Finally, the youngest of the commanders approached the aga, asking permission to speak.

"What is it?" demanded Zoar gruffly. "Can't you see I'm spending time with my son? What do you want?"

The young commander glanced back at the other officers.

This pleased Zoar. He wanted his soldiers to be afraid. Men fearing for their lives were easy to control.

"Well, speak up! Speak up!"

"Great Aga. One of our spies in Anqara has reported something that we think would interest you."

Zoar sat up. A servant immediately straightened the pillows behind his back. "You have found the secret hiding place of the banks?"

The young man, knowing better than to answer with a negative reply, simply dodged the question. Zoar asked so many questions he sometimes forgot. "One of our spies in Anqara reported that several nights ago two large beings of an unknown origin burst into the room of the High Priestess in the House of Magi."

"Continue." Zoar leaned forward, showing his interest.

"These beings were dressed as birds and flew into the High Priestess' room which sits at the very apex of the building."

Zoar laughed.

The commander did not smile.

"You really don't expect me to believe your fairy tale, do you?" asked Zoar.

"This particular spy has been extremely competent in the past and swears with his life this is true."

"Two men, dressed up as birds, flew into the room of one of the most revered persons in the world. Is this what you are telling me?"

"Great Aga, we have other reports of people seeing these strange birdlike creatures in the past several weeks. There is a butcher in Anqara who swears he was attacked by one."

Zoar waved the dancing girls away as the music died. He slowly sipped some shaybar—a boiled drink of borax blood and milk. "You know, this story reminds me of something." He placed his finger to his mouth, thinking, "But I can't think what."

He held out his hand. A servant wiped Zoar's hand with a warm cloth and then dried it. The aga held out the other hand. She wiped it clean.

"I would like to speak to this spy."

Smiling, the commander replied, "Great Aga, our man thought this so important he has traveled here to speak to you personally."

"Good. Bring him in."

The commander waved to the guards standing by the large tent flaps. They opened them carefully. Outside, a dust storm was raging.

A small, meager man stepped inside. He stood by the aga's favorite horses near the edge of the tent and shook the dust off his new clothes. Adjusting his eyes to the light, he soon saw the commander beckoning. He approached the young officer timidly. When he reached him, he spoke to the commander in a language unknown to Zoar.

The aga watched the spy carefully.

The little man realized he was standing before the Great Aga and kowtowed.

"Tell this little baggage to get up!"

The commander spoke in low tones. The little man shook his head and mumbled a reply.

"He says he is not worthy to look upon your greatness."

Zoar was pleased but did not respond. He called for more oil lamps so he could see better.

Servants with lamps and torches immediately stood beside the commander and the spy.

The commander spoke again to the little man.

The kneeling man responded at length, making various hand gestures.

Nodding from time to time, the officer kept encouraging the man to keep talking until the spy was through telling his story.

"Great Aga," said the commander, turning toward Zoar. "This man is Kaysian from the northern region of Kaysia. He has been in your service for over two years now. Several months ago, he was assigned to Anqara where he dresses as a beggar. His orders were to watch the House of Magi for any unusual activity. For the time he has been watching the House of Magi, nothing out of the ordinary had occurred until three nights ago."

The commander paused as if for effect and glanced around him, studying his comrades' faces. "Three nights ago, this man swears he saw two persons fly to the chamber of the High Priestess, hover in the sky without benefit of ropes or wires, and burst through the glass to the room."

The beggar spy remained kneeling with his forehead on the carpet.

Zoar interrupted, "Were they male or female?"

The commander turned to the spy and asked him, giving him a little kick.

The little man sat up and shrugged as he replied.

"He says he does not know for sure. He thinks male because they were so large."

"How large?" queried Zoar.

When asked, the diminutive man pointed toward the horses.

"As large as my warhorses!" exclaimed Zoar.

Frightened, the little man pressed his forehead into the carpet again.

Zoar ignored him. "What else did he say?"

"He says they stayed for half an hour and then left via the same window, flying due west," answered the commander.

The spy looked up questioningly.

"What happened to the High Priestess?"

"Nothing, as far as we know. He said he stayed until he was sure there was no death call."

"She could have been murdered, and the rest of those witches are covering it up," said Zoar.

The commander spoke again to the spy.

The spy shook his head, replying quickly while stealing looks at Zoar.

"He says there would be no reason to do that as the House of Magi has no known political or religious affiliations. The House of Magi is a house of study and intellectual pursuits. There is no reason to hide the death of the High Priestess."

"Why is she called the High Priestess if she is only a reader of dusty scrolls?" questioned Zoar.

The commander looked sheepish. "My lord, it is a type of joke. The scholars are given to whimsy."

Zoar mulled this over for a moment.

"Great Aga, women with the best minds from all over the world come to the House of Magi to study and contemplate."

"Just women?"

"Yes, sire. Mostly women. There are a few men."

"Do we have any contact with them?"

The commander consulted his comrades. "Great Aga, I am sorry to report that we have made attempts, but all of our applicants have been rejected."

"What about servants?"

"They use none."

"Slaves?"

The commander shook his head.

Zoar gave an astonished look to his son, who was listening carefully. "Who cooks? Who cleans? Who serves?"

"Um, they do. They apparently take turns."

"I understand that there is only one door and it's open all the time. Just have one of our people enter it." Zoar was growing agitated. He disliked the thought of smelly, old women getting the best of him.

"Several of our men disguised as scholars have entered just as you suggested. The doorway leads into a stone room where the only doorway is the one they've entered. We have not been able to discover an entryway into the main part of the building. Also, our men have reported that while searching, even in the dead of night, the priestesses appear out of nowhere and assault our men, chasing them from the building."

"Chase our men away? How did they manage that?"

The commander blushed. "They were hit on the head with brooms and pots, Great Aga."

"Brooms?" questioned Zoar. "Our men are chased away by gray-haired women swinging brooms?"

"Most of the women are young and quite strong."

"Brooms!" shouted Zoar. "My soldiers, my best spies, men in the prime of their lives, run off by straw and wood! Little man, have you been inside the House of Magi?"

The commander translated as the spy spoke rapidly. "He says that was never his assignment, Great Aga. But if you will give him the opportunity, he will find a way in."

"Who gives him his assignments?"

"He does not know. He finds written instructions inside his bread basket and burns the instructions as soon as he finds them."

"Someone is leaving written instructions in a bread basket so anyone can read them. I don't believe the imbecility of my network!" Zoar shouted.

Both the commander and the spy bowed low, moving out of Zoar's reach.

Zoar kicked over a fruit tray.

When a servant bent over to pick up the fruit, Zoar kicked him as well.

"Little man," said Zoar to the beggar spy. "I will make a deal with you. Find the way into the House of Magi and find out the secret of your flying birds, and I will give you your freedom and ten more of these." Zoar threw a bag of gold at him as the commander was rapidly translating.

The spy's face lit up at the sight of the gold. He greedily grabbed it, almost slobbering.

The man's lack of control disgusted Zoar. He turned his head and waved the commander and the spy away.

The commander grabbed the arm of the spy and dragged him from the room as the beggar spy continued speaking gibberish and bowing his head.

Wishing to calm himself, Zoar called for refreshments.

The musicians began to softly play again as the dancing girls floated in. They swirled in their colorful costumes while flirting with Zoar's men.

Zoar paid them little attention. He was thinking about what the little spy had said.

He was not alone.

In the dark shadows of the tent, KiKu was seething with rage. He slowly pacified himself with controlled, short breaths, a technique he had learned on his journeys. That man was *his* spy with orders to report only to KiKu personally. The little traitor would have to pay for his disloyalty, but not here, not now. He must bide his time. KiKu knew who the birds were. They were the Dinii, an almost mythical species told about in fairy tales to children. How strange Zoar did not see the connection. But he might soon enough. KiKu studied Zoar's face. He knew Zoar was deep in thought. It would be only a matter of time before Zoar realized who the Bird People were and determined their connection to the land beyond the mist.

KiKu must stall him until his own plans could be placed into effect. That must be done first. Then, KiKu had a little surprise for the beggar spy who would meet his death in a dark alley, but not before the cat played with the tiny mouse for a long time.

9

Iegani returned to Mehmet.

He visited when the moons were the weakest and the night was the darkest. At first, it was to check on the deciphering of the code. At least that's what he told himself even though Toppo was keeping watch on the priestess. However, as the passage of time lengthened, Iegani found himself growing very fond of Mehmet.

Months grew into changing seasons and seasons grew into years. A strong friendship developed between the two of them, which later blossomed into a romance. It was not easy for Iegani to make love to a fragile creature such as Mehmet, but they went very slowly, and he did his utmost to be gentle.

It was very different from mating with a Dini. Dinii females tended to be a passionate lot with strong, fierce emotions. Since the females were stronger, the males had to be careful. And Dinii mated while flying in the air, which is what Iegani preferred, but Mehmet had other qualities, which gave him just as much pleasure.

Mehmet had a quick wit, making Iegani laugh. She suited Iegani at his advanced age. He was glad she was not Dinii, although he strongly suspected what really interested Mehmet was that he was. This caused him to smile. She was incorrigible in her thirst for knowledge.

Over the years, Iegani regaled Mehmet with stories of Hasan Daeg and its people who were geniuses with plants, but he spoke very little of his own city and people.

Iegani's visits were more frequent lately as groups of Dinii, under the cover of night, smuggled in supplies to the House of Magi.

Zoar, frustrated that his spy network had been unable to ferret out the bankers' strongholds, finally laid siege to the city with the intent of starving the Anqarians into submission.

That had been seven years ago.

Anqara had resisted with splendid courage. The people of Anqara had spat from the tops of the city walls upon the heads of Zoar's soldiers as they tried unsuccessfully to storm the great stone barriers.

No outside enemy had ever taken Anqara in her five-thousand-year history. Even if the city's walls were breached, the enemy would be confused by the winding narrow streets. Not being able to march more than two men abreast would markedly slow the enemy's advance into the heart of the city.

But the citizens of Anqara had never encountered an enemy like Zoar. He was indomitable.

The underground of their city was honeycombed with secret exits into the countryside. Special agents were given the task of searching outside and bringing back foodstuffs.

Zoar discovered the secret exits, and the Anqarian military had no choice but to destroy them to keep his men from entering the underground passages.

Rebels from neighboring villages catapulted supplies over the city walls. They were quickly sought out and killed by Zoar's men.

Still, the people of Anqara were stout and resolute. During the spring months when the river ran high and wild, they cheerfully threw buckets over the walls into the moats surrounding the city and drew up water heavy with silt. Every available patch of yard, street, or alleyway was converted into a garden. Vegetables of all varieties were growing on balconies, rooftops, porches, wagons, troughs, and window boxes. Seeds became more precious than gold.

Carpenters made a small fortune constructing watertight rain barrels. The city's garbage was taken to the House of Magi where many of the reclusive scholars came out and showed the Anqarians how to make compost, recycle, and handle their own waste without contamination.

In response, Zoar constructed a great dam across the river and diverted its flow out of the city's reach.

Zoar personally admired the Anqarians' tenacity, even though his generals cursed them. They wanted to return to Bhuttan.

The Anqarians were a very intelligent people, by far his most worthy opponents to date, but Zoar would not be deterred. It was only a matter of time. After seven years, the city had exhausted its resources. The huge compost heaps surrounding the great portico of the House of Magi existed no more. Every scrap of available wood had long since been made into a water barrel or an arrow. Zoar constantly harassed the city with flaming coals shot over the walls. Over the years, anything not made of stone had burned to the ground. The people were reduced to wearing rags. Still, they resisted.

The plague broke out in Zoar's camp. He rejoiced. Special catapults were constructed so that plague-ridden corpses could be heaved over Anqara's walls. Sickness soon spread throughout the city.

The women from the House of Magi knew how to combat the plague, but they had no way of making the medicine they needed. They could only make the ill comfortable until they died. Mehmet sent word for the Dinii to stay away. Nothing could help them now as there were not enough soldiers to stand guard. Zoar would storm the walls soon. Yet Mehmet kept her window open just in case.

The next dark night Iegani appeared.

"Didn't I tell you not to come!" snapped Mehmet, although she was relieved to see him.

"The Dinii are not affected by your little illness," growled Iegani. "Is the code deciphered?"

"Code, code, that's all I hear from you. The world is burning, and you care for nothing but your little piece of bark."

"That's right. Have you discovered the meaning?"

Mehmet gave him a disgusted look.

Iegani suddenly felt ashamed and held Mehmet in his winged arms, enveloping her.

She loved the woodsy smell of him. Mehmet sighed as she laid her head against his feathered chest and listened to his steady heartbeat.

"I'm sorry, Mehmet. You are struggling to survive here, and I pester you month after month about the code. Look, I have brought food."

"Give it to the children outside," she chided, pulling away.

"No, you are more important."

"Will I be as important when I have finished deciphering the code?"

"You're speaking gibberish."

"Am I?"

"Sit down, Mehmet. I have something to discuss with you. For the past several weeks, I have been having secret talks with Queen Abisola. She has agreed to absorb fifteen hundred refugees from Anqara."

"What do you mean?" asked Mehmet, clutching Iegani's arm in

hope.

"Tomorrow night, two thousand Dinii will fly into Anqara and fly out fifteen hundred persons. It is a one-time operation. I dare not risk it again. Zoar never makes the same mistake twice. We think that, with careful maneuvering, most of us will make it. It will be raining, and we are hoping the thunder will cover the sound of our wings."

"But there are more than four thousand children in Anqara!"

Iegani paused. "We will take those we can, but not all. We are going to evacuate all of the scholars from the House of Magi. We will also be taking with us the bankers and their families. Whatever soldiers are left we will fly out, and finally the children."

"Monstrous!" cried Mehmet. "I will not be a party to this!"

Iegani grabbed her by the shoulders and shook her.

Mehmet looked at him with fear.

"Listen to me," he commanded. "We must rescue the most important resources. I know it sounds cruel, but that is how it must be. Your women must be the first flown out of here. Your minds, your knowledge, your logic must be preserved to fight Zoar. Do you really think Anqara would have withstood Zoar for seven years without you and your disciples? Anqara would have been starved out in two years at the most."

Mehmet turned her head away.

"You know it's true," said Iegani.

"Why the bankers?"

"Because of the money. In return for their lives, they will hand over to us the treasure of Anqara." Iegani searched for words. "Don't you see? Queen Abisola can use this money to trade with the Sivans to make a last stand against Zoar? It makes sense to take it. Why let it fall into Zoar's possession?"

"You are not taking this money for yourself?"

"Take a good look at me, Mehmet. We used to be the lords of this planet. We used to be great teachers and knowledge gatherers like yourselves. We were powerful like Zoar until we met the Lahorians. Our minds never recovered from the encounter. We now shun knowledge for intuition.

"Instead of great houses, we live on the tallest mountain in a city built of sticks plastered with mud. We have almost refashioned our beings into a true animal state. Our needs are simple. What would the Dinii want of the Anqarian treasure?

"It is for Queen Abisola so she may buy weapons. It will be she who makes the last stand. Your work is done here, Mehmet," he said, stroking her hair. "You gave us the time we needed."

"And what of the code?"

"If you cannot decipher the code, I will find another way to fight Zoar. I truly thought it was a riddle to the future. What matters is that you be ready with your women tomorrow night. You must wait for us on top of the roof."

Mehmet began weeping. "Oh, these terrible choices. What will become of those not taken?"

"If they are lucky, they will die quickly." Iegani kissed her forehead, sighing. "I know, I know," he whispered. "It is terrible." His eyes grew moist.

"Iegani."

"Yes, loved one."

"I know what the code says."

"What!" exclaimed Iegani.

"I have known for years."

"Why didn't you tell me?"

"Because we needed the Dinii's help. I thought that if I told you the truth, you would go away with the secret, and the medical and food supplies would stop being flown in. We needed them so desperately."

Mehmet went to the window and looked out. "I am an evil woman, I know. I realize the end is soon. Even with the plague medicine from Hasan Daeg, most of us will not survive. We are simply too weak. That's why I sent word not to come." Mehmet chanced a look at Iegani. "There was no reason to risk your life anymore. Please forgive me. I was trying to save my people, my city." She held out her hands in supplication.

Iegani fell on his knees and kissed the palms of her worn hands. "Mehmet, it is I who should beg for your forgiveness. I should have taken you away years ago."

"You tried," she laughed, "but I always stopped you. It would be the death of me. I would rather meet Zoar face-to-face than touch the clouds. Oh no, I am a land-bound creature. You are the one that wings to the sky." She laughed again. Hastening to her desk, she spread a scroll across the desk.

Iegani bent over to look.

"The writing you gave me is very ancient. I had to scour for many months in our library before I could find a comparison. I was correct about one thing. It had its basis in Lahorian. But I was looking for words. The code is not a message but a formula. These symbols are not words but numbers and chemical compounds."

"But what does it mean?" asked Iegani, quivering with excitement.

"What you see before you is an equation for extreme longevity. Perhaps even immortality. Just think of what this means."

"I am. Zoar must never have this."

"You don't think this equation could really work, do you?"

"I do. I got this code from a tattoo on the back of Princess Maura. Only the rulers have this tattoo, and all Hasan Daeg rulers are extremely long-lived." Iegani thought for a moment. "What are the chemical compounds?"

"Very rare protein compounds found in very evolved plant life. These compounds interact with natural hormones in a donor's body. Mutates them. If we were to take a sample of Queen Abisola's blood, I think we would find her blood altered from that of her countrymen. How do the rulers die?"

"They voluntarily die. They wait until their only child is forty years of age, and if the child is not defective, the ruling monarch abdicates and retires to a special compound in the forest. There, they meditate until they simply will themselves to death."

"If the child is unsuitable for the throne or simply dies, can the parent reproduce again?"

"Yes, but it has only happened once before."

"You have told me that the Hasan Daegian rulers are blue. Do you know of any plant that only they use and not the rest of the population?"

"There are ancient myths that the Hasan Daegian rulers once made a treaty with a plant that was self-aware. Complete rubbish."

"And this plant does not exist?"

"Never did. It is just a story," Iegani lied.

Mehmet rubbed her chin. "But we have seen evidence that the Hasan Daegians are gifted with understanding the uses of plants. Were they like this before they were relocated to Hasan Daeg?"

"We have no memory of it. They were slaves. Maybe under servitude they were not able to act out their natural tendencies and had to compensate."

"What are their origins?"

"They were of different stocks collected from all over the world."

"But the Hasan Daegians are not like the rest of the world. You tell me the females are on average two to three inches taller than the males and almost twice as strong. They are naturals with plants, which seem to respond to them in a positive manner. Plants grow very fast in Hasan Daeg and produce much more food than the same plant, for example, in Anqara. Right?"

"I have observed this to be true."

"And you don't think this is strange?"

"The Dinii females are larger than the males and stronger."

"But you are a bird. These are people!"

Iegani acted insulted.

Mehmet tried another avenue. "Don't you think it is a wondrous thing the Hasan Daegians claim their plants can talk to them?"

Iegani shook his head. "I don't think they mean the plants have an actual language. They mean to say that from intuitive thinking and observation, they understand the biological nature of plants. It is just the same way a Dini can read nature by observing natural phenomena."

"Oh, Iegani, open your eyes!" exclaimed Mehmet, frustrated with her lover. "Your race has had this mystery under its nose for centuries and never investigated. If you didn't know Lahorians were living in your territory for almost two thousand years, what else was going on that you didn't know? Maybe the Dinii should start hunting in the day instead of the night."

"There is truth to your words. We were negligent. As long as there was plenty of game to eat, we did not look too hard."

Mehmet sat in her chair and lit her pipe, smoking quietly until she remarked, "There is so much to do. I must rest awhile now."

Iegani knelt down beside her and held her hand gently.

Mehmet caressed Iegani's leathery cheek. "A plant could provide the compounds listed in this equation. Do you think such a plant exists, dear one? I believe such a plant exists, probably right under your nose, Iegani, Great Divigi from the House of Gitar. Take the scroll and go now."

"Everything is explained in this scroll?"

"Yes, all the compounds, the amounts needed, and how they should be introduced into the body are written on the scroll."

"Is there another copy?"

"No," lied Mehmet, eyeing Iegani suspiciously.

He handed her back the scroll. "You bring this with you. Have your women ready on the roof. They must dress warmly." Iegani turned to go. He turned back again. "How did you keep me from knowing? I scanned your mind periodically."

Mehmet took a long puff on her pipe and smiled. "Why do you think this is called the House of Magi? You're not the only one who can read minds, you know, or hide from scanning." She glanced out the window. "You must go now. It will be dawn soon."

"Be ready on the roof tonight. We will wait for no one. Understand?"

"Understood."

Iegani flew out the window and, with every beat of his wings, regretted leaving Mehmet and the scroll behind. He believed the rescue of her scholars would cause Mehmet to act with prudence and care. Iegani hoped nothing would befall Anqara before tonight's evacuation.

10

Zoar strode out of his tent.

He looked up and caught a glimpse of Iegani streaking across the orange sky. He watched until Iegani was out of sight. Whatever he thought of the huge bird winging through the sky, he kept to himself. Turning to his First General, he asked, "Is everything ready?"

The general snapped to attention. "Yes, Great Aga."

"Then we attack soon."

"Yes, Great Aga!" The general turned and strode off, screaming orders.

Zoar looked at the sky again, and turning, went back inside his tent.

By the day's end, Anqara would be his.

11

Most Anqarians were asleep.

They awoke to the sound of drums and ran to their rooftops or the city's parapet in their bedclothes to see what was happening. Many unashamedly groaned out loud, but mostly there was a deathly quiet amongst the Anqarians when they saw thousands of enemy soldiers in full combat armor standing like statues under the growing day sky.

Rows and rows of soldiers as far as the eye could see. Silent. Watchful. Deadly. An arrow was shot into the air. At its signal, all of the soldiers began beating their shields with their swords and shouting out war cries.

Many Anqarians covered their ears.

The sound was deafening.

Another arrow was shot into the air.

The soldiers in the front moved aside to let a massive platform emerge from the sea of men. Forty grunting slaves, twenty on each of the front axles, pulled the litter. On top of the platform sat Zoar on a golden throne encrusted with precious gems. He wore costly silk robes embroidered with the symbol of the dragon, his personal emblem. On Zoar's head was a wreath of flowers.

Beside him sat Dorak wearing a similar outfit.

Behind Zoar stood his two senior generals. Bright yellow plumes on their helmets danced gaily in the light morning breeze.

Musicians with drums stood on either side and followed the litter onto the plain.

At Zoar's signal, the procession came to a halt, as did all noise.

Zoar slowly stood. His gestures were exaggerated. "People of Anqara," he shouted. "I come in a last effort for peace. You must be tired and hungry. Open your gates to us. My men will bring food to your markets the likes of which you have not seen for years. Open your hearts to me. My healers will attend the sick and wounded. Let us put aside our differences. I am offering peace and prosperity. Join with me to build a great empire. Put your names alongside mine on the roster of glory."

Rude laughter erupted from a parapet. The mayor of Anqara, still dressed in his nightshirt, stood on a box so he could be seen by all. "Go to hell, you unnatural spawn of a demon's womb," the mayor shouted. "We'll not surrender on our knees. We'll die fighting like free men and women."

Zoar furiously threw off his flower wreath. "So be it, you cur. Their deaths," screamed Zoar, waving at the Anqarian people, "are on your head!"

"A pox upon you, Zoar. You would have slaughtered us anyway." The mayor spat in Zoar's direction and left the wall. He ran home to gather his armor and weapons, but he did not get far.

His wife met him at the parapet's steps with his gear. There was no use telling her to go home. He knew she would not leave his side. They smiled at each other, knowing they would be dead before sunset.

Meanwhile, Zoar threw off his robes. Steps appeared at the litter, and his armor and sword were brought to him.

The drums sounded again as his men marched into fighting formation.

Zoar kissed Dorak on the cheek. He turned toward his First Commander. "Place my son on the highest hill. I want him to witness the destruction of Anqara."

"Yes, Great Aga!" answered the commander, saluting.

Zoar turned to a waiting general. "We will begin as soon as Dorak is out of danger."

"Yes, Great Aga!"

Zoar started down the steps. He stopped and turned. "What is a hell?"

The general shrugged. "These people believe in only one god who will send them to a bad place if they do evil."

Zoar smiled. "And so he has." He jumped on his giant warhorse and rode back to his command post, his long black cape with the dragon's emblem flapping in the wind.

12

T he battle raged for many hours.

Yeti and Benzar flew high over the city and landed on a hill to the south of Anqara. The sky was already darkening with the coming storm. They quickly assessed the situation and flew back to Yesemek and Iegani, who were waiting impatiently for them.

"Well?" snapped Iegani.

"Zoar has committed his troops in earnest. He has brought in reinforcements from Bhuttan. He will either take Anqara today or he will die trying," confirmed Yeti.

"He is in full uniform. I think Zoar will lead his men into the city himself," Benzar reported.

"No one ever accused Zoar of being a coward," claimed Yesemek. She looked at Iegani. "Now what?"

Iegani shook his head. "We will have to keep to our plan."

"But, Iegani, they could all be dead by nightfall," asserted Yesemek, Empress Gitar's First Commander and Iegani's wife.

"I realize that, Yesemek, but if we go in now, we expose ourselves to Zoar. If Zoar doesn't pick us out of the sky one by one, the Anqarians will kill us thinking we are Zoar's minions abducting their prize citizens. No, we will have to wait for night and hope the sky is very dark." He muttered to himself, "And pray the Anqarians are very good fighters. They must hold on until dark."

Yesemek nodded in agreement. She turned toward Lieutenant MeNe. "Tell the others to rest quietly for now. We move out as soon as it is dark."

Iegani asked, "Yeti, did you see Toppo?"

"No, she must be hiding in the city until nightfall."

Iegani nodded and wandered off by himself. Finding an empty branch, he perched, going into a trance. Hoping that Mehmet was really telepathic, he sent her word to hold her position and wait. All through the morning, he sent his message until, exhausted, he fell asleep.

13

The fighting was fierce.

Zoar rained the city with treated arrows that exploded on contact.

The citizens found it hard to breathe with all the smoke within their city walls. Every Anqarian man and woman who could fight, carry water buckets, or care for the wounded was doing so.

Many of the children were rounded up and hidden in the tunnels underneath the city. A group of women were digging the rubble out of a previously blown-up tunnel with the hopes of getting the children out of the city. Sweat poured off their bodies. Many tore off their shirts, tying strips of material around their foreheads to catch the sweat and their hands to stop the bleeding. The older children helped by carrying baskets of rock and dirt to the tops of the tunnels.

One of the women stopped digging long enough to form the children into a line, each handing the next a basket filled with debris. None of the children cried, not even the smallest.

The Anqarian military fought bravely. Unexploded arrows were recycled to fit Anqarian bows and shot back at Zoar's men. The Anqarians could hear the enemy scream as the arrows exploded on contact.

Zoar countered with two huge scaffolds dragged by hundreds of his men. One was set against the northeastern wall and the other against the southwestern wall, thus splitting the Anqarian defenses.

The Anqarians tried desperately to set the scaffolds on fire, but Zoar had installed roofs of brass, which deflected anything the Anqarians tried. Once installed, Zoar's men swarmed up the scaffolds and stood in position. The roofs were pulled off by a system of pulleys exposing hundreds of soldiers. They held their shields over their heads to protect them from rocks thrown by the Anqarians.

Moving as a single beast, Zoar's army swarmed over the walls, climbing blindly until they were safely on the parapets. Immediately, they set their shields upright and began hand-to-hand fighting.

The Anqarians, weakened by years of deprivation, were no match for the battle-hardened Bhuttanian soldiers and soon fell back into the city.

There was hard fighting on both sides.

Zoar's generals soon found that any map they possessed of Anqara was false. They were fighting blindly as to their position inside the city. Much to their dismay, each street had to be taken one at a time. No more than two soldiers could march abreast in the tiny, winding streets. They were met with resistance everywhere.

Anything the Anqarians could set on fire, they threw at the enemy. They struck from balconies and windows, using the house rooftops as their main corridors, moving up and down at will.

Zoar, furious that his men were taking such a beating, ordered his soldiers up, only to find the stairwells booby-trapped. Soon the stairs were impassable with the corpses of his men.

Ropes were ordered so his men could scale the walls of houses. Once on the rooftops, the sheer number of Zoar's men overwhelmed the Anqarians. Many roofs collapsed from the weight.

This slowed Zoar even more. Without the roofs to use as passages into the heart of the city, he had to stop and begin digging the streets clear again. To make matters worse, it began to rain and continued raining the rest of the afternoon with the storm intensifying as night approached. He did not even hear the Dinii arrive from the western sky and land on still-standing rooftops.

The Dinii, in groups of twenty, flew in their regular V formation until landing was imminent. The V straightened to a single line, and they hovered in the air until the signal to land was given.

Iegani was the first to land on the rooftop of the House of Magi.

Mehmet ran and embraced him. The rain was pouring so hard she could barely see his face. Behind him, ten Dinii landed, forming two lines on the roof. Iegani shouted at Mehmet, "Are you ready?"

"Everyone was told to come here at dusk. If they are not here, they have died fighting."

The women behind Mehmet looked frightened. They knew of the existence of the Dinii, but only the High Priestess had ever had contact with them. They had never seen them. Many were silently praying.

Everyone could hear the fighting had made its way to the street below.

"Tell your women they will be blindfolded and placed in a harness. They will go through this line." He pointed to the waiting Dinii. "My hawks will place them on the edge of the wall where my flyers will swoop down and snatch them up by the harness. My people are strong enough to attach the harness in flight. This will allow them to fly with their hands free. If your women struggle, my warriors have instructions to drop them. I will not endanger my race any more than I have to. Do you understand?"

Mehmet nodded. She had her women form a single file. She told the first woman, "Close your eyes. Don't open them no matter what. Don't move unless they move you." She kissed the woman on the cheek. "Good luck."

The scholar looked at Mehmet apprehensively. The din of fighting and dying men groaning increased in the streets below. She took a deep breath and walked toward the waiting Dinii. She closed her eyes. The first two Dinii in line straightened her arms perpendicular to her body and pushed her forward. The second two Dinii roughly put her in a harness. The third pair of Dinii buckled the harness. The fourth pair blindfolded her. The last duo checked the harness and placed the woman on the edge of the rooftop. Within seconds, a hawk swooped from the sky, gathered her up, and was gone into the dark night. The remaining women heard their colleague scream as she was lifted up.

Iegani did not give the women time to think. "Move, move!" he yelled, pushing them forward. "Keep it going!"

Mehmet helped by repeating over and over again, "The blindfolds are so that you will not be frightened high up in the air. Don't struggle or they will drop you. Do as they say. It is your only salvation. Hurry! Hurry, my children! We must not fall into Zoar's hands!"

The scholars obeyed. After the first scholar, no one screamed. Any small sounds they made were muffled by the constant beating of the rain and roar of the thunder. During flashes of lightning, they could see Dinii on other rooftops doing the same. They wondered how many were going to get out that night. How many of them were going to die?

14

Zoar heard strange sounds.

He wiped the blood and dirt off his visor to scan the sky. He could see nothing, but he felt something was happening.

General Alexanee came up behind him. "The House of Magi is surrounded."

"Good," said Zoar. "Bring the ladders. What about the rest of the city?"

"The entire city has been surrounded. No one can get in or out without our knowing about it."

"And if they try?"

"They are being cut down on the spot."

Zoar grunted, "Take a platoon of men and search the catacombs. The treasure has to be somewhere near here."

"The catacombs are already being searched, Great Aga."

"Report to me immediately if anything is found."

Soldiers bearing ladders ran past Zoar.

He followed them.

The House of Magi had no windows save those on the top floors and only on one side of the building.

Since the Bhuttanians couldn't penetrate the building, they would have to start at the top and work their way down. The soldiers put the ladders up and waited. No resistance. A special team assembled at the ladders and ascended. Reaching the top of the ladders, they began climbing the walls as if they were rock cliffs. They slowly made their way up until they reached the first set of windows. They jumped inside the building.

Zoar waited until his men poked their heads out and let down ropes. "No one here," they cried.

Other soldiers began a system of pulleys to easily lift men into the building. Zoar wrapped his hands and feet around a stiff rope, holding on as he was lifted up. His men pulled him inside a window. "Search each room. Don't kill any of the women. I want to interrogate them. Leave things undisturbed," he ordered. He began searching each room himself.

His men split into two groups, one group searching downstairs and the other up.

Zoar went up.

15

The women had been evacuated.

Iegani turned toward Mehmet. "You go next."

Mehmet pulled the scroll out of her robes and handed it to Iegani.

Iegani's eyes lit up. He put it carefully in a pouch and handed it to a courier. "Give this personally to Empress Gitar. She will know what to do."

The courier bowed and flew off, heading directly into the storm.

Mehmet backed away from Iegani. "I'm sorry, but I can't go with you, Iegani."

"What do you mean?"

"I'm terrified of flying. If you force me, I will die of heart failure. I cannot go."

"I can't leave you here."

"I don't want to die, but I can't go. Not that way."

Iegani started to panic. He scanned her mind.

Indeed, Mehmet did not bother to hide her thoughts from him. It was true. She was almost beyond reason with fear.

"Mehmet, listen to me," he yelled through the beating rain. "You can't stay here. You're being irrational. Let me blindfold you. You won't be able to see anything."

She shook her head and continued to back away from him. "Zoar will not know who I am. I'll pretend I'm a cleaning servant."

Iegani took several steps toward her. "I can't leave you behind. You're too dangerous alive if you get caught by Zoar."

"I'll be careful."

"Is this your last word?"

"Yes. Go now before we're caught." Mehmet turned to run only to find Benzar standing behind her. She looked up at him with her eyes pleading.

Without any expression, he quickly broke her neck and gently laid her down on the stone roof. He waited for Iegani.

The old owl went over to Mehmet and knelt down. "Oh, Mehmet, Mehmet. Why did you have to be so stubborn? You could have flown with me. I would never have dropped you."

"Great Divigi, Zoar is in the building. We must go!"

"Retreat then. I will follow in a moment."

Benzar flew off.

Iegani patted Mehmet's hand in the rain. He could feel her heat already dissipating. He heard Zoar cursing loudly down below.

Reluctantly, Iegani flew around the House of Magi to Mehmet's window. Entering her room, he pulled her portrait off the wall, causing the door to the secret chamber to open. Iegani was stunned at the material in the secret chamber. How could Mehmet have hidden this room from him?

To make matters worse, Mehmet had not destroyed her valuable papers and correspondence. Had it been Mehmet's intention to betray him and make a deal with Zoar? Iegani didn't have time to ponder this.

He could not take the chance her notes would be deciphered. Like a mad man, he pulled all books and scrolls into the middle of the secret room, forming a huge pile. Seizing an oil lamp, he started to throw it just as Zoar burst into the room, his sword drawn.

Zoar and Iegani stood frozen, staring at each other.

Even in old age, Iegani was fast. He threw the oil lamp into the secret chamber, setting it on fire. Grabbing Mehmet's portrait, he jumped on the windowsill, ready to take flight.

Zoar roared, "What are you?"

Iegani grinned. "Your nightmare!"

Before Zoar could draw another breath, Iegani disappeared into the rain.

16

Despair.

It's what Queen Abisola felt as she stood on her private balcony watching with the rest of O Konya as the Dinii ferried in the last of the survivors of Anqara.

This was the first time many of her people had seen a Dini, let alone scores of them dropping terrified and screaming Anqarians from the sky into nets woven to catch them.

After the initial sweep of Anqara, many Dinii had volunteered to go back to the burning city, saving whom they could. Starved children, bleeding warriors, terrified adults were plucked from the streets and rooftops of the dying city only to be unceremoniously dropped into a refugee camp on the southern side of O Konya, closed off from the rest of the city.

Injured, angry, confused, hungry, and just ready for a good fight, the rescued Anqarians were anything but grateful.

They rioted.

Hasan Daeg's newly trained soldiers had to be called into the camp until the situation could be controlled.

Women from the House of Magi finally calmed down the frightened refugees by helping to ladle out bowls of hot soup. But bedlam broke out again as exhausted Dinii flew into the camp to receive medical treatment, eat, and sleep.

Several hostile Anqarians brandished large wooden spoons at the resting Dinii. An Anqarian soldier got too close to one of the Dinii hawks, who merely picked up the young lad with her taloned foot and threw him back into the antagonistic crowd. If the looks on the Anqarians' faces hadn't been so wild with terror, it would have been amusing.

The women from the House of Magi formed a barrier so the hungry Dinii could rest on constructed perches in peace while eating raw meat.

The Anqarians calmed down when they realized that *they* were not going to be the Dinii's dinner.

From her window, Abisola watched it all. She shook her head and wondered how they were going to assimilate the more combative Anqarians into the passive Hasan Daegian culture.

She received word from Iegani that all of Anqara had fallen. The intellectual center of the world had fought until she could no more. Abisola prayed for those who had gone to their graves bravely. She also prayed for herself. Abisola grieved over the eventual loss of the world as she knew it. She grieved over the loss of her child to the Dinii. She grieved over the hardships that were to come.

Abisola hated the changes that needed to be made if her people were to survive. But most of all, she grieved for herself and her husband. Queen Abisola had been contemplating suicide for several weeks. She even procured the powder needed to put herself and Iasos to death. She would not leave her faithful consort behind. She would give the powder to him in his nightly colla tea, holding him until he fell into sleep and then into death. After dressing him in his ceremonial robes, she would robe herself and, lying beside him, take her own life.

That had all changed. Several nights ago, an apparition appeared to Abisola and begged her not to take her life.

"We know what you are contemplating," declared the phantom. "This you must not do! It is imperative that you live."

"I have no faith left," answered Queen Abisola. "There is no spirit in this body. I am bones and nothing more."

"You must find courage!"

"My mind is in constant turmoil. I am a selfish woman. I want the peace only death can bring."

"This is not about what you nor I want."

Abisola waved her hand in front of her face. "Go away, spirit. Leave me!"

A gaseous form drew together into a vision of a woman gliding across the room as though riding a wave. Abisola, so despondent, did not even become alarmed at the sight.

"Look at me," commanded the spirit. "I am not as I once was." The spirit turned around. "Look in earnest at me. What do you see?"

Abisola observed the spirit carefully. "You are with child!" exclaimed Abisola. "How can a spirit, not of flesh, be with child?"

"I am not a spirit, although my species is evolving. I am still flesh and will give birth. Without your help, my child will never see his own children, nor will your daughter see hers."

The queen searched the specter's face for answers. "What are you?" she asked imploringly. "Who are you?"

The visitor now floated inside an orb made of moving water bouncing slightly off the floor. "Who or what I am is not important. What is important, Your Majesty, is that you take your place in history."

Abisola laughed.

The woman quickly held up a hand, in the middle of which was a closed eye. The eye opened at once and scanned the room.

Startled, Abisola fell back against her chair. She repressed a shiver.

"I will not lie to you," continued the woman. "I cannot. You will die before your time. It will be an ugly death, but only after you have seen all you love destroyed. It is not pretty what I see in the future. But neither is my future. My people will suffer as will yours. I will also die before old age takes me. But I will live until my child can carry on in my place and so must you!"

"My daughter is safe with the Dinii. They can fly from danger, taking my daughter with them."

The woman shook her head sadly. She winced as if in pain and then straightened her shoulders and clapped her hands over her belly. "This conversation is upsetting my offspring. I must hurry." Water inside the phantom's orb began glowing as its sides quivered. "Anqara will fall. Zoar will rip the city apart brick by brick, stone by stone, looking for the treasure of Anqara and the women from the House of Magi."

"I know this," spat out Abisola. "It was I who offered sanctuary. These women will be safe within my city as will be the treasure. Be gone, spirit. I am not afraid."

"Yes, you are, Queen Abisola. You are most afraid that you will not be able to make the sacrifices necessary to win this war. You are afraid of failure, afraid you lack heart. You want to run away and die a coward's death."

Abisola placed her face in her hands and wept. "It is true."

The specter continued. "Princess Maura is not safe. You and she hold the secret Zoar will one day lust after. You must see she completes her quest before he finds her or all will be lost."

"What secret?" implored Abisola. "I don't know what you are talking about." She pounded on the sides of the bubble. Water splashed on the floor. "What is it?"

"The secret is in Iegani's hands and yours," responded the phantom. The orb began to hum loudly and fade. "Seek out Iegani!"

Abisola ran after the bubble. "No, stop, don't go! I need more information. Stop!"

The phantom waved farewell as the bubble disappeared from view.

Falling to the floor, Abisola rolled on her side. Like a baby, she clutched herself and drew her knees up to her chest. Rocking back and forth, she softly sang lullabies to herself and did not notice when Iasos found her on the cold stone floor.

Alarmed, he picked her up, carrying her to his bedchamber. Once he had her in his bed, he called for help. While waiting for a healer to arrive, he called her name.

Abisola did not respond to him but continued rocking and murmuring.

A servant brought warm, wet cloths that Iasos applied to his queen's forehead and arms. He wiped the perspiration from her torso.

Iasos drew himself up, hearing the commotion of the guards searching for a possible intruder. Iasos suspected whatever had transpired with the queen was in Abisola's mind and not in the palace.

A healer, still dressed in her nightclothes, rushed into the bedchamber. The healer bowed and hurried over to Abisola.

Iasos related how he had found the queen and stood back.

The royal healer threw back the covers with the help of Lady Sari, the queen's old nurse and companion, and stripped off the queen's clothes.

She searched for any kind of marks, even examining under the nails of her hands and feet. She felt for the pulse and examined the eyes and mouth. The healer smelled the queen's breath and sex. After an exhausting examination, she turned to Iasos. "I am sorry, my lord, but I cannot help our queen. She has had a profound shock to her mind. There is nothing wrong with her body."

"What do you mean?"

The healer wearily put away her instruments. "I mean, sire, she is not right in her mind. I can give her sedatives to calm her and herbs to bring her out of the stupor," the healer paused, "but look at her. The queen has regressed to an infantile state. She will come out of it only when she has healed here," said the healer, pointing to her head, "and here," pointing to her heart. "There is nothing more anyone can do." She bowed to Iasos and departed with Sari, giving her instructions about the medicine she was leaving.

"Abisola," Iasos gently whispered. "What trouble have you gotten yourself into? You are so like a child. You want everything to be perfect, to be lovely. You live for beauty and when you see beauty will not last, you want to hide. As if that will make evil go away." Iasos held her hand. "When will you learn I love you for you. You are one of the bravest and truest persons I have ever met. Wherever you have gone, come back to me. I need you."

Iasos stroked her hair. Finding a gray hair, he plucked it out. "I don't think you can stand a gray hair and all this mess too," he teased. He climbed into bed with his queen and held Abisola until he finally fell asleep with exhaustion.

17

Queen Abisola did not rise.

She would not communicate with Iasos nor take the morsels offered by his hand. She just rocked, singing softly.

Iasos would not leave her side, falling asleep in a chair with his arms flung over the bed only to awaken in the morning and finding Abisola not there. In panic, he rushed to her chambers and found her dressed, eating breakfast.

"Good morning, darling," she purred. "We have a good many things to do. Will you help me?" Abisola asked, reaching out to him.

Iasos clasped her hand and sat beside her. "Are you well now?" he asked.

Abisola stroked his cheek gently. "I felt as though I was straddling a high wall, and no matter which side I fell upon, there was doom for all. I will never be well again, dearest, but you and I must act as though I am. I must do things now I don't think you will understand, but we need to move forward if our people are to be preserved. You must help me. Give me strength, I beg of you."

"I will always love you," declared Iasos. "I will help you wherever I can, I promise."

"You are such a comfort to me. You will never know how much." She looked away. "I start in motion a way of life that will not be undone."

"I trust you, Abisola," said Iasos, looking at her with an understanding she had not realized he possessed. "Whatever you think best, I will stand beside you and support you."

Abisola wept. "You are so good to me!"

"You are my queen and wife. I would die for you."

She hugged him closely and kissed his cheek, neck, and then his lips. "I want you to know no matter what happens, I will never leave you behind." She looked deep into Iasos's eyes. "Do you understand?"

Iasos did not look away. "I understand. My destiny is yours. Where you go, I will follow."

More tears gathered in Abisola's eyes. "Who would have thought of such devotion from one so young."

Iasos wiped her tears away. "Will you ever stop thinking of me as a mere boy?"

Abisola shook her head and laughed, throwing her arms around her husband. "To work now. Enough of this maudlin talk. I will assemble my advisors today. We must start as soon as possible."

"Finish your breakfast first," laughed Iasos. "Our people cannot have a half-starved crone sitting upon the throne."

The queen and her consort gazed at each other with tenderness.

Abisola smiled, pinching his cheek. "You are such a hen," she teased, stuffing her mouth full with a muffin.

Iasos returned his wife's smile, wondering if this happy breakfast might be their last.

18

Queen Abisola waited.

She had earlier sent word to all her ministers, governors, and nobles that there was to be a royal audience.

It had taken many weeks for all of them to arrive from various parts of the country. With great fanfare, they entered into the audience hall wearing billowing gowns, priceless adornments of precious gems, and rare flowers in their hair while holding large fans painted with their crests and stations.

They chatted politely with each other, each trying to glean information from the other since this was no ordinary summit. A royal decree had summoned them, stating they were to bring only five attendants with them and not their regular retinue. They were told to travel only on the north road and not announce their entrance into O Konya. Displaying their banners and flags was forbidden. Also, the southern parts of the city were denied to them.

O Konya, usually bright and cheerful, was quiet with its citizens rushing home by nightfall. The streets were dark and silent save for strange cries heard from the south side.

Many were sure the queen was going to announce an outbreak of the plague, but others had heard rumors of ghostly birds and war outside the wall of mist. All thoughts were put aside when trumpets blew, announcing the arrival of the queen.

Queen Abisola entered with Consort Iasos and Royal Consul Rubank. Wearing the royal colors of blue and gold, Abisola was resplendent as she proceeded to the marble dais to the accompaniment of drums and horns. Behind her large throne was a massive, stained glass window depicting the first Hasan Daegian queen, Rosalind. Shafts of light through the colored window fell on Abisola, giving her an ethereal quality. As she took her seat, Abisola gave Rubank the signal.

He nodded, and soldiers marched into the audience room. Never had soldiers entered the royal audience room in six hundred years. Once in position along the walls, the soldiers stood at attention, holding out their massive lances. Those soldiers near entrances shut and bolted the doors.

"What is this? How dare you! Open at once!" cried the court.

Queen Abisola sat upon her two-thousand-year-old throne as she waved her fan of royal authority with quiet dignity.

One by one, the crowd quieted down until falling silent and looking expectantly up at their sovereign.

"That is the last time you will be allowed to act with such impudence," announced the queen with resolve, her voice clear and strong.

The nobles and governors looked about at each other in confusion and glancing at the soldiers, determined the queen was going to enforce her wishes with violence if needed. It seemed the days of noisy protests and casual interaction with their Abisola were over. New rules were being put into play.

"Yesterday, we lived free from fear of want or tyranny. We knew such evil existed far away from us, but we were safe behind our veil of mist. But not now. Today, the world is a different place. The fear of war that we have not faced in six hundred years is now upon us and a wall of hypnotic fog is not going to save us. We must save ourselves. The unthinkable has happened. Anqara has fallen to Aga Zoar!"

The royal audience anxiously murmured to each other.

When the queen waved her fan, they quickly fell silent again, but an occasional sob could be heard. Many began sorrowfully wiping their eyes. While most of the court had never left Hasan Daeg, everyone knew that Anqara was the largest and grandest city on Kaseri. This was bad news. Very bad indeed.

"It is only a matter of time until the conqueror of Anqara turns his eyes west to us. Our current defenses will not keep this aga and his warriors out of Hasan Daeg. As he found a way to conquer Anqara, Zoar will find a way into Hasan Daeg, either through the fog or through the secret corridor in Siva. All it will take for our world to be destroyed is one rogue Sivan merchant with a loose tongue and a lust for gold.

"We must be ready. We must prepare. We must change and embrace this change or perish. And we have already begun.

"You all were ordered to enter the city by the north gate, because of sickness in the south side of the city. There is sickness on the south side of O Konya, but not as you were informed. On the south side of the city are refugee camps filled with survivors of Anqara. We endeavored to save as many of them as we could with the hope that they would share their knowledge and, in return for a new home, fight when the time came. We are currently caring for their needs while negotiating a treaty through the House of Magi."

The crowd gasped. Saving the women from the House of Magi and bringing them to Hasan Daeg was impressive. Many, who questioned Hasan Daeg's isolationist policy, were thrilled at having contact with outsiders. The hearts of others overflowed with loathing at the thought of foreigners tainting their "pure" society.

"If strangers are allowed in Hasan Daeg to fight, who else is expected to serve in this capacity?" challenged a high-ranking noble who forgot protocol in the shock of the news.

The nobles, afraid their pampered lives would be threatened, glanced anxiously at each other.

Stunned, the governors stood, wondering how they could implement changes in the general population.

Here was the one question to disrupt Hasan Daegian society more than anything else, but Queen Abisola could not avoid it and she must make her people accept it now.

"We have allies who must be bound tightly to us, but in the end, all of us, even our men, must learn to fight until this dreadful ordeal is over."

Pandemonium broke out. Everyone balked. Some had to sit down even in the royal presence.

"Great Mother," addressed one senior minister, pointing to the soldiers in the audience room. "You have increased the army five-fold and are now using it to support your policies, but the inclusion of males in our military will cause a great moral collapse. They simply will cause too much confusion."

Another one added, "They are not strong enough to handle our bows."

"Then make smaller ones they can use," rebutted Abisola patiently. "Just as long as they can kill something."

"They have no endurance. Our men cannot handle long marches."

"I don't think they will have to travel to meet the enemy. I believe the enemy will come to us." Abisola raised an eyebrow and scanned the waiting faces below her. She waved the guards into view.

In full body armor, they stood menacingly between the crowd and the doors. They lowered their lances.

"I will tell you what is to happen, and you must accept," demanded Abisola. "You will recognize my royal authority or die."

Iasos was shocked at this implied violence, but showed no change in his expression. He stood unflinching near Abisola in her carved throne on the dais.

There were gasps from the ministers and governors. The nobles glowered.

Abisola leaned forward. "I tell you this once. I am trying to save our people from being wiped off the face of this planet. You stand before me, whining like curs when they don't get their regular bones to gnaw on. You have become soft. Well, Zoar is not soft and soon he will know where we are. Do you think he will come in expensive clothes with fancy manners and flowers in his hair?

"No, he will come with thousands of battle-hardened soldiers swinging weapons we have never seen, much less know how to use. They will break through our defensive wall, and then they will slaughter every living being they can find. Those who are young will be sold as slaves or worse.

"If you love your sons at all, teach them to fight. Dying in battle will be much better than being raped and beaten to death. Maybe, just maybe, we can salvage something of our culture when the time comes, but allow someone else to convince you." Abisola motioned to her consul, who went to a side door and admitted a robed figure.

The Hasan Daegians gasped as the robed person bent over to enter through the tall doorway and then stood in front of Queen Abisola, a full seven feet in height.

"Behold, a Dini!" cried Abisola.

The figure threw off his robe and stood before the crowd in all his feathered glory. To illustrate what he was, he stretched out his ponderous wings and hovered just slightly off the floor. With graceful movements, he retracted his wings and sat on a chair placed on the same level as the queen's on the dais.

The crowd murmured angrily at this breach of protocol.

Queen Abisola held up her hand. "May I introduce Prince Iegani—Great Divigi and uncle to Empress Gitar, fourth in line to the throne of Hasan Daeg, first husband to Yesemek, First Commander to Empress Gitar. Ladies. Nobles. This is your true prince and ruler."

"What lie is this?" cried out one noblewoman.

The crowd hissed and booed, shaking their fists. "Who is this Empress Gitar?"

Queen Abisola stood angrily. "Quiet! Prince Iegani is our guest and will be treated with all Hasan Daegian hospitality!"

The angry crowd fell silent.

The guards, relieved, lowered their lances a tiny fraction.

"Prince Iegani, please speak to my people."

Iegani stood. Facing the crowd, he scanned their minds. He felt hate and great fear, and quickly decided how to appeal to them. "I know my presence must shock you, but now is the time for truth, not myths or rumors. As you must realize now, I am of the Dinii, the winged creatures who brought you here to safety two thousand years ago just as in your creation myths. However, we are not messengers of your goddess, Mekonia. We are creatures like yourselves.

"We are made of blood and bones. Underneath this," he pointed to his feathers, "we have skin like you. And like you now, we have a common enemy—the Great Aga, Zoar. He is coming this way and will be here before your youngest children grow up. The choice you need to make today is whether you want your children to live as free citizens or to live as slaves."

"Zoar won't be able to penetrate the mist!" one woman called out.

"Why not?" Iegani countered. "I penetrate the mist all the time. I simply fly over it. What if Zoar finds a way to fly or he spreads a pollutant in the air and the plants die? The plants could get a fungus or there could be a drought. Oh, a clever man can think of many ways to beat the mist if he is expecting it. Let me assure you, Zoar is a very clever man, and he does know about the mist. He doesn't know yet what is beyond the mist."

"What would he want with us? We are a simple people."

Iegani paused, clenching his teeth, before continuing. "Resources. As simple as that. Hasan Daeg is a breadbasket for one thing. The land is so fertile here that food easily could be produced to feed a population of twelve million. There are, of course, the virgin timberlands in the northern mountains and untapped minerals, such as copper, just waiting for someone to mine them. Shall I go on?

"Hasan Daeg is a country rich in natural resources. Fertile land, plenty of rain, timber, minerals, and a pacifist population thrown in for good measure. You can rest assured that if Zoar knew what is behind the wall of mist, he would sacrifice thousands of his men just to conquer a little part of Hasan Daeg. He would drool at the thought of it."

"Why do you care?" someone cried out.

"Because Hasan Daeg is my country, too. You are here under special treaty signed by your first ruler, Queen Rosalind." He turned and pointed to the figure portrayed in the window. "In Article Seven of the treaty, any population living in Hasan Daeg will declare war on any enemy of their benefactors, the Dinii."

The nobles shook their fists. The royal governors gathered in a group and argued among themselves. Most of the ministers kept their thoughts to themselves.

Iegani noticed it was the ministers who studied him with purpose.

The great gong sounded. The crowd grew quiet.

Queen Abisola stood beside Iegani. "I have seen this treaty. It is legitimate. We are allowed to live in Hasan Daeg in a symbiotic relationship with the Dinii as long as we cooperate within the guidelines of this treaty."

One noblewoman strode toward the dais. "Let's kill the Dini!" she cried.

A guard jumped in her way and knocked her down, placing the point of the lance at her throat.

Queen Abisola's heartbeat quickened but her expression did not change from one of stoic reserve. "I will let Prince Iegani address this issue."

Prince Iegani bowed to Queen Abisola. He jumped to where the noblewoman had been knocked down, pushing the guard out of the way. He picked the woman up and carried her back to the dais, holding her up by the throat. Spreading his magnificent wings, Iegani rose to the top of the ceiling and dropped the woman to the floor. "Leave her be," he ordered, fluttering down and resting his taloned feet upon the moaning woman.

Others stood in awe.

Iegani held out his hands and, with each finger, released a razor-sharp talon. "Take a good look at these," he boasted, displaying his hands to the assemblage. "Even with your current weaponry, there is neither shield nor armor that will protect you against these. Our females are ten times stronger than your most powerful female. We do not need fire. The cold and wet do not bother us. We rarely get sick. We can out run you, out jump you, out hunt you, out distance you, out endure you. Oh, did I mention that we can fly?" Iegani smiled for effect.

Stepping off the woman, he motioned for the guards to gather her. "She has only a couple of broken bones because I was just toying with her. What do you think I could do if I were angry?" Iegani placed a talon to his pursed lip. "I wager," he said, turning around sharply, "I could kill most of you in this room before you could kill me. No. I wager I could kill all of you before you could kill me." He sat down.

The room went cold with silence.

Abisola gave him a warning glance. He was going too far. She smelled the stink of fear in the room. "Let me remind you that we have lived with the Dinii for two thousand years without serious repercussions. In fact, our association, though a shock to many of you, has been extremely beneficial to our social and political development."

She looked appraisingly at Iegani. "Yes, the Dinii are tremendous in both strength and height, but until this day, they have never shown unwarranted aggression toward us. Most of you had never seen one and thought they were mythical."

Iegani returned Abisola's gaze. He knew when he was being reprimanded. He bowed his head slightly in acknowledgment.

One of the ministers approached the dais. "Great Mother, may I speak?"

Abisola nodded.

The minister stood on the bottom step of the dais and faced the crowd. "I am Jon, minister to Governor Petenptope in the northern state of Kinton. In our region, we have heard many stories of Dinii sightings for generations from our people." She glanced back at Prince Iegani. "Until now, I believed the stories were a product of an overactive imagination or too much ale. I also would like to state that Kinton receives more intruders than any other region. For the past five years, spies and deserters have encroached on our territory. As consistent with current policy, we have led them back out with plenty of food and water, but I want everyone here to understand that these newcomers are not like the wanderers and travelers of old. These new men are cruel and their nature is something unfamiliar to us."

Jon pointed back to Iegani. "I'm glad the Dinii are here. I'm glad they are fierce. I'm glad they are on our side. Let us keep the treaty. Our interests are compatible." Jon thanked the queen and stepped down.

Another minister stepped forward. "If we were to fight Zoar, how would this be accomplished?"

Iegani liked these ministers and was pleased with the intelligent questions rather than the high emotions running among the nobles. He answered, "Hasan Daeg has a military that is little more than an honor guard. You have not fought a war in six hundred years. However, your population density is high. You have over three million people. Your entire population will be turned into a fighting force.

"The Dinii have over ten thousand warriors. We have started a new breeding program. We hope to have twice that many in ten years.

"We will combine our forces and make a stand in Hasan Daeg at the border. We know the terrain. Zoar does not, and he is currently occupied tearing Anqara apart, which gives us time."

The queen, her stiff robes rustling, reiterated, "You see the importance of what we are trying to accomplish. The war is no more outside our country. It is here. It affects us now. No matter what doubts you harbor, this treaty is going to be honored. You will swear your allegiance to me now or you will die. The choice is yours." Abisola returned to her throne and leaned back. Sweat beaded on her upper lip.

Any of the nobles could have rushed the throne and killed her before the guards could intercede. She was a tempting target, except for Iegani beside her.

Iasos sensed danger also, but dared not change his position. Before coming into the audience room, he had inserted a dagger into his boot. He prayed that he would be quick enough to use it if needed.

The governors and ministers seemed resigned. They were known to be more progressive and favor change if it was for the good.

Iasos studied the faces of the nobles. There he registered anger, surprise, and shock. The nobles would resist, for they were the most conservative element of the population.

No one moved. No one spoke.

Finally, there was a cough and a rustle of stiff, rich fabric.

The audience moved aside for Riza, the most respected of all the queen's nobles as she hobbled forward leaning upon her staff. "I was a little girl when you had been queen for many years. We have had peace and prosperity all this time. If you say there is danger, then I believe you. You have never made strong demands before."

Riza struggled to kneel when several of the ministers helped her. "Therefore, I swear allegiance to you, Great Mother, and will do my utmost to save my queen and country, even at the sacrifice of my life or my children's lives." She bowed her head.

Scribes entered the room and took their places before Queen Abisola.

The ministers and governors kneeled one by one, pledging allegiance to Abisola.

The nobles were the last to swear their oaths, many scowling as they knelt.

After the oaths of fealty were given, Queen Abisola raised the royal fan. "Let this be entered into law. From this day forth, Hasan Daeg males shall have all the rights, privileges, and duties as Hasan Daeg females until the Queen's pleasure is withdrawn."

The great gong sounded.

"From this day forth, all persons from the ages of fourteen to fifty shall be conscripted into the military until the Queen's pleasure is withdrawn."

The gong sounded.

"From this day forth, taxes shall be raised one-eighth until the Queen's pleasure is withdrawn."

The gong sounded.

"From this day forth, the treaty with the Dinii shall be recognized and honored by the current population until the Queen's pleasure is withdrawn."

The gong sounded.

"This is law until the pleasure of the Queen is withdrawn."

At Queen Abisola's command, the guards raised their lances and retreated from the room. Abisola felt victorious. She felt Iasos place his hand on her shoulder for just a brief second. It comforted her. She rose and retreated from the room. Court was dismissed.

Iegani left for the City of the Peaks immediately. There was no grand farewell. He flew out a window as the court gasped in awe and fear.

19

Worry followed Queen Abisola.

It finally caught up with her on her private balcony. She gazed upon the twinkling lights of O Konya and heard Iasos enter her room. She looked at him questioningly as he joined her.

"It is really a beautiful place, isn't it?" he whispered as he gazed upon the city. He placed his hands on the railing and breathed deeply. "I joined the military today."

"You what!" exclaimed Abisola.

"Yes, this afternoon. I walked down to the headquarters and joined up. Of course, it took a bit of doing. They didn't believe I was serious at first, but I finally convinced them. It will be announced tomorrow."

"You're mad," scolded Abisola angrily. "Your place is with me, not in some cold barracks."

"No, my love. You are wrong." Iasos turned toward her. "My place is being an example. How can we expect others to do what we won't sacrifice ourselves?"

"Isn't our daughter a sacrifice enough?"

"What have we really sacrificed there, Abisola? That she is safe for the time being. That she is being trained to fight her enemy in order to save her life. Could we have done that for her?" Iasos shook his head. "We offer her nothing at the moment. Surely not safety. No, the Dinii are a blessing." He looked toward the heavens. "Maura is better off where she is. You know that."

Abisola stood beside her husband and kissed him. "How would I fare without you?" she cooed, smiling.

"Very badly, I expect."

"So do I."

Iasos returned her smile. "What now?"

"We need to contact that old buzzard, Iegani."

"He's an owl-man."

Abisola rolled her eyes. "You know what I mean."

Iasos laughed. "Should queens roll their eyes like school girls?"

"Only if they feel like it."

"Just tell the wind what you want. Iegani will come soon enough."

"Really?"

"Haven't you noticed, dearest? Ever since our contact with the Dinii, we have been under constant surveillance. Just tell the little songbirds what you want. Any bird will do."

Abisola swirled around and studied the walls of the palace. Nooks and crannies were filled with birds of all kinds. She was surprised and noted that security would have to improve. Abisola called out, "I want to speak to Iegani!"

A swirl of sparrows, twittering nervously, flew into the night sky in all different directions.

"Some will report to Gitar, no doubt," complained Abisola.

"No doubt," replied Iasos, pulling Abisola toward her chamber. "But the night is young, and Iegani might not come tonight, which leaves us time for other pursuits."

"That's right. I can't send a soldier off without a kiss."

"I was thinking of something more."

"Aren't you being bold for a male?"

"Well, now that I have equal rights with females, I might as well take advantage of them," Iasos crowed, pulling Abisola down on the bed.

Abisola rolled on top of him. "Almost equal, but not quite," she quipped, nipping his nose.

"It will do for now," teased Iasos as he blew out the lamp.

20

Maura was an enigma to her people.

She would swoop down upon the back of a great hawk, followed by falcon guards, who would drop her off on the roof of the palace.

At first, this unsettled the people, especially when the great Bird People tarried in the city—walking upright, speaking to frightened citizens in their mother tongue, drinking ale in taverns, and singing bawdy songs with drunken Sivan merchants.

The Sivans seemed to know the Bird People well and did not find the female hawks strange with their painted feathers, tattooed faces, or hands with retractable talons. They deferred to the Dinii.

Children also wanted to be with the Bird People. They loved to creep up behind a hawk, pluck a feather, and then run off screaming with delight. The purloined feathers were placed in the hair or worn around the neck in the form of a necklace. The children rebuffed fathers loudly if they tried to cut out feathers from tangled hair or untie a Dinii feather necklace in order to wash a dirty face and neck.

Scores of hawks and falcons of all colors and sizes entered the city frequently, flying in a V formation and landing right on the palace grounds. They would stay for months and work with the high-ranking officers of Her Majesty's army. They inspected storehouses, weapons, and fortifications. Then, they would strap nervous Hasan Daegian officers to their bodies and fly out into the countryside to study each small village's preparation for the inevitable conflict. They always would exhort in their high-pitched voices, "Not good enough, not good enough," to the dismay and frustration of the ministers and governors.

Only when the combat-hardened mercenaries, recruited by the

Sivans, trained the grumbling Hasan Daegians in the art of swordplay, ax throwing, and hand-to-hand fighting with a mace did the Dinii relax a little.

In the early days, the mercenaries taunted the observing Dinii to spar with them in front of their pupils.

A hawk would good-naturedly lumber over to some arrogant, over-muscled soldier of fortune and wait to be rushed. Hovering just out of reach from her opponent, the challenged hawk would jab at him with her taloned feet. Otherwise, she liked to catch his face and hold him at arm's length while he struggled to break free.

Yesemek issued a decree putting an end to the fighting when it was discovered the mercenaries nearly suffocated with each encounter.

The real reason the challenges stopped was that the mercenaries realized the hawk soldiers, especially the females, were too powerful and quick.

A new game of rivalry ensued soon after. Several mercenaries would attack a lone hawk in the streets, usually at night. The fight concluded quickly with one of the mercenaries being thrown into a wall or another landing on his head in a water tank. The attacked hawk or falcon would quietly gather a coin from the pocket of each of her attackers, salute, and saunter off to the nearest tavern to drink ale that the Dinii were becoming increasingly fond of.

The wounded mercenaries collected themselves and, with their heads aching, tried to figure out what they were doing wrong. As the years went by, the attacks became more elaborate and ingenious. Once in a while, they would successfully overtake a Dini and, as a symbol of their achievement, pluck out some tail feathers and proudly display them on their shields. It was very prestigious, but rare.

As Maura grew older, the presence of the hawks and falcons was more accepted in the city. She would join them in the streets to walk along the wide boulevards, look at fresh fruit in the bazaar, and sip colla water.

Behind her followed Queen Abisola's personal bodyguards, aware that their presence was superfluous. They could not hide their boredom. There was no fool born who would try to harm Princess Maura with a seven-foot birdwoman holding her hand.

Sometimes, she rode on the shoulders of the Dinii, giggling while taking care not to injure their wings as she leaned over to yank people's hair or pull their hats over their eyes. Of course, the hawks would get the blame as Maura innocently blinked her wide eyes and cried loudly if anyone persisted in scolding her.

Hasan Daegians took great pride in their appearance and were sorely vexed if hair or adornments were out of their proper place, but the sight of their future queen bawling in the street, even if she deserved reprimand, was too much for them.

Princess Maura and her hawks were soon given wide berth, much to her dismay. She did so like causing a commotion.

Every winter and spring, Maura came home to the safety and luxury of her parents' palace. And every year, she would have to be reintroduced to court etiquette.

While Dinii chicks were encouraged to be inventive and daring in their play, Hasan Daegian children were to be quiet and unassuming when adults were present, and even well behaved when they weren't.

"Don't wipe your nose on the tablecloth, don't pull ladies' dresses over their backsides, don't hide food in your pockets, don't spit at other nobles' children, don't burst into your mother's receiving room when she's conducting a private audience only to show her the morning's finds of bugs, don't laugh out loud if you think someone is funny looking, don't wear your father's undergarments on your head, don't, don't, don't!"

When her tutors and nannies admonished her, Princess Maura would look genuinely overcome with shame and hug them, saying with complete sincerity that she would never do it again. They relented by stroking her hair and giving her a treat. They couldn't help but spoil her.

At the City of the Peaks, life was different. Princess Maura was taught the knowledge of the outdoors. She grew astute in understanding the sights and smells of nature and their meaning. By the age of five, she could track any animal. By the age of eight, she could camouflage her body to match any surrounding. She was taught how to wrestle, throw daggers with deadly accuracy, and eat bloody meat without flinching. Even with the Dinii's exceptional sight, they sometimes had a hard time discerning her in a grain field or from a limb of a tree.

Maura grew accustomed to being outside in any kind of weather as were the Dinii. They spent most of their lives outdoors, so most of the buildings in the City of the Peaks were of a semi-permanent nature.

As a very young child, she wore very little until the Dinii found the sight of her naked, pale, indigo body without the covering of feathers almost obscene. Several of the craftsmen made a little leather shift and a plumed hat for her, taking feathers from their own bodies. They periodically replaced her clothes as she outgrew them.

When she came home to O Konya, her little brown shift and feathered hat were stored away. She was dressed in the finest robes, her hair washed with scented soap and braided with flowers, the most costly of oils rubbed into her skin, and her feet encased in the softest of shoes.

Maura was taught manners, geography, mathematics, history, herbal medicine, dancing, and military strategy. Above all, she was taught to rule.

Queen Abisola was away for much of the year, touring the country and encouraging her people during these stressful times, but she always made sure she was home for her daughter's visits.

Although Abisola was not a demonstrative parent, Maura sensed her mother's fierce pride in her. She realized her mother expected great things of her and was careful not to disappoint her. What these great things were, she did not yet know, but she guessed it had something to do with the uneasy pact between the Dinii and her people. Of course, being a child, she never thought about it long.

When Princess Maura wanted hugs and kisses, it was to her father, Iasos, she ran. He would always be there for her when she received scratches and bruises. He even defended her the time she caused a playmate to cry by practicing the Dinii death grip on him.

Iasos always stroked her dark bluish hair and gave her a big wet kiss. His eyes seemed moist most of the time, and there were evenings when he looked at her and could not speak. He was never harsh with her. Her father was a constant factor in her life with love, kindness, and understanding.

Maura also loved the Dinii and wondered at the confusion her people seemed to have when confronting them. She loved the rough way the Dinii smelled of leaves, trees, mountain air, and musk. She loved the softness of their feathers. When she wanted to sleep, she would just curl up against any one of them. Many Dinii mothers would find the sleeping princess nesting with their chicks. They would always let her remain. Everyone in the City of the Peaks, down to the lowliest servant, knew Princess Maura and protected her, fed her, and generally kept an eye on her, hoping to curb her mischievous ways.

The princess loved Empress Gitar, regarding the empress as her second mother. She loved Gitar's children whom she thought of as her siblings . . . especially Chaun Maaun, Empress Gitar's only male chick.

From the very beginning of Princess Maura's placement in the royal nest, Chaun Maaun seemed fascinated with the featherless chick who was blue and cried out loud. He would always scoot next to her, placing his little undeveloped wing over her arm. Chaun Maaun liked sharing the royal nipple with Princess Maura until she was given her own Hasan Daegian wet nurse. He did not understand why the wet nurse would shoo him away when he tried to nurse from her too. Chaun Maaun wanted to drink from the big, soft breasts with the pink nipples after smelling the milk on Princess Maura. He would become irritable, flapping his wings and hissing whenever the nurse approached Maura, but he never turned from the princess. He tried to share his regurgitated food with her always until Empress Gitar explained that Hasan Daegians could not properly absorb the already digested meat. They were used to plant matter, not meat.

Princess Maura, in turn, doted on Chaun Maaun. She would cry if separated from him for too long. She loved to play with his feathers as she outgrew her allergies. The smell of them calmed her so much that finally Queen Abisola was forced to ask Empress Gitar to collect Chaun Maaun's downy feathers so a quilt could be made for the princess when she was staying in the royal palace.

As they grew older, they became close companions, growing uneasy when apart from each other for very long. The years went by comfortably for Princess Maura as she grew into a strong-willed, powerfully built young woman.

When Maura received word that Empress Gitar and Chaun Maaun would visit O Konya for the princess's eighteenth birthday, she was overcome with excitement and joy. Running into her mother's morning room, she stopped short, gathered herself, and then continued gracefully to her mother's breakfast table on the veranda.

Queen Abisola sat regally at a handsome table carved with flowers and mythical beasts. Her robes were a shimmering blue, edged with beaten silver that formed a simple geometric design. Her hair was braided with rare flowers, as Hasan Daegian custom dictated, and was piled lustrously on her head.

Maura suddenly realized that her mother was no longer beautiful by Hasan Daegian standards. She had gray in her hair and her face was starting to line, but the princess could not take her eyes off her mother.

Queen Abisola seemed to radiate a beauty beyond the merely physical. Sitting there quietly in the morning light, Queen Abisola shined with an otherworldly glow, and power emanated from the Queen's skin.

WALL OF DOOM

Princess Maura thought to herself, *This is how I shall always remember my mother—dressed in beautiful robes, sitting on the balcony, overlooking her kingdom. Forever vigilant. Forever resolute.* Maura felt panic. How could she rule after a great queen like her mother? She feared she would never measure up.

"Maura, why are you staring at me?" inquired Abisola, gingerly picking up her colla cup.

"I'm sorry, Mother. I think you look so beautiful this morning."

Queen Abisola smiled warmly at her daughter. "That's very nice for you to say. I don't feel very beautiful." She sighed.

"Maybe we'll find the Mother Bogazkoy this year."

"Perhaps we shall. That would be a great blessing for us both," Queen Abisola said. "Our Bogazkoy is dying and provides little support to me now or I to it, I'm afraid. One day we shall talk about the Bogazkoy and its meaning to the rulers of Hasan Daeg. You did not run in only to say good morning to your mother. What news have you?"

Maura grinned. She handed her mother a letter, which her mother scanned quickly.

"So, the Dinii are learning to write."

"On no, Mother. Queen Gitar has hired a scribe through the Sivans to write all her correspondence."

"Of course, Gitar would never lower herself to become literate."

Maura paled at her mother's harsh words. "Mother, you know how they feel about written symbols. They are not stupid."

"How well I know. They are a very intelligent race." Abisola beckoned her daughter into a chair. "I'm sorry if I sound rude. In a few months you will go back to them, and the palace will seem empty for your father and me." The Queen shook her head. "I know I must sound bitter, but how would Empress Gitar feel if Chaun Maaun spent half his life growing up away from her in a strange land?"

Maura plopped her elbows on the table. "That's what I've come to tell you. Chaun Maaun and Empress Gitar are coming for the celebrations. Isn't that wonderful!"

Queen Abisola winked conspiratorially at Sari, who had just brought them fresh colla tea and fruit.

Sari stood behind her mistress, not wanting to miss any gossip.

"I know, dear. I too have a letter from Empress Gitar." She held up a beautifully written scroll detailing the date and time of the Dinii's arrival. "They will arrive tomorrow."

"Not much time for preparation," snorted Sari.

Maura replied, "They don't need much."

"If the palace were a forest, that is. We'll have to equip all the bedrooms with tree limbs and hunt down fresh game, beating the meat until it's nice and bloody, just the disgusting way they like it."

"That's enough, Sari," admonished Abisola. "We will be able to accommodate any special needs of the Dinii. Don't you worry, my dear," she said to Maura. "We will make them feel right at home." Abisola folded her napkin. "After all, they have taken such good care of Maura all these years."

As she rose, Maura bowed in respect.

"No, no, finish your breakfast. I need to start my day. I will see you later at dinner."

"Is my father coming home?"

Abisola's face softened at the mention of her husband. "Yes, with all haste. He sent word last night. Now I must go. I will see you tonight."

Princess Maura bounced in a chair, stuffing a pastry in her mouth. Cream smeared on the corner of her lips.

Sari glared at her.

"I don't care if you disapprove," argued Maura with her mouth full. "I tire of doing everything correctly and according to tradition. Blast tradition!"

"That's fine, little one, for now, but never let your mother see you conducting yourself so. She's spent the last seventeen years battling problems this country never anticipated, and it would not do her heart good knowing she was leaving her people in the hands of a willful girl who stuffs food into her mouth and slurps like a common Sivan merchant. You lack discipline!"

"I lack nothing, you old busybody," spat Maura, crumbs falling out of her mouth.

Lady Sari walked away in disgust.

Maura swallowed and wiped off her mouth. With great care, she sipped her tea and then gathered the crumbs off the table, putting them in a nice little pile on her plate. Peeling one of the green fruits offered by a servant, she graciously gave the man leave to go. Sitting very straight in her chair, she would occasionally wave to a passerby who would wave back with gusto. Although she was very happy about her upcoming birthday, Sari's words rang in her ears. Maura's growing fear that she was not made of the stuff of queens kept encroaching upon her happy thoughts.

I will do better, she thought. *I will make Mother and Father very proud of me. I will not embarrass them in front of dignitaries who already think I am a half-wild Dini. I will be the perfect Hasan Daegian princess.*

She smiled. The next week was going to be glorious, and she was not going to miss a single moment of it. She was going to eat, dance, laugh, wear gorgeous clothes, and, most of all, be with Chaun Maaun.

Soon she would tell her parents they intended to be married. Perhaps that's why Chaun Maaun was coming—to tell them himself.

She giggled, thinking of the wondrous days to come—of flying in Chaun Maaun's arms in the cold night sky, the stars their only companions, and joint-ruling the Dinii and the Hasan Daegians with him by her side. Maura dreamed of a future where both races intermingled in peace and prosperity.

Healers, scholars, musicians, writers, and great artisans would gather in the streets of O Konya. Together, she and Chaun Maaun would make Hasan Daeg one of the most beautiful places in the world. Everyone would love her and her king, and she would be the greatest ruler of all time. She shivered with girlish anticipation.

Princess Maura simply did not understand why her mother took everything so seriously and made life so hard for herself. With the characteristic self-involvement of the young, Maura's mind drifted to thoughts of pleasure. She changed her clothes and went to the archery range to practice. She wanted to show Chaun Maaun how good she was with a bow and arrow.

Yes, that was why Chaun Maaun was coming. He was going to ask Abisola for her daughter's hand in marriage.

Maura giggled.

Life was ripe.

21

The princess practiced archery.

Abisola went to her work chamber, a massive room filled with paintings and tapestries. Fresh cut flowers were cheerfully arranged in hand-blown glass vases standing on the tops of polished tables and chests. As always, two scribes, three personal secretaries, and one servant who tended to the queen's personal needs stood at attention.

The queen nodded to Consul Rubank. As with all consuls before him, his tongue had been cut out voluntarily. In order for him to advise Queen Abisola, she had to ask direct questions to which he could nod or shake his head. It was said that no Consul in the history of Hasan Daeg had ever divulged the confidences of his ruler—hence the absence of the tongue.

Abisola sat down in her chair behind the gleaming desk. "Are most of the preparations for my daughter's birthday ready?"

The consul nodded yes.

The queen looked pleased, asking the consul's assistants, "What is left?"

The consul motioned one of the young men forward.

"Well, Great Mother, everything is in readiness. However, we feel if Princess Maura is to ride in a parade through the city, security needs to be tightened. Of course, we recommend that she does not ride in the parade at all."

"The people need to see their future ruler, a young girl with vitality and strength. Not some aging relic as myself."

"There have been threats on her life. We do not think the parade a good idea."

"I know some of the nobles have formed a secret cabal sworn to bring this dynasty down and put their own queen on the throne."

"Why don't we just arrest them? It would make our job so much simpler."

Queen Abisola cocked her head to one side. "Because it would create sympathy among the rest of the nobles. We need their support. We need them to fight when the time comes. I can't afford to cause unrest among them right now. We must present a strong and unified front. They must think the throne is in strong hands."

"Great Mother, I don't mean to be disrespectful, but how long can you fool everyone that you are all right? Your health is failing. Your endurance is low. At this rate, you will not survive until Princess Maura's fortieth birthday," advised the assistant in low tones.

The consul gave the assistant a threatening look.

"I understand your concern. I am worried myself. We must find the Mother Bogazkoy. The ruler of Hasan Daeg must look in peak condition or the nobles will swoop down like the Dinii on an unsuspecting boaep." Queen Abisola paused. "That is my present concern. Empress Gitar will be arriving tomorrow and staying through the birthday celebration. We must make ready. I want everything perfect for her."

"Will the Dinii princesses be joining her?" inquired the assistant.

"No," replied the Queen. "Only Chaun Maaun."

The consul raised an eyebrow.

The queen studied his face. "Yes, I know," she replied to Rubank. "I don't like the looks of it either."

"I'm sorry, Your Majesty, I don't understand," confessed the assistant.

The queen looked away from Rubank. "It's nothing," she sighed. "Please make sure all beds are removed from their chambers. Have large tree limbs brought in and placed there instead. Make sure each room has an ample supply of straw and soft animal hair for their nesting. Lady Sari will help."

"I don't know if we can buy enough meat on such short notice," stated the assistant.

"Go through the Sivan guild here in the city. If I know the Sivans, they knew about this visit before I did. I'm sure they have in stock everything we need to make the Dinii comfortable. Just tell our cook their food is served warm but not cooked, and it must be bloody. Oh, and tell him the Dinii like the meat cut into ribbons."

The assistant nodded and motioned to the scribe to give him a copy of everything that had been said. With copy in hand, the assistant was given leave to finish his preparations for the birthday celebration.

Queen Abisola turned her attention to Rubank. "I want to examine yesterday's report again."

Rubank went to the opposite side of the room and unlocked a door, which led into a stone-lined archival chamber for important documents and reports. He immediately went to yesterday's report from the eastern border.

Queen Abisola took the report and slowly went over it again with a heavy heart. It was not good.

Zoar was advancing in an erratic line, looting city after city, always heading in Hasan Daeg's general direction. After being quiet for almost ten years, Zoar was on the move again, conquering with the same terrible swiftness and finality that marked his earlier campaigns.

Once conquered, the enslaved territories were assimilated into the Bhuttanian Empire. If the population resisted, it was decimated.

Queen Abisola hoped Zoar would break off before reaching her border, but in her heart of hearts, she knew he would keep marching. She was glad Gitar was coming, for she could share this burden with the Dinii empress.

Abisola looked up from the report. "The day after my daughter's birthday, Hasan Daeg will go on war alert. The armories are to be opened in O Konya, and all citizens are to be armed. Zoar is much too close to our borders to ignore his threat."

Rubank nodded.

"For the time being, triple the guards on the eastern borders. I will ask the Dinii to extend their patrols when Empress Gitar arrives. We must know every move Zoar makes. I find this report too vague. I wish for more detail." She handed the report back to the consul.

Rubank saluted and left the room almost at a run to execute Abisola's orders.

Abisola sat back in her chair, wiping the perspiration off her forehead. She wondered when Iasos was going to arrive. She needed to hear his soft voice and feel his velvet skin beneath her. Everything was becoming too much for her to handle by herself. She did not feel well. Abisola steeled herself. *I must survive until Maura can ascend the throne.*

She nervously rubbed her hands together. Gathering up documents from the desk, she signed several papers while her thoughts always went back to Zoar. It was just a matter of months now. She was sure of it, and she was truly glad Empress Gitar was coming. Maybe they could fly Maura back to the City of the Peaks until the war was all over? Deep in her heart, Abisola knew that was not going to happen. No one was going to be spared.

Least of all her daughter.

22

Empress Gitar flew into O Konya.

Residents of the city stood in the streets and watched as the Bird People entered with a precision that took the Hasan Daegians' breath away.

Falcons with black geometric designs painted on their wings flew in a cross formation, diving suddenly in single file as though they would crash into the palace roof. At the last moment, they arched upwards, creating a fan-shaped effect in the sky. The designs on their wings looked like pairs of eyes staring down at the people.

The thrilled Hasan Daegians in the streets below and on rooftops clapped enthusiastically.

The falcons jetted down again, spinning as if out of control until, at the last second, they flipped up and landed on chimneys of various roofs. They remained immobile and looked as though they were statues.

Next, the hawks entered. There were thousands of them. They flew in a giant star formation with the red hawks creating the form of a five-point star while the gray hawks formed the outline of the star. With the wing of one hawk touching the wing of another, they flew in perfect formation, all wings moving in unison. As the red hawks had white chests and bellies, the star was white and surrounded by the dark outline of the gray hawks' wings.

With one rotation, the red hawks rolled over and flew upside down, exposing their red wings.

People cheered and hollered with glee as the white star suddenly turned into a red one and then turned back again to white.

The Dinii flew off into the darkening eastern sky. As soon as they were out of sight, drums sounded from every rooftop in an almost deafening cacophony. Trumpets joined and heralded the arrival of the Dinii empress.

A thousand moving lights lit up the sky as more hawk, owl, and falcon Dinii soared, each holding a torch. They flew in a spiral formation. In the center flew their Empress surrounded by huge silver and white flags dancing gaily in the dimming sky. As the spiral approached the palace, the Dinii spun outward, creating an explosive effect. Empress Gitar dropped out of the center of the lights and landed with her party onto the roof of the royal palace.

Queen Abisola and Princess Maura approached the Dinii party and bowed. "We welcome you to our home," said Abisola. She could barely hear herself speak over the roar of the crowd in the streets below.

Empress Gitar smiled and nodded. She beckoned Queen Abisola to her side, and they stood together near the edge of the roof, waving to the people watching from below.

Empress Gitar spread her mighty wings. The diamond dust she had sprinkled on her feathers twinkled in the fading light. It looked like small bolts of light flashing.

The crowd erupted with cheers.

Empress Gitar turned toward Queen Abisola, and they clasped hands, raising their arms in a sign of unity.

The roar of the applause was deafening.

Queen Abisola smiled brightly. She beckoned to Princess Maura and the young girl shyly joined them.

Cheers sounded in the air again.

After much waving, the queens and their entourages moved indoors where they could speak. Instead of entering the throne room, Empress Gitar was shown to a private audience chamber where chairs and tree limbs were strategically placed.

Gitar turned to Queen Abisola. "How very thoughtful. We can sit as you, but not for very long periods of time."

Queen Abisola waved toward a limb.

"First, Your Majesty," said Gitar, "I would like to formally present my son, Prince Chaun Maaun, to you."

An eagle with markings like his mother's stepped forward and bowed low to Queen Abisola and Princess Maura. "Great Mother," he addressed Abisola, "the last time we met, I was quite young. I see Her Majesty's beauty still complements her legendary wisdom."

Abisola nodded to Chaun Maaun with pleasure. She loved compliments when they sounded sincere. Out of the corner of her eye, she noticed a strange gleam in Princess Maura's eyes as she gazed upon the striking royal son.

Queen Abisola did not think this a good omen, but she gave no sign that she noticed her daughter's apparent infatuation.

Empress Gitar did the same.

"Princess Maura," said Chaun Maaun, tenderly turning toward her.

Maura returned his gaze longingly.

"And, of course, you know my uncle, Prince Iegani, Great Divigi," quickly said Empress Gitar, trying to push down her anger with her son for his public display of affection.

Iegani stepped forward and bowed.

Queen Abisola extended her hand. "Always a pleasure, Prince Iegani," she lied.

Iegani caught the sarcasm and chuckled. He always liked Queen Abisola's candor.

She said to him, "I have prepared your usual room." Queen Abisola clapped her hands and asked the servants to bring refreshments.

Maura looked up and answered Iegani, who was sending her telepathic messages. "Yes, Great Divigi, I have been practicing as you taught me, but I still cannot send over long distances." She lowered her eyes. Of all her teachers, Iegani was the one who instilled fear and uneasiness in her. She greatly respected her mentor but never could relax around him. Maura was always afraid she would make a mistake, and she frequently did. His disapproval was keenly felt.

Chaun Maaun reached over and patted her hand. He frowned at Iegani.

Princess Maura felt relieved and looked appreciatively at the visiting Prince.

Chaun Maaun was not afraid of Iegani as she was. He was not afraid of anything.

Iegani pursed his lips and slowly breathed out.

Empress Gitar gave a warning look at both Chaun Maaun and Iegani as if to say, "behave!" She knew they were sending messages to each other telepathically.

"I can hardly believe Princess Maura will be eighteen tomorrow," teased Empress Gitar. "It seems like only yesterday she was driving me to fits with her constant crying as a baby."

Maura blushed, glancing at her mother.

"May we expect the Royal Princesses from the House of Gitar?" asked Abisola, tactfully changing the subject.

"Someone needed to stay behind and keep order," quickly answered Gitar. "My people are not responsible like yours," she said, referring to their combined troops. "My hawks have become too fond of ale and are smuggling kegs into the City of the Peaks."

Queen Abisola took a sip of her drink, noting that Gitar had spoken too quickly. She did not believe her. No, there was a specific reason that only Chaun Maaun was present. Queen Abisola started to speak, but the door to the chamber burst open.

"Father!" squealed Maura as she rushed forward to embrace her dirty and sweating father.

"Not too close," he said, laughing and holding his daughter at bay. "I smell as bad as a decaying borax."

Maura wrinkled her nose after getting a strong whiff of him.

Iasos bowed to Empress Gitar. "I've only just arrived and come to pay my respects to my wife and child. I did not know you were present, or I would have bathed before presenting myself. My apologies, Empress."

Empress Gitar stood up and towered over Iasos. "No apologies needed. Please excuse me. I need to rest. May your servants show me to my quarters?"

"Of course," replied Queen Abisola, rising. "It's been a long day for us all. Lady Sari will be your personal servant while you are present in O Konya. You have only to ask."

"You are so kind." Empress Gitar started to follow Lady Sari out of the room when she turned to Chaun Maaun. "Coming?"

Chaun Maaun bid his hosts good night and sheepishly followed his mother and great uncle to their quarters.

Once the door was closed, Abisola rushed to Iasos, branding him with a kiss and staining her splendid golden gown with dirt and grease. "I thought you would never get here," she confessed breathlessly.

Iasos returned her passionate kiss and, grabbing Maura, held them both tightly. "Nothing could keep me away from my daughter's birthday."

Maura looked at them both with delight.

Iasos smiled at his daughter and then returned Abisola's gaze.

Maura knew when it was time to leave. She politely excused herself and left her parents to their own devices. Her day would come tomorrow. She could wait for their complete attention. This night belonged to them.

23

Maura barely had time to change.

Looking sheepish, Chaun Maaun squeezed himself through the narrow window of her bedchamber.

She gaily ran over to him and they embraced. Maura loved the feeling of security and tenderness when he surrounded her with his broad wings. He was smaller than most Dinii, so Maura didn't feel overwhelmed by his size.

"Did anyone see you?" she asked.

"I don't think so," he whispered.

"You don't have to talk so low. I have sent everyone away for the night."

"Don't you think that will cause them to be suspicious?"

"No, I often sleep without servants or nurses. I'm not a baby anymore. They still try to treat me as such though," Maura pouted. "Besides, I'm a Hasan Daegian of legal age now. I may do as I please."

Chaun Maaun laughed. He picked her up and swirled her around. Her laughter joined his. Laughing and kissing, he took her over to the bed, placing her gently in the middle of it. "Do you think it will hold me?" he asked.

She nodded enthusiastically.

He cautiously joined her and snuggled closely.

"Did you talk to your mother?" Maura asked.

Chaun Maaun busily untied the blue ribbon to her nightgown. "I have tried for several weeks, but every time I tell her I need to see her, she has some excuse. I think she knows about us and doesn't want to talk to me. Tomorrow, I'll corner her and make her listen." He reached into her gown and pulled out a breast, slowly sucking on a nipple.

"Mmmmmm, delicious."

Maura giggled and pulled away. "We need to talk, Chaun. We need to make plans."

"Right," he said, leaning on his elbow and grinning. "Talk all you want. Did you tell *your* mother that we want to get married?"

Princess Maura looked apprehensive. "No. I tried. I really did. I just couldn't get the words out." She started chewing on the end of a ribbon from her gown. "I thought I would wait until Father got home. He's more reasonable, and I thought he could talk to Mother."

Chaun Maaun gave her an appraising look.

Maura snapped, "Oh, don't look at me so. This is not going to be easy."

"Doesn't she like me?"

"Oh, Chaun!" she said, scooting next to his face. "It's not personal. My mother will probably say that I should marry one of my own people, because I'm going to be queen one day."

"You could tell her by marrying me, the treaty between our two nations would be strengthened. Royalty from other countries marry for the same reason all the time." He rolled on his back and pulled her on top of him.

She lightly kissed his chin. "I don't think my mother is the problem. What if Zoar comes?"

Chaun laughed. "He doesn't even know we exist."

"Mother says he's moving west."

"He will come to the mist and, seeing nothing but his doom if he tries to enter, turn back. He will think it is the end of the world. He won't bother us, but if he does, the Dinii will take care of him."

"I don't know. Mother says he's awfully determined."

"I don't want to talk about Zoar. I don't want to talk about our mothers. I want to kiss you again and again and again." He kissed her passionately.

Maura responded warmly.

"The night is ours. Let's not waste it," he whispered, giving her a rakish look.

Maura grinned and put out the lamp.

24

Maura pushed Chaun Maaun out the window.

Neither of them saw Iegani standing in the window of the apartment across from them, watching silently in the darkness.

Chaun Maaun crawled contentedly into his room and fell asleep while Maura began preparing for her big day. The servants found her already bathed and brushing her hair.

Upon entering the chamber, Sari smelled both the foreign odor of a Dini and the familiar smell of lovemaking. She looked at Maura, but decided not to say anything. It was Maura's big day, and Sari did not want to spoil it. Besides, there was nothing anyone could do. Maura was of legal age.

Already she had left the Queen, who was terribly upset with a new report that Zoar was moving ever closer to their border. Iasos was dressing in the Queen's room, hoping his presence would calm his distraught wife.

Hurriedly, a message had already been sent to Empress Gitar that Abisola wished to have an audience with her immediately.

Sari wished to spare Maura this awful news and her parents' anguish. "Nothing is going to spoil this day for her little one," she muttered to herself.

"What was that?" asked Maura, looking at her strangely.

"Nothing, my wild bird baby."

"I thought you said something."

Sari shook her head and began supervising the dressing of the princess.

Maura donned a gown of white with gold buttons and trimming. Her headdress was a gold crown with a matching white veil, which was sheer and fell to the floor behind the dress. Her slippers were the color of gold and covered with Mother of Pearl. The design of an uultepe was on her right breast. She wore no jewelry. Her pale indigo skin gleamed under the various applications of oil.

Sari looked at her with satisfaction.

The girl standing proudly before her looked every inch a princess.

Sari felt tears come into her eyes. "Two Hasan Daegian queens I will have served."

Maura laughed while looking into a mirror. "I'm not a queen yet."

"You soon will be," said Queen Abisola, standing in the doorway. She walked toward her daughter. "I'm so proud of you. Here, let me look."

Maura twirled around in her dress.

Sari fussed at her. "Your hair!" she nagged.

"She looks fine, Sari," admonished the queen.

"Mother, what is it! You look like you've been crying."

Abisola held her daughter's hands. "Nothing that can't wait until after the celebration. You have your eighteenth birthday only once. Isn't that right, Sari?"

Sari nodded enthusiastically.

Maura looked suspiciously at her mother. "Something's wrong. I can tell."

"Can you tell that your father is waiting impatiently at the breakfast table with a big present for you?"

"He is?" asked Maura excitedly. Picking up her skirts, she rushed to the dining room.

Sari blocked her path. "Oh no, you don't," scolded Sari. "You are going to act like a princess all day, even if it kills you."

The queen winced at Sari's words, but no one noticed.

Sari and Maura glared at each other in a standoff.

Abisola coaxed, "For once, let's do as Sari wants. It would make her so happy."

"All right, Mother, but when I'm queen, no one is going to boss me around."

Lady Sari looked heavenward as though beseeching the great goddess, Mekonia.

"Walk slowly with your head held high," instructed Abisola. "Show the people they can have confidence in you. Go on. I will follow shortly."

"I'm going. You will come soon, promise?"

"Absolutely. I'll be there in a few minutes."

Maura turned and, with exaggerated slowness, walked out of the room.

Sari turned to her cousin in exasperation. "When is she going to grow up?"

"Soon," replied Abisola. "Very soon."

25

Guests rose.

Queen Abisola and Empress Gitar entered the great dining hall and took their seats at a massive table. On Abisola's right sat Empress Gitar looking as forlorn as her hostess. Moments before, they had discussed Zoar, and both knew war was imminent. The very thing they had been dreading was now upon them.

Empress Gitar had trouble focusing on small talk with the Hasan Daegian nobles and governors who had gathered for the breakfast. Her voice was higher-pitched than usual, and she sometimes lapsed into Dinii clicks.

Abisola gave the empress a reassuring smile.

Gitar brightened.

At the end of the table sat Iasos with Maura on his right and Prince Chaun Maaun seated across from her.

Prince Iegani sat uncomfortably between two ancient noblewomen, who complimented him on his still-powerful physique, attempting to stroke his lap under the table. He wanted to slap their silly over-powdered faces, but pretended he did not notice them. He was troubled about the report, but strove not to show it.

Stealing a look here and there, he saw that both Abisola and Gitar were pale and drawn. In the trying times ahead, Iegani hoped the two rulers would bond together as true sisters and not as rival queens. He looked to his left. Chaun Maaun and Princess Maura were enjoying the day. Chaun Maaun looked sleepy. *No wonder*, Iegani thought.

Maura looked fresh and cheerfully picked at her food, impatient to begin her official birthday procession.

Sensing Iegani was thinking of her, Maura looked up and met his eyes. He quickly turned his head.

Odd, thought Maura as Iegani's actions left her with a feeling of uneasiness. She became angry, for she did not want her day spoiled. With childish impudence, she threw her chin out in defiance.

The breakfast continued at a slow pace with people chatting gaily and loading their plates with food. Musicians played lively tunes. Servants poured drinks, running back and forth with platters laden with food from all parts of Hasan Daeg.

For Chaun Maaun, the meal dragged on with endless toasts to Maura and songs in her honor. He wanted to go out into the city and be away from these old relics—both Hasan Daegian and Dinii. He wanted to have fun.

A commotion sounded outside one of the doors.

Chaun Maaun turned and strained to see what was happening.

A guard emerged from the hallway and went to Queen Abisola. She whispered into the queen's ear.

Queen Abisola stood. "I'm sorry to leave this wonderful gathering, but duty calls. Please continue in my absence. I shan't be long."

The guests stood as Queen Abisola left the room.

A few moments later, a guard came for Empress Gitar and Prince Iegani, escorting them out of the dining hall.

The guests murmured anxiously among themselves.

Iasos continued chatting, even though his daughter looked at him questioningly.

Outside the windows, Maura could hear the dancers, acrobats, fire-eaters, illusionists, exotic animals, and escort guards lining up for the parade. She knew she ought to be in the courtyard and getting ready to mount the float decorated just for this occasion. Craftsmen had spent weeks designing the elaborate structure with thousands of flowers and topiary statues. She began squirming in her chair, desiring to be off. Her father gave her a stern look. Chastened, Maura remained quietly with her hands folded in her lap.

The guests made no pretense of small talk now. Everyone sat hushed, and either stared out the windows or picked at the food on their plates. Only the melodious tune from a lone flute sounded in the immense room.

A soldier strode into the room, saluted, and handed Iasos a note. Iasos cut the seal open with his plate knife and silently read it. Putting the note in his pocket, he returned the salute and gave the soldier leave. He stood and, for a moment, had to steady himself against the table.

"Father?" questioned Maura, rising to help him.

Iasos waved her away. "Countrywomen, kinsmen, honored guests, I have the sad duty to tell you that our day of joy celebrating with your future queen, Princess Maura, has been postponed to an indefinite date."

Iasos paused, trying to calm his nerves. "You are to gather your belongings, children, and servants, and make ready to return to your homes."

Everyone gasped.

Iasos continued, "Before you leave, Queen Abisola has commanded that you attend a royal audience inside the throne room within the hour. Those who do not attend will be imprisoned. I'm sorry for this—this inconvenience. You are dismissed until the bell strikes the next hour. Then we shall meet again."

Chairs were thrown back as guests rushed to their quarters to gather their husbands and belongings. Servants scurried beside their mistresses, receiving their instructions, and ran off to complete their tasks. Everyone noticed that the number of guards had doubled in the hallways, and Dinii hawks and falcons were standing at attention near any royal apartment.

The dining hall was empty except for Chaun Maaun, Princess Maura, and Iasos.

Sari entered the room from the servants' entrance. "Sire," she gushed with tears in her eyes, "Her Majesty wishes you and Princess Maura to change into military dress and join her in the throne room shortly before the new hour. Prince Chaun Maaun, you are to wait with Empress Gitar in her apartment. This is your mother's wish."

"What has happened?" Chaun Maaun croaked.

Sari shook her head. "All will be made known to you. That is all I can say." She turned to the stricken princess and took the young girl's hands in her worn ones. "I'm so sorry. It just could not be helped."

Maura stared at Sari's gnarled hands—hands which had bathed her, fed her, hugged her, kept her from danger, and helped her take her first step. She looked into Sari's moist eyes. "I know it must be something awful to cancel my celebration. I have something better than a parade or presents. I have my parents and you. What more is there?"

Iasos hugged his daughter and pushed her toward the door. "You'd better hurry if you want to change out of that garb."

Guards entered and escorted Chaun Maaun from the room.

Maura hurried out into the great hallway as well.

Alone in the room, Iasos fell into a chair and stared at the empty room. In a fit of rage he jumped up, sweeping serving dishes off the table and throwing crystal against the wall. He threw centuries-old china out the window, pulled apart massive flower arrangements, and hurled fruit at the large portraits of previous Hasan Daegian rulers and their consorts. When he came to the portrait of Abisola, he fell to his knees sobbing.

Servants, hearing the tumult, ran into the dining room.

Embarrassed, Iasos hurried out through a side door.

Aghast at the disarray the consort had left in the room, they began the awful process of cleaning and restoring order.

26

Yeti and Tarsus fell in step with Maura.

Tarsus made way for Maura through the ribbons of people streaming past in the great hallway.

"Panic is not a pretty thing," murmured Yeti, pushing people out of the way.

Maura felt a rush of air behind her. It felt unnatural, and she swirled around to see the blur of a silver blade coming toward her chest. A cry sounded, "No war!" Instinctively she parried with her forearm and felt something slice her skin. Hearing screams, she felt Yeti push her out of the way. Lying on the floor, she could see upward between the powerful legs of Yeti who was now standing protectively in front of her.

Tarsus had in his hands a youth struggling in vain against the powerful Dini. Tarsus held the boy's head in a lock and released his killing talon.

Maura mouthed "NO" in horror as Tarsus slit the boy's throat, throwing him against a marble wall, cracking his skull open.

The would-be assassin twitched several times and then fell still.

Tarsus picked up the boy's dagger and instructed the newly arrived guards to remove the body for examination.

The senior guard officer assessed the condition of the princess and ordered four of her soldiers to stay with the Dinii, while the rest dragged the body away. Many of the soldiers spat on the boy's body before touching him.

Yeti bent down and pulled up Maura who moaned as the hawk brushed her cut arm. She clicked to Maura in the Dinii language.

The princess nodded and walked behind Yeti, hiding her wound, with Tarsus following to Maura's private chambers.

Once inside Maura's suite, Yeti tore off the birthday dress, searching for other injuries while Tarsus bathed the cut in water. Maura acquiesced silently. Her beautiful dress was ripped and ruined with blood. The crown and veil were removed quickly as were the rest of her clothes.

"It's not so bad," announced Tarsus. "Just a few stitches and you'll be good as new." He tore apart some bed sheets and wrapped them around her arm. "This should stem the bleeding until your healer can attend."

Yeti shook Maura gently. "Maura, put this behind you. You need to join your mother in a few minutes."

Maura sat bewildered, trying to make sense of what had happened. "I know that boy. He is Baroness Mikkotto's son, Yubuto. I used to play with him. He is, I mean was, my cousin. Lady Sari is his grandmother." She looked pleadingly at Yeti. "Why did he try to kill me? I've never done anything to him. I liked him."

"There is no time for this. You must think on your feet. Remember all we have taught you. Here is your uniform. Get into it. Tarsus will help you."

"You shouldn't even be in here," snapped Maura.

Tarsus grinned. "I used to see you running naked from house to house in the City of the Peaks causing mischief. I doubt you have anything I haven't seen before."

"Oh, for goodness sake," scolded Yeti. "Maura, get in your uniform. Wash that makeup off your face. There isn't time for false modesty."

Tarsus went through many closets trying to find suitable underclothes. He did not understand how Hasan Daegians could stand cloth next to their skin. He ignored Maura's blushes as he and Yeti helped put on her pants and boots.

Yeti buttoned her top. "Maura, you will have to design a uniform that you can get into yourself. You need to be as independent as possible. Haven't we always taught this?"

"Yes, but my mother thinks it's unbecoming for a Hasan Daegian princess to dress herself." Maura stopped, realizing she was sounding like a fool.

Tarsus checked the dressing on the wound. It was holding. No blood showed through.

"We must go now," announced Yeti.

"I think we should go through the servants' hallways," cautioned Tarsus.

Maura got to her feet and followed Tarsus and Yeti out through her chambers the back way. She was relieved to find guards stationed at every door. This was a momentary comfort, for she realized that if the conservative nobles wanted her dead, they would find a way. Twisting and turning through a maze of corridors, Yeti and Tarsus finally arrived at the main hallway.

Seeing the nobles were beginning to arrive, Yeti placed Maura between herself and Tarsus. Spreading their wings as shields, they marched her into the throne room. Toppo and Benzar met them and escorted them to the conference room at the back of the chamber.

Inside, Gitar stood alongside Abisola, looking at a massive map of the continent.

Yesemek was pointing out spots on the map, explaining strategy to military staff that stood politely behind.

Maura scanned the room quickly.

Iegani sat in a corner with his eyes closed.

I know you can hear me, thought Maura. *Open your eyes, Great Divigi, and speak to me.*

Iegani opened the first set of his eyelids. The second set was still over his eyes, but almost transparent, so Maura could see his orbs vibrating.

Maura knew he was in a deep trance. She didn't care. *Why did young Yubuto try to kill me?*

He thought by killing you, your parents would be so distraught they would not fight Zoar.

That is the surface explanation. What is the deeper meaning?

We have taught you well, my daughter. Certain elements of the nobility do not believe we can win a war against Zoar. They wish to protect their interests by collaborating.

Why kill me? Why not try to kill my mother?

They perceive you to be the greater threat. You have been trained as a warrior. You know how to fight. Your mother does not.

Why was I trained as a warrior?

Because we were told to do so.

By whom?

Iegani did not respond to the question.

Who told you to make me a warrior?

Iegani closed his first set of eyelids, and Maura knew she had lost him for now. She would try again later.

Chaun Maaun entered the room and stood next to Maura. He nudged her. "Are you all right?" he asked. "Did the bastard hurt you?"

"You already know?"

"Everyone knows. When I think of what that lunatic might have done! I'm so glad Yeti and Tarsus were there to protect you."

"Yes, isn't it a fortunate coincidence they were standing right outside of the dining hall," she replied sarcastically.

"If they hadn't been there, you could have been killed."

"I can take care of myself," Maura shot back.

"If you were as good a warrior as you think, he never would have gotten near you. You would have sensed him."

"I'll be more careful from now on."

"You had better be or you might be dead next time," shot back Chaun Maaun, angrily. He left and joined his mother at the map.

Ashamed, Maura followed discreetly and placed her finger in the palm of his hand. He squeezed back gently.

Yesemek turned to Abisola and Gitar. "Are there any questions?"

"Yes," said Iegani, still sitting in the corner with his eyes closed. "Why don't we open the Forbidden Zone? Why have we not looked for the Bogazkoy there?"

Yesemek pondered this. She knew enough of her husband to know that his words always carried wisdom. She was open to discussing the idea.

Queen Abisola spoke, "We have always held the land to be a danger to our people. We have never ventured into the Forbidden Zone."

"Do you know why it is forbidden?" asked Iegani, opening both sets of eyelids.

"I do not know why. Perhaps someone from the House of Magi could tell us."

"They will not know. I know, but I will not tell you now—only this. There is no inherent danger to the people of Hasan Daeg or to the race of the Dinii in the Forbidden Zone. Beyond the Forbidden Zone is the sea."

"I have never seen the sea," responded Queen Abisola.

"March to the sea," advised Iegani.

There was silence in the room.

Yesemek turned to Queen Abisola. "Great Mother, we can discuss this matter later for we have other urgent matters at hand. You must speak to your people. They are waiting."

Queen Abisola adjusted her official robes and proceeded into the audience hall. She paused as she was announced and then made way to her throne. Consort Iasos and Princess Maura stood beside her.

Empress Gitar followed and sat in a chair made of rare wood one step higher than Abisola. Prince Chaun Maaun stood to the left of his mother.

Queen Abisola opened her fan, rose, and faced the agitated crowd. "It is my sad duty to inform you that last night Zoar, Aga of Bhuttan, camped just outside our border."

The court murmured.

"This morning he began sending soldiers through our wall of mist. The soldiers were met on the other side by our warriors. The Bhuttanian soldiers died quickly and without pain. Their armor and weapons have been confiscated, and their bodies removed for burning. The total of Bhuttanian casualties has been over seven hundred so far. We have suffered none."

The court gasped and moaned for the poor Bhuttanian soldiers.

Abisola lifted her fan for all to see. "I, Queen Abisola de Magela, Great Mother, ninth ruler of Hasan Daeg, Daughter of Queen Hagar, find the acts of Zoar, Aga of Bhuttan, to be of bold naked aggression against the people of Hasan Daeg. Therefore, it is my duty to proclaim war against Zoar, Aga of Bhuttan, and all other peoples who make war against citizens of Hasan Daeg."

The great gong sounded and it was made law.

Abisola took a step down on the dais. "I, Queen Abisola de Magela, do hereby formally petition Empress Gitar, Overlord of Kaseri, Queen of the City of the Peaks, to acknowledge the treaty between our two peoples and proclaim war against Zoar, Aga of Bhuttan." She turned and looked at Gitar.

Empress Gitar rose, keeping her eyes on those assembled. She motioned for her attendants. Several hawks brought two pairs of snowy white wings made with the feathers of royal eagles. "I have saved these royal feathers for many years to make these symbolic pairs of wings. I present them to you, Queen Abisola and Princess Maura, heir apparent, as symbols of kinship and enduring bonds between my race and yours. You are both now full-fledged members of the Dinii."

Both Abisola and Maura bowed to Empress Gitar and held out their arms so the wings could be slipped on over their garments. Abisola tried not to stagger under their weight. Both the queen and princess were instructed to pull a leather strap that allowed the wings to spread to their full glory.

The court erupted with delight.

Gitar, smiling broadly at the cheering crowd, cried, "I, Empress Gitar, Overlord of Kaseri, do acknowledge the ancient treaty between the Hasan Daegians and the Dinii. I also proclaim war. Thy enemies are my enemies."

The great gong sounded.

Gitar returned to her throne on the dais.

Abisola stepped forward. "I, Queen Abisola de Magela, do hereby sentence the body of Yubuto Sumsumitoyo, to be burned, and his ashes cast adrift with the wind. His mother, Baroness Mikkotto Sumsumitoyo is to be executed upon sight for the attempted assassination of Princess Maura de Magela. All properties belonging to the Sumsumitoyo family will be confiscated for the Crown. Baroness Mikkotto's children will be hung if found guilty of conspiracy."

Maura found her heart growing heavier with each pronouncement. She saw her future slipping away. She was beginning to doubt if she would ever marry Chaun Maaun. She stole a glance at him. From the expression on his face, she knew he was thinking the same. She would be expected to behave like a ruler of Hasan Daeg, sacrificing whatever was needed. No longer would she be able to fly with Chaun Maaun to some distant peak and spend the day lounging in a nest of down, watching the clouds roll past. Her destiny had finally caught up with her. Maura did not think she was going to like it.

27

Accept your destiny! Accept your destiny!

Iegani stood in the doorway.

Maura knew the message was for her and felt his eyes bore into her back. She refused to turn her head to look at him. Instead, she watched her mother proclaim edict after edict.

The great gong sounded each time with finality.

When Abisola was finished, she snapped her fan shut and returned exhausted to her throne.

Queen Abisola's First General, Kimtemee, addressed the worried governors and nobles. "It is Her Majesty's wish that you return to your homes and begin enacting the primary plan. Word will be sent to you regarding further orders. I wish you good luck! You are dismissed."

The crowd fled the room and hurried home to make ready for war. A few of the older noblewomen lingered and approached Queen Abisola.

She answered their questions and listened to their concerns.

One apologized for the actions of Baroness Mikkotto, but warned of unrest among the nobles. The others nodded their heads in agreement.

"Thank you for your warnings and kind support. They are greatly appreciated," answered Queen Abisola.

The ancient noblewomen said their good-byes and slowly left the throne room aided by their daughters or male servants.

When the chamber was empty, Rubank approached Queen Abisola, taking the heavy ceremonial fan and crown to storage.

Gitar turned to Abisola. "How do you think they reacted?"

Queen Abisola looked at Iasos. "I couldn't see everyone."

"I think the governors and ministers will back us totally. After all, the Crown employs them," said Iasos. "However, the nobles are another matter. The older families will support us totally. It would be treason not to do so, but the younger noble families are less concerned with honor than with money. Still, we have been preparing them for years. They ought to accept this war."

"What of the attack on Princess Maura?" asked Empress Gitar.

"We know that Baroness Mikkotto is behind the attack and used her son as a pawn. There are other conspirators. We are sure of it, but we only have suspects currently," replied Queen Abisola, watching the reaction of her daughter.

Princess Maura seemed to be studying the pattern in the marble floor.

"Could the boy have acted on his own?" Empress Gitar questioned.

"In our culture, it is rare for a boy his age to initiate an act of this magnitude unless he is insane. No, this was the act of a woman, a ruthless one at that! May her bowels be scattered to the buzzards while she still lives!" seethed Iasos.

Queen Abisola smiled at her husband's passion. "The baroness has fled. We shall apprehend her soon enough."

Maura ventured an opinion to Empress Gitar. "Mikkotto's lands are near the border where Zoar is approaching. She has much to lose if Zoar enters that sector. I think she will probably try to regroup with her personal guards and perhaps make a deal with Zoar. Mother, I think it is imperative we find her."

All those attending looked appraisingly at Maura. A new respect entered their eyes.

Iegani stepped forward. "So our little fledgling is finally spreading her wings. Good. Good. This is what I've been waiting for—clean logic. Not some prattle about a ridiculous party or a new frock that your mother had made for you." He turned to Empress Gitar. "See, all our efforts are reaping just rewards."

Empress Gitar's face fell into a sad expression. She turned to Abisola. "Our little girl is no more," she whispered. "Iegani, perhaps you do not understand something has happened here, which does not pertain to war, but is just as important to a mother. Something precious has been lost and, for all your wisdom, you do not even see it."

She leaned on Chaun Maaun. "I wish to go to my room to rest. I will talk with you and your generals later this afternoon before I fly back to the City of the Peaks," Gitar said to Abisola.

"I understand," answered Abisola.

"I know you do," replied Gitar.

Iegani bowed as his empress left the room with her confused son.

"Mother, what do you mean?" Chaun Maaun asked quietly so the others would not hear.

"Oh, my precious dear, our little Maura, who used to run naked through our streets, is no more. Princess Maura de Magela, future ruler of Hasan Daeg, Great Mother to her people, now resides in this palace of cold stone. I have lost a daughter and gained a rival." Empress Gitar could barely keep from weeping in the great marble hall as she walked back to her chambers.

Maura sorrowfully watched the Dinii depart. Throwing back her shoulders, she returned to the conference room with her mother and father.

The three of them began the business of war.

28

Zoar watched the sun set.

The wind gently blew from the west and played with the coverlet draped over his lap. He felt so cold these days.

Knowing his healer would scold him for being out in the brisk air rather than in his tent near a warm fire, Zoar stroked his beard and ordered his litter moved closer to the mist. If his healer annoyed him, he would just get another and then another, until he found one that would let him do as he pleased.

At the moment he was *pleased* to study the wall of mist which taunted him. For ten days he had sent men into the mist, and they had never returned. Over two thousand men had met their fates beyond the wall. *But what fate?* thought Zoar. *What is behind the wall? There is something there. I can feel it.*

He told his men to stop and lower his litter. They did not dare get too close. The mist made Zoar sleepy. He wondered if his soldiers had fallen asleep in the mist and died in a peaceful dream. Or were they met by some terrible fate? Perhaps paradise was behind the wall, and they did not wish to return. Frustrated, Zoar beat the arm of his litter chair with his fist. *If I weren't crippled, I'd go myself!*

Ten years earlier, a horse had thrown Zoar during the last days of war with Anqara and fell upon him. The carnage in Anqara had been so severe that it had taken Zoar's men several days to find him. By that time, Zoar's severely shattered leg could not be set correctly. Zoar swore he would be in the saddle in no time, but could not keep his promise.

As the years passed, Zoar's body betrayed him more and more until he was nothing but an arthritic old man who complained daily of aches and pains. A day did not pass when Zoar did not go over the events of that fateful incident. He had saddled the warhorse himself, checking the tack as always, and had kept the horse with him ready to mount. There was no way anyone could have gotten to the animal. Yet, there was a tiny cut on the girth, which caused the leather to finally pull apart and with it—Zoar. Suspicion remained with Zoar, ate at him, and totally consumed him. What if? What if?

Zoar pondered on his life as he watched ducks fly over the mist. He noticed they did not seem to be bothered by it. Back and forth went Zoar's thoughts from the mist to battles fought long ago, women ravished, and the feeling of invincibility he had once possessed. He wondered what would have happened had he had not been possessed by bloodlust. Would he have built instead of destroyed?

But he *was* building for the future, damn it! He was building a great empire with one central government instead of petty city-states or weak countries floundering in ineptitude and indecision. One culture, one language, one nation! That was his dream. And it took the flowing of much blood to make it happen! Now an old man, Zoar questioned not his dream, but his methods. "Too much blood," he muttered.

"What, Father?"

"Dorak, I didn't hear you approach." Zoar looked at his son.

Dorak had grown into a beautiful man, looking much like his mother. His skin was a honey caramel, encased in a tall frame. His hair was raven black, and it highlighted his dark, intelligent eyes and aquiline nose. His mouth was full and pouty.

How different from me, thought Zoar, who was short and squat.

"I've ordered the men to stop entering the mist. I don't see the need for wasting valuable resources."

Zoar noticed the hint of disapproval in his son's voice. "What would you have done differently, Dorak?"

"I would have sent scouting parties, but when they did not return, I would have come up with a creative solution."

"A creative solution? I do not know what that means. I do know whatever is beyond that mist can dispose of two thousand men without so much as a sound. I also know I can faintly smell smoke coming from the west. And where there is smoke, there is fire. That means there is man!"

"The fire could be caused by lightning."

"There hasn't been a thunderstorm in two weeks," countered Zoar. "No, Dorak, look at the mist." He pointed. "Follow the lines. They are not natural. It must be man-made. Always the same height, always without a break regardless of the topography. It's rather magnificent," he said with admiration.

"Father, do you remember those stories KiKu used to tell about singing plants and streams of different colors in a land to the west?"

"Yes, I remember his babble. I almost cut his head off for those lies." Zoar coughed phlegm into a vial.

"I've sent to Bhuttan for copies of any report suggesting these things, and none are to be found. But I remember quite distinctly being in the room with you when KiKu reported these wonders."

"It was during the last campaign before I was blessed with this broken body." Zoar thought back to the days when he was strong. Now his hair was shot through with gray, and his body was withered.

"But I did find reports about men dressed as birds who could fly. In fact, there is a report back in my tent which states you saw such a creature yourself at Anqara."

Zoar looked away. He did not want his son to see fear and confusion in his eyes. "Dorak, it was not a man dressed as a bird, but a man who was a bird."

"I don't understand. How can that be?"

"Nor do I, but it was not a costume. He was real. An immense creature who had the body of man, moved like a man, talked like a man, but had feathers covering him except for his feet, hands, and face. He had great wings on his back, and he flew out a window. I remember running to the window to see if he had fallen. I heard laughing and looked up, and he flew past me with the tip of a wing brushing my face. He said we would meet again. There was nothing mechanical or artificial about him. He was as real as you or I. Even now, the telling of it leaves me shaken."

Dorak was surprised at his father's intensity. "I'm sorry, Great Aga. I did not mean to upset you," he said with sincerity.

Zoar clasped his son's arm. "I will listen to any plan you may have. What are you if not a capable advisor? It is the reason for this one last campaign. You must proceed as you wish. The men must learn to trust you, and they will. It just takes time."

"Time is what we don't have. Our world is starving. The land is depleted. We must find fertile land to grow food until our fields recover."

"What do you propose?"

"I want to hear more about Anqara."

"Anqara?"

"Yes, it was after the campaign of Anqara that these reports dry up. No more leads after that. I think there might be a connection. Weren't you planning to keep moving west?"

"That's right," replied Zoar animatedly. "But my accident happened, and I was ill for a long time."

"How interesting."

"Yes, isn't it," replied Zoar grinning. "I think we should speak to KiKu, don't you?"

"There is a problem with that."

"Oh?"

"He is nowhere to be found. He has disappeared with the wind."

Zoar took this news in silence.

Dorak stood waiting.

"Son, that night in Anqara when I found the birdman in the room of the High Priestess of the House of Magi, he was attempting to destroy her writings. I had the fire put out, and the papers stored."

"Are there any other priestesses alive who can interpret the writings?"

"All the priestesses from the House of Magi disappeared that night. No trace of them at all."

"And you think this birdman had something to do with their disappearance?"

"I can feel it in my bones. I've often wondered what strong magic he possessed to steal those women past my men."

"Maybe he just flew them away," joked Dorak.

"Maybe he did," replied Zoar. "I have often wondered about the possibility." Zoar shifted in his chair and rubbed his hands together, blowing on them. "What do you propose to do about the mist, Dorak? We cannot sit here forever."

"I will send for the writings of this woman, and see if we can glean anything from them."

Zoar snorted in disgust.

Dorak maintained his position. "I'm not going to continue sending men into this fog."

"Perhaps, that is the reason why you should. Test the boundaries. Tie ropes around the men before you send them in. Do something. Our women back home are starving."

Dorak shot back, "You've starved women before, and it never seemed to bother you."

"If you are referring to your mother, I did everything I could. What did you want me to do . . . force her mouth open and pour soup down?"

"Yes, I did!" said Dorak fiercely.

"Ah, we've been over this a hundred times. She wanted to die and so she did. There was nothing I could have done."

Dorak started to speak, but thought the better of it. There was no use arguing about a terrible event that could not be changed. He motioned to the litter bearers to get up. "It's time to go inside now, Father. You must rest."

His father put up no resistance as the bearers led him down the hill to the campsite.

Dorak followed at a brisk pace. He would do well not to anger his father. He needed the old man's cooperation to gain power among the generals.

The campsite was spread over several hills with Zoar's tent in the middle. They followed the main trail to his tent.

Soldiers, who were polishing their weapons, sparring for fun, or playing dice, quickly stood and saluted as Zoar passed in his litter chair borne by four sweating and grunting men.

Zoar paid them no mind, for he was in pain again and wished to be in bed. The desire to conquer worlds left him as the pain grew stronger. As they approached, both Dorak and Zoar heard a loud commotion and screams coming from the aga's tent.

Dorak came to the side of the litter, ordering the men to stop.

The tent flap was pushed aside by two guards tenuously holding on to a woman who was fighting with all her strength. She bit the hand of one guard and as he let go, she swung around and punched the other guard in the face. Quickly grabbing the fallen guard's sword, she sliced both men.

The soldiers held their hands to their wounds, crying out.

The woman looked about and was about to flee when she saw the aga's litter. Realizing who was before her, she flung herself at the litter only to be repulsed by Dorak who threw himself in front of her. Dropping the sword, she fell to her knees.

Dorak strolled over, pulled her head up by her hair, and prepared to cut her throat.

"Great Aga!" she cried out. "Don't kill me! I come from beyond the mist!"

Zoar roared, "DORAK! STOP!"

Dorak's knife nicked the woman's throat before he released her. A thin line of blood trickled down her neck. The woman fell unconscious on the ground.

"Bind her wounds and bring her to me," Zoar commanded.

Dorak obeyed and called for a physician who had to push his way through a crowd of curious men gawking at the strange woman. Kneeling by her side, Dorak looked for concealed weapons.

The healer had the woman taken to a nearby tent where he could tend to her as well as the two injured guards.

While being examined, the guards told Dorak they had been following their routine, checking the aga's tent when they discovered the woman lurking inside.

"Explain to me how one woman can get past forty thousand men!" shouted Dorak. "Get that woman ready! I want to question her."

The physician bandaged the woman's neck and caused her to awaken with a horrible smelling solution he kept in a borax stomach.

She pushed the foul-smelling bag away, and sat up shaking her head as if to straighten her thoughts. Seeing Dorak out of the corner of her eye, she immediately became still and waited in silence.

He studied her coldly, and she turned to return the stare. He was surprised by her boldness.

The woman was in excellent shape for being middle-aged. She was very tall and muscular. Her clothing looked of rich quality, though now dirty and torn in places. She had all her teeth. Her hands were strong, but lacked the look of a manual laborer.

This is no peasant woman, thought Dorak. "Come, my father will see you," said Dorak. He motioned to her to follow. "Do you understand me?"

The woman nodded and swung off the table. Passing the soldiers she had wounded, she smiled patronizingly at them.

Obviously uncomfortable, they looked away.

Four guards fell into step, marching behind Dorak and the woman. They passed the aga's horses being brought in for the night, a small group of musicians, numerous advisors, attending guards, and servants bringing shaybar and cheese.

Zoar's concubines lounged on couches. They became alarmed when the strange woman was brought in.

Zoar was drinking shaybar–a bowl of boiled borax milk mixed with blood his healer had brought while having his feet bathed in scented water by a concubine.

Dorak knew his father was using this time to study the prisoner.

Finally, Zoar waved the healer away. He belched loudly and gave the bowl to a waiting servant.

The captured woman was forced to her knees by a guard.

Dorak approached his father and whispered in his ear all that he had learned.

"Who are you?" asked Zoar after listening to Dorak. "Can you speak my language?"

"I can speak Sivan, Great Lord," answered Mikkotto in the Sivan language.

A scribe, who could translate, hurried to the aga's side.

"Where do you come from?"

"Hasan Daeg, the land beyond the mist. My name is Baroness Mikkotto from the House of Sumsumitoyo."

"Why are you here?"

"I have come to serve the Great Aga."

"Liar!" shouted Zoar, his face turning red.

For the first time, the woman felt fear. "No, it is true," she stuttered. "I have come to serve you against the royal house of Hasan Daeg."

"Why would you betray your king?" asked Dorak.

"I've come because I want blood revenge. The ruler, Queen Abisola de Magela, killed my only son. I want her to die as well as her offspring, Princess Maura," Baroness Mikkotto professed maliciously.

"Why did the queen kill your son?"

"Because she wanted him as a consort and he refused her. Out of a jealous rage, she had my son murdered," lied Mikkotto.

Zoar and Dorak exchanged glances.

"Let's try another answer. If your son refused the advances of his queen, then he deserved to die. You would not betray your country over that. What is the real reason?" asked Dorak. "Be quick or I really will slit your throat this time."

Mikkotto's hands flew up to her neck. "I tried to have Princess Maura, assassinated, but my child was killed instead."

Zoar threw back his head. "Ah, truth finally enters the room. Pray, truth, be seated."

A chair was brought for Mikkotto and she gratefully sat.

"Why did you want the princess to die?" asked Dorak, fascinated by the woman sitting before him.

"I do not want war. I want to make a treaty." She stopped and caught her breath before continuing. "My lands are on the border and will be decimated. I stand to lose everything."

"And yet it seems you have," claimed Zoar.

"Perhaps not," Mikkotto implied.

"I will not deal with a woman. Where is your husband?"

Mikkotto bristled. "Our husbands do not deal with public life. That is reserved for the females. You will make your deal with me or better yet, let me speak to the woman in charge here."

Zoar's concubines gasped, staring at Mikkotto in awe. They had never heard of such concepts before.

Dorak's mouth fell open, but Zoar let out a lusty guffaw. "I like you, Baroness," he laughed. "You will provide me with much entertainment and information about this Hasan Daeg."

Mikkotto eyed Zoar suspiciously. "Only if we can come to some agreement."

"Even without an agreement. There are things worse than death, Baroness Mikkotto. And before your death, you would tell me everything I wish to know. But why such rancor? We can become friends. Come lie beside me on these comfortable pillows," he offered, pointing to his side.

"We will dine and listen to beautiful music sounding like a woman weeping when she is being made love to. After you have rested, we will talk like old comrades." Zoar paused for a moment. "What choice do you have, my lady?"

The baroness listened calmly to the translator knowing she was trapped. She smiled convincingly at Zoar. "Great Aga, surely you do not want me to lie next to you in these filthy rags? I am a woman of high rank—noble blood. I should dress accordingly."

Dorak motioned to the oldest of Zoar's concubines who rose and went over to him. "Arrange for Baroness Mikkotto to have suitable clothes for one of her station, and a private tent with a bath waiting for her."

The concubine nodded and left with several servants.

"May I compliment you on your choice of bedmates," remarked Mikkotto looking at all of Zoar's concubines.

Zoar laughed. "That's all they are, Baroness. Mates to keep me warm, and nothing more. But a man could make love to a woman like you even with only his mind. Come. Lie next to me. Talk to me," he cooed entreatingly. "Let us learn one from the other."

Mikkotto rose and sat down beside Zoar.

Servants placed pillows behind her so she could sit up without straining. Another pillow was gently eased under her neck. Women pulled off her boots and bathed her feet with warm water and oils. Mikkotto, used to being served, relished the attention. Her outer garment was pulled off and her hands were placed in bowls of scented water. The musicians played sweet music, almost lulling Mikkotto to sleep. She opened her eyes to find both Zoar and Dorak staring at her curiously. It startled her.

"I apologize for being so rude," uttered Dorak, "but we have never seen a woman so powerful as you. You are tall and almost as muscular as a man."

"All the women from my country are my size or larger. I find it strange that your women are so delicate."

"Why do you have no hair on your body?" asked Zoar.

"It is the custom of my country that both women and men shave all hair except for their heads."

"Even down there?"

Mikkotto caught Zoar's meaning. "Especially down there." She felt exasperated. She had expected to be talking about matters of war with the king, not the hygiene of her countrywomen.

Zoar and Dorak were conducting themselves like two adolescent schoolboys after their first kiss. It disgusted her, but she would answer anything they asked. As Zoar had put it, what choice did she have?

"What do the men look like?" asked Zoar.

Zoar's advisors gathered closer. They too were fascinated by the large woman, who moved like an experienced warrior. Even the servants put down their platters so they could overhear what was being said.

"Our men are beautiful and very graceful. They wear their hair long and usually braid it with flowers. They are smaller and taught in the ways of poetry, art, stewardship of the home, and lovemaking. That was until our queen decided to make them like women," lamented Mikkotto.

"And you think this is bad?" asked Zoar.

"I think it is unnatural."

"So you are a traditionalist in your country. A noblewoman who wants to preserve the old ways."

Mikkotto said nothing after listening to the translator.

"My dear, this conflict tearing at your heart caused you to sacrifice your son and risk your life entering the enemy camp, making you dangerous indeed for you are a fanatic! Fanatics will not listen to reason, and they are hard to control. I'll tell you something else too. I wager you have daughters, but you would not sacrifice them to assassinate the princess because you knew in all probability the assassin would be killed." Zoar took a drink from his goblet.

"Wanting to preserve my way of life doesn't make me a criminal or a traitor, but a patriot!"

Dorak stifled a laugh.

Zoar too was amused. "What is it that you desire, my pretty traitor?"

"I want to rule Hasan Daeg. I would be a much better queen than that hag who now rules," Mikkotto declared bitterly.

Zoar turned to Dorak. "You see, my son, that all things come down to greed, power, or lust. With a fanatic, it is usually all three."

The translator refused to repeat Zoar's words to Mikkotto.

Still, she knew she had been berated by Zoar through his tone of voice. Insulted, Mikkotto pulled her hand away from Zoar's touch.

"Baroness, why should I make you ruler over Hasan Daeg and not put one of my own governors in or even my son?"

Mikkotto licked her lips before speaking.

Dorak thought she had the look of a poisonous snake before it struck.

His hand steadied on the hilt of his dagger.

Mikkotto spoke slowly. "I want my country to be as it was before Abisola started meddling in our culture. I want to preserve our heritage. What she is doing goes against nature and against our religion. In return for allowing me to restore the natural balance, I will serve you loyally. I know your world is in desperate need of food and medical supplies. My country can supply these things in abundance. We can feed your world!"

"What happened to my men?" asked Dorak.

Mikkotto chose her words carefully. "The mist is a powerful narcotic spray emitted by the caromate plant when its leaves are disturbed. With caromate plant beds, we have put other plants that draw small animals, birds, and insects not bothered by the mist. There is constant activity in the plants due to the movement of the small animals, so there is constant mist."

"Go on," encouraged Zoar.

"Anyone who enters the mist becomes drowsy and disoriented. We are immune to the plant so we can simply enter and do whatever we want. Your soldiers were taken out and given a heavy sedative. They died peacefully in their sleep. I can assure you they were not molested or disrespected in any way. Their bodies were taken away and buried according to our custom." Mikkotto seemed pleased with the telling of the story.

Zoar's face grew red with fury. "You have denied my men an honorable death!"

"I don't understand."

"In our world, a good death is one in which a warrior meets his end fighting a worthy opponent. It ensures peace for the soul of the deceased. Allowing the men to die defenseless means they will walk the land without rest."

Mikkotto was alarmed. "I am sorry. We did not know. We thought we were being merciful." Mikkotto slid to her knees. "Great Aga, my country has not had a war in over six hundred years. We have forgotten the ways of the warrior. Do not place blame on my people, who thought they were doing right. Blame the bitch who brought this all about. Make me queen so I may serve you. You will not regret it."

"I already regret it. Get out of here. Go bathe. You stink. Then come back later. You will tell me more of your country." Zoar looked at her lecherously. "Maybe there are other things you can show me."

Mikkotto barely suppressed a shudder. "Sire, I am too old for you. I have spent a life of being pleased rather than one pleasing. I would not know what to do."

"As you are taking your bath, you may reflect. I'm sure you can think of something to benefit the both of us."

Mikkotto bowed her head and left the tent, eager to be away from Zoar.

Dorak turned to Zoar after she had left. "Surely, you are not serious about taking that odious woman into your bed. She would sooner kill you than look at you."

"I am too old and sick for such ventures, but she doesn't know that. I like to torment her. It gives me a new interest in life. I'll make her beg and say sweet things, knowing all the time she is retching inside," said Zoar, smiling sweetly.

"But why waste the time? Let's just torture her and get the information we need."

"Dorak, you have no instinct for sport. Besides, I don't want her tortured by anyone but me. She interests me. She excites me."

"She's the enemy. She ought to be treated like a prisoner of war."

"She's a woman. What real harm can she do?"

"Try asking the wounded guards."

"Luck. They were careless."

Dorak could not believe his father's stubbornness. "Father, she fought like a trained soldier. It was not luck bringing her to your tent. It was skill. She is very dangerous. Too dangerous for a bed toy. Please let me interrogate her."

Not wishing to continue this line of conversation, Zoar changed the subject. "Do you believe her? I mean, it sounds fantastic–a country run by women who have built a barrier from simple plants. Can it be true?"

"It sounds very much like KiKu's stories."

"KiKu," mused Zoar. "Yes, let's make every effort to find him. We have many things to ask him." Zoar flicked a moth off his sleeve. "You concentrate on KiKu and the spy network, and I will concentrate on the woman. Between the two of us, we should be able to overrun this Hasan Daegian queen within a full turning of the big moon."

Dorak did not believe in the methods of his father, though they usually had merit. If his father wanted to play with this woman's mind, who was he to say it would not be effective? He bowed and left the tent. He had much to do that night. He paused for a moment outside, looking at the mist looming in the distance. He made a silent vow that whatever was discovered beyond the wall, he would not let his father carve it up as he had other conquered lands. Too much waste and destruction for Dorak's taste.

He remembered the fall of Anqara. The city was still not inhabited. It was considered a place haunted by the dead. Thousands of people had been killed during the siege until the streets turned red with their blood. Many others had vanished. No, he would not let that happen to Hasan Daeg. Whatever was there he would try to preserve. And if it took working with the distasteful baroness to achieve it, he would do it.

Some soldiers began singing around a fire.

The singing caused Dorak to break his concentration. He regarded the soldiers for a moment, almost wishing he could join in their revelry. Pushing this thought from his mind, he headed for his tent with his way lit by several servants bearing torches.

29

Mikkotto bathed a long time.

A blue-green kimono and cork sandals were brought to her. "These are the clothes of a courtesan," barked Mikkotto in the Sivan language. "Bring me leggings and a tunic."

Zoar's concubine bowed low. "I am sorry, Baroness, but this is the court attire for a noblewoman. My lord would be most offended if I dressed you like a man. It would not be fitting."

"This foul country with its stupid practices," ranted Mikkotto, snatching the robe away from the concubine. "Get out. I can get dressed myself."

The concubine bowed low again. "I'm sorry. If you do not look presentable, I will lose my head. I cannot allow this to happen, so I must stay. You may kick me if it will make you feel better, but you will look presentable. After all, a kick is better than death. Do you not agree?"

Mikkotto looked at the concubine. "I have a daughter about your age," she said softly.

"That is good. Perhaps you will take pity on me and be kind," pleaded the concubine, putting ivory combs in Mikkotto's hair.

"In my country, women are treated with respect. We would kill a man who talked the way Zoar did tonight."

"Perhaps one day I will be allowed to visit your country. I would like once before I die to pick a man of my own choosing. Is that possible in your country?"

Mikkotto nodded.

The concubine smiled with great pleasure. "Baroness, you have given me something to dream about. I thank you for this great honor of serving a most independent female. Perhaps you will remember your most humble servant and call for me in the future?"

"We shall see."

The concubine lowered her voice. "Zoar has no intention of mating with you. He cannot. The most he can do is fondle. You can stand that, surely. It is Dorak you must watch."

Mikkotto did not respond to the concubine's words, but fussed with her hair. "What is your name, girl?" asked Mikkotto.

"KiKusan. I am the daughter of KiKu, the hetmaan for my master."

Mikkotto realized she had made a valuable friend. She smiled warmly at KiKusan.

KiKusan tied Mikkotto's sandals. "It is time for us to go," she announced.

The older woman followed the young concubine to Zoar's tent.

Mikkotto took a deep breath before entering. She was again assaulted by pungent odors. The smell of horse dung, incense, cooked meat, and body sweat permeated the air. She hoped she would not get a headache.

On the aga's couch lay Zoar with several of his women. The girls had already fallen asleep, but he was still awake and motioned to her.

Picking her way carefully through the various flung-out limbs of sleeping bedmates, Mikkotto made her way beside Zoar on her side, facing him.

Zoar appraised Mikkotto. "You look very handsome," he said in the Sivan language.

"Thank you," replied Mikkotto, knowing now that he had understood every word she had uttered. Zoar had never needed an interpreter. Still, she was grateful for his compliment. She knew she was not pretty, but striking in appearance. She pulled at the kimono folds.

Zoar raised up on one elbow, "No, don't do that. I want to look at you." He pulled the kimono apart. "Did you suckle your children?"

Surprised by the question, Mikkotto answered quickly, "Yes, I did. Only with the girls. My son had a wet nurse."

"There is something very pleasing about a woman who has suckled. These girls are all very beautiful. Their bellies are without blemish, their breasts high and firm, their lips eager to be kissed, but they bore me."

Mikkotto laughed, not believing him.

"No, it is true. I am bored with their beauty and youth. You told me you are used to being served. Then let me, Great Aga of the Eastern World, serve you. Let me stroke you. You need not respond if you do not wish to. Just tell stories about your homeland. What would you do if I made you queen? Talk about anything until you fall asleep."

Mikkotto did not move away, but her mind was full of astonishing thoughts. She did not feel repulsed as she thought she would. Instead, she felt lulled by the soft music playing, Zoar's murmuring voice, and the gentle snoring of the girls lying with them on the huge couch. She found Zoar's large rough hands soothing.

"It has been a long time since I have had pleasures such as this," she sighed.

"Tell me about your husband."

"Which one? I have had several."

"You tell me your story, and I will tell you about my wives. You remind me of my first wife."

"Did you have feelings for her?" asked Mikkotto, closing her eyes.

"I certainly love the memory of her. Now I have told you a truth about myself. You must tell me a truth."

"I married my first husband for dynastic reasons. He was an only child whose land doubled my holdings. I had my first child by him."

"And then you had him killed, right?"

Shocked, Mikkotto sat up, pushing Zoar away.

"Don't be so defensive. It only makes sense. You did not love him and, being an only child, he was probably a big baby. You could not bear the thought of spending the rest of your life with him, so he met with an unfortunate accident."

"No one knows," hissed Mikkotto.

"I do now. Your reaction tells me my guess is true. Lie back down, and I will tell you a secret about me. Come, come. Don't be shy. We are getting along so well." Zoar looked thoughtful and weighed his words before he spoke. "My first wife. I loved her desperately, but she did not love me. She was in love with another."

"You saw them together?"

Zoar shook his head. "She would never have betrayed me. She was very honorable. But I couldn't stand the notion that she thought of another when she was with me. It drove me nearly insane. One day we were out hunting and a borax attacked. I hesitated killing the animal, and that mistake cost her life. It was during her funeral, I realized I had wanted her to die, and that's why I had hesitated. Strangely, her death set me free."

Zoar paused and looked at Mikkotto. "I wish to love again, Mikkotto. Let me love you, and I will make you queen of Hasan Daeg."

"I have no wish to recapture your past with you and die as did your queen."

"I am an old man long past all such vanities. I know you would never love me as you are past such grand passions yourself. I wish only to love on a small scale. I want to touch this time with clarity, not the drunkenness of lust. I want to talk about old glories. I want a woman who wants to be pleasured instead of sniffing around me like a hound in heat. Give me a little passion, a little companionship, and I will make you queen of Hasan Daeg."

"It is such a tempting offer. I must say you are not as repulsive as I thought you would be."

Zoar winked. "Tell me the truth. Isn't this more pleasant than rotting away in some prison?"

Mikkotto smiled. "I accept your offer, Great Aga. May we both not live to regret this foolishness."

"Call me Zoar, please. Now move closer, my pet. Let me feel your belly. That is all the energy I will have left for tonight. If you need more, you must satisfy yourself."

Mikkotto moved closer and untied her kimono. "Maybe we can satisfy each other?"

Zoar grinned with anticipation. "We can try, pet. We can certainly try."

30

Dorak took a deep breath.

"Tell me again. Who are the Dinii?"

"We have been over this countless times. I am tired. I want to go to sleep," complained Mikkotto.

"Not until I understand."

Mikkotto sighed. "The Dinii are the Overlords of Hasan Daeg. They are the real owners of the land. We cultivate the land which attracts the wildlife upon which they feed."

"And they are birds?"

"Yes. No. Yes!" cried Mikkotto, exasperated. "They are birds, but they are people as well."

"Are they intelligent?"

"Extremely. They are a very old race and great warriors. Your shields and swords will be no match for them."

"Dorak, I don't see what good it is to go over the same information time and time again," interjected Zoar. He, too, was tired and wanted to go to bed.

The Prince held up his hand. "I must see if her information is consistent. Please try to be patient."

"Can't you see that she is exhausted?"

"Which is why I want to continue questioning her, Father, to see if there are any cracks in her story."

Mikkotto gave Dorak a vicious glare. "I've told you all I know. If you fight the Hasan Daegians, you must also fight the Dinii."

"If it is the Dinii's land, where did the Hasan Daegians come from?"

"I don't know. I just know it was the Dinii's land before we came."

"Where did you come from?"

"I don't know," spat Mikkotto.

"As you told us, Hasan Daegians have various ethnic appearances. Don't you think it strange that Hasan Daegians have different skin colors and hair textures from each other?"

Zoar said, "I don't see the point."

"Father, don't you see? In every country we have been in, all the people have looked similar except for the slaves, which were brought in from other places. This has always been consistent."

"We are not slaves," protested Mikkotto, very insulted.

"How do you know? You can't even tell me the origin of your own people. You could be manipulated by the Dinii and not even know it."

Zoar countered, "Suppose they are the descendants of slaves, how does this information help to invade Hasan Daeg? Tell me. I would truly like to know."

"We could use this information to help break the treaty between the Dinii and the Hasan Daegians," answered Dorak hoarsely, his throat feeling dry.

"Bah, this is silly." Zoar turned to Mikkotto. "Pet, how would you invade Hasan Daeg?"

Mikkotto tried to suppress a yawn, but could not. "There is only one river which enters Hasan Daeg from the east. Across this river, they run huge, stationary barges filled with dirt in which they have planted caromate plants. It is here the mist is the weakest. Have your men destroy the barges, and you will have a pathway into Hasan Daeg." She lay down by Zoar's feet and curled up. "Leave me alone now. I must sleep."

Dorak started to kick Mikkotto but Zoar caught his leg, shooting him a warning glance. Dorak bowed and went to the table to replenish his wine goblet. He did not like his father's fascination with this woman. For weeks, the army had remained stationary while Zoar amused himself with his new plaything. Their relationship interfered with Dorak's plans.

Outside a thunderstorm raged furiously. A thunderclap woke Mikkotto, and she groggily struggled to rise.

Zoar helped her.

Dorak thumbed through scrolls on the table and continued his interrogation. "Do you recognize this drawing?" He held up a picture.

"It is the Bogazkoy tree."

"What is that?"

"It is the rarest species of plant life in Hasan Daeg. There is only one specimen rumored to exist, and it is owned by the Crown."

"Why does Queen Abisola want this plant?"

Mikkotto coughed, "May I have some water?"

"Answer the question first," said Dorak.

"It is thought the Bogazkoy tree is used to prolong the lives of the rulers. It gives them and their offspring the blue color. The blue skin is a sign of royalty."

"True blue bloods, eh, Dorak," croaked Zoar. He thought it amusing.

"How does it do this?" asked Dorak, ignoring his father.

"I don't know. It is just a rumor of how the de Magelas got their blue skin. Probably superstition. You said I could have some water."

Dorak handed her a goblet of wine.

She drank greedily.

Zoar observed them both quietly. His intuition told him that Dorak was planning something unpleasant for Mikkotto. He would have to keep an eye on his son to prevent him from doing something that would cause misery between the two of them.

"You have seen this Bogazkoy tree?"

"No one has ever seen it."

"Then how do you know this picture is of the Bogazkoy?"

"That same picture is in our religious texts which we use to worship our goddess, Mekonia."

"Where is this tree planted?"

"Probably the palace, but I don't really know."

"You don't know. You don't know," mimicked Dorak. "You are worthless!"

"Stop it! Stop screaming those endless questions at me. It is driving me crazy, I tell you," shouted Mikkotto. She feared she was breaking under the strain of constant interrogation for the past four days and nights.

Zoar had done little to interfere.

She looked pleadingly at him.

"This is enough for tonight," said Zoar, motioning for his men to raise his litter.

Dorak started to protest.

"Enough, I said," countered Zoar forcefully. "What good is she to us if you drive her to exhaustion with your constant pestering?"

"But Father!"

"She has told you how to enter Hasan Daeg. Isn't that a start? Why don't you start planning a strategy to get us inside? Why are you asking questions about their culture, habits, their royalty? We will know all of that soon enough when we enter. Your questioning is wasting precious time. Fall will be here soon, then winter. I want to be back in Bhuttan by the first snow."

"Father, I only ask on your behalf."

"How is that?"

"If this Bogazkoy tree prolongs life, perhaps it can restore part of your vigor. Maybe your health entirely. Remember, these Hasan Daegian queens are renowned as healers!"

"Dangling a carrot on a stick, son? I know all about this Bogazkoy tree. I've known about it for years from the papers of the High Priestess from the House of Magi." Zoar pulled the coverlet closer to his chest. "The High Priestess was named Mehmet. She kept a personal diary, which was partially burned in the fire set by the Dini I witnessed in her room. She was found on a rooftop with her neck broken."

Dorak scattered through his scrolls, looking for a translation of the diary. "I have no such copy of this diary," he complained, puzzled.

"You were given none by my orders," replied Zoar, looking pleased. "I have the only copy and it is locked away. It took years to translate it. She had written it in no known language, but in her own coding system. This woman would have made a great spy," Zoar said admiringly. "Her code was finally broken two years ago."

"That's when you started planning this campaign."

"Correct. From the scraps of the diary, I realized the significance of the Bogazkoy tree. There was hope again that I would be able to walk." Zoar's eyes glowed with anticipation. "How the tree works, I don't know yet. But whatever happens, no one from the house de Magela will be killed or injured until I have discovered their secret."

Zoar pointed to Mikkotto leaning against the litter chair asleep. "And she is going to help me."

"She knows nothing."

"You do not give Mikkotto credit. She is a brave and resourceful woman. She is also connected to the royal house by kinship. This poor creature may know the answer to the Bogazkoy mystery, but does not realize that she does. That's why my method is more fruitful. If she is not intimidated, she will divulge more."

"Is that why you treat her kindly?"

Zoar stroked his beard. He regarded Dorak coldly, his voice ringing with deadly earnest. "I treat Mikkotto well because she is the key to Hasan Daeg and because I care for her."

"What!" exclaimed Dorak. "Surely you're joking?"

"No, Dorak. After the campaign, I intend to marry Mikkotto and make her my empress." Zoar mused, "With a little luck, she still might be able to conceive."

Dorak grabbed the table to steady himself, betraying his inner thoughts. "I don't understand. You have only known this woman for a few short weeks."

"At my age, that is long enough."

"But you cannot perform." Dorak felt as if he had been kicked in the stomach by a warhorse. His mind was quickly calculating the damage if Mikkotto were made empress and conceived. Could Zoar, in his ardent passion for Mikkotto, proclaim a new heir presumptive? No, Dorak could never allow this possibility. He and his mother had suffered too much.

"I am feeling better all the time. As I said, Mikkotto is a remarkable woman. Now I wish to retire." Zoar motioned for his bearers to lift Mikkotto into the litter chair. He stroked her hair absently while bidding Dorak good night and left for his own tent.

Sickened, Dorak fell into a chair. He brooded for hours and did not hear the trumpet herald the new morning.

His servants found him slumped over a table, his hands clutching scrolls. Gently they removed him to his couch and undressed him. Pulling the tent flap closed, they let him sleep until dusk. When Dorak awoke, his future course had been plotted. He knew he could not turn back.

31

It took weeks for the preparations.

The river was surveyed as much as possible while great rafts were constructed. Huge catapults were dragged into place on both sides of the river before the mist wall. Archers practiced shooting with their longbows the distance Dorak said would be required to set the barges on fire. Men, hand-picked by Dorak, spent hours swimming back and forth across the river. It was very difficult as some of the men lost their way and drifted into the mist. They became sleepy and drowned.

Foot soldiers practiced hand-to-hand combat while the cavalry ran their warhorses through daily exercises. The tanners made extra bridles and gloves. Armor and weapons were polished until they were blinding in the late summer sun and checked over and over again.

The Camaroon population was rounded up and interrogated. When Dorak was satisfied they knew nothing about what was beyond the mist, he used them as slave labor to gather firewood for his army, tend the animals, and satisfy his men at night. The captured Camaroons, crying out in agony, were heard by Hasan Daegian soldiers standing watch on the other side of the mist.

On the last night before the invasion was to begin, forty thousand men along with ten thousand servants, slaves, and camp followers celebrated Bhuttan's most sacred holiday, the mating of Bhuttu with Bhutta to create a new world order.

Tables, laden with food and drink, were stretched from one end of the camp to the other. Huge fires were built, and the soldiers danced feverishly around them.

Those in Zoar's tent were also celebrating. Paper mache replicas of phalluses were placed all around the tent. Zoar's concubines dressed gaily in bold colors and danced lasciviously in Bhuttu's honor. Some had fake phalluses attached to their costumes and pretended to mate with other girls.

Mikkotto watched the girls with quiet disdain and was glad when the food was brought in. It gave her an excuse to be distracted from the entertainment. She looked at Zoar and saw that his eyes glittered with excitement. She thought him an old lecherous fool.

Dorak strode into the tent, his face tense. He went up to Zoar. "Father, I thought there would be no spirits tonight."

"The men need something more than just water to wash down their food."

Dorak curbed his tone. "I realize tonight is a special celebration, but we are going into battle tomorrow. The men will need clear heads and steady hands."

"Tomorrow will pose no problem for us," laughed Zoar. "Mikkotto has told us everything we need to know about the Hasan Daegian army." He smiled sweetly at her. "We could go in with only twenty thousand men and mop up before dusk."

"I wish I could be so confident," said Dorak, lowering his voice. He smiled at the advisors and honored guests of his father's, not wishing to cause a scene.

"Relax, sit down beside me and enjoy the festivities." Zoar motioned for a servant to get some wine for Dorak. "You worry too much."

Dorak sat down, trying not to scowl. His brain was racing. He noticed Mikkotto was looking around Zoar at him. *Even she thinks this is ridiculous*, thought Dorak.

Zoar was stuffing himself with food and drink. He wiped his greasy hands on his robe. As soon as he was finished with one dish, Mikkotto offered him another and then another dish. She teased him, coaxed him, and baited him. Zoar laughed uproariously. He slapped his knees with mirth at performing clowns who juggled small boaeps. Suddenly he grabbed his middle and let out a loud belch. "I think I need to make water," Zoar announced.

Servants rushed over to help Zoar to his litter.

"I will go with him," offered Dorak, rising to follow his father being carried out.

The servants placed Zoar's litter by a tree and lifted his robe to allow him to relieve himself.

Dorak told the servants to leave. "I will call you when he is ready to go back in," ordered the prince.

The servants, always impressed with Dorak's concern for his father, gladly left Zoar in his hands. They wished to watch the clowns.

Zoar babbled incoherently, his mind befuddled by too much drink. He leaned precariously from his chair as he began urinating.

Dorak looked about. There was no one to be seen.

With the strength of a powerful warrior, Dorak quickly grabbed his father's face, placing his hands over Zoar's nose and mouth.

Zoar struggled hard, grabbing at his son's hands and twisting, almost causing Dorak to lose his grip.

But Dorak held on for what seemed to be an eternity.

Zoar's squirming slowed until it ceased all together. Finally, he slumped against Dorak's chest.

Dorak checked for a pulse. Finding none, he gathered Zoar gently in his arms and carried him into the tent. In a loud voice, he cried out, "My father's ill. Someone help!"

Tears of sorrow fell from Dorak's face.

32

Princess Maura could not sleep.

She stood staring into mist listening to the revelry from the other side.

Before dawn, her soldiers would slip through and attack Zoar's army. They would try to inflict as much damage as possible before they retreated beyond the wall again. It had been decided that the Hasan Daegians, even though well-trained, were no match for Zoar's crack troops and would have to resort to guerrilla tactics.

She looked behind her.

All through the forest, trees were filled with the darkened outlines of the Dinii who had perched for the night. Beneath the shelter of the trees and the watchful eyes of the Dinii camped thousands of Hasan Daegians, Anqarians, and mercenaries from other countries. They all looked asleep in their bedrolls, but Maura knew her soldiers were awake, listening to the sound of singing coming through the mist wall.

Chaun Maaun came up behind and placed his arm around her.

She rested her head on his chest, grateful for his small kindness. As always, Maura deeply inhaled his scent for she loved the woodsy smell of him.

He kissed the top of her head. "I guess I shouldn't be kissing the new commander-in-chief," he teased.

Maura said nothing. Since her birthday, they had spoken little, both realizing they had no future together. Saddened by the thought that they might die soon, Maura clasped her arms around Chaun Maaun and sobbed into his chest.

He held her tightly, rocking her back and forth with soothing sounds. "You mustn't cry," Chaun Maaun said softly. "You must stay strong for everyone's sake."

"I don't feel very strong," she hiccupped, tears streaming down her face.

"You want to know a secret? I'm frightened too."

"You, Chaun Maaun!"

"Even me."

"But you've fought before. You've even killed. I don't know that I can."

"When you see a double-edged ax coming toward your face, you'll kill without even thinking about it. Trust me on that. The instinct to survive will not let you down. Just let it guide you."

The princess wiped hot salty tears from her face. "Chaun, I have terrible fears that I will be a coward, hiding until the battle is over. How will I be able to live with myself if I dishonor my family?"

"Maura, you are not alone. I remember the first time I fought with a poacher. I was so scared. I had the same thoughts, but you cannot run away even as I could not. There is something inside us that won't allow it. Trust your instinct. Pull from your center all that Iegani has taught you."

"I wish my mother had never made me commander-in-chief. I begged her not to. Yesemek should have been in charge. She's a true warrior."

"Yesemek is not Hasan Daegian. She would never be able to inspire the people as you do. They will follow you, but will always have a seed of mistrust of Yesemek because she is a Dini. Your mother is correct about this and far-seeing in her choice."

"You are right. I am being a fool. It's a little late to have second thoughts."

Chaun Maaun laughed heartily. "That's an understatement!"

She joined with him laughing.

Yesemek flew down beside them. "Shh, do you want to alert the enemy?" she hissed angrily.

Princess Maura blushed furiously. "I am sorry, General Yesemek. It was most unwise of us, but as I am commander-in-chief, I will remind you not to publicly reprimand me again. Good night," she said brusquely. Marching to her tent, the princess left the general astounded and Chaun Maaun grinning.

Yesemek gaped after her and turned to Chaun Maaun.

He shrugged his massive shoulders and said, "I guess she's taking her new title very seriously."

The Dini general flew back up to her perch making clicking noises.
Suddenly the singing from the other side stopped.
Anxious cries could be heard.
Chaun Maaun listened carefully.
Maura ran back and joined him.
The entire Hasan Daegian camp got up from their bedrolls and waited.
"Get Yeti," commanded Princess Maura to a Dinii sergeant.
Within a few minutes, Yeti and Benzar appeared at Maura's side. "They are not celebrating anymore. See what's happening and report to me here," she commanded.
Yeti and Benzar flew off with barely a sound.
A stool and a blanket were brought for Maura.
Chaun Maaun and Yesemek stood beside the shivering princess, both of them realizing she wasn't shaking from the cold. They knew their presence brought her some measure of comfort.
Yesemek silently prayed that Maura's years of training with the Dinii would instill her with courage. She wished Iegani was present so that he could reassure the princess as he always did. He had flown off to some secret place for a retreat. He needed to communicate with his inner self, he had said. *What balderdash!* Yesemek had thought when he came to say goodbye. He was needed now, and no one knew where to find him.
Maura, Chaun Maaun, Yesemek, along with all the other warriors waited in silence.
Twenty minutes later, Yeti and Benzar flew into the camp. They were hot and panting, but they looked jubilant.
"What has happened?" asked Maura, standing abruptly.
Yeti cried, "Zoar is dead!"
"What!" echoed Chaun Maaun, stunned.
"Yes, he died this very night during the feast of their gods. The entire camp is in mourning. They think this a very bad omen."
"This means the attack will be called off!" exclaimed a jubilant Chaun Maaun. He shook his fists into the air and did a little dance, skipping and hopping around Maura and Yesemek.
"Is Dorak, the son of Zoar, still alive?" questioned Yesemek.
"Yes, he was with his father when he passed away," said Benzar.
"How did Zoar die?" asked Maura.
"They don't know for sure, but it is thought from natural causes. Dorak claims Zoar was relieving himself and grabbed at his chest as

though in pain. Zoar was dead by the time a healer could be called. There were no marks on the body."

Yesemek gave a deadly look at Chaun Maaun. "You say Dorak was with Zoar when he died?"

"Yes, General," answered Yeti.

Yesemek turned to Princess Maura. "It may be Dorak will take his troops home out of respect for his father. However, I would like to point out if Dorak does leave, he will lose face with his men and might never regain their trust again. If I were he, I would still attack, if only to remove the memory of the former ruler."

Maura inclined her head. She turned to Yeti. "You say the men are upset. Are they drunk?"

"Some are, Your Highness," replied Yeti. "It is certain that they are disoriented and low in spirit."

Maura pondered on this information. Everyone was looking to her for guidance. She felt her heart beating faster and not sure what to do. "I wish to be alone," she barked.

Everyone bowed and left except for Chaun Maaun. He looked at her expectantly.

"You too," she said more softly.

Looking hurt, he lumbered down the hill and joined Yesemek.

Pulling the blanket around herself, she slumped down. For a moment, she had the very strong urge to suck her thumb. She wanted to go home. Disgusted with herself, she put the thought out of her mind. Surely, Dorak would not attack with his father dead.

Closing her eyes, the princess struggled to meditate as Iegani had taught her so many years ago. Deeper and deeper she reached into herself until there was a blinding light flashing from behind her eyes. It caused Maura great pain causing her to double over. Through the light, she saw Iegani in a strange watery place reaching his hand out toward her.

"Trust your inner self," he said.

Maura held her head as she felt a grinding pain near her ears. She was sure she cried out. In the blinking of an eye, the pain released her and she slumped back into her chair. Sweat matted her hair, and her skin was covered with goosebumps. A strange tingling crept up her spine and then left her body through her eyes. She felt it dissipate.

Maura was unable to move. She tried lifting her arms, but could not. Finally, after some exertion, she could move her fingers. They felt as if they had been burned. The princess lowered her head toward her chest. Her hands and legs began to twitch. She tried to sit up, but couldn't. Straining, she tried to call, but this time no sound came forth. Suddenly she heard Chaun Maaun.

"Yesemek, help me! The princess is having a fit!" cried Chaun Maaun, rushing to Maura's side.

Yesemek blocked his way. "Let her be! She is on the Path of Seeking."

Chaun Maaun angrily pushed Yesemek aside, but too late. Princess Maura fell out of her chair.

The Dinii Prince fell to his knees to hold Maura, but felt a blow to the back of his neck. Bewildered, he swung around.

Yesemek warned, "Don't touch her. You don't want to be where she is."

Strong vibrations surrounded the trio. The very air seemed disturbed and unsteady. An angry buzzing noise sounded around the princess, then slowly faded.

Yesemek watched the young woman and knew her to be suffering.

Chaun Maaun sat back on his haunches, waiting until the spasms grew faint.

With her face still contorted, Maura slowly opened her eyes. Upon seeing Chaun Maaun, she struggled to talk.

Sensing the danger was past, he pulled her into a chair and called for a healer. He pulled hair out of her eyes and brushed leaves from her robe.

"I did not understand at first why Iegani left," confided Yesemek to Maura. "I thought it very odd. When I saw you go into a trance, I realized Iegani went to one of his special places of power. He was waiting for you, wasn't he?"

"She is not ill?" asked Chaun Maaun.

Princess Maura shook her head. "I was in a strange place. I wasn't really there, but then again, I was. It seemed like a spirit walk, but it was in water. Water surrounded me, and yet I could breathe and walk without hindrance. There was a bright yellow light, and I followed it. Before I could find the source of the light, Iegani stood before me encased in a huge orb. It shimmered in the light as water cascaded over its façade. He beckoned, telling me not to be afraid. I was going to be shown my destiny, but I would not be alone. His words calmed me until a strange-looking woman came up from behind and pushed him out of the way. Her hair floated in the water current, and she wore no clothes. I could see inside her body. I saw her heart pumping with blood running through her veins." The princess shivered, looking beseechingly at Chaun Maaun.

"Continue," encouraged Yesemek.

"The woman talked to me telepathically. She said she knew me and was going to show me a dark and terrible future if I did not fight. She said she knew I was thinking about returning to O Konya. From the corner of my eye, I saw Iegani struggle to move between us. The woman blew her breath at Iegani causing him to float away. Then she held out her hands. In the middle of each palm was an open eye, which moved independently from the other. She told me to look at the eyes.

"I said to her, 'No, I don't want to', but I could not look away. She took no pity on me. I was carried into the future, and it was a future without me. I knew I had been dead for a long time. The planet was scarred beyond recognition. Where once green valleys had nestled, there were now deserts. The land was cracked and scorched. Water was scarce and worth more than gold. Most of the animals were gone. People moved in bands, scavenging what they could. They were poor and ragged, without hearth or home to call their own. Everything that I had loved was gone. Hasan Daeg did not exist, nor did the Dinii. It was a world without hope because even the tools to rebuild no longer existed. It was a miserable existence for those who survived. I was glad that I was dead!

"The woman pointed a finger at me. 'You are responsible for this because you were weak. You did not take up the sword when needed, letting the enemy overrun your land. You could have stopped this. You are responsible!' Then I awoke." Maura mumbled again softly, "You are responsible." She stood unsteadily.

Chaun Maaun threw out a hand, but she dismissed it. She smiled gently at him. "I understand now what I must do. Please help me."

"Always!" cried Chaun Maaun alarmed.

"My dearest friend, you will not always understand my ways, but I beg of you to be patient with me. I am led down a path that I do not fully understand except I must follow it. The thought of turning my back fills me with such foreboding, I can do nothing else but go where I am called."

"I swear to you before all this company, both Dinii and Hasan Daegian, I give my personal fealty to you regardless of the relations between our two races." He bowed before Maura and kissed her hand.

Overcome with emotion, Princess Maura's hand flew up to stroke the feathers on his head before she summoned her soldiers.

"Get me Queen Rosalind's sword," she commanded of a servant.

The ancient sword of the first queen of Hasan Daeg with its jewel-encrusted hilt was handed to the princess. She raised the sword high over her head. In a loud voice she proclaimed, "I, Princess Maura de Magela, Heir Presumptive to the Royal House of Hasan Daeg, Little Mother of the Weak, Healer of the Infirm, do swear before this good company that I will fight and defend all that is mine and thine!"

"Aye! Aye!" shouted the crowd. "We love you, Princess. We will follow you unto death!"

Maura stood before the cheering crowd, her sword rising into the air, her legs apart and arms akimbo. Her eyes seemed ablaze. Her countenance was one of rapture. One by one, the soldiers began to bow down before her and proclaim their allegiance.

Maura turned to Yesemek and Kimtimee. "We attack just before dawn."

Yesemek snapped to attention and saluted. "Yes, everything will proceed as planned."

"Our goals are to knock out the catapults and rafts. After that is accomplished, kill as many as you can before retreating," said Maura.

Surprised, Yesemek ventured, "I thought we would only concentrate on military weapons systems."

"I have changed my mind," Princess Maura said, looking at her coldly. "Knocking out a few catapults is not going to change Dorak's mind about invading, but bloodshed might."

General Kimtimee offered, "Or it might make him angry."

"Do as you're told," snapped Maura.

Kimtimee and Yesemek bowed their heads and left to execute Maura's new orders.

Yesemek passed the word along to the Dinii. No one in the Dinii camp realized her concern about attacking the army itself. Were the Hasan Daegians ready for such bloody confrontation?

Chaun Maaun looked questioningly at Maura.

"You gave me your oath," she remarked bluntly.

"So I did and so I shall act," he replied. "I hope you don't lead us down the path of perdition."

"I don't know what that is," Maura retorted.

Chaun Maaun looked at the mist. "I imagine Dorak doesn't either." He turned and strode away, leaving her in the gloom of a dwindling torch.

33

All stood ready!

Princess Maura rode her pony, Beca, to the head of the soldiers anxiously awaiting her signal. Solemnly dressed in black leather, she sat stoically on the back of her prancing horse. Taking a deep breath, she extracted an arrow from her quiver and put the shaft in a cauldron of fire. With one swift movement, she withdrew the flaming arrow and notched it in the taut bowstring of her longbow. Deliberately, she raised the longbow to the heavens and, with a sudden cry of emotion, released the bowstring.

This was the signal to attack.

Watching as the flaming arrow arched upward over the waiting troops, the Dinii sprang into action. From the limbs of hundreds of trees, groups of Dinii flew in formation to scaffolds where Hasan Daegians awaited with small clay pots filled with burning oil. Each pot was in a leather sling with a long circular strap. The pots were hoisted up by the Hasan Daegians on tall poles. The Dinii would straighten out their formations into two lines, fly in low, snatch the flaming pot by the strap, and then regroup into their previous formations. With horrific battle cries, they flew by the hundreds over the wall of mist into the camp of the Bhuttanians. Once over their targets they simply released their slings with their burning fuel. So acute was their eyesight in the dark, they rarely missed snatching the slings or dropping them on their targets.

The Bhuttanians, demoralized and confused by the death of their king, stumbled out of their tents without benefit of armor or weapons. They stood perplexed, watching the catapults and rafts explode into flames as demon-like creatures flew across the dark sky. These creatures terrified them with hideous screams, their red eyes highlighted by the flames and sparks shooting into the air. Thinking their god, Bhuttan, was sending an army of banshees to avenge the death of Zoar, many of the soldiers ran screaming into the night only to die later as the Dinii hunted them down, one by one.

As soon as the first catapult was afire and gave enough light, several thousand male Hasan Daegian archers emerged from the mist. Taking aim with their small bows, they released a deadly rain of arrows, which found its mark in more than one man's chest. As soon as they released, they kneeled and began rearming their bows.

From behind stepped forward the female archers with heavier and stronger longbows. They lit their arrows and aimed for any target that would burn. Once they released, they kneeled and rearmed. The male archers then stood and began the process over again.

Step-by-step, arrow-by-arrow, they began to advance upon the encampment of Zoar until at last they were given the signal to retreat.

Out of the mist stepped Maura. Her dark hair framed her camouflaged face. The only mark of her station on her black uniform was embroidered uultepes encircling a Bogazkoy tree on her chest. Armed with a mace, sword, dagger, and shield she led her soldiers into battle with a mighty swing of her morning star mace.

The women, excited by the smell of blood in the air, cried out and descended upon the camp in a frenzied state. They were fighting for their land, their homes, and their children. They realized they would never have another opportunity like this again to destroy the enemy, so each blow must count.

Maura struck the first blow. A soldier, his eyes wide with fear, blocked her way. He swung at her with a sword. She parried with her mace.

The soldier, confused, hesitated.

Princess Maura immediately struck the side of his head.

He looked strangely at her, falling with the mace embedded in his skull.

She put her foot on his neck while trying to pull the mace out of the soldier's skull. Seeing another man approached from the left side, she whirled around, pulling out her sword. Falling to her knees, she placed her shield before her and thrust upwards with her sword. The stunned soldier dropped his ax and grabbed his belly.

A Hasan Daegian soldier came from behind and finished him off. She then helped Maura up. The princess murmured thanks and continued on.

Slashing, cutting, hacking, and thrusting, the Hasan Daegian foot soldiers made their way steadily deep into the enemy's camp. Behind them followed dismounted members of the cavalry, scavenging for useful weapons, carrying back their wounded, and killing any enemy soldier who was found still alive. Unable to bring their ponies through the mist, they were still eager for a fight until they saw the carnage left by Maura and her warriors. More than one was heard to say, "This isn't right."

Another soldier snapped back, "What do you think they would do to us, if given half a chance?"

By this time, the archers had moved around to the right of the encampment and, stepping out of the mist, they began their reign of terror over again.

Looking up, Maura gauged she only had about a hundred feet to go before her people would start making contact with the arrows. Coughing because of the thick smoke moving throughout the camp, she called to her next-in-command to signal a retreat.

The lieutenant shot an arrow with a red streaming tail into the air.

Dinii, watching from nearby trees, called to Kimtimee to retreat. She commanded the Hasan Daegians to blow the signal on their trumpets.

The trumpets sounded, and the Hasan Daegian women began moving back.

Bhuttanian soldiers from the rear of the camp had had time to dress and gather their weapons. Delayed by the stampede of borax and horses, they still made their way to the center of the camp where the Hasan Daegians were fighting.

Hearing a great cry from behind her, Maura swirled around, dodging a sword. She fell and quickly rolled to her left to bring up her shield. A heavy blow met it. She rolled to the right and threw up her shield. A blow rained down again and was so great that it split the shield. Sweat dripped into her eyes, making it hard to see. She parried her sword upward only to have it knocked from her hands. Rolling to her left, her opponent's sword struck the ground about her face. She rolled to the right and the same thing happened. Realizing her opponent was now playing with her, Maura charged forward only to be knocked down.

Breathing heavily and wiping sweat from her face, Maura glanced quickly about her. She was alone. Her soldiers and personal guards were fighting several hundred feet beyond her. Realizing she was captured, the princess pulled open her shirt and bared her throat to her victor. She would not be taken prisoner.

"Upon the brow of the goddess, it's the princess!" she heard a familiar voice cry out. "Look, see the blue skin!"

Maura looked hard at the small group of the enemy now encircling her. "Mikkotto!" Maura gasped. "You, here! Traitor!" Princess Maura spat at her.

"Tsk, tsk, is that any way for a royal princess to act?" baited Mikkotto, her eyes narrowing. "May I introduce your host to you? Prince Dorak, this is Princess Maura de Magela of the Royal House of Hasan Daeg. Princess Maura, the man with the sword at your chest is Prince Dorak. I am so sorry. I mean to say, Aga Dorak."

Maura shot a look at Dorak.

He slowly sheathed his sword, never taking his eyes off her. They were dark and seemed to penetrate her with their questioning stare.

Maura found she could not look away. And what was more, she did not want to.

He extended his hand to her.

She shook her head and stood on her own, feeling a little woozy.

"Please call off your warriors, Princess," requested Dorak politely, "I have taken you prisoner. It is considered very bad form to continue fighting after one's leader has, shall we say, fallen."

"You can't be serious," sputtered Mikkotto. "Kill her now and all resistance will fall in Hasan Daeg. Keep her and they will fight to the death to get her back."

"I don't believe you are on my staff of advisors, Baroness," Dorak warned coldly.

"Your father would have listened to me!"

"My father is dead, and you were nothing but my father's passing fancy."

Mikkotto's face grew red with fury. "Your father swore an oath to give me Hasan Daeg and she stands in the way!" The baroness, with lightening speed, withdrew a dagger from her sleeve and pushed past Dorak.

A black and white blur flew past her in front of Maura. Chaun Maaun stood facing the baroness.

Mikkotto gasped and stepped back. Even Dorak seemed unable to move, so frightening was the sight of Chaun Maaun towering over them.

"Here's something to remember me by, Baroness," Chaun Maaun said contemptuously. He reached out a taloned hand and scratched her left cheek. "Every time you look in the mirror."

Mikkotto screamed and, dropping the dagger, put her hands up to her face. Her hands were bloody.

Chaun Maaun smiled and, then stretching out his mighty wings, he took to the sky with Maura hanging on to his back.

Dorak watched them fly away until they were out of sight.

34

It was mid-morning.

Both sides were taking stock.

Dorak's camp was ravaged. Only a few hundred tents, out of thousands, stood. The armory tent, mess tent, and the medical tent were burned to the ground. Horses and borax that the Dinii had not slaughtered were scattered throughout the hills. A third of Dorak's men were missing or dead.

Patrols came back with horrid stories of finding their comrades, who had fled during the night, hanging upside down from tree limbs with their throats slit.

Each report made Dorak more livid until he thought his brain would explode. He sat exhausted on his father's couch, his head hung low. From the corner of the tent, he heard a low chuckle. "Go away from me," Dorak growled. "Torment some other poor fool!"

"A fool is what you are, Dorak," sneered Mikkotto. "You let an eighteen-year-old girl get the best of you. I wonder what your men are thinking of you right now. Are they saying Dorak is a great warrior like his father?" She laughed heartily. "Or are they saying that you are nothing?"

"Be careful how you tread, traitor," cautioned Dorak.

"Oh, you won't do anything to me. At least, not for a while. I'm too valuable. I know the terrain of Hasan Daeg. I know its people. I know the traits of the leaders. I know where the City of the Peaks is. No, you won't touch one hair on my pretty head."

"In my current mood, I would torture you for pleasure."

Mikkotto gave a tight-lipped smile before sitting on Zoar's couch, stretching out alongside Dorak.

Dorak thought she looked like a cat lounging in the summer sun.

"Dorak," she cooed, "have you any magic?"

"What?"

"Obviously, it has occurred to you that you might not be able to enter Hasan Daeg with brute strength, not as long as the Dinii are fighting with the Hasans. You need another tactical advantage."

"Such as?"

Mikkotto thought Dorak an idiot like his father, and tried to hide the irritation in her voice. "Maura won today because of the advantage of surprise. If your soldiers had not been so overcome by the loss of your father, they would have responded more quickly. That, together with their first sight of the Dinii and women as soldiers, unnerved them even more."

"The Dinii are a frightening lot."

"Your men are mentally prepared for them now. Haven't I heard you say time and time again that your soldiers are the best troops in the world? Don't you believe that still?"

Dorak looked at her, trying to see through his fog of despair. He felt lost and the guilt of his father's murder ate at him. Surely, Bhuttu was punishing him for his crime by this horrible defeat.

"Listen to me, Dorak," said Mikkotto, her voice taking on new authority. "You need to find a way to enter Hasan Daeg. Once inside, your soldiers can overcome any resistance."

She slid over to his side seductively and whispered in his ear. "Hasan Daeg is a jewel worth conquering. She is rich in minerals and precious gems. Her land is fertile, her timber virgin. Our cities are spacious and clean with wide boulevards and gardens with fountains. They are not like the crowded, starving, dirty towns of your world. Our population is tall and strong, free of disease. Treat Hasan Daeg well and she will lick your hand. Your father never conquered any country as rich in natural resources. You can really build your empire with Hasan Daeg's help, not some dogged villages with dirt roads patched together here and there, but a real empire. An empire to last a thousand years or more!" Mikkotto sat back and studied Dorak's face.

A vein in his temple pulsated strongly. He turned toward her. "Everything you say is true."

Mikkotto smiled smugly.

"And I despise you for saying it," he continued.

The baroness was startled.

"I despise the fact that you are a traitor. I hate you for being my father's woman and thus being a threat to me. I loathe you for daring to give me counsel."

Mikkotto began to move away from Dorak, but he grabbed her arm, causing her to wince in pain.

"But as you say, I need you. That, for the moment, is the only thing keeping you alive." He shoved her off the couch. "I will enter Hasan Daeg, and I will become her conqueror and king. You will be by my side the entire time. But I warn you, if you ever try to kill one of the de Magelas again, I will kill you by cutting one inch of your skin off at a time until there is nothing covering your body but muscle. How long do you think it would take, Mikkotto, slicing off skin one inch at a time until you look like a skinned boaep? Nod if you understand."

Mikkotto, terrified, nodded.

"That's a good girl. Now go run and play. Your lord and master needs time to think." Dorak leaned back on the couch and closed his eyes.

Mikkotto rose silently, tiptoeing out of the great tent. Her skin felt clammy as she breathed heavily. It was one thing to deal with a vain, pompous, old man. It was quite another to deal with a maniac. She would have to think long and hard about this boy.

35

Order was brought to the camp.

Throughout the day, Dorak's men managed to right their camp, even though they were constantly harassed during the morning by arrows shot through the mist wall. Dorak ordered the camp to move out of range and sent companies of men out foraging. What they could not buy or borrow, they stole. Some of the borax were found, and immediately killed and skinned to set on the roasting spits. At night the men readied themselves for another attack, and they were not disappointed.

The Dinii circled the camp and came up from behind, dropping a hail of rocks on the camp. As swiftly as they appeared, the Dinii flew off again, howling like night demons.

The camp was constantly harassed by arrows. More than one man died in full armor with an arrow through his neck.

Dorak sat in grim silence in his tent. He did not respond when his advisors begged him to retreat until reinforcements and supplies could be sent. He calmly drank his wine and watched his father's body being prepared for burial.

The next morning, Dorak, in full military dress, accompanied his father's body onto the battlefield in front of the mist. A handful of men erected a funeral pyre and carefully placed the body on it. Dorak ordered the men to join the other Bhuttanians, also in full armor, standing on a ridge watching.

Alone, he stood on the platform facing Hasan Daegians who stood at the edge of the mist watching. Dorak paid them no heed. The Dinii flew over the mist and roosted in trees away from Bhuttanian soldiers, but close enough to witness the funeral.

With great exaggeration of movement, Dorak snatched a large amulet from his father's corpse and set fire to the pyre. As the flames shot into the air, he took off his plumed helmet. Standing very rigid, he began to recite incantations as he began moving clockwise around the pyre. His voice became louder and more urgent. Round and round he walked gesturing to the heavens.

Princess Maura, flanked by Yeti and Benzar, stood in a cluster of noblewomen.

Chaun Maaun strode over, scattering women in his path. "What's he doing?" asked Chaun Maaun.

"I don't know. I wish Iegani were here," responded Maura with a worried look on her face.

Suddenly, a great dark cloud appeared in the clear sky. It rumbled loudly, and an occasional bolt of lightening struck the ground near Dorak.

"I don't like the look of this, Your Highness," pleaded Yeti. "Perhaps we should get behind the wall."

"No. I must see what is happening," Maura answered stubbornly.

Dorak reached up into the sky with both hands with the amulet encircling his fingers. Calling forth in a strange tongue, he threw the amulet into his father's pyre. A great cloud of smoke burst from the pyre, and from its midst emerged a man clad in a black robe and hood who stood on the burning body of Zoar. His face was hidden.

The Bhuttanians cheered loudly and beat their shields with weapons.

The man in black stretched out his dark leathery arms and rubbed his hands together.

"Oooohhh! This isn't good!" exclaimed Yeti.

Maura stood riveted by the sight of the man in the black hood. "General Kimtimee, do we have reports of the Bhuttanians using magic in battle?" asked Maura, fearing the worst.

"Not for decades. We have reports Zoar banished all wizards from his court for meddling in politics."

Yesemek fired back, "It seems he kept a spare."

Frightened, Yeti advised, "Princess, I don't think we should be standing here. This is black magic at work."

Maura agreed and ordered all her people back except for herself and her advisors.

Flames from the funeral pyre were now leaping about the man's face, but he didn't seem to burn.

The princess watched as a ball of purple and yellow light shone from the man's hands. Lightning continued striking about the black-robed man and Dorak, who commanded the figure to throw the ball of unearthly light at the mist.

"Here it comes," cried Yeti as she picked up Maura and flew way beyond the wall. The blast almost knocked Yeti out of the sky. She saw many of her feathers scattered on the wind. Looking back, she saw Chaun Maaun and Benzar carrying the rest of the small group to safety. She descended with the princess, but another blast hit and knocked everyone to the ground. The sky was filled with the acrid smoke of Zoar's burning body and waves of purplish, yellow light.

Maura crawled behind a crop of rocks yelling orders over the rumbling of the thunder and the explosions.

Yesemek managed to crawl to Maura's position. "Whoever he is, he's blasting a hole in the mist!" the general screamed over the continuing explosions.

BOOM! Another explosion hit.

Clods of debris landed on Maura and her company. She climbed up to look over the boulder.

There was a forty-foot-wide hole in the wall! The barges were sinking as bits of the caromate plants were strewn everywhere. There were holes on the riverbank where the ball of light had struck. Giant yagomba trees burned as their leaves withered.

Someone grabbed Maura's foot and pulled her down. She turned around and faced an angry Chaun Maaun. "What in the gods' names do you think you are doing?" he shouted over the din.

"The Dinii don't believe in the gods," answered Maura.

Chaun Maaun ignored her remark. "They are going to come through."

"I know." She turned to a dirty and frightened high-ranking officer. "Tell my generals to meet me by the north shore of the Sacred Lake. We will all rendezvous there. I will take this fight away from the population and into the great woods. Evacuate the people in the southeast corridor. They are to go to O Konya. Burn everything in Dorak's path. Leave nothing for the Bhuttanians to scavenge."

The officer saluted and turned to withdraw.

Maura grabbed her sleeve. "All soldiers! Go now. Hurry!"

"Yes, Your Highness," said the officer, now alive with purpose. She was gone in a flash.

BOOM! Another explosion hit.

Princess Maura ducked down and covered her face. She coughed from the smoke whirling in the air.

"Why are we retreating?" asked Chaun Maaun. "We should make a stand."

"It is too exposed here. Dorak still outnumbers us two to one."

BOOM! BOOM! The ball of light, the color of an angry bruise, came dangerously close to the crop of rocks. Everyone lay facedown on the ground. Clumps of dirt sprayed the Hasan Daegians and the Dinii, who wanted to fight, not hide behind stone.

Maura continued, "We need the cover of the forest. Dorak would decimate us on the plains."

Yesemek nodded in agreement.

Yeti turned her back to Maura. "Climb aboard, Princess. I'll have you at the lake in no time."

"I'll go with Chaun Maaun. You are to make sure everyone gets away safely."

Yeti opened her mouth to speak.

Maura interrupted. "Don't argue. There isn't time. Move out now!"

The princess held on to Chaun Maaun, gripping with her legs and wrapping her arms around his neck.

He spread his great wings and they took off. Yesemek followed closely behind. As they flew higher, Maura could see the first wave of her soldiers moving out, carrying supplies and the wounded as best they could. She smiled as she saw many Dinii, who had suffered no casualties in the fighting, take the injured and fly off to O Konya where medical treatment awaited. The Dinii, after dropping off the wounded, would report back to the north shore of Yappor Lake where their prince, Chaun Maaun, would await them.

36

Chaun Maaun reached the Sacred Lake.

He settled Maura on a moss-covered rock by a majestic waterfall. Tired and dirty, he dove into the crystal clear water to refresh himself. Hearing a splash, he found Maura swimming beside him, washing the day's dirt and sweat from her skin. Had this been another time, he would have indulged himself with her, but now he could only worry. He jumped out of the crystal clear water and lay out on a flat rock, spreading his wings to dry.

A few minutes later Maura joined him.

She sighed. "You think I'm wrong."

Chaun Maaun rose up on one elbow. "You let them enter the country. You are now fighting a war in your own territory."

"How could we fight Dorak's wizard? We have never seen power as this. We have only heard of such magic. His bolts would have destroyed us. At least this way, we still have an army to fight another day." She touched his cheek. "The Dinii can simply fly away. But my people can't outrun this wizard's power."

Chaun Maaun acknowledged the logic of Maura's thinking. "What do you propose to do now?"

"I have sent messengers to the High Priestess of the House of Magi. Until I get more information about this sorcerer, I don't know what I can do except delay Dorak as much as possible. I dare not confront him openly at this time."

Chaun Maaun leaned over and kissed Maura tenderly.

She returned his kiss ardently.

He stroked her hair and kissed her neck.

Maura climbed on top of him and they made love, slowly, wondering if this was going to be the last time. Again and again, they mated until hearing the beating of wings in the sky; they parted from each other and quickly dressed.

Yesemek descended accompanied by the rest of the generals, both Hasan Daegian and Dinii. In the rear of the group, four Dinii were bearing a specially constructed litter carrying an imposing woman dressed in a blue velvet cape. On her cape were gold buttons gathered together in the shape of constellations throughout the material. She had, on either side of her litter chair, leather bags stuffed to capacity. One of the Dinii helped her off the litter. She thanked the Dinii with calm regal authority and threw back her hood as the Dinii gathered her bags.

Princess Maura and Chaun Maaun approached the newly arrived guest.

The woman bowed. "Greetings, Your Highness and Good Prince. I bear messages from both your mothers." She handed them letters bearing the royal seal of Hasan Daeg.

Chaun Maaun looked hopelessly at his.

"I hope you understand the high level of anxiety they feel."

Princess Maura inclined her head. "Greetings, Noabini, High Priestess of the House of Magi. I appreciate you bringing us our mothers' salutations."

"I bring you more, Your Highness. Your mother is quite distressed that the enemy has entered Hasan Daeg, and our army has retreated before them."

Maura felt like a schoolgirl being scolded by her teacher. "There was no other plan of action possible," she declared.

"I quite agree," replied the High Priestess, "but, unfortunately, your mother does not."

Princess Maura stopped herself before nervously biting her lip. "What news do you bring of this wizard?"

"You are correct when you say wizard." The High Priestess opened one of her bags and went through it. "I have searched all of our records about Bhuttanian magic. The one who dressed all in black is called the Black Cacodemon. He is the most revered and feared of all of Bhuttu's priests, but seldom seen. He is known as the harbinger of destruction and is said to drink the blood of sacrificed victims during Bhuttu's high holy days."

"I have so many questions. Please be seated," said Maura.

The High Priestess looked around, and seeing no chairs, cheerfully sat upon a rock. "The Black Cacodemon was once a powerful person because of his dark magic. Zoar's father used him often to obtain control over stronger lords and gain territory.

"But Zoar was different. He felt the Black Cacodemon wielded too much power and wanted to loosen his grip. He did this by the most passive means without directly confronting the Black Cacodemon. He simply did not use him. Zoar really did not need help when it came to warfare. He could rely on his own amazing intellect and intuition to guide him. Over the years, the Black Cacodemon was seldom seen at court and his position fell into disuse."

"And now Dorak has brought him back," said Chaun Maaun.

"Yes. Dorak is young and has suffered a great military blow besides the untimely death of his father. He probably felt he needed the Black Cacodemon to solidify his position. And it worked. I am sure Dorak and his men are swarming through the hole blasted by his evil priest even as we speak."

"How can I fight such an opponent?" asked Maura.

"Somehow, the Black Cacodemon must be taken out of the equation," replied the High Priestess quietly. "You must make yourself impervious to the magic of this evil man."

"How shall I do this?" asked the princess, overwhelmed. It was one thing to fight a human enemy. It was quite another to battle a magician steeped in the arts of black magic.

"You must mate with the Mother Bogazkoy!" interrupted Iegani.

"Iegani!" shouted Chaun Maaun. "Where have you been?"

"Looking for the Mother Bogazkoy, impertinent boy!"

Maura felt relieved that Iegani was once again by her side. "You have found the Mother Bogazkoy?" she asked excitedly.

"It's no wonder we never found it," said Iegani. "It is in the Forbidden Zone in a cave underneath the sea. You must go to it and bind yourself with it. The Mother Bogazkoy is so potent that once you have mated with her, very little will be able to touch you. Not illness, not arrows, maybe not even death."

"How can she mate with a plant?" sneered Chaun Maaun.

"It's a figure of speech—a metaphor," replied Iegani disgustedly. Sometimes he wondered about Chaun Maaun's inability to grasp the obvious.

"You have seen the Mother Bogazkoy?" asked the princess.

"I have talked to her!"

"You have what?"

"She is waiting for you, Your Highness, and wishes your company very much. She needs to procreate. And without certain fluids from your body, she will be unable."

"She told you this?" asked the High Priestess.

Iegani nodded his head.

"I will leave at once. How long will it take me to get to the Forbidden Zone?" the princess asked, now anxious to be moving.

"If Chaun Maaun and I take you, almost a week to get there and back."

"Can I travel by the Seeing State?"

Iegani raised his eyebrow. "The Seeing State will not work. You must meet the Mother Bogazkoy in person."

"Your Highness, may I join your party?" asked the High Priestess. "I will not be a burden, and I may be able to help you along the journey. If I impede you, you may send me back at my own risk."

Maura looked at Iegani.

He nodded.

Noabini smiled, flashing large white teeth.

"Yeti and Benzar will accompany us," stated Maura.

"Good," stated Iegani. "Toppo and Tarsus are waiting for us just before the Forbidden Zone."

Without warning, a Dini courier swooped down out of the sky and crashed into the ground.

Chaun Maaun ran over to him and helped him sit up. The courier was badly wounded.

"Greetings, Prince Chaun Maaun and Princess Maura. I bring grave tidings." The courier stopped and took a deep breath.

"Take your time," Maura said, feeling alarmed. A sense of dread overtook her.

"O Konya is under attack, Your Highness. Your mother is trapped in the palace. Empress Gitar and many Dinii stayed behind in the city to fight. Other Dinii are picking up any Hasan Daegian they can find on the roads and flying them to the City of Peaks."

Princess Maura staggered a bit.

Everyone else cried out in shock, looking at each other in confused wonder.

Even Iegani looked bedeviled. "How can that be? It should have taken Dorak months to march to O Konya–not hours. And to overtake the city? A city like O Konya. It's impossible! You must be mistaken. It's just impossible."

"Magic, my lord. It's some form of magic. The Bhuttanians are moving so fast they look like streaks of colored light," gasped the injured Dini. "Who can fight against such an enemy? Even the Dinii are helpless before the Bhuttanians moving so fast."

Princess Maura fell to the ground and put her head in her hands. "How could I have been so stupid?" she moaned.

"You underestimated the power of your enemy," lamented Iegani, "as did we all. The Dinii have no knowledge of black magic. We possess no magic to fight this. We must wait until Dorak and his men come out of the spell and try to strike then."

"This spell must take an enormous amount of power. Dorak and his army will need to rest as well as the Black Cacodemon. We must be ready to fight," said Chaun Maaun.

"But what if you are wrong?" questioned Maura tearfully. "I've already made a huge blunder." She stood on her feet and yelled at the heavens. "I swear by all that is holy, neither I nor my kin will rest until the Bhuttanians are thrown out of Hasan Daeg. If I have to lie, cheat, murder, and commit the worst of atrocities, I will set my country free or the heavens may curse me for all time."

Wind swirled around the group as the sky darkened.

"Oh, do not make such a vow to the heavens!" beseeched the High Priestess. "It will doom us all."

"Not only shall I vow it, but so shall ye all. Vow it now, or I will curse each and every one of you right now."

"Maura, think of what you are asking of us. The Dinii do not make such oaths," implored Chaun Maaun.

"Vow it!" screamed Maura. "Vow it!"

Iegani lowered himself to his knees. "I swear." He looked around at the others.

One by one, they kneeled before Maura and repeated her words.

Lightning struck near them as rain pelted from the sky. The ground shook.

The High Priestess wept. Maura had uttered a terrible oath and the heavens had accepted it. She wondered what monster Princess Maura would turn into for uttering such a terrible curse.

Hearing a gasp, she turned and saw what others were seeing.

Before their eyes, Maura's being was luminous, flickering like an oil lamp before the wick burns out.

Maura turned toward her comrades. "It is done. The heavens had accepted our vow. I'm going to O Konya. The Queen and the

Empress must be saved. Do not try to stop me. The attempt must be made. Never fear. We will meet again soon, my friends."

Having said that, she climbed onto the back of Chaun Maaun. With wings outstretched, he flew into the foreboding sky, leaving the rest to go their separate ways to fight for freedom.

37

Chaun Maaun and Maura smelled smoke.

With his keen sight, Chaun Maaun saw buildings burning in the distance.

Maura could also discern an unholy light near the horizon. She sank her head between Chaun Maaun's shoulders.

Chaun Maaun beat his wings upon the night air faster and faster until he finally landed on the roof of the palace.

Maura rolled off the exhausted prince and stood riveted. Down below, the city's wondrous architecture was being put to the torch. The streets were blocked with the bodies of the dead.

Amidst the dying and wounded stood the Dinii fighting Dorak's men hand-to-hand, slashing as many throats as they could and throwing the bodies into heaps.

From other rooftops, Hasan Daegian archers rained arrows down upon the enemy.

But still Dorak's men came—waves and waves of them.

With a fury, Princess Maura unsheathed her sword and started down the staircase. She heard Chaun Maaun calling, but did not stop. Running as fast as she could, she reached the bottom of the stone staircase only to find fighting ensuing at the other end of a massive hallway. There she spied her mother, father, and several Dinii desperately fighting a group of Dorak's men.

Maura released a great cry of terror combined with anger, rushing toward the clashing throng.

Abisola, recognizing her daughter's voice, turned away from her opponent.

Seeing his opportunity, a soldier stabbed the queen through the shoulder, causing her to stumble and fall to the floor.

Iasos immediately threw himself on top of his injured wife, trying to protect her from any further blows.

Maura struck the Bhuttanian soldier nearest her, almost severing his head.

Smelling a Dinii next to her, she looked out of the corner of her eye and spied Gitar and Yeti fighting alongside her.

Gitar picked up a screaming soldier and, with one jerk, broke his neck. She then threw the twitching body at the on-rushing Bhuttanians.

Yeti began pulling Iasos and his wounded queen away from the fray.

Maura fought like a wild animal, snarling at her enemies and baring her teeth. Her skin glistened with blue sweat as red blood splattered on her. She did not think; just reacted, letting her instinct for survival take over.

It was just as Chaun Maaun said it would be.

"BHUTTANIANS, ALL WEAPONS ON THE FLOOR!" shouted a booming voice from behind the melee.

The Bhuttanians looked at each other in confusion and reluctantly dropped their weapons. The soldiers parted as Dorak emerged.

Dorak marched to the front of his men while sheathing his sword. Pulling off his dusty helmet, he revealed an exhausted face covered with the grime of battle. The dragon emblem on his chest was caked in blood, most of it still wet.

"Princess Maura, we meet again," Dorak chortled. He looked around the great hallway. "I see your party has dispatched more of my men. I'm afraid I will have to put a stop to that."

Maura said nothing, but watched his every move. He stepped closer to Queen Abisola, now being held upright in the arms of Iasos.

Maura and Yeti immediately blocked his way.

Dorak held up his hands in supplication. "I only want to speak to your mother," he implored. Looking past the princess, he said, "Queen Abisola, it is over. The city has been taken and is under my control."

Queen Abisola groaned.

Dorak continued in a soothing voice. "Your Majesty, I will give you the best terms for surrender. You and your family will not be harmed. Look, as you can see, my men have put down their arms." Dorak took a step closer. "It is not my desire to destroy this wondrous city. Your family may still sit on the throne as long as you pay homage to me as liege lord. My people need food. We need it desperately. Give me what I want and I will make Hasan Daeg a power to behold within the Bhuttanian Empire." Dorak took another step closer.

Maura brought up her sword.

Dorak walked up to the blade pointing at his throat. He stood so close that the point of the blade almost touched his skin. "Princess, I beseech you. Nothing can be gained from this last stand."

"I can kill you right now."

"Then you would sign your own death warrant. My men would kill you and your parents before you made it to the roof," Dorak replied softly as though calming a frightened horse. "You would be of no use to your people then, I assure you."

"But neither would you."

Dorak chuckled softly. "You are a most unusual young woman. What a queen you will become. I do hope I will be present to witness your final blooming, but it is up to you."

When Maura did not respond, Dorak turned his attention to the failing Hasan Daegian queen. "Queen Abisola, think about your daughter. Surely you do not want to see her die? Surrender. It is all you can do."

The queen struggled. She coughed and blood seeped from her mouth.

Iasos quickly wiped the blood away with his sleeve.

Holding tightly to her husband's arms, she wept silently. "You may take me into custody. But all of the Dinii, including Empress Gitar and my child, are to leave now." She looked up at Iasos. "My husband will share my fate with me."

"Mother, no!" insisted Maura.

"This is my final command. Start withdrawing. Now!" croaked Abisola.

"I am afraid I can not allow this," interjected Dorak.

Queen Abisola measured her words carefully. "Dorak, I am over three hundred years old. Only recently have I begun to age. Even your magicians have no spells to do this. Do you not want to know my secret? Do you not want to live for a long time? How long did your father live? He wasn't even fifty, and he was used up." Abisola took a deep breath, which made a wheezing noise. "Just think of what you could accomplish in three hundred years or maybe more. Let my daughter go with the Dinii, and once they are safely away, I will show you how it is done." She let her words sink in.

"She is lying. The Bogazkoy will never accept a male bonding," cried a female from the shadows.

"Mikkotto!" exclaimed Iasos. "You traitorous mongrel!"

Dorak swung around and, upon seeing Mikkotto, his eyes narrowed. "How did you get up here?"

Mikkotto laughed. "Well, the front entrance was wide open. There was no one to stop me. It seems everyone is dead." She moved closer.

"Stop where you are," commanded Maura, her skin prickling from the tension.

Mikkotto cooed, "Is that any way to talk to your cousin?"

Dorak shot Mikkotto a surprised look.

She grinned. "That is right, my dear Dorak. I used to play in these very hallways as a child. My mother was Abisola's first cousin and Lady Sari's daughter. I told you I was a kinswoman of the royal family. I just didn't tell you how close." She moved forward.

Dorak blocked her way. "I swear to you, Mikkotto, if you do not leave right now, I am going to kill you here with my own hands."

"I think you have forgotten we have a deal. I am to be queen of Hasan Daeg in exchange for certain services rendered."

"You, queen?" snorted Iasos in disgust.

"I have made no deal with you to be queen," denied Dorak. "I merely said I would let you live if you showed me the location of O Konya. I am sorry to say I regret my decision. I now have new plans for you."

Dorak, his expression one of hatred and anger, moved toward Mikkotto with deadly intent.

Realizing Dorak's intention, Mikkotto shoved Dorak into Princess Maura. "NOW!" she screamed.

Several soldiers pulled daggers from their sleeves and threw them at the royal couple.

One struck Abisola in the heart, killing her instantly.

The other hit Iasos in the stomach. He crumpled to the floor, his hands around the dagger, trying to pull it out.

Maura screamed, scrambling on the bloody floor. She threw herself across her parents.

At that moment, Chaun Maaun, having recovered from the arduous journey, rushed down the steps. He pushed his mother and Yeti behind him. Seeing Maura curled over the body of her mother and her dying father, he let out a muffled cry.

Dorak stood between the Hasan Daegians and his soldiers with his arms outstretched.

Other Bhuttanian warriors rushed forward to hold the men, who had thrown the daggers, prostrate on the floor.

Mikkotto was nowhere to be seen.

"No one move!" commanded Dorak, his voice like ice. Upon seeing Chaun Maaun's fury, he was moved to say, "I had nothing to do with this. Take your people and go. It is over."

Gitar leaned her head against Chaun Maaun's back while weeping.

Yeti stared in bewilderment at the fallen royal couple on the floor.

Chaun Maaun started toward Maura who was lying over her mother.

Dorak drew his sword. "It is over," he said again emphatically. "Take the empress and leave, Prince Chaun Maaun or I will kill Princess Maura. I swear it."

At Chaun Maaun's surprise that Dorak knew his name, Dorak said, "Yes, I know who you are. I know everything there is to know about this country."

"I will never rest until I kill you, Dorak. This I swear to you!" spat Chaun Maaun.

Dorak inclined his head in acknowledgment. "I will not harm her if you leave now. Go in peace."

Chaun Maaun picked up his distressed mother and swiftly left with Yeti covering his retreat.

Yeti looked back at the royal Hasan Daegian family she had sworn to protect, lying in a crumpled heap on the bloody floor. It had happened so quickly. "I will be back, little bird. Do not give up hope," she whispered.

She gave one last look at Dorak, who bowed to her as one honorable warrior recognizing another. Yeti turned and joined her group on the rooftop. "Can you fly, Empress?" she asked Gitar.

With great tears streaming down her face, Gitar clasped the hands of both Chaun Maaun and Yeti. "We must not blame ourselves. We did everything within our power to do. Dorak's evil magic was too powerful for us. There is no shame." She squeezed their hands. "Come now. We must live to fight another day."

Stretching out her mighty wings, Empress Gitar of the Dinii rose ghostlike into the night.

Chaun Maaun and Yeti followed, flanking her.

Empress Gitar flew about the city summoning the Dinii warriors to her.

One by one, they heard her call over the din of fighting and reluctantly joined her in the sky. When no more Dinii answered her lonesome cry, they flew toward the City of the Peaks.

A young Bhuttanian soldier, grieving over the loss of his best friend, lifted his longbow. With a quick release, he shot an arrow into the hellish night before he was cut down by General Alexanee, Dorak's first-in-command.

Dorak's conquest for Hasan Daeg was over.

But Maura had just started her quest for revenge, and she would not stop until she regained control of Hasan Daeg and Dorak was dead . . . or she was!

Wall Of Peril

The Princess Maura Tales
Saga of the de Magela Family

Book Two

Abigail Keam

Worker Bee Press

**Wall Of Peril
The Princess Maura Tales
Copyright © Abigail Keam 2018**

ALL RIGHTS RESERVED

No part of this book may be reproduced or transmitted in any form without written permission of the author.

This is a work of fiction. All characters are fictional and similarity to any living person, place, or thing is just coincidence unless stated otherwise. If you are seeing wizards, the Dinii, and other creatures mentioned in this book, then you should see a doctor.

Worker Bee Press
P.O. Box 485
Nicholasville, KY 40340

Acknowledgements

Thanks to my editors,
Patti DeYoung and Jacy Mackin

Artwork by Karin Claesson
www.sweediesart.deviantart.com

Special thanks to
Peter Keam and Betsy Meredith

Book Jacket by Peter Keam
Author's photograph by Peter Keam

Preface

The peaceful country of Hasan Daeg has not fought a war in over six hundred years. But the winds of conflict blow across their hidden borders.

From the eastern plains of Bhuttan, comes a nomadic horse tribe. The Bhuttanians, bent on assimilating all countries into their empire, are causing the world to fall into chaos.

Only the Hasan Daegians and the Dinii stand between them and world domination, and they pin their hopes on Princess Maura to save them.

After the Hasan Daegians and the Dinii wage a brilliant first battle against the Bhuttanians, Dorak, son of Aga Zoar, calls upon a dark wizard to use black magic.

Helpless against this evil, the Dinii and Hasan Daegians are forced to retreat, but before they can regroup, the Bhuttanians overtake Hasan Daeg.

As Maura desperately tries to save her parents, Queen Abisola and Consort Iasos, from capitulating to Dorak, Baroness Mikkotto enters the fray and deals a deathblow.

And so our story continues with Baroness Mikkotto.

Prologue

Baroness Mikkotto pushed open the doors.

Through the majestic brass doors of the royal palace, its gleaming white walls and floors now stained with blood, she entered cautiously. Bodies of Hasan Daegians and the Dinii were strewn throughout the hall and staircase. Mikkotto ordered her guards to move the corpses out of her way, fearful that a soldier might play dead and stab her as she stepped over. Soldiers who moaned when moved were quickly dispatched by an axe.

The horrible chunking noise of the metal striking bone did not bother Mikkotto, who calmly studied the carnage. Between the death throes of her countrywomen, Mikkotto listened for commotion in the palace. She knew Abisola and Iasos were nearby. Did they go downstairs into the bowels of the royal stronghold? Or were they on the rooftop waiting for extraction by the surviving Dinii?

It didn't matter. Mikkotto had placed guards at every exit point. She was searching for the royal family, and she must reach them before Dorak.

Dorak! She had to hand it to him. He had made an inspired play by recalling the Black Cacodemon and using magic to invade Hasan Daeg. By manipulating the wizard's powers, Dorak was able to conquer Hasan Daeg within hours rather than months or years. The Hasan Daegian army never stood a chance against the lightning speed of the Bhuttanian army in the grips of the wizard's enchantment.

As soon as Dorak took control of the capital O Konya, the spell disbursed, and now everyone moved normally. Mikkotto twisted her lips in annoyance. Too bad. She wished the spell had lasted until she could discover the whereabouts of her royal cousin.

Mikkotto jerked her head up. She faintly heard Dorak ordering,

"BHUTTANIANS! ALL WEAPONS ON THE FLOOR!"

She cursed knowing Dorak had found Abisola and her consort. Fortunately for her, she had placed men among various squads, giving them instructions to kill the queen and her husband if they came upon them.

Grinning, she relished the thought that they would obey her and not Dorak, paying them with gold and the promise of more coins and land to come if they carried out her orders. Greed was a great motivator to get the unpleasantries of life done by those who valued money above all else.

Still, Mikkotto couldn't take a chance. She scampered up the grand white marble staircase, jumping over slain bodies until she reached the second floor. Hearing screaming, she ran up another flight with her women warriors following behind.

Motioning for her warriors to wait, Mikkotto peered into a doorway and saw Dorak and a few Bhuttanians threatening Abisola and Iasos, who huddled on the floor before a small staircase going to the rooftop. Between them stood Maura, brandishing a sword. Behind her stood two Dinii with their talons exposed, looking very threatening.

The Dinii gave Mikkotto pause. She did not care to have her face slashed again nor die from a quick cut across her throat with their razor sharp nails. If truth be known, Mikkotto was terrified of them, but that fear had to be put aside. Victory was given to the bold, not the fearful.

Mikkotto studied the Dinii, thinking the taller one was Empress Gitar. She had seen her briefly at Maura's birthday celebration before her son bumbled Maura's assassination. Although the attempt on Maura's life had failed, Mikkotto had not flinched when told of her son's death at the hand of a Dini. She had little faith in her only son's ability and was only too glad she had not assigned one of her daughters to the task. Daughters were precious, but sons were expendable.

She motioned to her warriors to be quiet while she listened to the conversation between Dorak and Abisola. If Maura and her parents were killed, Dorak would make her queen of Hasan Daeg. If he decided to spare them, she would have to make a daring move and quickly too.

Moving closer, Mikkotto heard Dorak speak, "Princess Maura, we meet again." Dorak looked around the great hallway. "I see that you and your party have dispatched a few more of my men. I'm afraid I will have to put a stop to that."

Kill her. KILL HER! thought Mikkotto, hugging the darkness of the doorway.

Concentrating on Dorak, Maura did not see Mikkotto slinking closer and closer.

Dorak stepped nearer to Queen Abisola, now being held upright in the arms of Iasos.

Maura and Yeti immediately blocked his way.

Dorak held up his hands in supplication. "Princess, I only want to speak to your mother," he said calmly. Looking past Maura, he uttered, "Queen Abisola, it is over. The city has been taken and is in my control."

Queen Abisola groaned.

Dorak continued in a soothing voice. "Your Majesty, I will give you the best terms for surrender. You and your family will not be harmed. Look, as you can see, my men have put down their arms. It is not my desire to destroy this wondrous city. Your family may still sit on the throne as long as you pay homage to me as liege lord. My people need food. We need it desperately. Give me what I want, and I will make Hasan Daeg a power to behold within the Bhuttanian Empire." Dorak took another step toward Queen Abisola.

NO! NO! What is Dorak doing? I was promised Hasan Daeg by his father. Dorak can't do this to me, Mikkotto screamed in her head. She had to make her move soon.

Maura brought up her sword.

Dorak walked up to the blade pointed at his throat. He stood so that the point of the weapon almost pierced his skin. "Princess, I beseech you. Nothing can be gained from this last stand. It is over."

"I can kill you right now."

"Then you would sign your death warrant. My men would kill you and your parents before you made it to the roof," Dorak replied softly. "You would be of no use to your people then, I assure you."

"But neither would you."

Dorak chuckled softly. "You are a most unusual young woman. I do hope I will be present to witness your final blooming, but that is up to you."

When Maura did not respond to his words, Dorak turned his attention to the failing Hasan Daegian queen. "Queen Abisola, think about your daughter. Surely you do not want to see her die. Surrender. It is all you can do."

The queen struggled. She coughed, and blood seeped from her

mouth.

Iasos quickly wiped it with his sleeve.

Holding tightly to her husband's arms, Abisola whispered, "You may take me. But all of the Dinii, including Empress Gitar and my child, are to leave now." She looked at Iasos. "My husband will share my fate with me."

"Mother, no!" Maura insisted.

"This is my final command. Start withdrawing. Now!" Abisola croaked.

"I am afraid I cannot allow this," interjected Dorak.

Queen Abisola measured her words carefully. "Aga Dorak, I am over three hundred years old. Only recently have I begun to age. Even your magicians have no spells to do this. Do you not want to know my secret? Do you not want to live for a long time? How long did your father live? He wasn't even fifty and was used up." Abisola took a deep breath, which made a wheezing noise. "Just think of what you could accomplish in three hundred years or maybe more. Let my daughter go with the Dinii, and once they are safely away, I will show you how it is done." She let her words sink in.

Mikkotto knew it was now or never. "She's lying. The Bogazkoy will never accept a male bonding!" she cried from the shadows.

"Mikkotto!" exclaimed Iasos. "You traitorous mongrel!"

Dorak swung around, and upon seeing Mikkotto, his eyes narrowed. "How did you get up here?"

Mikkotto laughed. "The front door was wide open. There was no one to stop me. It seems everyone below is dead." She moved closer.

"Stop where you are," commanded Maura, her skin prickling from the tension.

"Is that any way to talk to your cousin?" Mikkotto cooed.

Dorak shot Mikkotto a surprised look.

Mikkotto grinned. "That is right, my dear Dorak. I used to play in these very hallways as a child. My mother was Abisola's first cousin and Lady Sari's daughter. For you see, Lady Sari is Marchioness Sari Sumsumitoyo and third in line to the throne. She gave up her title to serve the House of de Magela, stupid woman that she is." She moved forward.

Dorak blocked her way. "I swear to you, Mikkotto, if you do not leave, I am going to kill you with my own hands."

"I think you have forgotten that we have a deal. I am to rule Hasan Daeg in exchange for certain services rendered."

"You, queen?" Iasos snorted in disgust.

"I made no deal with you to be queen," denied Dorak. "I merely said I would let you live if you showed me the location of O Konya. I am sorry to say I regret that decision. I now have new plans for you." Dorak, wearing an expression of hate, moved toward Mikkotto with deadly purpose.

Realizing Dorak's intention, Mikkotto shoved Dorak into Maura. "NOW!" she shrieked.

Several soldiers pulled daggers from their sleeves and threw them at the royal couple.

One struck Abisola in the heart, killing her instantly.

The other hit Iasos in the stomach. He crumpled with his hands around the dagger, trying to pull it out.

Maura screamed, scrambling over the bloody floor and throwing herself across her parents.

Chaun Maaun, having recovered from the arduous journey, rushed down the steps. He pushed his mother and Yeti behind him. Seeing Maura curled over the body of her mother and her dying father, he let out a muffled cry.

Dorak stood between the Hasan Daegians and his soldiers with his arms outstretched.

Other Bhuttanian warriors rushed forward to restrain the men who had thrown the daggers.

Mikkotto scurried away with her guards running interference before her. They collided with a squad of Bhuttanians loyal to Dorak. Thinking quickly, Mikkotto pointed and barked, "Hurry, your master is in danger. The Dinii empress is upstairs and threatening Dorak. Save him!"

She and her women pressed against the wall, letting the heavily-armed men rush past her to the third floor as they all heard Dorak shouting commands and trying to gain control of the grave situation.

Not wanting to linger where Dorak could seize her, Mikkotto pulled free a lance sticking out from the gut of a Hasan Daegian warrior and knocked a Bhuttanian soldier off his warhorse with it.

Jumping upon the giant creature, Mikkotto gave orders, "Get yourselves horses and catch up with me at my estate. We will regroup and hide in Camaroon. There must be another way to the throne of Hasan Daeg, and I swear to you, my good women, I will find it!"

Mikkotto kicked the anxious horse and rode off.

When Dorak rushed out of the palace with his men, not a trace of

Mikkotto could be found even with a massive hunt looking for her.
It was as though Kaseri had swallowed her up.
Mikkotto was gone!

1

Dorak carried Maura to her chamber.

He laid Maura carefully on her bed and summoned a healer. As he waited, Dorak smoothed Maura's furrowed brow and held her hand. Gently, he kissed the tips of her fingers.

A guard soon appeared with Meagan of Skujpor. Her traditional white robe was soaked red with blood. Seeing the patient was the princess, Meagan rushed to the bedside and pushed Dorak out of the way. She examined Maura with great care. Finally, she sighed with relief.

"What is wrong with her?" asked Dorak, offended by the healer's brusque treatment.

"She's in shock," replied Meagan, pushing red hair out of her face. She pointed to the princess' skin. "This blood is not hers."

"How do you know?"

"Because it is red. Her blood is blue." She paused for a moment. "It must be her father's."

"When will she recover?"

The healer looked at Dorak with distaste. "When her mind can absorb the shock of this terrible day. Until then, she will stay as she is." Meagan stood directly in front of Dorak, confronting him. "I will come back to check on the princess, but now I must go back to the wounded. They need me more."

Dorak did not stop her as she moved toward the door. "I will send an escort with you and have my physician accompany you."

"That is not necessary. I have seen your healers in action and do not approve of their methods." Meagan turned as if an afterthought. "If you wish for us to treat your men, send them over. They will have a greater chance of survival with our medicine."

"You would help your enemy?" asked Dorak, confused.

"It is you whom I wish to kill," Meagan replied simply. There was a moment of unnatural silence between Dorak and the woman he knew could help Maura. "I will help any injured animal, including your men," said Meagan, breaking the angry quiet. Then she was gone.

Dorak, relieved that Maura had no serious physical injuries, went out into the hallway and found his second-in-command.

The commander, yelling orders at his men, immediately came to attention and pressed his fist to his chest.

"Are there any survivors from the court or noble houses?" asked Dorak.

"Yes, Great Aga. They are guarded in the royal stables."

Dorak raised an eyebrow.

The commander looked sheepishly at him. "Great Aga, this palace does not have a dungeon. I had nowhere else to put them."

"Get some of the noblewomen and have them stay with the princess—I mean, the queen—in her chambers. Then take the bodies of Queen Abisola and Consort Iasos to the throne room. Have women attend them." Dorak fell silent.

The commander waited a long time before Dorak spoke again.

"There is to be no looting. Tell the men that no citizens are to be harmed upon pain of death. Is that understood?"

"Yes, Great Aga. Your word is law." The commander waited to be excused.

"Send the Black Cacodemon to me. You will no doubt find him lurking around the dying."

The commander's eyes widened. "Yes, Great Aga," he replied in a weak voice.

Dorak strode away, leaving the commander to search for someone else to carry his message to the Black Cacodemon. He would rather face ten hostile Dinii than speak one word to that foul wizard who stood among the dying inhaling their souls as they departed their bodies.

Finally, he spied a young lieutenant and called him over. With a faint smile, the commander gave the young man his instructions and watched the color drain from the boy's face. With a strong push to his back, the commander sent the lieutenant off and proceeded to the stables.

Dorak returned to Maura's bedchamber. From the balcony of her room, he watched his men putting out fires in the city and restoring order. The dead were being collected and laid into long lines. Tomorrow, he would let the Hasan Daegians mourn their departed loved ones and put them to rest according to their customs. He would honor his own fallen with purifying fires in accordance with the Bhuttanian way. Then he would start building his empire. He looked at Maura. "The dead did not sacrifice in vain. Together, you and I will build a new order."

He leaned on the balcony railing, surveying the city. "The greatest the world has ever seen."

Maura did not hear Dorak. Dreaming, she heard only her screams as a dagger pierced her mother's heart. Again and again, the scene replayed itself until her mother, dead on the floor, opened her lifeless eyes and said, "Leave this place of death and rejoin the living. I will always be with you."

A shimmering woman appeared. She floated toward Maura and held her hands against Maura's temples. "Sleep. Sleep. Find comfort in the darkness. Morning will come soon enough." The horrible images slowly faded from Maura's mind as she drifted into a deep slumber.

2

Maura opened her eyes.

The first thing she saw was the royal physician in spotless white robes, bending over her bed with a puzzled look in her eyes.

"You look tired, Meagan," spoke Maura, noting the dark circles under Meagan's eyes.

Ignoring the remark, Meagan asked, "How do you feel, Your Majesty?"

Maura winced at the word *Majesty* and was overwhelmed with a flood of painful memories. "My mother?" she asked weakly.

The healer wiped a tear from her cheek and shook her white-capped head with wisps of red hair peeking out.

"Father too?"

"He died shortly after the queen passed away. I must add that he died without much pain. He wrote a letter for you, but I do not know what happened to it." The healer sat on the bed and patted Maura's shoulder. "I want you to know that they were treated with respect and honor as befitting your mother's glorious reign."

Maura sat up, alarmed. "How long have I been unconscious?"

"Nine days," boomed a masculine voice from the balcony.

Maura looked past Meagan, squinting her eyes and holding her hand up against the strong rays of the sun bouncing off the white balcony.

Silhouetted against the white-hot light, a dark figure emerged from the filmy curtains separating the room from the balcony. Dorak strode lazily over to the bed.

The healer bowed and left the room.

Dorak towered over Maura. He had a worried look on his face. He was unshaven, and his hair had not seen a comb for some time. Dressed in a black shirt with black breeches tucked into worn black boots, Maura thought he looked like a convict or, even worse, a privateer. His dark brooding look frightened her.

"I was very worried about you, Queen Maura," said Dorak, pouring her a glass of water. "I was beginning to wonder if you were ever going to open your eyes again."

Maura drank greedily. Her mouth felt hot and dirty. The cool water soothed her raw throat. "I wish I had never awakened," she spat.

Dorak gave her an appraising look. "You look awful."

"So do you," Maura replied, returning the stare.

"Never at a loss for words, are you?"

"Why are you here with me? Isn't there someone who needs butchering somewhere?"

"Your . . . *our* country is in safe hands. Its citizens are safe. Law and order have been restored. The fires have been put out."

"You mean after you murdered the lawful queen and invaded a peaceful nation to which you have no legitimate claim?"

Dorak grew angry. "I had nothing to do with the death of your parents. I swear to you before Bhuttu!"

Feeling her eyes tearing, Maura struggled to retain her composure. "You will never know how much I hate you! I will not rest until you and your cohorts are thrown out of Hasan Daeg!"

A wicked smile grew on Dorak's handsome face. "That will pose something of a problem since I intend to marry you."

Maura gasped and drew back.

Dorak's smile grew broader as he saw her panic. "I am going to leave now." He put out his hands as if to stop her from pleading. "No, my indigo queen, don't try to stop me. Matters of state. I am sure you understand."

Sneering, Maura turned her face away. "I'll die first before I marry you. You know I can make it happen."

Dorak pinched her cheek and laughed. He strode out of the room as if in good humor. Once out of sight, Dorak's expression grew serious. He motioned to the healer Meagan, who waited in the hallway with several noblewomen. Meagan's white robes fluttered in the breeze of the marble hallway as she went over to him. She bowed and waited for Dorak to speak.

He seemed confused and rubbed his temples as if in pain.

"Do you have a headache, my lord?" she asked.

Dorak ignored her question. "The queen is depressed. She threatened to take her life."

"That is understandable considering the circumstances."

"I have heard stories that Hasan Daegian rulers can will themselves to die."

"Anyone can will themselves to death if unhappy enough."

"I want the queen watched. Make sure she eats. Stop her if she tries to do anything foolish."

The healer raised an eyebrow. "Sire, you can rest assured that I will do everything in my power to ensure the queen's health returns. However, I will never help you enslave her."

"You people constantly surprise me. I would have anyone from my country executed who talked to me the way you just did. Since you are not Bhuttanian I give you allowance, but that will not last forever."

"Of course, my lord, but you came seeking us and not the other way around." Meagan bowed and briskly walked away, calling to her assistants who were struggling to carry her medical bags. She knocked on the queen's door before entering.

Behind her followed several noblewomen who had consecrated their lives to become healers. Gone were the necklaces made of precious stones. Gone were the flowers woven into the hair. Gone were the costly robes of rare cloth. Now they wore the stern black robes of the initiate, allowing only their family crest embroidered on their chest for adornment.

Hearing no reply, Meagan opened the door and peered into the room.

The queen lay on the bed in a fetal position with her eyes tightly shut. Maura did not stir.

Meagan checked Maura's eyes. Startled by what she saw, she called discreetly for Lady Sari so word would not pass to Dorak that something was wrong.

Lady Sari came as swiftly as her old bones would carry her. She hovered over Maura, wringing her hands.

"What is the meaning of this?" asked Meagan, pulling open Maura's eyes. The eyes had become a solid blue, blocking out any sign of a pupil or iris. The effect was chilling to one who had never seen it before.

Sari gasped at the sight.

"I have read ancient treatises that discuss the care and nurturing of the Royal House of Hasan Daeg. There is no mention that the queens' eyes ever turned a solid blue for any reason," Meagan stated.

"That is because we are not allowed to touch the body until it is over. By then, the eyes return to normal."

"Body? You talk as though this girl is dead."

Sari's face assumed a look of intense sorrow. "For all intents, she is. She has taken herself into the *death dream*. There is nothing more you can do."

"Hasan Daegian queens will only do that if they are over three hundred years old and have produced a suitable heir. She is neither old nor has she had a child."

Sari looked softly at Meagan. "You did not read enough. Hasan Daegian queens can will themselves to die if they are in terrible pain." She straightened Maura's coverlet. "And this child is in terrible pain. She does not have the will to go on."

Meagan blustered.

"You do not understand. They reach a certain nadir and this just happens. It is nothing they can control. Dorak must have said something to cause this."

"In most ancient writings, there is mentioned a tree as a giver of life to the Royal House alone. It is written that there is some sort of blending between the ruler and the tree." The healer took Sari's hand in her calloused ones. "You have been with this family all of your life. Do you know of such a tree? I have done all I can. I fear that if I do not bring her out of this self-induced coma, she will die this time."

Saying nothing, Sari went deep into thought.

Meagan was quiet. She was a healer, but she had been exposed to politics long enough to understand the significance of Sari's silence. "Do you know of a tree that can save this queen? Help me for I can do no more!"

The old woman shook her head slowly and clasped her hands in despair. She had the air of defeat about her. "There is such a plant, but it cannot help her. It is also dying."

"How does it work? I must try something." Meagan felt Maura's pulse. "If her heart gets any slower, we are going to lose her!"

"I will take you to it, but we must bring the queen."

"How can we remove her from this room without suspicion?"

Sari gave a weak smile. "Not all of our teeth are gone. We can bite a little yet. Follow me."

Confused, Meagan ordered her assistants to carry the limp queen.

Sari went to a wall and pressed a certain stone.

Silently, part of the wall opened into a small, narrow hallway.

3

Sari entered.

She poked her head back out of the passageway and motioned for the healer to follow her.

Meagan grabbed an oil lamp, lit it, and taking a deep breath, entered.

The black-robed women followed, carrying the moaning queen. One of the noblewomen placed her hand over the queen's mouth. The door closed, leaving the group feeling isolated and confined.

"Watch where you are going," Sari cautioned. "We will soon begin descending. The steps are sometimes slippery."

The group silently followed the old woman down the stone steps, their footfalls echoing loudly against the massive hand-hewn walls. Down and down they went, descending far below the city. They could hear the noisy hubbub of the market, and the traffic on the main boulevard of O Konya.

With Sari leading the way, Meagan held the lamp high above her head, so the light spread unevenly but brightly on the walkway. She was surprised that the ancient passageway was clean of debris. Her breathing was not impeded by mold or dust. She wondered who kept the underground passages clean.

Coming to the bottom of the stairs, the initiates placed Maura gently on the stone floor and rested, panting deeply. Some wiped the sweat off their foreheads and the back of their necks with the hems of their robes.

Sari motioned them forward.

Without complaining, they picked up their royal cargo and resumed following the older woman deeper into the passageway. There were many corridors, but Sari consistently traveled down the farthest left.

Meagan took careful note of this, as well as the presence of a gentle breeze in the corridor, a fact she tucked away.

Sari took another left and came upon double wooden doors with carvings of ancient, mystical, and religious symbols. Although they were not locked, Sari did not have the strength to open the massive doors by herself.

Meagan and several of the initiates pulled at the iron handles, which formed the image of pouncing uultepes.

Groaning, the doors opened an inch at a time.

One of the smaller women wiggled through a crack between the doors and then pushed from the opposite side as the doors opened out into the corridor. Frightened, she dared not look behind as strange sounds reverberated in the darkness. She was glad when the heavy doors opened wide, and lamplight spilled beyond her.

Sari and the Anqarian healer stepped beyond the doors into a voluminous chamber.

The older woman watched Meagan's face as she discovered the secret of the de Magela family. "Behold, the Tree of Life!" Sari whispered.

Meagan took everything in.

The cavernous chamber contained a small lake. Steam hissed from the water's surface, and Meagan could make out a small island of green rock at its center. In the middle of the island stood a blue plant with wide, flat tendrils extending beyond the rock and into the steaming water.

"There is a boat over there," Sari pointed. "You and I alone must take the queen. The boat will not hold all of us."

"That's the Bogazkoy?" asked Meagan, looking at the limp, unimpressive plant.

Sari barked a cruel laugh. "That's the Tree of Life or rather what is left of it. It may be too weak to do the queen any good now. It has not been used for almost ten years."

"That is when Queen Abisola started to age," commented Meagan.

Sari nodded. "Queen Abisola wanted what was left of its power for her daughter." Sari instructed the initiates to follow her and place the queen into a small rowboat.

Meagan looked skeptically at the rickety boat but tucked the hem of her robes in her belt determinedly. "Why is the boat in such poor condition?"

"As I told you. Queen Abisola did not want to use what was left of the Bogazkoy's power, so we rarely came down here. The hot water must have rotted the wood."

Meagan climbed precariously into the boat as it rocked back and forth. She tried to steady herself by grabbing the oars.

Sari climbed in after her and immediately sat down. She checked Maura's breathing. It seemed labored. Taking the wooden oars from Meagan, Sari began rowing toward the green island.

Meagan placed her hand in the steaming water, pulling it back quickly. "It's almost scalding!"

Sari nodded. "The lake is fed by a hot mineral spring. The Bogazkoy needs the minerals to survive. Taste it."

Meagan gingerly placed her fingertip in the water and then to her tongue. "It's salty, but we are hundreds of miles from the sea."

Sari looked at her with a knowing smile. "Yes."

Meagan thought she saw something move under the water and peered closer to get a better look.

"If I were you, I would not put my nose too close to the water," Sari cautioned.

"Is something down there?" asked Meagan, pointing to the black, bubbling water.

"I have never seen anything, but things do not feel right to me. Maybe it is because my nerves are so fraught. Princess Maura has never been here before—I mean the queen." Sari looked uneasily around the chamber.

Meagan shuddered and put her hands in her lap. "Do you think we are safe in this thing?"

Sari dipped the oars silently into the lake. "I don't know. I have never done this before."

"What?"

"I always stood back where your women are. I have never been across the water. I cannot swim."

Meagan blinked several times. She felt her left eyebrow twitch.

Sari grew silent and said no more, concentrating on rowing until the boat reached the rock island, scraping against it.

Meagan pulled the boat closer to the island dock and climbed out.

Sari handed her a battered rope with which to tie the boat.

Meagan stood on the wooden dock, noticing that many of its planks looked rotten. She whispered a prayer that the boards would hold. Leaning over, she helped Sari pull Maura from the boat.

Sari, not used to such a heavy load, almost dropped the young woman into the bubbling water.

Meagan heard her women cry out.

"Oh dear," was all Sari could muster, upset at her lapse, but became horrified when something went under the boat and raised it out of the water several inches.

With a heavy fog blowing in her face, it was hard for Meagan to see what circled the rowboat, but she knew it was large. Reaching down, she pulled with all her might and dragged Maura from the boat. She felt the wooden planks start to give under her. With a mighty lunge, Meagan jumped onto a small outcropping of rocks with Maura on her shoulders.

Maura slid off and landed with a hard thud.

Meagan then extended a hand to Sari. As Sari reached for the healer's plump but sturdy hand, the boat rocked a second time, and she lost her balance again.

Meagan saw a green motley creature swim away and turn, making its way to the boat again. "Lady Sari, hurry!"

The older woman looked over her shoulder and saw the monster swimming toward her. Her eyes wide with fright, Sari scrambled to the edge of the rowboat and jumped as the boat was smashed into pieces. A great wave of hot spray hit her.

Tearing at Sari's hair and clothes, Meagan pulled her up.

They both clung to the dripping rocks, catching their breath.

Sari's hands and face were bleeding where they had scraped against the jagged stones.

Meagan held a hunk of Sari's white hair in her hand. "Here, I think this is yours," she said, trying to put the hair back on Sari's head.

Both women broke into laughter.

Meagan's attention was diverted when she spied the Bogazkoy extending its blue tendrils slowly over Maura's body. She suppressed a shudder. "It's alive," she mumbled.

"It knows the queen is here," said Sari, her breathing relaxing.

"What do we do?"

"Let us pull her closer to the plant. Queen Abisola used to stand in the center of the island, and it would wrap itself around her."

Grasping the queen under the arms, Meagan dragged Maura toward the plant. If she stepped on tendrils, they would writhe upward as if in agony.

Sari followed, helping as best she could.

"Here! Here is the center of the tree," said Sari. They gently placed Maura at the foot of the main trunk.

Meagan folded the queen's hands.

"Step back," Sari ordered.

Meagan jumped over the moving tendrils and stood by Sari, reaching for her hand. They waited together, clasping their hands tightly.

Slowly, all of the Bogazkoy's tendrils retracted from the water and moved over the rocks, searching for the queen. Upon finding her, they wrapped themselves around the unconscious girl until Maura was not visible.

Alarmed, Meagan started forward.

Sari caught her arm and held her back. "This is what the Bogazkoy does."

"She won't be able to breathe," Meagan argued.

"Yes, she will. Let the Bogazkoy do its magic if it has any power left." Sari shrugged. "And if it cannot, what difference will it make for the queen to die anyway?"

Finding no fault in Sari's logic, Meagan sat on her haunches studying the Tree Of Life.

The tendrils wrapped themselves around Maura so tightly as to become a second skin. An acrid smell filled the air. Maura began to twitch inside her cocoon.

Meagan glanced nervously at Sari.

Sari smiled. "It is injecting its serum into our lady. It has some life in it yet."

"What kind of serum?"

"I do not know, but when the queen arises, she will have little puncture wounds over her body, and her orifices will be sore."

"All of them?"

"Yes," replied Sari, looking off into the rolling water. "That is why it is referred to as a 'mating.'"

"Oh," was all Meagan could comment.

The cocoon continued to jerk and twitch, seeming impervious to anything surrounding it.

Meagan soon gained the courage to touch the tendrils. They did not respond to her. Inside the cocoon, she could hear gurgling noises.

"Do not worry," Sari comforted. "This is normal."

"Did Queen Abisola ever complain about pain during this procedure?"

Sari grinned. "The only thing she ever said to me was that it was like being loved by six different men at the same time."

"Well, that could hurt," replied Meagan, feeling the conversation was taking on a disrespectful tone.

"Or it could be ecstasy. It depends on one's frame of reference."

It was Meagan's turn to snort. She continued watching, taking mental notes until she glanced forlornly at the broken pieces of the dock and the rowboat floating in the water. She would think about getting across the water later. Right now, she had a queen to save.

The initiates waited patiently on the other side, occasionally waving and calling. Some prayed to Mekonia, their nature goddess.

A loud wail came from the cocoon. The cry wavered and then fell silent.

Sari rushed to the blue-wrapped mass. "Help me!" she cried. "This is not right!"

Meagan helped Sari tear the tendrils from Maura.

They had become brittle and broke off, crumbling into dust. After removing many layers of plant wrap, they could see their queen. Her clothes were shredded.

Hastily, the healer pulled plant material from Maura's nose and ears. Realizing the tendrils had crumbled inside her mouth, she reached inside and scooped out the debris. She rolled the young queen over, trying to get her to expel plant material on her own. She hit Maura between the shoulder blades. Getting no response, she pummeled again and again.

4

Maura coughed.

She spat debris onto the rocks.

"Good," Sari encouraged. "Get it all out."

Exhausted, Maura stretched out, breathing heavily. There was a pile of dead Bogazkoy tendrils beside her. She opened her eyes and stared at Sari who peered down anxiously, and then at Meagan who was taking her pulse.

The queen's skin was a much darker hue and swollen with tiny punctures. There was another change in Maura that Meagan had a hard time deciphering, but the queen seemed to radiate life. An aura of soothing heat surrounded her. Meagan had the sudden urge to dry her wet clothes on Maura's skin.

"The Royal Bogazkoy is dead," Maura muttered. "It gave me all it had left." She began pulling dead tendrils from her hair. Laughing bitterly, she said, "Sari, you must not approve of how I look. I certainly don't look like royalty. How the nobles would fret over my lack of decorum."

Meagan and Sari laughed as well, both aware of the irony of the situation.

"Well, frankly, I have seen you look better," replied Sari, her eyes full of relief.

"I have news for you, Sari. Most of your hair is gone."

"Thanks to this heavy-handed know-it-all."

"That's the thanks I get for saving you from the creature," growled Meagan.

"What creature?" Maura asked.

Sari pointed to the water. "That thing there."

Maura peered over into the water and caught a glimpse of something skimming the surface. She was astonished. "My mother never mentioned anything about a creature in the water."

"I have never seen it before," Sari said.

Maura thought for a moment. "This must be some evil work of the Black Cacodemon trying to prevent me from getting to the Royal Bogazkoy." She looked appraisingly at Meagan and Sari. "Good work, women. I salute you."

"Why do you say that, Your Majesty?" Meagan asked.

"I did not put myself in the death dream of my own will. Something has been compelling me to do so."

Sari put her hand up to her mouth. "The Black Cacodemon again!"

"Sari, do you think I am so cowardly that I would leave my people at their hour of greatest need?"

"So much has happened. I have not had time to think."

Maura nodded her head. "How well I am beginning to know that feeling." She looked around and acknowledged the greetings from the initiates standing on the other side of the lake. "The question now is how do we get from here to over there?" She pointed to the initiates and carefully perused what was left of the dock and the boat. Then she spied the doors. "I wonder if those doors float? You, over there!" Maura shouted. "Get one of those doors and put it in the water."

The noblewomen looked at each other and then back to the little group on the island.

Maura motioned toward the giant doors. "Get a door off its hinges, and paddle it over here."

Sari argued, "Oh, Your Majesty, that is too dangerous."

"Do you want to swim? This is our only option at the moment, or we could send the women back for Dorak. I am sure he would love to know about the Bogazkoy and how the Hasan Daegian queens are so long-lived."

Sari bowed her head in acquiescence.

One of the noblewomen found a large rock and began beating at the lower iron hinge. The rock broke against it.

Another initiate found a larger rock, taking two women to raise it and strike against the rusty hinge. It took a great deal of sweat and effort, but the initiates finally removed the bolt out of the hinge. The door made a grinding sound as it shifted its weight.

The noblewomen then climbed atop one another forming a pyramid. The top two women lifted the rock over their grunting comrades.

They dropped the rock once and had to climb down to retrieve it. This process went on for what seemed hours, but finally, they managed to knock the last bolt out.

The door teetered toward the pyramid. One of the women lunged forward and pushed the door away from them. The sudden motion caused the precariously balanced women to tumble to the ground. At the same time, the carved door landed with a thunderous crash.

One by one, the women sat up, rubbing their heads and arms. They checked each other for broken bones, and when satisfied, they waved back. Only one woman was slightly injured, and the others improvised a sling for her arm.

Maura sighed with relief. "Thrust the door into the water. See if it floats," she called over.

The noblewomen laboriously dragged the door to the water. One woman ripped her skirt into strips and made a rope, which she tied on the door handle.

With a great push, the door was shoved into the water.

Meagan held her breath, and closing her eyes, she clutched Sari's hands, asking, "Is it floating? Oh, by the good Goddess, let it float!" She peeked with one eye and then immediately closed it again. "I cannot stand this excitement."

Sari retorted, "Quit your whining. Try this adventure at my age."

Maura leapt triumphantly in the air. "It works. It's not sinking!"

Remembering she was now queen, she composed herself. "Two of you women climb aboard and paddle over here," she commanded.

Two of the younger women sat on the rock's shoulder and jumped on the wooden door now serving as a raft.

The door rocked, and for a moment, Maura thought it would capsize.

The black-robed assistants quickly spread themselves out on the raft and steadied it so that it rocked gently on the boiling current. Once steady, they sat up and tore their skirts. Wrapping long pieces of cloth around one of their hands and arms to protect their skin from the hot water, they lay on the edges of the door and began paddling.

The women, remaining on the shore, yelled encouragement. One initiate, with a particularly loud voice, counted the stroke beats for them. Everyone else became quiet as the woman counted.

They were halfway across when Sari yelled, "LOOK OUT!"

A creature, with shiny green scales and barbed protruding teeth, rose out of the water, attacking the raft. It picked up one screaming woman and pulled her down into the murky depths.

Bubbles rose to the surface and diminished until there were none.

Then only stillness.

No one made a sound. Only the rolling of the water could be heard. The woman still alive on the raft was dazed and confused.

Suddenly, Maura pierced the stunned silence. "STROKE! Keep on. I am giving you an order, you worthless piece of flotsam. Stroke! Stroke! Stroke!"

The woman, responding to the firm voice, got over her shock and took up the count again. When she came to a piece of wood from the disintegrated rowboat, she used it as a paddle.

Nervously, Maura peered into the water. She could see no sign of the beast.

Sweating profusely, the initiate made it to the rock island without further incident. She threw the skirt-twisted rope to Maura who tied it around a large boulder.

The queen helped her climb up.

The initiate tried to bow.

Maura waved her away. "Go rest. Save your strength for the journey back."

The woman did as told, collapsing on the rocks.

Meagan checked the woman's burns from the hot water.

"You think we can get across with that creature?" Meagan asked, unwrapping the steaming bandages from the woman's arms. "It will be suicide."

Maura looked over her shoulder at the water. "She made it."

"With one dead."

"That is right," Maura replied. "Only one is dead."

"This is appalling," Meagan said, not quite believing their situation.

"Yes, you speak the truth. It is appalling that Anqara was burned to the ground. It is appalling that my parents are dead. It is appalling that my country has been invaded, and my crown taken. The list goes on and on. I can sit on this stupid rock and cry myself into oblivion, or I can go back and try to save something." Maura's eyes narrowed. "Healer, what do you suggest I do?"

Ashamed, Meagan bowed. She knew that she lacked Maura's resolve.

"Your Majesty, can you send for help?" Sari asked, thinking of the Dinii.

"I have no magic powers, Sari. The Dinii taught me to fight well, but I never could master telepathy long range."

"But I heard that Hasan Daegian queens can heal," Meagan ventured.

Maura regarded the worn-out initiate nursing her burns. "I dare not try it. I need all my strength to get back across." She sat down, her courage deserting her momentarily.

"But you are a good warrior."

Maura brightened. "Yes, Sari, I am a good warrior."

"Then get up, little sparrow, and fight. The day is not over, and I do not want to die on this barren rock pile." She smiled tenderly at Maura and held out her hand.

Maura pulled herself up and touched Sari's cheek. "If I must die, good Sari, it will be an honor to die at your side. But I do not think that will be today." She turned to Meagan. "As soon as your woman is able, we will gather what wood we can from the dock and boat."

"For what purpose, Your Majesty?"

"To make spears, of course. And we will need good rocks to grind the wood into points. Get busy. We have much to do."

Meagan walked away. "Why of course. We will just make spears," she muttered to herself in a mocking tone. "Why didn't I think of that?"

"I hope Dorak doesn't wander into your chamber to check on you," Sari mused, suddenly worried. "I do not think we could explain your absence."

"Let us hope matters of state keep him away for a long time," Maura said. The mention of Dorak brought back painful memories. For the first time, she thought of Chaun Maaun. She wondered if he was safe in the City of the Peaks. Realizing she missed him terribly, she pushed the thought from her mind and concentrated on the crisis at hand.

I can do this! she thought. Relaxing somewhat, she searched for a grinding stone. Daydreams and longing for Chaun Maaun would have to wait.

After several hours, the women had gathered many planks of wood.

Maura sharpened them into points, although she was sorry there was no fire to harden them, she would have to work with what she had.

Finally, they were ready!

The initiate bound her arms with rags again as did Meagan.

Maura and Sari sat in the middle.

Cautiously, they climbed onto the bobbing raft. For several hours, they had seen no sign of the creature and were not anxious to announce they were leaving the island.

The women quietly dipped their rough-looking oars into the rolling water and began paddling back to the other shore.

The initiates waited for them with hands folded inside their long black sleeves. Their faces were devoid of expression as they watched the raft make its way toward them. Suddenly, one of them cried out, "It comes! It comes!"

Maura jerked her head around and caught sight of something sliding under the raft. A large fantail sprayed hot water on them. "It's going under! Hold on!"

Picking up a spear, she leaned on the side where the creature emerged and jabbed hard into the water, striking deep into its flesh. The spear broke, leaving Maura with only a short jagged stick.

The beast submerged in the dark water.

Maura leaned from side to side looking for the creature.

"Paddle! Paddle!" Sari encouraged, her face white with fear.

Without warning, the serpent-like monster rose from the water with a deafening roar.

Sari clamped her hands tightly over her ears.

Gusts of scalding water sprayed the women as they clutched the raft now swirling around and around uncontrollably.

A long, black barbed tongue violently lashed out and struck Meagan in the face. Stunned, Meagan did not resist as the slimy band wrapped her head and tried to pull her into the water.

Seeing Meagan helpless, Maura repeatedly stabbed at the monstrous tongue until her spear sliced through the tough tissue. The creature released Meagan and began to submerge.

"Hang onto the tongue!" Maura shouted. She dropped her spear and grabbed the injured tongue oozing foul smelling blood. "Help me! I need to keep its head above water!"

Numb with fear, Meagan grabbed the odious band of tissue.

Sari got behind Meagan and helped to anchor her.

Now bucking with its fantail, the beast tried to flip the raft into the swirling water.

Maura frantically looked for her spear, but it had fallen into the water like the others.

The initiate threw to Maura the last surviving weapon.

Maura took careful aim and shoved the spear into the creature's left eye.

It writhed in pain. Hanging on, Maura thrust the spear in deeper until it reached its brain.

Giving one last cry, the sea serpent slowly sank into the murky depths of the lake.

Maura fell gasping on all fours. She looked at Meagan questioningly.

The healer nodded.

Maura took off what was left of her nightshirt, ripped it apart, and wrapped the rags around her hand. She lay down on her stomach and gave the order to paddle.

The initiate and Meagan put their arms into the hot water as well, as they had lost all of the makeshift oars. It took the battered survivors a long time to get to shore.

The waiting noblewomen greeted them somberly. One of the women tried to give Maura her robe.

Maura pushed the initiate's offer away. "Let me see your hands," she requested of Meagan, Sari, and the initiate. Maura placed their raw scorched flesh between hers and concentrated.

"Oh, my!" exclaimed Meagan. "It feels tingly." She looked at Maura with awe.

Sari mumbled a prayer and pulled her hand away, causing the bond to break with the other women. "That is enough, Maura. Do not waste your new strength on us."

Meagan studied her hands in astonishment. "I am almost healed. The blisters are gone. Just some redness and swelling left."

"Sari?" questioned Maura.

"I'm fine, little bird. Do not worry about me. I have more than enough energy to guide us home," Sari replied as she led them away from the lake.

Forming a single line, the women began the arduous journey back to the palace. No one said a word as they traveled through the corridors.

Reaching the stairs, they groaned with each step. Tired and hungry, they finally arrived at the top of the stairway.

Sari listened with her ear pressed next to the secret panel. Convinced no one was in the bedchamber, she cautiously opened the hidden door and entered Maura's room.

5

Sari opened the secret door.

The exhausted women crept into the bedroom.

"I hope you ladies had a good time on your journey," Dorak rasped as he lit a lamp in Maura's room.

Several of the women frantically turned around to seek shelter in the secret corridor, but the panel had already shut.

"And what is this? It is the good Queen Maura awake." He paused and took a hard look at the rags she was wearing. "I must say that is a fetching gown you have on there, Your Majesty. And what is that smell?" He sniffed the air. "It must be a new cologne, eau de sewer." He sat upright in his chair and crossed his arms. "You all smell that way. I guess that means you were together for a little escapade."

Maura, startled at the sight of Dorak, managed to calm herself. "You are in my private quarters, my lord. I am asking you to leave."

Dorak ignored her. "You know, Your Majesty, my top general, Alexanee, has been turning this city upside down searching for you. I told him—NOOOO, she has not escaped. Queen Maura is just taking a little sightseeing tour of the city. She will be back. Well, he did not agree." Dorak stood and approached Maura, pushing several noblewomen out of the way. He caressed her shoulder with his index finger.

Maura held her breath and dared not look into his dark, menacing eyes.

Like a lover delivering words of endearment, Dorak whispered, "You will never guess how many people he has interrogated since your disappearance."

Maura flinched but remained silent.

"You are not playing the game, Your Majesty. Guess how many people have been rounded up and interrogated by my soldiers. Now, when I say interrogated, we Bhuttanians do more than ask questions." Dorak stopped his caressing and gloated. "Nod if you understand what I am implying."

Maura inclined her head.

"I think the last count of the interrogated who did not make it through the entire session was eight. If you do not believe me, take a look outside your window."

Maura staggered to a window and peered over the balcony railing. In the middle of the courtyard was a small stack of corpses. Maura resisted the urge to scream by crushing her lips tight.

Dorak came up behind her and whispered in her ear. "There was no need for this carnage. Let it be on your head."

She turned and faced him. "I was not trying to escape, I swear."

"I will make that determination after I have questioned these lovely ladies."

Maura grabbed his arm. "I'm asking you not to do this. I was not trying to escape."

"What were you doing?"

Maura looked away and said nothing.

"All right, ladies, you are to follow me. I have some nice gentlemen waiting for you," Dorak announced, pointing a short sword at them.

"Wait! Wait!" Maura pleaded. "If you hurt them, I shall will myself to die."

Dorak paused.

Maura realized how fearful he was of that happening. "You know I can do it, Dorak. I can will myself to die before sunrise, and there will be nothing your black wizard can do about it."

She came closer to him until she was almost touching his chest. "Dorak, I am asking that no harm come to these women."

"Are you begging me, Queen of Hasan Daeg?"

She swallowed hard. "Yes, I am, Aga Dorak. I am begging for their lives."

He moved closer until his lips were touching her hair. "What about the woman, Maura? Is she also begging?"

Maura closed her eyes.

Dorak laughed and pushed her away. "You win for today. I am so happy to see you up and about that I will grant your wish."

There were collective sighs from the small knot of women huddled together.

"Of course, you will have new quarters. These rooms are now officially off-limits to you and your companions."

He laughed and flicked his sword at Maura's shredded clothes. "It pains me to tell you this, my lady, but I have never seen you clean. Next time you are in my presence," he pointed to her hair and face, "please do something with yourself. It is very depressing to look at you." He smiled a rakish grin and called for the guards. "Ladies, follow me."

Maura started forward.

Dorak waved her away. "I will keep my end of the bargain. They will not be killed or even tortured, but I am going to keep a very heavy guard on them."

He bowed very low to Maura. "You better start thinking about what you are going to give me in return for my generosity." He began leading the women out of the room.

"One more thing," Maura called out.

Dorak swirled toward her.

Just for a brief second, Maura could see deep anger welling in his eyes. "Yes, Queen Maura?"

"May I keep Lady Sari?"

Dorak looked at the old woman. "If it pleases you. I must take my leave. I have been up rather late and would like to sleep now."

"Where are the guards taking me?"

"To your new quarters. I know those rooms have no secret passages."

"And pray, where is that?"

Dorak yawned. "Right next to my chambers."

"That is impossible. It is not respectable."

Dorak gave Maura an irritated look. "Madam, do I look like I give a damn about respectability? I am going to bed. I do not wish to talk anymore. If you give my guards any trouble, they have orders to drag you by the hair of your head to your quarters. Good night!"

Dorak strode out of the room.

Bhuttanian guards entered and escorted Maura and Lady Sari to their new quarters.

As Sari hobbled after the queen, she thought about the day's events, but what bothered her were the looks that Maura and Dorak exchanged with each other. There was too much heat in them. Too much hate in their exchanges. Hate and love were opposites of the same coin. She knew the gaze of desire when she saw it.

Dorak wanted Maura to be more than just a political wife.

What caused Sari's heart to fear was that Maura wanted him too and wondered if the young queen realized it yet.

6

There was a pounding on the door.

Sari, who was sleeping on a pallet, got up and limped over to answer. Her old bones creaked as she pulled open the door.

A courier asked permission to see the queen.

Sari told him to wait in the next room, and the queen would see him when she had dressed.

The courier did as instructed.

When Sari closed the door, Maura jumped out of bed. "What does he want?"

"I do not know, but he is from Dorak. You must hurry."

Maura washed her face and dressed in a rush, but entered her private audience chamber calmly.

The Bhuttanian courier bowed in the Hasan Daegian manner and greeted her. "Salutations, Great Mother and Queen. The Aga of Bhuttan and Emperor of Kaseri, asks me to convey his invitation to dine in the main dining hall."

"I see."

The courier blushed. It made him nervous to be near a woman so tall. All the Hasan Daegian women made him nervous.

"What else?" Maura asked, sensing another agenda.

"Aga Dorak wishes that you be properly attired, freshly scrubbed, and clean-smelling." The courier lowered his eyes.

Maura could barely contain her anger. She wished to pull the courier's silly plumed hat down around his neck. How insulting this was, especially when the Bhuttanians rarely bathed, and the Hasan Daegians washed every day.

Sari leaned over and whispered, "Aga Dorak is trying to raise your color."

"Thank you, courier. You may tell Aga Dorak that the Queen of Hasan Daeg will be pleased to have the Aga of Bhuttan join Her Majesty in *her* dining hall for the noon repast. Make sure you tell him in those exact words."

The courier silently mouthed the message as he backed out of the room.

As soon as he was gone, Sari laughed.

"I don't think it is funny," Maura snapped. "He implied that I am dirty. I'm not going."

"Oh, yes, you are little one. Dorak thinks no such thing of you. He just wants to anger you into making a mistake so he can pounce. Oh, how I would love to see his face when the courier repeats your words."

"Then be quick and prepare me a bath. Bring me some of my mother's robes from which to select. I am going to dazzle that coarse, stupid man."

Sari gave Maura a strange look but did as she was commanded. She prepared a hot, steamy bath with herbs and scented oil. The queen's hair was washed several times and ironed dry. Sari took great pains weaving flowers into Maura's hair, which had grown back in black and long after being with the Royal Bogazkoy.

After several hours of primping, pulling, and preening, Maura de Magela stood before Bhuttanian guards awaiting entrance into the dining hall. She stood regally in a white gown with blue trim. Yellow and white flowers adorned her hair, and she carried a silk hand fan with a drawing of the uultepes on it.

An old man, in Bhuttanian dress of the long tunic over trousers, shuffled out and bowed to her. "Your Majesty, Aga Dorak will see you now."

Maura swept past him and glided into the de Magela's dining hall. She looked around the room. The last time she had been in it was on the day of her birthday celebration. Tears welled in her eyes as she stared at the chair in which her father had sat. He had been so proud and was the perfect host overseeing his guests' comforts. Her hand flew to her heart.

Chairs scraped the floor as Bhuttanian officers jumped to their feet. Each pressed a right fist to his heart, giving her the Bhuttanian salute.

"What is the matter, Your Majesty?" she heard Dorak say behind her. "Does the table not please you?"

Maura started. Why was he always out of sight behind her? She turned. "No, the room is lovely. It's just I feel very strange. May I sit down?"

Dorak motioned for a slave to bring a chair for the queen. He gazed about the room genuinely puzzled. Then his face took on a look of enlightenment. "You know it is much too stuffy to stay inside on such a pretty day. Why do we not eat on one of the balconies overlooking the city?"

"No, we mustn't," interjected Maura quickly. She did not want to be seen casually dining with Dorak by her countrywomen. They would get the wrong impression. "Why don't we eat in the kitchen?"

"The kitchen!"

"Yes, the servants have a nice room right off the kitchen, and we could eat at their table."

Dorak hesitated.

"Are you too good to sit at a servant's table, my lord?" asked Maura, fanning herself.

"Frankly, yes, but if you want to." Dorak gave the order that they would dine in the kitchen. He offered his arm to Maura.

Politely, she took it and walked with him.

"I hope this makes you happy."

"If you want to make me happy, leave my country."

Dorak chuckled. "I want to make you happy, not giddy."

Maura smiled at him. As she walked, she noticed all of his servants had iron collars about their necks and kowtowed as the royal couple passed. "What are those things around your people's necks? They look awfully heavy."

"Just adornments, nothing more."

Maura took exception but said nothing. She needed to cultivate his good will. She was planning to ask for a favor.

Dorak spun Maura around and looked her up and down. "Your Majesty, I must say you are stunning. And I see you have changed your hair color again. But not only the hair color but the length as well. You must have a skillful hairdresser."

The officers walking behind them murmured in agreement. Maura noticed the general called Alexanee kept quiet.

Maura ignored the comments about her hair. "Thank you. This robe was a favorite of my mother's."

The grin fell from Dorak's face.

Smiling sweetly, Maura tugged at his arm and led him down the hallway.

Catching sight of Maura and Dorak entering the kitchen, the servants flew into a flurry of activity.

Dorak glowered at the Hasan Daegians as they clustered around Maura in a tight group. He pursed his lips when Maura shook hands and even hugged a few as they greeted her.

They scattered when Dorak gave them a stern look.

"I see you have been down here before," Dorak said, following a servant to the kitchen dining room.

The Hasan Daegian queen laughed. "Yes. I think I have spent a good deal of my childhood with cooks and serving maids. Most of them helped raise me. I know more than once they hid me in the pantry to escape a spanking from Lady Sari."

"I find it difficult to believe that you ever required corporal punishment," commented Alexanee.

Turning, Maura stared at the impressive-looking general. She did not reply as he had spoken without her permission. She expected Dorak to reprimand Alexanee, but he didn't.

"Of course, they spoiled me with food. So when I was home, I would come down here and stuff myself with cakes and puddings," Maura said to Dorak.

"Were you away from home often, Your Majesty?" Alexanee inquired.

Maura ignored the general's question as she sat at the servants' table.

Tall goblets, filled with wine, were brought.

Dorak sneered at the ruby liquid. "What I am in the mood for is shaybar. Yes, milk with thick foam." He slapped his hand down on the table. He leaned toward Maura. "What is your pleasure, Lady of the House?"

The Bhuttanian officers remained standing at attention.

Maura was ravenous. "I want warm bread and cakes with lots of honey icing to start."

Dorak leaned back in his chair. Addressing a trembling Hasan Daegian maid, he ordered meat for himself.

Bread was immediately put on the table, as were several jugs of borax milk.

Dorak poured a goblet of milk for Maura as well as one for himself. He took a drink, made a face, and then swallowed. "I remember now that I hate this stuff. It's too wholesome," Dorak said smiling.

"My father would mix borax blood with milk or boiled water and drink it all the time. Most of the older Bhuttanians do. It is what my people once lived on."

Wiping the foam from her lips, Maura teased, "Not human blood? You disappoint me, Aga Dorak."

"We can't be savages all of the time. But when we do drink human blood, it should always be that of a virgin." He winked at the maid serving them and gave her a lecherous once over.

Maura gave him a disapproving look. "There is no need to frighten these people." She turned to the addled serving maid. "You may go now."

The girl bowed and hastily retreated behind a dark cupboard where she pulled her apron over her head.

"I thought all Hasan Daegian women were brave warriors," drawled Dorak, noting the maid's timid demeanor. He slapped butter on a hunk of bread.

Maura started to reply but thought better if it. She drank more of the milk to stall for time. She felt all of the eyes of the officers observing her, but it was Alexanee who gave her pause. She detested sharing a meal with Dorak and his men, but for the time being, she could not afford to alienate him. She would have to bide her time until she could make her next move. She looked up from her thoughts and was surprised to find Dorak studying her. "What are you looking at?" she asked sharply. Dorak always took her by surprise.

Dorak rubbed his chin. "I was just wondering how one's hair could grow so many inches overnight and turn black as night as well."

"It's a hairpiece," she lied, silently cursing for not cutting her hair to its former length.

"Is that so?" Dorak studied her intently as Maura tried not to squirm under his gaze. "Can you explain why you are not covered with puncture marks today?"

"I do not know what you mean." Maura bit into a hunk of bread Dorak had torn off the loaf for her.

Servants brought plates of steaming food and placed them on the table.

Maura eagerly began eating.

Dorak took a sip of wine from a goblet, having sent the milk away. "Last evening, it looked like you were covered with tiny wounds."

"As you can see for yourself, I am not."

"I can see that not only has your white hair grown dark in the last ten hours but your skin color is noticeably different. You were considerably paler yesterday."

"I appear darker in harsh light, just as you might turn redder."

"Where did you go last night?" asked Dorak, narrowing his eyes.

"I thought you asked me to dine, not to an interrogation," answered Maura, picking up the salt bag near his plate. She generously poured salt over her vegetables.

"As I understood my courier, it is you who invited me."

Maura took one look at Dorak's face and broke into peals of laughter. "So I did." Her laughter broke the tension at the table. She bade the officers to sit with them.

Comfortable with his men eating as well, Dorak engaged in more genial conversation. He talked of philosophers familiar to Maura.

Maura discovered that Dorak was educated. They argued over the Anqarian concept of zero, which the Bhuttanians could not fathom. Maura tried over and over to explain "nothingness" to Dorak, but he refused her explanations, saying there was no such thing as a complete void of something. She was having such an engaging time she forgot Dorak was her enemy until one of his men tapped the table to gain his attention.

"I am sorry," he said rising, "but I have matters that need my attention."

"One moment, please," Maura requested, folding her napkin.

Dorak waited for her to speak.

"I wish to pay respect to my parents."

"That can be arranged." As always, Dorak looked for signs of weakness. "Do you wish me to escort you to your parents' grave?"

Maura blanched at the thought of Dorak accompanying her to her ancestors' final resting place. Regaining her poise, she answered politely, "No, Great Aga. That will not be necessary, although you are kind to offer your assistance. I need only a small guard of Hasan Daegians to accompany me to the royal sepulcher."

For a moment, it looked as though Dorak was going to forbid Maura from leaving the palace without his guards, but he relented. He remembered the stricken look on Maura's face when she discovered the stack of corpses beneath her balcony window. He doubted she would try anything foolish, but he would have her followed surreptitiously just in case. "I will have a litter prepared for you," he said while summoning a slave.

"If it pleases you, I would like to ride my pony to my family's sacred grove. That is if my pony has not been slaughtered."

A little vinegar with the honey, thought Dorak. He smiled. "I find it very amusing that you Hasan Daegians prefer to ride your little pet ponies as though they were horses. Your feet almost drag the ground when you are astride them."

The Hasan Daegian queen returned the smile. Maura was not going to rise to his bait. She wanted to visit her parents' grave, and she was not going to do anything Dorak could use as an excuse to stop her.

Dorak continued, "Your Majesty, I do not know if your pony survived, but if alive, it will be waiting for you in the courtyard. If it has met with misfortune, one of my horses will be given to you to compensate your loss. Now you must excuse me." He turned abruptly to leave.

Maura clutched at his sleeve.

Dorak spun around, half-expecting to encounter a dagger. He met only with Maura's pained expression.

"I sincerely thank you for allowing me to visit my parents and for their honorable burial. It is decent of you."

Dorak winced at her words. "Decency is not just a Hasan Daegian trait, my lady. Even Bhuttanians can be honorable." He stopped short and grinned rakishly at her. "At least, some of the time."

Before Maura could reply, Dorak bowed and rushed out of the kitchen with his men, leaving Maura alone.

7

Maura dressed in a white gown.

Her face covered by a blue mourning veil, she rode through the streets of O Konya in a palanquin. Her pony, Beca, could not be found, and she was wary of the Bhuttanians' warhorses.

The queen's guards, bereft of weapons, marched proudly beside her. They still made an impressive sight as they carried the royal blue banners with the crest of the uultepes on them.

Maura opened the curtains of the sedan so she could wave to the people.

The citizens of O Konya stopped whatever they were doing and ran to pay homage to their new queen. A few of the citizens spat as she passed.

Taking note of this, Maura's face did not betray her keenly felt sorrow that some of her people thought her unworthy to be their sovereign, but she could not blame them.

Her mind raced over the events of the past several months: the death of Zoar, the great Hasan Daegian victory at the border, the resurrection of the Black Cacodemon, and the fall of O Konya into the barbarians' hands. Her mind rejected the notion that there was anything she could have done to resist Dorak's dark magic.

Was the rest of her country still fighting? Without her scouts and her spy network, she was blind and deaf. She felt helpless. Still, hoping to give her countrywomen encouragement, Maura smiled and waved until she could stand it no more. Drawing the curtains, Maura shut out the light and the curious faces staring at her. By the time she reached the royal grove of her parents' final resting place, Maura had grown sullen and withdrawn. She barely looked up as she was helped from the palanquin. Ordering her guards to wait, Maura gathered her mother's ancestral sword and prayer book after accepting a small torch from one of the guards.

While following the pathway leading to the ancient sepulcher of the Hasan Daegian queens, she recited the litany for the dead. As there were no other mourners present, she read both the invocations and the responses. Feeling more despondent with each step and verse, Maura reached the ornate marble building that housed her ancestors. She tucked the prayer book in her sleeve and ascended the steps leading into the great hall.

In the middle of the atrium were the sarcophagi of her mother and father. Traditionally, consorts were never placed with their ruling mates but laid to rest in a lesser building in the grove.

Tears sprang to Maura's eyes.

This was a great honor for Iasos to be placed here.

She realized Dorak was responsible and was grateful that he had allowed her father to be at the side of his beloved wife for eternity. Though she might have wanted to, Maura would never have defied tradition in this manner.

Dorak was immune to such observances.

A flood of tears ran down Maura's face as emotions that had been pent up for so long could now be vented freely. Maura pulled at her hair and unabashedly cried out. She tore at her veil. "Mother! Father!" she shrieked, choking over the words. Overwhelmed with her loss, she rent her mourning robe and fell to her knees sobbing. Maura pounded the sides of her head with her fists.

A hand shot out and grabbed one of Maura's arms.

Startled, Maura jerked forward and almost toppled over, but was caught in powerful arms.

"Shh, shh," whispered a male voice. "You must not harm yourself. It will do no one any good."

Maura swiftly leaned her head down and bit a tattooed hand.

The man yelped and lessened his grip somewhat, allowing Maura to bring her hands up and force her captor's arms from her. She immediately rolled to her side and viciously kicked the strange man in the gut.

The man crumpled over and fell to his knees. Though winded, he tried to kowtow and show obeisance to the queen. "Please, Your Majesty! Have pity. I was trying to save you from harm." The man placed his forehead on the cold marble floor.

Panting, Maura gathered her torn robe about her and stood over the man. She kicked him again for good measure. The stranger grunted but did not move his position. "Have mercy, Queen Maura!"

Feeling in control of the situation, Maura picked up her mother's sword and unsheathed it. She placed the sword on the neck of the man prostrate before her. "Who are you?" she demanded.

The man peered upward. "May I speak freely to the queen of the Hasan Daegians?"

"You may sit up, but move very slowly or I will kill you," Maura replied, furious that an intruder had desecrated her parents' resting place.

The man straightened his back but remained on his knees. He was deliberate in his movements, making them slow and exaggerated. Clasping his hands behind his back, he said, "My name is Prince KiKu of the Hittals, fifth in line to rule after my mother and the last surviving female heir. Along with my twin sister, I was taken to court as a hostage at the age of eight by Zoar. My sister was forced to marry Zoar when she became of age, and I was kept in the Bhuttanian royal household as a means of ensuring her obedience.

"Zoar, thinking he could control me, had me trained in the arts of secrecy and duplicity. I rose through the ranks until I was made the hetmaan, Zoar's spylord. I was put in control of his vast network, and it is through this spiderweb that I learned of Hasan Daeg. I wished to live in your land, and I entered your country as a Sivan merchant after years of careful planning and finding the secret corridor from Siva into Hasan Daeg."

"You left your sister alone with Zoar?"

"My sister perished in a hunting accident. She was gored by a wild borax bull." He paused for a moment as if remembering the incident. His face hardened, and his eyes dulled with hatred. "Because of my loathing for Zoar, I became a spy for Queen Abisola and returned to Zoar's court."

"You are my mother's secret spy in the court of Zoar?"

"Was," KiKu replied, becoming animated.

"You are the one rumored to have cut the cinch on Zoar's saddle after the battle of Anqara."

KiKu inclined his head. "The same."

"And did you?"

"Your mother gave the order for Zoar's mishap in Anqara. She thought it would either kill him or slow him down, which it did."

Maura lowered the sword. "Why that particular time?"

"My usefulness to Queen Abisola was running out. There had been too many leaks, and my absences from the court were getting harder to explain. I believed Zoar was growing suspicious and planning to assassinate me. It was a scenario of now or never."

"Why did my mother wait until the fall of Anqara to unleash you?"

KiKu cocked his head to one side. "It was a simple case of logic. If the Anqarians won, then the threat of Zoar would be over, and life would go on as before. If they lost," KiKu shrugged, "your mother would have the treasure of the Anqarian banks plus the House of Magi with which to defeat the Bhuttanians."

"She never planned on the Black Cacodemon?"

"The Bhuttanians had not used magic in over twenty-five years. There was no reason to believe Zoar would start again. He disliked magicians. But we did not count on his untimely death and that Dorak would unleash the dark wizard upon the world."

"How did you gain access to my mother?"

"Your mother liked to breakfast in the royal garden. I dressed as a gardener to gain access."

"It was that easy?" asked Maura, appalled that the palace security had been so easily breached.

KiKu gave her a quick smile. "It was for me."

"And you just ambled up to my mother's table and began to chat with her?"

"I watched for many days, approaching the table closer and closer, until the queen and her guards became used to me. One morning, while pretending to prune a sinjo bush, I flung myself at her feet and gave her a pouch that would prove my claim."

Although Maura did not believe KiKu's story, it was fascinating nevertheless. She made up her mind not to kill KiKu yet, but to listen to his story. "What was in the pouch?"

"The gold seal from the hand of the statue of Bhuttu in the temple located in Bhuttan."

Maura snorted. "Anyone could have a reproduction made."

KiKu shook his head. "There is only one seal such as this in the world. Your mother knew it was genuine."

KiKu waited for Maura to question him further but when she remained silent, he continued. "The seal can be identified in two ways. There is writing on the band that is invisible to the naked eye until heated. It also has a secret compartment known only to the senior priests of Bhuttu and, of course, to myself.

"What is in the compartment?"

"I never knew. The seal could be broken but once. Your mother had the seal opened by my instructions and read the inscription.

Whatever the message was, it was enough to convince her that I was whom I said. We reached an accord. I would return to Zoar's court and act as a double agent. When my service was over, I would be allowed to return to my country and live out my days in freedom, something I had not known since a small child."

"Do you have a theory about the inscription?"

"I believe that the inscription had information concerning the fall of the Overlords at the hands of the Lahorians."

"You know of the Lahorians?" Maura gasped. This was only the second person to speak to her of the Lahorians. Iegani was the first.

KiKu nodded his head.

The mourning queen sifted through KiKu's story for inconsistencies. There were many pieces of information missing, but perhaps the spy thought he had little time and wished only to provide the highlights before they parted. "What do you want of me?" She wondered if this man had been planted by Dorak to trick her.

"Your father told me to meet you here and present you with this." KiKu handed Maura a letter.

This was the letter of which Meagan had spoken. Maura took the parchment and eagerly broke the seal.

Dearest Daughter,

It is my gravest wish that you are alive and in good health. The man who brings this letter is KiKu. He is a spy and has worked for your mother many years. It is he who caused the cinch on Zoar's saddle to tear, thus causing his accident. It gave us ten more years to prepare. He is to serve as your advisor, and you may use him as you see fit. It is the last gift your mother and I can give you.

I have not much time. I do not mind. I already miss my wife terribly and wish to join her as soon as Mekonia deems it. My only regret is that we leave you behind.

Daughter, be strong. Survive so that you may fight another day.

To prove that KiKu is as he says, he will give you a sign; the one I talked of so long ago at the City of the Peaks. I must go now. It is time. All my love.

Your Father,
Iasos

Maura wiped tears from her eyes so they would not stain the parchment.

"Is that not your father's handwriting, Your Majesty?"

Maura nodded and looked up at KiKu with tenderness. "I thank you for this."

"We must burn it."

"No!" cried Maura, clutching the letter to her breast.

KiKu was stern. "We must."

She hated to part with the letter but knew KiKu was right. The letter had to be destroyed immediately. Maura reluctantly threw it in the flame of the torch she had placed in a stand. The letter was reduced to ashes within a few seconds.

Sighing, she gently patted the sarcophagi of her parents before turning to KiKu. "What else do you have of my father's?"

KiKu slowly reached inside his dirty tunic and pulled out a crumpled piece of cloth. He handed it to her.

Maura unwrapped it and let out a small gasp. It was her father's betrothal ring that signified his status in court and his relationship to her mother. "How did you get this? My father never took this ring off."

"Your father told you that if he ever needed to get a message to you, he would send this ring."

"I had forgotten, and I had promised him that I would not." She had to control her anger. If indeed, this man was sent by her father, she could not squander such a precious resource. "What do you propose to do, KiKu, Hetmaan of the Spies?"

KiKu resisted wiping the sweat from his upper lip. He could have killed this girl easily many times during their talk and disliked being the target of her swordplay. He realized she was the key to his dreams and that he must make her trust him. He wanted to break the Bhuttanian Empire. This young flower before him was needed to help plot against Dorak.

"The western regions of Hasan Daeg have not surrendered to Dorak. He has given these areas little attention while keeping the main part of the army in O Konya."

Maura thought this tactic strange. "Do you know why?"

"He seeks the women from the House of Magi. Dorak secretly interrogates them. Those scholars who have managed to flee the city have taken refuge in the cities west of here or with the Dinii in the City of the Peaks."

"What is he after?"

"He seeks knowledge of the Mother Bogazkoy."

Maura fell silent.

KiKu studied the young woman's blank face, which offered no

insight as to her thoughts. He sighed inwardly, knowing this relationship with this young woman was going to be trying. He did, however, admire her courage and could sense a keen intellect behind her blue-tinted eyes. KiKu thought Maura had the same strange alien beauty he had found in her mother. He needed to know if she could be as ruthless as Abisola. Maura needed to be if she were going to outwit the cunning Dorak.

Maura finally spoke. "I am allowed no contact with my advisors nor any of my staff, except for Lady Sari. I have not heard from the Dinii. I have had no messages from Iegani. If I do anything that looks suspicious, Dorak rounds up my people and executes them. How can I fight Dorak when I can't find my warriors? I am in a desperate situation."

"I can act as courier to your army and to the Dinii, but first, you must find the Mother Bogazkoy and mate with her."

Footsteps sounded on the marble stairway leading into the atrium.

Maura turned and saw several Bhuttanian soldiers coming toward her. Frantically, she spun around, but KiKu was nowhere in sight. Realizing her actions would make the soldiers suspicious, she began wailing and pulling at her hair.

"Your Majesty, are you all right?" asked a young officer wearing an elaborate metal helmet with many red plumes.

Maura looked up from beneath her tangled hair. "What do you mean by disturbing my mourning? How dare you invade my privacy? Get out! Get out!" she screamed. "I will inform Dorak of how you disturbed me during my time of grief. He will no doubt hang you for your lack of respect."

The officer's expression froze at the mention of Dorak. "My apologies. Please forgive us. We only feared that something had happened for you to tarry so long. Please excuse us for our ignorance of your ways." The officer bowed and quickly backed out of the atrium and ran down the marble steps.

Maura followed the soldiers to the edge of the steps and saw that her guards had been surrounded by armed Bhuttanians. She looked at her shamed women with disgust. "You could have at least warned me," she yelled. Deciding she would deal with them later, Maura returned to the atrium where she studied the room.

"KiKu. KiKu," she called softly.

No response came from the marble hall.

After waiting about an hour, Maura relented and left the final resting place of her beloved parents, leaving her grief to reside with them.

8

Lady Sari stood quietly.

She watched a Bhuttanian slave comb and braid the queen's blue-black hair.

Sensing that Sari wished to speak to her, Maura dismissed the slave when the braiding was finished. As soon as the door closed behind the departing girl, Maura swiveled in her chair to face the older woman. She did not give Sari leave to sit down.

Lady Sari took note of this but was determined to speak. "May I talk with you, little sparrow?" she asked, barely able to contain her frustration.

Maura nodded with reluctance.

Lady Sari squared her shoulders. "It has been many months since you have visited the final resting place of your parents. Since that time, you have been close with your thoughts. You have confided with no one. I have seen little effort being made to throw the enemy out of our country. Instead, you dine with Dorak, hunt with Dorak, talk with Dorak, and listen to music at night with Dorak. You permit Dorak to stroke your hair in public." Sari hesitated a moment out of fear but threw caution to the wind. "Do you not understand how this looks to the citizens of O Konya? Many think you are consorting with the very man who brought such unhappiness to our land?"

"What are your thoughts, Sari?" asked Maura, her voice cutting like sharp flint.

"I wish to guide you away from folly. Perhaps because you are so young, you do not grasp the significance of your actions."

"I understand exactly what I am doing," Maura replied. "Let me just remind you of who I am."

Maura rose from her cushioned chair and stood only inches from the trembling advisor. "I am your queen. It is your sworn duty to obey me in all things. If you ever question my loyalty or duty to my country again, I will have you beaten. I swear it, old woman!"

Sari's lips quivered, and her shoulders slumped with defeat. "I am sorry. I have overstepped my place. Please forgive me." She knelt as fast as her advanced age would allow.

Maura turned away and sat in her chair before a dressing mirror. She closed her eyes briefly and calmed herself with the techniques Iegani had taught her. For the past few months, Maura had been receiving telepathic messages from him imploring her to come to the Forbidden Zone by any means possible. Lately, however, she had difficulty making out his words.

She wanted desperately to join Iegani at the foot of the Mother Bogazkoy and receive her blessings. Since she had been with the Mother Bogazkoy's offspring, the Royal Bogazkoy, she had felt the ancient Mother Tree call to her over and over again. The Mother Bogazkoy desired to reproduce and needed Maura to achieve this goal.

All Maura could think of was to get to the Mother Bogazkoy as soon as possible, but she could not even stray from her chambers without Dorak having her watched. She had not heard from KiKu and had no idea where he might be or even if he were still alive. She had to gain Dorak's trust so he would lower his watch on her. That was the only way she was going to escape the palace walls.

It stung Maura that even her old nurse and trusted companion doubted her. Still, she would not give up. She must find a way to the Forbidden Zone without implicating those near and dear to her. "Get up and fetch me some cool water," she commanded. "The morning is warm."

Sari, after bowing as low as she could, gladly left the room.

The queen looked hard at herself in the mirror. Her face was no longer that of a young woman. Her features had set and hardened. Instead of twinkling eyes, hers now glared like hard stones found on a pathway.

Dorak allowed Maura to exercise, and she worked steadily on strengthening her muscles. Her arms and legs were wiry and muscular while her stomach was flat and hard. Maura's breasts, thought ample by Bhuttanian standards, were not voluptuous by Hasan Daegian measures. Her hips did not flare out as those of the ideal Hasan Daegian female. Maura had to admit she was no great beauty as she looked in the mirror. Her tinted blue skin only added to her alien look.

She wondered what Dorak thought as he looked at her. Did he desire her? Or was she simply someone he must endure on the way to securing the Hasan Daegian throne? Maura sighed.

Her thoughts went back to long summer evenings spent with Chaun Maaun under a brilliant star-lit sky. She missed him pleasuring her body. Wondering if he was well, Maura's head drooped as memories of passionate lovemaking spilled over. Would she ever know tender moments like that again? Maura purged such thoughts from her mind.

She could not afford to wallow in the past if she was going to deceive Dorak. Dealing with Dorak required all of her concentration.

A sharp knock at the door broke Maura's thoughts. She bade the person to enter.

A slave crossed the room bearing scarves for the queen to select for the day's apparel. The woman was unknown, and this immediately put Maura on guard. Her brow knotted, thinking the new slave might be a spy placed by Dorak. Yet, there was something familiar about the woman.

Maura studied the slave while pretending to select one of the muted-colored scarves. The woman was too tall to be a Bhuttanian but was too flat-chested to be Hasan Daegian. Finally, it came to her. "Good morning, KiKu," Maura whispered.

The slave raised her eyes, and the corners of *her* mouth turned slightly upward. "I think Your Majesty will find this scarf suitable for your ride today," said KiKu. *She* held out a scarf to Maura, who reached for it. "You must hold it to the light in order to see the intricate pattern," recommended the slave.

Maura did as instructed and held the scarf up to the window. Inside the scarf's design was a message written in Anqarian script.

She returned the delicate material to the servant. "I do not think so," she replied, picking up a muted blue and green silk scarf. "You may go now," she ordered the servant. "I have what I need."

KiKu bowed and gave Maura a knowing look. He silently quit the room, passing undetected by the guards at Maura's door.

A few hours later, Maura found herself riding on a Bhuttanian warhorse in the forest behind the palace.

The very size of the Bhuttanian mounts had, at first, caused Maura concern. But once on the broad back of one of the mares, Maura relaxed as she realized the mare's temperament was not at all different from her beloved pony. She liked riding high on the beast's back as she went through a series of exercises to determine the animal's capabilities.

Though powerful and sturdy, the Bhuttanian horse could be outmaneuvered by the smaller Hasan Daegian ponies. It was more difficult to redirect the massive bulk of the Bhuttanian warhorse quickly.

She thought of uses other than war for the animals. These robust steeds could till fields all day and never fatigue. Maura made a mental note to discuss the possibility of a breeding program with Dorak.

At a reasonable distance behind the queen rode her guards on their small ponies. Behind them trotted Bhuttanian soldiers assigned to make sure the queen was safely delivered to Dorak, who was overseeing work on a new aqueduct he wanted to show Maura.

Riding deep into the forest, Maura twisted and turned her mare among giant fern trees and briar patches. Looking back, she found she had eluded her guards. Giving the horse a vicious kick, she spurred it into a meadow. Galloping at full speed, she heard the Bhuttanians call after her in the distance. Kicking her horse even faster, Maura dropped the reins around its neck, took her feet out of the stirrups, and lifted her arms about her head.

A whoosh sound came from above, and Maura was lifted into the sky. She glanced at the talons clutching her. They were of a red Dini hawk. A warrior. It could only be Yeti.

Maura relaxed as the Dini wound skillfully through the dense foliage in the forest and came to rest on the strong limb of a mingo tree.

Yeti placed Maura carefully on the broad limb.

Hearing the familiar click of the Dinii language, Maura slowly sat down as instructed. Looking about, Maura saw Yeti confer with another red hawk who she knew to be Iegani's apprentice.

The Dini hawk approached Maura. She bowed low and said, "Greetings, Great Mother, Maura de Magela, tenth ruler of Hasan Daegian, Healer of the Infirmed. I was sent by the Great Divigi to speak with you."

Maura brightened at the mention of Iegani. "Greetings to you, Toppo. What news have you?" She ignored the fact that Toppo had remained standing and was towering over her. This was against Hasan Daegian protocol.

"I see the Hittal was successful in getting to you our message."

"Yes, KiKu is most ingenious, but I do not need to tell you that my absence is most dangerous. If I am missing very long, Dorak will start rounding up citizens and killing them."

Toppo's narrow face relaxed. "Ah, that explains much." Toppo sat on her haunches so she was eye level with Maura. "May I, Great Mother?"

Maura gave Toppo permission to sit.

The red hawk paused for a moment while chewing on some mingo leaves.

Maura could tell Toppo was gathering her thoughts. She waited politely as the Dinii often took a long time between sentences. The Dinii were a precise race and wanted to get every nuance perfect to explain their meaning. When dealing with the Hasan Daegians, the Dinii took longer than usual as they were speaking in a second language.

This fact notwithstanding, Maura needed to move this meeting along. "Do you wish to speak in Dinii?" she asked.

Toppo nodded. "My master, Iegani, wishes to know why you do not come to the Mother Bogazkoy."

Maura was taken back. She was not in the habit of explaining herself, and it was the second time this morning she had been confronted by those making demands on her intentions. She reflected on the implications of the question. "Answer this first, please. Why has Iegani stopped communicating with me? I have not heard from him for many days."

Toppo smiled, exposing her large teeth stained with yellow mingo juice. "My master has been communicating with you every day. Since he has not felt your presence, he thought you might be terribly ill or that..."

"Or what?" questioned Maura, growing impatient.

Looking uneasy, Toppo replied, "He thought that perhaps you might have learned to stop him from communicating with you."

The queen pursed her lips. "Why would I do that when I am dying to learn some news? Dorak has cut me off. I can get nothing out of his servants. Bhuttanians simply do not gossip with Hasan Daegians," explained Maura, exasperated with her situation.

Toppo bowed her head. "My pardon, Great Mother. I can see now Iegani has been thwarted by the Black Cacodemon. Even the Lahorians have been trying to reach you telepathically."

"Lahorians!" cried Maura.

Toppo realized her mistake in mentioning the Lahorians and

steered the conversation away from them. "I was sent to tell you that you must come to the Mother Bogazkoy. Her cycle to reproduce is almost finished. Without you, there is no hope, and without her, there is no way you can shield yourself from the magic of the Black Cacodemon." Toppo stated emphatically again. "You must come!"

"I cannot," Maura pleaded. "If I leave, Dorak will start killing my people in retribution."

"The few must be sacrificed for the good of all."

Maura was horrified. "Surely, you do not mean that. So many have died already."

Toppo's ears perked. "The soldiers are coming. There is not much time." The red hawk extended her hand to help Maura rise. "You must find a way to come to the Forbidden Zone soon. You have only three cycles of the moon left." Toppo fixed her steady gaze on the queen. "You must come! There is no other way." With those words, she spread her wings and flew away.

Yeti jumped down and, with an extended talon, began ripping Maura's clothes.

"What are you doing?" exclaimed Maura.

"We must make it look like you fell from your horse. When I put you down, make sure you rub dirt on your face," advised Yeti.

Satisfied with Maura's tattered appearance, Yeti picked up the queen and flew her to the ground, allowing Maura to fall with a hard thud. Yeti flew back to the tree and blended in with the branches.

Even Maura with her keen eyes and tracking ability had a difficult time discerning the Dini's location.

Bhuttanian soldiers reeled into the meadow. The warhorses came bearing down on the queen with such speed that, for a moment, she wondered if they would be able to stop without trampling her first. The horses pulled up several feet short of Maura, causing her to let out an audible sigh of relief. She tried her best to look rattled, which was not hard to do.

An officer jumped off his great stallion and knelt by the queen. "Your Majesty, are you all right?" he asked, trying to keep the exasperation out of his voice.

"I think so," Maura replied timidly. "I could not control my horse, and I fell off—as you can see." She pointed deep into the forest. "I think he went that way."

The young officer looked skeptically at the queen. He knew what an accomplished horsewoman she was, but she made a convincing sight with her torn clothes and dirty, sweaty face. However, she should at least know the difference between a mare and a stallion. His eyes scanned the forest for possible intruders.

"Can you help me up?" asked Maura innocently.

Reluctantly, the officer tore his eyes away from the dark, intimidating woods patched with silver mist and was secretly glad the Hasan Daegian queen had been thrown in a meadow. Bhuttanians were from the wide, open steppes and considered forests unnatural places. He helped the young woman stand.

As Maura placed weight on her feet, she winced from pain. "I think I twisted my ankle during the fall."

The officer knelt and examined Maura's legs. "It does appear that your left ankle is swelling."

At this time, the Hasan Daegian Honor Guard rode into the meadow. Angry that the Bhuttanian soldiers reached their charge first, the women could barely hide their contempt as they jumped off their ponies and pushed the Bhuttanian men aside. "We will take care of our queen," said the highest-ranking Hasan Daegian.

The Bhuttanian officer, wishing to avoid a confrontation with the women, bowed to the queen and asked permission to withdraw.

Maura nodded.

He saluted the Hasan Daegian officer in Hasan Daegian fashion and got back on his horse. "I will leave six of my men to help escort your queen to O Konya. I will send back a litter so that it might ease her journey."

The Hasan Daegian guards glared at the Bhuttanian as he rode off with several of his men. One of her women asked, "Great Mother, do you think you can ride?"

Maura nodded.

A Hasan Daegian officer brought her pony over and helped the queen on. Walking beside the animal, the officer turned it toward O Konya and began the long trek home.

Dorak's aqueduct would have to wait.

Maura dared not look in the trees but could feel Yeti's eyes upon her group. Determined to comply with the Mother Bogazkoy's wish, Maura knew she had to escape to the Forbidden Zone.

The question was how!

9

Maura waited patiently.

She sat with her hands folded in her lap as Dorak paced angrily before her. She stifled a yawn. By now, she was used to his ranting and was fairly confident she could persuade Dorak to see things her way. Her calmness only served to make Dorak more furious.

"I do not believe your horse threw you. I personally selected a very gentle mare."

"Even the best horses have bad days. She threw me as I said. I am not used to handling such a large animal," defied Maura, looking straight at Dorak.

Dorak snorted in disbelief. "I find it hard to believe that you could not handle this horse, let alone one of the more spirited stallions."

Maura smiled inwardly at the compliment. "I was thrown as you can see for yourself."

"How can I tell if you are bruised with that blue skin?"

She pointed to the darker places on her arms. "Look here. You can see the bruises."

Dorak stomped over to her and peered down at her arms. He unexpectedly grabbed Maura by the shoulders, pulling her out of the chair. "If you are lying to me, you'll be sorry," he warned.

Maura caught her breath at the dark menace in Dorak's voice. She pushed him away. "I am sick of your threats. Go ahead, round up the entire city, and kill them all. I do not care anymore. You treat me like one of your slaves. I am not allowed to speak to anyone. I do not know what is happening outside this city. It's driving me crazy, you understand!" she screamed at Dorak. She fell back into her chair, sobbing.

Dorak, surprised at her ferocity, gently touched her shoulder. "Did you meet anyone?" he asked quietly.

Maura shook her head adamantly. "I did not meet any of my people or yours in the woods," she answered truthfully.

Dorak studied her for a moment. "I believe you," he said. He pulled up a chair and straddled the seat. Dorak lifted Maura's chin.

Tears streaked her face.

He pulled a handkerchief from his pocket and wiped away her tears. "Here," he said, giving her the cloth. "Blow your nose. You look awful."

Maura took the handkerchief gratefully.

Suddenly, Dorak leaned over and kissed Maura softly on the mouth.

Startled, Maura pulled away.

"Don't," he said quietly. "Maura, I am not like my father. I will not lay waste to lands just because I can. I want to build a great empire with roads and cities that are centers of learning and trade." He gently touched her cheek. "I do not want to kill anymore. I want to build."

Dorak moved closer to her. "Do you not see that the two of us could create a wondrous civilization? We are alike, you and I. We are cut from the same cloth." Dorak's eyes took on an intense, dreamy look. "Believe in me as I believe in you."

Maura stared into Dorak's black eyes and felt herself slipping into them. "This cannot be," she said, resisting his pull. "We can never be on the same side. We are enemies. You defeated me, and my honor will never permit me to forgive you."

Dorak took her hand and began lightly kissing her fingers one at a time. "An honorable person knows when she has been defeated fairly and to accept the situation."

"But you did not defeat me fairly," hissed Maura, her fingers tightening hard around Dorak's hand. "You used evil magic which even your father refused to seek."

Dorak kissed Maura's thumb and took it into his mouth.

Maura drew in a sharp breath and exhaled slowly. Her eyes closed.

"Then meet me on the field of battle, just you and I," cooed Dorak. "If you win, I will leave Hasan Daeg. If I win, you will become my wife of your own free will." He kissed the palm of her hand with light, flickering touches. His face was crimson with passion. Dorak pulled Maura toward him and held her in his strong arms. "Tell me your answer."

Maura seemed dazed.

Dorak shook her hard. "Tell me, woman!"

"No tricks?"

Dorak held up his hand to his heart. "Upon my honor as a Bhuttanian."

Maura felt her heart quicken.

"I want to be more than your liege lord, my gracious queen. I want to be your husband. I want to be your partner as we build a world of grace and beauty."

"What are the rules for the combat?" asked Maura.

"Hand to hand with any weapon you choose."

"Until death?"

Dorak laughed and released Maura from his hold. "No, my queen, only until one corners the other. There will be no death with this fight. I will not kill you, and I hope you will return the favor."

"If I fight, I will try to kill you," Maura said defiantly.

Dorak's brow furrowed. Disappointed, he stood back from her. "As you wish. Try to kill me if you can, but I am going to win and make you my wife."

"And I am going to win and regain my throne."

"You have your throne already, and with my help, you can gain the throne of the world."

"I will have none of you," Maura spat.

Dorak raised his hand as if to strike the rebellious woman, but dropped it harmlessly against his side. "Be stubborn, Maura, but I will win, and you will be my bride!" He stomped out of the room.

"Tomorrow at noon in the courtyard," Maura called after him.

Dorak slammed the door after him.

Even through the thick wooden door, she heard him cursing down the hallway to his rooms.

Maura ran into her bedchamber where Sari awaited and fell at her feet.

Sari stroked Maura's hair. "I heard, little sparrow. You must not fight him. If he wins, you will lose your honor."

Maura looked up at Sari through her tears. "If I win, he will be dead, and I will have freed my country."

"Then why do you cry so much? I heard him say he will not kill you in this fight. He has already given you a great advantage. The both of you are about the same height. It will be an evenly matched contest. You can kill him easily."

Maura hid her face in Sari's lap, mumbling something.

Sari lifted the queen's face. "I cannot hear you."

Maura's eyes had a wild look of despair. "I said I do not want to kill him. I want him to live. I have feelings for him." She shuddered with shame.

Sari wrapped her arms around Maura, rocking her gently. "I know this. I think he has feelings for you too. That is what makes this situation so awful."

Maura was momentarily lulled by the familiar comfort of Sari's arms. She closed her eyes and let Sari soothe her. "Tomorrow, I will kill Dorak and all of this will be over," Maura whispered.

10

Dorak waited.

Dressed in black, he waited for the Hasan Daegian queen on the cobblestones in the courtyard. He wore a red strip of cloth around his dark hair. It was hot, and already he was sweating. He ordered chalk and dipped his hands into a bag that a slave brought. *Where is that woman?*

The courtyard was empty except for Alexanee acting as his second and one slave boy.

Bhuttanian soldiers and officers hid in the recesses and windows of the courtyard, as did their Hasan Daegian counterparts, to cheer on their champion.

Maura stepped into the courtyard wearing black as well with gold uultepes embroidered on the back of her shirt. She wore a leather vest with braces on her forearms, and her head was shaved.

Dorak gaped at Maura's bald head. He silently cursed her for pulling a stunt that threw his concentration off. Dorak also admired her for doing so and wished he had thought of something so visually startling. For the first time in many months, Dorak thought he saw a ghost of a smile on Alexanee's face.

Seeing Dorak's confusion, Maura threw him a big grin. Behind her walked Sari, who was in turn followed by Rubank carrying a blue pillow. On the pillow lay two immaculately polished swords. Maura halted before Dorak and bowed.

Dorak returned the gesture.

"If it pleases the aga, Consul Rubank has chosen two weapons he finds satisfactory for combat." Maura waved Rubank forward.

Rubank held the weapons for Dorak's inspection.

"I hardly think the word combat is correct for betrothed persons such as ourselves. I would just call this a lovers' tiff," replied Dorak, winking at Maura.

The soldiers hidden in the walls' recesses laughed out loud while the Hasan Daegians twittered.

Maura pretended not to notice Dorak's brashness or hear the laughter.

Alexanee picked up one of the swords and inspected the blade. "Both weapons seem in splendid condition. If I may, I would prefer this one for Aga Dorak," he said, slashing the sword through the air. "The balance seems better."

The sword whizzed near Maura's ear, but she did not flinch. "If we might start, Great Aga," she said sweetly. "I would like to dispatch you before my noon meal."

Alexanee seemed astonished at Maura's boldness. He looked questioningly at Dorak.

Dorak merely gave her a rakish smirk. "The only thing that will be killed today, Queen Maura, is your arrogance." He looked about him. "I feel like a victor."

"So do I," replied Maura, stretching her legs.

Dorak bowed again and turned to practice with his sword.

Maura continued stretching her taut muscles, keeping a close eye on Dorak's movements. She nodded that she was ready and signaled for chalk to be poured into her hands.

Sari handed her a towel, and Maura wiped sweat from her face.

A cloth similar to Dorak's was placed on Maura's head. Out of the corner of her eye, she saw something white flutter in the breeze. She turned sharply and observed Meagan the Healer sitting with a Bhuttanian soldier guarding her. Meagan looked paler and thinner but otherwise seemed fine. She sat beside her medical bag and gave a small wave.

Maura sighed with relief.

Dorak had kept his pledge.

Maura understood the appearance of Meagan. It was Dorak's way of saying that he had honored his promise, and he did intend to marry her. Maura shuddered both with pleasure and horror at the thought of becoming Dorak's wife. Realizing she was losing *her* concentration, Maura silently cursed Dorak and searched for him.

He was lounging against a railing, studying her.

Rubank went to the center of the courtyard. He bowed to his

queen and then to the aga, motioning both of them to come near him.

Dorak was not familiar with the dueling statutes of the Hasan Daegians. He could find nothing about warfare in the royal library and was suspicious that this was the first duel in centuries. Maura was probably making up the rules as she went along. The Bhuttanian way was far simpler. Each opponent stood at opposite sides until a horn sounded and then rushed toward each other until one was dead.

Dorak masked his anger when Rubank searched for hidden weapons on him. When Rubank finished, Dorak motioned for Alexanee to search Maura.

Maura stood expressionless as Alexanee patted her down. He even had Maura take off her boots so he could look at the bottom of her feet.

Sari stamped her foot at General Alexanee's impudence.

When finished, Alexanee merely grunted to Dorak.

Maura motioned for Rubank.

The consul knelt on all fours behind the queen so she could sit on him while Sari helped her with the boots. Now ready, the determined queen picked up her sword and balanced it in her hand. She nodded to a servant, who rang a centuries-old bell that was suspended above the entryway.

Upon hearing the bell, all Hasan Daegians left their tasks and went into the streets. Facing the palace, every Hasan Daegian woman, man, and child knelt and began praying to Mekonia, their nature goddess.

Curious, Bhuttanian soldiers and Sivan merchants followed the Hasan Daegians into the streets watching the seldom seen ritual of Tsnsuni.

The Bhuttanians asked the Sivas in the Anqarian language if they knew what was happening.

The desert merchants shrugged their shoulders and replied they had never witnessed such a sight before.

While the Bhuttanians were taken back by Hasan Daegians kneeling in the streets, the Sivans became bored and lumbered back to their caravans or taverns.

The Bhuttanians stayed and watched. They knew fervor when they saw it. This was something they had in common with the Hasan Daegians.

11

T he wizard opened his greenish eyes.

Feeling a shift in the atmosphere, the Black Cacodemon rose from his pallet only to don black gloves over his pale skin. A fine dust rose up from his parchment-like flesh as he moved.

Sensing something was happening, the wizard left his dark, narrow room in the cellar of the palace and hurried to the roof. There he saw thousands of Hasan Daegians kneeling to pray. He stretched out his arms, testing the air only to find he did not like the vibrations.

Hurrying to the other side of the roof, the wizard peered down. There he saw the Hasan Daegian queen and the Bhuttanian aga ready to engage in a duel.

Why was he not informed of this? Anger shot up the wizard's spine. What fool thing was Dorak doing?

He would have to stay in the burning sun and watch, making sure the little Hasan Daegian witch did not harm Dorak. The young aga was too important to his plans.

Dorak and Maura stepped into the middle of the courtyard.

Rubank held up a blue and gold scarf.

The rulers crossed swords.

Maura never took her eyes off Dorak's, which seemed blacker than ever.

Rubank dropped the scarf.

Like lightning, Maura spun around and brought her sword to Dorak's head.

He parried, just barely missing the blow.

Acting as the aggressor, Maura pummeled Dorak with blow after blow.

Dorak avoided being struck by the sharp edge of the sword.

Maura sliced his clothes, nicking his skin. Moving to his left, Maura stepped out of his range. "Why are you not striking back?" she cried, lowering her sword.

"I am too damned busy trying to keep my head intact," Dorak yelled. "Here I come," he cried, running toward her. At the last moment, Dorak veered off to the side and hit Maura on the buttocks with the broad side of his sword. "As I said before, your death by my hands is not my intention," cooed Dorak, leaning on the sword hilt with his feet crossed. He gave the stunned queen an arrogant smile.

Maura was speechless. She felt fury rush over her face. "How dare you insult me like this," Maura hissed. "Come back and fight!"

"I bow before your prowess with a sword, my lady. You possess as much strength as two men. I do not remember you being this strong when last we fought. Perhaps you have had communion with a spirit . . . or a magical tree."

He shifted his feet. "It might interest you to know, my little Hasan Daegian treasure, that I surveyed the caverns beneath the palace.

"It took me days, but my men found a huge underground lake with an island. On this barren island, they found debris of a rotting plant. My best men examined it, and they tell me that the dead thing has remnants of Hasan Daegian hair and blood on it. Now, don't you think that is interesting? A plant with human blood. Blue blood, that is. Well, it has all sorts of interesting implications." Dorak blew the queen a kiss.

Maura did not charge the boasting aga but stood her ground. She knew Dorak had succeeded in making her too angry to fight effectively.

Iegani had taught her that angry warriors make dead warriors.

She scanned the courtyard with her peripheral vision, placing everyone. She wanted to make sure some assassin did not sneak into the courtyard and kill her with an unseen dagger while Dorak taunted.

The Black Cacodemon, realizing that Maura would spy him, touched a medallion on his chest, causing him to become invisible.

Maura remained stationary as Dorak circled her. Without warning, she advanced upon Dorak with stunning speed.

He barely had time to lower his sword before she was thrusting at him. Dorak turned and parried too late.

Maura had pushed her sword into his side.

Grunting with pain, Dorak reached down and felt his side. His hand was bloody. Dorak looked at Maura in disbelief. "You have cut me to the bone!" he cried out bewildered.

Maura raised her sword to make the final blow. Convinced of victory, Maura started down with the sword. She would make Dorak's death quick and painless.

Suddenly, the avenging queen felt a ball of intense heat descend upon her shoulders as though the sun had exploded. She cried out in surprise more than pain. The heat became so intense Maura dropped her sword and fell to her knees. She held her hands over her eyes to shield them from the blinding light.

Dorak, clutching his bleeding side, hovered his sword over Maura's neck. He deftly nicked her and watched the blue blood ooze from her skin. Angry, Dorak kicked Maura's sword away from her. Hearing someone plead for Maura's life, he turned and saw Sari begging on her knees. With his sword still at Maura's neck, he raised his face to those assembled. "Before all present," Dorak shouted, "before the rules of combat, I claim this woman to be my wife. She will marry me at the time and place deemed proper by me. If she refuses to honor her oath, then she, with her kith and kin, shall die by Bhuttanian custom."

Dorak dropped his sword and began to wobble. Feeling the world spin about him, Dorak was unconscious before hitting the ground.

Both Bhuttanians and Hasan Daegians ran to their rulers.

Meagan of Skujpor pushed everyone out of the way and began administering to the fallen warriors. She applied a compress to Dorak's side and instructed Alexanee to maintain pressure on the bandage.

Turning Maura over, she gasped. Maura's face and hands were scorched with large, angry blisters forming while other parts of her skin were seared as though she had been roasting on a spit. "The queen has been burned! Quick, we must get her out of the sun. Hurry! Hurry!"

The soldier who had been guarding Meagan helped Rubank carry the Hasan Daegian queen to the kitchen, the nearest set of rooms off the courtyard.

Dorak was carried by Alexanee.

Both of them were placed on tables in the kitchen where Meagan's initiates had scattered the cooking implements on the floor. As soon as Dorak and Maura were put down, the women went to work cutting off the their clothes.

Alexanee chased the servants out of the kitchen and placed guards at the doors. He silently cursed himself for allowing this duel to take place, but the general had not taken it seriously. Believing that Maura would not have the courage to harm Dorak, he dismissed her. He knew that Dorak's fondness for this woman would restrain him.

He had underestimated both their passion and determination to win. Even if they both survived, the fact that a foreign man had cut their queen would not sit well with the Hasan Daegians. And there was the question of how the queen became burned.

To all appearances, Alexanee seemed collected when he gave the orders for martial law, but his heart was racing so fast he thought he might faint.

If the Hasan Daegians rose up in rebellion, the Bhuttanians would quash them, but Alexanee would be battling an uprising thousands of miles from home with several hostile countries lying between him and Bhuttan, cut off from reinforcements and all communication. With odds like that, only a small percentage of his men would ever see home again.

Sari stayed outside in the courtyard with Alexanee's officers investigating the walls and recesses. She saw nothing to explain Maura dropping her sword when victory was so near. Believing something unnatural had happened, Lady Sari searched the courtyard, finding nothing out of the ordinary. She swore, though, as did the Bhuttanians warriors, that she could hear a distant laughing.

12

Maura sat up.

She was in a makeshift bed located in the kitchen. The fire in the great stone fireplace, where gleaming kettles hung and meat for the Bhuttanians roasted on spits, was out. The bustling kitchen staff, in their blue aprons dusted with flour and netted turbans wrapped around their heads, was absent as well. Only nervous guards and busy healers were in attendance.

Too bad the Dinii did not know of this moment. It would be the perfect time to strike.

Looking over to the other side of the room, Maura spied Meagan bending over Dorak. Seeing him bloodied, Maura winced and let out a small moan.

Sari, who had been sitting in a wooden rocker by the queen's cot, awoke from her fitful sleep. "Your Majesty, you have awakened," said Sari smiling. "I will get Meagan."

The young woman shook her head. "There is no need," Maura replied, prying off bulky bandages from her arms and hands.

Sari tried to stop her. "You mustn't! You have been burned."

"I was burned, but am no more."

Sari shot her a disbelieving look.

"Truly, I am healed. Help me, and you may see for yourself."

Lady Sari gingerly unwrapped the queen's bandages. Opening her mouth in astonishment, Sari exclaimed, "I see nothing! The Bogazkoy, though dying, still gave you much power." She turned Maura's hands over and peered closely at the skin. "There is not even one scar. It is a miracle! Mekonia be praised!"

"What's this on my head?" asked Maura, fingering goop that had been plastered on her face and scalp.

"An ointment of Meagan's for burn injuries."

"Hand me a towel."

Sari hesitated.

Again, Maura reassured her. "My face will not be burned as you see my hands are not."

Sari handed her a kitchen towel which Maura took and vigorously rubbed the heavy ointment off her face.

Maura turned her head for Sari's inspection. "What is happening?" Maura asked, looking toward the healers at a large table on which Dorak lay.

"Dorak is dying. You struck him a fierce blow before you fell."

"I must not let this happen. Help me up. I must go to him."

"Let the dung-eater breathe his last. He has brought us nothing but unhappiness. With his death, we shall be free again. Isn't that what the duel was about?"

"I cannot let him die now. His people will say that he won fairly. The Bhuttanians will accuse us of some foul complicity and go on a campaign of retribution. His people will see his death as murder, not from an honorable duel. If only he had fought me in earnest instead of playing. The Bhuttanians have taken all of our weapons. We cannot defend ourselves. I must save him!" Maura swung her legs around the side of the little cot. Her head felt woozy, and her legs were unsteady.

"Look what he did to you. He did not win the contest fairly. If he does not die, you will have to marry him. Please, let him join his dead father," Sari pleaded.

"He did not harm me. I am sure. Tell me, did you see anything? A strange light?"

"It was very odd. You were starting to bring down your sword to deliver the deathblow when you just went down. Nobody could understand why you fell. It was only after we turned you over that we saw the burns. The air felt so hot we could barely stand it."

"But not around Dorak?"

"No, little sparrow."

"And you saw nothing?"

Sari shook her head.

"And you heard nothing?"

The loyal servant paused for a moment. "I lingered outside searching for clues and to make sure the Bhuttanians did not tamper with any evidence. I saw nothing out of the ordinary, but thought I heard a strange squealing sound. It was very high-pitched. It sounded almost like laughing to me."

Maura reflected on Sari's words for a moment. "I have no doubt he was laughing."

"Who, little sparrow?"

Maura ignored Sari's question. "Iegani was right. I will have to be with the Mother Bogazkoy before I can face the Black Cacodemon. He is too powerful for me."

Sari gave the little band nursing Dorak a black look. "I want him to die."

"Dorak must live for now. Help me to him."

Meagan of Skujpor, hearing whispering, turned and saw the Hasan Daegian queen rising. Flustered, she ordered the Bhuttanian guards, "Put that woman back!"

The queen's guards, who had been watching their sovereign and Sari from the corner, sprang up ready to sacrifice their lives.

Maura ordered, "Stand aside."

Her guards parted and fell in beside her.

Maura pointed at the Bhuttanian soldiers. "If you dare touch my person, I will have you killed as is my right. Now out of my way."

The confused Bhuttanians looked at Alexanee.

Stress lined Alexanee's face.

If they touched the Hasan Daegian queen and harmed her, news of it would spread throughout the city like wildfire. This towering woman may not be as popular as her beloved mother, but she was still revered by the population. The reports of Hasan Daegians praying in the streets proved that. The general motioned for the Bhuttanians to step aside.

Leaning on Sari, Maura went over to Dorak. She sensed the Bhuttanian soldiers were placing their hands on their swords as she approached their aga.

Meagan bowed as did her initiates. "Great Mother, you seem to have recovered," she commented with one eyebrow raised.

"Is that your apology for ordering commoners to touch the Royal Queen of Hasan Daeg?"

Meagan's green eyes, red with strain and worry, blinked once and then boldly made contact with the strange blue ones of the Hasan Daegian queen. "If it pleases you, you may take my life when this little drama is over."

Ignoring her remark, Maura asked, "Dorak?"

Meagan wiped her forehead with a clean towel. "You struck him in the side. It missed his major organs but I cannot stop the bleeding. I think he is hemorrhaging inside."

"And?"

"If I cannot stop the bleeding, he will be dead in a few hours," Meagan replied with finality.

Maura looked at the Bhuttanian physician assisting Meagan.

He nodded in concurrence.

Taking a deep breath, Maura declared, "I can save him."

The Bhuttanian healer protested vehemently.

The soldiers drew their swords while Maura remained very still.

Meagan motioned for everyone to be quiet.

Turning to Alexanee, Maura appealed to the stone-faced general. "It is well known that Hasan Daegian queens can heal when it so moves them. Look at me. Was I not covered with burnt flesh? I have healed my own skin. My skin is as normal as yours." She held her arm out to Alexanee.

"It could be a trick," cautioned a Bhuttanian soldier.

"Quiet, you cur," ordered Alexanee, chastising the outspoken warrior. The bedeviled general asked the Bhuttanian physician, "What is your opinion?"

The healer shook his head in amazement. "These people show wonderful recuperative powers. I have read their medical texts in detail. There are recorded stories of Hasan Daegian royalty saving those who are even in worse condition than our aga. There is historical precedent. Whether this queen can," he bowed in deference, "I do not know. But her burns should not have healed for many months, and there should be evidence of heavy scarring."

"What do you have to lose?" Maura asked. "He is going to die anyway. I might be able to save him."

Alexanee looked at Meagan.

Meagan nodded her head, and then looked at the Bhuttanian physician, who concurred.

Alexanee walked over to a window and looked out. He was quiet for a long time. "Why save him when you tried to kill him?"

"If the aga dies now, your soldiers would decimate my country before returning to Bhuttan. They would do so because they would think he was murdered instead of perishing in a fair contest of arms. And you would be the one to give the order, thus consolidating your power. But all the Bhuttanian generals would be vying for power, and there is a good chance you would be assassinated on the way home."

Alexanee pondered her words. Finally, he spoke to Maura, "If you fail, you will die."

"I accept your condition."

"Great Mother, do not do it. He's not worth it," Sari begged.

"The aga must live, Sari," replied Maura, pushing the woman's pleading hands off her arms.

Meagan moved out of the queen's way but stood where she could watch.

The Bhuttanian physician tiptoed beside her.

Alexanee stood by the window, his shoulders heavy with tension. He gave Maura leave to proceed.

Maura bent over Dorak and studied his face. His mouth twisted from suffering. "Dorak. Dorak," she called.

"Can you hear me?" She gently wiped the grime from his brow. "I am going to place my hands on your wound. You will feel heat. Do not fight it. Blend with it. It is healing and will make you well." Maura placed her hands carefully on his wound.

Dorak moaned at her touch.

Alexanee's hand tensed over the hilt of his dagger.

Maura closed her eyes and concentrated. She felt a strong surge of energy come from deep within her bowels and move through her spine. It flowed up through her arms and out of the palms of her hands. A glowing light emanated from her fingertips and melted into Dorak's flesh.

Dorak turned his head, crying out.

"Do not fight it," whispered Maura, "or we shall both be dead."

Dorak relaxed at the sound of her voice and lay still. The light emanating from Maura's hands became stronger and brighter.

Everyone moved back as sweat poured off Maura's face. She felt a towel wipe her face. The sweat on her arms sizzled and hissed as it rose as steam. Maura lost herself in the healing of Dorak. She began to feel her consciousness merge with his. Frightened that she would lose herself, Maura pulled back and hurled herself from the table, hitting her head on the flagstone floor and was dazed for a moment.

Several hands reached down to help her up but pulled back after touching her scorching flesh.

A chair was brought. Maura fought back nausea as she rolled to her knees and pulled herself up on the wooden chair. Smoke rose where her hands touched the wood. Standing uneasily, Maura caused her mind to dampen the blinding light, and as a torch that runs out of oil, her inner light dwindled until it was extinguished.

Squinting, Maura saw several of her guards examining their hands.

They looked at her in wonder.

"It feels wonderful!" one exclaimed.

"It both warms the skin and soothes. I can't describe it," a guard muttered to Meagan.

"Yes," confirmed another. "It feels like . . . youth."

Unsteady, Maura hobbled over to Dorak's table again. She glanced over the Bhuttanian physician's shoulder as he busied himself examining Dorak's wound.

"I do not know what Her Majesty did," the physician said to Alexanee, "but this wound has stopped bleeding. I see signs of healthy tissue already growing back." He turned to Maura. "If you were not the queen, I should like to study you."

Alexanee, relieved that he was not going to have to issue an order for the annihilation of the Hasan Daegians, pushed the Bhuttanian doctor out of the way. He examined Dorak. The aga's color had returned, and his pulse seemed strong. Alexanee had seen enough battle injuries to recognize a healing wound.

Dorak's eyes fluttered open. The first person he saw was Maura peering down anxiously at him. "I told you that you would not be able to kill me," he said huskily.

"I did my very best," replied Maura chuckling.

Everyone joined her.

Dorak's puzzled look only caused more laughter. He was very suspicious that the joke was on him, but he did not care as he had won the hand of the Hasan Daegian queen in marriage. The secret of the Bogazkoy could not be very far behind.

Lady Sari sensed a strange presence in the room. Looking behind her, she caught a fleeting glimpse of a black-robed figure descending one of the staircases leading to the cellars. She shuddered at the recognition. She remembered looking out her window the night of the invasion during the battle in the courtyard and seeing the Black Cacodemon fluttering over dying Hasan Daegian warriors waiting for the moment of their deaths.

How long had the Black Cacodemon been watching?

13

Maura rested.

At dusk, she rose from her bed.

With the help of young noblewomen acting as servants, she bathed and dressed in a simple green robe with a woven hem dyed light blue.

At Sari's insistence, Maura ate only a light dinner of fruit and bread. Afterwards, she sat on her balcony overlooking O Konya.

A servant lit incense, and a young boy, sitting in the corner, played the lute softly.

Citizens of O Konya were already lighting their oil lamps for the coming evening. The city twinkled and shined like a precious gem.

The air smelled sweet while distant mountains rumbled like a hungry gootee. Rain was coming.

Lulled into deep meditation, Maura pondered on the terrible war and the cost that Dorak had inflicted upon her people because he needed to feed his own. Could he not have accomplished this with trade?

That had not been good enough for Zoar or Dorak. They were men who needed to dominate women, treasure, land, water, objects that fed their insatiable lust for power. Otherwise, these men would drown in self-doubt.

Maura became aware of someone listening to her thoughts. She created an aura of protection about her mind to lock out the intruder... a simple trick Iegani had taught her. This procedure left her disoriented for a few seconds. Maura pinched her earlobes so her senses would clear. She scanned the palace walls searching for anyone who might be spying on her. Seeing no one, Maura studied the boy musician.

Feeling the queen's gaze, the boy stopped playing and looked up at her with large, questioning eyes.

Deciding that he was just a little boy with a gift for playing the lute, Maura smiled.

The boy relaxed, returning to his strumming. He had thought his playing had displeased the queen and that his ears were going to be boxed for it.

Finding no evidence of an intruder in her chambers, Maura could only surmise that the telepathic interloper had been the Black Cacodemon. She scowled at the thought of the dark-hearted magician.

He had seldom appeared since the invasion of O Konya, but Maura was quite sure he had ventured into the light to cause the sea creature to attack at the underground lake and to produce the mysterious burns during the duel, even though Dorak denied that the wizard was still in O Konya. Maura pondered what to do. Squaring her shoulders resolutely, Maura left her chambers to see Dorak.

In the hallways, she had to raise her skirt to avoid debris strewn about by the Bhuttanians who were in the habit of throwing their trash wherever they stood. There were fruit rinds, dirty cups, parchment scraps, and muddy boot prints on the wide marble corridors.

Maura noted that the hems of costly tapestries were filthy from being used as towels or handkerchiefs. She tried not to show her disgust and wondered if much of O Konya was still as beautiful as it was before the invasion. Or were the Bhuttanians slowly turning the garden city into a sty as they were the palace?

Since Dorak's compartment was next to hers, Maura reached it quickly and stood patiently as Dorak's guards searched her for weapons under the watchful eyes of her honor guard. Both sets of soldiers eyed each other with contempt.

While the Bhuttanian men still regarded the female Hasan Daegian guards as nuisances, they had acquired a begrudging respect for the tall women who so zealously protected their sovereign, even though they might only use their hands as weapons. The Bhuttanians had curtailed their abuse of the female guards since discovering that these women would do more than slap faces when offended.

More than one Bhuttanian warrior had found his nose bitten or his ear torn off when he had acted aggressively. These Hasan Daegian women were not submissive like their wives at home.

The Bhuttanians opened the massive doors to Dorak's chambers and let the Hasan Daegian queen enter.

A slave showed the queen to Dorak's bedchamber, and there she found him sitting up in bed, sipping broth from a cup held by a Bhuttanian slave girl. The girl wore the Bhuttanian traditional low-cut tunic over pants. Her dark, lustrous hair was undone and hung down her back instead of being in the usual braid worn by the Bhuttanian women. Her feet were bare and jangled with the many brass ankle bracelets she wore.

Upon seeing Maura, Dorak dismissed the girl.

She bowed low.

Maura was sure that from Dorak's vantage point, he was able to see all of the girl's assets. She wondered if the slave did more for Dorak than just feed him. She felt a stab of jealousy and was surprised by it.

"Your Majesty, how nice that you honor me with your presence," Dorak declared.

Maura returned his smile and was happy that he seemed genuinely glad to see her. "I have come to discuss the wedding," she said mildly. She pointed to a chair. "May I sit?"

Dorak pushed maps and reports out of the way, making room for her on his bed.

Another slave scurried to pick them up and left the room.

The aga patted the bed. "It is very nice here," he said grinning. "It will strain my neck if you sit farther away."

Maura sat on the edge of the bed and spread her skirts about her. "I see your bandages are smaller. You must be healing nicely." She sniffed the air. "No stink of infection."

"I'm doing rather well. I must thank you formally for not finishing me off."

"Not every day is perfect."

"I hope all of our arguments are not so costly," uttered Dorak smiling, "or so painful."

"Once married, I doubt we shall speak at all."

"Why would you say that?"

"You will be returning to Bhuttan."

"I have no intention of returning to Bhuttan, and if I did, you would go with me."

Maura gave Dorak a charming smile. "Once married, you will have the key to Hasan Daeg. You need not stay, and why would you? The Bhuttanian Empire is immense. Hasan Daeg will become just another small fiefdom paying tribute to the Bhuttanian aga."

"There is you," replied Dorak, lowering his bedcovers, thus revealing a muscular chest.

Maura almost broke into laughter. Men were all alike, forever playing the coquettish bed toy.

"Besides, I like it here," continued Dorak. "I might make O Konya the new seat of my government."

Maura bristled at the last comment. "That is ridiculous. We will marry, we will bed, and then you will return to your homeland."

Dorak put his hands behind his head. "You make it sound like such a cold arrangement."

"Our marriage will be a political arrangement. That is all!" snapped Maura, weary of his sexual posturing. She wanted him to put some clothes on.

"It doesn't have to be."

"Surely you jest. What else can there be between us?"

Dorak began playing with the fabric of her skirt.

Maura jerked it out of his hands. "Perhaps I should call your slave girl back. You seem in need of a cold bath."

"Why should I call her when you can give me one?"

Maura snorted with anger. She turned away from Dorak.

"Don't be angry. You might not want to please the aga, but would you please your husband?" Seeing that Maura was still offended, Dorak changed the subject. "Let us discuss the wedding."

"Hasan Daegian couples marry before all their kith and kin."

"As do Bhuttanians," replied Dorak, wondering where the conversation was going.

"Yes, but the Hasan Daegian couples do so naked," said Maura with a straight face.

Dorak could not keep from laughing and held on to his wounded side. "You do not, little liar. Besides, it would take more than standing naked in front of a bunch of old ladies before I would pull out of this wedding."

Maura smiled. "Well, we do invite all of our kin, and I would expect that we observe my customs of marriage since you are marrying me in my country."

Dorak looked suspiciously at Maura. "There is a lot of me and mine in that statement."

"It is the bride's wishes that are followed, not the groom's."

"I see. What if I elect to follow Bhuttanian customs?"

"It will be as you wish, Great Aga, but you are too good a politician to realize that doing so would greatly displease the Hasan Daegians you now rule, not to mention your future wife. You do want to make me happy, don't you?" Maura fluttered her eyelids.

Once again, Dorak burst into laughter. "You almost kill me to win your freedom, and since you've failed, you are trying another tact." He grabbed Maura and kissed her firmly on the lips.

Maura liked the musty smell of him and returned his warm kiss without thinking.

"You are a wonder. What children we shall have."

Blushing, Maura pushed him away. She was not used to Dorak's rough handling. Chaun Maaun had always been gentle.

Still, Dorak's touch electrified her while Chaun Maaun's had merely soothed her like a warm summer shower. Passionate images of coupling with Dorak rose in her mind. She found herself studying the black hair on Dorak's chest. It had been a long time since she had been with someone, and she missed being touched.

Dorak let his finger wander down Maura's neck and chest until it came to rest between her breasts. Her cleavage felt warm and moist. He gently removed his finger and sucked it.

Maura took a sharp breath.

Leaning toward her, Dorak's eyes became heavy with desire.

Maura placed her hands over his encroaching arms and held them firmly. "Give me the wedding I desire and what is due to me as queen of Hasan Daeg."

"You shall have it," growled Dorak, "but you must be ready for me. Whatever I want, you must give to me without question."

Maura returned his heated gaze boldly. "I understand."

Dorak shook her. "To understand is not enough! You must want me!"

The young queen felt the blood rush to her face. "I will want you, Dorak, and all that comes with you."

"I want you to wear a gown of white without blemish." Dorak's hands began to roam Maura's body. He touched her breasts and kneaded her stomach. His breath became labored. "I do not want you to bathe before I come to you."

He grabbed her hair and pulled her face closer. "Your hair must be worn loose." Dorak leaned forward, kissing her cheeks. He then bit her lips lightly.

Maura kissed him back roughly.

"What else do you want?"

"Can you love me?"

Maura drew back. "Love?"

"Is that too much to ask?"

Maura bowed her head in confusion. She never once entertained the idea that Dorak would want love.

Disappointed by her response, Dorak hid his feelings. "We will take it one step at a time. I feel tired. Please go now. Make the arrangements as you wish."

Maura rose from his bed and moved toward the door. Stopping, she turned. "Dorak?"

"Yes," he murmured, his head already on the pillow.

"Do you think you could love me?"

"Who will have time for love when one is ruling an empire?" Dorak responded, hoping to hurt her as she had just injured him.

Maura quietly left the room. Tears welled in her eyes, but Dorak did not see them.

He was staring at the ceiling when the door closed. "Yes, I could love you," he whispered to no one in particular.

14

Maura fumed.

A conclave of administrators, military personnel, and advisors sat around the royal dining table squabbling about the correct protocol for the royal wedding.

Bhuttanians sat on one side fuming, while the Hasan Daegians sat on the other, glowering at their queen.

Maura had long since abandoned the idea of making the Hasan Daegians and Bhuttanians sit next to each other.

The Hasan Daegians, a particular and fussy people, could not stand the crudeness of the warring Bhuttanians who blew their noses on their shirtsleeves and freely spat on the carpets.

To show their disdain of the conquering nomads, the Hasan Daegians had come with perfectly combed hair decorated with flowers and immaculate flowing gowns of elegant designs.

The Bhuttanians arrived in full military dress with their weapons prominently displayed.

The Hasan Daegians, seeing the Bhuttanians swagger into the dining hall with their daggers and swords, immediately badgered their queen to dismiss with the proceedings altogether.

To avert disaster, Maura firmly replied that the Bhuttanians were merely showing respect by wearing their dress uniforms and weapons. War was all they knew, and their entire culture and protocol were built around it.

This explanation did little to soften the Hasan Daegians attitude toward the Bhuttanians. As far as the Hasan Daegian women were concerned, their queen was being forced into an undesirable marriage with a brute. Their only hope was that one day the Bhuttanians would be thrown out or, at the very least, the offspring from this hated union would blend both cultures together. They did not even guess that perhaps Maura secretly wished for the marriage, that her feelings for Dorak were deep and complex, and her heart raced upon seeing him.

The Bhuttanians were confused by all of the fuss. The verbal abuse from the Hasan Daegians did little to make the Bhuttanians agreeable, even though most of them did not understand the Hasan Daegian language. They did, though, understand the gestures the women used. It only stiffened their resolve not to negotiate with women at all. "Where are your husbands?" they demanded in Anqarian. "We must negotiate with the men in charge!"

Maura slammed her fist down on the table. "THAT IS ENOUGH!" she commanded in Anqarian, the universal language. "You have been in this country long enough to understand that our men are homemakers and do not handle matters of state."

The large, gruff Bhuttanian men snickered at this, but with a very stern look from Alexanee, the smirks quickly disappeared from their faces.

The queen turned to the Hasan Daegian women and spoke in their language. "You must stop this constant arguing with the Bhuttanians. They don't understand it. You must show them respect."

Maura slowly rose from her chair so her words would have more impact. "Aga Dorak and I wish this wedding to take place a week from now with all honors befitting a royal marriage. If we are disappointed, we are going to identify those who have wronged us, and the punishment for our displeasure will be of the same severity for both Bhuttanian and Hasan Daegian. Do I make myself clear?" She repeated her warning in Anqarian and Sivan.

Both the Hasan Daegians and Bhuttanians nodded or murmured their acquiescence.

Alexanee motioned for a servant to come to him. With great deliberation, he unsheathed his sword and handed it to the servant with orders to place it by the entrance. He then gave a stern look at his subordinates. Reluctantly, the other Bhuttanians stood and removed their various weapons and threw them in a pile by the main door.

Everyone knew the Bhuttanians kept several knives in their boots, but the Hasan Daegian women were diplomatic enough not to mention this.

The women were pleased and would no longer hold up the negotiations. They understood the symbolic gesture of the Bhuttanians and gave their queen the signal to proceed.

Matters of food, invitations, and flowers were discussed.

The Bhuttanians, not knowing the fine art of Hasan Daegian weddings, kept silent during the lively discussion.

Whatever the Hasan Daegian queen wanted was fine with them. It was only during the subject of security that the Bhuttanians became animated. No Hasan Daegian warriors would be allowed to accompany the queen nor guard the palace. The matters of security were to be entirely in the hands of the Bhuttanian army.

"What if Mikkotto tries to assassinate me during the wedding?" Maura fumed.

The Bhuttanian officers, including Alexanee, merely shrugged. They were concerned with the safety of the aga and would permit no armed Hasan Daegians near him.

"Without my personal guards, my safety is compromised."

The Bhuttanians took offense, and their backs straightened in their chairs.

"Your Majesty," Alexanee said. "We shall protect you as one of our own during the festivities."

The angry queen dismissed his remarks with a wave of her hand. "We all know that Mikkotto infiltrated the Bhuttanian ranks before and made traitors with some coin. I want my own guards."

The officers' faces reddened at the implied insult.

"You say you do not know where Mikkotto has fled. She could be enjoying sinjo tea with the Black Cacodemon at this very moment for all I know."

Not rising to the queen's bait, Alexanee stressed, "With as many people as you are inviting, our security must be tight for your sake as well as our aga. We simply cannot allow armed Hasan Daegian soldiers, who have not pledged their oath of loyalty near Aga Dorak!"

"DO AS SHE COMMANDS!" boomed a voice from the doorway. In strode Dorak wearing a flowing grey cape with a black lining, his hair glistening from rain droplets.

Maura knew he had been exercising one of his great warhorses.

Everyone immediately jumped to his or her feet except for Maura.

The Bhuttanians pressed their fists to their chests while the Hasan Daegians merely inclined their heads.

Maura shot a warning glance at the Hasan Daegians. They reluctantly gave stiff little bows.

"I have come to find my bride-to-be and discover her entangled with a bunch of petty bureaucrats who are wasting her valuable time with nitpicking and complaining." Dorak gently placed a hand on

Maura's shoulder. "I wish the pleasure of your company for the noon meal."

"Your wish is my command, Great Aga," replied Maura, pleased at his touch.

"I would make this suggestion," advised Dorak, glaring at the audience still standing. "Form committees and have them make recommendations by tomorrow. Once you have decided, they will be responsible for carrying out your plans, or we shall carry them out feet first the day after the wedding. I wish to be the only one who monopolizes your time."

Maura had been trained to lead through a more diplomatic process than Dorak. However, she could not deny that such blatant threats had a very quick and mobilizing effect on the intended. She always took note of how Dorak handled his violent and stubborn men.

Lady Sari, who had been standing behind the queen's chair along with Rubank, approached Dorak, "Great Aga, may I speak with you?"

Dorak had long taken note that Sari, though of no official capacity, was of great importance to the royal family. Her advice was sought by the young queen. This alone made the woman important to Dorak.

At his command, a chair was brought for Dorak. Motioning to Sari, Dorak gave her leave to speak freely.

"When Queen Abisola was married, I was greatly involved with the wedding and oversaw many of the details myself. Of course, I was younger then, but I think I could still do it."

Dorak had not expected Lady Sari to offer her help and glanced at Maura.

The blue-skinned queen sat quietly, but her face was frozen with fear. He knew immediately that Maura had no prior knowledge of Sari's offer. "Why would you wish to help with this wedding since we all know of your feelings regarding me?"

Sari blushed to the roots of her tidy white hair. "I have not changed my opinion. However, Hasan Daegian queens mate for life, and if this wedding occurs, you will be our king. My thinking is that if you are pleased with the wedding, you will treat the queen well, and your heart will soften toward the Hasan Daegians who are under your control."

Dorak pondered her words as Maura stirred uncomfortably in her chair. "Has my reign been that awful for the Hasan Daegians? Your possessions have not been stolen. Your children have not been sold into slavery. The population goes about its daily life largely untouched by my soldiers."

"I am an old woman. I have nothing to lose by speaking my mind."

"There is your life."

"My life, for all intents and purposes, is over. I am living on borrowed time and know it."

"Then speak freely as long as your words are not treasonous."

"Great Aga, it is true that our buildings are being rebuilt to their former glory. Families have not been torn apart. We are not starving as is much of the world. Life in the city goes on as it had before the invasion. However, certain leaders of our community have disappeared, never to be seen again, such as the women from the House of Magi."

"They simply fled O Konya."

Maura stirred and tried to gain Sari's attention.

"I do not accept this," Lady Sari replied in a bold tone. "I have heard rumors that they are being detained by Bhuttanian soldiers somewhere in the city."

Dorak rose from his chair and faced Sari. "Are you calling me a liar, old woman?" Dorak asked, his voice sizzling like water over hot coals.

Maura prayed that Sari would tread more softly.

Sari smiled sweetly. "Of course not, Great Aga. I am merely suggesting that you may have forgotten where you put them."

Dorak started to speak and then halted abruptly. His gaze moved from Sari to Maura's amazed countenance until he threw back his head, laughing. "You may not like me, Lady Sari, but I like you very much indeed. I wish I had twenty diplomats like you. I would not need an army."

Dorak bent forward and kissed Sari's withered hand. "You may indeed be in charge of the wedding. Do as you please as long as it satisfies my intended bride."

He turned to Maura. "I will give you your wedding present now, my love. All detainees from the war will be set free on the day of the wedding, even those corrupt women from the House of Magi. I am sure I will be able to remember where I have put them by then."

Maura slid out of her chair and kneeled before Dorak. "Thank you, Great Aga. This is most gracious of you."

"I do not understand your strange attitudes toward war. Prisoners are taken all the time, and nothing is thought of it."

"That is until you have been taken prisoner yourself," replied Maura, looking up at Dorak with a sour smile on her face.

15

Maura appraised herself.

She gazed into a large standing mirror in her chambers at her blue and gold wedding gown trailed by a sheer white train encrusted with pearls. Her black hair had grown back and was held in place by a simple circlet of white rooshars, a rare marsh flower. She wore her mother's emerald signet ring, which was now hers as ruler of Hasan Daeg. On her feet were dainty gold sandals. A blue gem-encrusted belt encircled her narrow waist.

Maura despaired when she saw that her maid had applied too much makeup. Not wanting to hurt the girl's feelings, Maura sent her for some water. After the maid left, Maura patted her face lightly with a damp towel. Too much makeup on her blue skin gave Maura a bizarre appearance. Satisfied, Maura turned toward Sari who hurried into the room, limping and using a cane.

Alarmed, Maura bade Sari to sit and helped ease her into a chair. "Is all ready?"

"All is in readiness, Your Majesty," informed Sari, wheezing.

"You seem out of breath."

Sari held up her hand. "I will be fine."

"You should not run at your age."

"The hallways seem longer these days, and my feet swell," complained Sari, good-naturedly pointing to her cane. She clapped her hands together in glee. "Little sparrow, wait until you see everything. It is all so beautiful. If only your mother were here."

"I do not think she would want this for me," lamented Maura, thinking sadly of her mother.

"How stupid of me!"

Maura patted her on the knee and got pillows on which to rest Sari's swollen feet. "It should be a happy day."

"How can it be happy when you are marrying someone you do not love? Hasan Daegian queens always marry for love. That is one of the reasons they live so long."

Maura laughed. "Is it? I was always under the impression that it had something to do with the Royal Bogazkoy."

Sari raised her hand up to her lips. "You must never say that out loud. Dorak has spies everywhere."

"You think Dorak does not know about the Bogazkoy? I know that within days after my visit with the Royal Bogazkoy, he found its remains and knew everything there was to know about it."

Sari moaned. "Why him?"

"It could be worse. It could be Zoar who would be my groom today. At least Dorak is handsome and intelligent. He is also sensitive." Maura paused for a moment. She started to fiddle with the hairbrush on her dressing table, not wanting to look Sari in the eye. "Maybe I can bring him around to my way of thinking."

"Do not think for one moment that you could ever tame Dorak. He is a wild thing, a law unto himself. Even his own people don't understand him. They say he is strange because he is only half-Bhuttanian. I will grant you he has been good to our city, but we do not know what he has done in the countryside. He may have destroyed entire towns and villages."

Sari looked bitterly at Maura's reflection in the mirror. "We are blind. We have no knowledge of the outside world." The flesh on Sari's face stretched with anger, giving her skin a puckered look that was unbecoming. "Dorak can never be trusted. Never!"

Maura looked at Sari's reflection in the mirror. Sari's eyes cast a weary look. "I know," Maura sadly replied to her. "He is the enemy, and I can never trust him."

A knock sounded on the door. It was abruptly opened by a Hasan Daegian guard.

A Bhuttanian escort guard stepped inside. A young officer dressed in his nomadic finest marched smartly up to Maura and bowed very low. "We have come to escort you, Great Mother," he announced gravely.

Maura followed him into the hallway where stood the marriage palanquin. At the poles supporting the chair were two Hasan Daegians accompanied by two Bhuttanians. All looked approvingly at the young queen, who studied the decorated chair.

"Does it please you?" asked Sari anxiously.

Maura smiled. "Yes, Lady Sari. It is lovely."

Sari's wizened face broke into a radiant beam.

Maura approached the palanquin and touched some of the hundreds of blue and yellow flowers so expertly woven on its structure. The poles were wrapped in gold foil. Fragrant aroma wafted on the gentle breeze throughout the hallway, which Maura inhaled deeply. The scent was glorious.

"Hurry," Sari cautioned. "We do not want the flowers to start wilting." She helped the queen step into the lovely wedding chair.

"Your mother had one just like this to carry her to the binding ceremony," she said absently-mindedly.

"Thank you," said Maura, close to tears.

Sari pulled a handkerchief out of her sleeve and discreetly gave it to Maura.

"I have nowhere to hide it," Maura said.

"You will not need to. I will be by your side," Sari replied, putting on her ceremonial robe. She motioned for servants to pick up the gilt poles.

Both Bhuttanians and Hasan Daegians picked up the litter on cue and did not jostle the bride.

The queen's guards automatically fell into place by the palanquin. They were attired in full dress uniform of blue with gold trim. Their weapons had been restored to them by Dorak for the day and hung proudly by their sides.

Behind the marriage palanquin marched the Bhuttanian guards hand-picked by Dorak. Each member of the guard knew that this was the most dangerous time for the queen. There were both Hasan Daegians and Bhuttanians who did not wish for this wedding to occur.

The fact that an assassination attempt had not yet been made only increased Dorak's anxiety that someone would strike at Maura as she was escorted to the ceremony.

Hundreds of guests had already filed into the palace. Dorak waited expectantly in the antechamber behind the large court hall where the wedding was to take place.

Couriers ran back and forth relaying the status of the queen's progress to the wedding hall. Three couriers had come back with good news.

So far so good, thought Dorak.

Maura had only five more hallways to negotiate.

Dorak grunted and continued his pacing, his dark eyes marking his pensive mood. He must marry this girl. It was vital to his plans. Feeling a draft in the room, he turned and watched Rubank, Maura's advisor, approached him.

Rubank seemed to glide like a silent apparition in his long maroon robe with the crest of the Bogazkoy and the uultepes on it, but then Rubank was always quiet. The royal consul was the only official position in the queen's court to be open to Hasan Daegian males.

Dorak did not understand how a person could advise when he couldn't speak, but then he thought all Hasan Daegian customs strange.

Rubank bowed. Standing patiently with his hands folded across his beautiful robe, Rubank waited for the aga to address him.

Dorak always found Rubank irritating, so he decided to have a little fun. "Rubank, how nice of you to join my officers and me. Have you come to wish me good fortune in my marriage?"

Lacking a sense of humor, Rubank had learned to endure Dorak's jesting. All Bhuttanians were great jokesters and loved to slip a marsh bloodsucker in someone's bedroll or unbuckle a saddle cinch. It seemed that for something to be funny to a Bhuttanian meant that someone needed to scream, gasp for breath, or fall off a horse.

Dorak loved to play with the hidden meaning of words.

Rubank understood that Dorak wished to catch him in his crosshairs. If he did wish Dorak good fortune, Rubank could be cited as a traitor, for this was going against official Hasan Daegian policy. If the consul did not wish Dorak good fortune, then he would displease the aga, which might cost him his head. Desiring to do neither, Rubank raised his eyebrows, indicating that he did not understand the question. He would continue with this gesture until Dorak tired of his game.

Seeing Rubank's reply, Dorak realized that he would not be able to trick the cagey diplomat today, so he opted for the true nature of his visitation. "Do you bring word from your mistress?"

Rubank nodded.

"Does it concern her location within the palace?"

Rubank nodded.

"Is she ready for the ceremony to proceed?"

Rubank nodded.

"Is she safe?"

Rubank nodded.

"Should we start now?"

Rubank nodded.

"Is there anything else you were ordered to communicate?"

Rubank shook his head.

"You may go," replied Dorak, hoping that his headache would depart with the royal consul. Slipping into an outer chamber, Dorak had his appearance checked again by his valet and then followed the High Priest of Bhuttu into the great throne room.

Hundreds of guests waited in anticipation.

Many of the Bhuttanian nobility, summering in Kittum, had arrived that morning. Most had balked at Dorak's instructions that all Bhuttanians wash before donning their finery. Yet, there they grimly sat, bathed and perfumed, next to Hasan Daegian women and their smaller husbands. Many of the Bhuttanian nobility gawked openly at the sturdy, muscular women with the voluptuous figures who did not cower before their blatant stares.

In turn, the Hasan Daegian men discreetly peered over their fans at the Bhuttanian women who were of similar stature. The females, covered from head to toe, were dark with small, trim figures. They looked older than their Hasan Daegian counterparts as they lived outdoors most of the time in harsh weather and did not have the custom of applying soothing creams to their skin at night.

Some of the younger Hasan Daegian men were intrigued by the petite women, but the older Hasan Daegian men concurred behind their decorated fans "not enough to mount."

For good measure, the Hasan Daegian women, most of whom had served in the war against the Bhuttanians, glanced at their counterparts' thick thighs and taut buttocks. They wondered how it would feel to run their cheeks across a hairy chest instead of trying to run a sword through it. More than one Hasan Daegian female closed her eyes, hoping to think of less taxing subjects.

After all, the Bhuttanians were the enemy. Still, being squeezed so tightly in a room with them was more than some of the Hasan Daegian women could bear.

More than cultivating their crops, the Hasan Daegians liked to make love and were considered by the Bhuttanians to be very hedonistic. Lovemaking was a favorite pastime, and all lovers were treasured. Many Hasan Daegian women instinctively knew they would not be cherished in return by Bhuttanian males, and this thought cooled the ardor of numerous Hasan Daegian females.

Without fanfare, Dorak assumed his place on the dais as he had rehearsed many times before the previous day.

The guests stood. Only the very old or the infirmed were allowed to sit as was the Hasan Daegian custom.

With a slight nod of his head, Dorak acknowledged the audience's obeisance. Turning to the High Priestess of Mekonia, he bowed deeply.

The High Priestess regarded him with frosty detachment.

Trumpets sounded, and the main doors were flung open. A cool breeze entered the hall just ahead of the queen's palanquin.

Delicate flute notes floated on the very breeze which now cooled the wedding guests. As was custom, the bride's litter proceeded through the center of the throng.

This part of the ceremony caused Dorak pause. He, along with many guards, scanned the audience looking for anyone with a weapon. After several tense minutes, the marriage palanquin emerged from the crowd without incident.

Dorak relaxed as guards brought the palanquin up the steps and onto the dais. Deeply inhaling the sweet fragrance of the litter, he watched as a Hasan Daegian guard helped his future bride to her feet.

Maura de Magela, tenth ruler of Hasan Daeg, looked striking as she stepped gracefully from the palanquin.

Sari, dressed in gorgeous finery, helped arrange the long sheer train on the steps.

The palanquin was removed to where Sari stood along with the Hasan Daegian Honor Guard.

Bhuttanian soldiers moved to Dorak's side.

Each group of guards turned toward the audience, scanning for trouble.

As Maura approached Dorak, she noticed his eyes were glimmering like black river pebbles in shallow water.

Reaching for Maura's hand, Dorak turned to the High Priestess of Mekonia.

Maura did not hear what the High Priestess said nor the words Dorak repeated. She did not recognize her voice responding. She saw her hands moving slowly toward Dorak to place a flowered wreath on his head.

All she heard was the voice of Chaun Maaun calling to her from a distant place. Perspiration broke out on Maura's forehead. Her limbs felt cold and useless. Chaun Maaun! Chaun Maaun! She was betraying him!

She was not being forced into this marriage. Perhaps as a queen, but not as a woman. Maura blinked back her tears.

Would Chaun Maaun ever understand? How could he understand something that she herself did not? Feeling Dorak's firm hand on hers, she looked up to see his concerned eyes searching her face. Maura gave him a reassuring smile.

Dorak turned his attention to the High Priestess once more.

The peal of the great bell resounded, acknowledging that Maura and Dorak had been married according to Hasan Daegian law and custom.

The High Priestess of Mekonia retreated to the back of the dais.

The High Priest of Bhuttu and High Priestess of Bhutta stepped forward.

Maura braced herself for the ceremony to follow.

Sari moved up the dais and removed the train of the dress, exposing Maura's back.

Beautiful backs of Bhuttanian women were considered desirable and thus shown to gain honor for the groom.

Maura's skin had been oiled and glistened in shafts of light from the morning sun.

The Bhuttanians murmured appreciatively.

The queen's back was straight, even, and without blemish except for its strange tattoo.

Sari held up the de Magela ancestral fan denoting their royal station and snapped it shut.

Maura closed her eyes as she heard the clicking sounds of fans closing one after the other throughout the great hall. She was glad Dorak did not understand the significance of the gesture which meant extreme disapproval.

Hasan Daegian women did not humble themselves to honor men. Some of the Hasan Daegians were dabbing their eyes. It was a sad day to see their queen marry outside of her people.

Maura was aware of the commotion her bare back was causing. She tried to focus her attention on Dorak, who was removing some of his clothing.

He took off his shirt and donned a ceremonial vest. She noticed how dry his olive skin was, even though it was hot.

The High Priestess spoke in the Bhuttanian language.

Maura tried to concentrate on the proper sequence of movements in which she had been coached. She repeated words she did not understand after which the Priestess handed her a sharp knife. Maura's hands were shaking as she reached out for Dorak's arm.

Dorak covered her hands with his left one and guided the knife to his wrist. "Be calm. Let me guide you."

Grateful for his intervention, Maura let Dorak guide the blade across his wrist, which made a shallow cut and dropped the knife on a pillow held aloft by the priestess.

Drops of blood seeped from Dorak's arm.

Feeling woozy in the stifling room, Maura glanced about the hall. Weren't the windows open?

She caught Lady Sari's eye.

The Hasan Daegian advisor with her elaborate hair and beautiful gown looked calm and composed. She didn't seem to be suffering from the heat. Sari gave her a quick wink.

Out of the corner of her eye, Maura saw Dorak take a similar knife from the High Priest. Hearing Dorak ask for her arm, she turned, but his voice sounded muffled and far away. When she did not respond, he gently lifted her arm from her side.

"Just a few minutes more," he cajoled. "Then it will all be over."

Maura jerked as she felt the knife nick her skin. Looking down, she saw blue blood drip onto the floor.

The High Priest said something to her, and Maura extended her arm to Dorak.

The Great Aga placed his bleeding wound over hers, and the High Priest of Bhuttu bound their wrists together with a leather cord. Then the cord was cut.

Maura knelt as she had been instructed, and Dorak stepped back a few paces.

According to Bhuttanian custom, brides were to crawl to their husbands as a symbolic gesture of their total supplication and their husband's dominance over their lives.

After moving one knee, Maura remained still as if made of stone.

Dorak could see fury twisted across his bride's face.

Tension gripped Maura's entire body.

Dorak knew the proud queen would never come to him this way. With quick intuition, Dorak realized that Maura had been pushed as far as she was capable. She would not be humiliated before her people.

Dorak's mind jumped about for a solution. Without the last part of the ceremony, his people would not accept the marriage as legitimate.

Dorak decided to do the only thing he could. He fell to his knees and crawled toward his shivering bride. Holding out his arms, Dorak whispered to her, "Come to me as I come to you."

Maura moved toward Dorak without thinking. She quickly covered the distance between them and fell into his arms.

Dorak cradled his new bride for a moment and then helped Maura to her feet.

The ceremony was over. They were married to each other according to both Hasan Daegian and Bhuttanian laws and traditions.

Feeling relieved, Maura felt Dorak kiss her on the cheek as they both turned to face a stunned audience.

Never had a Hasan Daegian queen knelt before any consort, and neither had a Bhuttanian groom crawled before his bride. Both Hasan Daegians and Bhuttanians were appalled for different reasons.

Only the Bhuttanian women were secretly pleased. They hoped that Dorak and Maura's marriage would set a precedent for their daughters' weddings. Maybe they could save their daughters from the servitude they had suffered under their demanding husbands.

At Dorak's signal, the great gong sounded.

The hands of the High Priestess trembled as she placed a crown on Maura. She waved her hands over Maura's head mumbling incantations that warded off evil. From beneath her robe, she produced a gnarled wand made from an ancient yagomba tree with which she sprinkled holy water. "Behold, these two are joined as husband and wife, which only death can sever."

"Which only death can sever," rejoined the Bhuttanians.

A gong sounded within the palace and bells heralded the marriage to the general population standing outside in the streets.

Dorak turned toward his bride. "I promised you that once we were married, I would set free all political prisoners in O Konya. This very moment, they are being released."

Maura's face lit up as she touched his arm. "Thank you," she replied gratefully.

Smiling broadly, Dorak cried in Anqarian, "As I have taken a Hasan Daegian bride, it is my wish for my people and hers to become one. There is no longer Hasan Daegian or Bhuttanian. We are one. To signify our desire for both peoples to become united, I not only take this woman to be my wife but my empress as well. She and I will rule over our people, and one day, our child, of both Bhuttanian and Hasan Daegian blood, shall rule over a united kingdom! So be it!" Dorak led his bewildered bride back to the center of the dais.

There awaited the High Priest of Bhuttu with a crown that resembled a bull's horns carved from gold and onyx.

The High Priestess of Bhutta brought out a similar crown.

The High Priest placed his crown on Dorak's bowed head. Taking a vial of blood from his robes, he held it over the royal couple. "This is the blood of Bhuttu, who in human form sacrifices his life with the eternal copulation of Bhutta," he cried out. The priest, in his costly robes of gold, carefully opened the vial and poured a small drop of blood in the center of his palm. With his index finger, he smeared a design onto his hand. "As Bhuttu sacrificed himself, Bhutta breathed everlasting life into his nostrils." The priest smeared blood on Maura's forehead and then on Dorak's. "From your joining must new life spring."

The Hasan Daegians stood quietly as they were not sure what to make of the unexpected coronation.

Maura's eyes swept past a beaming Dorak and over the cheering Bhuttanians.

The Hasan Daegians were quiet, but she could see the glimmer of hope in many of their eyes. If their queen were empress of the Bhuttanian Empire, she might have influence over the political process that controlled their country. One by one, the Hasan Daegians realizing this advantage, patted Bhuttanians on the back and clapped their hands together.

For the first time in over a year, Maura began to feel a surge of joy. There was hope where there had been none before. She felt giddy and wanted to dance. Maura turned to Dorak. "Bless you for this."

Dorak looked at Maura with intense longing and pulled her against him. He held her in his gaze for a very long time.

Embarrassed, the new empress looked away. Out of the corner of her eye, she spied a strange woman sitting next to a Bhuttanian nobleman, staring at her with a menacing intensity. Maura recognized the look. It was hate. Hate such as she had never seen in the face of another being.

The woman was an Anqarian with pale skin and yellow hair. She wore expensive but simple clothes of Anqarian design. Something about the pattern in the woman's dress struck Maura as familiar. Her hair was bound by luxurious combs. Judging by her appearance and seating, though Anqarian, she was obviously a person of great importance to the Bhuttanians.

Returning the stare, Maura was surprised to find that the Anqarian did not look away, but continued to scrutinize with great malevolence. The woman's gall unnerved her for just a second. Maura narrowed her eyes at the Anqarian.

The woman's escort, seeing Maura's displeasure, bent his head and whispered into the woman's ear.

Reluctantly, she lowered her eyes.

The man tried to take the woman's hand, but she pulled away.

On the other side of the pale Anqarian sat a little boy. He was about the age of five and had black, curious eyes like Dorak's. The little boy looked at the reigning couple with a blank expression on his face.

It occurred to Maura that the woman may have been a favorite concubine of Zoar's, and the boy was Dorak's half-brother, perhaps the only one who had survived. It was rumored that all of Dorak's male siblings had met with fatal accidents.

Noticing that his new bride was taken with something, Dorak followed her gaze. Seeing the Anqarian woman, he froze, and his smile was replaced by dark hostility.

The blonde woman, feeling Dorak's eyes, looked pleadingly at him. She put her hand protectively upon the boy's head.

Dorak pulled Maura closer to him.

The woman's face crumpled. Her mouth became pinched and drawn. Leaning her head against the shoulder of her escort, she closed her eyes.

The tall elderly man put his arms around her and leaned his chin against her head. He murmured to her as one does a child. It seemed to soothe her.

Maura turned toward Dorak, but he was no longer concerned with the pale stranger.

He was smiling and waving to the cheering crowd. She was feeling too happy to be concerned at the moment, but Maura would recall the stranger when she was alone.

Dorak led Maura out onto the balcony overlooking the city.

Beneath them stood throngs of people who had come to give their best wishes to the new bride and groom. Already, the story of their queen's coronation was making its way throughout the city.

The only ones unimpressed were the Sivan merchants, who merely shrugged and stated that Dorak could have done no less as it was certainly in his best interest. The Sivans were a practical people.

The Hasan Daegian women banged on drums, children tooted whistles, and the men of households clanged pots.

Prisoners, who had been set free that very hour, were carried through the streets on the shoulders of strangers.

The surviving women from the House of Magi made their way through the crowded streets as best they could. Many of them limped from the effects of torture. Several were so ill they had to wait in the streets until litters could gather them to their new residences that Dorak had established for them.

As they were considered holy women by the Hasan Daegians, no one dared touch their persons. Instead, Hasan Daegian men brought out heaping bowls of soups, platters of bread slathered with melted cheese, and wine. They watched over the starving women as they gobbled the food, making sure no Bhuttanian soldier pestered them.

Hasan Daegian children gave Bhuttanian soldiers on duty flowers. Not knowing what to do with the flowers, but not wishing to offend, they stuck the flowers in between the wedges of their leather chest guards. The children laughed good-naturedly and tried to explain that the flowers were to be worn in their hair.

The soldiers, not speaking Hasan Daegian, merely nodded and continued with their patrols.

The newly-crowned empress laughed also watching the antics of the crowd gathered below the balcony.

Dorak noticed that Maura's crown had become lopsided and straightened it.

The mere touch of his hand sent a thrill up Maura's spine. All of her senses exploded with color, sound, movement, and touch. She felt as though the nerves in her body had awakened from a deep slumber with every sensation heightened. Her sight and hearing gathered information more quickly than her mind could assimilate. She felt dizzy and clung to the railing of the balcony festive with flags and garlands of flowers.

"Are you all right?"

"I feel glorious," Maura gushed, shielding her eyes from the mid-day sun.

"But it is all too much?"

"At times."

"Are you sorry?" asked Dorak, watching her expression intently.

"If our marriage can bring peace, then I am not sorry. You have been most generous today." Maura placed her hand inside Dorak's.

His fingers pressed around hers.

"It is time we see to our guests," Dorak spoke cheerfully.

"Are we not going to the wedding parade?"

Dorak chuckled. "The Lady Sari has seen to all of the arrangements. We are going to have our wedding feast in a pavilion. We shall be able to see all the floats from there."

"And eat, I hope. I am very hungry," said Maura, feeling her stomach growl.

"I see you did not eat breakfast, either. I guess we were both nervous."

Maura nodded enthusiastically in agreement. They waved once more to the cheering crowd and went back into the palace.

Both Hasan Daegian and Bhuttanian guards escorted them to a blue and gold pavilion tent with brightly colored banners hanging from the sides. The tight security inside the pavilion was obvious and gave Maura pause. She realized what a bold thing she had done by marrying Dorak, and as a result, both Bhuttanian and Hasan Daegian factions hated her.

Dorak was despised as well and had his food tasted by others before he ate. His physician discreetly followed him everywhere with a medical bag full of poison antidotes.

The wedding party made its way to a large platform where tables awaited them.

There stood Sari directing servants and rearranging goblets and silverware. Sari hoped the Bhuttanians would follow Dorak's example and use napkins instead of their sleeves. She also put out the word that she did not want to see meat bones thrown on the ground. Seeing her queen, Sari smoothed her hair before bowing.

"You have outdone yourself, little nanny," Dorak called out so that all could hear. "My bride and I are grateful."

The frown lines on Sari's face softened as she basked in the public praise. She knew she would have little to fear now from any Bhuttanian, as it was clear she was a favorite of Dorak's. There would be no more sulky looks from disgruntled slaves or jostling in the hallways by Bhuttanian soldiers wishing to frighten an old Hasan Daegian woman for pleasure. She would breathe easier.

Maura sat beside her groom. She looked down the length of their table. The only family representing her was her father's sister, Everlynd, Duchess of Enos, who sat on Maura's left. The rest of the royal family had long since passed on or had been killed during the invasion.

For a moment, Maura's happiness was dampened as she became painfully aware of how alone she was in the world.

Her other family, the Dinii, were denied to her. How she wished Empress Gitar and Iegani were present to wish her well. Of course, that was adolescent thinking. Even if they could have come, the proud Dinii, once the Overlords of Kaseri, would have refused to bow to Dorak. And how would she have been able to face Chaun Maaun?

Maura blinked back tears as thoughts of Chaun Maaun raced through her mind. The empress looked around the room quickly, hoping to find something to divert her attention. Her eyes moved across the tent, searching for some juggler or mime that would amuse her. As she scanned the pavilion, Maura again spied the strange woman with the white skin and yellow hair.

She was with the dark-haired little boy with the wide black eyes and the doting elderly Bhuttanian. The woman was seated among those of very high rank in the Bhuttanian party.

Other Bhuttanians came to her table and gave her the Bhuttanian salute while speaking to her in low tones. Many left small gifts for the boy, which he ignored. He looked sleepy and put his head on the table until his mother gently shook him. He yawned and was given some peeled fruit to eat. The little boy smiled greedily and began to eat the fruit as though ravished with hunger.

The empress turned toward Dorak who was engaged in a philosophical conversation with the High Priest of Bhuttu. Finally getting his attention, Dorak smiled at her. "Husband, who is the Anqarian sitting over there with that Bhuttanian nobleman? She keeps staring at me as though she knows me," spoke Maura. "Should I know her?"

Dorak casually glanced at the table his bride indicated. "The Anqarian way is strange. Pay her no heed."

"I thought everyone not saved by the Dinii had been killed at Anqara or taken as slaves. This woman seems to be important."

Dorak seemed disinterested. "Not everyone," he answered in a husky voice.

"But who is she?"

"A nobleman's wife, nothing more," stated Dorak in a dismissive tone.

"Is she married to that nobleman?"

Dorak was silent for a moment. "No," he said.

"But . . ." Maura continued.

Dorak cut her off. "If the woman bothers you, I will have her removed," he replied, trying to hide his irritation.

"No. I do not wish to cause any reason for discord today," Maura answered dejectedly.

Dorak grunted and returned to his conversation with the High Priest, who was proceeding to make himself drunk on Sivan wine.

Maura looked back and saw the woman with the boy leaving, but not before the Anqarian shot her an undisguised look of loathing as she quit the tent.

The Duchess of Enos leaned close to Maura's ear. "Who is that dreadful woman leaving?"

Maura, not taking her eyes off the retreating Anqarian, whispered, "I do not know, but I'm going to find out."

The Duchess sighed. "Well, I am glad she is going. She's frightful."

Maura nodded in agreement.

At that moment, Dorak leaned over, and in Sivan recited to Maura's aunt a ribald joke that he had just been told by the High Priest.

The duchess, fond of bawdy humor, rolled back her eyes and let out an impolite snort of laughter. She then related the joke to a translator, who whispered it to Alexanee who was sitting next to her.

The general started to laugh and then stopped short. Frowning, he scolded the duchess in Anqarian, "Women should not know of such things!"

Astonished to find the ruthless general a sexual prude, the duchess turned to the translator, "Tell the honorable Alexanee that he would be surprised at the things I know concerning this subject." She winked seductively at the Bhuttanian.

Flustered, Alexanee sipped his drink, trying to regain his composure.

Later that afternoon and into the evening, a bored Dorak and an enthralled Maura listened to poems and ballads in their honor. The new empress especially liked poems regaling epic deeds, but noticed that Dorak squirmed during the long epics.

Poetry was new to the Bhuttanians, even educated ones like Dorak, but all Bhuttanians loved music. They liked to clap their hands and sing along. Even if they did not know the words, they would make up their own lyrics much to the chagrin of balladeers, trying to perform their compositions.

While listening, Maura ate with relish. Careful not offend anyone, she ate something from both the Bhuttanian and Hasan Daegian dishes presented to her. There were also Sivan and Hittal side dishes. She knew all of the cooks were watching in the wings and anxiously awaiting the opinions of the royal table concerning their elaborate, ethnic dishes.

Dorak ate as well, even handing Maura tidbits on his knife, but only after the food-tasters had consumed from each dish. Under the tablecloth and away from curious eyes, Dorak rubbed his hand over Maura's thigh.

The feel of Dorak's rough hand pleased Maura, and she was glad when it finally came time for the royal couple to excuse themselves for the night. As she walked with her honor guard and a silent Sari trailing behind, Maura could still hear the revelers singing and dancing. The wedding feast would go on for several more days, as was the Hasan Daegian custom. She hoped there would be enough food and patience to go around.

Sari escorted Maura to the bridal suite.

Dorak had the entire set of rooms repainted and new drapes installed.

The Bhuttanians were not much for colors, favoring browns and greys, but Dorak had the walls painted a delicate green. About the rooms were potted ferns and small trees, allowing an outdoor feeling. Soft yellow and pink knickknacks accented the plush emerald furniture.

Maura went from the sitting room to the bedchamber.

A bed with a blue canopy trimmed in gold sat in the middle of the room. The new bride rested on it, sinking into the moss-stuffed comforter and mattress.

Turning, Maura spied her nightgown hanging next to a full-length mirror encased in an exotic wood. It was as Dorak wanted. A simple gown made of common cloth, white and unblemished.

It reminded Maura of a mourning dress except for the blue trim on the bodice. Next to the gown was a robe, carefully folded and made of the same cloth with blue slippers embellished with the uultepes and the Bhuttanian dragon. On closer inspection, Maura could see that the dragon looked as though it was going to bite off the head of one of the uultepes. Maura smirked. Of course, this was Dorak's idea of a joke, or at least she hoped it was.

Across the room was a dressing table holding her toiletries and perfumes. Dorak had thought of everything.

Or perhaps Sari had. As though Lady Sari had overhead Maura's thoughts, she entered tentatively into the room, accompanied by several female noblewomen. "May we help you disrobe?" Lady Sari asked softly. The older woman seemed tired, and her lips were drawn back from her teeth.

Maura noticed she leaned against the doorjamb and righted herself as an afterthought. "You go to bed at once," Maura scolded. "You need not stay with me. It will be all right."

"But . . ." Sari resisted.

"There is nothing more you can do for me," interrupted Maura, looking intently at her friend and protector. "I must face this alone. You must go now and rest. I will need you in the morning."

Sari's shoulders slumped.

The girl was right.

There was nothing more she could do this night.

Maura must meet with Dorak and face him as best she could.

Sari could not help but fear for Maura but did not let it show on her frazzled face. "As you wish, Great Mother. But if you need anything, you may send for me. I will place a runner outside your door."

Sari's meaning was not lost on Maura. Bhuttanian husbands were known to become violent on the wedding night to assert their dominance.

Although Maura did not believe Dorak would treat her in such a manner, the possibility was unnerving.

It was so un-Hasan Daegian. Hasan Daegian brides and grooms passed their wedding night making love and giving each other gifts that would be treasured throughout their lives together. It was unthinkable to strike a loved one, let alone on such a special night.

The older woman gave the attending women last-minute instructions and exited the chamber, hobbling on her cane.

While the noblewomen attended to her, Maura quietly told one of them to fetch Meagan of Skujpor for Sari.

The woman bowed and slipped out of the room.

The others helped Maura remove her crown. They placed it inside a lockbox. Turning the key, they gave the box to Dorak's man, who retrieved it under guard and left the room.

The noblewomen began undressing the empress, never saying a word due to nervousness on everyone's part. The bridal gown was carefully folded and taken to the laundry room where it would be freshened and then hung on display in the main ceremonial hall.

Hasan Daegian boys of noble birth would file into the hall so they could touch the gown for good luck in hopes of catching a rich and caring wife. It was an honored custom.

Maura studied herself in the mirror. Her eyes seemed too large for her oval face. They had an intense quality that was not pleasing. Brides should have warm and loving eyes, Maura thought. Hers were apprehensive.

The assisting women laid her carefully on a table and massaged oil into her skin. One brought over a warm cloth to wipe her skin down, but Maura forbade it, thinking of Dorak's wish. The woman seemed surprised but said nothing. Above the reclining empress, the noblewomen glanced at each other.

Relaxed and warm after the gentle and soothing massage, Maura sent the servants away. She donned the nightgown by herself. It felt soft against her skin. Putting on the slippers, she unfolded the robe and put it on as well.

At her night table, the fatigued empress brushed her hair and powdered her face. She looked appraisingly at the haunted reflection staring back at her. "Well, this is the best it is going to get," she remarked.

A knock sounded at the door.

"Enter," called Maura, her heart pounding.

A Bhuttanian slave entered with a tray of finger foods and mulled wine.

Not looking at the empress, the slave put the tray down and kowtowed, waiting for the empress to grant permission to withdraw.

Disappointed that it had not been Dorak, Maura nibbled on a piece of fruit and began humming a tune. Not knowing what to do, she drifted into the sitting room and picked up one of the various manuscripts left on the table.

Startled at the contents, she picked up another. Each one she opened contained love stories with strong erotic overtones. Some even had explicit drawings accompanying them. The love stories were from Hasan Daegian myths, but the drawings were a new element.

Hearing loud footsteps in the hallway, she dropped the drawings and fled into the bedroom, ashamed of herself for being embarrassed. Maura had to smile.

Such sexual material was usually reserved for older married Hasan Daegian women who collected love stories and shared their contents with their younger and shy husbands.

However, was she not the empress of the Bhuttanian Empire? She could read what she wanted.

Maura could not sit still. The stories and their illustrations had inflamed and aroused her.

More footfalls sounded in the hallway. Listening intently, the echoing sounds passed her suite.

Disappointed, Maura sank into the fluffy mattress and listened to the night sounds of the city.

"You are not asleep, are you?" asked Dorak, languishing in the doorway.

Maura jumped. "I did not hear you come in," she said, her words rushing together.

"I know," grinned Dorak.

Maura frowned. She hated the way he kept her off-kilter.

Dorak turned around in full circle. "You like?" he asked, pointing to his outfit. He was wearing a loose-fitting tunic made of the same material as her gown. His long black hair was loose from its usual tight braids and brushed to a lustrous shine. This only added to the allure of his penetrating eyes outlined in kohl. Dorak's feet were encased in simple peasant sandals, but Maura could not help but notice that his toenails sparkled with designs made of gold foil.

Maura looked at Dorak in surprise.

These Hasan Daegian gestures of male beauty were considered decadent for a Bhuttanian warrior.

Behind him, Dorak dragged a little cart laden with beautifully wrapped gifts.

Maura stared stupidly at the gifts.

"I was told the bride and groom exchange gifts on their wedding night. Is this not correct?"

"Yes, yes, it is," stammered Maura, "but I didn't expect you to follow this custom."

Dorak pretended to pout. "Does this mean you have no gifts for me?"

Flustered, Maura began fiddling with the bows on her robe. "I have only one gift."

"Well," said Dorak, looking about the room. "Where is it?"

Maura went to the dressing table and held out a small pouch beautifully embroidered with the uultepes and the Bogazkoy tree.

Dorak stared for a moment at the uultepes entwined around the Bogazkoy. "There is that interesting shrub again. Like the one of which I found the remains in the cave under the palace." Dorak squinted at

Maura, whose face became impassive at the mention of the Bogazkoy.

Maura forged a beguiling smile.

Dorak frowned. "You are simpering again," he replied, feeling the weave of the pouch. "Not your style at all."

Chastised, Maura plopped down onto the bed and sank into the moss-filled mattress.

Dorak laughed as he took a running jump and landed down beside her.

For a few seconds, they both bobbed on the soft, springy bed.

Dorak let out a raucous laugh. He gave his new bride a little shove on the shoulder. "Oh, don't be so serious. I'm not going to hurt you," he declared. Dorak winked. "At least, not tonight," he said, his eyes casting a smoldering look at her.

"That is reassuring."

"I should think you are damned lucky that I made you my wife and empress to boot and did not throw you in the dungeon."

"That would be hard as we have no dungeons in Hasan Daeg."

Dorak raised an eyebrow. "An oversight I will have to correct."

Maura grimaced at his suggestion.

"I do not wish to discuss gloomy topics tonight. Being seated next to that boring priest for most of the afternoon was punishment enough. We have the rest of our lives to test our wits against each other, my dear wife. Let us enjoy each other tonight. Tomorrow will bring what it will."

"Agreed," said Maura, somewhat relaxed. She extended her hand and grabbed Dorak around the wrist. "Not enemies tonight."

Dorak grabbed her by the wrist and shook firmly. "Friends tonight and lovers in every sense of the word."

Blushing, Maura withdrew her hand. "Go ahead and open it," she urged, glancing at the pouch.

Dorak pulled open the pouch. He emptied the contents into his hands.

Out fell a ring. It was small but exquisite in workmanship.

Dorak leaned into the lamplight to get a better look at it.

Maura reached over and snatched the ring from Dorak's palm. She gingerly placed it on each of his fingers until she found one that it fit. "This was the ring my mother gave my father on their betrothal. Do you like it?"

"I am touched that you would give me a gift of such importance to you," replied Dorak, admiring the ring. "What did the ring represent to your parents?"

"The emerald represented my mother and the smaller ruby, my father."

"No," laughed Dorak. "The emerald should have been the man. You Hasan Daegians get everything backwards." He smiled warmly at her. "I am very honored. Thank you."

Maura eyed the wagon full of gifts. "What did you get me?" she asked with childlike glee.

Struggling to climb out of the spongy bed, Dorak was helped by his bride who pushed on his backside. Laughing, he tiptoed over to the wagon and pulled it close. Dorak piled gifts in Maura's lap.

"Which one should I open first?" asked Maura, picking up boxes and shaking them.

"This one," coaxed Dorak, handing her a gaily-wrapped package.

Maura tore open the wrapping and discovered a beautiful sheer negligee inside.

Tiny seed pearls were sewn onto the sheer black material. "It is wonderful!" exclaimed Maura, holding it up to her torso. "Oh," she said, disappointed. "It makes my skin look too dull."

"Nonsense," said Dorak, gently stroking the material. "It makes you look sensuous."

"Does it, Dorak?" She blinked at the gown. "Somehow, I think this gift is more for you."

"I hope we can both enjoy it." He grinned widely. "Open another one."

Unwrapping a small box, Maura discovered a pair of simple earrings carved out of plain wood.

"These were my mother's," explained Dorak upon seeing Maura's bewildered expression. "This was the only possession she was able to take from her village when she was kidnapped by . . ."

"Your father," Maura finished.

Dorak nodded. "Yes. She wore these nearly every day of her life. One moment, she was a simple girl minding her father's young borax calves in the pasture, and the next, she was wrenched onto a snorting, stampeding horse while watching her village torched. Then she became the Empress of Bhuttan. End of story." Dorak looked saddened by his tale. "I know they do not have the worth of your betrothal ring, but the sentiment is the same."

"Why did she not come to the wedding?"

Dorak smiled bitterly. "She died years ago."

Maura wished to inquire further, but she could see that talking about his mother was difficult for Dorak. She needed him to be in good spirits tonight. Taking out her garnet earrings, she replaced them with the wooden posts. "How do they look?"

"Like they belong to an empress." Dorak smiled, not a mischievous grin or a lecherous glance, but a warm, expressive smile that was without guile.

Maura was overtaken by the masculine beauty that gave Dorak an aura of being strong and true when not posturing.

Dorak took Maura's hand. "I know that we have talked about nothing but our differences. We have argued over policy and debated over political issues. During all this frustrating time, never once did I tire of seeing your face. Never once when you were shouting at me did I wish to be gone out of sight from your angry eyes. I never wanted to send you away."

He stared down at the ring. "It would have been safer and easier for me to banish you or to have you killed." Dorak leaned down and kissed Maura's hand. "But I swear on my mother, I never seriously considered it. I desired you near me as I desire you now." He leaned over and softly kissed his bride on the lips. "Will you have me of your own free will?"

Maura heard herself say, "Yes, I take you of my own free will." Her words inflamed Dorak, and he kissed her more passionately. He stopped abruptly, looking at Maura with wondering eyes.

"Kiss me again, please, Dorak."

Dorak took Maura in his arms. He gently kissed her forehead, cheeks, and throat. Turning her head, he gave baby kisses down the back of her long neck. Encouraged by her soft moans, Dorak continued down Maura's spine, kissing through the fabric of her robe.

Reaching up under the gown, he massaged her buttocks, slowly working his way between her legs.

Maura remained still as her breathing became heavier. She called out his name, her voice raspy.

Able to stand it no longer, Dorak tore the robe and gown off and began caressing Maura's bare skin.

Maura turned toward him, returning his fondling. Roughly, she pulled off his tunic and reached for his manhood, pulling him toward her.

Dorak groaned and followed her commands.

Pleased, Maura pulled Dorak on top of her and began to tease him with the grinding of her hips.

For hours, they made love play, teasing, licking, kissing, and murmuring endearments. Long into the night and early morning, they pleasured each other with touch only.

Finally, Dorak could endure no more and entered Maura.

Maura raked her fingers through his long, dark hair.

Abruptly, Dorak stopped and seemed bewildered.

"What's wrong?" asked Maura, confused at the interruption. "Are you hurt?"

Dorak's face was sour as he put his head down on her shoulder. "No. Let us continue," he answered, his voice vague and troubling.

Realizing Dorak had changed, Maura tried to see into his eyes.

Dorak turned his face away and began moving upon her.

She tried to stop him, but he refused until he gave a strangled cry of release. He collapsed away from her.

Perplexed, Maura reached out to him, but Dorak jerked away. "What is it?" asked Maura in a hurt tone.

"Nothing. Go to sleep," replied Dorak coldly.

Her emotions tangled in a knot, Maura rolled over. Hot, salty tears ran down her face.

Why did Dorak change? All through the night, he had been a caring, considerate lover.

Maura felt his emotions had run deeper than she had anticipated. Then he abruptly changed to a cold, almost hostile partner. Her mind raced over the events of the night. She could think of nothing to cause this reaction.

What had she done?

Exhausted with worry, Maura finally drifted into a restless sleep.

Hearing her rhythmic, ragged breathing, Dorak turned toward her. He touched her damp tresses fanned out on the pillows, thinking of the yellow-haired woman from Anqara and her flaming eyes of hate. Dorak looked at Maura tossing in her troubled sleep and wondered. Would Maura come to hate him as well?

He stroked her cheek lightly, knowing that she would never forgive him for humiliating her so. "You little fool," he said softly. "Why didn't you tell me?"

16

Maura awoke the next morning.

Dorak was not beside her.

Swinging her legs over the side of the bed, she groaned. Pulling a rope, the new bride slumped back against the massive wooden headboard carved with the royal crest of the House of de Magela.

The Bhuttanian girl who had nursed Dorak knocked on the bedroom door and entered. She looked around the room sullenly and bowed.

Bhuttanian custom dictated that she should have kowtowed, but Maura chose to ignore the insult. "Please call for Lady Sari," Maura commanded in an even-handed tone. "I wish for a massage."

The slave girl did not cast her soulful eyes to the floor, as was the custom for all Bhuttanian women, but looked directly at the empress. "Sari has been put to bed by the female doctor. She is not allowed to move for several days."

"You may address my nurse as Lady Sari, as is her title. She has a lineage the likes of which your family has never seen, nor will. You are to address me as Great Mother or Empress Maura. If you dare to look at me directly again, especially with those impertinent eyes, I shall slice off a bit of your ear and feed it to you."

The slave scowled at Maura.

They were both the same age, but Maura easily towered over the little nomadic female. Maura knew that even reclining in a bed, she looked imposing.

Still, the girl had courage and spoke her mind. "The Great Aga will not let you touch me!" she spat defiantly.

Maura's fears that this sapling of a girl had been Dorak's bedmate were confirmed, or the little wench would never have dared to speak to her in such a manner. Feeling a spasm of jealousy, Maura swallowed the bile rising from her stomach. "The Great Aga is not always around. Accidents can happen. He would hardly chastise his wife and empress if a slave girl's ear, or worse, got in the way of my dinner knife." Maura let her words sink in. "Think about it, my dear. Make life easy on yourself," said Maura smiling sympathetically at the fuming slave.

The girl, so filled with anger, could not utter a word and stormed out of the room.

Sighing, Maura donned her robe and went into the hallway where her guards stood.

They snapped to attention as soon as they saw their queen.

Pointing to the young slave muttering as she stomped down the hallway, Maura said, "That girl is never to come close to my person or food again. If she does, kill her."

Several of the female soldiers ran down the hallway and stopped the slave, who protested vehemently. They stored the frightened girl's height, weight, features, and coloring in their memories. As soon as they had burned her image into their minds, they apologized for detaining her.

The girl ran down the hallway, stumbling over jugs and water bags left by the Bhuttanian guards on watch the previous night.

Maura's guards returned and waited for further instructions.

"Inform my servants that I wish to have a bath prepared for me. I want my breakfast tray now."

One of the guards stepped forward. "Perhaps the Great Mother has forgotten that a wedding breakfast has been prepared and is awaiting only the attendance of the bride."

Maura's face went momentarily blank and then took on the expression of one who has received a piece of bad news. "Yes, I had forgotten. Thank you for reminding me," said Maura slowly. "Have my servants attend me. I should make haste. Please relate to Aga Dorak that I have risen and will attend shortly." Maura tried to act nonchalantly. "Where is Aga Dorak?"

"He awaits you in the dining hall, Great Mother. He is talking with guests."

"Of course," Maura responded.

Seeing Bhuttanian soldiers march down the hallway, she hurried inside the apartment and waited for her servants. It wasn't long before her Hasan Daegian attendants scurried into the room to wait upon their newlywed empress.

Being Hasan Daegian, they liked to talk about acts of love but were disappointed when Maura said nothing regarding her wedding night. According to Hasan Daegian custom, the bride would relate anecdotes regarding her husband's prowess in bed. It was considered a sign of respect to boast about one's bedmate.

Hasan Daegian bridegrooms looked forward to hearing the gossip of their mating feats that would follow for weeks after their wedding night.

It was very *Bhuttanian* of Maura to be so reticent and even considered rude.

Although they knew the new empress would have to compromise here and there, the noblewomen hoped she wasn't going native on them.

Maura was soon ready and hurried to the dining hall.

A gong sounded her entrance as she proceeded into the great chamber, looking calm and poised.

With two guards flanking her, Maura acknowledged well wishes and made her way to the royal table. As she did so, she scanned the room for Dorak. Locating him next to her aunt, the Duchess Everlynd, she smiled broadly.

As Maura approached the table, he sprang to meet her and extended his hand to help her into her chair. Maura studied Dorak closely. The anger that she had felt from him last night was nowhere to be found on his handsome face shining in the morning sun. Confused, Maura sat. Seeing Dorak so radiant, Maura could not but suffer that her husband was more handsome than she, causing her to compare herself to a molting Dini chick.

Dorak tapped his goblet with a jewel-encrusted knife that had been brought from his father's tent.

Everyone became quiet.

"You may be seated," Dorak said good-naturedly as he stood next to Maura. "I hope all of you had more of a restful evening than I did."

The Hasan Daegian guests politely twittered as the Bhuttanians remained stone-faced.

The laughter inspired the aga to continue. "I wish to take this time to express my great happiness with this union, both personally and politically. I arose early this morning to compose a song for my bride."

Dorak looked expectantly at Maura. "I did not have time to write any words, but here is the melody. I hope it expresses what I feel."

Dorak motioned for the master flutist to approach the royal table.

The flutist wet her lips and raised an oiled-smoothed instrument to her mouth. She began playing a lovely song that was both sweet and sad. The notes turned and twisted in the air, hanging for a few captivating seconds before they floated up to the stained glass windows and out into the busy city.

Maura closed her eyes, thinking of beautiful bubbles shining with iridescent color as they circled shafts of sunlight and then dissipated into the fresh morning air. She opened her eyes only to discover Dorak staring at her with his brilliant eyes seemingly violent in their intensity. Maura quickly looked away. Did she imagine the last disappointing moments of their lovemaking? Perhaps that was the way with Bhuttanian men. *NO! NO! I must trust my instincts,* Maura thought. Dorak had been angry with her. She was sure of it.

Blonde hair swirled before her, and Maura focused on the Anqarian woman who had surfaced in public again. The woman's eyes looked dull as if she was drugged, and her jaw fell slack, giving her mouth a droopy appearance.

Dorak's elderly cousin was with her, but paid little attention, as he seemed enthralled with the music. He noticed the empress looking at their table and gave a friendly smile as he nodded. Then he turned his attention back to the flutist. Finally, the musician finished.

The Hasan Daegians clapped politely while the more enthusiastic Bhuttanians pounded the tables with their hands and whistled.

Realizing that words of appreciation were expected from her, Maura rose. "Good people, it is glad I am that you are present to share my joy. I thank my husband for another wonderful wedding gift. My head is reeling from all that he has bestowed upon me the last several days, especially last night."

Dorak's smile froze on his face.

Maura continued, "But I know that you are hungry, so I will not detain you further by remarking on my husband's amazing attributes, so let's have the morning feast."

Servants brought out trays of freshly baked flatbread, bowls of cooked grain, buns, and morning cakes. Pots of boiled gootee eggs and trays of ripe fruit were so heavy that several women were needed to carry each one out to the awaiting guests.

Jugs of shaybar, the Bhuttanian staple of boiled milk mixed with borax blood, were poured. The Hasan Daegians politely took a sip of the shaybar, quietly gagged, and then returned to their wine and fruit juices.

The breakfast dragged on with the Bhuttanians giving toasts to the couple and singing old Bhuttanian love songs, which sounded like war stories to the more cultivated Hasan Daegians.

As the morning sun drifted into the afternoon sky, Dorak made his excuses for them both and escorted Maura out of the great hall. Once in the back corridor and away from prying eyes, Dorak handed Maura unceremoniously over to Rubank, who had been waiting patiently.

"Where are you going?"

"I have duties to attend," Dorak replied flatly.

"We need to talk,"

"About what, my lady?"

"Last night, our future, everything," retorted Maura, frustrated at Dorak's coldness.

Rubank retreated to a discrete portion of the hallway.

"There is nothing to discuss."

"There is everything to discuss."

Dorak shot her an angry look and, taking her by the elbow, jerked her farther down the hall. "This is not the place nor the time to discuss anything. Nor will I be shouted at by a woman who acts like a fishmonger's wife even if she is the empress."

"How dare you speak to me like that!"

Dorak leaned close to Maura's face. "I shall talk to you any way I like. I am now your husband, and you no longer have rights, but those I grant you."

"That is not true. I am the queen of Hasan Daeg. I have independent rights."

Dorak sneered. "You have nothing, my lady. You should have studied Bhuttanian customs a little closer. You accepted being my empress; therefore, you lost all rights concerning Hasan Daeg. I am now the legal ruler here."

"You bastard!" declared Maura, her fists clenched at her side, ready to strike. Instead, she grabbed his arm, pushing Dorak against the wall with her weight. "That is why the coronation was a surprise!"

"Such tender words from a devoted wife." Dorak motioned to Rubank. "Escort the empress to her chambers and keep her company. I will return this evening to do my husbandly duty."

Rubank looked nervously between Maura and Dorak, not knowing what to do. His face was heavy with confusion.

"You mean to rape me. That's all you Bhuttanians know. Rape.

Destruction."

"Are you implying that you were raped last night?" Dorak's face turned crimson, and his lips curled back, giving his face a snarling appearance. "It would be a hard contest to violate you, my lady, when your legs are so readily open."

Maura gasped and struck out.

Dorak caught her hand and encircled her wrist, squeezing mercilessly.

Maura grimaced at the pain, but would not cry out.

Dorak brought all his strength to bear upon Maura. "On your knees before me," he rasped, his voice lined with hate.

The blood rushed from Maura's face and, for a few seconds, her face was as pale as any Anqarian's. The transformation startled Dorak enough to loosen his grip, allowing Maura to break free. Breathlessly, they glared at each other with eyes filled with disappointment and deep pain.

Embarrassed by his lack of control, Dorak pulled his leather gloves from his belt and again waved to Rubank. "Take your mistress to her rooms," he commanded, trying to insert normalcy in his voice.

"How like a Bhuttanian to use a servant to vent his anger upon," sneered Maura. "Do you not see, Rubank, that we both have been ambushed? This is a little game Bhuttanians like to play. If you obey Dorak, then I will kill you because it means you have changed your loyalty. If you disobey, Dorak will have you killed for not following his orders as he is now legally the sovereign of Hasan Daeg, or so that is what he claims. Still, if nothing occurs, your loyalty to me will be in doubt, and I will never trust you again. I will be asking myself why you were waiting in this particular hallway? Why did Dorak single you out to escort me back to my rooms and not my guards? Were you to assassinate me? Put a quiet little knife in the back of my neck?"

Stricken, Rubank lowered his eyes and shook his head, seemingly more from sadness than denial.

Dorak laughed bitterly. "I am not the only one who plays games, eh, my sweet?"

Maura tore her gaze from Rubank's grief-lined face. "I do not know what you mean."

Dorak twisted a twig of Maura's hair between his thumb and index finger. "I think you do, but we will discuss it tonight. I have to go."

Maura pulled away. "Go then. And let the devil take you."

Dorak feigned surprise. "How very Anqarian of you. It must have been the House of Magi's influence upon you."

Before Maura could deny his subtle accusation, Dorak began whistling the composition he had written for her and jaunted down the hallway.

Maura turned her fury upon Rubank, who stood shivering.

Without hesitation, Rubank began undressing and threw his robes, one by one, at Maura's feet.

She picked them up and examined the costly robes carefully, looking for hidden weapons.

Standing naked before her, Rubank lifted his genitals showing his queen that he had not hidden any weapons or poisons and then turned, spreading his buttocks apart.

Satisfied that his anus did not appear swollen or glisten with lubrication, Maura called Rubank over to her.

He knelt before her and opened his mouth. Wrapping the cloth from one of his robes around her finger, she examined Rubank's mouth, looking for pouches or strings tied to one of his molars. All that was in Rubank's mouth were his teeth.

Both of them, stunned at Dorak's treachery and their mutual fear, remained still as though transfigured into stone.

Maura felt Rubank's lips upon her feet, the Hasan Daegian gesture for forgiveness, and jerked away from his touch.

Rubank let out a sound from his tongueless mouth that would cause pity even in the heart of the bravest Bhuttanian warrior. His cry was one of agony and of dreams shattered.

Ashamed, Maura fled Rubank and, upon entering her private chambers, crouched in a corner and cried until the bodice of her dress was drenched with her blue-tinted tears.

Hours later, her servants found her lying on the floor and put Maura to bed.

Meagan of Skujpor was summoned. The healer ran so fast that her cumbersome bosom bounced painfully, but no one laughed as they saw the Magi physician racing toward the empress' private rooms with one hand holding her breasts in place and the other gripping her medical bag.

Even the Bhuttanian guards stepped out of the way for the out-of-breath healer, whom they had grown to respect for saving so many of their own.

Hearing that the empress was ill, Dorak's slave girl ran to Maura's quarters to check for herself. Poking her head inside the bedchamber, she spied Maura looking drawn and pale. Delighted, the girl pranced out of the room and gleefully went about her duties for the rest the day, not aware that a Hasan Daegian guard was shadowing her every move. In the evening, she was found in a laundry basket with her throat slit.

The news of the slave girl's discovery was whispered into Maura's ear. Immediately, Maura's eyes fluttered open, and the empress struggled to sit up. Her throat parched, she greedily drank from a goblet that Meagan held to her lips. Seeing that the empress wished to speak to her in private, Meagan shooed everyone out of the chamber.

"Where is Dorak?" croaked Maura, her voice hoarse.

"He went to visit the army's encampment beyond the city. There are rumors that the Bhuttanians are preparing to move out."

"To where?"

Meagan replied, "I was bandaging the leg of a captain who has gout. He did not realize that I speak Bhuttanian, and I overheard him talking to his next-in-command. He didn't seem to know. He just knew the bulk of the army was going to relocate."

"So Dorak lied to me the entire time."

Meagan lowered her voice. "Maybe not. Perhaps it was this morning's altercation that brought about a change in his mood."

"Does everyone know of our lover's spat?"

"The Bhuttanian girl who nursed Dorak followed you and saw the entire disagreement. She lost no time in telling Bhuttanian servants who then related the story to those Hasan Daegians who understood Anqarian. Of course, we don't know for sure what she related was true, but the fact you were rolling on the floor again would indicate some of what she was spreading might be true."

"I am glad the little bitch is dead."

Meagan merely shrugged. "I certainly won't lose any sleep over her absence. She never changed Dorak's bandages properly. It so irritated me that she would not follow my instructions."

"Poor Rubank. Dorak and I have disgraced him."

"Rubank is a servant of the Royal House of de Magela. He is used to sacrificing."

Maura interjected, "Will he ever forgive me?"

"Forgiveness may not be coming for a very long time, but what choice did you have? You can trust no one. You are now the wife of the Bhuttanian Aga, the most powerful and hated man in the world. A lot of people want to see you dead. And if you die, what will happen to the Hasan Daegians? There is no offspring to take your place. You are the last of the de Magelas. You must survive! It is imperative!"

"Trust no one. Not even you, Meagan of Skujpor?"

Meagan returned Maura's sad gaze. "No one," she mouthed silently. After a short pause, she turned to the business, which was foremost on her mind. "Why do you go into a sort of coma every time you have an altercation with Dorak? These trances must stop. You must be able to rouse yourself quickly after a stressful episode with this man. These fits put you in danger."

"I do not think they have anything to do with Dorak. He may only be a conductor."

"What do you mean?" asked Meagan who forgetting protocol, as usual, sat on the edge of the bed.

"I do not put myself in these trances. I feel compelled to slip into the dream world. I am convinced the Black Cacodemon is on the palace premises somewhere so that he can be close to me. I think he acts through Dorak without Dorak's knowledge. As I said, Dorak acts as a conductor. The wizard feeds upon my fear. He uses my own emotions against me."

"The palace has been searched. The Black Cacodemon is not inside the premises. No one has seen him since the fall of O Konya."

"Sari thought she heard him laughing in the courtyard after the duel."

Meagan looked at Maura doubtfully.

"I am telling you that he is somewhere on the palace grounds." Maura struggled to get out of bed and fell back against the headboard. Rubbing the sides of her temples, she tried to clear her head of the fog that seemed to impede her thinking. "What time is it?"

Meagan rubbed the empress' body with a soothing lotion. "It is after dark."

"Dorak will expect me to be in the bridal chamber."

"You are still going to meet Dorak after this morning?" asked Meagan, alarmed.

"I cannot give him an excuse to imprison me. I must not let him see me defeated. Help me please."

Meagan gave Maura a stimulant, which would help her to move without sluggishness. With Meagan's help, she dressed and combed her tangled hair. Squaring her shoulders, the determined empress entered the hallway and, moving in step with her guards, returned to the bridal suite where she knew Dorak would come for her sooner or later.

The empress waited in the chamber.

For two days, Dorak did not appear. On the third day, Dorak returned. He sauntered into the bedroom with an air of jocularity until he spied the wagon full of gifts still unopened. "You have not opened these," he said.

Maura gave him a look of disgust. "As if they mean anything."

"If they do not, it is because of your treachery!" Dorak cried. He seemed on the edge of losing control as he paced about the room.

Maura studied him.

His face was unshaven, and his clothes were stained with dollops of food.

"I don't understand you, Dorak. One moment, you seem calm and at peace. The next, you are babbling nonsense." Maura went over to him by the window and gently touched his shoulder. "I thought our night together was special. We were like a real husband and wife. You were so gentle and caring that I thought . . ."

Dorak interrupted, "You thought what?"

Maura took note of the warning in Dorak's voice. "That perhaps we could care for one another, but you turned on me. I know not what for. You hurt me. Look!" Maura rolled back the sleeve of her gown and showed the bruises, which colored her arm.

Dorak winced when he saw the bruises and turned away, looking upon the city. "I am sorry that I hurt you. I was angry."

"But why?" asked Maura, who could feel the beginning of tears in the making.

"You were not a virgin!" cried Dorak, slamming himself against the wall. He sank down to the floor and put his head into his rough-looking hands. "By Bhuttanian custom, I should have you executed."

Maura stood rooted to the floor, stunned.

Dorak moaned and pounded his leg with his fist.

Maura came out of her stupor and grabbed Dorak's hand, placing it between her breasts.

Dorak let out a small sob.

"I do not understand, Dorak. Please help me."

Dorak lifted his face. There was no malice or cunning stalking the lines of his face, only pain. "Bhuttanian law requires virgin females for all husbands, especially the royalty. Any woman found not to be chaste is stoned to death by her husband's relatives. This is how we ensure the bloodline through the male."

"I am not Bhuttanian." Maura sank beside Dorak and leaned

against his shoulder. "I never told you that I was a virgin. You never asked me."

"You were the only daughter of the ruling queen. I assumed you were unspoiled."

"Dorak," said Maura, trying to keep her voice even. "Ruling queens don't marry until after the age of three hundred. Did you expect that there would be three hundred-year-old virgins?" Maura started to laugh. "I mean, just think of it, who could stand living like that? Besides, we expect the males to be virgins . . . not the females." Maura threw back her head and let the laughter escape unchecked.

Dorak shook her angrily. "This is not a game. You could lose your life over this."

Maura could not stop laughing. She felt hysterical. "I am not killed for trying to destroy you. I am not killed in battle. I am not killed because I am queen. I am not killed because I pose a threat to your throne. My death will be because I had sex before I met you." Maura broke out in new peals of laughter. "Oh, this is too much. I mean, I don't know what stoning is, but I imagine that it has to do with rocks that are used in a most unpleasant way. Ha, Ha, Ha!"

Dorak held Maura close and rocked her like a small child. Laying her head against his chest, she was comforted by the musky, outdoor smell that always accompanied him.

"If you are going to kill me, then let me at least die as a warrior. Let me end my life with honor." She hiccupped. "This custom of yours is most cruel and barbaric. To demand of women that they not make love until they wed is hideous. Most hideous."

"It has been the way of our people for centuries." Dorak kissed the top of her head.

Maura felt his warm breath on her skin.

"Who knows of this lover?" asked Dorak.

"I do not know who knew. We were trying to keep it a secret until after the war."

"That is good that it was hidden. Tell me your lover's name."

Maura stiffened in Dorak's arms. "If I tell you, then it would not be a secret any longer."

"You would protect this man even if it means your life?" asked Dorak incredulously.

Maura pushed her way out of Dorak's arms and faced him. "You have no intention of killing the queen of Hasan Daeg. Without me, there would be total insurrection. You need me, and we both know it.

You want to know his name for your own reasons, to hurt someone I love. I will not let you hurt anyone that I love ever again!"

Dorak pulled Maura to her feet and threw her across the room. She landed with a dull thud. Defiant, she continued, "I am Hasan Daegian. Your laws did not apply to me until after you conquered my territory. If you kill me, it will be seen as murder, but you don't care about any of that. You are just crazy with jealousy!"

"Was it Chaun Maaun? Was it?" Enraged, Dorak fell upon Maura and pounded his fists upon her chest and stomach.

Pinned down by Dorak's weight, she reached behind her and felt for an object. Picking up something heavy from the floor, Maura swung and hit Dorak in the forehead.

The blow stunned him long enough for Maura to lift her leg and kick Dorak hard in the stomach.

Grunting, Dorak fell back with a loud thump.

Knowing she could not risk seriously harming Dorak, Maura scrambled for the door only to have Dorak tackle her. Maura flipped on her back so she could have her hands free to block his punches.

"You crazy spawn of a bastard. You show your true colors at last! You are insane!" Maura cried out. Tasting blood in her mouth, she spat in Dorak's face, infuriating him more.

He grabbed her hair and began banging her head against the floor.

Believing that Dorak was angry enough to kill her, Maura could hear her guards pounding on the door. She had to stay alive until they could get into the locked room. She wrapped her powerful legs around Dorak's waist and flipped him over as she grabbed onto his nose and gave it an awful twist.

His nose ring ripped through the fleshy part of his nostril. Dorak howled with pain. His hands flew up to cradle his bleeding face.

Losing no time, Maura hit him in the neck to disable him, but the blow was not strong enough to put him under.

Reeling from Dorak's pummeling, Maura crawled away from him and pulled herself up on a divan. Out of the corner of her eye, she saw Dorak make for her again. She swung around and kicked him in the groin as hard as she could.

Dorak stumbled but still came at her. There was murder in his eyes.

Maura had never felt so terrified, even in battle.

Battle was impersonal, but Dorak wanted to kill her, his wife, in a blind rage over what she considered a trifle.

Maura flung herself at the door and twisted the knob in desperate hope. It would not turn. She was trapped. Turning, she faced Dorak as he stalked her. His face was dark and menacing, wild with confusion. "Dorak, please don't," Maura pleaded. "You do not know what you are doing. If you kill me, the entire city will rise. O Konya will be as Anqara, and all of your work will be for naught."

Dorak halted at the sound of her terrified voice. His face became unclouded as his black eyes focused on her swelling and bloody face. His face felt wet as he wiped his hand across it. It was smeared with red blood . . . his blood. Dorak's mouth fell open in disbelief. He stepped back from her. "What am I doing?" Dorak gasped.

The Hasan Daegian guards burst into the room through the balcony on ropes tied from the rooftop. Seeing their queen flattened against the door, they ran to her, throwing furniture out of the way. More Hasan Daegian guards dropped onto the balcony and quickly surrounded Dorak. One of the guards took out a dagger hidden in her boot and started to approach Dorak.

"NO!" cried Maura as she blocked the guard's arm. "Leave him be. Just get me out of here. Take me to Lady Sari."

The largest of the guards picked Maura up in her arms and carried her away.

Hearing Bhuttanian boots rushing on the stone floor, the guards ran the other way toward Sari's quarters.

Watching them flee, Dorak slumped against the door jamb, bellowing, "MAURA, DON'T LEAVE ME!"

17

Sari's apartment was not spacious.

Still, it was of adequate size and comfortable with plush furniture. A young girl of eight opened the door as the guards rushed in carrying the queen. The little girl's eyes widened, and she hurried to Sari's bedside crying, "Oh, my lady, the empress is here to see you! She looks as though she has had a fall!"

Sari had been resting comfortably in her bed when she heard the commotion in the next room. She rose quickly and put on her robe with the little girl's help. With the aid of a cane and the girl, Sari hobbled into her sitting room. The old woman clutched at the collar of her robe when she saw the queen, battered and beaten, sitting in one of her rocking chairs. "What happened?"

Maura dismissed her bruises and cuts with a wave of her hand and bade Sari to sit.

The Hasan Daegian guards faced the door, ready for anything amiss. They would not fail their mistress as they had in the sacred grove of her ancestors.

The little girl gave several of them a start when she came up behind them and began fondling their clothes and armor, her mouth opened in amazement.

"Nani, get away from those women. You bother them," Sari scolded.

Nani returned a mischievous grin that showed her missing several of her front teeth.

One of the guards smiled back at her, but only for an instant.

The little girl skipped over to Sari's chair, where she casually plopped down at the woman's feet.

"Who is this?" Maura asked.

"This is my adoptive daughter, Nani, who will take Mikkotto's place as head of the family as my grandchildren have been disinherited. Nani is a distant kinswoman and has Sumsumitoyo blood."

Maura hid her surprise that Sari had spoken Mikkotto's name.

Sari, who had abdicated her position as matriarch of her family to serve the de Magelas, had not spoken her granddaughter's name to anyone since Mikkotto had thrown down the family's ancestral fan in the Council of Elders and Nobles.

Maura grunted her approval in Bhuttanian fashion and paid the girl scant attention.

"Dorak do this?"

"If you think I look bad, you should see him," replied Maura, trying to sound jovial.

"This attack," asked Sari, putting her words together carefully, "was unprovoked?"

"He hit me first if that is what you are asking."

"Then perhaps nothing more will come of it. It was just another Bhuttanian husband chastising his wife."

"This was a beating," corrected Maura, touching her left eye, which had swollen shut. "Dorak has had opportunity to use force with me before, but he has always chosen the quieter path. This is a rash act, even for him."

Sari thoughtfully folded her hands in her lap as she considered the situation. "Perhaps now that he is your husband, he thinks he may do as he pleases."

"I think he intends to kill me."

"For what purpose?" inquired Sari, not believing Maura's theory. "With you, he has everything. Without you, he will struggle to hang on even with the help of the Black Cacodemon."

Maura leaned forward in her chair. The hair stood on her arms, and the moist air suddenly seemed chilled. "You did not see his eyes, Sari. He was truly mad."

Sari unfolded her smoking pouch, offering some to her queen.

Maura made a cheroot from the herbs and various papers presented for her selection.

Sari made herself one, which Nani gaily lit.

While considering her predicament, Maura watched the smoke drift toward the wooden beams that supported the ceiling. She waited for Sari to speak.

"I am not a wise woman like those from the House of Magi, but I have lived for many years. Dorak's actions are not what they appear." Sari drew on her cheroot. "Perhaps there is another explanation."

"What do you mean?"

"I have discovered the identity of the blonde Anqarian woman." She paused for effect.

"Well?"

Sari settled back in her chair. "The woman is Princess Jezra. She is one of the few survivors from Anqara before the siege started. Her father was one of the most distinguished bankers until he fell in disgrace."

"Why is that?"

"He is said to have left Anqara with his family and all his belongings several weeks before Zoar showed up at the city gates."

"Could be a coincidence."

"I hardly think so with the man's daughter appearing at the marriage ceremony. Many say that her father loaned much of the his wealth to Zoar to finance wars, and with this, he bought the safety of himself and his family. Jezra was his only child and is rumored to be like her deceased father, intelligent and ruthless."

"But why would that cause her to look at me with such hate?"

Sari was very tired by all the palace intrigue. "Little sparrow. Dorak has addled your brain. I said she was called Princess Jezra. Anqara has no royal family. The city was ruled by a democratic council with a mayor at the head. One is only a princess by birth or by marriage to a prince."

Maura realized the implications of Sari's words, and the knowledge screamed through her mind like a howling banshee. "She is Dorak's wife!"

"Yes," said Sari sympathetically. "And the child with the dark river eyes is Dorak's firstborn. He is the child Jezra wishes to see ascend to the throne of Bhuttan. Make no mistake, she is your dangerous opponent, and she is not bound by the honor code of a warrior."

Leaning back in her chair rocking, Maura inhaled deeply the sweet smoke of her cheroot. "I don't feel my heart anymore."

"It's a shock, I know."

"You think Jezra put Dorak up to this?"

"No," Sari said emphatically. "I think it is a possibility she may have slipped something in Dorak's wine to make him aggressive, but I do not think she has any influence over him. He did not seem pleased to see her at the wedding."

"Whatever the reason, I must be away from here," said Maura, her voice sounding odd.

"You must go to the Mother Bogazkoy."

"Yes, you are right," the empress murmured, gazing at her hands as if in a drunken stupor. Her mind reeled from the day's events. Images of Iegani and Gitar whistled through her mind. She saw Yeti taking her out flying over the high cliffs and then dropping her thousands of feet with only a nervous Tarsus to catch her as she fell through the clouds. That was to make her tough and trust the Dinii as she trusted nothing else. She saw her mother observing tutors as they worked with her, and her father teaching her to lace her sandals. So many people had spent countless hours teaching her to become a noble warrior, an astute politician, and a worthy queen. How had she repaid those who had been selfless with their time and knowledge? How many had sacrificed their lives for her? There were her parents and many more. Maura felt a deep and unrelenting shame.

"Sari, will you help me?"

"Yes, little sparrow," said Sari, observing the changes upon Maura's face.

"Even if it means great peril or the supreme sacrifice?"

Sari paused for a moment. Her face became mottled with emotion. "I live only to serve the House of de Magela."

18

Dorak put the torch out.

"You have come."

"Yes," was all Dorak could reply.

The Black Cacodemon moved about the small windowless chamber. Dust floated beneath his black robe and drifted about the hem. "And she thinks you are mad and going to kill her?"

"Yes."

"If not you, then your harpy of a first wife. By now, word of her identity should have spread throughout the entire palace." The wizard chuckled under his foul breath.

Dorak could smell it from where he stood.

"It was brilliant to bring that woman to the wedding. I am surprised that Jezra did not scratch the Hasan Daegian bitch's eyes out the moment she saw her." The Black Cacodemon's shoulders fell as though disappointed that she hadn't. "And the whining that you didn't mean to hit her was a masterful touch."

Dorak said nothing, staring belligerently at the eerie being in the black robe. He could see very little of the wizard's features. Just a sliver of cheekbone, a knotted finger pointed in the darkness, and a glimpse of pale, thin lips. Dorak restrained from shuddering.

"You have regrets?" asked the Black Cacodemon softly, his face covered by the black cowl of his robe.

Again, Dorak was silent.

"Ah," replied the Black Cacodemon. "I sense the truth unspoken in this room. You have feelings for this girl."

"She is not to be harmed," spoke Dorak forcefully, his dark eyebrows arching.

The Black Cacodemon hissed a long drawn out breath. Droplets of moisture were illuminated by a shaft of moonbeam that fell through a crack in the mortar. "I cannot guarantee this. If General Alexanee finds out that she is not a virgin, he will have no recourse but to kill her."

"The only way he will know that is if you tell him. He is going back to Kittum soon, so I don't see that as a problem, do you?"

"Still, it was a good reason to put her on guard. Let us hope she runs tonight."

"If she does, all we will do is follow."

The Black Cacodemon made a conciliatory gesture with his hand. "Of course, we can restrain ourselves until she reaches the Mother Bogazkoy, but then she must be stopped. She must never touch the flesh of the Bogazkoy. How she is stopped is up to you, Great Aga. It may call for an arrow through the heart." The wizard circled Dorak and whispered in his ear. "Are you up to it?"

Dorak leaned away from the odious being who made his skin crawl.

The Black Cacodemon became still. "Shh, can you hear it? She is healing herself. Hear the buzz?" The black-robed man raised his head and sniffed the air. "She is healing the old one as well." He raised his hands in the night air. "Minor ailments, but it will sap her energy and slow her down."

It was Dorak's turn to laugh. "I have yet to see that."

The wizard, not liking to be mocked, spoke sharply, "This would all be unnecessary if the code from the tattoo had been broken."

"The design does not match any description found in writings from the House of Magi. I think Abisola had the royal tattoo altered to confuse us. She knew we would locate the secret in ancient manuscripts sooner or later."

The wizard inhaled the dark, moldy air deeply. "A worthy woman she was, but her triumph was small and will not last. In the end, we will learn the secret of the Bogazkoy, and its power to grant immortal life." He ran his hand along the damp walls, his long ragged nails scraping against the stone. "What of Mehmet's journals?"

"Nothing," lied Dorak, his face throbbing where Maura had hit him.

The Black Cacodemon chuckled. "She was worthless as an informant. All those years on your father's payroll, and he didn't even know she had taken a Dini as her lover. What makes the story amusing is that she spent years secretly helping your father's opponent." The wizard snorted. "Your father had such a way with women. No doubt he bedded Mehmet roughly in his youth, and she turned on him because of it. She was originally from Bhuttan, was she not?" He spread out his hands. "It would only make cosmic justice."

Dorak, not wishing to hear of his father's lovers, changed the subject. "I'm positive Maura thinks the Mother Bogazkoy will infuse her with the same power the offspring gave to Abisola. Nothing more."

"That is good. It would not do for her to realize its true potential. She would fight like a demon to gain this power."

Through the gloom, Dorak thought he could see something that might have resembled a smile, but looked like an angry slash that revealed dirty, chipped teeth. "What will happen if she does reach the Mother Bogazkoy first?"

The Black Cacodemon's head tilted toward Dorak. "We shall have to kill her immediately and drink her blood as it flows from her veins. The effect on us will not be as potent, but it could extend our lives by five hundred years, give or take."

Dorak pressed against the wall. "I will not do that!"

"Dorak, I am surprised. You have killed before. You even murdered your father while he was taking a piss."

"How do you know that?" Dorak hated this room and the stench that reeked from its walls.

"Dorak. Dorak. I know everything." The Black Cacodemon raised his cowled head and peals of laughter rippled from his throat. The cowl fell backwards exposing the wizard's misshapen, scarred head.

Dorak shrank back against the wall. He turned and blindly felt for the door. His clumsiness only encouraged the Black Cacodemon to laugh harder—high-pitched squeals combined with snorts that sounded like an animal being strangled. Dorak discovered the door lever and wrenched the door open.

As he ran down the hallway, he heard the wizard call after him, "Next time, don't be so long between visits! I do so love our little chats."

19

A drunken Bhuttanian was enticed.

He followed a half-dressed Hasan Daegian guard calling to him sweetly into a horse stall. Several minutes later, the guard emerged with the dead Bhuttanian's clothing.

Other Hasan Daegian guards stepped out of the darkness and buried the Bhuttanian under a mound of straw. In the warhorses' drinking buckets, they mixed a golden liquid with water, causing the horses to slumber. Finished with their macabre business, the guards left as quietly as they had come and melted into the darkness.

An hour or so later, the empress, wearing a hooded cloak stepped from Sari's room and, with her guards, began stealthily negotiating the palace hallways.

The Hasan Daegian women unsheathed swords that had been stolen from the armory and quickly dispatched any Bhuttanian soldier on duty with cunning and speed. The group made their way down hallway after hallway to the first floor of the palace, leaving a legacy of bloody carnage behind. Before them stretched the expansive courtyard and the garden.

If they could make it to the end of the garden, they would escape through a hidden door the Bhuttanians knew nothing about and melt into the city.

Cries of alarm sounded in the palace.

The Hasan Daegians realized they had been discovered. They bolted for their lives through the courtyard just ahead of advancing Bhuttanian soldiers.

The empress, in her hooded cape, stumbled and fell to her knees.

Two guards immediately pulled her up and began running with her.

One of the guards took an arrow through the heart and fell. Another guard immediately took her place at the side of the empress.

Several guards took the rear, acting as shields knowing they would be cut down any second as they ran over the rough cobblestones of the courtyard.

The stones were slick from rain, reducing the Hasan Daegians' speed as they strained to reach the secret door.

Only the empress knew of its precise location, and if luck prevailed, they needed only a few more minutes.

Without warning, Bhuttanian soldiers, roused from their sleep, rushed at them from the left.

The Hasan Daegian women surrounded their queen and faced the oncoming enemy. They fought valiantly but could make no headway toward the secret door. One by one, the combatants fell until both Hasan Daegians and Bhuttanians were strewn about the courtyard like broken toys.

Alexanee, dressed in his nightshirt, pushed his way to the front and held up his hand.

The exhausted Bhuttanian soldiers pulled up their swords.

"Will you surrender?" he cried.

The hooded queen spoke nothing but shook her head vehemently.

The Bhuttanian Commander ordered his men to move away from the small knot of women and their quivering queen. He sent a runner to find Dorak. "Great Mother, I cannot permit you to leave. Please, please do not commit this folly," he begged. His hand was firm upon his sword as he looked over his shoulder to see if the aga was coming.

The hooded empress began inching her way toward the courtyard wall.

Bhuttanian soldiers moved to intercept but made no attempt to strike at the women.

At once, the general had a brilliant idea. He laid down his sword and ordered the rest of his men to do so.

The Bhuttanian soldiers reluctantly followed suit.

The general displayed his open hands as he slowly moved toward his new empress. "Great Mother," he said to the dark-clad woman. "Have mercy on me. Do not make me the only Bhuttanian in history to strike down his ruling lady."

The Bhuttanian empress remained motionless inside the tiny knot of Hasan Daegian guards.

"HALT!" a voice boomed from the darkness. Dorak swept out of the blackness and into the timid light of handheld torches. "Maura, stop this! You are surrounded and cannot escape. Think of your women." He seemed more irritated than angry.

The empress did not move.

After several minutes, Dorak grew impatient. "Either surrender at once, or I will cut your guards down."

Again, the cloaked empress did not move.

Dorak turned to Alexanee, "Kill them, but leave my wife untouched."

The Hasan Daegian guards moved into a closer knot around their queen.

Alexanee picked up his sword, as did the others.

They outnumbered the Hasan Daegians four to one.

The Bhuttanian soldiers scowled as they waited for the order to attack. They couldn't help but think this was outright butchery. And what if one of them slipped on the wet cobblestones and struck the empress instead?

General Alexanee raised his hand and looked beseechingly at Dorak one last time.

Dorak stared straight at the cloaked empress, who did not return his gaze.

With a final sigh, Alexanee lowered his hand. The Bhuttanians rushed the little group of women.

The women did not flinch but waited as the silent men overcame them. As they struck swords with the Bhuttanians, they cried out, "FREEDOM FOREVER!"

The men made quick work of the remaining Hasan Daegian guards, causing their deaths to be as painless as possible. The Hasan Daegians looked at their killers gratefully before closing their eyes one last time.

The soldiers, wiping blood from their swords before sheathing them, looked at their general with wide, questioning eyes.

Alexanee, understanding the unspoken request, nodded.

Four Bhuttanians stood with each slain Hasan Daegian guard. With a solemnity reserved for one of their own, the Bhuttanian soldiers picked up each Hasan Daegian woman. Two holding the legs and two more raising the body under the shoulders, the Bhuttanians slowly marched the bodies over to where a crowd of Hasan Daegians from the palace stood watching the sad spectacle. The soldiers turned the bodies over to the Hasan Daegian servants and stood with the bereaved group as Dorak faced the defiant and silent empress.

Dorak was beside himself with fury. He was not sure if it was because Maura had placed herself in such a dangerous situation or that her attempt to escape had failed. "There is nowhere to go," Dorak said, his voice swollen with anger. He started toward Maura.

The empress flinched and stepped back.

Dorak ran and caught the flailing woman in a bear hug. He felt like crushing her in his powerful arms. Dorak began squeezing Maura.

She gasped out loud.

Dorak let go. Something was wrong.

The woman felt too soft.

Fearing he had been duped, Dorak pulled back the cloak's hood.

Staring back at him with huge, fearful eyes was not Maura.

"Sari!" cried out Dorak. He violently shook the old woman. "Where is she? Tell me or I will torture you until you don't even know your own name," he threatened.

Sari struggled with Dorak. Pushing him back, she stumbled to the ground. Her hand came upon a short sword. "I'll tell you nothing, you bastard!" she cried as she fell upon the sword.

Dorak rushed to stop her but felt her warm blood rush upon his hands as he reached for her. Pulling the sword out, he tried to staunch the bleeding. "Sari, no! Sari!" he kept calling, but the old woman was already dead.

20

Meagan was binding wounds.

The Hasan Daegian guards had killed over fourteen Bhuttanian combat soldiers and wounded fifteen before they entered the courtyard.

Tears flowed down her face as she tended to the living. She was both horrified at the savagery of the Hasan Daegian attack yet proud of the damage they had inflicted.

Many Bhuttanians had been mutilated upon the face and genitals. Some had been castrated.

Meagan barked, "What is this?"

Her assistant lurched as though she would vomit.

A soldier had been brought in with his face cut into ribbons with bits of bone exposed. This made the third Bhuttanian soldier whose face the Hasan Daegian women sliced away.

Meagan felt for a pulse.

There was a faint one.

She looked at her initiate. "Compose yourself. I need caromate," she said without rebuke.

The initiate took dry herbs out of the medical bag and placed them in a clean cloth. Taking the cloth between her hands, she ground the fabric to break the herbs inside. Taking a short whiff, she nodded to Meagan and placed the cloth over what remained of the mouth and nose of the soldier. He struggled for a few seconds and fell into a deep sleep.

Meagan took a blue liquid from her bag and put a few drops on the soldier's tongue. He fell into a painless death. "May Mekonia have mercy on your soul," Meagan said.

"And ours," echoed the young initiate.

Meagan moved over to the next soldier who also had a bloody mask for a face. "It looks like they started on this one but didn't finish," remarked Meagan as she took a cloth with ointment to wipe the blood off.

The soldier's hand reached up suddenly and grabbed Meagan's hand in a vise grip.

"What's this?" exclaimed Meagan, feeling alarmed.

The grip on her hand tightened.

Meagan peered closer.

The skin of the soldier had tints of blue.

Meagan reached over to her bag and pulled out a surgeon's knife.

Holding on to the soldier's hand, she pricked a finger.

A tiny drop of blue blood oozed from the small nick.

Meagan immediately wiped the droplet from sight and put a bandage on the finger.

"Help one of the others," said Meagan to her initiate. "I don't need you with this one."

"But . . ." argued the initiate.

"His vitals are stable. I'm just going to put him to sleep and attend the worst ones until I can get back to him," she said, breaking some herbs under the soldier's nose.

"But it looks as though he has been castrated," persisted the woman.

Meagan gave the novice a stern look.

The initiate wandered over to another table where the flesh from a sword wound was being sewn together.

Dorak, following soldiers carrying the body of Sari, staggered in.

Sari was placed neatly in a row of the dead awaiting funeral preparations.

Dorak stared numbly at the row of dead Bhuttanian soldiers, Hasan Daegian guards, and Sari. He seemed bewildered.

For a moment, Meagan almost pitied him. She leaned down to the ear of the soldier in her care and whispered, "Dorak is here. Move not if you care for your life."

An officer addressed Dorak, which caused him to come out of his stupor.

The officer was ordered to search high and low for the empress. Every room in the palace was to be searched as was every house in O Konya. The officer pressed his fist against his chest and hurried off.

Seeing Meagan, Dorak stormed over. "I don't suppose you would know where your empress is?" he asked Meagan sarcastically.

"I'm sure the empress will turn up, most likely under our noses, Great Aga."

"What is wrong with him?" asked Dorak, pointing to the soldier whose face was swollen and black-blue from massive facial cuts.

Meagan was suddenly very afraid. She looked timidly at her feet. If Dorak knew, he would strike them all dead.

"Well, speak up," demanded Dorak, his patience wearing thin.

"Some of the soldiers had their faces disfigured, and some were castrated." She pointed to the groaning soldier. "This one they started but didn't finish."

Dorak seemed taken back. "Is it customary for Hasan Daegians to disfigure their enemies?"

"No, Great Aga."

"By the eyes of Bhuttu, I thought Sari was enough, but this!" Dorak waved to the dying men in Meagan's care. "This is most vicious."

"Great Aga, these men must be removed to the hospital in O Konya. There simply is not enough room or medical supplies to care for them properly in the palace."

"Take them to the infirmary near the barracks."

"Your soldiers have taken over the infirmary for living quarters. These wounded men need help quickly."

"Fine, fine," answered Dorak impatiently. "Move these men where you will. Supply them anything they need."

"Yes, Great Aga. I will move the men immediately to the hospital," replied Meagan relieved. She snapped her fingers at the waiting servants and Bhuttanian slaves who would carry the wounded to wagons and on to the city hospital.

Her assistants gathered their instruments and walked alongside the stretchers, comforting the wounded while pushing the Bhuttanian physicians out of their way. Hasan Daegian medicine had been deemed superior to the Bhuttanian way. Even Dorak did not interfere with the Hasan Daegian healers, giving them free reign.

This caused many of the Bhuttanian physicians, who were little more than temple priests, to protest vehemently. However, the wiser of the Bhuttanians, who tired of their patients dying from infection and blood loss, began studying the techniques and philosophy of Hasan Daegian medicine.

Meagan had grown weary of these meddlesome old men who peered constantly over her shoulder and dirtied her clean instruments with their unwashed hands. She knew that one of the reasons she was not in prison was due to teaching Bhuttanians things as simple as washing one's hands before touching a patient.

The death rate of Bhuttanian infants had gone down drastically under her supervision. Meagan could not help but think she was contributing to the demise of her people by helping the Bhuttanians.

Now before her lay the Hasan Daegian queen disguised as a Bhuttanian warrior with a badly wounded face. Meagan was going to get her off the palace grounds and into the city, even if it meant her death. This act was going to be her redemption. Meagan breathed easily as she felt the weight of guilt lift from her shoulders. She even began enjoying herself as she followed Maura's stretcher outside and loaded it onto the wagon carrying other patients. So, as not to call undue attention to the queen, Meagan tended to other soldiers in the wagon.

The driver made short work of the trip to the hospital, located in the middle of O Konya. Built a century before, it was one of the tallest buildings in the garden city. The first floor housed the sick and injured, and the second and third were used for lodgings and research.

The women from the House of Magi had taken over the top floor when they had come as refugees to O Konya and lived there still—what remained of them.

As Hasan Daegians rarely got sick, the lower floor was used to treat injuries from accidents. Much of the time, it had been empty until the war came.

Now it was always busy with Bhuttanians due to this and that. Much of the illness was caused by the lack of hygiene. Simple cuts became infections, colds turned into pneumonia, and rotten teeth became poisonous to the entire body. The most common medical problem suffered by the Bhuttanians was blindness caused by the lack of certain nutrients in their diet.

But Meagan pushed all of these worries from her mind as she jumped out of the wagon, shouting orders concerning her patients. She waited by the main entrance until all of the patients were unloaded and taken inside.

Then she ordered patients to specific rooms, putting the empress in a room with a dying Bhuttanian—a boy really.

Meagan placed the queen over by the window and leaned over. "The boy is unconscious. He can hear and see nothing. He will die very soon."

The woman on the table did not respond to Meagan's reassurances but moaned like a soldier in great pain.

Meagan pressed her hand against the shoulder of the disguised woman, saying, "May Mekonia be with you," and left the room.

An hour later, she came back with her white gown covered in blood and her face dirty.

The young boy was dead as Meagan expected he would be.

The bed by the window was empty.

And the window was open.

Queen Maura, tenth ruler of Hasan Daeg and Empress of the Bhuttanian Empire, had escaped into the black and moonless night!

Wall Of Glory

The Princess Maura Tales
Saga of the de Magela Family

Book Three

Abigail Keam

Worker Bee Press

Wall Of Glory
The Princess Maura Tales
Copyright © Abigail Keam

ALL RIGHTS RESERVED

No part of this book may be reproduced or transmitted in any form without written permission of the author.

All characters, locations, and things are fictional and similarity to any living person is just coincidence unless stated otherwise.

Worker Bee Press
P.O. Box 485
Nicholasville, KY 40340

Acknowledgements

Thanks to my editors,
Patti DeYoung and Heather McCurdy

Artwork by Karin Claesson
www.karinclaessonart.com

Book Jacket by Peter Keam
Author's photograph by Peter Keam

Preface

Centuries ago, the Dinii, Overlords of the planet Kaseri, were defeated by the Lahorians, an advanced race from the sea island of Lahore.

Despondent, the Dinii retreated to Hasan Daeg, their homeland. Unable to care for their slaves, they released them from bondage while continuing to watch over them in secret.

Believing that their former masters had abandoned them, the Hasan Daegians developed into a prosperous, agricultural society, having all but forgotten their origins with the Dinii. For centuries they lived in peace, thinking their world was secure.

But to the east of Hasan Daeg, a warlike aga of Bhuttan rose—Zoar. His most burning desire was to become Overlord of the planet at any cost, thus plunging Kaseri into a wasteland.

The Lahorians, threatened by Zoar's plundering, emerged from their underwater retreat to contact their former enemies, the Dinii. Able to see into the future, the Lahorians persuaded the Dinii to establish contact with the ruling family of Hasan Daeg.

The Dinii were instructed to take the Hasan Daegian queen's only heir, Princess Maura, and train her as a Dini warrior to defeat Aga Zoar, thus allowing the Lahorians to continue their evolution into beings of pure energy.

Zoar's army finally reached the border of Hasan Daeg.

Princess Maura, commanding an army of Hasan Daegians, Anqarians, and Dinii, won the initial battle against the Bhuttanians.

In desperation, Zoar's son, Dorak, who had become the sovereign of the Bhuttanians, conjured the Black Cacodemon, an evil wizard to spin magic against the superior Hasan Daegian forces.

Unable to withstand the wizard's powerful spells, Hasan Daeg fell, and Princess Maura was taken prisoner.

Desirous of the Hasan Daeg throne and wishing the people to see his rule as legitimate, Dorak connived to marry Princess Maura while unintentionally falling in love.

Regardless, Dorak forced Maura to marry him. He also had Maura crowned Empress of Bhuttan, thus rejecting his offspring with another woman, Jezra the Anqarian.

Maura returned Dorak's love but did not trust him.

Unable to influence Dorak, Maura makes a dramatic escape and journeys to Atetelco, the ancient capital of the Dinii. There she must "mate" with the Mother Bogazkoy, a tree of mysterious abilities, so she may gain power to defeat the Black Cacodemon and set her country free of Bhuttanian dominance.

Thus our story continues with Maura fleeing O Konya.

1

Maura rushed to meet KiKu.

As a child, she had covered every inch of the city with the Dinii, memorizing every sewer hole, forgotten gate, and musty stairway in the garden city.

They planned to leave the city through an old caravan gate originally built for the Sivans that had not been used for centuries.

KiKu winced when he saw her. "Great Mother, your face is falling to your feet," he complained, watching her flesh drop to the ground.

"Just a piece here, a piece there," Maura mocked.

The alarm on KiKu's face did not vanish.

"It looks worse than it is," she said, trying to comfort him.

"You are injured! We cannot travel with you like that," KiKu insisted. He was not one to panic, but the empress' injuries were most unfortunate and ill-timed. He looked about, searching for a place to hide.

The city was being torn apart in the hunt for her. At any moment, the Bhuttanians could stumble upon them.

Maura pushed the tall man aside and mounted a Bhuttanian warhorse. "Listen, KiKu," she said. "Listen to the sound of a city being destroyed. It is all a ploy. I was meant to escape."

She donned the helmet that was hanging on the saddle horn. "How many people are going to die tonight because Dorak wants the Mother Bogazkoy? Hundreds? Thousands?" She paused, looking at the city. "Do you know what I did, KiKu? I had my women cut off the manhood from Dorak's men. I did some myself."

She pointed to her face. "This is not my blood. My blood is blue, not red. This is the blood of Bhuttanian men who stood between freedom and me. I needed a disguise to escape the palace, and those faceless men provided me one. I now know the true meaning of ruling. It is rule or be ruled. Kill or be killed."

Maura lowered the visor on her helmet and slapped the horse with the end of her reins.

The stallion whinnied and galloped off, aware that an unyielding hand controlled it.

KiKu jumped on his horse, wondering if the woman he followed had become worse than the aga he had betrayed.

2

They rode all night.

When chancing upon any Bhuttanian search parties, KiKu spoke for them, saying they had been on leave in O Konya and were now returning to their garrison in Qatou.

If any soldier questioned the blood on KiKu's partner's clothes, he would answer that O Konya was under martial law, and they had helped detain many citizens before leaving for their garrison.

Each time the bands of soldiers let them pass, not realizing that the tall Bhuttanians were the empress and Zoar's former spylord.

Before dawn, KiKu led them to a small cave on a ridge just large enough to conceal them and their mounts. Two fresh mounts waited inside with needed provisions.

Maura jumped off her horse and collapsed on a bedroll that KiKu provided her. She was exhausted both physically and mentally.

KiKu handed Maura hardtack and a cup of water. "There will be no fire tonight," KiKu apologized. "Sorry about the rations, but I had only a few hours to arrange for this little escape of yours."

Maura grunted in agreement. "It is good that your cohorts can move so quickly and easily." She pondered for a moment.

"Getting these warhorses was no small task. How many Bhuttanians still work for you, KiKu?"

KiKu blinked while leaning against a rock munching on some hardtack. "The beauty of my system, Great Mother, is that if caught, you will never have any information to divulge to Dorak that could threaten my loyal followers."

She chortled. "In other words the less I know, the better."

"Correct, Great Mother."

"What do you get out of this if I win?"

"Your mother promised me my kingdom. I wish to gather my people if there are any left."

"My mother's wish is now my command, KiKu. I swear to you that if we prevail, you will have your kingdom."

"Upon your oath as Great Mother?"

"Upon my oath as Empress Maura de Magela."

"Then indeed we shall prevail." KiKu swallowed some water and rested his head on his chest.

Thinking KiKu had fallen asleep, Maura got up to care for the horses.

KiKu stuck his foot out and shook his head while still resting his closed eyes. "I will see to the horses in a moment, Great Mother. You must sleep."

Maura gratefully returned to her bedroll and was dreaming before her head came to rest.

3

Maura awoke.

She found KiKu squatting before the entrance of the cave surveying the valley below. "Any sign of trouble?" she asked, rubbing her sore muscles.

KiKu shook his head slightly. "Search parties were down in the valley. They have left to go on to Qatou, I suppose." He looked at Maura intently. "Your face doesn't look any better," he commented.

She felt her features with her hands, as there was no mirror. "Some of the cuts are starting to get infected," she said. "I feel feverish."

"Can you do anything about it?" KiKu asked.

Maura shrugged her shoulders. "I guess I could heal myself before we leave tonight."

"Great Mother, may I suggest that if you can do so, you do it now. We may have to flee at any moment, and it would not do to have a sick woman on my hands."

Maura rubbed her face and did not answer KiKu.

"Great Mother, I know you are feeling sad about the death of Lady Sari, but being a ruler sometimes involves knowing when not to put your servants in needless danger."

Maura flinched at the mention of Sari and began to weep silently. "You know about Sari?"

"Before you came to the wall, one of my contacts made a brief visit. She told me that an imposter posing as you had committed suicide rather than be taken. I guessed it was Lady Sari."

"And my guards?"

"It is correct that you cry for them. It shows you still have a heart, and you honor them with your tears."

"If I had a heart, I would not have let them die."

"What else was to be done? You had to flee the city, and they willingly gave their lives to ensure that you could. They knew what they were doing. It is our way."

Maura gave KiKu a long, hard look. "Who?"

"Those who serve, Great Mother. We know our lives are expendable, and we accept our lot in life." His expression was one of acceptance and regret.

Maura left KiKu with his memories and moved to the back of the cave where she relieved herself. When finished, she perched upon a rock in the cave and began healing her face.

KiKu did not watch but gazed upon the valley, watching a hawk soar in the sky. If he could have escaped being spotted, KiKu would have contacted the hawk to take a message to the Dinii, but it was too much of a risk to call out.

An hour later, Maura jumped down from the rock and washed her face from a small tin of water. "How do I look?" she asked KiKu.

He studied her face, looking for marks or cuts. "You look like a young woman again, but you have the blue face of a de Magela."

KiKu walked to the opposite side of her, again studying her face. "I have heard of your regenerative powers, but this is the first time I have witnessed them for myself. It is amazing. Have you still the fever?"

"See for yourself."

KiKu cautiously extended his hand and touched her brow. "Dry and cool. No fever," he pronounced happily. "We will be able to travel tonight."

Maura nodded in agreement. "Where do we go from here?"

"We will travel south into Siva. There we will pose as a merchant with his obedient and humble wife."

Maura teased, "Are you going to pose as the wife?"

KiKu smiled a toothy grin.

For the first time, Maura noticed that KiKu was a good-looking man and not as old as she had believed. She wondered if he had a wife stashed away somewhere. "Why don't we head north to the City of the Peaks?"

KiKu's smile vanished.

Alarmed, Maura grabbed his arm. "Why do you look like that? What has happened?"

KiKu bowed his head. He did not want to see her face as he told her. "The City of the Peaks is no more. Burned out."

Maura cried, "How? The city is impregnable!"

"Magic," was KiKu's reply.

"The Black Cacodemon!" Maura spat on the ground. Her face contorted as though she were struggling to find the right words. "What of the royal family—Empress Gitar and her children?" she asked quietly.

"I don't know. I suppose some got out."

"Why?" Maura felt as though someone had gutted her with a knife.

KiKu rubbed his unshaven face. "Dorak did not want the Dinii to help you if you fled. He put them on the run. I think you are right in that this is a trick, too. Soldiers should have been swarming over that west wall. We did not see any until the road patrols. Easy enough to fool them. I think the hitch in their plans was that your disguise was too good. You threw them off, and now they've got to find you."

"To follow us!"

"Correct," KiKu said. His respect for the girl had increased. She was not stupid and, judging from her masquerade, was resourceful as well as ruthless. He had not recognized her at all when she first approached, and he was a master of disguises. "Dorak wants the Mother Bogazkoy."

"She will not accept him. He is not suitable for her purposes."

"Perhaps he doesn't know that or he doesn't believe it. Perhaps the Black Cacodemon has promised him the mating will work."

"Perhaps, perhaps. I need facts. I need to know who remains of the Dinii. I need to know where my western army is. You are supposed to be my spylord. Tell me something of value," she prodded in frustration.

"No one has seen the Dinii since the attack. We do not know where they have gone. They could have left the country."

"No," challenged Maura. "Chaun Maaun would never have left me. Never!"

"Chaun Maaun could be no longer, and you did marry someone else."

Maura's face drained of color. She looked almost pale. "I was forced into marriage!"

KiKu gave a look that challenged the veracity of this last statement.

Maura buried her face in her warhorse's long mane, weeping. "That's a lie. I wanted to marry Dorak." Tears ran down her cheeks as shame illuminated her face.

The spy was moved to pity her. "We cannot help with whom we fall in love."

"But I loved Chaun Maaun and hated Dorak, at least in the beginning."

"Who knows the will of the heart? It can love many people in many ways. It can also hate and love at the same time. Zoar loved my sister, but he let her die in a hunting accident. Dorak both loved and hated his father, and yet he murdered him."

Maura wiped her tears away. "Dorak killed Zoar?"

KiKu nodded solemnly.

The horse on which Maura leaned shifted and nuzzled her arm with his nose. "I don't know why, but that news makes me feel better."

"Misery abides company?"

"It explains Dorak's suffering." Maura scratched behind the ears of the contented horse. "I am content that he suffers as I do."

"I think Dorak suffers a great deal. If he had been born with better parents, such as mine, he would have been a great man."

"Like you?"

KiKu ignored her sarcasm. "Dorak has the seeds of greatness within him, but with Zoar as his father, he didn't stand a chance to grow without being twisted in some fashion. Dorak was right to kill him."

"Who am I to judge Dorak when I allowed my beloved Sari to be killed?"

"You still do not realize."

"What?"

"Dorak is not the man to fear, nor the Black Cacodemon. It is Alexanee who must be watched."

"Why him?"

"Dorak will make a mistake that will cost him his life because he is impetuous." KiKu picked up some pebbles and flipped them back and forth between his fingers. "Like Dorak, the Black Cacodemon must be dealt with, but he is not invincible. His fatal defect is his ambition. Sooner or later, a spell will backfire, or Dorak will tire of him and do the bastard in with one thrust of a sword. They are capable but flawed men who will perish from their own miscalculations."

KiKu put a pebble in his mouth and began to suck on it. "Alexanee is different," he continued after he spat out the small stone. "He has no weaknesses. He does not gamble. He stays away from women. He is not a religious fanatic. Alexanee is highly intelligent, a brilliant strategist, even better than Zoar in his heyday. He is a man of moderation, both spiritually and emotionally."

Maura was intrigued by KiKu's analysis of Alexanee. She had never given him much thought. "It does not matter what attributes Alexanee has. He can never be aga."

"You are wrong, Great Mother. Only three people stand between Alexanee and his gaining control of the Bhuttanian Empire. Dorak, Jezra's son, and you."

KiKu lowered his voice. "Alexanee is Zoar's first child, born on the wrong side of the blanket you might say. His mother was a Bhuttanian noblewoman who was much older than Zoar. The details of Alexanee's birth remained quiet, but when his mother died, Zoar brought Alexanee to court to serve as an officer in his army. Since Alexanee's parentage was not known, Zoar spared his life when killing the rest of his sons in favor of Dorak."

"Does he know?"

"Neither Dorak nor Alexanee know. I became privy to this information when Zoar and I were watching Alexanee train once. Zoar said, 'There goes the best one of the lot, and I can't acknowledge him.'"

"And then you did some digging on your own?"

"Yes."

Maura remained silent while stroking the horse.

KiKu realized she did not wish to talk further. The hetmaan spent the remainder of the day resting near the mouth of the cave, though deep sleep eluded him. Noticing that he could no longer see the sun, KiKu looked outside. It was growing dark, and soon it would be safe for them to leave. He saddled the horses.

Maura, who had been resting quietly on her bedroll, fell into step with KiKu to help with the horses and gather their gear. When finished, KiKu told the young empress to wait outside with their new mounts.

The young queen was sad for she knew the fate of the two still-exhausted horses they had ridden from O Konya.

KiKu could not let them roam loose as their discovery would give away the direction of their escape.

Maura took the reins of the fresh mounts and walked a bit from the cave. She held her breath waiting for a panicked whinny or scream but heard nothing.

KiKu soon joined her, sheathing his knife. Taking his reins and a hank of mane, the lithe man pulled himself upon the warhorse.

"I have killed many a man, but I can't abide hurting an animal." He put on his helmet. "Don't you think that strange?" Without waiting for an answer, he kicked his horse and started down the mountain.

Maura followed behind, ever alert for trouble.

They had traveled several miles when Maura heard a rustling in a nearby tree and looked up, her hand upon her sword.

Yeti sat upon a limb calmly eating a hedgepear. She looked happily at Maura and waved, "Greetings, Great Mother. I have been sent to fetch you!"

4

Yeti took another bite.

"Yeti!" exclaimed Maura, turning her horse around. She jumped down and tied the horse securely to a low branch.

Yeti threw away her pear and glided down gracefully. Standing in the moonlight, she towered over Maura. She fluttered her massive wings in greeting and smiled a wide, sloppy grin.

The horse shied nervously, but Yeti spoke to it soothingly and patted its roan neck.

The stallion settled down and began munching on grass.

Maura asked excitedly, "How did you find me?" She grabbed Yeti's hand and squeezed it with genuine affection.

"We heard that you had escaped. Iegani sent us out to find you and take you to the Forbidden Zone."

"I am ready now."

Yeti held up her hand. "You cannot travel with me. It is too dangerous. I can only guide you."

"I don't understand," Maura said, her heart sinking.

"It is the Black Cacodemon," said KiKu, steadying his horse.

"Greetings, Hetmaan of Queen Maura," Yeti said, her wings fluttering.

KiKu noticed the Dini did not refer to Maura as empress.

"You know his face?" asked Maura incredulously. "The identity of the hetmaan should be known only to a certain few."

"It is the first time I have seen him, but the Dinii know of the lord who worked as a double agent for Queen Abisola. Otherwise, how could I have rendezvoused with you in the meadow for our last meeting? He sends messages to us via the gootee." Yeti bowed in respect. "A master of disguises. I almost mistook you both for Bhuttanian soldiers and was going to kill you, but then I saw you were not Bhuttanian."

KiKu raised his eyebrows. "How is that?"

"Bhuttanians ride with their knees higher and heels turned downward. You ride with your feet level."

Yeti turned toward Maura. "You ride well, but you look uncomfortable, as though you are unfamiliar with handling such a big animal. Nothing I could see directly. Just what I felt when I saw you."

"Lady, you are most observant. I could use someone like you. Would you like to be a spy?" KiKu teased.

Yeti laughed easily. "I don't think I could easily blend in with the common folk."

KiKu jumped down off his horse and joined Yeti and Maura. He handed Yeti a waterskin from which she drank sparingly, due more to good manners than lack of thirst.

"I heard you say that you were sent here to fetch the empress," KiKu commented.

Yeti handed the waterskin back to him and nodded. "You are headed toward the border of Siva. There are bounty hunters and bandits waiting for you to cross."

KiKu whistled. This was a mighty blow to his plans. "Is there a reward?"

"Yes, but not from the Royal House of the Aga. It is offered by Baroness Mikkotto. She has put up the money."

"Mikkotto!" Maura ranted. "That murderous bitch."

Yeti, undisturbed by Maura's ire, continued, "The baroness has resettled on her estates with impunity. Other than answering to Dorak, she fears no one and is a law unto herself. Her estate is guarded by Hasan Daegians loyal to her cause and Bhuttanians who serve as mercenaries."

Maura seemed stunned and wove a bit on her feet as though she were about to faint. She rubbed her forehead. "That would mean Dorak gave her permission to resettle. It means my parents' death by Mikkotto's plot was a ruse. He was going to kill them anyway, and he used her as a tool."

"It would seem so," replied Yeti, thinking kindly of Abisola and Iasos. They had been worthy rulers, and she was sorry they were gone.

Maura cast a wicked eye upon KiKu. "Did you know of this?"

KiKu shook his head and looked questioningly at Yeti. "None of my sources have mentioned Mikkotto since last spring. I find this information surprising."

Maura slapped KiKu hard across the face, almost knocking him off his feet. "You had better not be lying to me. If you fail me again, I will kill you."

KiKu's face remained hard and impassive, but it was evident that he was struggling to control himself. He took off his corselet of chain mail and dropped it on the ground, then put his hand on his sword.

Yeti stepped forward, but Maura grabbed her arm.

KiKu unsheathed his sword and presented its hilt to Maura.

She took it.

"I have offended thee. I am dishonored. Take my life so that I may die with honor, or permit me to die by my hand," he begged.

"I will neither kill you nor grant you permission to die by suicide," said Maura coldly. "You have treated me like a child since we met. I will forgive you since I have indeed acted as a child who could not see beyond her nose. But now I am truly the Ruling Lady of Hasan Daeg. Do you know why?"

Maura tapped on her chest as she spoke. "Because in here, there is no more a child, only a queen who needs your help getting to the Mother Bogazkoy so she may fulfill her destiny." She pointed the sword to the ground. "Pledge your allegiance to me."

KiKu fell to his knees, his face red with shame that he had failed his sovereign. He prostrated himself before Maura. "I pledge with my life and honor that I will live to obey you in all things and to serve the House of de Magela."

Maura asked, "Upon your life?"

"Upon my life!"

"Rise then and serve me well. We will never discuss this again."

KiKu rose from the ground and dusted off his clothes. He seemed genuinely chastised.

Yeti wondered if she would eventually have to kill him to protect Maura. It would be a pity as KiKu was such a valuable resource.

She sauntered over to a kokobo tree and pulled a small pouch from a knothole, handing it to Maura. "You are not to go by land to Siva. You are to go to the Sacred Lake of Yappor. There the Lahorians will take care of you."

"The Lahorians again," scoffed Maura, opening the pouch. She handed the contents to KiKu who held them up to the moonlight so all could see.

Yeti waved him away. "I can see in the dark without light," she said.

Inside the pouch was a map drawn on leather with berry juice. Maura was surprised and looked at Yeti. "Did you do this?"

Yeti smiled. "I can also read and write. Empress Gitar decided everyone needed to read, so we all learned. Badly at first, but better as time goes on."

She fingered the outlines on the map. "Here is an old hunter's trail that you will take to the Sacred Lake. From there the Lahorians will transport you and KiKu to the Forbidden Zone."

The hairs on the back of Maura's neck stood up at the mention of the Forbidden Zone, a place not visited by any Hasan Daegian since prohibited by Mekonia, their nature goddess.

"Why can't you fly the empress to the lake?" asked KiKu.

"Is empress your title now?" asked Yeti.

Maura lowered her eyes. "There is only one empress, and she is Gitar."

"Yes, that is what she thinks. She would want me to remind you," Yeti replied.

Peering at the map, KiKu asked again, "Why can't you transport her to the lake?"

Yeti lowered her head to study the bald man. "Because you will have a better chance of making it if you remain disguised as Bhuttanians. With me, there is too great a risk that we would be shot out of the sky. The Bhuttanians have been ordered to shoot anything larger than an eagle flying. I only travel easily when the sky is pitch black. There is a full moon tonight. We would make an easy target."

"Makes sense," said KiKu as he folded the map. He seemed to have forgotten the unsettling reprimand he had received only moments before.

"What of Gitar and Chaun Maaun?" asked Maura, her heart slowing down to take the shock of any bad news.

"I cannot tell you where they are, but they are alive," Yeti replied, her face lined with sadness. "Empress Gitar has aged with grief. All her daughters were killed when the Black Cacodemon destroyed the city."

Maura groaned.

"Chaun Maaun lives. He never leaves his mother's side." Yeti handed the pouch to KiKu, who placed the map carefully inside his tunic. "He wants to see you, Maura."

Maura's eyes widened with apprehension. "Where?"

"He would not say. He wanted me only to tell you that he will see you but at his discretion."

Maura's heart raced as her eyes took on a strange light.

Yeti placed her hand on Maura's shoulder.

"Don't expect too much, little sparrow. He has changed and is not the same Chaun Maaun that you knew before. It has been terrible for him. He lives now only to hate the Bhuttanians. He is consumed with it."

"Does he wish to harm our queen?" KiKu asked, wondering how he was going to subdue a Dini. Without waiting for an answer, KiKu pleaded with Maura, "You must not see him."

Maura shamelessly brushed a tear from her cheek. "Tell Chaun Maaun I will see him on his conditions."

"You must not!" KiKu reiterated. "If he is that angry, he might try to kill you." KiKu looked at Yeti for support.

None was forthcoming.

"I will give him the satisfaction of calling me a traitor."

KiKu said, "What if he tries to kill you? Not even you can fight a Dini!"

Maura whispered, "Do you think that is the worst thing he can do to me?"

Yeti grunted with approval.

KiKu was desperate. "Yeti, help me. Persuade her not to see Prince Chaun Maaun."

Yeti shrugged her shoulders. "Chaun Maaun was her betrothed. His love was as pure as the water in the Sacred Lake of Yappor. She betrayed him for a human who was a murderer and butcher of both Hasan Daegians and Dinii. Now he wants satisfaction. It is the Dinii way. Maura was raised with the Dinii. She will follow our customs in this matter."

"You knew about us?" asked Maura.

"Little sparrow, everyone knew. The young hide their love not well at all." Yeti looked at the night sky. "You must hurry now. Every minute counts. I will follow you when I can. If anyone comes after you, I will kill them. Remember—take the short cut to the Sacred Lake of Yappor."

"What happens once we get there?" asked KiKu.

Stand at the edge of the lake. "The Lahorians are waiting for you and keeping watch. Once you arrive, they will transport you to the Forbidden Zone. You must do as they say."

"Can they be trusted?"

Yeti smiled. "As much as an old enemy can be. Their survival depends upon you at the moment. They will keep you safe enough."

Maura hugged Yeti warmly, inhaling her musky scent.

Yeti rested her chin on the top of Maura's head and brought her wings around to encircle them. "You smell like a barn, Yeti," whispered Maura.

"That is what you have always said, little sparrow," cooed Yeti, embracing Maura with her powerful wings. Yeti gave her one last tight squeeze before retracting her wings. "You must go now. Be careful." Yeti cuffed Maura under the chin.

"Chaun Maaun?"

"I will tell him that you will meet with him. Now go!"

Maura jumped onto her horse and sped off, following KiKu.

Yeti watched them until they disappeared deep into the forest and then flew back to her hiding place in the tree.

Tarsus handed her another hedgepear. "She looks good for having gone through so much."

"The young always recover fast."

"That was a very inventive lie about Mikkotto and Dorak," Tarsus commented.

"It is Iegani's doing, not mine. It's a dirty business, but I see no benefit for lying to Maura." Yeti threw the hedgepear away in disgust.

"Will Iegani let her see Chaun Maaun?"

Yeti wiped her mouth with her forearm. "Not even Iegani can control the prince. Chaun Maaun will have his way eventually."

Tarsus grunted and leaned back against a limb, quickly falling asleep.

Yeti watched the moon. She felt deeply for the woman she had held as a baby and guarded. She remembered the times she had picked up the child who gurgled and laughed as she pulled on Yeti's feathers. Yeti felt a stirring in her heart that she did not quite understand but accepted.

She loved the girl and felt Iegani was wrong to deceive her. Nothing good would come of it. Sooner or later, it would catch up with him. Hopefully, Yeti would be far away when that happened.

5

KiKu and Maura rode hard.

Just as they thought they were safe, they ran into a patrol coming off the plains.

The leader, a rough looking Bhuttanian, did not believe KiKu's story about rejoining his unit after a leave in O Konya. He ordered KiKu and Maura off their horses.

Just as he was going to have his men take out their weapons, Maura struck his horse with her hunting knife and gutted it. The warhorse screamed as it staggered and fell, crushing the patrol leader underneath.

Maura jumped at another horse that sidestepped out of her reach.

The rider swung his baton, striking Maura on the side of her head, crushing the side of her helmet.

Blood swam into her eyes. Years of training came to the forefront, and Maura countered a deathblow aimed at her neck.

Maura scurried under the trained horse that snorted with anger and fright, striking at her with sturdy legs and hooves. Pulling off her helmet, she reached up and swung her sword, cutting the soldier's leg and stirrup off at the ankle.

The soldier shrieked with pain, falling to the ground in shock.

Maura made quick work of him.

KiKu was surrounded by three angry soldiers who did their best to punch him. Like a butterfly, he flitted out of their range, countering their blows with savage leg kicks. His fight was entirely defensive as he had left his sword in the chest of a nameless opponent and couldn't pull it out in time to defend against his three new adversaries. Using his peripheral vision, KiKu scanned for Maura and caught a blur moving beneath a horse. He heard someone scream but couldn't identify the source. He inwardly prayed that Maura would come to his rescue as he was getting tired, and one of the three men would soon breach his defensive strategy.

Unexpectedly, the man on his left grunted and threw up his hands, dropping his sword. He fell backwards with a heavy thud revealing Maura standing behind him.

She immediately turned her attention to the dead man's comrade who charged at her in a fury.

Maura smiled coolly at him.

The lifeless smile gave the rushing man pause, and he veered off at the last moment.

Unfortunately for him, his path was not wide enough.

Maura struck out with her sword and caught him deep in the side.

The man grabbed his side and cried out, stumbling to the ground. She leaned over him and finished him with a jab to the neck.

KiKu pummeled his last opponent with lightning-quick blows with his fists and legs. KiKu thought beating a man to death took an awfully long time for both the victor and the soon-to-be-dead man. He knocked the man unconscious and mercifully broke the man's neck. KiKu fell to the ground, breathing heavily. He looked about him and saw the bloody remains of five men and two horses.

The other horses, including their own, had run off but he could hear them snorting nearby. They were trained not to go far.

Maura walked toward KiKu and stood over him peering down. "You are getting too old for this," she said reproachfully.

KiKu watched her calmly wipe her sword clean on the grass. "I have many good years ahead of me. You have the strength of the Bogazkoy that gives you an unfair advantage."

"That unfair advantage just saved your life."

"I'm not complaining," said KiKu, extending his hand.

Maura reached down and pulled him up.

They both looked at the cooling corpses on the ground.

"We need to hide them."

"We don't have time. Besides, Yeti will come along and take care of this," Maura said.

KiKu wiped the sweat from his forehead. "I don't know. Another patrol could come along and find them."

Maura grew impatient. "We don't have time to dispose of five men and two huge horses. Let us be off!"

She strode with purpose to where she heard the horses grazing and quickly caught the reins of one. She mounted and caught the reins of the other horses. "We will bring them along with us," she said, starting off.

KiKu jumped on one of the horses, secretly glad he would not have to kill any more animals. He rummaged through its saddlebags and found rolled bread and meat paste. He caught up with Maura and shared his bounty with her. They both tore ravenously at the bread, which tasted like a bland pancake, but were grateful for any food.

The young empress rode through the night as though propelled by some deep and unfathomable force.

Occasionally, KiKu caught her lips moving silently as though she were communicating with someone or something. Her face had taken on a darker pallor.

The hetmaan worried about the warhorses. Even though they had been bred for endurance, KiKu knew they were starting to tire.

Every hour, he and Maura would switch mounts while still moving. He cautioned her that they were wearing out the horses, but she paid KiKu no heed and rode on.

At dawn, they rested for only an hour or so.

Maura sensed they were near the Sacred Lake of Yappor. As a child, Iegani and Yeti had brought her to the lake's placid shores and sat with her while Iegani instilled in her the potential of her destiny. He had only mentioned the Lahorians once, a mystical race of people of supreme intellect who lived beneath the lake and would contact her as needed. Over the years she had forgotten the Lahorians as Iegani had told her many parables. It seemed that this was one story she should have remembered. Try as she might, Maura could not remember what Iegani had said to her.

Now Maura felt a burning desire to reach the lake as soon as possible. Her throat was parched. She was constantly sipping from her waterskin, ignoring KiKu's pleas to quit drinking and to slow her horse down. She sensed her name called over and over again.

Watching KiKu out of the corner of her eye, she knew he had heard nothing. She answered with her mind, "I am coming! I am coming!" urging her tired mount forward.

They pounded into a clearing with a brook running through it.

Maura stopped her horse and dismounted, guiding her horse and several others to water.

KiKu remained mounted and studied their surroundings. He

thought the clearing was an unnatural manifestation in the middle of the forest.

Suddenly, Yeti swooped down, causing the horses to bolt.

KiKu cursed as he lunged forward trying to catch the reins of the horses. "I'll be back," he called as he galloped after the fleeing horses.

The fact that Maura trusted Yeti was no reason he should trust the Dini. He thought her sudden appearance somehow staged as if to intentionally frighten the horses. He pulled his horse to a stop and turned it around, riding back to the clearing.

Both Yeti and Maura were gone.

6

Yeti set Maura down.

The yagomba tree limb was so broad several people could walk abreast comfortably on it. At the joint where the limb sprang from the trunk of the tree stood Chaun Maaun.

Chaun Maaun nodded to Yeti, and she flew off, leaving Maura alone with him.

Maura was startled at the sight of Chaun Maaun standing in the dark crook of the tree. Forgotten feelings rushed back to claim her heart. She started toward him, but he held out his hand, staving her off.

"Chaun Maaun," she whispered feverishly.

Chaun Maaun stepped out of the shadow of the tree, allowing Maura to view him closely.

She recoiled without thinking.

The Dini prince scowled. "What's the matter, Maura? You don't like the way I look now?" he asked, venom dripping from his words. "The night of the invasion when we were supposed to leave in peace there was a lone arrow in the sky. Isn't it pretty?"

He was wearing a large patch that covered his left eye as well as part of his cheek. He turned the left side of his face toward her and pointed. "This is what your husband did to me!" He pulled off the leather patch, exposing his face. Chaun Maaun's left eye was gone, and a deep scar was carved in his cheek.

Maura whimpered, "Oh, no!" and reached out to touch him.

Chaun Maaun retreated out of Maura's reach.

Regret and longing squeezed Maura's heart. She fell to her knees and put her head in her hands, weeping. Maura reeled from the heartache that her beloved Chaun Maaun spurned her—even hated her!

"Do you think your tears will save you?" asked Chaun Maaun, sneering. His one good eye swam with tears also, but he blinked them back. He would not give her the satisfaction of seeing the pain he had suffered due to her. His voice took on an icy tone. "I want to know why!"

"Why what?" asked Maura, looking up at him. Her face was streaked with salty tears, and her nose was dark blue and swollen.

"Why did you marry him?"

"It was a challenge of combat. If I won, the Bhuttanians would leave Hasan Daeg. If he won, I would have to marry him."

"And you lost?"

Maura nodded. She looked pleadingly at him. "Please understand, Chaun Maaun. I never stopped loving you." Her face contorted in agony. "I was alone. My parents were dead. I did the best I could. I thought you were safe in the City of the Peaks. I thought he was honoring the peace."

"Dorak and that corrupt sorcerer of his destroyed it, Maura. You wouldn't even recognize it now." Chaun Maaun drifted off, thinking of that terrible day. "We truly live like animals now. Always on the run. Without proper food, without comfort. Dorak has scared off all the game. We are slowly starving to death."

Maura got to her feet and wiped her face with a sleeve. She bravely stepped toward Chaun Maaun. She knew that he could strike her dead or throw her off the tree limb, causing her to break her neck in the fall. "Please believe me. I did not know this was occurring. Dorak had me watched night and day. I had access to only a few advisors who were as blind as I. If I stepped out of bounds, he rounded up my people and tortured them."

Maura stepped closer to him. She could feel his breath and smell his woodsy smell. "You are not the only one who suffered. Please, Chaun Maaun, I can't bear this! Let us forgive one another for events over which we had no control." She embraced him, resting her head on his chest. She clung to him as if her life and sanity depended on it.

Chaun Maaun relaxed. He took a deep breath. He smelled her feminine scent, and it brought back memories of loving and being loved. His jealous rage subsided as he relived his life before the war when Maura was his.

Maura looked older now, and her eyes had taken on a hard, bitter look. There was nothing soft about them except for the few times she had looked at him, pleading with him to understand.

He understood all too well. Much of his rage was at himself for not being able to save Maura. He should have defied Dorak that night in the palace and taken her with him.

He knew that he could have grabbed her before Dorak stopped him, but Chaun Maaun had been afraid for Maura. It seemed too great a risk at the time. Now he bitterly regretted his decision. If he had taken her out of the city that night, Maura could have joined her western army and resisted Dorak.

No, that would not have been the outcome.

Chaun Maaun winced at the memory of that night. If he had flown with her out of the city, Maura would have died, as he would have dropped her when the lone arrow sliced through his eye.

Chaun Maaun shook his head. He bent down and kissed the crown of her head. No, he did the right thing by leaving her with Dorak!

Maura responded to his kiss by embracing him tighter and melting into his arms.

"What will you do now?" he asked.

"I go to join Iegani in the Forbidden Zone."

"You are going to be with the Mother Bogazkoy?"

"Yes, I think she is hidden in the Forbidden Zone near the sea."

"And if you survive, will you come back to me?" Chaun Maaun's face was warm and tender.

Maura bowed her head and pulled away from him.

Chaun Maaun felt as though he had been struck in the face. "You will not come back to me," he said with finality.

"Things are different now. We are not the same people," Maura said, her voice low and husky.

"Once the Bhuttanians are gone, we can forget."

Maura shook her head slowly. "I am their ruler now. I cannot desert them."

"You can't be serious." Chaun Maaun grabbed Maura's shoulders.

She tried not to flinch at the pain.

"Do you think Dorak intended you to be his empress? He wanted to find out the secret of the Mother Bogazkoy. He used you. If he ever discovers it, you will be as good as dead."

"No!"

"What is this!" exclaimed Chaun Maaun. He picked Maura up into the air until she was face to face with him. "You dare to defend

Dorak!" He shook her hard.

Maura's teeth rattled.

"Do you have feelings for him? Do you? Damn you," he hissed. "I ought to kill you."

"Sire, I am asking you to put her down. NOW!" demanded Yeti, standing behind Maura.

Chaun Maaun's good eye was wide with rage. "She betrayed me! She betrayed our love!" he bellowed.

"No, my lord, Maura betrayed no one. If you don't put her down, I will have to disable you. I brought her to you as you commanded; now I must take her away. Iegani is waiting."

Chaun Maaun laughed like a crazy man. He swung her over the limb.

Maura was filled with terror as she looked down. She was a hundred feet in the air. Even with her recuperative powers, she wouldn't be able to survive the fall without massive injuries.

"My Prince and Lord, listen to me. I am bound by a sacred oath to protect Maura. I will kill you if I have to," cautioned Yeti, watching his every move.

She knew Tarsus waited below to catch Maura if she was, indeed, thrown over.

The agonized Chaun Maaun placed Maura back on the limb.

Maura fell into a crumpled heap and looked up at his towering figure. "I am everything you think I am."

"I don't want to hear this."

"No, listen to me so you can purge me from your heart. I have become a different woman."

Chaun Maaun shook his head in disbelief.

"It is true. I went to Dorak willingly," Maura shared.

Chaun Maaun trembled.

"I don't know why. He was never like you. I don't understand my feelings, but I do love him in some strange way."

"NO MORE!" Chaun Maaun roared. He fell beside her, a broken husk, and sobbed openly. "He must die. You understand that, don't you?"

Maura nodded her head.

"Then you can come back to me."

"We can never be."

"Why?"

"I will never heal from this terrible thing that has been thrust upon me. I could never be a true mate to you. After this war is over, you must marry from your own people. This is best for both our races. We can't think of ourselves anymore."

"You would still think of him?"

Maura said nothing and looked away.

"So you love him more."

"I love you deeply, but I am married to him. If things were different, I would want to be with you."

"I could make you forget him."

"That is impossible."

"Give me a chance."

"No, it is the principle. It is everything I stand for."

"Is principle more important than your love for me?"

"My duty to my people is more important than my love for you. And so it should be with you. But, yes, I love him more."

Chaun Maaun pushed off his feet. "Then have your principle and your love of Dorak. From this moment forward, I am your enemy. Do you understand?"

"Remember your oath to me."

"I renounce it."

"I have a reprieve until the Bhuttanians are defeated?"

"Then I will kill you."

"You can try." Maura squared back her shoulders.

Chaun Maaun took one final look at his lost love and flew off the yagomba limb, his heart breaking, never to be mended again.

7

Yeti quickly moved to Maura.

"That was a bold strategy you played. I thought Chaun Maaun was going to drop you for sure."

Maura placed her hand on the black armor protecting her belly. "Now that he has spared me, I have to stay alive until after my baby is born. She must be next in line to the throne of Bhuttan."

"What!"

Maura sorrowfully watched Chaun Maaun disappear into the sky. She replied softly, "I am carrying Dorak's child."

8

Yeti placed Maura down.

Benzar waited patiently on the shore of the Sacred Lake of Yappor with KiKu, who looked a little green around the gills.

KiKu smiled with relief when he spied Maura and rushed to her side.

"Are you all right?" he asked. He didn't even wait for an answer. "This thing," he said, pointing to Benzar who regarded KiKu with cool disdain, "swooped out of the sky and pulled me right off my horse."

Maura smiled weakly at Benzar.

Benzar acknowledged her by bowing very low. "It is good to see you again, Queen of the Hasan Daegians."

"Thank you, Benzar. It is good to see my old companion." She always thought it odd that Benzar was formal with her even though he had changed her diapers as a baby.

She turned to KiKu. "I'm fine. We may continue the journey. But what about the horses?"

"We are taking care of the horses. They will be put to good use," Yeti replied.

Maura understood Yeti's meaning. The horses were to be eaten by the Dinii.

Knowing KiKu was fond of horses, she wished to divert attention away from them. "This place looks vaguely familiar," she said.

"Should we be out in the open like this?" KiKu questioned.

Yeti took a quick look around the lake. "Dorak has diverted all his extra soldiers to the ruins of the City of the Peaks." She directed her comments to Maura. "He rightly assumed that you did not know the city was destroyed and would go there first. We have left suitable tracks for him to follow."

"The Black Cacodemon will not be fooled long by such tricks. He will use his magic to find me."

Yeti replied, "So far he has used his magic to track the Dinii only. We have spread what remains of us along the western portion of Hasan Daeg. With each little group, a Hasan Daegian woman has been placed to confuse him. I would say we have done a good job keeping him busy looking for you. He is not searching for two renegade Bhuttanian soldiers."

"Well done," commented KiKu. "I could not have succeeded better myself."

Yeti bowed to KiKu, seemingly pleased. She loved praise. It was her one vice.

"What now?" asked Maura, feeling tired.

"We will wait until the Lahorians come," replied Yeti, looking at the crystal clear water.

KiKu followed her gaze upon the vast lake. "When will that be?"

"Whenever they are ready," Maura said.

KiKu suggested, "Perhaps they do not know we are here."

Maura laughed. "They know, all right. They are simply biding their time."

"What do they look like?" KiKu asked.

Yeti shrugged her shoulders. "I do not know. I have never seen one."

"Are you sure Dorak is nowhere near us?" asked KiKu, disliking having no contact with his spy network.

"We have patrols throughout this area. It would be unlikely that Dorak could get by without our seeing him," answered Benzar.

KiKu gave him a disdainful look. "If it were only Dorak, I would rest easy, but the Black Cacodemon is another matter."

"You fear him?" Benzar asked.

"Yes, I fear him and so should you, my feathery friend, if you wish to stay alive."

"We had no knowledge of this sorcerer before the invasion," Yeti said, thinking this was a fine opportunity to get KiKu to talk freely. "Had you dealings with him before?"

"I saw him several times as a youth when he served as the main advisor to Zoar's father, Tnpothar. Then Tnpothar died, and Zoar made use of him for several years. That was when the Bhuttanians started on their quest for more territory. After that, the priest seemed to have vanished. I had forgotten about him."

"Zoar always headed west?" Yeti asked.

"Yes. My country was the first to fall under Bhuttanian aggression after Tnpothar unified all the steppe tribes. Hittal fell completely under their domination, and then Tnpothar stopped. He thought enough territory had been subjugated. He wanted to spend the remaining years of his life training promising candidates as bureaucrats to govern the new territory."

"But he was not successful, was he?" Benzar inquired.

KiKu shook his head. "The Bhuttanians are not suited to the intricacies of statecraft. Their culture is based solely on warfare. They can conquer, but once they take the land and its people, they don't know how to assimilate them other than by terrorizing them into submission."

Sighing, KiKu said, "That is what happened to my people. We were hard to vanquish and Zoar, after his father's death, just ground us into the dust until we no longer resisted. Of course, by that time there were very few of us left. Still, the Bhuttanians are more sophisticated than they once were."

Maura tried not to grimace, thinking of the dirty stink hole her palace had become with the Bhuttanians staying there.

Seeing Maura stifle a bitter smile, KiKu added quickly, "It is true, Great Mother. The Bhuttanians have come a long way. Look at how Dorak managed Hasan Daeg once he invaded. It was much less bloody than the old days, I assure you."

Maura turned her head away at the mention of Dorak's name. She did not want them to see her distress.

"Then what happened?" asked Yeti, not wishing KiKu to be diverted from his tale.

KiKu resumed his saga. "Zoar continued the policy of expansion."

"Never south or north or east, for that matter," Yeti stated as a matter of fact.

"It was always to the west."

"Do you know why?" Maura asked.

KiKu shrugged his shoulders. "It was the omens." He looked at the group's confused faces. "The priests of Bhuttu always deemed the west as fortuitous."

"And the Black Cacodemon is the High Priest of Bhuttu," spat Maura, her hands balling into fists.

"Until he was banished from court by Zoar," concurred KiKu. "As

I said before, this was the first time I had seen him since I was a child. I was surprised that Dorak summoned him. He must have been quite desperate."

Yeti thrust back her shoulders with fierce pride. "We are a hard race to defeat."

KiKu looked up at Yeti. "Madam, with that, I will give you no quarrel."

"Enough of this talk. Wake me up when the Lahorians decide to meet with us. As for me, I am going to take a nap," said Maura, strolling over to a tree that provided shade. She curled up in her armor on the ground and was soon asleep.

The hetmaan hid in a bush close enough to keep an eye on things while remaining out of sight.

Benzar and Yeti assumed places high in surrounding trees.

Yeti was disappointed that the conversation with KiKu was halted so abruptly. She felt Maura had done so on purpose. *Life is circles within circles*, thought Yeti as she watched over the Hasan Daegian queen and the enigmatic spylord.

9

Dorak angrily entered his tent.

The trail to the City of the Peaks had proved false, and he had wasted precious time searching for Maura. He threw off his gloves and kicked over a small table. Hearing a titter, Dorak looked toward the back of the tent.

The Black Cacodemon was just visible in the shadows, lurking there with his hands folded in the sleeves of his black velvet robe.

"What do you want?" barked Dorak, irritated at discovering the wizard in his private tent. "Have you found my wife?"

The Black Cacodemon solemnly nodded.

Dorak's heart beat faster at the answer. "Where? Tell me, you spawn of a demon! Where is she?"

"Do you wish to find her because of what she can give us or because you still fancy her?" the sorcerer rasped.

"My motives do not concern you," replied Dorak hotly.

"I think they do, young master. For the use of my powers in conquering Hasan Daeg, you are in debt to me. It would not do to have you take pity on this wretch of a queen simply to placate your sense of morality."

Dorak growled, "I owe nothing! You are but a lowly servant to Bhuttu. It is through Bhuttu that you are granted powers, and Bhuttu has blessed me, not you."

The wizard bent over as though he suffered from pain. His black robe quivered until he threw back his head, snorting short bursts of sound.

Dorak realized the wizard was laughing.

"Oh, that is precious," giggled the sorcerer. "You actually think there is a Bhuttu, a god, who if placated, will grant your wishes. Dorak, I thought you were of different stuff, but you truly are just a superstitious peasant like your mother. You should have learned more from your father. He never believed in Bhuttu or in any god for that matter. Zoar thought it was all rot, stuff for the masses to swallow. He would have none of it. That's why he sent me away. He couldn't stomach the sight of me and refused to use my powers. He had his own power—the power of a strong will such as the world will never see again. He didn't need me ever."

The Black Cacodemon circled Dorak. "But you are made of weaker stuff. The Dinii and the Hasan Daegians routed your army like children breaking sticks. You couldn't think of how to destroy the wall of mist without magic. I could think of several ways to break down that sleepy border, but you panicked."

Dorak turned away from the magician.

The Black Cacodemon chuckled. "Yes, you panicked and summoned me to help you. Now you are in my debt and pay me, you shall."

"Or what?" asked Dorak hotly, lightly touching his sword's hilt.

"I will expose you as the murderer of your father."

"You can never prove that," Dorak contested fiercely.

The wizard waved his hand.

Before Dorak appeared the image of him murdering Zoar. His father struggled as Dorak, looking grim but determined, slowly suffocated him. Dorak turned away from the awful sight. "Stop tormenting me, you fiend!" he whimpered.

The wizard waved his hand again, and the image disappeared. "I may have done many evil things in my life, but I have never committed the crimes of patricide and regicide. Your soul must be very dark, and knowing how your father loved you, the guilt must be unbearable."

Dorak grabbed the wizard by the throat.

The Black Cacodemon touched his amulet and vanished, leaving Dorak holding only air.

Hearing a gootee-like snort, Dorak swirled around.

The wizard was calmly sitting in a chair with his legs crossed under his black robe. "You cannot kill me," declared the Black Cacodemon. "You are, how should I put this, trapped, my dear boy." He uncrossed his legs and leaned forward. "Because I am so fond of you, Dorak, I am willing to make a deal that will outshine your love for this girl."

"I'm listening."

"I have lived for a long, long time, but I wish to be young in the flesh once again. The Bogazkoy can offer that. I do not want to remain in this decrepit body for my remaining years, which even without the Bogazkoy are many. You are haunted by your crime to the point that it is driving you slowly insane. I can help you with that."

"How?" asked Dorak, suddenly interested.

"Get me to the Bogazkoy and help me persuade the plant to accept me as the bonding mate rather than the girl, and I will give you not only her, but I will erase any memory of your crime. It will be as though you never committed it. You will believe that Zoar died of natural causes like everyone else. You will live the rest of your life with the woman you treasure, sitting on the throne of the aga. You will be happy, secure, and without any painful memories to rob you of sleep in the middle of the night. Just think of it, Dorak. I'm offering you a freedom that all men dream about—freedom from one's past mistakes!"

Dorak stood, thinking the offer over carefully. It was very tempting, but could he trust this magician?

The wizard leaned closer and fingered the leather of Dorak's leggings. "Who knows, Dorak, when I am young again, we may find common attraction."

Dorak moved away from the wizened old man. "I choose my own bedmates, and you shall never be among them."

The Black Cacodemon shrugged his shoulders. "One can never know. Circumstances make strange bedfellows. Your job now is to find the Bogazkoy before the girl does."

"I thought you didn't know where she is."

"I do. She is at the Sacred Lake of Yappor. Look on your map. It is an insignificant lake in the middle of nowhere."

"The Hasan Daegians think it is inhabited by their nature goddess Mekonia. I wonder what Maura is doing there?" said Dorak, pouring over his maps.

"I do not think the Bogazkoy is there, but it is apparent she is waiting for something or someone."

"It will take days to get there from here."

"Get something to eat, rest while there is time, and gather your best men. I will prepare a spell to transport you. I must find out why your wife has gone there."

Dorak strode outside his tent and told Alexanee to gather twenty good men with horses and to wait by his tent in two hours time.

Alexanee pressed his fist to his chest and hurried to carry out Dorak's orders.

Hailing a slave, Dorak ordered food and drink brought to his tent. When Dorak reentered his tent, the Black Cacodemon was gone. It did not surprise him.

Just as well, thought Dorak, while pushing on the backside of a servant pulling his boots off.

10

Yeti shook Maura vigorously.

Maura struggled to open her eyes and leaned her head on her elbow.

"Get up! They come," said Yeti, pointing to the lake.

Maura sat up and shook the cobwebs from her head. "I don't know why I feel so sleepy," stated Maura as she struggled to get up. Her muscles were stiff and sore after sleeping in her armor.

"Did you drink from the lake?" asked Yeti, helping Maura to her feet.

"No, just from your waterskin."

Yeti glanced suspiciously at the sleeping Benzar snoring loudly and dangling upside down from a high branch. "I told that idiot to get water from the stream, not the lake."

"But it looks so clean and pure."

"And it puts you to sleep like the caromate plant does a foreigner."

"I've never slept so well in my life."

Yeti pointed to the lake. "Enough of this. Behold! The Lahorians come!"

KiKu joined Maura and Yeti on the sandy shore of the lake.

Despite the darkness that had fallen several hours ago, KiKu could see the water rolling and turning as though boiling in a kettle. Light streamed upward from the bottom of the lake. He had seen many wondrous things in his life, but he hoped his courage would not fail now as he watched hundreds of strobing, colored bubbles pop up from the surface and gently roll toward them.

Maura was both excited and fearful as she watched large spheres emerge from the turbulent water. She stole a glance at Yeti.

The proud hawk's human face was contorted by fear as she beheld her race's ancient enemy.

Maura realized that it required every ounce of Yeti's training to remain composed and firm in her stance.

Yeti stepped in front of Maura protectively as did Benzar, who had awakened and flown beside them.

Knowing this was not the time to confront the Dinii's protective attitude, Maura satisfied herself with a view stolen between the hawks as they stood akimbo in front of her.

She heard KiKu move to protect her flank. Giving him a quick look, she saw he had his sword out and was studying the forest behind them. Not wishing to have anyone with a sword near her back, she pulled out her dagger just in case.

As if hearing her thoughts, KiKu sheathed his sword but still watched the dark outline of the tall forest.

Yeti let out a sharp trill, and within seconds, fifty Dinii flew out of the forest and stood in a defensive ring around the Hasan Daegian queen and KiKu.

Maura smiled. She should have known Yeti would have more Dinii around in case there was trouble. Many of the Dinii she recognized from her days of living amongst them.

They did not turn in her direction but kept watch on the approaching bubbles. Each Dini had his or her deadly razor-sharp talons exposed.

Maura wondered if they blamed her for the destruction of their home or if they held Dorak responsible. She pushed the thought from her mind and concentrated on the bobbing orbs and the deafening thunder overhead. Rain began to pelt them in earnest.

The largest of the orbs rolled to the shore. It slowly dissipated, exposing a woman in its center. The woman stood naked with long brown hair covering her breasts. Neither her hair nor skin was wet from the tumultuous water crashing about her mid-thigh. The Lahorian woman looked like a Kaserian, except parts of her flesh were translucent, exposing her veins, ligaments, and muscles.

"Empress Maura, why do you hide behind the Dinii? Why do you insult us with your fear?" the woman shouted over the thunder.

Feeling ashamed, Maura pushed Yeti and Benzar aside and stepped in front of them.

The Lahorian woman bowed her head. "Greetings, Great Mother," she said, beckoning. "We are happy to meet with you at last, but we must hurry. The black-robed one knows of your presence and will soon approach now that we have arrived. Come with me so I may transport you below."

"What assurances do I have that you are a friendly force?" Maura shouted back over the howling wind.

"We are one." The woman held up her hands, revealing a single, blinking eye in each palm. "We have from the beginning orchestrated your upbringing." Her hair blew upward with the howling wind, exposing pendulous breasts.

Several spheres landed beside her and fell away, leaving two men standing on the water. They too held up their hands, exposing eyes in their palms.

Maura saw that their penises and testicles were small.

"You and your friend must come with us quickly. The Dinii are to join Iegani in the Forbidden Zone."

Yeti cried out, "We will not leave her unescorted. We must come with her!"

The woman shook her head. "We cannot accommodate any more than three. There is simply not enough oxygen. You may come, but you must order the rest of the Dinii to fly to the Forbidden Zone."

"My orders were that you were to smuggle her into Siva and then to the Forbidden Zone," yelled Yeti, testing her.

"That was the man named KiKu's plan. We will take her directly to the Forbidden Zone. The magician now knows where she is and is approaching fast. We must hurry." The woman beckoned to Maura again. "Join me!"

Maura looked into the stormy sky and at the chaotic water that was cresting high. She was fearful that she would drown but stepped toward the woman as water lapped at her leather boots. "You are taking me to Iegani?"

"We are taking you as far as we can in the Forbidden Zone. There, at a rendezvous spot, Iegani will have Dinii fly you into Atetelco."

"What is Atetelco?" Maura asked, pushing back the hair whipping in her face.

"It is the ancient capital of the Dinii. Iegani waits for you as does the Mother Bogazkoy."

Maura was not convinced.

The Lahorian woman looked into the sky, sensing the coming of Dorak and his minions on the wings of a spell. Time was running out. "Call for Iegani and see for yourself," the Lahorian cried out as a forceful wave crashed around her.

Maura, sensing the urgency of her decision, drew upon her inner strength. *Please don't fail me, Iegani*, she pleaded.

Go with her. Do all that she instructs. Hurry! The Black Cacodemon is coming with Dorak!

Maura heard Iegani's voice as though he were standing next to her. Her head snapped back, and her eyes rolled over in their sockets. She felt strong hands catch her.

Yeti knew Iegani's message had been powerful. She had no doubt it was Iegani who had touched the mind of Maura with such force. She had seen Maura in such trances before. Yeti lifted the girl in her arms and stepped up to the Lahorian woman, placing Maura at the woman's feet.

Without waiting for an invitation, KiKu jumped next to one of the men who held a hand out to the hetmaan. An orb enveloped them while riding out into the lake.

Yeti hated water, but still strode out to the last remaining man. She stood knee deep in water when she felt something slide under her feet and raise her up. Sides of an iridescent bubble encircled her. She shouted to the rest of the Dinii, "We will meet in the Forbidden Zone!"

The words were no sooner uttered than the Dinii spread their wings and flew west.

Satisfied that her subordinates were safely on their way, Yeti began to investigate the bubble. She crunched her wings behind her and bent over as its structure was confining. "May I touch it?" she asked the amused Lahorian male who watched her expressions with curiosity.

"Gently," he clicked in the Dinii language.

Yeti made sure her talons were safely retracted before she gingerly placed the palm of her hand on the orb's transparent surface. It gave with a push. Slowly it began moving toward the center of the lake. Yeti saw the lit globe with the Lahorian woman and Maura descend into the water.

KiKu was also watching from his iridescent sphere and looked to Yeti for reassurance.

She smiled bravely and waved.

The sphere began bobbing over the steep waves. The jostling threw Yeti against the side while the Lahorian man remained stable. Sensing Yeti's discomfort with water, he sought to comfort her by speaking, "Perhaps it will help if you sit down."

Yeti agreed and slid down the flexible, iridescent sides of their globe. She heard a grinding sound and noticed the orb moved at right angles and wondered if something was pulling it. Exploring the transparent floor, Yeti thought she might discover a chain or rope but could see nothing.

"Where are we going?"

"We travel directly to the rendezvous spot to meet with the Divigi while bypassing our city."

"Why is that?" Yeti asked.

"Because we will be under attack in a few seconds, and we wish to draw conflict away from our homes." The Lahorian man pointed to the sky above them.

Yeti looked up through a circular window. The sky was no longer streaked with lightning as before, but now had a strange green and purple hue. She had seen the sky like that before. She threw herself against the sphere. "We must get out! The Black Cacodemon is here!"

The Lahorian male touched Yeti's arm, and she fell silent. "There, there," cooed the Lahorian soothingly. "We will be safe."

"We will?" Yeti asked incredulously, feeling ashamed at her outburst.

The Lahorian male nodded and said, "We are one, and we are powerful together. He will not breach us. I must join the others now. We must concentrate." He closed his eyes and held up his closed palms, which slowly opened to expose its eyes.

The frightened Dini watched KiKu's sphere disappear into the murky depths. Her sphere kept moving on the surface until it reached the spot where the other bubbles had disappeared. With a low humming sound, it slowly began to descend.

Yeti could see glowing balls of a purplish green light explode in the water, lashing against the sides of the orb. Yeti peered toward the shore. She made out the figures of Dorak astride a prancing warhorse, and the Black Cacodemon standing in the water hurling angry-looking balls of energy.

As water rushed to cover the top of her descending bubble, Yeti smiled and whispered, "You lost again, Dorak."

11

Maura came to her senses.

Halfway down to the bottom of the lake, she sat up with a start and looked around. The first thing she saw was the legs of her benefactor. The Lahorian's legs were hairless, and her paper-thin skin was covered with shimmering oil. Maura could plainly make out the woman's muscles and veins.

Maura shuddered and drew herself into a ball so she would not make contact with the Lahorian who was deep in a self-induced trance. Wiping condensation off the inside wall, she peered outside.

Hundreds of spheres were moving in the water. They were different colors and sizes—each creating its own illumination and transporting Lahorians. Smaller bubbles of pale blues and green hovered about the spheres, providing light in the now dark murky water.

Maura moved around the Lahorian woman. She could plainly see the two orbs carrying KiKu and Yeti, both of whom had hunkered down trying to find room in a bubble that was too small. They both looked miserable but determined.

Yeti glanced in her direction, and Maura waved to her. Yeti waved back and cupped her hands over her mouth yelling something.

Maura put a hand to her ear, trying to indicate that she could not hear.

Yeti began pointing frantically to the bottom of the orb.

Maura looked down.

To the right, at the bottom of the lake, was a collection of illuminated spheres stacked on top of each other. Covering the entire structure was a giant bubble with multi-colored veins that blinked off and on. The conglomeration of stacked bubbles resembled fish eggs.

Maura could see outlines of people moving around inside in various compartments. As she wondered if her group was going to the strange Lahorian city, her bubble veered off to the left. The other orbs floating beside moved also. They picked up speed and descended ever deeper into the lake. Maura could see large schools of fish dart about trying to get out of the spheres' way.

Occasionally, a monstrous fish with large sharp teeth would deliberately swim to the bubble, trying to bite into the sphere's fabric. Disgruntled, the large predators swam off only to attack a smaller bubble, which acted as a decoy.

Yeti did not like these fish and bared her teeth at them, making a great commotion in her bubble.

Still, the Lahorians did not awaken from their self-induced trances.

Resigned to her fate, Maura lay down on the floor and contented herself with wondering at the various life forms that swam past the speeding orbs.

Without warning, bolts of purple energy sliced through the deep water. Some of the bolts hit the orbs with great force, causing them to vibrate violently.

Maura feared they would start leaking, but they did not. She looked back and saw many of the spheres hit by angry lightning, but these attacks did not disturb the spheres' progress. Maura discerned the distant city was under attack also. A blanket of green light enveloped the city and furiously lashed out in the shape of a fist at the stacked spheres, trying to find a weak point.

Whoever the Lahorians were, they were risking their lives to save her skin. Maura was grateful and wished she could help her companion, but she knew that her ministrations would be weak help indeed.

She would just have to wait.

12

Dorak jumped off his black steed.

He hurled himself at the Black Cacodemon, hitting the old man with such a blow that they both fell to the ground.

The sorcerer opened his eyes under the hood of his cowl, exhaling loudly. Angrily, he sat up and raised a finger that released a short blast of energy at Dorak.

Dorak could not rise.

The lances of Dorak's soldiers pointed immediately at the wizard's heart. The Black Cacodemon smiled and lowered his hand, sitting very still.

An officer helped a stunned Dorak to his feet.

"Dorak, we almost had her," the wizard whined.

Dorak shook the dirt off his pants and tunic, not bothering to hide his disgust. "We were only to find Empress Maura."

"It was my plan to capture her and make her lead us to the Bogazkoy."

"By drowning her?"

"I don't need that bothersome girl anyway to accomplish my task. I know how to manipulate the Tree of Life."

"But I want her, you idiot! Alive and well. Not lying dead on the bottom of some lake."

"Details," chirped the wizard, fluttering his hand like an injured bird.

Dorak paced back and forth studying the lake while the violent rain stopped.

His soldiers scouted the shores and reported back to him. Others made makeshift rafts and, guided by the light of oil torches, paddled their way across the lake and back.

Dorak leaned against his horse. "Tell me, Magician, did you think you were going to find the empress in a soap bubble with naked people?"

The soldiers had allowed the Black Cacodemon to sit on a leather-folding stool but watched him warily. He turned his head from the lake toward Dorak. Dawn was coming, and the sun was emerging from behind the forest trees, casting a soft yellow glow.

"I must admit that I am confounded," confessed the Black Cacodemon.

Dorak seemed surprised at the wizard's candor and was about to speak when several of his scouts appeared.

The scouts fell to their knees. "Great Aga, we have navigated the lake."

"What did you find?"

"Nothing. No horse tracks but ours, though we did see footprints of the Dinii."

"It was expected they might be here. What else?"

"The lake is not a closed system. There is an underground river which flows to the northwest."

"The west," murmured Dorak. "Always the west. Does the river ever surface?"

"Yes, Great Aga. If our maps are correct, the river should surface in about a hundred miles."

"That is where we shall probably pick up their trail," Dorak reasoned excitedly. "Don't you agree?" He turned toward the Black Cacodemon, but the magician was no longer sitting placidly on his stool. He was nowhere to be seen.

Dorak roared, "Blast it! He's gone on ahead—that snake charmer." Jumping on his horse, he spurred it, causing the horse to spin into a gallop.

The tired and famished scouts had no choice but to follow.

13

Maura must have fallen asleep.

When she awoke, she was still in the orb, and the Lahorian woman was kneeling over her.

"You are pregnant," the Lahorian stated flatly.

Maura nodded. "It is the aga's child."

"That is good. We were worried you might conceive by the Dinii prince."

Blushing deeply, Maura tried to hide her embarrassment by looking out of the sphere.

"We are in the river system now," said the Lahorian.

Maura turned her head and gaped. Realizing the Lahorian woman studied her as well, Maura stammered, "I . . . I am very sorry. I didn't mean to stare."

The Lahorian sat down beside the young woman, leaning against the back of the humming sphere. "It is all right. We know we appear strange to you. My name used to be Rakel. Now we are simply known as the Lahorians to you."

Maura was pensive for a moment but brightened. "You no longer have an individual identity?"

"Correct, Great Mother of Hasan Daeg. We used to be separate, but now we are one."

"Why are you helping me?"

"We are reaching the end of our journey to a spiritual union. We do not wish this process to be interfered with by outsiders. It's in our best interest to help those who would wish us well on our journey."

"How does that involve me?"

"With you as ruling empress, there would be policies that could protect our homeland. You have not seen the destruction in the mountains. The Bhuttanians have great need of timber and have been stripping entire mountains of trees. The dirt from the slopes contaminates the streams, which feed this lake. See for yourself. The river used to be clear. For now, we have enough muscular strength to build the machines needed to cleanse the river before it spills into our lake, but it will not always be so. Even now our arms atrophy."

It was true. Maura noted that the Lahorian's arms looked weak compared to her muscular ones.

"The Bhuttanians must assimilate into the Hasan Daegian culture, or they must be destroyed," Rakel said emphatically. "You must join with the Mother Bogazkoy. Only then will you have the power to fight the one known as the Black Cacodemon."

"My mother fused with an offspring of the Bogazkoy, and she did not have the strength to fight Dorak and his pet sorcerer."

"The Royal Bogazkoy was ill and dying. The Mother Bogazkoy is a thousand times more potent than her offspring. Only you possess what the Mother Bogazkoy needs. Neither the Black Cacodemon nor Dorak will suit the needs of the Mother."

Maura struggled to talk about the Bogazkoy. She remembered being enveloped by the plant's tentacles, which had probed her every orifice. She sighed with pleasure at the thought of the plant's leaves caressing her skin and feeling tiny pinpricks as the leaves moved over her skin only to inject a blue substance into her skin. It had given her a feeling of euphoria she had never known.

"I don't understand. Why my family? Why not any female?"

The Lahorian smiled softly. "It is my guess that the Mother selected your ancestor out of personal preference. The Mother was attracted."

Maura was confused. "How can a plant have preferences?"

"This is not just any plant. It is a Bogazkoy."

Still not understanding, Maura's mind raced, trying to connect all the Lahorian was telling her and what her mother had said.

The Lahorian looked at her as though watching her child take a first step.

Maura felt entirely stupid. She was not connecting the information. Maura was shocked by her lack of knowledge.

"You see, the title Mother Bogazkoy is a misnomer. It is both a she and a he." The Lahorian stopped to let this information sink in. "And it needs a Hasan Daegian queen's egg to reproduce."

Maura's eyes lightened with understanding. "My egg?"

The Lahorian placed her hand tenderly on Maura's shoulder. "My dear, it will need most of your eggs."

14

Maura's brow furrowed.
"My eggs! You surely jest."

The Lahorian woman's eyes saddened. "You are young, and this news is a shock. I am sorry, but this is the way of the Mother Bogazkoy. We all have to sacrifice. That's why Hasan Daegian queens have only one child. The Bogazkoy only leaves the donor two eggs."

"You mean the Royal Bogazkoy was half Hasan Daegian?"

"The plant takes plasma from the queen's unfertilized eggs. The Bogazkoy is nothing more than a highly-evolved, sentient plant."

Maura instinctively put her hands on her belly. "What about my baby?"

Rakel spoke her words tenderly. "I do not know. Tell the Mother you are pregnant and ask it to be merciful. It was always our plan that your baby should live and rule both Hasan Daeg and Bhuttan, but with the Mother Bogazkoy, who knows."

"I won't go. I won't do anything to hurt my baby!" Maura barked stubbornly.

"If this is your wish, no one can force you. You must go willingly to the Bogazkoy or else it will not accept you. However, if you don't, then the Black Cacodemon will surely intercede with magic and deceive the Bogazkoy to gain the plant's injection of its sap. No one will be able to stop the Black Cacodemon then. He will be too powerful. This unholy union will plague our descendants for generations to come until our people die out. The planet will be uninhabitable, and no one will survive but those the Black Cacodemon wills. Is this what you want for our future? For your child's future?"

Maura slid down the wall of the pulsating sphere and cried softly.

She threw off the comforting hand of Rakel.

The Lahorian did not touch her again, leaving the young woman alone with her private thoughts.

Terrible images ran through Maura's mind as she tried to sort through her options. All she knew was that she wanted to run away and hide from Dorak and the Lahorians. Both of their needs were too great for her to bear. She did not speak to Rakel. Around and around Rakel's words spun in her head. *We all have to sacrifice!* Maura could stand the silence no longer. "What have you sacrificed, Rakel?" she asked sarcastically.

The Lahorian wiped condensation off the side of the sphere and touched Maura's forehead with the cool wetness. "This sphere was damaged during the attack by the Black Cacodemon and is no longer watertight. There is just enough oxygen to get you to the rendezvous spot, but I will not be able to return home."

Maura was alarmed. "The Dinii will fly you to safety."

The Lahorian shook her head slowly. "I'm afraid not. My people have not left the water for over three hundred years. Our bones are brittle. No matter how careful the Dinii are, this frail body would never survive the journey home. Without the sphere, we cannot survive outside of our city."

She folded her hands together. "It does not matter. We have foreseen this death before you were born. We even discussed it with Gitar."

"You visited Gitar?"

"She came to us years ago. We showed your adoptive mother the future. She knew the death of her world was imminent. She was frightened as you are now, but she was determined that you should survive to carry out your destiny. Now you must take up where she left off. Let us show you how it could be." Rakel extended her arms and held her palms up. The eyes in the middle of her palms opened their lids sleepily and blinked several times. "Look into the future and see your destiny."

Standing transfixed, Maura stared into the seeing eyes of Rakel. Deeper and deeper she felt pulled until she was no longer in the sphere but sitting on a horned throne in the middle of a massive pavilion. Torches held in brass sconces lit the dank leather shelter giving it a shadowy and smoky atmosphere.

Standing by Maura's side was an older Yeti whose feathers were tinged with grey. A young girl whose skin was pale blue and whose hair was ebony stood on the other. She had Dorak's black, probing eyes. The young girl slowly turned her head and looked at Maura.

She saw herself smile at the girl and then turn her attention to the multitude prostrating themselves before them: Bhuttanians, Hasan Daegians, Sivans, Kittium, Hittals, and other races that Maura did not recognize.

That is my daughter, Maura heard herself say somewhere in the distance.

That is the daughter that could be, if only you would speak to the Mother Bogazkoy, she heard Rakel speak into in her mind.

The image blurred and wavered as though it was a mirage in the desert. Then it disappeared.

Maura stood unsteadily in the cramped sphere. She placed her hands on her belly and locked eyes with Rakel. "Do not be afraid, Rakel. I will have this baby, and then I will restore order to Kaseri."

"You know what you have to do to gain the throne?"

"I understand my destiny. I know what it is that you would have of me."

"It will be a sorrowful occasion."

"What do any of you care except that I do as you wish? Was that not the reason for my birth? To do everyone's dirty work for them?"

"I am truly sorry, but what you say has merit. No one else could have gotten close enough to the aga, whether he be Zoar or Dorak."

"But then the Black Cacodemon intervened."

"He was unforeseen by us. He managed to keep his presence a secret from us."

"Clever," mused Maura. "But I was to marry Dorak and conceive his child."

Rakel beamed a strange smile. "Well, conceive Zoar's or Dorak's child anyway."

Maura's eyes darkened. "It didn't matter if I were forced."

Rakel's face paled as she looked away. "It did not matter to us how the child was conceived."

"The only thing that mattered was that an aga and I meet, conceive, and bear the child who would one day rule over Hasan Daeg and Bhuttan, thus ensuring friendly policies to the Lahorians. And if I had to kill the child's father, so be it," Maura spat into the sphere. "You Lahorians are really smarmy."

Rakel ignored the insults in Maura's words. "It is more complicated than you imagine. We are but a spoke in the wheel."

Maura growled, "But something went wrong with your plans. The great all-seeing eyes failed in projecting the future because the Black Cacodemon eluded you. You didn't foresee that I would fall in love with Dorak and would shudder at the thought of harming him."

"We did not foresee that he would fall in love with you."

"You mean he loves me?" Maura clasped her hands together.

"That does not change what you must do."

"If I could talk to Dorak without the Black Cacodemon, I could make him see. We could do away with that wicked man."

Shaking her head slowly, Rakel began to tremble. "It is not possible. You are thinking like an impetuous girl, not a queen."

"You mean I am thinking with hope?"

"The hope in your love is not possible. You are thinking without clarity. Once Dorak takes you back to Bhuttan, it would only be a matter of time before you and the child are assassinated. The Bhuttanians want a Bhuttanian for their queen."

"But Dorak has never married a Bhuttanian. He first married that Anqarian woman."

"And as you saw with your own eyes, he did not acknowledge her or his first son."

"That was because of me."

"NO! You must listen to us. He has never acknowledged her publicly nor his son for he does not want this child to rule."

Maura put her hands over her ears. "Lies! Lies! He loves me. He will not hurt me. You said so yourself."

"We said he loves you. We did not say he would not harm you. He has never been honest with you."

"It's not true. Not true."

"You know it is true. No matter how much Dorak loves you, he is ambitious and desires to rule above all else. He will not let his love for you interfere with his ultimate goal."

Maura faced the Lahorian. "Tell me one thing. Did Dorak know that Mikkotto had set a trap for my mother?"

"We cannot lie. Dorak had no knowledge of Mikkotto's treachery."

Sighing with relief, Maura mumbled, "Thank you for that."

The orb lurched forward, throwing both Maura and Rakel off balance and causing them to fall against the side of the sphere. It twisted and spun, finally ramming itself into the soft mud of the riverbank.

Maura fell on Rakel and immediately pulled herself up. She instinctively felt her stomach and, sensing that everything was fine, turned her attention to Rakel.

Rakel's face twisted in agony.

Maura realized that Rakel had taken a nasty fall.

Murky water seeped into the sphere.

Kneeling down, Maura felt for any broken bones or injuries to Rakel.

The Lahorian woman groaned with each touch.

"I'm sorry," Maura said as she continued to explore the woman's body.

"I have not been touched since I suckled my child," moaned Rakel.

"How long ago was that?" asked Maura, trying to keep Rakel talking.

"Sixteen years."

"Why does that not surprise me," retorted Maura, checking the woman's arms.

"We are not affectionate with the flesh. Just the mind."

The water in the sphere was rising higher until the tops of Maura's boots were covered. "Let me heal you," Maura offered.

"Too much damage. Will weaken you. You must get to the Forbidden Zone."

Maura held the woman's head out of the water. She could see that Rakel was hemorrhaging from the lungs. Blood seeped under the skin of her chest and spread into her abdomen.

Rakel coughed, and a thin trickle of blood appeared at the corner of her colorless lips. "Save yourself," she implored.

Righting herself, Maura felt the sides of the sphere. Sunlight poured through the crystalline bubble. Maura recognized part of the sphere was out of the water. If they could break out, land would only be a step away. Maura pounded on the top of the bubble. "How do we get out of this thing?"

Choking on water rising over her mouth, Rakel struggled to point her finger at something but dropped it from exhaustion.

Maura hunkered down again and pulled Rakel up into a sitting position.

Rakel cried out from the pain. Her entire chest was red, and the crimson stain was gathering in her belly.

Maura knew Rakel's end was coming.

Rakel struggled for air. "The walls are giving way and will collapse. As I die, so does the sphere."

"You mean this thing is alive?"

The injured woman nodded weakly. "Do not fear. The others are on their way."

"Do you realize that you have been saying 'I' instead of 'we'?"

Smiling faintly, Rakel coughed, spewing out a spray of blood.

Maura tried to wipe the blood from the woman's face, but Rakel weakly pushed her hand away. Her lips began to pull back from her teeth, and her eyes were becoming dimmer. "It is a bit of vanity that I allow with my passing." She locked eyes with Maura. "May Mekonia be with you on your difficult journey. I can be of no more help."

Maura started to reply when Rakel shook with the death rattle and lay still. She gently closed the Lahorian's eyes and wiped the blood from around her mouth. Grateful that Rakel did not suffer long, Maura turned her attention to the orb. Taking a dagger out of her boot, Maura stabbed the sphere repeatedly.

Water began to pour in rapidly, and Maura now stood waist deep in it. The sphere shook and shuddered as Maura tried to twist its skin off. The bubble began to lose its iridescent illumination, but its sides still would not yield.

Maura breathed deep gulps of air even though she knew she was using up her oxygen supply.

A large object bumped into the sphere, knocking Maura over into the pooling water. Hearing shouts, Maura yelled in response as she tried not to step on Rakel's body.

Dark forms climbed over the top of the orb and tore at it. Finally, a razor-sharp talon ripped the top of the sphere, and Yeti's head appeared through the opening.

Seeing Maura was safe, her face lit up until she spied the dead body of Rakel. "My oarsman told me she had died, and you were unable to open this contraption because it had died with her."

"Oarsman?" echoed Maura.

"That's what I call the Lahorian. Come on. I'll help you out," Yeti said, extending her hand through the torn skin of the sphere.

Maura tried to pull Rakel out of the water. "Help me with her!"

Yeti waved her hand. "Leave her be. Each Lahorian has an orb in which they are buried. The Lahorians will take it back with them. Come on. She's beyond our help now."

Maura hesitated.

"She knew she was going to die on this trip. She foretold it many years ago to your mother just as she foretold your mother's death."

Maura reluctantly let Rakel's body slide back into the cold water.

She stood on her toes catching Yeti's hand and was pulled up. Once through the hole and outside, she sat on top of the bubble while her eyes adjusted to the bright light.

"It's early morning. We've traveled all night."

Maura cupped her hand over her eyes and scanned her surroundings. "Where's KiKu?"

"Here I am, Great Mother," greeted a relieved KiKu, standing on the riverbank.

"The woman is gone. She bled to death."

"Yes, we know. The other Lahorians felt her death. We were following at a distance and hurried as fast as we could."

"Where are the Lahorians?"

KiKu pointed toward the middle of the river. "They are mourning their companion."

Maura's gaze followed the direction of his finger to where two large glittering spheres bobbed in the river. She could barely make out the darkened forms of two men who seemed to be chanting.

"They will take her back when we leave," said Yeti, watching them also.

"Should we stay and help them?" asked Maura, uncomfortable with leaving Rakel's body submerged in the water.

"They are waiting for us to go. They do not wish us to observe their death ritual. Besides, we have a journey of our own." Yeti looked up into the sky. "We must be off if we are to meet Iegani at the rendezvous point."

Maura looked at Yeti, disbelieving. "This isn't it?"

Yeti answered calmly. "We are in the Forbidden Zone but several miles short of our destination. Your orb ran into a log and got snagged. The Lahorian was hurt so she couldn't maneuver it out." She shrugged her massive shoulders. "So here we are."

"Can you fly us there, Yeti?" asked KiKu.

"Not at the moment. My wings are cramped from being inside that tiny thing for so long. I would probably drop you."

Maura jumped off the top of the sphere and onto the shore. Her legs had muscle cramps, and her leather clothes were becoming extremely uncomfortable after being exposed to water. She took her dagger and split the sides of her pants and then stretched her leggings around her legs.

After KiKu handed her a waterskin, she took a long drink. Sheathing her dagger, Maura massaged her calves and then straightened. "Let's be off," she ordered with determination, trying to ignore her growling stomach.

"This way," Yeti advised as she set off at a brisk pace.

Glancing back at the spheres in the water one more time, Maura set off after Yeti with KiKu following her. They stayed close to the riverbank, making sure they never lost sight of it. After several miles, they finally came to a small clearing.

Yeti stopped and surveyed the trees.

Maura and KiKu hid in the bushes until Yeti gave them the signal that it was safe.

Satisfied, Yeti stepped out into the clearing and began stretching her wings. "Ah, that feels good," she said to no one in particular.

"Where are the others?" asked KiKu, surveying his surroundings suspiciously.

"We are to be picked up here. We simply wait," replied Yeti, scanning the sky.

KiKu merely grunted and fished in his pockets for some biscuits, which he shared with Yeti and Maura. Stale though they were, Maura was grateful for anything to eat.

They had not been waiting long when Yeti heard the familiar flapping of great wings from the western sky. It was mid-afternoon. "Right on time," she said, checking the position of the sun in the sky.

Three hawks settled lightly on their feet.

Though KiKu should have been getting used to the sight of the Dinii, they nevertheless astonished him. He unwillingly took a step back.

All three Dinii bowed very low to Maura and greeted her with various hoots and whistles particular to the Dinii language.

Maura inclined her head toward the hawks while a frown spread across her face. "Greetings, Toppo," she said, thinking of their last encounter. "I hear you have the makings of a divigi."

Toppo blinked heavily. "You are most kind in your praise."

"Benzar. Tarsus."

"Always a pleasure, Great Mother."

Yeti interrupted. "We must be off. Benzar, you take KiKu. Tarsus, take Her Majesty."

Maura strode behind Tarsus.

He had a harness that she put around them both and buckled around his middle.

Maura placed her hands around Tarsus' neck and nestled between his wings as they took off with astounding speed.

Toppo took wing after them, protecting their flank.

KiKu searched the sky and saw more Dinii diving from cloud cover and quickly surrounding Tarsus and his passenger.

Grinning, Benzar went over to KiKu and turned his back, pointing to a harness.

KiKu paled, and his knees buckled. "I don't think I can do this again."

"You are the hetmaan who tricked Zoar. Surely, a ride on my back is nothing compared to dumping Zoar off his horse," needled Benzar.

"As long as I do not end up like Zoar."

"That's enough," commanded Yeti. She gathered some tall grass and quickly wove a strip that was long enough to go around KiKu's eyes and tied it behind his head. She did not even give KiKu a chance to protest. She covered his eyes and lifted the protesting KiKu into the harness. Seeing that he was becoming more and more agitated, she struck him sharply in the head, knocking him unconscious.

Benzar laughed.

Angry, Yeti swung Benzar around. "The last person who was afraid to ride a Dini had her neck broken. Don't you remember?"

Benzar's laughter suddenly stopped as he lowered his head. "I remember Mehmet," he said softly. "I meant no slight."

"Make sure this one arrives alive," snapped Yeti, her nerves frayed. The responsibility of Maura's safety was a heavy burden.

"Yes, Yeti," replied Benzar, his head cowed. He checked the harness and made sure KiKu was safely buckled in before spreading his wings and flying toward the western horizon.

As soon as Benzar was out of sight, fifty Dinii dove from under cloud cover and reported to Yeti. They brought water and food. Once Yeti satisfied her thirst and hunger, she rested in a large tree with the Dinii acting as guards. The first rest she had taken in many days was like a balm to her racing mind.

Night fell too quickly, and a guard awakened her. Groggily, she shook her head and splashed water on her face from a waterskin hanging on a branch. She shook her wings trying to work out the kinks and cramps until she was ready.

Standing in formation, the fifty-one Dinii took off in perfect unison and flew to join Iegani, the Great Divigi, waiting in Atetelco.

15

It grew bitterly cold.

Tarsus flew over the mountains that divided Hasan Daeg and the Forbidden Zone where Atetelco stood.

Huge goosebumps rose on Maura's skin as her teeth chattered. The wind howled in her face as she began to lose feeling in her extremities.

Hearing her moan, Tarsus thought he might lose her to the cold elements. He signaled to the other Dinii flying in formation with him, and they landed on a mountain. The Dinii carefully unbuckled the nearly unconscious Maura and laid her on the ground. Tarsus dug a hole in the snow while other Dinii rubbed Maura's skin vigorously. When they finished with the pit, several Dinii climbed in, and Tarsus lowered the shivering woman to them. They laid her on top of them as other Dinii climbed in and surrounded her, spreading their wings over her wet, cold body. Tarsus packed dry snow around them, leaving several air holes. Then he and the other Dinii buried themselves in the snow to wait for better weather.

Several Dinii hid among the mountain boulders to keep watch. They knew Iegani would be furious with this delay, but a late queen was better than a dead one.

As soon as dawn broke, Toppo lifted up from her shallow pit and faced the morning light. It was snowing heavily. She found that her water had frozen. Toppo broke the ice with her fist and she, along with several Dinii, breathed on the waterskin until the ice turned to slush.

Taking a pink powder from one of the many pouches hanging around her hips, she mixed the powder with the icy slush. The novice divigi located the spot where Maura was buried and dug until she unearthed the small group that was keeping the queen alive with their body heat.

The Dinii sleepily opened their eyes and yawned.

Toppo and Tarsus pulled them out of the pit along with the groggy but warm Maura.

Maura struggled to open her eyes as the Dinii gathered around to shield her from the extreme wind and the blanket of snow that was quickly covering them.

Toppo grabbed Maura's face with her powerful hands and compelled her mouth to open. Pouring the pink ice water into Maura's mouth, Toppo stroked her throat forcing the liquid down.

Struggling for a moment, Maura swallowed and soon fell into a deep sleep. Checking the young woman's hands and feet, Toppo was satisfied there was no damage from frostbite and helped Tarsus harness Maura onto his back.

"Will she be all right?" Tarsus asked, more than a little concerned. He hated to face Iegani's wrath.

"She is warm. The powder will make her sleep the rest of the journey. She will not suffer from the cold anymore."

"Do you think KiKu is still alive?"

"I'm going back to find Benzar's party and see."

"Who would think these creatures would be so susceptible to a blizzard?"

Toppo wiped the snow from her eyelids. "We should have thought of it, even someone with Maura's strength."

All the other Dinii hopped around and shook the snow and ice from their wings, preparing to fly northwest. They stretched and rubbed their wings.

"As soon as they can accompany you, take off and don't stop until you reach the city," Toppo commanded. "We have only one more day."

Tarsus nodded, realizing the severity of the situation. He looked very concerned.

Toppo smiled, giving him a knowing look. "Don't worry. We will prevail." She patted his hand. Approaching an overhang, she spread her wings and took off into the howling wind.

Tarsus could not see her in the blinding snow but sensed her flying steadily into the wind. He turned and barked orders.

The other Dinii quickly gathered into formation. With the snow falling around them, they spread their mighty wings and flew into the western sky. Next stop would be the former capital of the Dinii. They were all determined to get there or die trying.

16

Maura awoke.

Her vision clouded as she struggled to focus on something white and fuzzy near her face. Finally, she relaxed and breathed a sigh of relief. "Hello, Iegani," she greeted huskily, her throat parched from her journey.

Iegani gently lifted her head and placed a bowl of warm water to her lips.

She drank greedily. When satisfied, she laid her head back on the pillow and closed her eyes.

"None of that," spat Iegani, shaking her shoulders. "Arise, young de Magela and face your destiny."

"What, no breakfast first?"

"Your Majesty, time is almost up. You must proceed to the Mother Bogazkoy now!"

Maura raised herself up on one elbow and squinted at the blue-robed figure wringing her hands behind Iegani. "Ah, Noabini, the High Priestess of the House of Magi. How nice to see you. I wondered what had happened to you during all these months while your women suffered at the hands of the Bhuttanians." Maura leaned back down on the pillow and turned over, pulling the fur covers over her ears.

The High Priestess from the House of Magi and Iegani exchanged anxious glances.

Iegani tore off the cover and gave Maura a sharp kick in the leg. "Get up, you impertinent child. The future depends on our actions today."

Maura laughed, which soon turned into coughing. She spat a wad of pink phlegm, which landed precariously near Iegani's feet. She wiped her mouth with the back of her hand. "Don't you dare order me about, you old fraud. You lied to me about Dorak."

The priestess reacted harshly to Maura's words.

"Do I offend you, Priestess, when I tell you this nasty old birdman is a liar and a manipulator?" Maura spat.

Iegani gave her a withering glare.

Maura stretched out on the bed designed as a nest. "So this is the Forbidden City of the Overlords. I should say 'past' Overlords."

Iegani reached down and grabbed Maura by the hair.

"Stop!" Familiar hands pulled Maura away.

Maura blinked several times before she realized who held her. "Empress!" she whispered.

Empress Gitar kissed Maura's cheek and then held her tightly in her arms. "My lost chick. You've had to endure so much," she cooed. She cradled Maura in her strong arms and rocked her as though she were still a baby. "I'm sorry. Many have died and for what? A crazy man's ambition. It is so senseless." Setting Maura upright on her knees, Gitar extended her talons and began raking the tangles out of Maura's hair.

"The Lahorian, Rakel, is dead," mumbled Maura, leaning against Gitar. Maura enjoyed the touch of a familiar and kind hand.

Gitar stopped combing for a second and sighed deeply. "It is as she foretold."

Maura turned toward Gitar and grabbed her hand. "Did you know about the Mother Bogazkoy?"

Her large yellow eyes were full of pity as they locked with Maura's. "Not until years after we made the pact with the Lahorians. Rakel told me some of the mysteries of the Mother Bogazkoy, but not all."

"There is more?"

"Yes, more than you can dream of."

Iegani pointed a finger at Maura, whereas Gitar shot him a look of extreme displeasure. He ignored her stare and addressed Maura. "If you hate, then hate me. If you must have vengeance, kill me. I am the one who has brought much of this to pass, not Gitar."

Pushing Gitar's gentle hands away, Maura stood defiantly before Iegani. "Once my teacher. Now my enemy."

Iegani peered down at Maura. He tucked his wings submissively. "I am not your enemy, but I am not your friend. I have protected you, taught you, yes, even manipulated you. Not because I loved you, but because you were needed. Why, might you ask? I have no great faith in slave flesh."

Maura stiffened at the mention of the word "slave."

"Iegani," cautioned Gitar, "you go too far."

"You are the descendant of slaves we conquered and took to Hasan Daeg after the Lahorians defeated us. We needed beings to cultivate the land and tend to the forests so we could be free to pursue whatever we fancied. And if game was scarce, your kind nourished us." Iegani paused and took in the silence of the cavernous room. "As your kind developed, we granted you more privileges, but never doubt this," he waved a finger in Maura's face, "we were always in charge."

"You are hideous." Maura seethed with white-hot anger.

"No, I am practical."

"Why are you saying such things?" Gitar lamented. "Hasan Daegians have not been eaten for centuries ever since we made the treaty with them. Why do you try to inflame her?"

"Because I am sick of her sniveling and crawling before the Bhuttanians. Somewhere there is a queen inside her." He threw a goblet at Maura, spilling its contents and almost hitting Gitar in the shoulder. "A queen who will fight!" he roared. "Not this coward, this whining mass of putrid skin. She is playing games because she is mad at me. Well, you shame us. You shame your mother. You are nothing like her. You are a disgrace to Abisola's memory!"

Maura flailed her arms trying to get at Iegani, but Gitar held her fast. "I'm not a coward! I want to save my baby. And I'll tell you one thing, I never saw my mother out on the battlefield. It was me taking risks, putting my neck on the line!"

"Do you think the Black Cacodemon will let you have your baby if he finds you? You stupid child. He'll rip that baby from your womb and eat it with relish."

"And the Mother Bogazkoy might kill my baby as well."

Gitar tried to calm Maura down. "You don't know that."

"Can you guarantee that it won't?"

Gitar was quiet for a moment and then spoke carefully. "No, I can't. The only thing I know for sure is that the Black Cacodemon will soon be here, and if he reaches the Bogazkoy first, all is lost. For your baby, for my son, for everyone."

Gitar slowly knelt before the young queen. "I am begging for the lives of my people as well as your offspring. Take the one chance offered to you and mate with the Mother Bogazkoy. Please!"

Maura could not stand to see her mentor and sovereign on her knees. "Don't, please," she pleaded, helping Gitar to rise.

She turned to Iegani standing by watching, unmoved. "You think me a worthless queen, a young woman whose mind and heart have been muddled by selfishness and cowardice. My mind has been strained, but not by weakness. I thought I could reach Dorak."

Maura could see she was not influencing Iegani. "You don't understand. Haven't you ever been in love? Are you so old that you have forgotten its hold on the heart?"

Iegani was so taken aback by the questions that his feathers ruffled on his shoulders. He decided to ignore the subject. "You have been trained from birth to do your duty in anticipation of this very moment. The Lahorians foresaw you with a child. There is every reason to believe that the Mother Bogazkoy will not harm it. But we must go now!"

Maura felt Gitar standing protectively near her.

"Maybe there is another way?" said Gitar.

Iegani bellowed, "There is no other way! If there were, don't you think I would have thought of it?"

Resigned, Maura put her hand on Gitar's arm, restraining her. "I have always done my duty. Regardless of what you think, Iegani, I am a good queen. Someday, I will be a great queen. You need only stay alive long enough to witness it."

Maura saw her sword and dagger on a table and went over to gather them. She turned and faced Iegani squarely. "I am ready," she said with finality.

There was a gleam of triumph in Iegani's eyes. He summoned Tarsus and Toppo.

They hurried into the room carrying a golden sedan with carved outstretched wings attached to two long poles. Bowing low, they glanced at Maura and sensed great hostility coming from her.

Iegani motioned to the chair. "They will carry you to the Mother Bogazkoy. Empress Gitar and I will follow to witness the union."

Saying nothing, Maura lowered herself into the portable throne. She signaled to Toppo and Tarsus with a nod of her head.

Grasping the poles, they lifted the chair and hurried out of the room, running into a massive hallway made of stone blocks where hundreds of Dinii stood pressed close to the walls like statues.

At the end of the hallway was a pair of the largest carved doors that Maura had ever seen. They must have stood sixty feet high. The mammoth doors were slowly swung open by Dinii pulling on large ropes looped through holes in the handle design.

Toppo and Tarsus ran toward the door as it was opening and flew out into the sky with Maura sitting in the golden chair.

She turned to look at the doors again. She could see little as Gitar and Iegani were following close behind with the rest of the Dinii contingent.

Turning forward in her seat, Maura gazed upon the Forbidden City of Atetelco, the long-lost capital of the Overlords of Kaseri.

Gigantic buildings mounted on marble and granite pillars stood everywhere. The main floor of each building stood at least forty feet off the ground. Each building had one main entrance, but Maura could see neither windows nor other exits in any of the structures. The buildings vaguely reminded her of descriptions from scrolls brought from the House of Magi.

Maura strained her eyes to see everything. Some buildings possessed no walls, just a roof. Maura guessed these structures had been open-air markets. Below were overgrown gardens and remnants of pathways. Creeping vines covered most of the Dinii statues spotting the grounds of the city.

Camping underneath many of the buildings or in the gardens were Hasan Daegian soldiers from the western division of her army. Tents and cooking fires were strewn all across the eastern side of the city along with laundry hanging from makeshift clotheslines.

Maura was startled to see shirts and diapers flapping in the breeze. Then she realized the Dinii were housing not only her army but also the western Hasan Daegian population.

Atetelco had become a refugee camp. Many of the buildings her people were lodged in had ropes and ladders hanging from the first-floor entrance. Women scurried up a ladder or pulled some heavy object up on a rope. Others, living on the ground, were putting out their campfires and tearing down their tents. Soldiers were lining up in combat formation.

Maura peered closer. *They are getting ready for battle!* she thought. She strained to look beyond the eastern part of the city. In the distance, a thin line of dust could be seen approaching the city. DORAK IS COMING WITH HIS ARMY!

Maura waved to catch Toppo's attention. Cupping her hands to her mouth, Maura yelled, "Fly lower around my soldiers. They must see me."

Toppo signaled to Tarsus, and they descended near the busy Hasan

Daegian soldiers.

Looking up at the approaching Dinii, many of the Hasan Daegians did not recognize their queen. Maura straightened herself in the golden sedan and tried to look every inch a sovereign worthy of them. She waved and called, cheering them on to victory. Slowly, the people acknowledged her.

The Hasan Daegians, depressed from months of deprivation and isolation in the Forbidden Zone, took heart when they saw Maura waving to them. She looked well and strong. As her manner gave them hope, they cheered and clapped each other on the back. Others danced little jigs, so happy were they to see her.

Receiving a reproach telepathically from Iegani, Toppo finally veered the chair away and headed toward the very western part of the city near the sea.

Maura looked behind.

Iegani and Gitar followed with many Dinii warriors in tow. The rest of the Dinii stayed with the Hasan Daegians to fight Dorak's steadily encroaching army.

They descended toward an inlet between the shore and a tiny island. Deserted boardwalks, dilapidated docks, and empty storehouses along the shore of the city gave testimony that the Dinii had once been a potent force at sea as well as on land.

Maura still could not get used to the size of the buildings, all of which were built several stories off the ground. She wondered if the Dinii had once been a taller race of beings as the entrances to the building were immense.

She thought about the City of the Peaks, which had existed on the highest mountain in Hasan Daeg. Though adequate for a Dini's needs, the stick and stone buildings possessed none of the architectural wonders with sculptures and mosaics that she witnessed in the Forbidden City. She did not have long to ponder as Toppo and Tarsus began guiding the chair precariously through streets and finally onto one of the docks. They gently laid the sedan down.

"Are you well?" Toppo asked with great concern.

Maura reassured her with a quick nod.

Tarsus helped Maura out of the chair and held her while she tried to steady her shaking legs.

"I much prefer the solid back of a Dini to that of a golden throne that might fall apart," said Maura, holding onto Tarsus' hands.

He snorted his approval.

Maura found her land legs and looked at Tarsus. "Now what?"

Toppo answered her. "It is only a little further." She pointed to a small cliff with steps carved near the bottom leading to the sea. "You must climb down this cliff to the stairs. Follow the stairs to the sea. There will be ten more steps underwater. At the bottom of these steps is a small tunnel, which you must swim through. You will come up into a rock chamber. Follow the hallway from the chamber, and you will eventually come to the Mother."

"What about you?" asked Maura, shivering in the sea breeze.

"We have to dive from another angle to gather enough momentum to swim under the sea." Toppo pointed to her feathers. "Did you forget they are water repellent?"

Tarsus and Toppo murmured, "Good luck," and bowed low. They spread their wings and flew high into the sky where Iegani and Gitar hovered as well as the Dinii warriors following them.

Maura tied back her black hair with a leather thong torn from her clothes. Securing her dagger, she climbed down until she reached the slick steps. Once she came to the bottom step, she tentatively stuck her foot into the water. Feeling the icy cold through her leather boots, she placed her hand over her womb. Maura closed her eyes and calmed herself. "Baby," she whispered to her unborn child, "if you want to live, stay strong." She gently patted her stomach. Taking a deep breath, Maura plunged into the green water. The shock of the water's cold forced the air out of her lungs, but she managed to acclimate herself. Losing the outline of the steps, she came back up for air and found the first step in the water. Taking another deep breath, she dove underneath again, this time taking care to follow the outline of the steps.

Maura counted carefully and swiftly followed the steps down to the tenth one. There she felt for an opening and found the small tunnel. She entered it quickly as she was running out of air, and her lungs were burning.

Hearing a crashing noise behind her, Maura realized the Dinii had entered the water. This encouraged her to keep going. Ahead, she saw light streaming through the water and swam toward it until her head popped out in a small opening. Maura grabbed the sides, trying to pull up, but coughing and spewing water so hard she fell back. Again, she struggled and managed to dig her heels into the side of the tunnel's slick wall, finally pulling herself onto a marble floor. Hearing commotion, she leaned down into the water's opening. Seeing feathers, she reached down into the dark water and, grabbing a fistful of them, pulled Toppo toward her.

Toppo grabbed the side of the hole and hoisted herself into the chamber. "I almost couldn't get through," she wheezed. "The tunnel is so small!" Catching her breath, she leaned down and helped Maura look for more struggling Dinii.

Seeing the outline of the royal black and white feathers, Toppo submerged her torso into the icy water and hauled a gagging Gitar out. Gitar stumbled into a corner to catch her breath.

Tarsus emerged from the tunnel hole without any assistance as did Iegani. As males, they were both smaller and were not as distressed. Spreading their wings, they shook themselves off with vigor.

Yeti and Benzar emerged, followed by the rest of the Dinii.

Maura backed off to get out of the way of the water spray. She was shivering and rubbed the goosebumps on her arms and legs vigorously. Once her teeth stopped chattering, Maura checked her dagger. Then she explored the chamber.

It was a natural cave, but the floor was enhanced with rare green and white marble. Delicate reliefs had been carved into the walls by superb artists.

Maura went over to them. Tracing their outlines with her fingertips, she studied the reliefs closely. There were carvings of past Dinii empresses pinning down beings of strange-looking races with their taloned feet. Some of the empresses looked as though they were about to tear off their captives' heads.

Beside each relief, there were lines of pictographs. Maura recognized many of the symbols. "Look here!" she said excitedly. "These marks are ancient Anqarian!"

Toppo and Tarsus joined her at the wall and examined the carvings.

Iegani and Gitar glanced at each other.

Standing behind, Iegani reminded Maura. "The Mother Bogazkoy awaits." He helped a reluctant Gitar to her feet. "Down this way," he said, pointing to an ancient passageway that led from the chamber.

Maura peered down the passageway. "I won't be able to see in the dark."

"Follow me," said Iegani. "I have visited the Mother Bogazkoy many times since coming here. She is anxious for you."

"I know what the Bogazkoy is. The Lahorian, Rakel, told me about it."

"Rakel only told you part of it, I am sure," replied Iegani. He started to explain when a green light suddenly flashed through the tunnel opening into the room. Malevolent looking fingers of light crept about the floor as though searching.

Gitar wailed, "The Black Cacodemon. He has found us!"

Not losing a moment, Iegani grabbed Maura's hand and began racing down a corridor.

Maura stumbled and fell in the dark but felt Iegani's hands drag her to her feet. Looking back, she could make out Gitar and the rest of the Dinii running behind her.

"Keep going," Gitar mouthed, her eyes wide with fright Maura hardened her resolve and began running as quickly as Iegani. Realizing she was keeping pace with him, Iegani let go of Maura's hand and concentrated on taking the correct passageway in the myriad of honeycombed corridors. Like the underground pathways in the royal Hasan Daegian palace, the corridor on the left was always the one taken.

Glancing back, Maura could see the faint glow of a pulsating light in the hallway. A terrible boom sounded in the passageway, shaking the walls about them. The Black Cacodemon was getting closer.

Iegani took one last left turn, and Maura followed him into an open chamber. He stopped suddenly.

Maura followed suit and looked about. She was in the chamber of the Mother Bogazkoy. As she expected, it was almost identical to the chamber of the Royal Bogazkoy in the Hasan Daegian palace, except there was no boat. Across a rolling lake of seawater was a small rock island on which abided the Mother Bogazkoy.

Making out a small blue lump on the rock, Maura turned toward Iegani. "Surely that small thing can't be the Mother?"

As soon as Maura spoke, the Mother Bogazkoy unfurled its magnificent leaves from the tight ball it slept in. A robust blue-green trunk emerged from the rocks with long green tendrils, which unfurled into the water.

"I hear the voice of my beloved's child," sang a melodious voice that was neither male nor female. Tendrils emerged from the water and quickly crept around Maura's body before she had time to move. "Centuries ago, your ancestor Rosalind came to me and helped to rejuvenate my kind. I would have been lost without her. Since then I have pledged myself only to her offspring and, in return, have given them my precious gifts of health and long life, small tokens of my esteem. Be my love now. Come to me."

Maura pushed away a probing tendril. "I am with child. I will not help you if you harm my baby," she shouted, amazed that the plant was sentient and could communicate.

The tendril stopped moving about Maura and loosened its grip on her.

Gitar and Iegani held their breaths.

The Mother Bogazkoy spoke after a long pause. "Your joy is my joy. Blessed is this union of human love. I will give your offspring the greatest gift of all. Everlasting life!"

"Everlasting? That is a curse, not a blessing," Maura argued.

A great pounding sounded in the hallway.

Realizing she did not have any more time, Maura dove into the hot salt water and swam for the Mother.

Tendrils gathered around Maura's waist while others entered the water. Together the tendrils lifted her out of the steaming lake and onto the rock home of the Mother Bogazkoy.

Without hesitation, Maura pulled herself up by the Bogazkoy's tendrils and hurried to the trunk of the plant. Fine hair covered the trunk of the plant, which now looked almost like skin.

"You are my beloved mate. I will not hurt you. You will know ecstasy with me. From your body, I will extract the eggs I need. My issue will replace me as I am getting old." The Mother's voice seemed to come from every direction at once.

"The Royal Bogazkoy never produced an offspring."

"Only I have that capacity, but now my long life is nearly spent. I must provide an heir to take my place."

"If the Royal Bogazkoy did not need to reproduce, why did it allow only one royal child?"

"Its gift to the queens was too powerful. It is the pact Rosalind made with me. In exchange for long life and power, only one child to each ruler. A second child could be born, but only under special circumstances. The secret had to be kept and not abused."

Maura placed her hand on her stomach. "Save my child."

The Mother Bogazkoy assured, "The baby will not be harmed if you do as I say. Move not unless I move you. Resist not and I will go nowhere near the child. Move and I cannot be responsible. Simply yield unto me. Do you understand, my love?"

A great crash sounded across the lake, but Maura did not look. She realized what had happened.

The Black Cacodemon had gotten through and was now in the

chamber. Wide strobes of green, purplish light flashed on the walls as did long beams of a bluish white.

Maura threw herself at the center of the Mother Bogazkoy and immediately limbs from the base of the trunk rose and encased her. For a moment, Maura struggled as she heard her clothes slashed by sharp tips of the tendrils and thought for a moment that she might suffocate in the tight encasement, but relaxed as the plant sprayed a soothing mist near her face. Her body became limp as she felt its limbs tighten on her skin. Inhaling the mist deeply, she found herself aroused. She did not protest as small leathery tips emerging from the side of the branches began probing her orifices. Maura welcomed their intrusion into her body. The memory of the Royal Bogazkoy shot through her mind, and Maura gave herself willingly to the plant.

She felt her legs pulled apart as several probes gently entered her anus, urethra, and finally, her vagina. Maura lifted her buttocks to help the probes until she heard the Bogazkoy remind her not to move. Her bottom felt wet and slippery. The living tissue of the probes issued a jet of mucus-like sap that lubricated her orifices and coated her skin. It even lubricated her tear ducts as the branches spread their tendrils across her face and entered her ears, eyes, and nose.

Maura forgot about the pleasure of the Bogazkoy as the tendrils merged to become a blue mask on her face, finally entering her mouth. Maura resisted, but the branches issued another cloud of mist, and she immediately sank into a stupor of intense physical pleasure.

Feeling her lips open, something sweet pried Maura's teeth apart only to wiggle down her throat. Being stroked and tweaked in every conceivable manner, Maura abandoned herself to the touch of the Bogazkoy. Her nipples and womanhood were rubbed and pulled upon until she was not able to contain herself. She arched her back and heard herself cry out in culmination. The probes in her anus and vagina intensified their manipulation as one tiny probe found her left ovary and injected a hollow tube into its fleshy sack to suck out tiny eggs.

Feeling a sharp pain in her abdomen, Maura squirmed and began to gag. The entire encasement of tendrils raised tiny needle-like hairs, pricking the skin on her body. A blue substance spurted into her skin and bloodstream. Maura felt her bowels loosen as the small jets of blue liquid shot into her veins. Now she could feel the eggs in her other ovary taken as her heart pumped faster, and flashes of blue and yellow light exploded in her head causing her to momentarily lose consciousness.

Then it was all over.

Instinctively, Maura knew the mating was completed. The Mother Bogazkoy had what it wanted from her. Slowly the tendrils began to withdraw, leaving Maura covered with a glistening blue slime and her own wastes. She felt the tendrils of the Mother Bogazkoy help her sit up as it massaged her forehead and neck.

Maura slowly opened her eyes. At first, she was so dazed, she could not comprehend the chaos in the room. As soon as her head cleared, she reached for her belly.

She gasped. Her hands and belly were dark. She rubbed her skin with her fingers. Standing, she checked the rest of her body. Her skin was ebony, but not the ebony of night as she first had thought, but rather the black of the darkest blue and rich with the power of the Bogazkoy. Only the nails on her toes and fingers appeared pale.

"Maura, help us!" came a cry from across the water.

Maura's head snapped up as her eyes scanned the chamber.

A wounded Toppo was trying to drag the unconscious body of Gitar behind a boulder out of harm's way.

Yeti, Tarsus, and Iegani plus many other Dinii were forming a barrier before Gitar.

The Black Cacodemon stalked back and forth in front of the Dinii. His cowl was pulled back, exposing a pale, enlarged head with tired wisps of hair straggling about his ears. The top of the Cacodemon's head was misshapen and bent with red, ugly scars running down the back of his skull as though something had struck his head many times. Magical incantations were tattooed on the scars.

Believing her end was at hand, Toppo screamed and flung herself over Gitar.

From behind the Black Cacodemon, a battered Tarsus threw himself at the wizard but bounced off an energy field.

As the light from his hands grew stronger, the Black Cacodemon's eyes took on a gleam that was akin to madness. He let out a sharp little bark.

Seeing her friends harmed, Maura threw her hands in front of her and cried out, "STOP!"

The Black Cacodemon diverted his eyes and stared at the Hasan Daegian queen standing defiantly in front of the Mother Bogazkoy whose tendrils waved in an agitated manner. His eyes narrowed as he took in the filthy, soiled woman standing naked before his power.

"I'm going to kill your silly friends, and then I'm going to come after you," he taunted, envious of the gift of the Mother Bogazkoy.

"Or maybe I should kill you first," he spat out, thrusting his hand into the air.

A bolt of ugly drab green light shot at Maura. She ducked while holding her arms before her face. She felt a strong sensation like wind surround her and then dissipate. Surprised that she was not hurt, she looked questioningly at the Mother Bogazkoy.

The Mother Bogazkoy had tucked its branches near the base of the trunk.

Maura could hear the plant hissing with anger. "We are one?"

"Yes," replied the Mother Bogazkoy. "You now have the strength of a hundred Dinii. He wishes to drink of my sap, my lifeblood. Feel your power. He wants what you have. Kill him before he destroys us both."

The Black Cacodemon forgot about the Dinii. He exhaled a gaseous cloud, which drifted about his feet. Stepping on the cloud, he floated across the water toward Maura and the Bogazkoy.

The wizard's excitement at being so close to the Mother Bogazkoy was barely contained. He had searched the world over for it. He had killed, schemed, and endured patiently for this very moment. The Black Cacodemon's eyes were wide with anticipation and desire for the gift of a long and healthy life.

A tendril of the Mother Bogazkoy waved wildly.

Maura could sense the plant feared the Black Cacodemon as she did. Maura ran to her scraps of clothing and searched through the pile trying to find her dagger. Sighting it, she grabbed it quickly and ran to the edge of the rock, determined to stop the sorcerer from stepping upon it.

The Mother Bogazkoy slipped several tendrils into the water in the hopes of pulling him down into the water, but to no avail.

The protective field surrounding the Cacodemon was too strong.

The Mother Bogazkoy withdrew its tendrils, wrapping its trunk tightly, and sank into a rock crevice, leaving Maura to do what she could.

The Black Cacodemon reached the base of the rock.

Maura moved to intercept the magician, but he merely waved his hand, throwing her out of the way.

Angry, the Mother Bogazkoy emerged halfway out of the rock crevice and faced the Black Cacodemon. "Do not hurt my beloved!" the Bogazkoy demanded, trembling with rage.

The Black Cacodemon merely shrugged. "Give me what I want, and I will leave in peace, hurting no one else."

"What would that be?" asked the Bogazkoy in its strange hissing voice.

"The same as she," the wizard whispered, pointing to Maura. "Immortality, life, health, invincibility."

"I don't understand," the Bogazkoy lied, hoping for more time.

The Black Cacodemon raised his hand and shot another thunderbolt at Maura. She raised her arms, covering her face as before and was spared the worst of the blow, but still was shaken.

"STOP AT ONCE!" shouted an angry voice from across the water.

Both the Black Cacodemon and Maura turned.

"Dorak!" Maura cried.

From beneath his bronze visor, Dorak's eyes took in his wife. He was shocked by her filthy, naked appearance. Her hair was long and disheveled and hung in great tangled mats. Her skin was black and glistened from the strange glow of the lake. Yet she stood defiant and proud before the Black Cacodemon.

The Black Cacodemon smiled painfully. "Dorak, I'm so glad you are here at last." He pointed to Maura. "She reached the Bogazkoy before I could."

As the wizard faced Dorak, Maura began inching her way toward him with her dagger hidden behind her back.

Dorak scanned the scorch marks on the rock walls and the bleeding Dinii, who were breathing heavily, but watching him with steady eyes. He recognized the black and white feathers of one of the Dinii, whose tips were dyed with purple as the sign of royalty. He bowed. "Empress Gitar, we seem destined to meet under the most insidious circumstances possible."

Dorak reached down and, placing his hands under her arms, lifted Gitar up and leaned her against a wall. He was amazed at how heavy she was. For just a second he wondered how she could fly so gracefully.

"Thank you, Dorak. Now, if only you had been this considerate at the City of the Peaks," Gitar said, struggling for breath. She placed her hand upon her chest as her eyelids fluttered.

Dorak saw that she was bleeding from the side of her head and hoped she would faint, sparing her any more pain or discomfort. He raised the visor on his helmet. "War is war, Madam. It was nothing personal."

"Ah, that is where you are wrong, Aga Dorak. The loss of my daughters and my home is very personal."

Dorak's lips pressed into a thin line. He said nothing but turned toward his wizard who was waving his hand to attack. "Don't do it, Zedek Sadjin!"

The Black Cacodemon gasped in surprise. "How do you know my name?"

"I know many things about you, spellweaver. I know centuries ago you were a mere stable boy until the magician Knoxel took you as an apprentice. You served him for twenty-two years until you stole all of his secrets and then murdered him."

The Black Cacodemon held his hands up beseechingly. "Dorak, we had a pact. This girl can give us what we want. She can give you the power you've always dreamed of."

"It is very tempting, but I have decided to change our little deal."

"How did you get into the city?" Maura asked of Dorak.

"With a very large army that I hope is, at this moment, cutting yours to pieces," answered Dorak, watching the Black Cacodemon. "So it would be to your army's benefit if you joined me and together we both tell them to cease."

Maura laughed. "Do you think I endured these hardships to listen to your lies?" she asked, slowly inching her way closer to the Black Cacodemon. "How could you move your army so quickly?"

Dorak removed his chain mail gloves. "He's not the only one who knows a little magic," said Dorak, wagging his thumb toward the Black Cacodemon. "I'm willing to forgive and forget as you must."

"I know why you want me. You want to kill me and secure the power of the Mother Bogazkoy for yourself."

"Just what is this power? This maggot of a man has manipulated armies and kings to get to this smelly cave where that hideous blue plant lives. All for what?" Dorak demanded.

"For invincibility," Maura rasped.

"You see! I have not lied about the power of the Bogazkoy," cried the Black Cacodemon. He pointed at Maura. "She knows!"

"Shut up. No one was speaking to you," snarled Dorak, raising his sword in irritation. He began pacing back and forth, trying to decide what to do. He would have to wait for the rest of his men so they could make a raft and go over to get both Maura and the Black Cacodemon.

The Black Cacodemon, seeing Dorak's attention diverted, threw a green ball of fire at him.

"Dorak, watch out!" cried Maura as she jumped at the Black Cacodemon. She was thrown back, but Maura focused her mind and sprang at him again. She had power now. She had to believe in herself. This time she penetrated his swirling aura and stabbed him in the side.

The Black Cacodemon twisted in pain. His black eyes had no bottom, like the blackest tempest.

Maura struck again, sinking the dagger deep into his bosom.

The wizard howled as he clutched his medallion.

But Maura tore the medallion from his neck and struck again at his chest. As he yielded to his death, the Black Cacodemon fell to his knees, grabbing Maura's legs. She shook his clammy hands off and kicked him for good measure. He looked at the Hasan Daegian queen standing defiantly over him one last time, opened his mouth to weave a spell before falling into a quiet death.

Maura looked across the water. She had not been quick enough.

Dorak had been hit and was lying very still. There was the look of death about him.

Feeling her heart shudder, Maura dove into the water and, after a minute's swimming, pulled herself onto the other shore. She groaned.

There was neither Dorak nor any of the Dinii.

Flipping her dripping hair back from her eyes, Maura rose haphazardly from her knees and made her way to the corridor.

No blood or water spotted the floor. Returning to the Mother Bogazkoy's chamber, she examined the walls and floor for another way out. She dove into the water and searched the bottom, thinking they had tried to get across and perished in the water. There was no sign of them.

Hours upon hours, she searched. Up and down the corridors she went, calling their names, looking for a sign of the Dinii and her husband. Finally, having exhausted all possibilities, she admitted defeat before the Mother Bogazkoy, which hummed sympathetically and let loose a terrible, lonely cry.

The Black Cacodemon must have uttered a spell before he died while she stood in false triumph over him. The spell banished her companions and the man she loved, leaving only his sword.

Maura fell to her knees and beat her breast in a steady rhythm as she wailed the death chant for her lost love and friends. For a few brief moments, she went mad with blinding grief.

Weaving down the stone hallways, Maura called out Dorak's name until she felt as though she was a mere shadow thrown upon the walls. She felt herself become smaller and fainter in her mind.

Finding herself in the entrance chamber again, she fell to the floor and clutched her arms about her. She was alone in the world. Even Dorak was no more. The Dinii were gone. Her family was destroyed. At the realization of her terrible aloneness and the numbing pain of her despair, Maura's mind went quiet and finally blackened into nothingness.

A cold draft blew through the halls of the Mother Bogazkoy's chamber. An unseen hand gently pushed the hair out of Maura's eyes and silently murmured her name, "Maura. Maura. Listen to the secret. Find me. Play the song for me. I've been waiting all these years for you. Play the song."

Maura opened her eyes, catching her reflection in the polished marble. The front lock of her black hair was streaked with grey, and there were grim lines about her mouth. She gently touched her battered face with stained, grimy hands.

"Who are you?" she whispered. "You are not the sweet girl who wanted to marry the dashing Chaun Maaun. He will not even see you now. You are not the consort of Dorak, Aga of Bhuttan. He is gone, and you will never know if he ever really loved you. The answer to that riddle will forever haunt you. There is no one left. I alone know the secret of the Bogazkoy." She bent forward and kissed the lips of her countenance in the marble reflection. Clumsily, she pulled herself up and searched the passages until she came to a relief carving of the uultepes.

Play the song, thought Maura. *Were the symbols on her back musical notes and not words?*

Maura tapped the symbols carved into the torsos of the uultepes as portrayed on her tattoo. Musical sounds emitted from the carvings similar to that of a lyre.

Maura stood away from the wall.

Slowly, the figures of the uultepes changed color until they were a dark red, causing their outlines to glimmer. Brighter and brighter, the uultepes glowed as the wall shook and rumbled. The outlines of the uultepes rippled as though unseen muscles were awakening from millennia of sleep. Growling, two uultepes stepped off the carved wall and stood before Maura in flesh, bone, and sinew. They positioned themselves on either side of the Hasan Daegian queen never to leave again so long as Maura lived.

The carved walls continued rumbling until one part of the wall pulled apart from the other, leaving a secret chamber exposed. There stood an ancient throne surrounded by rusted swords and dull shields. Large trunks stood everywhere, filled with fading parchments, mold-covered scrolls, and locked caskets.

On the throne sat a collapsed skeleton. A golden crown was haphazardly resting on its side by the skull, which lay on the throne's seat while bits of bone from the hands along with the feet were strewn across the dusty floor.

Maura went to the skeleton, searching among the dust pile. After several moments of brushing aside bone fragments, she finally cried out in triumph. In the crumbled remains of Rosalind, Maura found an ancient gold ring with the seal of the Overlords of Kaseri upon it. It was the ring given by the Dinii to Rosalind, the first queen of Hasan Daeg and lover of the Mother Bogazkoy.

Laughing, Maura kicked away the rest of the skeleton, which landed upon the steps of the ivory and marble throne. The large uultepes took their places beside the throne. One began licking its matted fur. The other lay down and closed its eyes, seemingly at rest.

Hearing a disturbance of the water beyond the chamber, Maura rested Dorak's sword on her lap and faced the entrance with her arms akimbo.

She knew Dorak's men were coming. Using her hair, she wiped away her tears as she waited to meet them. Pulling her grief deep inside, she assumed a mask of power and arrogance.

Her naked black-blue skin began to glow as she felt the power of the Mother Bogazkoy pulsate within her. She did not fear Dorak's men. They would see what she wanted them to see, and she would remain the Bhuttanian Empress as she carried the aga's child.

But more than that, Maura had the golden seal of the Overlords. She was now the most powerful being on Kaseri.

Regent Empress Maura de Magela, Aganess of the Bhuttanian Empire, Tenth Queen of Hasan Daeg and Great Mother of Kaseri had a world to govern. After all she had endured, one thing she learned was that one takes power. It is not given.

She was born to rule.

And Maura intended to rule the Bhuttanian Empire.

Wall Of Conquest

The Princess Maura Tales
Saga of the de Magela Family
Book Four

Abigail Keam

Worker Bee Press

Wall Of Conquest
Copyright © Abigail Keam 2018
ALL RIGHTS RESERVED

No part of this book may be reproduced or transmitted in any form without written permission of the author.

All characters, places, or things are fictional, and any similarity to any living person is just coincidence unless stated otherwise. This book takes place in a fantasy world. Relax, read, and enjoy.

Worker Bee Press
P.O. Box 485
Nicholasville, KY 40340

Acknowledgements

Thanks to my editors,
Patti DeYoung and Jacy Mackin

Artwork by Karin Claesson
www.karinclaessonart.com

Book jacket by Peter Keam
Author's photograph by Peter Keam

Preface

Centuries ago, the Dinii, Overlords of the planet Kaseri, were defeated by the Lahorians, an advanced race from the sea islands of Lahore.

Despondent, the Dinii retreated to Hasan Daeg. Unable to care for their slaves, they released them from bondage while continuing to watch over them in secret.

Believing they had been abandoned by their former masters, the Hasan Daegians developed into a prosperous agricultural society, having all but forgotten their origins. For two thousand years, they thrived in Hasan Daeg, by retreating from the rest of the world and emerging into a pacifist society. Hiding behind a wall of hypnotic mist, they considered their world secure from outside influences.

Unknown to the Hasan Daegians—Zoar, the powerful Aga of Bhuttan, arose in the east. His most burning desire was to become Overlord of Kaseri. His policies of conquering and plundering threatened to transform Kaseri into a wasteland, never to recover.

The Lahorians, threatened by Zoar's marauding, emerged from their underwater retreat to contact their former enemies, the Dinii. Able to see into the future, the Lahorians persuaded the Dinii to again establish relations with the ruling Hasan Daeg family to counter the threat from Zoar.

The Lahorians instructed the Dinii to take the Hasan Daegian queen's only heir, Princess Maura, and raise her as a warrior, who could defeat Zoar, thus allowing the Lahorians to continue their evolution into pure energy.

At eighteen, the young Maura, commanding a combined army of Hasan Daegians, Dinii, Anqarians, and mercenaries, won the first battle against Zoar's more experienced Bhuttanian army, but total capitulation of the Bhuttanians eluded her grasp.

Dorak, Zoar's son, succeeded upon his father's death and now the Aga of Bhuttan, realized he would be unable to defeat Princess Maura unless he used magic. He called forth the Black Cacodemon, an evil wizard.

With aid of the dark arts, Dorak won the war and conquered Hasan Daeg, banishing the Dinii.

Desirous of the Hasan Daegian throne and wishing the people to see his rule as legitimate, Dorak connived to marry Maura. Unexpectedly, he fell in love with her, but his ambition overshadowed his love.

Maura grew to love Dorak but remained wary of him. Realizing she could never influence Dorak regardless of their feelings for each other, Maura fled. She escaped and fled to Atetelco, the ancient capital of the Dinii. There she underwent a "mating ritual" with the Mother Bogazkoy, a primeval sentient tree with the ability to impart mysterious powers.

The Black Cacodemon, Dorak's malevolent wizard, learned of the Mother Bogazkoy's power. Betraying Dorak, he hastened to Atetelco and discovered Maura deep inside the Bogazkoy's secret lair.

To save Maura, Dorak followed, but during the confrontation, the wizard cast a spell, sending Dorak into a dark netherworld. Maura battled the Black Cacodemon and destroyed him.

Grief-stricken, Maura fell into despair until a mysterious apparition appeared and came to her aid. The spirit of Queen Rosalind, the first ruler of Hasan Daeg, led Maura to a secret throne room where Rosalind's bones had been in repose for centuries.

Our last story ended with Maura seated on the ancient throne of Rosalind, awaiting the arrival of Dorak's troops.

Thus our new adventure begins.

1

Maura de Magela looked unhappy.

This pleased Timon not one bit, but he could say nothing until his master, the Consul Rubank, whose palanquin he trudged alongside, beckoned.

The empress tapped her fingers impatiently on the arm of her carved throne made from bones of those vanquished by previous Bhuttanian rulers—and by her as well. The empress had anyone who opposed her leadership executed, including Hasan Daegians.

The throne sat upon a carved wooden dais, decorated with Imperial flags and resting upon a massive painted wagon pulled by a team of festive borax wearing plumed headgear. A detachable canopy of rare wood carved with images of dragons and other Bhuttanian symbols covered the rolling platform.

One had to be alert not to stumble under it and be crushed for it could not stop in haste.

The empress motioned to her consul who waved for the wagon to stop.

Timon, who acted as Rubank's scribe, kneeled as did others.

Fanning herself, the empress stepped down onto the dusty ground.

The young scribe did not like having close contact with the empress. She frightened him with her blue skin and fierce expressions. Her mercurial moods were such that he always waited for a calamity to fall. Timon wished he had remained a nameless scribe in the guild for he despised his duties as royal scribe, but Rubank had handpicked him.

If Empress Maura noticed Timon's discomfort, she did not show it.

They were on their way to Bhuttan so she could officially assume the reins of government in the capital city of Bhuttani. She was the mother of Princess Dyanna, heir to the throne of the Bhuttanian Empire, and would rule as Dowager Regent until the child became of age.

Timon chuckled when he thought of the empress relinquishing power she had ruthlessly fought to gain. He doubted she would voluntarily turn over control when the time came for the child to ascend to the throne.

Get out your tablets, commanded Rubank with the sign language Timon had devised for the consul to communicate with him.

Previously, Timon had to guess what the consul wanted or wait for him to write his instructions down. Timon's thoughts that a tongueless advisor to a ruler benefited no one and Rubank was too old to be of any real use were kept to himself.

How many times do I have to tell you that you must be ready for the empress at all times! Rubank loved his new way of communicating and was quite adept at it.

Timon shook his head. He regretted that he had designed the hand language, for Rubank never shut up now.

As Timon unwrapped moist clay tablets from his leather pouch, two uultepes jumped off the royal platform with singular grace. The great beasts, conjured by magic, constantly stayed near the side of the empress. One pressed close to Timon, knocking him down. It circled, taking care to look Timon in the eye.

The strong odor of the brindle animals mingled with the dust of the marching army caused Timon to erupt in a fit of coughing. He brought his fist to his mouth, hoping to stifle the hack rising from his chest. He glanced up red-faced to see if the empress had noticed his breach of protocol.

She had not.

Timon immediately stood up, and grabbed his tablet and stylus, ignoring the snickers of the guards, who watched as the uultepes circled again pressing even closer. Timon, ready this time, took the sharp end of his wooden stylus and stabbed a paw of one of the giant cats.

The uultepe's eyes widened. Angry, it trotted toward its mistress after giving Timon a malevolent glance.

Timon smiled. Brushing off his dusty knees with several quiet groans, he reluctantly followed. Timon made a mental note to speak to Rubank about a transfer again as he stumbled along. Fumbling with his stylus and wet clay tablets, he dodged an army trudging in the opposite direction.

Scribes used beeswax, wood, and cloth, but clay tablets were preferred on a military march. The wet clay was never allowed to dry out and could be used over and over again.

Timon thought the heavy clay tablets a nuisance and hated working with them, but then Timon hated everything about his life at the moment. Oh, he longed to escape.

Empress Maura strode steadily toward the rear of the army with her hands clasped behind her back.

Two lads-in-waiting struggled to keep the costly embroidered train of her light blue and gold gown out of the dirt.

Underneath the skirt of her gown, Timon could see leather boots and heavy, twined cotton pants commonly worn by most Bhuttanian soldiers. He was sure there would also be a dagger or two tucked away somewhere on her royal personage.

Timon was aware the empress only donned the beautiful gown to please the more conservative elements of her court. She wore the soldier's clothes to please herself. On a second's notice, she could rip the gown off, becoming a skilled combatant. She had become the deadliest woman in the Bhuttanian Empire, which no one could best, regardless of their proficiency with weapons.

There were others who were more dexterous in swinging an axe or lighter on their feet with a sword, but she possessed brute strength and lightning fast agility.

Perhaps a Dini possessed sufficient skill and strength to topple the empress, but the Dinii were seen no more.

The empress rested her eyes upon Timon, as she inclined her head. "What is the name of you, boy?"

Timon blinked and heard himself replying, "My name is Timon Ben Ibin Moab. My people are from the Steppes of Moab named after the first of my ancestors." He bowed his head.

"We will cut through the Steppes of Moab before we reach Bhuttani."

Timon continued to stare at the ground. "Yes, Empress. My home is only a week or so from here."

"You have been in the consul's employment for how long?"

"Many moons."

He's unusually clever, Great Mother, Rubank wrote on a tablet for the empress. *He has an impressive talent for symbols and language.*

Maura considered this information for a moment after reading the tablet. "He must be, Consul, as I do not see your usual interpreters with you."

She addressed Timon directly. "Timon Ben Ibin Moab, you will come to my tent after the evening meal and show me from whence you came on my map," commanded the empress. She turned her head from the consul and the lowly scribe, who realized he had just wet himself.

Luckily, Timon's long woven tunic covered his disgrace. He touched his fingers to his heart and then his lips with a theatrical flourish. Seeing Rubank was displeased, Timon gave the usual Bhuttanian salute of the fist to his heart. With a wave of her hand, Maura dismissed both Rubank and Timon.

Timon reluctantly followed the silent Rubank and helped him into his palanquin. The years of war between the Bhuttanians and Hasan Daegians had strained the royal consul's heart. Rubank did little these days to be of real use to the empress except give her occasional advice.

Still, the empress showed Rubank respect by letting him keep his title and honors. In fact, Timon noticed she rarely let Rubank out of her sight.

Timon pinched the side of his face. *It is regarding things which are none of my business that got me noticed by the empress today!* thought Timon, but still he pondered the reasons why Maura de Magela, Dowager Regent, Aganess of the Bhuttanian Empire, Tenth Queen of Hasan Daeg, and Great Mother of Kaseri, might need an old man who was past his prime.

Timon had heard Rubank served Queen Abisola, Maura's mother, for much of her reign. *That would make him—let's see—past one hundred, maybe older,* Timon thought as he counted on his fingers. Timon shook his head in disbelief and hurried to catch up with Rubank's palanquin.

These Hasan Daegians lived a very long time.

2

The army followed the same routine.

Before dusk, the empress had her husband's favorite horse saddled and brought to her. With only the uultepes for company, she rode behind the main body of the army where she awaited scouts, who had been sent in search of stray feathers that might have fallen from the elusive Dinii.

Upon their return each day, she'd excitedly go through their pouches full of feathers with eager anticipation until she dropped the last feather in disappointment at finding no Dini feather.

"Maybe tomorrow," she murmured to the sweating couriers. "Go. Get something to eat." Empress Maura would then gaze at the distant horizon until darkness.

Timon was so bored with this daily scene, he thought he'd scream. To ease his frustration, he played games in his imagination, waiting for the empress to return to her wagon.

Sometimes, he looked at Rubank, imagining him dressed as a fool, complete with a purple face and a green nose. This would cause Timon to smile. Other times, he pictured the empress on her knees begging him to make love to her.

"Timon, why are you grinning?"

Timon's eyes widened as he realized the empress was standing before him speaking.

"Are you dim-witted?"

"No, Great Mother. My mind drifted off. A hundred pardons."

Maura's eyes narrowed as her jaw tightened. "That could be a foolish mistake, which might cost you your life, Royal Scribe."

Timon's face flushed. He bowed very low. "A thousand pardons. It will never happen again."

"I'm not talking about me causing you harm, boy. An assassin could make straight for me, and if you are not alert, you could fall right in her pathway. Death by mere association. Beware!" Grumbling to herself about Timon, the somber empress strode off on foot in haste.

One of the uultepes turned and snarled a warning before following her queen.

Timon mouthed an oath under his breath at the uultepe. Struggling to hold his tablets and writing sticks, Timon hurried after the empress, dropping a stylus here and there.

Maura made way to her tent, which was hurriedly being prepared by many servants. Out of the corner of her eye, Maura saw flickering lights on the northern horizon as eventide approached.

No troops of hers were straggling in from that direction.

Maura speculated on who it might be and wondered how her scouts had failed to inform her of approaching strangers in the area.

All the local people had given their fealty to her, so she knew it was not an opposing force. "You there," she called to a Bhuttanian. "Help this boy up."

The soldier immediately ran over to Timon and intertwined his hands together. Timon clumsily swung a foot in the soldier's hands and climbed atop his shoulders, straining to get a look at the entourage approaching the army.

"What do you see?" called Maura.

"They ride Bhuttanian war steeds. There are numerous wagons as well, so there must be women and children, but their banners are too far away. I can't make them out." Timon jumped down with his pens spilling upon the ground. He thanked the embarrassed soldier helping to pick them up.

"Let's hurry to my tent. A courier awaits with news, I'm sure," she called to Timon.

"I hope so, or it will be someone's head," muttered Timon, breaking into a run.

As expected, an out-of-breath courier waited in the tent as the empress strode in.

"Is it an emergency?" she asked the courier.

The stalwart courier shook her head, struggling to regain her breath.

Maura smiled. "Good. You may tell me as I make ready for dinner."

The courier followed the empress into her private quarters.

Lads-in-waiting stood eagerly.

Maura washed her dusty face and hands. Grabbing a towel, she sat as one of her servants pulled off her boots and washed her feet. "What news do you have, woman?" Maura grunted as one of the servants tried to coax her unruly hair into a braid.

"Prince KiKu of Hittal humbly requests permission to enter the perimeter of Her Majesty's camp."

Timon shivered when he heard the name KiKu.

"KiKu! Here?" asked Maura as she reached back, grabbing the annoying comb out of the servant's hand and hurling it across the room.

Maura stood, and two servants immediately began unbuckling her pants and shirt. A beautiful pale green lounging gown with gold trousers was produced for her inspection. Pleased with the embroidered flower designs on the gown, she nodded yes. The empress stood with her arms extended. The servants removed her tunic and wiped down her arms, chest, and back. Stepping out of her trousers, her legs and buttocks were cleansed as well.

The lads, delighted the empress approved their selection, dressed her.

The courier stood at attention and stared at the tent wall, never looking at the empress.

Sensing the courier was embarrassed at being in the presence of the empress while dressing, Maura gave leave for the courier to retire.

Relieved, the courier backed out of the chamber while bowing.

Maura turned to Timon, who was kneeling in obeisance with his forehead pressed against a carpeted floor. "Ask Prince KiKu to join me for dinner this evening. Tonight, he will set his tents outside the perimeter, but tomorrow, he may place his tent next to mine."

Timon was about to remind the empress his guild only allowed him to write messages, not deliver them but thought better of it. He rose to his feet and bowed.

"Be early for dinner to take notes and work with my map," Maura ordered sharply as she rotated on her stool to face the blushing Bhuttanian.

Timon salaamed and backed out of the chamber. Once outside, Timon grimaced as he pondered how he could shuffle this duty onto someone else. He did not want to be around the infamous KiKu, let alone speak directly with him.

Obviously, no one else did, either.

He asked several officers, but they declined harshly, backing away from his annoying request.

Mustering his courage, Timon commandeered a pony cart with a servant holding a torch and trotted over to the dancing strobes of light from paper lanterns that signaled KiKu's rapid advance toward the Bhuttanian army.

While the empress was the most dangerous woman in the Empire, KiKu the Hetmaan was the most dangerous man in the Empire.

Timon hoped he would be able to recite the empress' message and leave.

One never knew with the renowned and loathsome KiKu.

One just never knew.

3

Maura sat on a high dais.

Along with Rubank and the High Priestess of Magi, Maura sat upright, sipping colla tea Hasan Daegian style. She listened politely to poetry offered by a minstrel, but when the singer began reciting about love, the empress waved her off. She would rather hear about epic deeds of long-ago heroes.

Love poetry only made Maura sad. She had lost both of her loves, Dorak and Chaun Maaun, and did not want to be reminded.

The minstrel strummed on her lyre while singing a ribald song about a countess and her stable boy.

The Hasan Daegian women of Maura's court thought the song amusing, but their husbands found it demeaning.

The Hasan Daegian males had fought hard to win legal and social rights. They finally had a matriarch who was sympathetic to their plight, and they disliked anything that detracted from their honors won fighting the last war, where they had made bold strides toward equality with women. The Hasan Daegian males studied the empress with interest.

Her eyes narrowed.

Many of the Hasan Daegian men turned their heads, so their wives could not see their smiles of relief at their ruler's displeasure. As Maura's eyes grew bright with anger, the men relaxed and leaned back in their chairs. Some even snickered at a particular verse. If the men hadn't had so much to lose, they might have thought the song was funny as well.

The minstrel, sensing the empress was not interested in her choice again, switched to peasant tunes she had learned from the Bhuttanians.

The Bhuttanians had no talent for art or music. Their songs tended to be uncomplicated, repetitive verses that demanded a call and response accompanied by a drum. But these songs would do until the minstrel could think of something else. As it turned out, she didn't have time.

The great gong sounded.

The minstrel was quickly escorted away.

The ancient Keeper Of The Palace waited for everyone to become quiet. It did not take long. "Great Mother," she boomed with her loud, steady voice. "Prince KiKu of Hittal asks permission to enter."

Maura nodded.

The High Priestess of Magi and Rubank rose to meet Prince KiKu, the famous spy who had helped topple the mighty Aga Zoar.

The Bhuttanians, after glancing at General Alexanee who gave a signal, also rose. They refrained from spitting on the spylord, who had betrayed their aga, though mutters and oaths could be heard throughout the tent.

"*I can't believe he would show his face here.*"

"*I hope for his sake he doesn't sleep too soundly.*"

"*May all his children see a painful death before his old age.*"

"*He should be skinned alive.*"

"*May his son sleep with his mother and his wife sleep with a borax.*"

Timon, who was sitting below the royal dais, could feel the electric charge in the air. He tucked his feet under his gown. For once, there was going to be excitement on this dreary march, and he was not going to miss it.

The High Priestess, overhearing some of the remarks, thought it folly for the empress to receive Prince KiKu publicly. Did the empress not realize the Bhuttanians hated KiKu, and their hatred of anyone always ran white-hot? She chanced a glance at Maura.

The face of the empress remained as impassive as carved stone.

The flap of the great tent opened. A tall, wiry man stepped forward into the smoke-filled pavilion of the empress.

Timon held his breath. Although he had delivered the empress' message, he had only seen a shadowy figure, who turned his face away. Timon was relieved that the spylord had taken no interest in him. The man had said nothing until Timon got the idea he should leave, which he did with haste. Timon scratched his chin in surprise. Now the great KiKu was before him, and he was as tall as any Bhuttanian.

Prince KiKu had harsh, black eyes, which darted about quickly. He sensed the hatred of the Bhuttanians. KiKu stifled a laugh. For years he had served the dreaded Zoar while watching his sister disintegrate under her marriage to him. Sweating and toiling under the hateful Bhuttanian yoke, KiKu was able to throw it off. Now he stood before the most powerful woman on Kaseri, who ruled over the despised Bhuttanians, his sworn enemies. It gave him great pleasure that she was not even Bhuttanian.

And the empress liked him—was even beholden to him. No Bhuttanian dared touch him on pain of losing his head. KiKu chuckled to himself. This afforded him better security than having a hundred guards. Abject fear had its uses.

Followed by four women, KiKu strode toward the dais. His eyes fell upon some familiar faces. He remembered Rubank, a senior advisor to Maura's mother, Queen Abisola. KiKu was surprised at how Rubank had aged in the two years since he had last seen him. Recognizing the indigo robes of the High Priestess of Magi, he did not know the face. He would think about her later. Out of the corner of his eye, he spied General Alexanee. He would have to watch that one carefully.

Finally, he looked upon Maura herself, feeling heat rising from her skin. It was like the sun's summer warmth.

The empress radiated a blue glow while emitting pale beams of gold and pink light from her hands and head. The power of the Mother Bogazkoy had not deserted her. The empress seemed a goddess. No wonder the Bhuttanians followed her.

KiKu breathed out slowly.

SHE MUST HAVE THE BOGAZKOY WITH HER!

The former hetmaan halted before the dais and knelt in keeping with Bhuttanian custom, folding his lush burgundy gown beneath him. "Greetings, Great Mother," he called out.

"Greetings, Prince KiKu of Hittal. Rise. I wish to see your face." Maura waved her fan impatiently while KiKu struggled to his feet. "I see you have acquired bad knees, Lord KiKu."

KiKu motioned to one of his companions to help him. "Old age, Great Mother."

"As well as too much rich food and wine," replied Maura, referring to KiKu's little potbelly.

Twitters arose among the court.

KiKu spoke quickly. "The gods have been good to me, Great Mother."

"What wind blows you here?"

"I have longed for the companionship of my empress and ruling lady. I wish only to bask in your infinite glory."

"As if there were any truth in those words, but never mind. May we be introduced?" the empress asked, pointing to the women standing behind KiKu.

"Great Mother, may I present my wives?"

Maura snapped open her fan, which meant approval in Hasan Daeg.

KiKu gestured to the oldest of the group.

A middle-aged woman stepped forward, looking frightened. Her eyes seemed to bolt everywhere, but one could sense a keen intelligence behind her plain face. The woman offered a silver box. Gently laying it on the first step of the dais, the woman spoke. "Great Mother, my name is Madric. I was taken prisoner seven years ago and sent to work as a tutor for a wealthy Camaroon in the Bhuttanian district of Zipei until I was liberated. I wish to present a token of gratitude for my release and reunion with my family." She stepped back.

One of the guards made her way to retrieve the box until the empress stopped her. "I'm sure it will give Madric great pleasure to open the box herself," purred Maura.

KiKu's face gave a faint impression of a smile. He had taught Maura well.

Death could easily be delivered in the guise of a gift by a friend. Madric stepped forward again and quickly gathered the silver box. With deft fingers, she undid a tiny silver clasp. "Great Mother, I present precious amber from my homeland."

She turned the box over, and large pieces of yellow amber tumbled onto the carpeted steps of the dais. "Purported to heal certain illnesses, amber can also be used in magic. It is my deepest hope that my humble gift will be acceptable to the woman who set me free from the terrible, dark place in which I had lived for so many years."

"It was not just I who has set you free, Madric," replied the empress. "Thousands have sacrificed so the yoke of tyranny could be thrown off."

The faces of the Bhuttanian officers grew dark at the implied insult to their former ruler but said nothing.

"Your gift will be accepted. I need earrings for my daughter. A small portion of this beautiful amber will do nicely."

Madric beamed at the suggestion that her amber would be used as jewelry for Princess Dyanna. She stepped back to her place behind

KiKu.

KiKu motioned for another wife to approach the dais.

A woman in her late thirties with rough-looking hands offered a large leather bag. Opening it, she exposed hundreds of small vials filled with colored liquids. "My name is Pearl. I am a healer from the Qiowa river region. My specialty is fevers. I was taken five years ago from the city of Peygen and forced to work in Bhuttan. I first worked as a servant in the house of one of the officers who raided my home. A pox, unknown to me, overtook the city in which I had been placed. The wife and daughter of the officer to whom I belonged contracted the illness. I saved them, but the wife still sent me away as her husband began to love me. I then worked as a common laborer in the fields." She smiled briefly, revealing several missing teeth. "I escaped and made my way to Hittal where I met Prince KiKu. He honored me by marrying a poor one such as I."

Pointing to the vials, Pearl continued, "These are all the ointments and oils I use in the treatment of my patients. I give them to you to add to your medical knowledge." She handed a servant a scroll. "This is to be kept with the vials. It contains all the information needed to use them." Pearl bowed and returned to her place in KiKu's retinue.

The empress remained silent.

KiKu wondered if the empress was displeased with his wife's gift.

The empress spoke. "I am sure I speak on behalf of our learned physicians when I say your gift is most precious and generous. I thank you from the bottom of my heart."

Pearl's face lit up.

Though KiKu's face remained unreadable, he felt relieved. The gifts of his wives were accepted with much honor. KiKu was sure he had not lost favor with the empress. He motioned for the last two remaining wives. They were of similar stature and looks.

The empress surmised they were sisters and the youngest of the wives.

They bowed graciously, and one could see they were suppressing giggles behind their pretty pink mouths.

The empress was slightly amused.

"I am Tippu," announced one of the girls. "This is my twin, Tippa. We are distant cousins of Prince KiKu. Most of our family died during the great famine. Prince KiKu found us and took us in. We are here to present you with a token of our esteem."

They laid down the heavy object they had been carrying and pulled off the shimmering cloth covering it. "We are artists, and we carved this out of obsidian."

The empress leaned forward to observe the statue. "May I ask the interpretation of this piece?"

Tippu's face flushed. "The woman in the carving represents you, Great Mother. At her breasts are two starving children suckling. The children represent—well," claimed Tippu, waving her hand at the congregation, "US!"

Maura had a servant bring the statue to her so she could touch it. "Again, I am delighted with a gift presented to me by the wives of an old comrade." She patted the statue. "I will take this with me all the way to Bhuttani, and place it in the official gardens of the aga's palace, where it will remain for the pleasure of all agas to come after me."

She turned to KiKu. "Thank you, Prince KiKu. Couches have been prepared for you. Ask anything you need for your comfort, and it will be given to you."

Timon smiled to himself as he watched KiKu being led away.

Not even the empress dared to incur the wrath of the Bhuttanian nobles by asking the traitor to dine on the dais with her.

Prince KiKu bowed, his face reflecting nothing of displeasure. KiKu followed a servant who made room for him near the Hasan Daegians and away from the hostile glares of the Bhuttanians. As he turned, KiKu met Timon's stare. His eyes, unsettled at the sight of Timon, did not betray recognition of the young scribe.

Timon gave a start and looked away. Composing himself quickly, Timon lifted his eyes to confront the infamous man, but KiKu was already escorting his wives to their couches. Timon felt his heart pounding in his chest as he watched the former spylord approach his old comrades.

It did not go unnoticed by the Bhuttanians that all of the Hasan Daegians stood as KiKu had made his way toward them. To the Bhuttanians, he was a traitorous servant of their former aga.

To the Hasan Daegians, he was an honored servant of their people.

Such was the business of war.

Sooner or later, one of the Bhuttanians would kill him, but not tonight with the Imperial Guards watching. The Bhuttanians turned their heads and resumed eating their meals. They were doubtful that KiKu would be alive for much longer.

4

The gangly scribe waited.

Timon stood with a little knot of impatient men wishing to petition the empress. He usually sat behind the empress, alongside Rubank, during court, but as the empress had invited him, he was to be treated as a guest. The wait gave Timon ample opportunity to study the proceedings without being noticed. Typically, all he saw was the back of the empress' head or the floor, as he could not directly gaze upon Maura. He missed all the subtleties of body movement and eye contact. And he was so busy translating for Rubank and waiting for the consul's responses, he missed the inflections of voice. He could now study the expressions and countenance of his betters.

He noted Maura cut an impressive figure sitting on her throne of bones, fixed on a rough-hewn dais covered with mats woven with intricate designs from Hasan Daeg.

Yellow flowers were interwoven into the braids of Maura's black-blue hair with its one lock of snow white at her widow's peak. Although her bearing was regal, Timon observed Maura's features to be average. She offered a severe expression with her blue-tinted eyes and their darker blue orbs, making her face resemble a mask. One could only guess what she truly thought.

Timon glanced about for KiKu. He was nowhere to be seen. The empress had not invited him to court. Timon tucked this information comfortably in his mind. He would retrieve it later when he could study the day's events in private.

On a lower level of the dais sat the High Priestess of the House of Magi with several other priestesses in their severe, dark blue-green robes. With their hands folded, they sat silently while their expressive eyes darted back and forth, surveying all things around them. Once in a great while, an older priestess dozed off for a few moments, but that was rare.

It was Timon's contention this was a ploy to put people off-guard. He was puzzled, as he could never discern the women's true purpose. They rarely advised the empress, and none of the information they collected was ever shared with the military or other advisors. They spent most of their time scribbling in huge books, cataloging everything they saw and heard on their journey to Bhuttan. He thought them a waste of the empire's money.

Behind the empress, on her right, was Rubank sitting with one leg on a small stool. He had problems with gout and had been placed on a strict diet by the royal physician. Rubank was the last of the older Hasan Daegian advisors who had survived the Great War, except for the fabled KiKu.

Surrounding this tight little group languished various military advisors and generals, both Hasan Daegian and Bhuttanian. They stood with their countrymen according to rank and did little to interact with each other.

The empress had forbidden fighting between Hasan Daegians and Bhuttanians, showing no partiality when sentencing to death those who disobeyed. So the former enemies had as little to do with each other as possible. They talked with their backs turned, chatting intimately among themselves reviewing the day's events.

Timon took in all of the little dramas of court. He found Rubank, as all Hasan Daegians, to be vain about his appearance.

The Hasan Daegians seemed an even-tempered people with occasional bouts of excitability when confronted with small, irritating matters such as a lack of clean water for baths. He thought their obsession with cleanliness to be ridiculous, though he had to admit the Hasan Daegians seemed to be sick less often than their Bhuttanian counterparts—and certainly smelled better.

Timon felt the hair on the back of his neck rise. He suddenly realized the empress was watching him observe the court. He forced his eyes up to the dais and met hers quickly. He salaamed by pressing his right palm against his forehead and lowered his eyes, but not before he saw her motion to one of her guards.

He waited obediently until the guard fetched him and brought him before the empress. Timon bowed very low, keeping his head pressed to the ground until the empress gave him permission to look up.

"I see you are wearing a new robe, Master Timon," commented the empress, studying his tunic's fabric.

Timon blushed, not knowing how to reply. It embarrassed him that the empress took notice of what he wore. He could feel Rubank's worried eyes upon him and hoped he had not shamed his benefactor. It would only mean trouble for him later. Timon pointed to the detailed borax design embossed on the front of his robe, stammering, "Uh, this work is done by the women in my mother's village. They take great pride in their workmanship."

"Pray, tell me, where is your mother's village, good scribe?"

"My mother is from a remote village on the Plain of Moab. Less than four hundred people live there."

Maura leaned back and considered the young man standing before her. Tall and gaunt with spindly arms, Timon was anything but a soldier, only he was too young to realize it. She knew he dreamt of glory and chafed under his current position. Maura also knew he would be killed within minutes on the battlefield. Timon was so lacking the skills of a warrior that Maura could lean across the space that divided them and crush his throat with her bare hands before he realized what was happening to him.

The empress blinked and unclenched her hands. She motioned to a nearby servant, who spread out an old map. "Show me your homeland," she commanded Timon. "You may sit," she added as a servant brought a small stool.

The thin scribe blanched, leaning over the map. It was a detailed depiction of the known world drawn on animal parchment.

Timon's eyes followed the lines of the mountains to the rivers, which flowed near his home. He could not fathom why the empress would be interested in his tiny village. "It is here," he lied.

"Tell me about your homeland."

"What shall I tell you, Great Mother?"

"Anything. What did you do as a child? Do you love your mother? Who owns the spoons in the houses—the men or the women? Who is the most respected person in the village and why? Anything. Anything at all."

A thoughtful servant handed Timon a drink, and he took a sip while collecting his thoughts. "My people are nomadic. In the summer, we travel to the base of the mountains with our horses and grazing animals. There we live in small tents made of felt and leather. During the winter, we travel down to the steppes and live in houses made of stone." He looked at the empress.

She was quiet.

"Pray, continue," chimed in the High Priestess from the House of Magi.

When the empress did not stir, he continued. "I am the baby in my family with two elder sisters. I used to see them every summer when they came to the mountains. We do not speak of personal things, as it is not allowed between unmarried men and women. I do not know what the lives of my sisters have been like or how they feel."

"Very interesting," commented the High Priestess.

"What is, High Priestess?" Timon asked.

"The fact there is no personal conversation between the sexes."

"As I have explained, we are a simple people. Our needs are few. There is not much to discuss besides the weather and our livestock." Timon twisted uneasily and added, "There is no need for us to talk. It only leads to trouble."

"How is that?" asked the High Priestess.

"Forbidden feelings. Taboo."

The High Priestess rebutted, "My young man, one does not need conversation for love if that is what you are referring to. One only needs to behold another person. To connect in the eyes to connect in the heart." She studied him, trying to discern his age. She smiled thoughtfully. "You are too young to understand. Continue with other matters. How were you brought here?"

"When Zoar came through our region on his way to Hasan Daeg, I joined his army." Timon added quickly, "I worked with the horses until my superior noticed I had an aptitude for symbols and numbers." Timon sat up proudly upon his stool. "I have a way with words—written, of course—and I picked up the language easily once in Hasan Daeg."

"Zoar was searching for people who had a head for symbols?" asked Maura, scowling at the bottom of an empty glass. It was immediately filled with colla tea.

"Yes, Great Mother. He was searching for these kinds of people. I was treated well and given lots to eat even though I trained many hours a day. I stayed in the ranks of the scribes until the royal consul sought me out and brought me thus."

"But you are not a true Bhuttanian," stated the empress, studying Timon's expression.

Timon's face grew red, and he blustered, "I am Bhuttanian, Great

Mother!"

The Hasan Daegians noticed the Bhuttanians watched the royal party intently. The entire tent grew quiet except for the bustling noises the servants made.

The High Priestess said, "No offense was intended, Royal Scribe. The empress only meant to clarify that the Moabites were absorbed by the Bhuttanian Empire before Aga Tnpothar's reign. According to oral history, the Moabites were a nomadic people akin to the Bhuttanians. They did not worship Bhuttu or Bhutta, but only one god who has no name. When the Moabites did not pay their annual tribute one spring, the Bhuttanians made war upon them. I make this comment because people of similar stock worship similar gods. Your people's god is much like that of the Anqarians—a god who is neither he nor she and has no name. It is only fodder for the mind."

Timon stiffened. He had made a terrible blunder before the empress by expressing umbrage at her words. Timon's mind swirled with avenues of protocol to ease him out of this difficult situation, but he could not choose one. He slid off his stool and lowered himself before the empress, who studied him without expression. "Great Mother, please excuse my outburst! I spoke without thinking. You did not offend me. I am unused to being in such close proximity to your person in direct conversation. It caused me to be nervous and err like the peasant that I am."

"Rise, Timon. I take no issue with you. I wish to hear more of your country," replied the empress without rancor.

Alexanee, the highest-ranking Bhuttanian general, approached the royal dais. "Great Mother, may I speak on this matter?"

Maura nodded, curious that Alexanee involved himself. She waved Timon back onto his stool and motioned with her fan for another one to be brought for the general.

Alexanee had a recent leg injury, which had not yet healed, and was grateful. "Great Mother, my mother's grandfather fought in the campaign to chastise the Moabites. There was only one great battle. As the Moabites were herdsmen, we quickly overtook them and placed our own man in their tent."

"Do you consider his people to be Bhuttanian?" asked the High Priestess.

"It is said the Moabites and the Bhuttanians were one people many years ago, but that overpopulation caused the tribe to split and go their separate ways. If we are not from the same fathers, then we are very close cousins." Alexanee turned toward Timon and pointed. "Notice the high cheekbones. The same ruddy, dark skin. He is a tall man like every Bhuttanian male." Alexanee grinned. "Not yet filled out, but he soon will be if the gods are kind."

The High Priestess spoke, "It is true these are hallmarks of Bhuttanian bloodlines."

The empress nodded thoughtfully and stroked the amulet around her neck.

Timon spied the amulet conspicuously, as did everyone else when she touched it. It was rumored the necklace had belonged to the Black Cacodemon Zedek, who used it for his most powerful spells. Many whispered that the amulet produced magic from other worlds if one had the courage to use it.

"Tell me about your god," Maura commanded softly as she motioned for the musicians to play.

The musicians bowed and obliged by softly playing sad Hasan Daegian love songs.

The empress frowned at their selection.

The musicians quickly changed to a more upbeat tempo.

"It is just as I told you, Great Mother. Our god has no name."

"What powers does your god possess?"

Timon shrugged his shoulders. "One cannot say. Perhaps none, perhaps infinite."

"Where does your god live?" asked the empress.

"Legend has our god living in a lake on the steppes, but we have never seen it. It is only a rumor."

"Is your god male or female?" asked the High Priestess, rearranging her skirts.

Timon looked baffled. "I do not know." He paused for a moment. "I would say our god is neither, yet both."

"Did life begin with your god?" asked Maura.

"Yes, Great Mother."

Maura stated, "Then your god must be female."

"But one cannot deny that the spark of life begins with the male, Great Mother," pointed out the High Priestess.

Maura pondered for a moment. "Having a female goddess makes the most sense, but this boy says his god may be both."

"An oddity perhaps," murmured the High Priestess.

"No," said Timon, shaking his head. "It—he—she is everything. We are part of it. We are one."

Maura straightened up, as did the High Priestess. The other priestesses began writing in their journals. "What did you say, Royal Scribe?"

Timon timidly looked at the tall and imposing empress sitting erect and stroking the huge uultepes lounging beside her with their eyes closed. "We are one."

"Why did you say that?"

"I—I don't know," stammered Timon. "It is something I have heard since my childhood."

"You have no priests or interpreters of your god, do you? No intermediaries?"

"Great Mother, we interpret for ourselves. We are one with this god; therefore, we listen to the god within us."

The empress leaned forward in her chair. "Tell me, Royal Scribe—and take care—do you feel your peoples' deaths without warning?"

One of the uultepes opened an eye and fixed it upon Timon, now squirming upon his stool.

"I feel sorry for anyone's death."

"No, no, no," scolded the empress, frustrated. "If a cousin of yours died, let's say, in a distant land, and you had no word, would you know she had died?"

Timon shook his head, seemingly confused at the question.

Maura sighed and fell back into her chair. Ever since she had heard of the Moabites and their strange god who lived in a lake, she wanted to get close to a Moabite and learn all she could.

Timon would do.

She could see she was frightening the young man, and decided she would let him retire from the dais to sit with the pretty girls who waited on the High Priestesses. Only Hasan Daegian male virgins and older widowed noblewomen waited on the empress. "You may go," she said, waving her hand in dismissal.

Wrung out, Timon was only too happy to escape the piercing glare of the empress. He bowed very low before the empress and salaamed gracefully.

Maura took no notice, as she was deep in thought. Suddenly feeling weary, the empress stood. Her uultepes immediately followed, yawning and stretching. One of them playfully swatted at the High Priestess.

She turned disdainfully, slapping the big cat on the end of its nose.

Maura did not reprimand her as the uultepes tended to rip, bite, eat, tear, or gnaw anything they could find. She did not blame the High Priestess for taking issue with her bodyguards. She did not even understand their presence, though she had called them forth from the Mother Bogazkoy's secret chamber, guarding the remains of the beloved first Hasan Daegian queen, Rosalind.

Everyone rose to their feet. Bowing, they bid their empress good night. Though Maura had adopted many Bhuttanian customs, she did not like to sleep on couches in the middle of a tent with others, as had the former agas. She retired to her private chambers where a soothing bath and her lover for the evening awaited. The same person rarely entertained her twice, but mostly, she sent them away after questioning them about their lives.

Tonight, though, she wanted to feel the pressure of hands on her flesh, have sweet words whispered into her ear, and enjoy cool lips on her neck. Maura entered her private bedchamber and smiled salaciously at the man who waited for her. Perched precariously on a chair, he appeared nervous.

She had chosen a Bhuttanian who had been a high-ranking official under her husband, Dorak. He was a tall and rough-looking man with several wide scars across his face. The Bhuttanian seemed jittery and at a loss for what to say. He asked Maura if her day had gone well.

Astonished, Maura regarded him. "Do you care if my day went well?"

The Bhuttanian shrugged his shoulders, not knowing what else to say. "I thought it might ease the strain if you talked about your day," he answered sincerely.

"Do you think I have tiresome days like other people? Like you, for instance?" she asked sarcastically.

"Of course, Great Mother," he replied, using the Hasan Daegian salutation. "You more than anyone." He paused for a moment. "Have I offended you, Great Mother? Perhaps I was at fault in comparing you to mere mortals?"

Maura went over to the Bhuttanian and stood before him. "Am I not like other mortals? What is the talk in the camp?"

Hesitating, the Bhuttanian finally peered into the empress' eyes. "They say you were once mortal, but you have mated with a devil tree, and now you are like one of the gods."

Maura gave a small laugh. She curtly dismissed her servants and poured her lover a cup of wine. Handing the cup to the man, she asked softly, "Does the fact that I may not be mortal frighten you?"

Happy that his hand did not shake, the lover revealed his tumultuous thoughts. Thinking he could not deceive her, he told the truth. "It frightens me very much, Great Lady. I do not know why you bothered to choose me. I am not young anymore." He shook his head in wonder and felt his face. "In fact, my countenance has little to admire. My wealth has been taken from me by misfortune. I have nothing to offer a queen, not even a gift such as a trinket."

"I think you have much to offer."

The Bhuttanian squared back his shoulders. "Though poor and broken, I will give what I can."

"Then I ask this of you. Make love to me as though I were a normal woman, one whom you desired." Maura felt the heat rise to her cheeks. "Can you do this for one night? I'll not ask more of you." She took the Bhuttanian's large, battered hands and pressed them to her breasts.

Realizing the empress might be lonely, the Bhuttanian took pity on her. "This I can do." He tried to hold her. "If only you will tell me how."

Seeing his stricken face, Maura laughed.

The Bhuttanian relaxed and laughed along with her.

She leaned forward, kissing him passionately.

He responded in kind and, picking her up, carried Maura to the bed.

"You will not find me ungrateful," Maura whispered. "In the morning, your property and more will be returned to you once you have pledged your loyalty to me."

The Bhuttanian lowered the empress on the soft bed. He was flushed with desire.

"I have one more request of you," said Maura.

"Ask, my lady, and if it is in my power, it is yours."

Maura looked deeply into his battered, questioning face. "Do not be gentle."

5

Maura climbed out of bed.

She donned nothing but Zedek's necklace. Touching the center of the amulet, she slipped behind her guards, going out the servant's entrance. Past dying fires and sleeping men, she sauntered unconcerned if one of them should awake. It mattered not for they would not be able to see her. She was invisible and would remain so for several minutes, the time needed to enter KiKu's chamber. She thought her entrance to KiKu's chamber easy until she saw the hetmaan sitting in a chair with only a small oil lamp casting a faint, warm glow about the tent.

KiKu gestured for Maura to approach when her unseen hand opened the flap to his private chambers.

Maura wrapped a blanket around herself and sat on a stool.

KiKu waited, seemingly undisturbed that an unseen force had entered his sleeping room. Finally, the spy could see faint features of Maura's face in the flickering of the oil lamp as she slowly became visible again. Her face was severe.

He waited for Maura to speak.

"Why are you here, KiKu?" she asked.

"I went back to my country, but there was no country to be found. The land was there, but my people had been scattered across the wastelands of Kaseri. Most of them are dead. The multitudes who have taken over my country are refugees from other places, and bitter ones at that. They have their own king and do not wish a Hittal to rule them. I have no army to force them." He paused.

"Is it my army you want?"

"For what purpose? To conquer a people who will always be in constant rebellion after your forces leave? I must face facts. They don't want me. They don't know the Hittal ways. It would be futile."

"Then why are you here amongst your deadliest enemies?"

He leaned toward Maura and whispered in her ear. "I have news that will interest you."

Dancing shadows thrown by the small oil lamp flickered across Maura's face.

KiKu thought her face was both cruel and beautiful, but it was her eyes that spoke the most to him.

Maura could not hide the longing in her blue eyes. KiKu knew she wanted Dorak still. Not even death could spoil her love for him. "Speak! Speak before I lose all manner of patience with you," she hissed.

"The Dinii have been seen!"

Maura grabbed KiKu's arm and squeezed.

KiKu patted her hand while trying to coax her constricting fingers from around his pained flesh. "Maura, you are cutting off my blood," he said, using her personal name.

Maura immediately withdrew her hand. She lowered her head to her chest, trying to dispel the anguish rising from her bowels. "Tell me quickly," she begged.

"I have heard strange rumors from among the priests of Bhuttu. Strange bird-like creatures have appeared before several priests as apparitions begging for release at the great temple in Bhuttani."

"Release from what?" Maura pressed her hands together in agitation.

KiKu shrugged. "This is all I know, but I have been theorizing."

Maura looked at him in anticipation.

"What if the Dinii and Dorak did not leave the chamber of the Mother Bogazkoy of their own volition?" KiKu shifted in his seat and wrapped his cloak closer about him. "You told me that as you struck the death blow to the Black Cacodemon, you could not see what was happening on the other side of the cave."

"That's right," confirmed Maura.

"What if you didn't kill the bastard quickly enough? What if, between the first blow and the deathblow, he had time to utter one last incantation? He was still wearing the amulet you now possess. We do not know of all its powers. What if he willed the Dinii and Dorak away to a magical place, a realm of spirits?"

"KiKu, it would explain so much. It would give an explanation to these horrible dreams I have been having since that terrible day."

"Dreams? You never spoke to anyone about dreams."

Maura smiled a twisted grin. "Do you have spies even in my tent?"

KiKu ignored her question, saying nothing.

Maura took it as a sign he did and congratulated herself on always assuming so. She continued, "I dream of Dorak crying out. I can barely see him except for his eyes, which are wide with fear. He calls to me, pleads for release from what I do not know. I see nothing, but I know he is in a dark and foreboding place." Tears, tinted blue by the gift of the Mother Bogazkoy, fell from her eyes. "I never accepted he was dead." She clutched at her blanket. "I never believed it."

"Then make haste to the temple of Bhuttu. If the Dinii are being seen there even in spirit form, there must exist a portal from which they can return."

"Perhaps this is why they are being seen now. They can make contact, but cannot leave for some reason."

KiKu pointed to the heavy necklace around Maura's neck. "I would expect the amulet you possess is the missing piece. Take the necklace to the temple. If you must, torture the priests until they tell you its secret. Someone there must know something."

Maura looked thoughtful for a moment. "Or you could go."

KiKu shook his head sadly. "My spying days are over. Your balladeers have made my exploits too well known throughout the land," he claimed, not without pride. "I would be discovered."

"A former contact perhaps?" Maura asked, pressing him for a commitment.

"All of the priests know each other well. They would not speak boldly before a stranger."

"How did you find out about the rumors then?"

"I cannot tell you without risking lives, but there are others besides the priests who have witnessed these phantoms."

Maura thought for a moment. "Perhaps we can train someone for a special mission? Someone who is educated and well-versed in literature and religion." She turned to the tiring spylord. "Could you train a person for this mission?"

KiKu rubbed his sleepy eyes. "Yes, but not around here. I would have to take this person to a secluded spot and train him for several months. It could only be done with careful planning."

Extinguishing the small oil lamp, Maura prepared to leave. "You are tired, and I have much to think about."

The prince barely made out the young woman in the dark now. "Great Mother, there is something else I want to tell you."

"What?"

"An old friend awaits you in Bhuttani," he said.

Maura scoffed. "I have no friends in Bhuttani. Of whom do you speak?"

KiKu leaned forward, clasping Maura's mouth with his hand so she would not scream. Softly, he breathed, "Mikkotto!"

6

Maura decided upon a plan.

The army marched forward. The next several weeks were tedious with boredom. Each day, the army journeyed farther and farther from the northern mountains down into the southeastern hill country, finally making its way to the broad band of plains that stretched for almost six hundred miles to Bhuttani, the ultimate goal of the empress. To secure her crown and that of her child, Maura needed to control Bhuttani, the capital and heart of the Bhuttanian Empire. And she needed to capture Jezra, who had fled with the child she had borne Dorak.

Then there were the matters of state. Once Bhuttani was captured, it was not certain whether Hasan Daeg would be assimilated into the Bhuttanian Empire or remain autonomous. It was the hope of most of the Hasan Daegian nobles that Hasan Daeg would remain independent with only a loosely drawn treaty linking the two nations.

The more conservative elements of Hasan Daegian society wanted to retreat again into isolation, hoping the world would forget them a second time. They wanted nothing to do with the Bhuttanian Empire with its many conflicts and problems. Every day, the Hasan Daegian nobles quietly pursued their goal but were extremely careful in handling the empress.

Assassination was ruled out. No one could get close enough to Maura because the ever-present uultepes stayed steadfast at her side. More than once, a zealot had rushed Maura only to be summarily dispatched by the giant animals' massive claws and lightning fast reflexes. Long-range assassination techniques were abandoned too as having even less chance of success. The empress had been hit many times with poisoned darts. Not only did she survive, but Maura would pull out the darts and, in several minutes, be quickly healed with her aura radiating, shining more brightly than before.

The rays emanating from Maura and her swift healing only roused the Bhuttanians' worship, portraying her to be a demi-goddess. They would leave no stone unturned searching for the assassins.

Then Maura would sit upon the aga's throne, made from the bones of enemies of years gone by, and watch the captured assassins twitch after being hung from the nearest tree. Their boiled white bones would be added to the aga's throne to yellow with age along with the others.

Regardless of the attacks on Maura, the pestilence, the dust and grime, and the uneasy alliance between the Hasan Daegians and the Bhuttanians, the army moved forward. Perhaps at a snail's pace, but still they marched–and wherever the army passed, the countryside began to recover from the terrible toil it had taken under Bhuttanian rule.

The Hasan Daegians immediately began working with farmers and loggers, teaching them new techniques. Sivans were recruited to bring in people who were familiar with the raising and breeding of livestock. Refugees were only too happy to find new homes and work their trades under peaceful conditions. Slowly, the countryside began to recover from the slash and burn policies of Zoar.

Trade was reestablished, and the economy flourished. The Sivans were permitted to barter freely where the empress had established order but were forbidden to trade with those not yet under her control.

The Sivans, believing the Hasan Daegian queen would reign over most of the caravan routes one day, did nothing to betray her confidence, but privately shook their heads as they passed starving people who remained outside Maura's protection. They felt sick in their hearts when they knew where warehouses full of food were stationed, but dared not betray their loyalty oaths. Helping when they could, they took in many a child from a pleading mother on the roadside. They adopted these children into their clans while Maura looked the other way. Privately, they admitted Maura was made of sterner stuff than her mother, Abisola.

The Sivans were officially apolitical. Their entire culture and economy were based on trade. No other country had been as successful as the Sivans in delivering goods intact and on time. They had become the lifeline for many nations, who depended on them for needed goods and foodstuffs. Sivans were so respected, bandits usually left them alone, but would attack a caravan led by another group traveling right behind them.

When the Hasan Daegians chose isolation and retreated behind their wall of mist created by the caromate plants, it was the Sivans who transported their harvested crops through a corridor specially created for secret trade.

For centuries, the outside world had been using Hasan Daegian medicinal herbs, hemp ropes, paper, cloth, and food, which they thought originated in a faraway land beyond the water known only to the Sivans who kept the secret. Their discretion was legendary.

Siva was a desert country with borders left unguarded. There was no land to be tilled, timber to be harvested, minerals to be mined, or slaves to be gathered. The few times Siva had been attacked, the Sivans burned everything in sight and committed suicide when captured. While it had not been a happy ending for the hapless victims, it certainly deterred future conquerors from thinking they could find anything of value in Siva.

Throughout the ages, the Sivans had been left alone to do what they did best, which was to distribute the world's wealth and resources through trade.

Like Hasan Daeg, Siva was a matriarchal society. The strange thing was no one outside Siva had ever seen a Sivan woman. Husbands, sons, sons-in-laws, and brothers were sent out into the world to trade while the powers-that-be stayed at home.

The men sported three brands, denoting the clan, the family, and the woman to whom they belonged. Once the brands were seared into the flesh, nothing could revoke those ties except death. There was no divorce in Siva. To ease tension resulting from unhappy marriages, Sivan men took foreign wives in distant lands. No one complained as everyone turned a blind eye and pretended the second wife did not exist. But it was understood by all, the first wife could have the second family eliminated if she so wished.

Happily, most Sivan women were understanding and kind, so all breathed easier under the strict Sivan social codes. Once in a while, a first wife became so enraged that her husband would return to his second home finding it burned to the ground with his family destroyed in the blaze. These men, so filled with grief for their lost families and shamed at having embittered their first wives, committed suicide. It was a rare occurrence but did happen from time to time.

The Sivan men were quiet, industrious, intelligent, and hard negotiators. No written contract was needed with a Sivan. His word was good as gold. It was getting the Sivan to agree in the first place that was usually the sticking point.

It was among a group of Sivans that Timon found the empress. He had asked for his release from service the prior evening, but Rubank refused. To show his displeasure, Timon was late. Now he was worried Rubank would say something to the empress about his pouty behavior.

Maura was on the gigantic platform talking animatedly with Sivans. She motioned to Timon.

At her side was the ever-silent Rubank, surveying all with his pale gray eyes. Rubank looked up at Timon briefly and continued monitoring the conversation between his blue-skinned ruler and the caramel-skinned Sivans. Timon knew Rubank would need him to translate, as everyone was talking much too fast for the old man to keep up. Rubank, upon taking service with Queen Abisola, had voluntarily cut his tongue out so as not to divulge the queen's secrets. Now that he was older, his hearing was going as well.

Summoning a servant to bring him fresh clay tablets, Timon sighed and hurried over. Kneeling and giving her the Bhuttanian salute, Timon took his place beside Rubank and made mental notes of what was worthy in this conversation to write down. To his surprise, the Sivans were speaking of Bhuttani, having left there many months ago.

Timon studied the Sivans standing before the empress. The men wore beautiful, long-flowing robes of white with finely detailed, embroidered belts and colorful headgear.

Young men wore veils, leaving only their dark, long-lashed eyes exposed. Many a young woman's heart beat faster when she looked into the soulful eyes of a Sivan merchant, but flirt and suggest as she may, nothing would come of it.

One had to be married to a Sivan man to see him let his black hair down the tawny skin of his muscular back and receive kisses from the full, moist lips that graced his face.

But the empress cared not for the beauty of the Sivan men standing before her. Her eyes snapped alive at their mention of Bhuttani. She leaned forward and inhaled every word the Sivans were saying. They were duly upset at the chaos surrounding one of the largest cities in the world and their best markets.

"Great Mother, it is a disgrace. There is no order, even with the White Queen present in the city," complained the elder Sivan, speaking in Anqarian.

"There is only one queen," hissed the High Priestess of Magi, standing behind the empress.

The Sivan merchant paled and bowed very low. Heavy breath expelled from his nose as he lowered his veil. "I express a thousand apologies, Great Mother. I should state Jezra claims to be aganess and her son the rightful heir to the aga's throne. I only repeat what she has stated."

Maura waved his apology aside. She knew her claim to the aga's throne hung tenuously in the balance.

Jezra had as much legal right to claim the Bhuttanian Empire for her son by Dorak as Maura did for Dorak's daughter. Maura was determined to beat Jezra at all costs. She just had to be cunning and keep those Bhuttanians, who remained at her side, loyal to her cause. All in all, Maura believed it was going to be fate that determined if she entered Bhuttani as aganess or found her head on a chopping block. Maura would do anything to ensure her daughter's future, and gaining absolute power was the only means to prevent her daughter from being hunted down and killed by Jezra.

Maura asked, "Why do you call Jezra the White Queen?"

"The Buttanians refer to her as the White Queen because of her golden hair and fair complexion, and you are the Blue Queen due to your blue flesh. The common people use these terms for it is easier for them to remember rather than formal titles. No disrespect is intended by either name."

"None taken. Go on," instructed Maura impatiently.

The Sivan looked cautiously at the empress before continuing. "The city is divided into three parts with Jezra controlling the largest area. She has power over the palace, the oldest sections of the city, the west gate, and the temple of Bhuttu. Cappet, a petty thug, controls much of the eastern part of the city. His part includes the river docks. He has access to food and oil."

"Wait!" cried Maura, holding up her hand. "What of the temple? Is the temple building intact? What of the priests?"

The eyes of the Sivan merchant revealed surprise. "Great Mother, I was not aware you had become a follower of Bhuttu."

Maura flinched. How stupid of her to show interest in the temple. There could be spies listening to this conversation. She had to be more patient. "I worry for the sake of my people, half of whom are Bhuttanian now. They revere their god, Bhuttu."

The elder Sivan merchant breathed easier. He disapproved of the harsh and cruel faith of Bhuttu and would not have liked to report to his superiors he suspected the new empress might be a follower of the ancient dark religion. "The temple has suffered very little damage, but the priests have been conducting strange purification rites for many months. There are rumors the temple is possessed."

"Tell me more about this Cappet."

"He is an opportunist. He saw a gap in Jezra's control and took advantage of it. I hate to say this, but he seems to be an able administrator. Of the three sectors, his people are the best fed and suffer the least."

"And the third section?"

"Controlled by a venerated general of Zoar's, a man named Prosperot. He controls little that is important and is in a weak position, but he is respected by all and is left alone."

"I know him. He was one of Zoar's main generals, along with Alexanee. He fled after Aga Dorak went missing. What does he control?"

"He guards the bones of Zoar and his ancestors."

Maura started to laugh. "A graveyard. He protects dead men." She paused for a moment. "The Bhuttanians do not bury their dead. They burn the bodies and scatter the ashes."

The Sivan merchant looked about him sheepishly. "Great Mother, the Bhuttanians are very involved with ancestor worship where their nobles are concerned. Bones of high-ranking persons left from the funeral pyre are taken back to one specific location where they are interred into the special crypts. That Prosperot would take this assignment without being ordered speaks very highly of his esteemed character."

Pulling a strand of blowing hair away from her face, the High Priestess said, "I thought Zoar was cremated in Camaroon outside the Hasan Daegian border. The empress saw him being burned."

"Oh no, Wise One, his bones were taken back immediately after the ceremonial fire," replied the elder Sivan merchant, who stealthily nudged his companion. He had thought the Magi scholars were all-knowing. This mistake of the High Priestess would prove to be valuable information to the Sivans in the future.

The empress took in the subtle nudge of the Sivan merchant to his companion and wished the High Priestess would keep her mouth closed. She, herself, had already made a costly blunder during this interview, and now the High Priestess had made another. "I wish to speak with the Sivans in private," she said abruptly.

Timon wanted to kick the High Priestess, who now looked very contrite as she climbed down off the platform. The conversation was becoming interesting, and now he would not be privy to it. He waited until the very last second before the guards pushed him toward the stairs. Blast it! For once, he genuinely wanted to be involved with the empress and was losing his chance. He thought of shouting the suggestion that he remain and take notes but caught the empress' icy glare. He hurried along with Rubank and the other advisors. Pushed away from the rolling platform for at least ten feet, Timon could hear nothing.

The empress had leaned very close to the Sivans and used a fan to cover her mouth. Now no one would be able to read her lips.

Squinting against the late summer sun, Timon saw the Bhuttanian cavalry approaching. He scampered out of the way of the great warhorses only to be scolded by a sullen cook, who was trying to navigate his wagon out of the way as well. Whirlwinds of dust were stirred up by the massive hooves of the giant steeds.

Timon, choking, called to a water boy. Holding up the leather bag, Timon took a long draught of the water, not letting the bag touch his lips, as was the custom. The water was clear so it must have been purified by Hasan Daegians. They refused to drink cloudy water.

Making his way back, Timon found the empress gone from the platform. He looked frantically about him. Grabbing a soldier trudging next to him, Timon asked, "Have you seen the empress?"

The foot soldier, weary from many miles of marching, pointed his lance at the western horizon. "I saw that dark head of hers go over there. She was walking with two Sivans."

"Thanks, my good man," said Timon, flipping the soldier a copper coin.

The soldier caught the coin in mid-air. "Anytime," he replied, waving a chipper goodbye.

Timon trotted through a column of marching soldiers, ignoring officers cursing him for causing their soldiers to falter. The hurrying scribe called out his apologies, only to be met by fierce growls from a commander getting his men into marching rhythm again.

While dodging soldiers, he came upon Hasan Daegian scouts returning to give their reports.

Astride their small ponies, the Hasan Daegian riders looked ridiculous next to any Bhuttanian mount, which was almost three times the size. But the Hasan Daegian ponies were gaining respect among the

Bhuttanians for their hardiness and the way they could maneuver during a battle.

Timon waved to some of the Hasan Daegian riders he knew and darted in between the horses.

A mangy murex caught sight of Timon and ran after him, trying to bite his ankles. A small girl ran up to the murex and, after spanking him for being naughty, put the chastised animal on a rope and led him away.

"Serves him right," muttered Timon.

Through a haze of wagons filled with wives, children, and servants belonging to various Bhuttanian officers, Timon could see the empress walking with the Sivan merchants. Timon strained his neck, searching the crowd around her.

Rubank and the High Priestess did not follow at a discreet distance. In fact, he didn't see them anywhere. Only the Imperial guards were present, and they were busy keeping pesky animals and curious children from bothering the empress.

The uultepes were lying down on a small mound, eyeing the women and children who were watching them. One of the uultepes yawned and rolled on its back, stirring up dust. It sneezed and rubbed its face with its paw.

Timon walked carefully around them at a great distance. He had never seen them attack anyone without cause, but it never hurt to be careful.

Suddenly, a company of thirty Hasan Daegian horsewomen with two riderless ponies rode up to the empress.

The uultepes were immediately by her side.

The horses, smelling the great beasts, whinnied and pawed the ground nervously. Their riders had a hard time controlling them.

Timon saw the empress give something to one of the Sivan merchants. The merchant took the object and tucked it in his robe. Both merchants bowed and allowed themselves to be helped in mounting the small Hasan Daegian ponies.

The Sivans, being natural riders, had no problem controlling the skittish horses. They waved goodbye to the empress, turning their ponies to the west. The rest of the riders surrounded the merchants and galloped away at high speed.

Timon's curiosity was piqued. The tall scribe approached the empress, coming to rest six feet from her. "May I approach the empress?"

Maura turned. Her face seemed strained but, at the sight of the young scribe, relaxed. "Yes, Timon, you may come closer."

"Does the Great Mother need anything?"

The empress thought for a moment and smiled. "I don't know what you mean, Master Timon."

Timon shifted his weight. "Do you need me to record your meeting with the Sivans?"

Maura laughed out loud. "Oh, Timon, you should be more subtle if you wish to discover something."

Feeling the blood rush to his face, Timon could not help but return her smile. Maura's laugh was infectious.

"How old are you, Timon ben Ibin Moab?"

"Seventeen, Your Majesty."

"You are not much younger than I." Maura cocked her head to one side as if to better study the youth. "Do I seem very old to you?"

"Well," Timon paused, not knowing what he should say. Her face was unlined but seemed old much like his mother's.

"Tell the truth, young scribe. How old do you think I am? Really."

"My age, Great Mother."

"Timon, you are terrible at flattery. The truth is I'll be twenty-three at the next full moon. The war started on my eighteenth birthday." Maura's smiled drifted away. "I would wager you still feel young. I would give almost anything to feel that way again. Enjoy your youth and innocence, Timon, while you can, because in one heartbeat, something could happen to make you feel old and corrupt."

Maura held up a finger. "Just one heartbeat."

7

T he army marched.

Scouts from Jezra's rebels could be seen in the distance, taking progress reports on the moving city that was the enemy army. Maura never had them pursued, letting the wary spies watch as if to say they were too unimportant for her to be concerned about.

Across the steppes, the army traveled at a leisurely pace from one paltry waterhole to the next. Maura was disgusted with the water on the plains. It was brown and dirty with a strong sulfur odor—not like the clean, pure water at home that glistened under the warming sun. Her countrywomen were alike in their abhorrence of the natural conditions outside their homeland. Any water the Hasan Daegians or their animals consumed had to be strained and purified with herbs. Hasan Daegian physicians warned the Bhuttanians not to drink the water without purification, but the Bhuttanians would laugh good-naturedly and then come down with a case of dysentery.

Fleas and lice were other problems repelling the tidy Hasan Daegians. They were forever rubbing ointments and lotions on their skin, trying to preserve some semblance of grooming while ridding themselves of parasites living on their bodies.

The Bhuttanians shaved the hair from their bodies, following the practice of the Hasan Daegians, and rubbed zelkova juice everywhere. While the juice had little effect on lice, it did repel the biting flies and good company as well.

Timon succumbed to the prevalent practices and shaved his entire body, except for his head. While he would wear the potent Bhuttanian juice to repel crawly things from his warm-colored skin, he also tried some of the Hasan Daegian lotions, which at the moment were not working. He slapped the side of his neck and, catching some gnats, squeezed them between his fingers. He wanted desperately to reach under his tunic and scratch his unmentionables but didn't dare. Timon had caught the empress scrutinizing him now and then, and he certainly did not want to be found scratching his backside or worse when she glanced his way.

The tall, lanky scribe wondered why the empress should show any curiosity in him whatsoever. Her interest in him had grown with the arrival of KiKu. He wondered if it had anything to do with the growing tension between the empress and KiKu. The prince of Hittal could no longer hide his dismay with the empress for never publicly asking him to dine with her or to be in her general company. It would be a great slight for any royal person, and the fact the Bhuttanians now openly laughed at him caused the wound to cut deeper. Though KiKu's tent was still next to Maura's, most people regarded this as the empress protecting KiKu from his many enemies while in her care and nothing more.

KiKu became less guarded with his emotions and could be seen scowling at the empress, which was immediately reported to her.

Maura merely tossed her head and snorted, but Timon knew that these incidents would cause further estrangement between the former allies.

When the empress organized a celebratory dinner for her birthday and did not ask KiKu to join, it was more than the Hittal prince could endure. He packed up his goods, his wives, and servants, leaving the camp in a huff one morning.

There was talk among the Bhuttanians they should go after him, as KiKu did not ask royal permission to leave the encampment. But the empress said she was glad to be rid of him, and they should not waste their valuable time on a petty, deposed potentate. Within hours of his departure, KiKu was forgotten and life went on as before. Only Timon seemed to ponder the strange relationship between KiKu and the empress.

The empress studied local maps as before, questioned Timon endlessly about his life and his homeland as before, took loveless lovers as before, fed the uultepes from her plate as before. She seemed relatively unconcerned about KiKu's hurt feelings.

Timon shuddered at the thought of KiKu. He would not like having the spylord angry with him.

KiKu was said to have a hundred disguises, which he could assume and move about anywhere undetected. He could be the washerman who cleaned one's shirts. He could be the servant who filled one's goblet. He could be a Sivan merchant trading rare cloth. He could be the soldier standing guard at the door. He could be the woman who enticed unsuspecting men into "her" tent.

And he had a hundred ways to kill his victims. The shirt could have a poisoned needle in the cuff. The goblet could be laced with a potent drug. The rare cloth could suffocate without notice. The soldier could kill with a single blow from his sword and melt into the confused crowd. The "woman" could use her hands to snap a customer's neck as he removed his clothing.

Timon dug into his pockets, rummaging for a writing stick while he considered KiKu's potential for danger. No, he would not like the spylord to be angry with him for any reason.

The empress, concerned the animals needed a well-deserved rest, stopped near the original tribal border of Bhuttan before its expansion into an empire.

Her Bhuttani soldiers were anxious to see their families again, but waited patiently with characteristic Bhuttanian sentiment—a great deal of cursing and complaining. They realized exhausted horses were no good to them in the battle that was surely coming.

The Hasan Daegians were content to use the time to bathe, rinse their hair, and wash their clothes. Their servants ignored the snide comments of the Bhuttanians as they hauled water from a nearby river. "At least we don't smell like a whore's backside," the Hasan Daegians sniped.

This comment would only make the Bhuttanians roar with laughter. "I'd like to have the money a good whore would have," a foot soldier yelled back, "and if that meant that I have the stink of twelve men on me—so be it."

"That's what you Hasan Daegian women need—a good Bhuttanian man to cover you like a stallion covers a mare," cried out another Bhuttanian.

A Hasan Daegian servant, who was drying his lady's hair in front of her tent, bellowed, "Our women don't need dirty Bhuttanians when they have refined, cultured men to marry."

The Bhuttanians hooted and hurled clods of dirt at the Hasan Daegian's tent. "Who said anything about marrying? We just want a quick poke and then be on our way."

The Hasan Daegian woman, who was having her hair dried, threw the towel off her head in disgust. She stood with her arms akimbo. "Quick, indeed. I'm sure it would be as Bhuttanian men cannot 'hold' for very long just as they cannot hold their liquor." She held up her pinky finger and wiggled it. "Of course, I hear there is not much to work with."

A Bhuttanian stood up from his fire and began raising his tunic. "I'll show you what a real man looks like, not those runty lap dogs you pillow with."

The Hasan Daegian woman pulled her sword from its scabbard hanging from her chair. "Hold it there, soldier, or I'll have you for dinner in more ways than one."

Other Bhuttanian soldiers, watching the exchange, burst into laughter and threw more clods at Hasan Daegian women now gathering in force. Brandishing a sword or dagger, the women began advancing on the mouthy Bhuttanian soldiers.

The Bhuttanian men, seeing their Hasan Daegian comrades were serious, stopped bantering. "They can never take a joke," complained one soldier. "They are always so damned serious."

"Our honor is not a subject for your entertainment," retorted one Hasan Daegian woman, dressed in her archer's uniform. "Apologize for your insulting remarks to my countrywoman or draw your weapons."

"I would rather stick my head in a bucket of borax shit," sneered the Bhuttanian, pulling his tunic down. His hand rested near his dagger's hilt. He moved in an aggressive swagger toward the knot of Hasan Daegian women.

"Halt, you stupid swine!" roared a Bhuttanian officer, who was hurrying toward his tent to change into ceremonial armor. "The royal consul is approaching. Be sharp about your manners."

Immediately, those present hid their weapons and scanned their surroundings for Rubank, worried that word of their argument had already made its way back to the empress. All knew they could lose their heads for wrangling in public. The empress kept a tight rein on any quarreling amongst her soldiers, especially now they were entering Bhuttan proper. The Bhuttanians quickly scattered while the Hasan Daegian women stood at attention, waiting for the worst.

A small pocket of dignitaries, dressed in the blue robes of the Hasan Daegian court, made its way toward the small knot of women. Next to an impressive older man walked a youth dressed in the brown robe of a scribe. He was speaking to the older man. The Hasan

Daegian women bowed low as they recognized the Royal Consul Rubank and the Royal Scribe Timon.

Rubank stopped in front of the Hasan Daegian warriors and peered into the sky. He placed his hand over his eyes and scanned the horizon. He wrote on a wet tablet given to him by Timon, who translated every word loudly so all could listen easily—even those hiding in their tents.

Timon addressed the other officials standing with them. "My Lord Rubank says he is baffled. He thought only a moment ago he heard the distant rumbling of an unfortunate storm, but now the sky is perfectly clear without any angry countenance. He asks his learned friends to account for this."

The other officials tried to appear very serious and not smile at the sight of the Hasan Daegian women straining their necks to listen.

One elderly man spoke, "I would venture, my Lord Consul, that an unexpected calm front came into the area, breaking up the current tumultuous weather pattern."

The officials glanced out of the corners of their eyes and saw frightened Bhuttanians peeking from their tents, after having sent their slaves out to work so they might better hear and report back.

The consul wrote again.

Timon read out loud, "My Lord Consul wishes to express calm weather will be expected for the duration of our march." Timon watched Rubank mark his reed in the wet clay. "And he thinks anything else would not be tolerated by the empress, not even the most innocent of breezes."

Rubank resumed his walk down the lane flanked by rows of tents. The other officials followed suit.

Timon turned his head toward the Hasan Daegian women and winked. He hurried his steps to catch up with Rubank.

The Hasan Daegian women relaxed their stance and breathed easier.

Rubank glanced back and shot them an icy stare.

The women gasped and rushed into their tents, not appearing again until nightfall when they shared food with their Bhuttanian brethren as a friendly gesture.

The Bhuttanian men were not keen on the feast, which consisted mainly of vegetables. They liked meat, but they ate the dishes nonetheless, and many found them not unpleasant. They, in turn, gave the Hasan Daegians small tokens that they would give to their wives or mistresses, not knowing what else to give a woman.

The warrior women looked down upon their gifts of small coins or scented handkerchiefs in disbelief. These were not proper gifts for comrades in war. They would rather have had sandal laces or a grinding stone to keep their weapons sharp, but wishing to keep the peace, they graciously thanked the Bhuttanian men.

The Bhuttanians sheepishly stared at the ground, wishing to be anywhere but with the large and imposing Hasan Daegian women. They were glad their females were petite —easier to control. Still, they stole glances at the Hasan Daegian women's full hips and breasts, wondering.

Timon, finished with his official duties for Rubank, strolled through the camp again. He studied the hide-covered tents of the Bhuttanians, which dulled next to the brightly colored cloth pavilions of the Hasan Daegians. He pondered how the Hasan Daegians kept themselves from getting wet during a heavy rain, but the tents were always dry on the inside no matter the weather. In fact, Hasan Daegians usually looked very healthy, and it was a known fact most of them kept all of their teeth until their deaths. Timon thought that was amazing. He put his finger in his mouth and felt the gaps between his back teeth. He wished he had beautiful teeth like the Hasan Daegians, but at least his were not rotting like most of the older Bhuttanian men. *Bad diet*, thought Timon.

As he passed, many people, both high and lowborn, nodded or hailed him. Most people knew of the young Bhuttanian from the outer steppes of the empire who translated the thoughts of Rubank, consul for the empress. Some believed Timon might be an important man one day and went out of their way to make themselves known to him. Timon, being without guile, thought they were being friendly and responded in kind. He didn't realize he was being sought out and cultivated on purpose.

A young courier trotted on a well-worn path, perusing the throng of soldiers, cobblers, cooks, slaves, and animals mingling back and forth. Spying Timon talking with a young Hasan Daegian woman, he scampered over to Timon and pulled on the scribe's long sleeve. Timon pushed the young boy away, continuing to flirt with the young Hasan Daegian archer.

"Master, Master, you must come! The empress has summoned you!" breathlessly exclaimed the boy.

"What?" asked Timon, incredulously.

"You must hurry," repeated the young boy. "She wants you to come quickly."

Timon swallowed hard and bid the Hasan Daegian archer a hasty goodbye.

She waved sympathetically.

No one wanted to be summoned by the empress. Maura was predictable only in that her moods ranged from a simmering quiet to a raging tempest. She was not known for her good temper. A sullen, withdrawn woman at most times, she lacked the grace of her cunning but ruthless husband Dorak.

Even Dorak's enemies thought he had possessed a certain charm, which seemed to make his evil less—evil.

While the empress was certainly more honorable than her former husband, she was not much of a wit or biting satirist—behaviors which made court life bearable for most Bhuttanians. A capable but boring monarch was a burden no one wanted to share, least of all Timon, as he hurried toward the royal tent. What could she want of him?

Stumbling through the entrance of the royal pavilion, he was waved back into Maura's private room by the chamber attendant. Straightening his tunic and smoothing down his hair, he asked the guards to announce him. He was told to wait as the empress was bathing her daughter. A chair was brought for Timon, and as he waited, he cleaned the dirt encased between his toes. A servant, bringing a clean cloth, chided Timon for not changing his sandals.

"I didn't have time," hissed Timon. "Hold your tongue, or I'll make you eat this mud!" he snapped at the woman.

The servant sniffed the air as though a foul stench had been emitted and turned her heels on Timon.

"Servants," muttered Timon, exasperated.

One of the lads-in-waiting came out and bade Timon to enter. "She's in a good mood," he whispered close to Timon's ear. "You are fortunate."

Timon nodded his thanks and entered.

Maura was sitting on her bed in a loosely tied robe playing with Princess Dyanna.

As she bent over her daughter, Timon could see her breasts sway. They were full and firm. Embarrassed, Timon inspected his clean feet.

Maura ignored the presence of Timon as she tickled her daughter's tiny feet and pulled the squirming princess away from the edge of the bed. The baby started to pout until the empress blew on her fat belly, causing the princess to squeal with delight. The happy mother hugged her daughter and then handed her over to a nurse.

When Maura turned to Timon, there were no remnants of the happy, contented mother he had witnessed just seconds before. Maura showed her calculating, mistrustful expression always given to the public. The sudden change in Maura's countenance chilled Timon.

The empress stretched out on the bed like one of her uultepes lounging on the floor. "Timon, I am bored. I wish to go out on a hunt tomorrow. Since you claim to know this area, you will act as my guide."

"What shall be the object of your hunt, Great Mother?"

"I want to kill something big, something we can eat later that day; something the minstrels will sing about."

"Then for game that big, we shall have to go toward the foothills. It will take more than a day to reach our destination."

"Won't that take us deep into Jezra's territory?"

"Not if we go due north. As long as we don't turn east, we shall be all right, if Your Majesty's scouts are correct in their assessment of Jezra's movements."

Maura cast him a sidelong glance. "To suggest my scouts might be wrong would be to suggest I might be wrong." She turned away from him. "Even when I'm wrong, I am right."

"I understand your meaning, Great Mother."

"To understand my meaning is good for the only son of a poor widow from an obscure village in the middle of nowhere."

"Great Mother, I am no one."

"It still seems strange to me that you were selected by Zoar out of thousands of boys placed in his service."

"I am grateful to the gods."

"I thought you believed in only one god."

"I was speaking figuratively. Perhaps I should say I was born under a lucky star."

"It would seem you were, Timon. A very lucky star." Maura paused and tightened her robe about her. "Come here. I want a better look at you."

Timon ventured closer.

"Closer. The light is dim." Timon moved toward the empress silently, hoping the uultepes would not attack him. One of them growled in a subdued manner.

The empress bade Timon to stop. She studied him as though trying to discover a secret. The way she leered at him made Timon feel naked.

"Have you a woman?"

Timon stood at attention—his heart pounding in his ears. Timon blushed to the very roots of his hair. He wanted to say yes—many women, but she would know he was lying. "No, Great Mother, I have never known the pleasure of a woman's bed."

"Or a boy's?"

"No, Great Mother."

"Are you an ascetic?"

"My mother made me swear an oath of purity until I was married."

Maura reached up and stroked Timon's black hair. She leaned over and took a deep smell of him. "Why would your mother make you take such an oath?" She tenderly kissed his earlobe.

"My mother was concerned there not be any paternity entanglements." The empress' hot breath on his skin made Timon both angry and woozy with desire. He wanted to be gone from this temptress.

"Why would a peasant woman care about such a matter? Only nobles worry about such things." Maura slowly rubbed Timon's chest.

"My mother is a chaste and virtuous woman, even though a peasant," spat out Timon, his upper body heaving heavily. He gave the empress a look of disdain.

"I see I have insulted you, Timon. It was not my intention, I assure you."

"Your Majesty has not insulted me. As you have so said, even when you are wrong, you are right."

Maura clasped her hands to her heart and feigned a blow to the chest. "You have injured me with my own words. Serves me right. Keep your virtue for now, Timon. There is no way I want to go against a righteous mother. I will catch up with you after a Hasan Daegian maiden has tumbled you." She picked up a goblet and took a drink of colla water. "You may go. I will see you at dawn."

Timon bowed low and retreated from Maura's presence. Once outside her chambers, he ran to his own tent.

Upon hearing Timon's hasty footfalls, Maura chuckled to herself.

From a darkened corner of Maura's room appeared the High Priestess of Magi. She gathered her bluish-green robes, waiting for the empress to address her.

Maura looked at her with bright eyes. "I don't know whether to congratulate his mother for his chastity or be insulted at his scorn."

"I think he is a most congenial choice, Great Mother."

"I pray to Mekonia he is the right one."

"I am sure you have made the correct selection."

"He'd better be, or I shall ride into Bhuttani without backup."

"I know this is a painful topic, but perhaps you should accept Dorak might be dead."

Maura threw the goblet against the wall of her chamber. "NEVER!"

The High Priestess bowed her head. "I have caused my sovereign grief. May I be excused, Great Mother?"

"Get out." Maura sank into a chair. She moaned in despair, her features contorting in misery. "Dorak," she whispered to drifting currents of air. "If you hear me, have faith. I will come, never fear. I will come. I will come for you."

8

The Great Divigi winced in pain.

He tried to spread his wings but was met with resistance from his companion.

"Get those damn feathers out of my face. I can't breathe," Dorak muttered.

"So sorry," mumbled Iegani, the Great Divigi, "but if we don't move them every so often, we get severe cramps in our shoulders. They are heavy, you know," he said, referring to his massive wings.

"And useless to us here."

"I agree my wings have been of little use since we arrived, but who knows about the future?"

"If we have a future."

"That's pitiful to hear from the Great Aga, Master of the World. One would think you would exude a little more confidence."

"The devil take thee, Iegani."

Iegani raised an eyebrow. "How Anqarian of you, Dorak."

Dorak chortled. "The influence of my first wife, I'm afraid."

"Ah, yes, Jezra. For such a moral and brave people, I would bet you were a little disappointed in Jezra's behavior after she arrived at court."

"That's an understatement. It was thought an Anqarian bride would be a positive influence. Little did we know," Dorak said before breaking off.

"Jezra would take an interest in the black arts," filled in Iegani. "You can hardly blame her for indulging. After all, you were dipping into the pot so to speak."

"I hardly thought my wife would team up with my wizard and try to usurp my throne."

"Oh, you thought she would be on your side," retorted Iegani, "especially after Zoar burned her city and killed her father. Of course, she welcomed you with open arms on your wedding night."

"Her father committed suicide," replied Dorak with grim brevity.

"That makes all the difference."

Dorak spat, "Are we going to quarrel again? After all, your hands are not without blood on them. Weren't there rumors you murdered your lover?"

"I did not want to. She left me no recourse."

"Oh, well, that makes all the difference."

"Shut up, you puny little man. You know nothing. You are nothing but a blight upon the world." Iegani's eyes flashed like molten gold.

Dorak's anger swelled like a tight ball in his stomach. He curled his fist and struck Iegani under the chin.

Iegani's extended his hand, and a razor-sharp talon was released from under his skin. He moved in for the kill.

"STOP THIS!" Gitar, Empress of the Dinii, stood several feet from the dueling Dini and the aga. "I GAVE YOU BOTH A COMMAND!" Her voice boomed and reverberated off the walls of their prison.

Reluctantly, Iegani retracted his long nail. He glared at Dorak.

"I understand you two argue to take your minds off our problems, but it is wasted energy. One of these days, you will both go too far, and then where shall we be?"

Dorak nodded in agreement and bowed very low. "My lady, you are correct as usual. The pain we cause each other takes our minds off our greater anguish."

"And guilt?"

"Yes, Empress Gitar, but my guilt is my burden that I do not wish to inflict upon you," responded Dorak.

"Then do not do so, Lord Dorak. I have enough to contemplate," said Gitar. She turned toward Iegani. "Have you been able to establish contact with Maura?"

Iegani shook his head. "She just has vague impressions. At present, Maura is acting on gut instinct. As long as she thinks Dorak might be alive, she will search for us. You must stay alive, Great Aga. If she thinks there is a chance for your survival, Maura will stop at nothing to find you."

Dorak closed his eyes, thinking of sweet memories with Maura.

"That you must go into the fires of hell to find me, be it so, Maura."

Exchanging glances with Gitar, Iegani said, "See, I told you he was turning into an Anqarian."

"Just keep him alive, Iegani. It is your meddling that got us into this situation in the first place."

Iegani winced at the words of his niece.

Gitar watched a priest burn incense upon the eternal flame to Bhuttu. She reached out to touch his arm, but her hand went through his flesh. "How strange. We stand beside them watching their every movement, but they can neither hear nor see us," remarked Gitar.

The priest looked up, feeling an unexplained draft. He shivered and tightened his shawl around his shoulders.

Dorak took out his dagger and stabbed the priest in the chest.

Feeling a sharp twinge near his heart, the priest murmured an incantation before running away. Dorak swung around laughing. Seeing the stark eyes of Gitar, he stopped short.

"We are even less than the wisps of ghosts," complained a forlorn Gitar. She sat glumly on the steps leading up to Bhuttu's bronze statue.

Dorak went over to her. "My lady, we are not without hope. Maura will come for us. I know it. And Iegani says she continues to wear the amulet."

"But will she make the connection? We never taught her about magic. We didn't believe in it. The Dinii know nothing about such arts."

The aga patted her on the arm. "She's a quick study."

Sitting on the marble floor and leaning against a massive column, the weary Dini empress looked as small as a child.

Dorak felt a stab of pity that a creature so noble as she should be reduced thus. He leaned over to comfort the empress when Iegani grabbed his arm.

"Did you hear that? Shhhh."

Dorak and Iegani peered into the darkened recess of the temple sanctuary. They had learned only the area in which they stood was illuminated. The rest of their prison remained dark and forbidding. Creatures, other than themselves, were caught up in their world and not all of them were friendly.

"What is it?" asked Dorak, unsheathing his dagger.

A slithering sound emanated from one corner, and Iegani saw something move behind the massive statue of Bhuttu. "There!" he said, pointing.

Dorak squinted his eyes. While the base of the statue was clear, the top portion was cloudy and out of focus until it receded into a thick grey mist. Dorak pulled Gitar to her feet. "Lady, I think it is time we should rejoin the others. There is safety in numbers."

Gitar, towered over Dorak, confused. "I am so tired, Dorak. Won't you let me sleep?"

Iegani pulled on one of her wings. "As they say, there is no rest for the wicked."

The regal Dini snarled. "I am not wicked. You are not suggesting that, are you, Iegani?"

"No, my niece, it is a figure of speech. We both know that of the two of us, I am the evil one."

"I would say evil is too harsh a word. Well-intentioned gone mad is more correct."

"You are very kind, Empress."

Gitar gave a lop-sided grin. "Of course, we both know the real evil here is Dorak."

Dorak bowed very low to them both. "You mark me well, Lady. That you would have me in your presence reflects your tolerance and graciousness."

Narrowing her eyes, Gitar took a sharp finger and poked Dorak in the chest, "Little man, I do believe your words carry more than one meaning."

Iegani sneered, "This is the most fun I have had in days, but something behind the statue sounds very big, and I am a coward in my old age. I wish to leave now and join the others."

Dorak turned to Gitar. "I think he is being sarcastic."

Iegani reattached their ropes of woven feathers to each other's waists, so they would not become separated in the darkness into which they would have to flee. He had not quite finished when a slimy green-scaled creature with great black lines on its back emerged from behind the statue into the open sanctuary.

Iegani caught only a glance of a moving green streak while wrapping the rope around his wrist. He pushed Gitar into the darkness. "Run," he cried, "and don't look back!"

Gitar and Dorak did not need to be told twice. They ran into the dark where they would be able to hide from whatever was hunting them, or, at least, they hoped. Each felt a tug on the other end where the rest of the outcast Dinii awaited for them.

As he ran, Dorak yanked back a signal code. The rope was being quickly reeled in, helping to guide the great aga and his bird-like companions. Because of their large size, Gitar and Iegani were more cautious in their escape than the quick and agile Dorak. They were in a building not designed to accommodate the legendary Dinii and their massive wingspan. Doorways were not wide enough, the floors were too slippery for their taloned feet, and the ceilings were too low. Though they could pass through stone and wood in their present form, they had great difficulty doing so. It gave them headaches.

Gitar looked back to gauge their escape. She spied the snake-like creature behind them.

It reared up and opened its gaping mouth, exposing hundreds of razor-sharp teeth. Gitar had never seen a creature so hideous in form and gasped in outright fear at its horrible appearance. She had never known fear such as this, not even that ghastly night when Dorak's minions swept into City of the Peaks, destroying her home forever.

Stumbling, Gitar could not regain her balance and fell on the cold marble floor. She cried out as the creature loomed over her. Empress Gitar, long astute in the ways of killing, and now fearing she was about to be devoured herself, instinctively exposed her talons and bared her teeth. If she were going to die, she would try to take the hideous creature with her, thus saving her friends. "Prepare to die!" she hissed at the drooling and loathing viper.

The serpent lowered its head as a foul stench emanated from its mouth.

Gitar spat at it and cursed its birth. Swinging her powerful arms at the snapping serpent, she raked her razor-sharp talons across the bridge of its nose. The creature seemed startled and sensing its hesitation, Gitar swung again, digging in deeper. Glancing out of the corner of her eye, she saw Dorak rush the creature and plunge his dagger into the viper's fetid skin while Iegani stood on the other side of the creature thrusting with his talons.

Purple syrupy liquid gushed forth from the creature as it rose higher, howling in pain.

A flash of light exploded, blinding Gitar and the others. Dorak covered his eyes with his left arm but kept stabbing until he felt the flesh of the creature no more. Confused, he lowered his arm and blinked heavily. He heard Iegani stumble to Gitar and ask her if she was all right.

Helping the empress to her feet, Iegani felt the last of his strength taxed. He wished desperately to sit down somewhere. Confident his niece had not been injured, he turned toward Dorak only to find the aga trembling, his dagger hanging limply at his side. Iegani followed Dorak's gaze and gasped.

On a shimmering, gaseous cloud, hovering off the floor, stood a spectral vision of Zoar, Dorak's father!

For a few seconds, Iegani stood stunned until he managed to find his voice. "Why aren't you dead?"

A small chuckle issued from the transparent form of the former aga. "Perhaps I am dead, and you are dead with me."

Iegani pondered this for a moment. "I don't think so," he said, although he was not sure.

"My father is dead. YOU ARE NOT ZOAR!" cried out Dorak.

"You betrayed me, son! Do you not feel the evil of your deed has undone our people?" snorted Zoar, fixing his withering gaze upon Dorak.

"I KILLED THEE!" shouted Dorak. "IT CANNOT BE!" Dorak trembled with fear and loathing.

Both Iegani and Gitar looked askance at Dorak. Iegani stepped beside Dorak, placing his hand on Dorak's shoulder. "The apparition is not he. Do not fear this bloated shadow of corruption. We cannot speak with the dead, my son."

Instantly, the milky semblance of Zoar disappeared, and a new form took its place.

"Zedek!" cried out Dorak, oddly relieved at the wizard's countenance.

"I always did like to make a grand entrance," announced the Black Cacodemon, irritated his disguise was seen through so quickly. "Did I give you a fright, Dorak?"

"What do you want with us?" asked Gitar, pushing Iegani aside. "Where are we?"

The Black Cacodemon's thin lips broke into a smile. "You are where I have put you."

"And where is that?" repeated Gitar, breathing heavily. That she was under the control of such an odious man made Gitar furious. As she talked, spittle flew out of her mouth.

"My dear Empress, there is no use getting yourself worked up into a lather. No one would be here at all if Maura had not stabbed me in the heart and stolen my amulet." The wizard waved a hand slightly, and his cloud floated closer to them. "I had only a few seconds to mumble an incantation, but without the amulet, one can only do so much," he said, shrugging. "I could only get this far, which was fortunate."

"Why is that?" asked Dorak, barely being able to hide his contempt for his former ally.

"I was trying to send you all to the bowels of hell," he smiled viciously. "Yes, the Anqarians are right about hell, but I digress. We were all thrown in together." He looked about him. "Otherwise, I would like it here. I was in need of a rest anyway, and this would have been the perfect hiding place to recuperate until I could re-emerge. Of course, life is not without its problems. All of you followed. Or I followed you. Now the mere presence of so many beings in the in-between-world disturbs the harmony." The wizard peered closer at Gitar. "The vibrations are not what they should be."

"I am so sorry," Gitar replied sarcastically.

"Ah, well."

"You have not answered me. Where are we?" asked Dorak impatiently.

The wizard winced, "Dorak, I never thought you were very perceptive. It should be obvious where we are." The wizard stared at Iegani. "I would wager that you know."

Gitar and Dorak looked at Iegani. The owl-like man sighed heavily. "Apparently, in a state of flux."

"Speak clearly, man," barked Dorak.

"Dorak, you said this place was the temple of Bhuttu. An actual place with people coming and going who we can see and hear, but not touch or contact. They can neither see, hear, nor touch us as well. They do not know we exist." Iegani held out his hands helplessly. "We are neither dead nor alive, but somehow we exist in the spirit world. We are in the Nether Realm."

The Black Cacodemon snapped his fingers. "Correct," he hollered. "It has only taken you years to figure that out."

"Years?" gasped Gitar. "We have only been here for a few hours."

Howling with laughter, the Black Cacodemon grabbed at his stomach. "Oh, dear Lady, you have been here for two years—almost three." He laughed again. "This is so rich."

Dorak advanced upon the wizard's cloud with his dagger pitched forward. "Do not laugh at her confusion. You are not even fit to speak to her."

The wizard feigned surprise. "You are defending the honor of the Dini empress? Are you not the one who destroyed her home and was responsible for the death of her daughters?" Putting a finger up to his lips, the wizard pouted. "Yes, I think you are the very one."

Dorak stopped short.

"The truth hurts, doesn't it, son?" the wizard cracked.

"It was war," Dorak said.

"War is a great excuse for murder and general mayhem. One can kill, plunder, destroy, do things one would not think of doing during peacetime. As long as the term war covers the crimes, it's all right." The wizard sneered at Dorak. "You are such a hypocrite. Even now, you try to hide your sins. You murdered your father, betrayed both of your wives, and disowned your son. Quite an impressive record for such a young man."

"I did what I thought was necessary. The boy is too much like his mother. I took no pleasure in it."

The Black Cacodemon bent down close to Dorak. "It doesn't matter how you feel. It only matters what you do."

"Dorak, do you not see what he is trying to do?" snapped Iegani. "He's trying to demoralize you—make you doubt yourself."

The aga dropped his dagger. Dorak felt sick to his stomach and dropped to the floor, sitting on his haunches. He moaned lowly.

"Get up, Dorak," said Gitar, not without feeling. She felt confused by her simultaneous loathing for the man who had killed her daughters and her need for his support during the present crisis.

Dorak asked, "Do you know what happened to Maura?"

Iegani moved over to Dorak. He shook him violently. "You are not to listen to him. He will lie and cheat us if he has the chance. He is the father of all lies."

"I will be glad to tell him of his lost love," interrupted the wizard, his figure beginning to disappear into the darkness.

"You will say nothing, you black-hearted demon!" Iegani cried.

"Maura died while giving birth to your daughter," said the Black Cacodemon.

Iegani interrupted, "That's not true. I can feel her presence."

"But you have not seen her, have you? You can't make contact with her, Birdman. That's because she is dead," the magician sneered.

"A daughter?" asked Dorak, snapping his head up.

The magician was fading fast into the darkness of the hallway until only his lips could be seen. "Jezra took care of her, if you guess my meaning."

Dorak muffled a cry and felt the floor rushing up to meet him. He had the vague impression someone was laughing, and another person was crying. Then darkness overtook him.

9

Timon awoke before dawn.

He stumbled out of bed and, still half-asleep, pulled on his tunic and leggings. He opened the flap of his tent and daintily stepped outside into the mud, his feet protected by the wooden clogs he had made for this purpose.

The waterboys had already filled everyone's bowl and pitcher for the morning wash.

As a Bhuttanian, Timon preferred to shun all of this excessive grooming, but the empress could smell dirt and body odor ten feet away—and she didn't like it. He didn't see why he had to wash when he was just going to sweat atop a horse anyway.

Resigned, Timon plunged his hands into the icy water and vigorously rubbed his face, neck, and ears, cursing the entire time. With his damp towel, he reached underneath his tunic and wiped his armpits. Satisfied with his ablutions, Timon took a ragged comb and raked the tangles out of his thick, black hair, braiding it into a luxurious tail down his back in Bhuttanian fashion.

Going back into his tent, he wiped his walking boots off with a dirty rag until they were presentable and then pulled them on. Around his forehead, he tied a bright red band. This signified to other hunters not to mistake him for the prey. Going over to a casket, he opened it carefully. The brass casket with its leather hinges had been his father's traveling box where he had kept his personal items. Sifting through the various items, Timon found a small bundle of twigs secured by a leather thong. He selected one and pulled it out.

Timon sifted again through the box and found a precious looking glass encased in brass. Holding up the mirror, Timon took the twig and began cleaning his teeth by rubbing the end of the twig around his gums. Between cleaning, Timon swished his mouth with stale wine and spat it out on the dirt floor of his tent. The scribe took one last glance in the mirror and smiled. His teeth were still presentable, white and straight, even though there were gaps here and there in the back. He did not cover his mouth when he smiled like so many Bhuttanians. His strong teeth were a sign of good health.

Leaving the warm comfort of his tent, Timon hurried to the royal pavilion where he knew the empress would have a breakfast buffet for the hunting party. He was not disappointed when he entered the gaily-decorated tent. In the center of the room, a table groaned from all of the breads, cakes, cheese, and dried fruit placed upon it. Happily, Timon stuffed his pockets with bread. On a wooden plate nicked with use, he piled elegant breakfast cakes the empress liked to eat. If they were good enough for a queen to eat, they were certainly good enough for him. Waiting for the Bhuttanian general, Alexanee, to peruse the table in front of him, Timon finally managed to get to the honey pots where he liberally dabbed honey on his cakes.

Sitting by himself in a quiet corner, Timon gratefully accepted a cup of hot colla tea from a serving lad and contented himself by stuffing his mouth while watching the rest of the party assemble.

The High Priestess of Magi was seated on the dais and giving Rubank a good tongue lashing over something. When anyone walked by, the High Priestess would stop talking and glance surreptitiously around the room. Timon determined she was acting strangely, but thought no more about it, as all of the women from the House of Magi were a strange-acting lot.

One of Maura's lads-in-waiting came from her private chambers and filled a gold platter with food from the table. Everyone made way for him. Though he was polite, the youth plainly reveled in the fact the much taller and heavier Bhuttanian men made way for him, as did his larger countrywomen. Satisfied his platter was filled with a complete selection for the empress, he nodded to another servant to follow him with a pot of hot colla tea.

Timon wiped crumbs from his mouth with his sleeve. So the empress was going to eat in her private chambers. Thinking that odd, Timon dipped another cake into the pool of honey on his plate and stuffed it into his mouth with relish. Next, he attacked a big slab of orange cheese. With his pocketknife, he cut off the green residue on the outside of the cheese, putting some in his pocket before taking great bites off the chunk left on his plate.

Belching loudly, he apologized to the Hasan Daegian noble women who were seated near him. They nodded their acknowledgment of his apology and began to eat their meal. Watching them, Timon wondered about the prodigious amount of food that had to be provided each day for the army. Not only for the soldiers, but also for their families, visitors, servants, slaves, and laborers who made the camp function, and that did not even include the animals.

Many towns and villages were happy the army moved in their direction as the empress had a reputation of paying for supplies she needed whereas other rulers might have stolen them. Farmers were cash poor and only too happy to see their beet crops taken if they had a little jingle in their pocket after the soldiers left.

Timon shuddered. Who liked beets anyway but Hasan Daegians and peasants? He had to admit the Hasan Daegian cooks had a way with vegetables even the meat-eating Bhuttanians could stomach. Many Bhuttanians were now eating fruits and vegetables of their own accord, even when meat was plentiful.

The young scribe was an astute observer. He could see how the two cultures were subtly blending, even against the wishes of the sterner conservatives from both sides. Timon had to hand it to the empress. She was a visionary. Perhaps she could bring about peace. Roads would be repaired. Roaming bands of thieves and murderers would be imprisoned. Schools would reopen and new ones built. Aqueducts could be constructed and dams erected. His people might even pick up their old nomadic way of life knowing the steppes were safe again.

The young scribe sighed. It was just a pipe dream. The empress would probably be murdered before they reached Bhuttani, and Jezra would reign in her son's name. Timon made a face. Jezra was neither a visionary nor an astute politician. She would bleed the Bhuttanian Empire dry rebuilding Anqara, her beloved razed city.

A gong sounded, and the empress entered the room. All stood.

Maura had donned black leather trousers and a tan twilled shirt under a black leather jacket. Her hair was braided with feathers entwined in the braids. After greeting everyone, she asked about the weather. One of her scouts felt a storm was brewing, and the hunt should be canceled. "Nonsense," snorted Maura. "Royal Scribe, what say you?"

Timon cautiously made his way through the crowd until he was in the immediate circle of the empress. He noticed the scout was scowling at him. "I'm sure your learned women of nature know what is best in matters of weather," he replied. He felt the scout return a kinder gaze in his direction.

"You know this area?"

"Yes, Great Mother. I have hunted here before but as a child."

Acting as though she didn't hear Timon's subtle warning, Maura turned to one of her generals. "Have there been any reports of Jezra's forces in the area?"

General Alexanee shook his head, "No, but that doesn't mean there is no danger."

Choosing to ignore Alexanee's warning as well, Maura declared, "Well, there seems to be nothing to stop me then. If it rains, I will merely take cover the best I can."

The High Priestess broke in, "Servants could follow with a makeshift tent and provisions, Great Mother."

"Thank you, my lady, but we shall have ample provisions. The hunt should take several days," said the empress.

"Yes," Timon replied. "We are going high into the hills to hunt borax. As long as we take guards and provisions in case we don't kill anything to eat, we shall be fine." Timon flinched under the steady gaze of Alexanee, not to mention the Hasan Daegian and Bhuttanian officers.

The Bhuttanian general tried to persuade the empress again. "Let me send in a large party to survey the area."

"And scare the game?" Maura shook her head. "I am bored and am in need of diversion. I want to hunt."

The Hasan Daegian officers, who stood in a little knot, were horrified. Not only was their sovereign leaving the protection of her army, but she was doing so to hunt, an activity they thought a barbaric trait taught to Maura by the Dinii.

Maura pointed to Timon. "He says he has hunted there plenty of times, and there has never been a problem."

Timon began sweating heavily. He realized if anything happened to the empress, he would be blamed.

Frustrated, General Alexanee clamored, "Great Mother, this is most unreasonable!"

The room became still.

Maura narrowed her eyes into bright slits. "Are you implying I am unreasonable?"

Alexanee lowered his eyes to the floor. "I am sorry, Great Mother, if I gave offense. It is not my intention. I mean only to protect my sovereign from any possible harm."

Maura grabbed a riding crop from a servant, and moving outside the tent, she called over her shoulder. "No offense taken, General. Since you are afraid for my safety, you may accompany me." She tapped the side of her boot impatiently with the quirt.

The general inwardly groaned. He did not want to gallop over the countryside looking for wild borax. He wanted to sleep and make love to his wife, whom he hadn't seen for several years. He was within a few days of his country estate. Instead, he smiled and replied, "Nothing would give me greater pleasure, Great Mother."

"Good. Shall we get started? You there," Maura said, pointing to Timon. "Do not leave me." She strode outside the tent where horses awaited. Maura mounted a beige Hasan Daegian pony and motioned to the one next to hers. "There, Timon. You shall ride next to me and tell me what you know of the region."

"Great Mother, I am afraid my knowledge has been depleted long ago in our talks," replied Timon, trying not to show his distaste for the small Hasan Daegian pony, unlike the impressive Bhuttanian warhorse. The fact that he was afraid of the giant horses did not enter into his thought processes. All he valued was that a man cut an imposing figure on a Bhuttanian horse while one looked like a fool on the smaller, but tougher Hasan Daegian ponies with one's feet almost dragging the ground.

"Nonsense. You have not even begun to educate me."

"That would be like trying to outshine the sun," teased Timon, holding his breath. He knew the empress disliked empty flattery. Perhaps if she were angry with him, she might command him to stay in the camp.

Maura smiled as though she knew what the royal scribe was trying to manage. "That may be so, but you will try, good scribe, or I will give Rubank a bad report when I return." She spurred her horse and galloped away, leaving Timon and the rest of the hunting party in a flurry of flying clods of dirt.

The Imperial guards immediately started after their empress while a small group of little girls with their woven grass dolls waved goodbye to them.

Alexanee nudged his pony next to Timon. "I do believe Her Majesty expressed her desire you ride with her."

"Yes, General," concurred Timon, not wishing to incur the wrath of this Bhuttanian general, who was already exasperated with this expedition and now with the small horse underneath him. Timon kicked his pony, and it took off following the guards who were already out of sight. He finally joined them several miles across the plain.

The royal scribe was no horseman, but he managed to keep his seat. After several hours, his thigh and calf muscles ached. He wished nothing more than to be in his tent alone and snoring. "Your Majesty, this is where we turn off the main road," he said, reining his horse a hard left. The main road was but a tired little brown scratch on the ground and the path that Timon took was barely perceptible.

Maura signaled to the other horsemen to follow her lead as she turned her horse. She had said little during the journey, as though something weighed heavily on her mind.

Timon regaled Maura with tales of past hunting trips. He told of times when his father had brought him. In the telling, he relived the happy memories of his boyhood and his deceased father.

"You must have loved your father very much," stated Maura.

Timon searched Maura's face to find any hint of mockery. He found only sympathy. "Yes, I did," replied Timon. "He was a great man."

A shadow passed over Maura's face, and she turned away. "No more talk of fathers," she said abruptly, spurring her horse forward.

Confused, Timon slowed the pace of his pony. He wondered if the empress had been close to her father. He decided he did not care about the empress and stopped thinking about her. His mind wandered to past scenes of home when his father had lived, and his mother had been much younger. He remembered the laughter and the love. The recollections warmed Timon's heart, causing him to chuckle.

The hunting party rode a good portion of the day until late afternoon. They came upon a large blue lake nestled at the foot of the Messaad Mountains, which ran northwest of Bhuttani. Scouts had been recruited to monitor for any sign of Jezra's men but found nothing. Mostly, they discovered hill villages deserted for a very long time.

Within her web of protection, Maura watched for signs of borax. Without notice, she would jump from her horse and anxiously push away fallen leaves from the damp earth. If she discovered an animal print, she would smell and taste the dirt forming it. She constantly sniffed the air. Finding spores or droppings, she inhaled their odor.

"Several days old" or "a female boaep in heat" Maura would pronounce with authority.

Maura's hunting affectations irritated Timon, as he was exhausted. The sooner he climbed off his wretched little pony, the better he would feel.

The scouts, however, followed behind the empress, study a gnawed branch or scratches on bark, and nod their heads in unison with her decrees.

As if reading Timon's mind, the empress asked Alexanee to make camp near the lake.

The chef immediately raced ahead to stake out a suitable spot where she could cook for the empress and her party.

Alexanee reigned in his horse, sighing with relief. He assigned guards around the campsite and sent several men on ahead to stand watch in the hills. Hasan Daegian women guarded the empress while the Bhuttanian men took the outer perimeters of the camp.

Stiff from the ride, Maura jumped off her pony and stretched. She informed her guards she was going to bathe in the lake. Shedding her sweaty hunting clothes, Maura was clad only in her undergarments with a dagger hidden in her shirtwaist. Diving into the water, the empress found it bracing. She stayed only long enough to wash the dirt and sweat off. Upon her return to shore, she found a warm towel, fresh clothes, and soft sandals, which she donned with pleasure. It was good to be out of that tight leather.

Maura hurried over to the campfire where she discovered Timon sitting near the flames with his feet immersed in a bucket of hot water.

Timon immediately tried to stand.

Maura bid him and the rest of the officers to remain seated. "Feet hurt, Timon?" inquired Maura.

"Great Mother, I am not accustomed to riding a horse this long. I usually walk."

"Then I would think another part of your anatomy would be affected."

"That hurts as well, Great Mother." Timon grinned sheepishly. "I guess I am not much of a horseman even though I am Bhuttanian."

"Do you know of this lake?" asked Maura, changing the subject.

"Yes, Great Mother. It is called the Lake of Forgotten Dreams."

"Why is that?"

"It is said a person who has a deep and abiding regret can come here, drink of the cool waters, and forget. Thus the Lake of Forgotten

Dreams."

"I wish life's decisions could be that easily forgotten," interjected Alexanee. He had grown up with silly stories about this lake and wished Timon would be quiet. This part of the Bhuttanian Empire made him uneasy with its eerie silence and strange shadows.

The empress joked, "If that be true, we should all drink buckets full."

Everyone laughed heartily except for Timon and Alexanee, who watched the remaining swath of sunlight turn the water into a fiery haze. Night fell quickly in the forest, and as soon as Maura had eaten, she bid her company goodnight and retired to her tent.

Timon followed the empress' example and turned in early. As soon as his head hit his saddle, he fell into a deep sleep, unlike the empress who tossed and turned in her tent.

Unable to rest, Maura sat up and swung her sturdy legs over the cot. She wiped the sweat from her brow and tasted it. It tasted of fear. "Please, Mekonia, do not let me fail tomorrow," she whispered before falling into a dreamless state that vaguely resembled death.

10

The empress rose.

She called to her uultepes. They had been sleeping in tree limbs overhanging Maura's tent and sprang down upon hearing her voice. Purring, they entered her tent and sat obediently in front of their mistress. If one chanced upon this sight, she would swear the woman and the cats stared at each other as if they were playing a peek-a-boo game and nothing more passed between them, but a wise person would know better.

The uultepes followed Maura out of the tent and immediately went over to a tree for the express purpose of sharpening their claws. They would stop now and then to inspect their razor sharp nails. Satisfied, they licked them clean until light reflected off of them.

The sound of the uultepes ripping bark off the trees caused Timon to groggily raise his head to see what was causing the fuss. He sneered at the menacing beasts.

Aware they were being watched, the uultepes stopped their grooming.

Timon swallowed hard. He would have sworn to a priest in a sacred oath the uultepes smiled at him. It lasted only for a few seconds before they returned to scratching the tree, but he was convinced they had actually smiled, and the smiles were not kind. Timon jumped up from his bedroll and stumbled away, nearly running into General Alexanee.

"The latrine is that way, boy."

Sheepishly, Timon followed the general's thumb toward the latrine. He nearly stumbled into the hastily dug hole in the ground. As he relieved himself, he glanced up into the trees and choked. One of the uultepes sat watching him. Timon spat at the fearsome cat. "Get away, you spawn of a demon," hissed Timon, pulling his tunic down.

Startled it had been discovered, the cat jumped down and hurried out of sight.

Before Timon had time to compose himself, several guards joined him, hastily removing their codpieces. They sighed in unison. Timon wasn't sure if the chorus of sighs was due to their relief at being off duty or emptying their bladders. Timon left the guards still sighing and realized he was hungry. He washed in haste at the lake's shore, rebraided his hair, and then made his way to the cook's wagon. Mush and day-old sweetbread was served along with hot colla tea. He waited patiently as the senior officers filled their plates and stuffed their pockets before he got in line.

As he ate, Timon checked the sky. It looked dark, as though a storm brewed in the west. Clouds threatened the sky, and the treetops bent in the strengthening breezes. Catching the eye of General Alexanee, Timon winced. He, too, had been checking the atmospheric conditions. His stony glare at Timon only convinced the youth the general held him responsible for the coming bad weather. Losing his appetite, Timon inwardly groaned as he watched the general head toward the empress' tent. He prayed to the nameless god of Anqara that Alexanee get his way, and the hunting party return to the army.

Several minutes later, Alexanee stormed out, running his hands through his thick hair. He sat grumpily on a stump, snapping at his servant to comb his hair. When his grooming was finished, Alexanee stood and called out, "We hunt today. Saddle your horses. Be quick about it. She wants to leave before the storm hits." Everyone scurried to the horses as the servants broke camp. Striding over to Timon, Alexanee puffed heavily, "Scribe, Her Majesty wants you to ride beside her at all times." The general grabbed Timon's arm. "Nothing had better go wrong."

Knowing a warning when he heard one, Timon nodded as one struck dumb. He knew if any unpleasantness befell the empress, Alexanee would make him the scapegoat. Timon braced himself mentally. Nothing should happen. Nothing must happen!

The empress strode out of her tent dressed in a forest green hunting outfit. She carried a Hasan Daegian bow and a quiver filled with Hasan Daegian style arrows. Her dark hair fell loose about her shoulders and blew gently in the breeze. For once, Timon thought Maura looked young.

The empress mounted her pony and smiled expectantly at Timon. "Lead the way, young man," she commanded softly.

Realizing she was speaking to him, Timon stiffly mounted his pony and led the way up a path, which would eventually open to a field where wild borax often grazed in the soft early morning light.

Maura signaled for only a few guards to follow her. She did not want the game to be frightened away by the trampling of too many horses.

After an hour of rigorous travel, the small party finally emerged into a soft meadow where a small herd of borax grazed quietly. The animals immediately became alarmed at the arrival of the hunting party. Massive heads lifted from the grass as the borax began snorting and pawing the ground. Large pointed spikes emerged from the humps on their backs, which ran from the tip of their heads down their spines while their shaggy heads brandished an impressive set of horns.

Maura was surprised at the immense size of the wild borax and momentarily cautious. She had seen only domestic borax, which had purposely been bred smaller. She whistled to Timon and motioned that he was to circle on the outside of the meadow until he reached the opposite side to await her signal.

Timon moved his pony along the outskirts as Maura walked her pony in the opposite direction.

Slowly pulling out an arrow, she notched it in her bow, guiding her pony with only her knees while holding the reins in her mouth. She placed the bow into a striking position, her arm expertly cocked and right eye centered on the largest bull in the herd. Giving out a loud war cry, Maura urged her pony into the midst of the herd.

Guessing this must be the signal, Timon kicked his horse forward and ran at the herd causing it to split. Timon hung onto his pony as best he could, realizing he would be trampled to death if he fell off.

The borax scattered, running in confused circles. Bellowing loudly, many borax charged Timon's pony, but he deftly managed to outmaneuver them. From the corner of his eye, he spied Maura shooting an arrow into the large bull, which enraged the animal into a bitter fury. Her horse circled around the animal as Maura notched another arrow and took aim. The bull, bleeding from his shoulder, charged Maura with surprising speed and rammed her pony. Maura's arrow shot upward, missing its mark. Before she could replace the arrow, the borax rammed the pony again, causing it to stumble. This gave the bull the time it needed to lower its head and slam into the pony with its spiny head.

Jumping off, Maura hit the ground, rolling away from her fallen pony. Satisfied the pony was no longer a threat, the bull skirted to the other side where Maura was and charged. Seeing Timon was too far away to help, Maura picked up her fallen quiver and bow and ran into the woods with the bull in full pursuit.

Timon's worst fears had been realized. The empress was now running for her life from an enraged borax bull that would undoubtedly gore her to death.

Knowing his life would be forfeited if that happened, Timon whipped the neck of his pony with his leather reins, spurring the animal after the fleeing empress. Acting on instinct, Timon drew his hunting sword from its scabbard as he raced into the woods. Ducking branches, he was momentarily blinded by stinging twigs slapping his face. Feeling wetness on his brow and cheeks, he realized his face was bleeding. He pushed that concern aside. Wiping blood from his eyes, Timon urged his pony deeper into the dense forest, but the pony pulled up and pranced nervously.

Timon looked about him. He had lost sight of the empress. He twisted in his saddle, turning his head in every direction listening, hoping to catch the sounds of the borax, only to hear a scream coming from the right. "Oh, Nameless One, let it not be so!" he cried as he pushed his pony into the dense foliage. He rode forward using his arms to protect his face from treacherous briars striking him.

He rode into a small clearing where he spied the empress. At her feet lay the borax bull being disemboweled by one of her uultepes.

Maura looked at him as Timon entered the clearing, pulling up his horse. Her face was drained of color.

Timon was reminded of an animated death mask. Suddenly, Timon was knocked out of his saddle and hit the ground with a heavy thud. Trying to rise, Timon felt a strong hand push his face toward the ground.

Someone pulled Timon up to his knees and stuck a rag into his mouth. Before Timon could fight back, his arms were quickly bound. He blindly kicked, causing him to fall forward.

Feeling vomit move up his throat, Timon gagged on the cloth in his mouth. Momentarily closing his eyes, Timon tried to focus on what was happening, but he didn't have time.

Something screamed, and it sounded human.

Timon snapped his eyes open and searched for the empress. He saw her standing near the borax.

She was drenched in blood.

Before her lay an unconscious man dressed exactly as himself. Maura uttered to the man, "I am sorry." With that, she signaled to the uultepes sitting atop of the carcass of the dead borax.

A uultepe sprang forward and effortlessly crushed the man's thorax with its massive teeth.

Death was swift.

Sensing its prey was dead, the uultepe took its claws and raked the face of its victim.

Timon moaned, turning his head away. Almost senseless, he felt himself being lifted and thrown over a saddle—a Bhuttanian warhorse saddle. He was tied to the horse. The horse shifted its weight, causing the ropes to cut into Timon's flesh.

"Hurry," he heard Maura say.

Someone else grunted in reply.

Maura pulled Timon's head up by his hair and peered anxiously into his face.

Timon slowly opened his eyes.

"You had to be the one," she whispered. "There was no one else." Her face swirled before Timon as he tried to pull his head out of her grasp. Gently, Maura kissed him. "Good luck to you, Royal Scribe."

"We must be off," a man grunted.

Timon could feel Maura's breasts brush against him as she checked the ropes binding him. Soft leather was inserted between his skin and the ropes.

"There is no time for that," barked the man. "Give it to me, and I'll be off!"

Maura tore the amulet from her neck and placed it into the man's outstretched hand. "Take care," she said, slapping his horse on the rump.

The man rode off, leading Timon's horse into the dense forest.

Hearing her guards calling, Maura broke off a leafy branch, wiping out the man's tracks. Satisfied, she ran over to the fallen borax and scooted herself under its heavy hooves.

When the guards came upon the clearing, they found their empress unconscious—just the way she had planned.

11

Timon was oblivious to time.

He did not know if it was night or day. The gag was removed, and he was given water occasionally. Timon's left eye was swollen shut, and he spat blood when he wasn't drifting in and out of consciousness. Finally, he felt the horse jolt to a stop. Several pairs of hands undid his bindings, easing him gently to the ground. His hands and feet were freed. Timon tried to open his good eye, but a blinding sun blotted out everything with its yellow brightness. Cool hands wiped his brow while another pair of hands removed his clothes.

In other circumstances, Timon would have struggled, but he lay passively, grateful the unseen hands were gentle on his burning skin. He heard a woman say, "He is awfully bruised. He will need rest and tending."

A man replied, "There wasn't enough time to treat him like a baby. He put up more of a struggle than I thought he would. I had to get him out of there before one of those damn cats attacked him."

"The empress?"

There was a pause before the man spoke. "It does not matter if she was hurt. She can heal herself."

"I wasn't talking about her body."

"She is more Dinii than she is Hasan Daegian. Her practical nature will see her through this."

"Her true nature is that of a Hasan Daegian. She will struggle with this."

"That's her problem. The man was an animal who murdered women and children for pleasure. He was scheduled to be executed anyway."

The woman sighed. "I suppose."

Timon's head was tilted back, and small fingers pried open his mouth.

"This will help you to sleep the rest of the way," Timon heard a woman say.

Timon obediently drank a bitter draught. He fell into a deep sleep and did not open his eyes again until he was jostled awake. He realized he was in a wagon struggling to get its wheels over a deep rut in the road.

A woman bent over him, peering anxiously into his face.

For a brief second Timon thought he recognized her, but the thought swiftly fled, leaving him confused.

The woman patted his shoulder. "Go back to sleep," she said softly. "We are not there yet." Timon did as the woman commanded and fell back to sleep.

12

Birds twittered happily.

A stream gurgled like a laughing child. Horses snorted contently grazing on thick grass.

Timon sat up straight. Still groggy, he looked about with half-opened eyes. He was in a well-made traveling wagon with all of the comforts of a nobleman. Timon pushed a warm coverlet off. He was naked except for oils and herbs covering his body in a thick poultice. Timon realized someone had cared well for him.

Feeling his bladder threatening to burst, Timon struggled to get up. His hands fumbled upon a container left by his bed for that purpose. Timon used the vessel, anxious that it might spill over, but its contents came right to the rim and no farther. Timon studied his urine and smelled it. It was a pale green and possessed an acrid odor.

"I will take that," said a female voice.

Timon's head jerked upward.

"Don't be embarrassed. I am a healer." The woman took the filled vessel from Timon's hands. She smelled the urine without hesitation and tasted a drop of it from her finger before handing it to someone outside the wagon. She smiled tenderly at Timon. "I need to examine you. It will only take a moment, and then you may dress if you like." She knelt down beside his pallet and with quick, efficient hands, the healer examined Timon's body, even checking his ears and throat. She leaned her head against his chest and counted his heartbeats. Satisfied with his recovery, she smiled.

"I know you."

"I am flattered you remember."

"Why have I been abducted, Lady Pearl?"

"Why indeed?" said KiKu, entering the wagon. "I see you have recovered with my wife's help."

"She has taken admirable care of me, but I wonder for what purpose?" Timon tried not to show fear at the sight of KiKu.

KiKu gave his wife a knowing look.

She rose and left the wagon, leaving them alone.

KiKu sat down on a stool. "Your clothes are over there," he declared, pointing to several robes hanging on wall pegs.

"Those clothes are too costly for a mere scribe."

KiKu smiled. "There is no need for subterfuge anymore, Prince Bes Amon Ptah. You must have forgotten I was in attendance at Zoar's court when your father first brought you with your older brother. I could not forget such frightened boys, who were pledged as collateral for your father's good behavior. You see, the same thing happened to my sister and myself."

"I don't know what you are talking about," replied Timon stubbornly.

"Yes, you do, but I will refer to you as Timon, if you wish it. I will wait for you outside. Please hurry. There is much to discuss." KiKu left.

KiKu's two youngest wives entered with towels and a tub of warm water. "Do you wish assistance with bathing, Prince Bes?" asked Tippu. "It would be both our pleasure and honor to help you." Tippu giggled behind her tiny hand.

Unhappily, Timon shook his head. "My name is Timon."

"Perhaps we can help you to stand?"

"Yes," answered Timon, extending his arm. "I am a little unsteady on my feet."

Tippa brought over a chair and turned its back toward Timon. "Use this to steady yourself. We will wait just outside in case you call."

"You are most kind," replied Timon sincerely.

The twins bowed and left the wagon.

Timon heard them chatter excitedly near the door while pulling himself up using the chair. He bathed slowly and dressed in the fine undergarments left for him.

Still woozy, he called for the twins, and they finished dressing him. Tenderly, they massaged Timon's head and combed the tangles out of his freshly washed hair. Tippa shaved him after rubbing fine oils into his skin. Soft leather slippers were placed on his feet and costly earrings on his lobes. After their skillful ministrations, Timon felt that he could function and made his way out of the wagon, carefully stepping down the worn painted steps.

The sun was waning, and KiKu, with his first two wives, was studying its descent over the mountains. "Ah, you truly look like a prince now," said KiKu admiringly. He motioned for a servant to bring a traveling chair for the prince.

Still weak, Timon sat. He gratefully accepted food from another servant. Timon hesitated a moment before eating.

"It is not poisoned," reassured KiKu. To show Timon the food wasn't tainted, KiKu stole a morsel from the plate and ate it.

Timon appeared unimpressed. "Why am I here?"

"That will take some explaining."

"I have nothing but time."

"That is precisely what you don't have."

There was no need for pretense now. KiKu had remembered him. Timon took stock of his abductor. "Are you threatening me?"

A deep laugh rose from KiKu's belly. "No, Prince Bes. I am merely stating a fact. I will start at the beginning. Please hold your questions until I finish." KiKu shifted his weight to a more comfortable position. "Have you ever heard of the Lahorians?"

Timon shook his head.

"The Lahorians are the reason you are here, my friend. Many generations ago, when the Dinii were the Overlords of our world, Kaseri—when your Bhuttanian ancestors were just another poor nomadic tribe roaming the steppes, when my people were just beginning to coalesce into a nation, a people from another world came to live on islands off the shores of Hasan Daeg. We called them the Lahorians. The Lahorians were truth seekers, wishing only to evolve until they joined the Great Truth."

"What truth is that?" interrupted Timon.

KiKu shrugged. "Who knows what they mean? Perhaps they mean the Creator. The important thing is they came here seeking a place to live. A great flood occurred, covering the islands on which they lived and causing the Lahorians to escape to the closest high land. Unfortunately, they ended upon land, which was the Dinii's territory. As natural predators, the Dinii immediately tried to conquer the desperate Lahorians and subjugate them.

"But the Lahorians possessed great power and were not easily defeated. A terrible war ensued. There was much loss of life and destruction on both sides. Realizing they could not conquer the

Lahorians, the Dinii fled to Hasan Daeg, taking their slaves with them.

"The war was cataclysmic for the Dinii culture. They had lost everything, even their confidence, their sense of self. So shaken were they, the Dinii pretended that the war had never occurred. Future generations were not taught of their history except for only a few nobles. Within a few generations, the knowledge died away, and the existence of the Lahorians was forgotten."

"But the Lahorians survived?"

"Yes, well enough they could propagate their species and carry out their original mission."

"Which was?"

"As I explained before—to follow their destiny and join with Truth," KiKu replied.

"Uh-huh."

"By your expression, Prince Bes—I mean Timon—I don't think you believe me. It is indeed a wondrous tale."

"Fantasy is a better word. My mother told me fairy stories that were more believable."

"I don't blame you, but I know it to be true. I have seen the Lahorians and their magnificent underwater city. The story is no more ridiculous than that of a young prince, known only to a few, hidden away in the recesses of the Zoar's palace as a royal hostage. A prince who decides to take advantage of Zoar's death to hide, so he may one day escape back to the Steppes of Moab. But fate takes a cruel hand. He is hustled into the Bhuttanian army by those unaware of his identity and spends years wasting away as a lowly bureaucrat. Finally, he gets close to his home again only to be chosen by the royal consul to become his personal scribe. Now his every moment is accounted for, and he cannot slip away in the night without having the Imperial guards after him by morning's light."

The scribe did not know how to respond. It was useless to deny his identity any longer.

Kiku continued with his eyes burning into Timon. "I was hoping to impress upon you the importance of our mission, but I will explain things in a more mundane fashion for your benefit." KiKu reached for a small scroll inside his vest and handed it to Timon. "You are to journey to the temple of Bhuttu where you will apply for training as a votary. There you will seek to discover the meaning of sightings by the priests."

"What sightings?"

"There are rumors the Dinii have been seen by the priests. You are to confirm any sightings and do whatever you must to free the Dinii."

Timon refused to take the scroll from KiKu. "I am not a spy. I am not a soldier. I have no idea of how to proceed in such matters. What you ask is impossible. I won't do it." Timon pressed his lips together into a tight thin line, allowing his eyes to brighten with defiance.

KiKu rose and dropped the scroll at Timon's feet. "Then your mother, your sisters, their husbands, and children will be tortured and killed. Every living animal your people possess will be confiscated so they may starve to death."

Jumping to his feet as a man released from a paralyzing dream, Timon struck KiKu with his fists, putting the full force of his body behind him. KiKu let Timon hit him several times and then expertly grabbed his arms. Like lightning, KiKu twisted Timon around, choking the young man. Try as he may, Timon could not get KiKu to release his hold from around his neck. KiKu squeezed tighter until Timon struggled no more.

KiKu whispered into the boy's ear. "Take my advice, young cub. Take up the struggle and join the rest of us who are fighting to preserve life on this planet. Are you forever going to hide among those eunuch scribes like a coward?" KiKu released the gasping prince.

Wiping blood from his mouth, KiKu sneered in contempt at Timon struggling to rise from the ground. "Perhaps the empress was wrong about you. She said you were untested clay who could be molded into a man of courage and tenacity." KiKu roared, "I SEE NO SUCH MAN HERE!"

Timon's face was clouded with pain and doubt. "I am not a coward!"

"I am not the one on my knees with my balls hanging out of my clothes like some boy whore in the back streets of Bhuttani." KiKu kicked the scroll over to Timon. "Read the scroll. If by morning you do not willingly assume your task, I will send word of your refusal to the empress."

"You can't do that. My people will die!"

KiKu spoke in soft tones. "Yes. They will die, but you will exist many years so you may live with your shame and guilt each day. You will be disgraced, a man without family or friend or tribe. All will curse your name and shun your company. No one fails Maura without a sorrowful price to pay."

"Then I have no choice," said Timon bitterly.

"You have a choice. You may take up the sword and fight, possibly dying like a man, or you can let your kin die a terrible death by saving your own skin. But let me tell you one thing, my friend, you will never be allowed to commit suicide if that occurs. You will be forced to live with your terrible pain the rest of your natural life." KiKu's voice dripped with disgust. "I told the empress you would be useless. Even the Hasan Daegian men, as small and effeminate as they are, fight like demons to protect their own. No one has to threaten them to put down their painted fans and pick up a sword." KiKu began to walk away.

"KIKU!" cried out Timon. "I am afraid."

KiKu turned and studied Timon for a moment. "So am I, Prince Bes. I sweat with fear every night, but in the morning, I face whatever the day brings. There is no shame in my heart. Good night, Prince Bes." KiKu's wives followed him with their heads bent down.

Timon wiped away tears staining his face. He struggled to his feet to make his way back to the wagon when he stepped on the scroll. Gingerly, he picked up the dirt-smeared parchment. Allowing one of KiKu's servants to escort him to the wagon, Timon did not resist when the man helped him out of his fine clothes. Timon rested on his bed. "Bring the lamp over to me, then leave," ordered Timon. The servant quickly left after handing the lamp to the young prince.

With trembling hands, Timon broke the Royal Hasan Daegian and Bhuttanian Imperial seals and unrolled the parchment. He scanned the writing quickly, trying to comprehend every word.

Prince Bes Amon Ptah,

You will be reading this after several intense days. Your feelings may range anywhere from anger to surprise to fear. Everything that has happened was necessary, I assure you.

The hunt was a ruse to stage your death. A convict with your coloring and body build was selected to switch places with you. Everyone had to be convinced you were dead. I could not take a chance that your people would look for you if you were thought to be missing.

I have known who you are for a long time. You have been under surveillance, as have other noble hostages of Zoar. Rubank thought it most ingenious of you to hide among the scribe guild. He thought your resourcefulness most impressive. Of course, KiKu confirmed your identity when he saw you at my court.

I have a mission for you. You are to proceed to the temple of Bhuttu posing as a nobleman's son seeking entrance as a novice. KiKu and his wives are to pose as your servants. Once there, you are to confirm reports of any unnatural sightings in the temple. I am hoping you will send word that you have sighted the Dinii. If you do confirm the Dinii are hidden away in the temple, you are to use whatever means possible to free them. There is a possibility that they have been bound by magic.

KiKu and his family have pledged their lives to protect you. If they fail, they will die. If you fail, your family will die.

It is a harsh edict, so leave no stone unturned. I wait for your successful return.

Maura de Magela

Timon burned the scroll in the lamp. Grabbing a robe, he hurried to KiKu's wagon. "KiKu, let me enter," Timon called out.

One of the twins opened the door and bade the Prince to enter. KiKu was in a dressing gown lounging on cushions with his wives. He seemed surprised to see Timon so soon after their confrontation.

"I thought you had retired. You must take care not to tax yourself," Pearl cautioned.

"You did not tell me your life would be forfeited if I refused. Would she really do that to you? I thought you had saved her life," blurted Timon.

"If by 'she' you mean the empress, yes. She is not in the position to do as she wants, but as she must. That is what you do not understand. Do you think she wanted to kill that man in the meadow? She didn't have a choice in the matter. She is trying to locate the Dinii, powerful allies, who will save thousands of lives if they fight with her again. She is trying to overturn an ancient feudal system, which has left much of our world in tattered rags with half of its people dying from starvation and poisoned water. In that context, what is the consequence of one life such as mine or even yours?

"You stand there self-righteous and condemning, but you have been a bystander for years hiding away while others have made the hard choices. She does not have the luxury of worrying about morality. She must be practical and cunning or all will be lost."

Madric interrupted, "Tell us, Timon, which queen will serve the Empire better, Maura or Jezra? You were at court with Jezra. You have spent more than a year with Maura. Which one would you chose?"

Timon did not know how to respond. Wasn't Maura like any other ruler—cruel with an impossible obsession for power?

KiKu sighed at Timon's lack of insight. "Let's start with the obvious," said KiKu, looking to his oldest wife for support. "Maura is uniting two vastly different cultures that had been warring with each other only years ago. Why do you think it is taking the army years to reach Bhuttani? She wanted time to unit the Hasan Daegians and Bhuttanians into one people. Jezra could never have achieved this. Jezra would not even see the need to do so."

"You must realize Jezra is just a woman, but Maura is a true queen," Pearl interjected.

"And you are willing to die for her?" questioned Timon.

KiKu's voice quivered with emotion. "I am willing to die for what she believes in, for it is the same as I believe."

Timon held out his hands. "That's my problem. I don't believe in anything."

"But you do, Timon," said Pearl. "You believe in love for your mother and your family. You believe in your people. It is a beginning."

"It does not matter what he believes in," snapped KiKu at his wife. "Maura has removed all political and religious obstacles from your path. She is using the oldest of all persuasions—fear. If you do not go to Bhuttani and fulfill your mission, those you love most in the world will die a terrible death. You can live a coward's life, or you may try to save them. As it is, they are dead already, practically speaking. She is giving you a chance to bring them back from the hall of death," admonished KiKu, pounding his fist in his hand, "and it can be done!"

Timon spat, "I will go to Bhuttani and do as you ask. I will tell you with all honesty I think this is a fool's errand."

KiKu's face split into a sadistic grin. "A fool can be the most dangerous enemy of all."

13

Alexanee pulled off the shroud.

He examined the torn and tattered remains carefully. A Bhuttanian healer stood in the corner anxiously watching. "Tell me something I don't already know," requested Alexanee, peering hopefully at the healer.

The healer stepped forward into the light. He replied, "Wounds were caused by claws. The boy's throat was crushed by an animal."

"He suffocated?"

The healer shrugged. "Whether he bled to death or suffocated is only a matter of seconds." He waved his hand over the shredded body. "There was not much with which to work."

"What kind of animal?"

The healer glanced up in surprise at Alexanee's frowning face. "The uultepes, of course."

"It couldn't have been the borax?"

"No, General Alexanee. If it had been the borax, the body would have broad puncture wounds from the borax goring with his horns. A borax cannot cause this kind of damage to the throat. No, this was the work of a powerful predator."

Alexanee pondered for a moment.

"If I may be so bold, General Alexanee, I have seen the work of the uultepes before. This is their doing."

"Is there anything unique about this attack?"

The healer smiled—several of his front teeth were missing. "Yes, my lord. This goes beyond what a uultepe would need to do in order to kill its victim, even if it was a fierce confrontation."

Alexanee went over to the carcass of the borax and squatted beside it. "What can you tell me about this animal?"

"It was a male bull in its prime weighing about three thousand pounds. Death was caused by a crushed thorax as well." The healer pulled back hanging skin to expose a gaping wound.

"What about all of these claw marks?" asked Alexanee, pointing to the rows of long rakes on the body.

"They were made after the animal was dead."

"Really!"

The healer puffed up his chest with pride. He could hardly believe he was talking to the exalted Alexanee as an equal. "You can see, General Alexanee, there is hardly any blood from these wounds. That would indicate this damage was done after the heart had stopped beating."

Alexanee stood and rubbed his chin. "Where are the clothes of the man?"

The healer called for a servant, who brought a bundle of bloody rags. Alexanee took the bundle.

Unlike his master, the servant was only too happy to leave the general. He did not like being so close to a noble who could have him put to death on a whim.

Alexanee, oblivious to the servant's consternation, patiently sifted through the remains of a tunic, gloves, leggings, a loincloth, and gnawed hunting boots. "Is this everything?"

The healer nodded. "This is everything on him except for the boots. They were knocked off his feet during the attack, I guess." The healer shuddered. "I imagine he did not suffer very long. He probably went into shock at the beginning of the attack and knew nothing after that." The healer glanced down at the shredded rags and let out a low whistle.

"There is nothing else?"

Curiously, the healer replied, "No, my lord."

"There was no red hunting headband?"

"No, my lord."

"You would stake your life on it?"

The healer's eyes grew wide into startled pools. "Yes, my lord. There was no red hunting headband when this man was brought in. I saw to the remains alone. No one else has been near him or his clothes."

"What about your servants?"

The healer shifted his large frame uneasily. He did not like being questioned about the honor of his household. The healer was a proud man and was known for his competence. "I can vouch for all of my servants. No one had access to this body except for me and my assistant, whom you just saw. He has been with me for twenty years. I trust him completely. He cannot be bribed."

Alexanee grunted with satisfaction.

The healer grunted in reply, as was the Bhuttanian custom.

"Is this the body of the scribe Timon?"

The healer pondered the implications of the question. He spoke cautiously. "The body is the same height and weight of the royal scribe. Hair is the same as any Bhuttanian boy. This is the remains of a young Bhuttanian male with nomadic breeding, but . . ." the healer paused.

"But what?"

"His face was obliterated during the attack. The skin and cartilage have been shredded. The eyes destroyed. Without a face, there is no way I can be positive." The healer folded his arms and rocked back on his heels. "This reminds me of something."

Alexanee waited patiently.

"I was one of the physicians attending the Aga Dorak during the siege of O Konya. The night the empress made her escape, there was a terrible battle in the palace. Some of the Bhuttanian soldiers killed had their faces disfigured."

"That is correct," affirmed Alexanee.

"The faces of the Bhuttanian soldiers were ravaged by dagger cuts, and a few had their noses sliced off."

Alexanee closed his eyes for a moment. "I remember. We were tearing the city apart trying to find the empress. None of the soldiers in the city were disfigured. Just those in the palace."

"I had always thought it strange the Hasan Daegians were so vicious that night. They had never desecrated an enemy soldier before. They had always been respectful of our dead. It was unlike them." The healer thought how ironic life was. The woman, who had been hunted like an animal that awful night, now commanded them and, with one word, could have them all hung.

Alexanee cleared his throat.

Realizing he had drifted, the healer snapped to attention and bowed low. "Is there anything else I can do for you, General Alexanee?"

Alexanee pressed gold coins into the healer's hands. "I don't need to tell you that our conversation is private. I want nothing said of this.

No report."

Without searching the general's penetrating dark eyes, the healer lowered his head in acceptance.

Alexanee grunted, "Good. I am sure we understand each other. I am pleased with your work. You may resume your duties now."

The general returned to his tent, happy to be away from that dreadful sight. He sat on his cot thinking for a very long time before a servant entered, bringing a lamp and a tray of food.

Alexanee glanced up in surprise. "Is it night?"

"In a very short while, my lord," assured the servant. "There is still enough daylight to walk the camp without a torch."

The general stood at the entrance of his tent, thinking.

After finding the empress under the hooves of the borax, the hunting party had returned posthaste to the encampment, while Alexanee and several of his men had remained scouting the area and waiting for wagons in which to retrieve the bodies of the dead scribe and the borax. Since returning, he had not even changed his offensive clothing but waited for the healer to examine the bodies. Realizing he stank, Alexanee called for a hot bath and gave his clothes to the servant to burn.

Seeing the servant's face flicker before returning to its usual stoic reserve, Alexanee hid his smile, also. Even the servants were taking on the Hasan Daegian custom of bathing. He pondered the blending of the Bhuttanian and Hasan Daegian cultures. He was no fool. He could see what the empress was trying to achieve with subtle machinations here and there.

Alexanee wondered what his fellow officers would think if they could see him relaxing in a wooden tub filled with bubbling water as his feet stuck precariously over the edge. His keen mind raced with a thousand different thoughts, but like threads of lightning springing from the same thundercloud, they merged into one mighty bolt of light—the lifeless body of the Bhuttanian male waiting for cremation was not the royal scribe, Timon!

The empress had made one mistake. Where was the red hunting band Timon had worn when he chased after the Maura and the charging borax? It should have been with the body. His men had retraced Timon's steps, and not even a shred of red material could be found. Even the dead boy's mouth had been examined, as well as the contents of his stomach and those of the borax. Perhaps the uultepes had swallowed the headband during the attack? By now, the fierce cat-like animals should have passed anything in their system. Alexanee's men had found nothing while searching their droppings. Why was the headband missing and where was it?

The tall and powerfully built Alexanee pounded his chest, hoping to relieve the anxiety he felt. In doing so, dirty water splashed over the sides of the tub, falling in great pools spreading on the carpeted ground. What was the inscrutable Maura up to? The general closed his eyes and slid deeper into the warm water, only to rise from his bath when the water cooled. Calling a servant to help, Alexanee dressed hurriedly and followed a guide bearing a torch, leading him through the camp to the empress' tent. Without hesitation, Maura's servants granted General Alexanee admission into her private chamber.

Looking pale and weak, the empress lay propped up by pillows on her bed. Near her side stood the High Priestess from the House of Magi and personal physician, Meagan of Skujpor, who was taking the empress' pulse.

Alexanee had to quell an impulse to laugh. If anyone didn't need a healer, it was Maura de Magela. Even at the site of the hunting accident, he didn't think she needed much medical attention.

"Great Mother," said Alexanee, bowing very low.

Maura waved him closer to her bed with a slight move of a finger.

The High Priestess slinked into the dark shadows of the room until she was almost invisible.

"I see you have made a safe return, General Alexanee," uttered the empress in a small voice.

"I am distressed that you have taken to your bed, Great Mother."

Maura ignored the small hint of sarcasm in the general's voice. "I am grateful I have not suffered any major injuries."

"As we all are."

"It is the shock of seeing young Timon torn so." She closed her eyes. "It has unsettled me. I feel so responsible."

"I understand, Great Mother. No one likes to see such a young life taken in such a manner."

Maura's dark eyes snapped open. "What manner would that be, General Alexanee?"

Meagan of Skujpor pulled the blanket higher around Maura's waist as one might tuck a child into bed. She gave a warning look to Alexanee as not to tire the empress with questions.

"I was wondering, Great Mother, if you happened to pick up the red headband of the boy during the struggle or perhaps it got caught on your boots?"

"Why do you ask?"

"Timon's hunting band is missing. I can't find it anywhere."

"I'm afraid I don't remember much of the attack. I do know Timon's horse was gored by the borax, causing Timon to fall. Then the borax turned on me, and I saw Timon running toward me. I fell beneath the borax, and that is all I remember." Maura winced as in pain.

Alexanee continued, refusing to acknowledge Maura's implied pain. "Timon's body had many deep cuts, apparently caused by an animal with sharp claws, not hooves. Do you think—in all the excitement—the uultepes could have attacked him by mistake?"

"Are you implying the borax did not kill Timon?"

"No, Great Mother, it is just his face has been erased, so to speak. I don't think even a borax could have caused such damage."

"It is possible the uultepes could have mistaken Timon for an attacker."

Alexanee grunted. "Do you think Timon could have been trying to attack you?"

"I think Timon an improbable choice for an assassin, but as I have said before, I don't know what happened. I hit my head when I fell underneath the borax and blacked out."

A lad-in-waiting carried over to General Alexanee a carved box and laid it at his feet. Alexanee hesitated.

"Allow me, General," offered Meagan of Skujpor, knowing Bhuttanians dislike for opening strange boxes or trunks. More than one Bhuttanian had been killed by opening a booby-trapped receptacle. She untied the leather straps holding the box closed. Carefully, she opened the lid. "I saved all of her Majesty's clothes for your inspection. I knew you would want to make a full report to the Council of Nobles."

Alexanee grunted.

Meagan grunted using the female Bhuttanian response of two sounds instead of one. She pulled out the empress' tattered green hunting outfit. The pants were split up the back and on the left side. The shirt was covered in blood, but otherwise seemed in good shape except for the right sleeve, which had been completely severed.

Alexanee examined the clothes closely and smelled them. They had a female musk odor to them that could not be obliterated by the smell of dried blood and dirt. For a second, Alexanee thought of his wife, who was waiting impatiently for him in their warm and cozy home. Sighing, the general took the boots handed to him by Meagan. He reached inside one and felt something lodged in the toe. Tugging, he pulled out a red headband. Dropping the boot, Alexanee pulled open the cloth.

"It seems we have found the hunting band, Great Mother," said Alexanee.

"Is it what you are searching for?" asked Meagan.

Alexanee ordered, "Hand me that bowl."

Meagan meekly handed Alexanee a washing bowl filled with clean water. Alexanee gingerly put the filthy cloth into the water and swished it around several times. Squeezing the water out, Alexanee examined the headband under a lamp. The cloth was a dull red with no markings on it as Timon had worn that day.

"This looks like it could be the scribe's hunting band. With your permission, Great Mother, I would like to take this and study it."

"Of course, General Alexanee. I realize how this accident may hang heavily on your shoulders, but you are not at fault. Take what you need."

Alexanee bit his tongue in order not to respond to the implication he was somehow to blame for the hunting accident. "I worry about the safety of the empress always, as do all of her most loyal subjects."

Maura patted Meagan's sleeve. "I'm in good hands now. There is no need to worry."

Alexanee bristled at the implied insult. He felt the blood rush to his hawk-like face. "Just one more thing, Great Mother."

"Yes."

"We could not find your amulet." He watched Maura's face.

Remaining stoic, Maura replied, "That is because I was not wearing it that day."

"I see. I say this only because you have worn it every day since Atetelco."

"You will see it again."

"I just wanted to make sure I had not overlooked anything."

"The amulet is safe and in my keeping. Thank you, General Alexanee."

Bowing very low to hide his distress, Alexanee backed out.

With the general safely gone, the High Priestess emerged from the shadows. "Do you think he suspects?"

Maura threw her covers off. "Yes. Alexanee is a shrewd man, but he can't prove anything for now. He will bide his time." Maura turned toward the High Priestess. "And I will bide mine."

14

Jezra studied maps.

They were placed on the table with great care. Her pale hair hung down, clinging to her graceful shoulders. Her forehead furrowed as she poured over the current location of Maura. "Why is she moving so slowly?" complained Jezra.

"Perhaps to cause you to be impatient and make a mistake," answered Mikkotto, looking like a well-pampered lizard lounging on a couch covered with costly material. A servant massaged Mikkotto's strong hands as the baroness stared at the elaborately painted ceiling depicting strange mythological creatures.

"She could have been here months ago, and this would have been over. I hate this waiting."

Mikkotto sighed. She disliked the young aganess who possessed no finesse for either politics or war. She thought Jezra stupid. No, stupid wasn't the right word to use; imperceptive was a better choice. "Meanwhile, you solidify your position in power here more each day, and the warehouses are being stocked with grain. You can withstand a siege indefinitely."

Jezra pushed her hair behind her ears. "I think we should venture out and engage her."

Mikkotto closed her eyes and sank deeper into the couch. "I think we should stay right where we are."

"I can't stand this waiting."

"My dear, you will find that most of life is spent waiting," replied Mikkotto, shifting her position so the servant could massage her other hand. "It would be better not to get into a huff about something you cannot change."

"What can't I change?"

"You cannot change Maura's progress. She has her own agenda. You can only watch, observe, formulate, and prepare to take action when finally needed." Mikkotto sighed under her breath. She thought this woman was truly tiresome since everything needed to be explained. "I have tried to kill her twice, and each time she has escaped. Maura was either born under a very lucky star, or she is a very capable person." Mikkotto lowered her eyelids.

Jezra seemed unimpressed. "Perhaps you are not as great a warrior as you claim. We might try different methods this time."

Mikkotto did not rise to the bait as much as she wanted to backhand the insulting wench standing before her. She had thought Anqarians to be sophisticated and knowledgeable, but this person was a mere trifle, an annoyance at best.

Under heavy lids, she watched Jezra turn back to her maps and study them again. Indeed, Jezra was a beauty. Mikkotto could easily see how a very young Dorak would have been infatuated with Jezra's pale hair, cornflower blue eyes, and pouty lips. Still, even after having Dorak's child, Jezra's figure was ripe and luscious with wide hips that accentuated her small waist, and full breasts, which swayed invitingly when she walked.

"How old were you when you married Dorak?" asked Mikkotto impulsively.

Jezra looked up from her maps. "Sixteen. He was seventeen."

"How old are you now?"

"How old are you?" snapped back Jezra.

Mikkotto smiled slowly. "I am forty-eight."

Jezra appraised Mikkotto's muscular body. The Hasan Daegian was a tall, powerfully built woman with long black hair. Her face possessed intelligent, dark eyes that darted beneath arched brows, like a predator hunting its next meal. Full, sensuous lips softened the sharp angles of Mikkotto's cheekbones.

If Mikkotto's face had belonged to a man, Jezra would have been more at ease with it. It was odd to see such blatant ambition and arrogance in a woman. Jezra thought back to her people. She had seen such a countenance on the faces of women from the House of Magi, who walked about the city in long blue-green robes. They had been respected and honored among the Anqarians. There were no such women among the Bhuttanians. *I have lived among the Bhuttanians too long*, thought Jezra. *I have forgotten the power of women.*

"I am twenty-six this year," confided Jezra.

"Ah," cooed Mikkotto, disappointed Jezra had not commented on her youthful appearance.

Interested in telling her story, Jezra was glad for a chance to talk to someone, even a Hasan Daegian. "My father owned the largest banking house in Anqara. It was he who serviced the Aga of Bhuttan with loans used to underwrite the expansion of Zoar's power. My father would meet Zoar secretly at the border of Anqara and Bhuttan, because he was afraid of what the other Anqarians would do if they knew he conducted business with Zoar."

Mikkotto inspected her hands after the servant had finished massaging them. She rolled on her stomach and bade the servant to rub her feet through the soles of her slippers.

Hatred welled up in the servant's eyes but died as soon as Mikkotto glanced in her direction.

Jezra witnessed the servant's momentary indiscretion, but did not rebuke. She could hardly scold a servant for feeling the same way she did. "You are not paying attention to me," chided Jezra. She was not used to being ignored.

"I have listened to every syllable you have uttered," answered Mikkotto, trying to hide a yawn. "I want to know how you became Dorak's wife."

Jezra was pleased Mikkotto had asked her to continue. "It wasn't long before Zoar owed my father a vast fortune. The expansion had not yielded the fortune Zoar thought he was going to make. My father, seeing opportunity, agreed to forgo part of the debt."

"You were to marry Dorak and become part of the royal family," Mikkotto interjected.

"Yes, that is correct," retorted Jezra, looking a little miffed Mikkotto had stolen her thunder.

"So old Zoar kept his word," expressed Mikkotto, thinking of her former lover.

"In a manner of speaking."

Mikkotto lifted her head from the couch. "I am waiting," urged the Baroness.

"I was promised to Dorak as a child and returned to Anqara to live with my father. Coming of age, I was reunited with Dorak and expected to act as his wife and he my husband." Jezra paused as if reliving painful memories.

"But you were not made princess royal."

Jezra shook her head as though unable to speak. She finally dropped into a chair next to Mikkotto. She had a defeated look about her.

"This is a very old story. I can finish it for you." Mikkotto rolled over and placed her arms behind her head. "Time passed. You had a baby. Dorak lost interest in you, and because you were not made princess royal, he could afford to ignore you. You pleaded. You begged. You threatened. The more you shouted, the less he paid attention to you until he paid no attention at all. In fact, you had become an embarrassment to him, a little nobody without money and power."

"Sounds about right," Jezra affirmed bitterly, while watching a slave light the oil lamps.

"And then he met Maura, and you realized you had lost him for good." Mikkotto licked her lips. She liked inflicting pain, especially on someone like Jezra, who displayed every emotion on her pretty but uninteresting face. Mikkotto compared it to watching clouds casting a dark shadow across a sunny meadow filled with flowers. The baroness knew she shouldn't give the aganess any cause to dislike her, but Jezra was such an easy target, Mikkotto found it hard to resist attacking.

"I hate her. She took my place. She must hate me, too."

"I doubt Maura feels anything about you one way or the other."

"What do you mean by that?"

Mikkotto shrugged. "I doubt Maura could even describe to someone what you look like. This is not a personal contest with her. She is coming to secure the crown for her daughter and to ensure that Bhuttan never regains superior military strength over Hasan Daeg."

"That's absurd! She knows the army has been split in two, dividing the Empire. Maura could have easily kept the Bhuttanians in her camp loyal to her banner and slept easily at night knowing that we are coping with a civil war within the walls of the city. We have neither the time nor resources to traipse back across this continent to reconquer Hasan Daeg."

"What you say is correct for now, but sooner or later, someone would win and then begin rebuilding the army. Without conquered land, Bhuttan cannot exist. All of her resources have been exhausted. Bhuttan would have to expand its territory down the road. It may take twenty years, maybe forty, but Bhuttanians would again one day stand at the borders of Hasan Daeg."

Mikkotto was many things, most of them unpleasant, but Jezra had to admit the older woman was a cunning tactician. The aganess saw possible uses for Mikkotto, other than being a nuisance who abused the slaves in her palace. She realized that Zoar had seen this, too, in Mikkotto and had taken her for his mistress for reasons other than pleasure.

Taking no notice of the aganess' scrutiny, Mikkotto continued, "You, however, fight Maura for personal reasons. That is why you will make mistakes."

Jezra huffed, "You make her sound like an old soul who has walked the wheel many times. Maura is younger than me!"

"She has mated with the Bogazkoy."

"That stupid tree is nothing but an old wives' tale. Zoar looked for it for almost two decades without finding a shred of evidence to support its existence. We have spies telling us everything that goes on in Maura's camp, and in two years, not one of them has seen or heard anyone talking about this Bogazkoy."

"It does exist."

"Have you seen it? Has someone brought you a piece of its bark or made a tea from its leaves? I tell you it is a lie!"

"How do you explain Maura's blue skin?" asked Mikkotto angrily, feeling that her honor was questioned.

"The blue skin is created by vegetable dye she puts on herself. If you like, I can be green tomorrow and purple the next."

Mikkotto snorted at the suggestion.

Jezra laughed. "I can't believe you accept those tales as truth. It's mumbo-jumbo. Now, this is real power." Jezra extended her hand and pointed a finger at Mikkotto. A slender bolt of blue light surged from her index finger and flashed toward Mikkotto, who barely dodged it.

Jezra giggled while inspecting her finger. She found it bruised and dark. Sucking on it for a few seconds, she rubbed her finger on her dress.

Mikkotto inspected the hole the blue light had made in the couch. A small swirl of smoke drifted from the burnt opening. She smelled the cushion and placed her finger in the hole. Regarding Jezra, she sneered, "Well, aren't you full of surprises?"

Smug, Jezra replied, "I have my moments."

"I'm just wondering where a nice little girl like you learned something like that?"

"I had to do something to fill in the time with Dorak gone so much."

Mikkotto threw the cushion out the window. She paused for a moment and then walked around the couch, standing before Jezra. Taking Jezra's chin in her hand, Mikkotto squeezed until she was hurting the self-proclaimed aganess.

Jezra gasped from Mikkotto's tight grip. She thought it audacious that the Hasan Daegian woman dared to touch her. Bringing her hand up, she pointed at Mikkotto, but the stronger woman grabbed her hand, pointing it at the ceiling. A weak beam emerged from Jezra's finger only to sputter and die. Mikkotto cautiously turned Jezra's hand toward her so that she could inspect more closely. Patting down the aganess arm, Mikkotto tore open Jezra's sleeve so she could feel the younger woman's armpit, rib cage, and chest.

"No apparatus," muttered Mikkotto, talking to herself. "You feel normal."

"Let go of me!" Jezra commanded through her teeth.

Putting on a sly smile, Mikkotto gave Jezra a shove while releasing her.

Rubbing her wrist, Jezra spat, "How dare you touch me!"

Mikkotto plopped down on the damaged couch and crossed her legs. "You've got yourself a little talent there, Aganess. What else can you do?"

"Are you mocking me?"

"On the contrary, I am quite interested. I would like to know what else you can do."

"That is my secret."

Mikkotto shook her head. "I'm sorry, my dear, but it is our secret. You see, I didn't travel all this way to be put off by a mere banker's daughter. You will tell me your secrets, or I will show you my talent. It is unique, but quite unforgiving when applied. I have a gift for inflicting pain."

Cracking her knuckles, Mikkotto gave Jezra a smile that sent tremors down the young woman's back.

"Do you wish to see what I can do?" Mikkotto continued with silky menace.

"I can have you executed for threatening me."

Mikkotto laughed, showing her white, straight teeth. "Your people won't execute me. I was Zoar's mistress and his intended empress. They would never harm me to protect you. It's just not their way." The baroness stretched. "Too bad he died so unexpectedly, but I guess that was good news for you. One step closer to the throne, or so you thought. That was before Dorak married Maura. Now everything is askew."

"What do you want of me? Why are you here?"

"No need to get hostile. I don't want your throne. I hate Bhuttan and everyone in it. These people are barbarians." Looking as though she wanted to spit on the floor, Mikkotto refrained. "I want Hasan Daeg. All of her. Give me Hasan Daeg, and I will help you to the throne of Bhuttan."

Jezra felt overwhelmed by Mikkotto's indomitable will and force of character, but she was shrewd enough to realize the Hasan Daegian could be of immense value to her. "You will have Hasan Daeg as long as you open the borders to free commerce, and you ship me a thousand wagons of grain each harvest."

"We could have a crop failure."

"That's your problem."

Mikkotto mulled over the idea, but Jezra knew the baroness was bluffing. Jezra could not show she was intimidated by the older woman. "Take it or leave it," she barked.

Clapping her hands together in triumph, Mikkotto sprang off the couch and extended her hand to Jezra.

Jezra clasped Mikkotto's forearm in agreement.

"There is one more thing."

Jezra wearily sighed. "What is it?"

"I want the head of Maura brought to me."

Jezra returned a cheeky smile to Mikkotto. "I thought you said this was not personal."

"I lied."

"Of course, I would never think of interfering with a guest's pleasure. It would not be considered hospitable."

The baroness, dressed in solemn black, lowered her head and kissed Jezra's hand. "To the Aganess of Bhuttan."

Jezra inclined her head in reply to Mikkotto's kiss. "To the Queen of Hasan Daeg."

Mikkotto looked at Jezra. "To the death of Maura!"

Jezra smiled. "To anyone's death who stands in our way."

Mikkotto understood Jezra's sly meaning and wondered how long before she had to kill Jezra. She hoped it wouldn't be long.

15

Timon stood in a little cluster.

He tried to blend in the crowd of arguing merchants, mingo drivers, soldiers of fortune, and the general rag-tag of men and women who followed wherever mayhem and tragedy existed, seeking their luck.

The guards, who manned the western gate, looked tired and forlorn as they gazed over the clamoring knot of humanity pressing their claims to enter the city of Bhuttani. The guards carefully considered every person's papers while searching cargo for contraband that might be sold on the black market. The only time the guards' faces relaxed a tiny bit was when they dealt with a Sivan, who always waited patiently with hands folded into a neat bouquet upon his belly.

Noticing how the guards were easygoing with any Sivan, Timon moved his position behind some mercenaries and stood near a small group of Sivans. He turned to tell KiKu to follow him, but the master spy and his women were behind Timon, standing mute with their hands folded, imitating the Sivan merchants.

Timon smiled at KiKu. He should have known that the sharp eyes of KiKu would have missed nothing.

KiKu's face remained expressionless.

"You there!" commanded a guard, poking Timon in the shoulder. "What do you want?"

Timon's head snapped around, catching sight of a huge Bhuttanian looming over him. This soldier was even large by Bhuttanian standards. Timon felt his throat constrict involuntarily.

"I am Timon de Berechiah from the Qued Zem province," stated Timon, surprised that his voice sounded steady. "I have come to seek entrance as a novice to the temple of Bhuttu." He handed the guard his papers.

"That's all we need, another religious fanatic," harrumphed the guard. He read the papers and then squinted at Timon. "Who are they?" he queried, thumbing at KiKu and the women.

"My servants," replied Timon calmly, even though his heart pounded.

The swarthy giant of a guard strode over to KiKu, who did not flinch as the Bhuttanian breathed on his head. Instead, KiKu looked up and confronted the guard with his hypnotic eyes.

The guard gasped slightly and stepped back a little from KiKu. "By the beards of the gods, he is a Bilboa."

"Yes," said Timon, stepping closer to distract the tall fellow. "I got him in Salamanca."

"I've only seen a few. Their eyes always give me the jitters," stated the guard, referring to KiKu's glowing red eyes with several black squares for twin pupils in each eye.

Timon felt the sweat break out on the back of his neck. He replied, "That's why they are so valuable. They can see just as well in the night as in the day."

The guard turned and spat on the ground. "Exactly. This man should be working as a scout for the army. He is too valuable to be working as a mere servant. I am going to confiscate him."

Timon moved to intercept the guard. "If you would check his papers, you will find he has been released from all military duty as he is physically unfit. He is damaged in the head."

The guard grunted and motioned to KiKu to remove his turban.

KiKu remained impassive.

Timon quickly intervened again. "They will respond to only one master. Allow me," said Timon stepping between the guard and KiKu. "Take off your turban and allow this man to touch you."

The Bilboa dutifully took off his turban, causing dark red locks to fall on his shoulders. He bowed his head toward the soldier.

The guard took out his dagger.

Timon became alarmed.

The guard, seeing Timon's dismay, said, "He could have lice," and went through the Bilboa's head, tapping with the blunt side of the dagger until he found a metal plate on the right side of the servant's head. He tapped it harder until it gave a little ring.

KiKu popped his head up, looking a little worse for wear.

Grumbling, the guard affixed a wax seal on Timon's papers.

Timon grunted his thanks and started to move through the gate.

"Young one," called out the guard. "You'd be better to go to a whore house. You'll not be happy at the temple. Strange things are going on there. Beware!"

As Timon thought to question the guard, KiKu gave him a push forward. "Better not test your luck or my head again," he hissed through his teeth.

Timon marched through the spiked gate with his servants following obediently behind him. He was stopped again on the other side of the massive wall but with little fanfare this time. Another guard looked at the wax seal, still warm, and pressed a wooden stamp on it. He grunted, and Timon went anxiously on his way into the vast city of Bhuttani, capital of Bhuttan.

While a Sivan caravan blocked his way to the main thoroughfare, Timon took time to study the buildings leading out into the main part of the city from the western side. The buildings were constructed of sandstone with immense wooden beams acting as supports. Solidly built, each building—many having as many as five stories—served as a mini fortress. Some were obviously private homes with laundry hanging from the upper windows, safe from dust stirred up by the myriad of feet and hooves below. Each home was the same with the first floor used as a stable and the second floor as a storage facility with rooms for servants. The upper floors were for the owner and his family where dust, odors, and bugs would be less of a problem.

Timon was bowled over by the putrid stench in the street. Holding his travel shawl up so that he could cover his mouth and nose, he quickly observed what was creating such a horrible stench. On either side of the dirt-packed street, he saw a ditch had been dug to accommodate each house's dirty water, food scraps, and body waste.

Timon remembered crying as a boy being carried though the wretched streets of Bhuttani by his pale, solemn father to meet the aga. He remembered pinching his nose and begging to be taken home because "everything stinks here." Timon shook the unpleasant memory from his head.

A small group of Sivans passed Timon's little entourage. with their elaborate headdresses covering their entire faces except for their eyes. Timon strongly suspected that all of the Sivans had herbs wrapped in the cloth near their noses to protect them from the smell and illness caused by the refuse in the streets. Timon wished he had the foresight to wear a similar costume.

Only KiKu seemed unaffected by the foulness. He stood patiently as only a Bilboa could, waiting for his master to command him. Even a swarm of biting flies passing through the street did not cause KiKu to move a muscle.

After slapping the obnoxious flies away from his eyes and nose, Timon exclaimed, "This is awful! We must find an inn." Timon hurriedly marched down the street, pushing his way through the throng of people, and occasionally asking where a respectable inn might be found. Most ignored him, but a kind man stopped and gave Timon the name of a good inn and directions. Timon profusely thanked him as the man briskly went on his way. No one liked to tarry outside for long if they could possibly avoid it.

As Timon swiftly negotiated the streets of Bhuttani, he was reminded again of his entry into the city as a child and his final emergence ten years later as a young man, marching with the aga's army, hoping someday to escape to his home. He had not seen his mother those ten years; the only contact with her were letters written full of love and longing. He doubted he would know her if he spied her on the street. Timon vowed if he survived this mission, he was going home to see his mother, and nothing would be able to stop him.

Deep in thought, Timon motioned KiKu to move to the head of their little group so the inn would be found more quickly, since the streets were not marked. After many twists and turns, KiKu found the inn, and waited outside with the exhausted women until Timon returned after making arrangements with the corpulent innkeeper.

They were shown two adjoining rooms on the second floor. There was only one bed and no chairs. When Timon complained, the innkeeper shrugged and said nothing else was available.

"Take it or not," the innkeeper snarled in a squeaky voice. "It's all we have."

Seeing the innkeeper was telling the truth, Timon threw him a gold coin. The innkeeper caught the coin with his apron and left the room with a happy smile on his whiskered face.

Pearl opened the shutters of a little window, which offered the only ventilation in the room, and peered out. "It could be worse," she said. "We could be stuck on the first floor with the animals."

The twins groaned while throwing their belongings on a dirty rug that covered the floor of their room.

There was a knock on the door. A maidservant entered with an arm full of reeds. Looking around for a good spot, she threw them on the floor, and then covered them with clean coverlets. Since the women lodgers appeared to be menials like herself, the maidservant did not curtsy as she left the room.

Pearl took a vial from her little satchel and turned back the coverlets on all of the pallets and the only bed in Timon's room, sprinkling a liberal amount of green liquid on them until everyone complained about the acrid smell. "Well, now you won't have to worry about bed bugs," she muttered defensively.

Exhausted from the journey, Timon spread out on the bed, ready to take a long nap. A shadow passed over his face, causing Timon to wearily open his burning eyes.

KiKu stood over him with a disgruntled look on his face. "I hope you are not thinking of resting now that we have entered the city."

"It will be dark in several hours," answered Timon. "It is too late to go to the temple."

"That is correct, but you will need to get ready for tomorrow. You will need to have your clothes washed. A bath for us is in order. If we don't tell the innkeeper now, the hot water will be used up. Someone will need to provide food and drink."

Timon flung himself from the bed. "All right, all right. I will take care of these matters." He opened a pouch full of coins. "You see about the water, and I will procure food. The women can wash my clothes. Uhm . . ." Timon stopped short as KiKu violently shook his head.

"My wives are tired and have suffered much on this journey. They need all the rest they can."

Timon nodded in agreement. They were so good at acting he sometimes forgot they were not servants. "You pay for the water, and I will go out into the city and get food. I will be less likely to be recognized, even though you do look like a Bilboa. There is no reason to take any chances."

KiKu bowed very low and salaamed, pressing his palm to his forehead. "Your will, my lord."

"My will, my arse!" complained Timon as he stomped out of the cramped room and down the dusty steps to the street door, holding onto a leather pouch. A doorman opened the entrance for him after Timon asked questions about where to purchase fruit and fried bread. The doorman told Timon the inn was serving roasted borax that was only a day old. Timon drooled at the thought of meat, but ventured out into the city anyway because the twins ate only vegetables or fruit. He would buy some meat for himself though, he thought happily. And off he went.

16

Timon returned.

He lugged a pouch stuffed with ripe fruit, followed by a slapdash of a boy whose arms were loaded with cheeses and several types of bread. As there was no table, the boy merely dropped his load on the floor and waited patiently for his promised reward.

Hearing commotion stemming from Timon's room, the women knocked and rushed in. Seeing the food on the floor, they cried out with both pleasure at the sight of it and disgust that it was lying on the dirty floor. They laid a clean shawl flat on the floor and arranged the food into an appealing display.

The young boy tried to help the women, but they pushed him away, crying that he was too dirty.

Pearl gave the boy some fruit and told him to stand by the door.

The boy smiled at Pearl wondering at her kindness.

Timon gave him a large hunk of bread and a small copper coin. The boy's eyes lit up as he shoved the bread in his mouth while running out of the room. He feared the young man might change his mind and ask for the coin and food back.

Timon sat on his bed and KiKu on his pallet as they watched the women fuss with the meal.

In addition to arranging for hot water, KiKu also garnered several skins of wine, which the women placed along with the bread.

Timon noticed the women's hair was wet so he assumed that they had already washed off the fetor of the road. They smelled fresh. Hittals were like Hasan Daegians—they loved to take baths.

The women clicked along at a furious pace in their language. Timon liked hearing their happy chatter. Glancing at KiKu, Timon assumed he liked to hear it, too, as KiKu's facial expression relaxed watching his wives prepare their supper.

Finally, the women waved the men over to the colorful shawl. In true harem fashion of Hittal, the women massaged the feet and shoulders of the men as they ate and drank wine. And in true male fashion of Hittal, KiKu and Timon ate quickly and retired to their beds so the women could eat.

The women took a leisurely dinner that included eating, laughing, and talking while occasionally stealing glances at the men who seemed to have fallen asleep. Before retiring to their rooms, they wrapped the remaining food in clean cloths and stored them in leather bags, which were kept at the foot of Timon's bed. They then dragged in a wooden tub filled with water and a pitcher from their room. After making sure everything was in its place, they went to their own compartment and shut the door.

As soon as their door closed, Timon sat straight up and, leaning over the side of the bed, rummaged through the leather bags tearing off a hunk of bread and cheese.

"Throw me some, too," said KiKu, also sitting up.

Timon learned that caring Hittal husbands did not make their hungry wives wait long for their meals. They would eat enough to satisfy the women, but not enough to satisfy their stomachs. After the women retired, KiKu was always sneaking off in the dark to eat more, as were Hittal husbands the world over.

"Why don't you and your wives dine together?" Timon asked.

KiKu seemed appalled at his question. "The man is head of Hittal family. It is disrespectful not to serve him first."

"Then why don't we just have dinner instead of sneaking off into all hours of the night trying to get something to eat?"

"It is unkind to make women and children wait to eat when they are hungry."

Timon tried again. "Why don't we put food in our pockets to eat later?"

"The women would see and be upset if they thought we were not eating until we are full. It would cast dishonor upon them."

Timon finally understood the Hittal logic. "And it would cast dishonor upon a man if he ate while a woman stood by hungry."

KiKu nodded enthusiastically. "Men eat until the edge of hunger is taken off and then let women and children eat till they are full. Men eat later, but mustn't let women see, or they will be dishonored. Everyone knows everything, but if you don't see, you are not dishonored. All Hittal men wait. It makes little sense anymore, but no one knows how to end it without casting aspersions, so we cope." KiKu flashed a big grin. "It is a small thing for me to wait."

Timon smiled back.

KiKu was right. It was not a burden. At times, he even liked to play the game, but tonight, he was ravenous and stuffed cheese into his mouth while reaching for the wineskin.

After eating his portion, Timon lay in his bed, patting his belly. He hesitated for a moment, looking at the tub, only to turn over after deciding that he would bathe in cold water tomorrow morning. Before he could delve into a deep sleep, he felt tapping on his foot. Timon opened one eye.

"What are you doing?"

"I am going to sleep," replied Timon, wondering what KiKu wanted now. He was beginning to annoy Timon.

"We must go soon."

"Go where?"

"To rendezvous with our contact. Usually, I would go alone, but if I die, you must know how to reach the temple contact."

"Can't this wait until morning?" pleaded Timon, eyeing his pillow.

Exasperated with Timon, KiKu huffed, "NO!" He thought the boy lazy at times. "We must meet tonight before you go to the temple in the morning."

Timon knew better than to argue with KiKu. "Wake me up when it is time." He turned over.

KiKu hit his foot again. Timon raised his head a little. "You have not washed your clothes or your body yet. It must be done now."

"Can't you do it?"

KiKu sat on his pallet. "Not my clothes, not my body."

Timon jumped off the bed in a foul mood. "Now I know why you took the disguise of a Bilboa. They never bathe."

KiKu never heard the scribe as he was fast asleep on his pallet with his hand on the hilt of his dagger.

Resenting the fair ladies and KiKu for making him perform menial tasks, Timon grumbled and muttered as he washed the outfit he was going to wear to the temple. He also mended a little hole he found in the jacket. Afterwards, he gave himself a sponge bath and washed his hair. He braided his long, dark hair and tied it with a leather thong. He put on a dark pair of trousers and a dark shirt from his bags to wear for the night. Weary from his tasks, Timon fell asleep for what seemed only for a few minutes before he felt KiKu's strong hand on his shoulder giving him a tight squeeze.

"Time to go."

17

Timon opened his eyes.

A shaft of moonlight feebly entered the room, outlining KiKu so that his eyes glowed like coals. The glowing red eyes in the darkness startled Timon, even though he knew they were a disguise.

KiKu moved silently across the floor and gracefully slid through the window, disappearing into the night.

Timon sighed and tried to cross the floor as quietly as KiKu. It seemed to him every floorboard squeaked. Remembering that a storage floor was underneath him and not other guests, Timon breathed easier. The young prince-turned-scribe-turned-spy pushed his frame through the narrow opening, getting several splinters from the wooden jambs. He silently cursed, but slid through and climbed down to the ground. He landed with a heavy thud. Looking around, he could not find KiKu.

A large hand reached out from a dark corner and pulled him in. KiKu clasped a hand over the mouth of a surprised Timon. "Shhh. Be quiet. You make more noise than a band of drunken freebooters. Remember your training."

Timon breathed deeply as he had been taught by KiKu and controlled his intake of air until his breathing was silent and steady. As trained, Timon stopped narrowly focusing on his surroundings and began to "see." He began with "splatter vision," which used his peripheral sight and focused his hearing. There was no one in the street. Timon's eyes shot up the surrounding buildings, studying the windows. Why would people get up in the middle of the night? Ask the important questions, KiKu always coached, then you will get the important answers. Timon thought, *A person would be up to get a drink of water, comfort a child, get fresh air, or relieve themselves.* No one appeared to be at a window getting air. He did not hear the squalls of any child. The street seemed deserted. Did his gut tell him the street was empty? Yes, it did.

KiKu, the true master of penetrating the unseen, slid out of the corner shadow and effortlessly glided door to door down the street, hiding in the dark recess of their entrances. Timon followed suit, but was sure he was making noise while KiKu seemed like a specter drifting on moonbeams. Every so often, KiKu would stop and take in his surroundings. If he felt nothing was askew, they continued.

After what seemed a long time, Timon's thighs burned from squatting in doorways. They finally came to a street where people spilled out onto its cobbled pathway, talking loudly and acting rambunctiously. Timon had never been to this part of the city, but he recognized a pleasure district when he saw one.

KiKu stepped out into the street, weaving slightly as though he was mildly drunk.

Timon immediately assumed the role of a companion assisting his sodden friend to negotiate the winding street. Light splashed out of the taverns' doorways, which helped Timon step over drunken soldiers asleep in the middle of the street. From the upstairs floors, women's laughter that sounded both lascivious and empty drifted down like a soft breeze. They could hear the not-so-quiet murmurs of men and women talking in deep husky tones and sometimes the slapping, wet noises made by frantic lovemaking. Boys, with painted faces and wearing handsome gowns, called out to him from windows.

Timon hoped the light coming from the taverns and doorways was weak enough to hide his shamed face. He was embarrassed to be in such a place, even though he was on a mission. No person of any character would hire a companion for such purposes. Only the meanest of spirit and the poorest in society would willingly expose themselves to lovemaking such as this. At least that was the way in his world. His mother had been very firm about that.

Halfway down the street, a curvaceous woman wrapped in a heavy shawl and veil approached them. "You there, would you like a tumble?"

Irritated with her presence, Timon was about to send her away when KiKu brusquely pushed the woman back against a wall. He lowered his pants as the woman wrapped her legs around his waist. KiKu jerked his head toward Timon, "Kiss her, you fool. A patrol is coming!"

Timon hurried over to the thrusting couple doubly embarrassed by the grunts KiKu was making. The woman cupped her arms around Timon. "Kiss me." Seeing Timon's reluctance, she added, "Act as though you are kissing me."

Timon bent his head toward the woman and could smell expensive perfumes on the woman's hair and skin. The scent was intoxicating. Without thinking, he touched her skin with his lips and then covered her mouth. Much to his surprise, she kissed back. Much to his surprise again, he kissed harder. He opened his eyes and saw the woman had open hers as well, but her eyes were searching the street behind him.

Timon heard the patrol marching and closed his eyes. His heart pounded from fear, and his knees felt weak. He kissed the woman harder.

An iron hand with a spiked knuckle band gripped Timon's shoulder and swung him around. Timon's eyelids snapped open to reveal a grizzled Bhuttanian combat soldier with a bulbous nose, who seemed very disturbed that he was on patrol so early in the morning or so late at night, considering his viewpoint. The soldier's one good eye swept over Timon. He called to his companions, "He's not one of us." The soldier pushed Timon out of the way as he tried to pry KiKu from the woman, who was making all sorts of gasps and grunts.

KiKu pulled out a short knife with one hand as he held onto the woman with the other. He jabbed near the soldier's gut. "Can't you see I'm busy!"

For a moment, the soldier seemed stunned and then grinned, slapping Timon on the chest. "A man after my own heart," he said laughing. "A man should be able to fight and screw at the same time. Take note from your comrade, young friend."

Timon nodded weakly and resumed kissing the panting woman. The soldier rejoined his patrol, as they heaved passed-out drunken soldiers into a large cart, dragging them back to their quarters where they would be sobered up and sent back to their tasks.

KiKu made a strangled cry as though he had climaxed and lowered the woman's legs to the ground. "Take my place," said KiKu pulling up his pants.

Timon looked at him horrified. "I can't. My tribe is very strict about these things."

The spylord's face grew angry, and he thrust his hands out toward the younger man in such a menacing way that the woman quickly pulled Timon to her and began untying his trousers. "It's just play acting," she whispered into his ears. "Hold me up to give me support," she said as she wrapped her legs around Timon's bare middle. Timon was relieved to feel cloth between him and the strange woman. Slowly, Timon began moving between the woman's legs as KiKu kissed and fondled her.

"Master, you have come at an auspicious time," she whispered between tiny cries of faked pleasure. "The sightings are occurring more frequently and with greater clarity."

"When was the last sighting?" KiKu whispered under his audible grunts and curses.

"Night before last. The priest came to me, his mind much disturbed. He had seen a strange beast—a human covered with feathers like a bird and possessing giant wings. The creature knelt before the priest and begged for release. Then the vision disappeared like a puff of smoke."

"Where had he seen this vision?"

"When he was lighting the oil lamps in the main sanctuary for midnight prayers. He felt something brush his head and looked up. Right over him was the creature kneeling upside down. It gave Onxor quite a fright."

"Did he try to communicate with the Dini?"

The woman shook her head. "He was too alarmed."

"Then how does he know the creature begged for release?" asked Timon, puffing away.

"Because the creature was on his knees with his hands in supplication," explained the woman as though Timon was a simpleton. "The creature's mouth moved very slowly. Onxor could make out what he was saying."

"Is that all?" asked KiKu.

The woman nodded.

"Finish up," he said to Timon. "We need to go. It will soon be daybreak."

Timon copied KiKu's motions and let out a strangled cry. He smiled. "I thought that was rather good," he said of his performance. He let the woman's legs down gently and tossed her a few coins.

"You might even enjoy the real thing one of these days," teased the woman.

No longer embarrassed, Timon looked at the woman's eyes peering at him over her veil. She had the most beautiful green eyes he had ever seen. He stared at them with the strong sensation he was falling.

KiKu nudged him. "Let's go."

"I'll follow you," answered Timon, unable to tear his eyes from the woman's face.

KiKu pushed Timon into the middle of the street only to have Timon swirl around and throw the woman a kiss.

She was nowhere to be seen.

Disappointed, Timon followed KiKu glumly back to the inn. As it would soon be daybreak, bakers, wine merchants, and beggars were already getting ready for the day's business. KiKu and Timon did not attempt to conceal their journey back to the inn.

Exhausted, Timon fell asleep the moment he touched his bed and snored loudly as KiKu lay awake on his pallet of straw. His eyes moved restlessly, panning the walls as he planned the release of the Dinii.

Even though Maura was fond of him, KiKu had no doubt she would carry out her threat to kill his family if he failed.

The Dinii must be released from the temple of Bhuttu!

18

Alexanee watched.

The Hasan Daegian women practiced the military moves he had taught them with their ponies. For the past several years, he had come to appreciate the agility of the small ponies and wondered how he could use them to their best advantage.

The main problem was that the rider was easy prey to enemy foot soldiers. She lacked the advantage of sitting high out of harm's way as one did on a Bhuttanian warhorse.

Still, the horses had their uses. He had been thinking about using the horses as a quick way to transport soldiers to a certain area in a battle where they would dismount to fight on foot. The horses would be trained to a series of whistles to return behind the battle lines. Alexanee was wiping the grime from his brow when he sensed a presence behind. He swung around, his hand on the hilt of his sword.

"Good afternoon, Lord Alexanee," Maura said.

Alexanee's eyes darted about the hillside.

Maura was alone except for her uultepes.

He bowed most graciously and clasped his fist to his chest.

Maura inclined her head.

Alexanee claimed, "I am afraid you startled me, Great Mother."

"How could I, a mere woman, startle the great general who conquered almost an entire continent?"

Alexanee's eyes narrowed. "Maura de Magela has never been a mere woman and will never be one. I did what I could for the service of my country."

Maura searched his dark, leathery face. Though still considered a young man by Hasan Daegian standards, Alexanee's face had deep creases that appeared like lines on a map. She could not find mockery in his dark eyes or the firm lines around his wide mouth. "I'll take that as a compliment, General Alexanee."

"As it was meant to be, Great Mother."

Maura smiled.

Alexanee was startled. He had never seen the empress give a genuine smile. It took him aback as she looked like a slip of a girl, innocent and pure, and not the feared despot she had become in recent years.

Maura's smile faded as she noticed his reaction. An expressionless face replaced the happy grin.

Alexanee regretted seeing her countenance change. This young woman should be worrying about what dress to wear and how many babies to have instead of whose head needed to be severed from his shoulders. His wife had given him a daughter, and he realized it wouldn't be long before his beautiful child would be Maura's age.

No woman should have been placed in a position of power so young, but Maura had been bred and trained to rule since the day she was born. She was not a normal young woman.

"Has the Great Mother come to watch the exercises?" he asked diplomatically. He hoped she would not bring up the hunting accident. It was nearly forgotten by all except for him. He had not been able to discover what Maura was planning, but he had not stopped trying to find out her secret.

"I want you to stop."

Alexanee's heart dropped. It was as he feared. She knew about his persistent inquiring about the scribe Timon. "I don't know to what you are referring, Great Mother," he bluffed.

Maura pursed her lips with impatience. "You have good men around you—experienced, loyal, bright. It would be a pity if unfortunate things began happening to them." She looked at the Hasan Daegian women practicing on their ponies. "For example, falling off a horse and breaking their necks. Don't you agree that would be horrible, General Alexanee? Men, in the prime of their lives and so needed to fight in Bhuttani, dead and burned to ashes on the funeral pyre in this cold and barren land."

The general blinked against the strong light of the sun. Holding his hand up to shade his eyes, Alexanee realized he was getting a reprieve, and his men were being spared. "That would be most unfortunate," he agreed.

"Let's hope fate does not take such a turn."

"It will not," replied Alexanee, bowing. He felt gratitude toward her.

Maura turned back toward him. "One more thing, General Alexanee."

"Yes, Great Mother?"

"I have taken the liberty of sending for your wife and daughter. They should arrive this afternoon."

Alexanee stood speechless as though rooted to the ground.

"I can only guess how you must miss them. I thought we could both enjoy their company. After all, Jezra might send an assassin to your home."

A pale Alexanee bowed. "I thank the Great Mother for her kindness."

"We wouldn't want to find either one of them with a dagger in their back, would we?"

"I will guard them with my life."

Maura smiled one of her "Empress" smiles. "That's what it may take. Come," she called to her uultepes.

They stood and swished their long tails at Alexanee as if to say, "See, there is more than one way to skin a general."

19

The Bilboa pounded harder.

He repeatedly banged on the grand metal doors guarding the entrance to the temple of Bhuttu, the war god of the Bhuttanians. He continued hammering until he thought his fists would turn into bloody hocks of meat. Defeated, he turned and slumped against the wall, shaking his head in defeat.

"There must be another way in," said Timon, disbelieving the priests would fail to answer their door even during a civil war.

"I know a way," a little voice piped.

Timon looked down.

Standing beside him like a lost borax calf was the young boy who had helped carry the provisions to the inn the other evening. Timon smiled at the scruffy urchin. "How is that, young man?"

The little boy puffed up his chest, trying to seem larger than he was. "If I show you, you must give me food and lodging for seven days." He peered eagerly up at Timon.

"I will give you enough coins for seven days," Timon agreed.

The little boy shook his head. "No. I don't want money. You must give me food and lodging for seven days," he replied firmly.

Puzzled, Timon turned to KiKu.

The spy was studying the young boy very carefully but said nothing.

The dirty scamp shrugged his shoulders. "You can pound here all day long, but no one will open the door. The doors have not opened since the civil war started."

"How do they get their supplies?" asked Timon, taking a very keen interest in the boy's knowledge.

The boy pointed to the walls. "They hoist everything they need over the walls."

Timon leaned his head near KiKu's ear. "There must be a door available if your contact got out last night."

"We cannot very well enter by the servant's door if you are applying as a novice," spat out KiKu, obviously irritated with the current situation. "We have to enter by the front. Since the front door is closed, it means they have ceased contact with the outside world, and they are not taking any more novices. This is a bad omen."

Timon asked, "How do the people worship Bhuttu if the temple is closed?"

The boy looked incredulously at Timon. "No one worships Bhuttu but by their death. He does not need live worshippers. He desires the sacrifice of life." The boy cocked his head at Timon. "Are you sure you are at the right temple?"

"That remains to be seen," muttered Timon, throwing out his hands in despair. Timon turned his back on the boy, staring at the mammoth doors. He had to get in, and he had to do it the proper way. He realized that if he entered by the servants' entrance, he would be chased off, therefore harming his chances of completing his mission. "What if we pose as merchants or servants, and then change our clothes once we get in?" he whispered to KiKu.

"We have already been spotted," KiKu answered. "I am sure someone from the temple is watching us even now and would guard against any possible intrusion. Also, that man sitting by the well could be a spy for any number of factions within the city. We must carry this out in our current disguises."

Timon knelt down as though he was trying to get a pebble out of his boot. He glanced surreptitiously at the well and did, indeed, see a man dressed as a peddler, flirting with servant women as they came to the well for water. He also watched the servant women, especially one who kept glancing in his direction. Timon concluded most of the women worked for businesses on the street, as most private homes had wells. Timon stood up and turned to KiKu. "I think there are two of them working together. The woman with the blue shawl seems very interested in us."

For a second, there was the note of satisfaction in KiKu's glaring red eyes. "Give the boy what he wants. We must get in."

Timon protested, "What if he gets in the way?"

"Then I will kill him."

Timon's mouth fell open and quickly closed. "If he serves us well, his life will be spared," Timon said firmly.

KiKu grunted.

Turning to the little boy, whose face was scrunched up trying to discern their whispers, Timon tousled his hair until he saw there were bugs. Not knowing what to do with his hand, Timon wiped his palm on his pants. "I will give you seven days lodging and food if you can open this door. However, I will sell you as a pleasure slave to the first soldier I see if you lie or steal from me."

The little boy nodded his head vigorously. "You do not need to worry, my lord. I will be very useful. I will be back. Stand there. Don't go away," he called as he ran off into the busy street. After a few minutes, the boy returned with a sharp rock and a stick. Kneeling by the temple doors, he dug a little rut in the dirt, going as far as he could underneath the thick metal. "I will need a gold coin," he said to Timon.

Reluctantly, KiKu handed the boy a coin.

The boy put the coin in the depression and, with his stick, pushed the coin farther and farther under the door. Pressing his ear on the metal, he waited.

KiKu also pressed his ear on the door and thought he heard scratching sounds from the other side.

The boy knelt and searched under the door. "I will need another coin."

KiKu kept giving him coins until five coins had disappeared under the metal doors.

Timon was about to give the boy a swift kick in his tiny backside when a side door, previously hidden to both KiKu and Timon, squeaked open just a tad.

A hoarse croaked, "What dost thou want?"

Peering at the shadow framing the doorway, Timon said, "My name is Timon de Berechial. I come from the province of Qued Zum. I have traveled a long way to apply for the priesthood in the service of Bhuttu." Timon waited for a reply. There was silence from the doorway as Timon felt more than one pair of eyes studying him.

"Thou art a long way from home, brother," screeched a higher, younger voice from the doorway.

"Yeeesss," stammered Timon, losing his nerve. He felt KiKu's bony finger poke him in the back. "I have traveled for many months and endured many hardships. I come for nothing more than to serve

Bhuttu and learn his ways."

"That is asking much from our Lord," replied the younger voice again. "What dost thou have to offer Bhuttu?"

"My mind, my body, my servants, and my wealth."

There was a long silence until the door slowly creaked opened. "Enter!" was the only response.

Timon, followed by KiKu and the boy, entered the dark doorway leading into the great temple of Bhuttu. Standing in a little alcove, they had to wait for their eyes to adjust to the darkness. Timon jumped a little when the door behind them slammed shut, causing all light to be extinguished. As KiKu stood behind him, Timon could not ask "his servant" if he could see anything, but he already knew what KiKu's answer would be.

The spy might be posing as a Bilboa, but that did not mean that KiKu had the same natural gifts as one, such as seeing in the dark. This thought caused Timon to stiffen his spine. Those watching would expect the turbaned Bilboa to see and act accordingly. "My servant might be able to see, but I assure you that I cannot nor will I command my servant to act if I cannot see where he is to step," said Timon into the darkness.

Utter silence answered Timon's words. He stood still and erect, trying to discern the tiniest movement. There was none. They waited until Timon gauged they had been standing almost three-quarters of an hour when an inner door opened.

A man, holding a lamp, stood barring its passageway. "Place thy weapons on the floor," he commanded.

Timon placed his dagger on the floor.

"Thy servant has one knife hidden in his turban and another stowed away in his boot."

Timon heard the clatter of metal fall to the stone floor followed by the unwrapping of cloth and then another clatter.

"May we now enter?" asked Timon, doing his best to sound authoritative.

"Thou mayest."

Timon strode through the door, glad to be out of the tiny little dungeon of a room. Bright sunlight struck like a hidden snake in the bush, causing Timon to shield his sensitive eyes with his hands. "Please wait a moment," he called to his guide walking on ahead. "My eyes must adjust. This light is blinding!"

"Thy servant might be able to guide thee," replied the man, retracing his steps to Timon's side.

"I would rather guide myself and not be led like a blind man," snapped Timon, holding his head down away from the glaring sun. "I refuse to go forward until I can see."

After several minutes, Timon opened his eyes tentatively and shielding them with a hand, glanced around. They were standing in the middle of a large courtyard. Hot air moved in waves across the paved walkway.

He blinked until his eyes adjusted to the almost white sunlight, though he could not stop squinting. "I've never seen such bright sunlight," he commented. He could see the outline of the man standing before him, but he could not make out the details of his face. Timon kept seeing black spots where the eyes should have been.

Turning, Timon saw his companions standing not too far from him. He tried to make eye contact with KiKu but immediately sensed trouble.

Because KiKu was supposed to be a Bilboa, KiKu had not lowered his head in the blinding sunlight, acting as though he could see, but Timon perceived KiKu's eyes were not making contact with anything. *He's blind!* thought Timon. He snapped his attention back to the man standing before him. Starting to panic, Timon's mind went blank.

"I'm frightened," said the little boy to KiKu. "Hold my hand."

The boy placed his hand in the tall spylord's hand and tugged. "Master, may we go? This place frightens me."

"Be quiet!" barked Timon, acting as though he was irritated with the boy, but pleased the urchin had engineered an excuse to hold KiKu's hand and guide the tall spy out of the disturbingly bright sun. Sensing the boy understood their predicament and was trying to help, Timon said to their guide. "I am ready now."

The guide grunted in Bhuttanian fashion and led them across the courtyard to a magnificent building made of marble and alabaster. He knocked quietly on one of several doors. The door opened, and the guide bade them to enter.

They came into a long corridor. "Proceed to the end of the corridor," ordered the guide. "There you will find a door. Enter it."

The three adventurers did as they were told and found themselves in a lovely garden, which was lit by a more natural and subdued sunlight. Since no one appeared to greet them, Timon sat on a bench while the boy led KiKu to stand under a large tree where there was ample shade. Occasionally, KiKu would blink, indicating his sight was slowly coming back.

Timon lowered his head as though he was praying. Besides their guide, they had seen no one, though Timon could faintly hear chanting in the distance. He assumed they had arrived during morning devotionals. After what seemed an hour, Timon heard a door open and footfalls coming toward him. He did not stand, but continued with his praying. Out of the corner of his eye, he could see sandaled feet waiting patiently for him to finish. Making the sign on his chest of the eternal circle, which represented life, Timon rose to his feet, trying to look like a devoted servant of Bhuttu.

Before him stood a handsome middle-aged man dressed in a spotless yellow robe with only gold pendant earrings to adorn his person. The man was not dark like a Bhuttanian but fair like an Anqarian, though his hair was braided in Bhuttanian fashion.

Timon bowed very low. "My name is Timon de Berechiah. I come from Qued Zem. I am seeking entrance into the service of Bhuttu."

"My name is Onxor. One does not need to come here to order to serve Bhuttu. What else might thou want?"

"Your wisdom is great, my lord. I harbor the thirst of ambition, which I thought might be quenched here."

"Rise, so I may see into thy eyes." The priest studied Timon for a long time. "Ambition in itself is not a fault, if tempered with logic and humility. Ambition can help a man ascend to great heights; however, ambition, without introspection, can be deadly for the man who harbors it and for the people around him as well." The priest peered over Timon's shoulder at KiKu and the young boy. "Thy servants are most unusual."

"The boy was not in my care until several hours ago. As he helped me gain entrance, I promised he would be in my keeping for seven days as reward for his services."

"Ah, he is most likely a street whelp." He turned away as though pained by the sight of the frail little boy. "Life in Bhuttani has been disrupted since the death of Aga Zoar. The people lack discipline in their duties. Orphans and beggars run amuck in the streets. The city is divided into factions that fight needlessly against each other, instead of uniting to fight the Deceiver, Maura." The priest lowered his excited voice. "But thou hast come to seek thy future, not to listen to a sermon about our society falling apart. Please follow me."

"Where are you taking me?"

"Thou art to stand before the judgment of the High Priest,

Hilkiah."

Although Timon didn't like the sound of that, he trailed the priest meekly out of the garden and through a maze of sumptuous corridors, until they came before two richly carved doors of rare black wood highlighted with gold relief. Timon glanced behind. KiKu and the boy followed at a respectful distance.

The priest tapped softly on the door. "I will take my leave now."

"Where are you going?" asked Timon, grabbing the priest's sleeve.

"Thou art to stand here until the door opens. That is all thee needs to do."

"How long will I be here?"

"As long as it takes the door to open. I must take my leave now. I hope I may see thy face again." Onxor turned and walked past KiKu and the boy, sharply turning the corner and then vanishing.

The boy tugged excitedly on KiKu's sleeve. "Did you see that? Did you see that? One moment he was there. The next disappeared. Just like that," said the boy, snapping his fingers.

KiKu scanned the hallway and studied the walls, saying nothing.

The boy wondered why he did not seem impressed.

KiKu signaled to Timon to turn around with a small motion of his finger. Frowning, Timon stood before the door awaiting entrance.

After several hours of waiting this time, Timon grew impatient. His legs were tiring, and he wanted to sit. His stomach growled. Angry that he was being made to wait so long, Timon tried one of the door handles and pushed. The door swung open just a little bit. Ignoring KiKu's warning cough behind him, Timon pushed the door open, stepping inside. Timon found himself in a beautiful, spacious garden filled with exotic flowers of bold colors. In the middle of the room meandered a bubbling stream spanned by a wooden bridge. A pale blue bird with yellow spots on its wings flew past Timon and landed on a strange tree, moving as though a wind was blowing its dark green-striped leaves. Timon wet his finger and held it up in the air. Just as he thought. There was no breeze.

Timon crossed the bridge, peering down into the stream. There were small colorful fish swimming between carefully placed reeds and ornamental water lilies. A tiny rock wren landed by Timon's hand on a rail, sounded a few peeps, and then dashed off. Timon could see that it flew into a stand of bamboo.

KiKu cautiously entered while the boy ran on ahead.

"Look at this!" exclaimed the boy, holding up a rock.

KiKu peered beneath the rock and held up several large gems worth a fortune in the outside world. He put them back and ordered the boy to replace the stone.

"Why don't we take them?" asked the boy. "They are doing nobody any good under a rock."

KiKu ignored the shrill plea of the boy.

"Why doesn't thee indeed?" a voice inquired.

Timon and KiKu swiveled around.

A man in a peasant tunic and trousers of coarse woven black cloth stood on a large boulder.

Timon had to remember to close his mouth for he had never seen another being that looked quite like the one standing above them. The man's skin was white as snow as was his close-cropped hair with his dark clothing serving only to create more of a contrast with his unusual skin tone, which Timon was sure the man intended. Timon found his voice. "Do we have the honor of addressing the High Priest, Hilkiah?" asked Timon, bowing very low.

KiKu and the boy followed suit.

"Thou dost. And the temple of Bhuttu has the honor of addressing Timon de Berechiah from Qued Zem. Welcome, fellow traveler. I hope thee hath enjoyed my private garden," he cooed, waving his hand.

Timon smiled. "It is most illuminating."

"In what way?"

"One may interpret this garden as the supreme garden, which we all hope to enter upon our deaths. Here is everything we are missing in our county. Fresh water, bountiful land that can grow a variety of plants, animals that can be harvested, and an aga's wealth in gems. Everything here is symbolic of our current deprivation; everything we need and desire."

The High Priest's face beamed with pleasure, mostly emanating from his shiny pinkish eyes. "That is exactly what I tried to accomplish with this garden; to make a model that would exemplify all that Bhuttan must have to be great. But let us not leave out beauty. I have tried to make it a place of wonder and color as well. As thou may knowest, many of our brethren have remained cold to aesthetics," he uttered, shrugging his shoulders a little. "But I have always been interested in pleasing sights." Hilkiah paused in speaking.

There was silence in the room, as Timon did not know how to respond at first. "If it pleases you, perhaps someday you might honor me with reciting the names and origins of these wondrous plants?" requested Timon, who thought this a most unusual interview.

"A servant of Bhuttu will guide thee to my office for a more personal conversation after thee hast rested. I see the whelp is in need of a bath."

The boy flinched at the mention of a bath, a most unusual custom for a Bhuttanian, but then priests were considered strange by the rest of the population. "Rooms have been provided for thee and thy servants."

"I and my servants must humbly thank you for your hospitality," replied Timon, bowing again as did KiKu while pushing the boy's head down.

When they looked up, Hilkiah was gone.

Timon and KiKu did not seem surprised, but the boy could hardly contain his excitement. "They must be magicians or something!" he exclaimed. "They are better than the ones who perform in the market squares. I wish I could do that!"

"Hush!" commanded Timon, who was trying to organize his thoughts. He wanted to explore the garden and find the trap door Hilkiah disappeared through, as well as the one in the hallway. He wondered if the entire complex was honeycombed with secret passageways.

A lad, several years older than the street urchin, entered the garden. He wore a brown robe and had a shaved head. He bowed very low and politely asked Timon to follow, which Timon did as well as KiKu and the "whelp."

The street boy, dazzled that another boy near his age could be in the temple of Bhuttu, asked him endless questions while fingering the material of the robe.

The temple servant ignored him, except to pull his clean robe from the boy's dirty fingers.

KiKu tapped the street urchin on top of his filthy head and ordered him to behave.

The boy folded his arms and sullenly marched behind KiKu, making faces behind the Bilboa's back.

The temple lad showed Timon to a spacious compartment that provided a balcony overlooking the western portion of the city and the plains beyond the city's walls. As the lad showed Timon his room, several other youths entered with hot water, towels, and bathing oils. A tray of fruit and beverages was provided, as well as a small tunic made of fine cloth and small leather slippers. Timon gave the older of the youths a gold coin, requesting that he wished to make a small donation to Bhuttu for the kindness the priests had shown.

The servant boy tucked the coin in his robe, assuring Timon it would be given to the priest in charge of donations. Timon was sure the coin would find its way to the temple's coffers. The priests of Bhuttu had a reputation for scrupulously honoring their word.

Timon washed his face, hands, and feet. Taking off his clothes, he shook them over the balcony rail to remove the city's dust. Lounging in his loincloth, he ate while watching KiKu struggle to give their young ruffian a bath.

Exasperated, KiKu scraped off much of the city grime with the oils and a bathing pumice. He then examined the boy while drying him. "He seems healthy enough," huffed KiKu, pulling a clean tunic over the boy's head. "No deformities I can see. His teeth are quite good. Still, Madric and Pearl should take a look and examine him for parasites."

"There is nothing wrong with me, Master," pouted the boy. "I'm strong. I will not be a burden. You will see."

"What I see is a very weedy boy whose knees are knobby from the want of good food and whose hair is full of bugs," replied Timon casually.

"Not anymore," boasted KiKu, showing Timon a basin filled with dirty water, which was lined with dead lice and grime.

"Loathsome," replied Timon, motioning for KiKu to remove the basin. He had picked up the Hasan Daegian dislike of anything crawling on the skin. KiKu threw the water over the balcony.

The boy looked disapprovingly at Timon, but remained quiet. He realized he had to stay in Timon's good graces. He tried pulling on his slippers, but couldn't quite get the hang of it since he had never worn a pair of shoes.

KiKu picked up a sharp knife used to cut the fruit and grabbed one of the boy's feet. With the expertise of a skilled surgeon, KiKu began carving away the boy's long and unsightly toe nails while dodging kicks from the other foot. "Be still!" commanded KiKu. "You want to put your new shoes on, don't you!"

Wiping a few tears from his eyes, the boy nodded and remained still for the remainder of the nail carving.

"What's your name, boy?" Timon asked.

"I dunno," replied the boy, not taking his eyes off KiKu wielding the knife.

KiKu shot a small glance at Timon.

"What would you like to be called?" asked Timon, feeling sorry for the boy.

The boy's face lit up. "Something that sounds important."

Timon smiled. "How about Akela?"

KiKu stopped his grooming in surprise.

Akela was Timon's older brother. He had been killed during the siege of Anqara.

KiKu threw the boy's slippers at him. "Our Master has done you a great honor by giving you the name of Akela. Make sure you do not disgrace it."

Akela looked at the grave face of KiKu. "I promise," he replied with much sincerity. "This has been the most wonderful day of my life. On this day, I have a new tunic. I have shoes for the first time in my life. Now I have a name. I belong somewhere." He hugged KiKu's hand.

KiKu jerked his hand away. "You will probably be an ingrate who will show the hangman how to slip the noose over our heads."

Akela shook his head. "I know what this name means. It means honor of the house. It is given to the eldest son in a family," he boasted with pride.

Timon did not see the light in the boy's eyes, as he had turned toward the wall, silently grieving for the loss of his beloved brother.

20

Dorak watched the new arrivals.

Iegani, the Great Divigi of the Dinii, accompanied him.

In the corner of the room sat Timon, KiKu, and a small boy. Recognizing KiKu through his disguise, Dorak seemed puzzled about the other two Bhuttanians.

"Who is the young man?" asked Iegani.

"I haven't seen him since he was a mere lad, but I am positive he is Prince Bes Amon Ptah. I don't know who the little boy is."

"Why would this prince be with KiKu?"

"I don't know. His family is from a powerful tribe living on the Plain of Moab. They have been strongly influenced by the Anqarian culture for centuries until they are not considered true Bhuttanians any longer. His people are monotheistic. They do not worship Bhuttu or any of the lesser gods, so I would say that his presence here is a ruse."

"Undoubtedly," said Iegani, studying KiKu. "That is one of the best disguises I have ever seen him assume."

Dorak grunted. He respected KiKu for his adaptability and skill, but hated him for his betrayal of Zoar and himself by becoming a double spy for Queen Abisola, Maura's mother.

Sensing Dorak's hostility, Iegani said, "Put away your anger, son. We do not have the luxury of it in this place. If KiKu can help us get out of here, then let us not impede his efforts."

Ignoring Iegani, Dorak spread his arms out and closed his eyes. "I feel power."

Iegani shook his wings. "That's because KiKu has Zedek's amulet hidden between his butt cheeks. I can see it in his mind. I wonder why the priests don't realize the amulet is here?"

Dorak's eyes popped open. "We must not let Zedek get close to him!"

"Zedek cannot influence him any more than we can. KiKu is very safe from that old buzzard." Iegani made a few clicks in Dini language and then reverted to Hasan Daegian, which Dorak spoke fluently. "It is the physical world that must be manipulated, and only KiKu and these two boys may do that. Let us hope the gods are with them."

"You don't believe in the gods, Iegani."

"I have been proven wrong about many things in my lifetime. Perhaps I am wrong about the existence of a god."

"May any god take pity on us."

Iegani shrugged. "Or, at least, may She not take pity on Zedek."

21

Timon began his training.

After several days of fasting and passing several oral examinations on religion, Timon was allowed to don the orange robes of a novice. His head was shaved, as was his entire body. He was given a small cell on the bottom floor of a dormitory where older initiates stayed. Timon coped as best he could with the flies and gnats that infested his thin bedding.

Akela and KiKu worked in the kitchen where they proved to be inept and were then made to scrub floors. This is exactly what KiKu wanted as he could closely inspect the hallways for hidden chambers and passages without drawing attention to his crawling around on his knees and tapping the walls. So far he had found three passages, although he had not had the chance to search them.

When opportunity presented itself, he taught Akela some of the techniques of discovering a secret panel or hallway.

Since Akela had the soul of a scoundrel, he picked up information quickly, which pleased KiKu to no end. KiKu thought that if the boy did not betray them or die during the escapade, he might adopt the little urchin since he had no son of his own. His only daughter was grown, and he had not seen her for many years. And so the master spy and the street orphan worked side by side, washing away the dust from polished corridors as they waited for something to happen.

Timon would pass the two, almost envious of their labor, as he was bored to death with the life of a novice. Hour after hour, he studied the religious dogma and traditions of Bhuttu and Bhutta, while forcing his body to obey the rigorous demands of ascetic life. Always, he had been celibate, quiet, and astute. Being a political hostage in the court of Zoar had taught Timon to be unobtrusive and invisible. Timon took pains not to draw attention to himself. He did what he was told and blended in with the other votaries as much as possible.

But life was difficult. Votaries were given only four hours to sleep each night, and their food was mainly fried bread and overcooked legumes. At the end of the day, he was hungry. Timon felt his mind start to go numb from the daily grind, dull food, and deprivation of sleep. Weakened and finding it more difficult to keep his mind on his real objective, Timon wondered if the food was salted with drugs that stupefied his thinking. His already lean body was growing thinner.

Passing KiKu in the hallway one afternoon, Timon sneezed with the dust KiKu and other workers were stirring up. A sneeze was the signal KiKu and Timon had agreed upon if one needed the other.

Reprimanded for making noise, Timon was sent to his cell early that evening without dinner to contemplate on making his body a servant of his mind, not the other way around. Timon weakly crawled onto his pallet and waited for KiKu.

Timon must have fallen asleep for he was awakened by a hand clasped over his mouth. Startled, the votary blinked involuntarily in the darkness as his body tensed, ready to fight. Slowly, the hand loosened until it pulled away.

In the gleam of a single shaft of moonlight illuminating the cell, Timon caught a quick glimpse of KiKu's face. Into Timon's hand was thrust a pouch, and then KiKu was gone.

Timon tucked the pouch between his legs where it was hidden by his manhood, and he bound his loincloth tighter. Its mystery would have to wait until morning when he could see plainly.

Comforted by KiKu's visit, Timon fell to sleep and dreamed he was in Maura's tent sitting on the dais with the empress feeding him from her table of plenty. She even took her napkin and dabbed crumbs from the corners of Timon's mouth. If one chanced upon Timon at that moment, he would have seen a young man curled under a thin coverlet, smiling in his sleep.

22

A sliver of light entered the cell.

It landed on Timon's eyelids. The novice fluttered open his eyes and immediately rooted for his pouch. He had only a few moments. Turning over on his stomach and away from any possible prying eyes, he lifted the pouch to his face and opened the thongs, moving as little as possible. With deft fingers, he pulled out a folded piece of fabric and gingerly undid it.

Written in blood, it read.

DANGER! FOOD POISONED! TAKE MEDICINE.

Timon turned over the material.

Nothing was written on the back.

Disappointed, Timon cursed, "May his wives have evil odors between their legs." Then Timon thought better of his outburst for he respected KiKu's wives. He wished no harm to them. "May his pecker never straighten to the sun."

Feeling better, he muttered, "No instructions on how to take the antidote or even what it is." Timon gently poured the contents of the pouch into his hand. Out rolled the amulet and several small beeswax pellets wrapped in leaves. He put the powerful amulet aside. He was more interested in something to put in his empty stomach. Timon picked up one of the pellets and smelled it. Unwrapping one, he discovered gray dust. He smelled it again. "Here goes nothing," said Timon as he popped one into his mouth. He collected his saliva and swallowed it. It tasted like mud. Disillusioned, he placed the amulet and the pellets back into the pouch and returned it between his legs.

He hoped his superiors would not search him or the other novices for contraband as they sometimes did. Scrunching up the cloth, he put it in his mouth, and after chewing it, he swallowed it whole as well. The thought that he was putting someone else's blood in his body did not disturb him in the least. Its iron could only help him in his present predicament.

The temple gong sounded, and a whisper of collective moans could be heard from the other cells down the corridor. Each novice staggered out of his small cell and trudged down the hallway with his robe slung over his shoulder. Coming to a larger annex, each man relieved himself in buckets left by the wall and then shuffled over to a long water trough where they shaved their faces and heads.

Drying himself off with his clothes, Timon hurried to the temple where morning devotions were already underway.

Scurrying through the door meant for new votaries, Timon took his place at the back of the temple. Bowing his head and kneeling, he began reciting the liturgy required for morning prayers while sneaking glances here and there. He needed to spend hours in the main temple to study it and perhaps open contact with the lost Dinii. But in his heart, he thought it useless.

For the three weeks he had been training, no one had mentioned any unusual events in the temple complex. No disembodied voices, no ghostly pleas from forgotten overlords of the planet—nothing.

There was neither gossip nor any sightings because this was a wild gootee chase. Resentful that he was being drugged and half-starved, Timon realized he was thinking more clearly. His keen mind was actually working again. Timon attributed it to KiKu's homemade pills.

Timon studied the other devotees milling around him, unfolding their prayer rugs and laying them neatly out on the marble floor. They were also thin like him, and their eyes had the glazed look of a stunned boaep caught in a lamplight. Timon concluded everyone was being drugged. Timon grunted. This was the time in a novice's life when he ceded his property to the temple. It was obvious the priests deliberately clouded their minds, so the novices would not have second thoughts about signing their wealth over. When the novice awoke from his drugged state, it would be too late. His property would be under the control of the temple, and his relations with the outside world severed. One either complied or committed suicide.

Timon admired their cold and calculating system. Because he had worked as a scribe dealing with property deeds, reports, and accounting records, Timon began to concede that his trip inside the bowels of Bhuttu might not be wasted. If he could locate their records, he could report to the empress the sites of Bhuttu's most important properties where strongholds of rebels could be in hiding. This was something he could use to bargain for his people's lives. Timon's heart leapt. He had hope again.

Hilkiah emerged from the shadows and ascended the altar. He was wearing his priestly robes of black with his elaborate horned headdress with gold feathers. Another priest wearing a saffron-colored robe walked about the kneeling priests and novices, swinging burning incense, which created a great deal of smoke.

All kneeled on their rugs and smudged themselves with the holy incense as the priest moved past them.

"Peace be with thee, brothers," Hilkiah said.

"Our peace will be found in death," answered the congregation.

"May Bhuttu accept thy final sacrifice."

"May He be kind to thee as well," rejoined the crowd.

Timon felt a tickle on the back of his neck. He ignored it.

After a few minutes of Hilkiah droning on about a priest's responsibilities, Timon felt a tickle again. He twitched his neck a little, hoping to discourage flies. Then Timon felt it again. He was sure he felt the unmistakable breath from another being upon his neck.

Timon searched to the left and right of him. No one was observing at him. Timon reached out slowly behind him, but felt no one crouching behind.

Perhaps KiKu's pellets were inducing hallucinations.

Curse that KiKu! Timon's anger welled up. He decided not to pay any attention to whatever was happening. He did not want to be punished for any indiscretion before he was ready to search for the records hall.

Then something Hilkiah said caught Timon's ear.

"Though only days from our city gates, we, as Bhuttu's servants, must remain calm and meet the nonbelievers with courage and steadfast loyalty to our traditions."

The blood in Timon's veins pulsed faster.

"We will remain in the confines of the temple walls, showing partisanship for neither side. Politics are not our concern except that our faith remain untainted by new ideas and our ways of worship go undisturbed." Hilkiah turned toward the statue of Bhuttu and bowed his head while the acolyte swung his canister of incense around the altar, creating a dreamy effect.

Timon was stunned. He thought he would have more time. Damn that food. It had kept him in a daze, not allowing Timon to work to his full potential. Now Maura was within days of the city, and he was without any proof of the existence of the Dinii or any plan of action! His body felt chilled. He had failed, and his people would be slaughtered!

The former scribe-turned-spy closed his eyes and began formulating plans to outmaneuver the empress. Running away would do no good. She would just take her anger out on his people. His tribe could escape to a new land! No—his people would stand to meet their enemy only to have Maura mow them down like a herd of wild borax browsing on summer grass. Even if he could convince his people to flee, the empress would find them and carry out her threat of annihilation.

Timon had only two options. He must find the Dinii or change Maura's mind if he failed. The problem with the first solution was that he did not believe the Dinii were contained within the walls of the massive temple complex. Maura was simply under a delusion produced by her grief over the loss of her husband.

Without warning, a priest, praying near the base of Bhuttu's statue, let out a blood-curdling scream and threw himself down the altar steps.

Hilkiah sharply turned around. His pink eyes threw off dangerous sparks as he wrapped himself in a protective cloak of angry, red energy.

Timon's lips parted and formed a partial snarl at seeing the protective orb. His people had a deep loathing of magic. Until now, the veneration of Bhuttu had been non-magical and harmless, even with its showmanship and trickery, which could be easily duplicated by any con-man employing his trades in the street. But the swirling cloud about Hilkiah could not be anything but true magic. The sight of it made Timon break into a cold sweat. The use of sorcery was unnatural to him.

The priest, prone on the steps, began babbling.

Its effect on Hilkiah was interesting to Timon. The red cloud surrounding Hilkiah dimmed momentarily before the priest twirled off the altar and into one of the side chambers.

The older priests tried to comfort the frightened priest, who was now gesturing in the air. Many of the novices huddled together in fearful little groups, whispering among themselves.

Timon would not be surprised if some of his brethren would flee into the night if given a chance. The babbling priest was creating a great deal of commotion, and others seemed cowed.

Seeing that no one was paying any particular attention to him, Timon slipped over to the side of the hall and scurried behind tall columns, which supported the stone roof until he was near the massive altar. Peering from behind an ancient tapestry, which divided the altar and the nave, Timon got a good view of the jabbering priest who was still pointing to the ceiling. He looked up to where the priest was pointing and gasped, seeing a disembodied face of a man hovering above him.

Distorted and foggy, it peered downward from the ceiling, and although it seemed to be mouthing words very slowly, nothing could be heard. Pale as Hilkiah, the face's whiteness had an unhealthy likeness to faded parchment, not like skin at all.

The vision grew fainter and fainter.

Everyone gathered in a confused throng at the altar, staring up at the ceiling.

Timon took this opportunity to step out from behind his hiding place and mingle with the rest of the crowd. He pushed through until he reached the rug of the priest, who had first sighted the vision. Hunching down, he pushed feet out of the way and pounded his fist on bare toes to get people to step off the rug. Using his fingertips, he felt the fabric. Nothing unusual there. Next, he lifted up the corner of the rug trying to balance himself against the jostling of the crowd. Knowing he had only a short time before the priests collected themselves and took control again, Timon frantically searched for anything that could explain the vision. Then his hand felt something soft. Pulling it out, Timon tucked it into his robe.

The older priests gathered into a tight little knot and hurled balls of blue energy at the distorted face, which was now barely visible. The blue orbs exploded with a loud blast into the face of the vision. The vision's eyes blinked several times as though surprised, and—then poof—like a puff of smoke from a fire-eater's mouth in the village square, the vision was gone.

Timon rubbed his face and stared at the ceiling, straining his eyes. The vision had indeed disappeared, and nothing remained of it.

The older priests returned their attention to the congregation. They gave the signal to disburse.

Timon had no choice but to leave the sanctuary, but he did not return to his dull little cell. He went to find KiKu. He did not have long before a strong hand reached out from behind a tapestry and pulled him down a secret passage. Timon did not cry out, as he was used to KiKu pulling him into mildewed dark rooms, cold pantries, and stale passageways to talk with him. He thought KiKu gained a perverse pleasure from stealing him out from under the very noses of the watchful priesthood. He merely acquiesced and waited for KiKu's chuckles to die.

Timon usually would not give KiKu the satisfaction of knowing that every time he pulled this stunt, Timon's heart fell to his knees, but Timon was really irritated this time.

"I suppose you know about the vision in the sanctuary." He was tired and wondered if KiKu's medicine was going to sicken him with a side effect.

KiKu's breath was short for he had run very fast. "As soon as I heard the commotion, I came and hid in the sanctuary. There is a spy hole in one of the walls. I saw the last part of the vision."

Timon wiped a spider's web from his ear. "Well?"

"We might not have confirmed the presence of the Dinii, but we have evidence of Zedek."

"Who?"

"The Black Cacodemon, my boy! That was his face you saw. He lives! The empress will not be pleased about this."

Both KiKu and Timon were quiet. KiKu was the first to break the stupor of their private thoughts. "I saw you investigating a rug."

"Oh yes," replied Timon, excitedly. He reached into his robe and searched among the folds. "I found something underneath it."

"What is it?"

"I can't seem to find it," said Timon as he patted himself down. "I must have dropped it in the hallway."

KiKu fell to his knees, searching the floor.

"Wait a minute. Here it is." Timon pulled out a long white feather that had been dyed purple at the very end and sparkled from diamond dust.

KiKu gasped. "By the gods! It is Empress Gitar's." He grabbed the distinctive feather from Timon's hand and smelled it. "It is the genuine article. Smell it," said KiKu, excitedly holding the feather to Timon's face.

Timon wrinkled his nose. "It smells like a marsh."

"Exactly," said KiKu, dancing a little jig. "We have found the Dinii. We have found the Dinii!!!"

"Then we can get out of this hellhole?"

KiKu retorted, "Not exactly. This is but half of our quest. We must now free them, and let us not forget that the Black Cacodemon is with them, wherever they are. If we free them, we might also have to let loose that demon."

"I don't like the sound of that," replied Timon worried. "That's not a good idea. If we let him loose, might Jezra get her hands on him and use him against the Great Mother?"

"We have to take that chance." KiKu was quiet for a moment. "I will send the boy with this feather to my wives. He can slip out of here easily. We have already discovered several tunnels, which lead out of the temple complex. Meanwhile, you and I can work on the means of setting the Dinii free."

Timon shivered. "I do not see how you stand this worrisome intrigue every day. It leaves me cold."

KiKu grinned, but his smile displayed sad overtones. "It's a living."

23

Akela took the torch.

He pressed his thin body through the mouth of the tunnel. Akela had been entrusted with a pouch, and he kept touching it to make sure it still hung by his side, even though KiKu had tied very secure knots to his clothing. One would have to strip the boy naked to snatch the cheap cloth pouch that was an everyday lunch sack. Of course, it was only a decoy. The real feather was tucked in his undergarment, but if anyone bothered to check there, Akela would have more to worry about than just a theft.

Akela made his way along the dirty corridor, occasionally stopping to listen for noise. He passed several doorways while hunting for any telltale signs of recent use. He did not know how he would be able to explain his using the corridor if chanced upon by a priest.

Although his child's mind was surprisingly sophisticated, it was still that of a child's. Akela had to blink away the tears falling from his long eyelashes. He could not remember his mother, but he understood the concept of succor, and to him, that now meant KiKu's wives. He was going to get to them as fast as his little legs would take him. And that was fast by anyone's standards.

He came to a stairwell and paused, listening for anyone coming. Hearing nothing but the sound of his heart beating, he descended, taking care to avoid the crumbling parts of the steps. Reaching the underground floor, he followed the corridor under the bowels of the temple, his feet slapping noisily in the water that bathed the floor. Here the walls were slimy and the air foul smelling. He slipped twice on the grimy mud that had built up century after century upon the stone floor. Akela's feet sank at least an inch into the smelly muck and made a sucking noise as he yanked his foot out of its terrible pull.

Thankfully, the frail boy finally came to some stairs, which took him up another level, but not entirely out of the belly of the temple complex. He had studied with KiKu time and time again the layout of the underground tunnels KiKu had mapped out so far. Akela kept repeating his instructions under his breath until finally he came to a wooden door. Fishing in his pocket, he pulled out a pick KiKu had fashioned for him. With the skill of a professional locksmith, Akela manipulated the lock until he heard a click. He pushed his weight against the door, and to his relief, it creaked open.

Akela quickly found his way through the maze of corridors and out onto the streets of Bhuttani. With the speed of a small bird, he ran through the crooked streets until he came to the inn housing KiKu's wives. He tossed small pebbles at shutters, hoping the women had not moved since he was last with them when he had delivered food with Lord Timon.

Pearl opened the shutters and peered out.

Recognizing her, Akela waved.

Appearing not to notice the small boy, Pearl closed the shutters.

Akela climbed the limbs of an old battered mingo tree and rested in a crook of a limb until the doorkeeper of the inn opened the courtyard door. He shuffled out into the street, dodging carts delivering wine and bread for the morning meals. He grabbed Akela's dangling foot and shook it. Startled, Akela almost fell, but steadied himself. "The lady told me to gather you and feed you breakfast," mumbled the doorkeeper.

The boy eagerly jumped down and ran through the doorway.

Tippu was waiting for him in the main hall with food.

Akela raced to her table and began grabbing gruel with his grimy hands, stuffing it into his mouth.

Tippu watched Akela gobble his gruel while getting a good deal on his face. She noticed that his body looked as frail as ever. "Don't they feed you in the temple?"

"Very little," mumbled Akela, before he shoved more food into his mouth.

Tippu left the table and returned with a bowl full of shaybar, the traditional Bhuttanian drink of boiled milk with borax blood. "Here," she prodded, "this will make little skinny boys fat."

Akela did not need to be coaxed twice. Shaybar was a delicacy that he rarely had in his short life. He gulped down the red shaybar, wiping his mouth with the end of his tunic, and then went promptly back to his gruel, smacking his lips with obvious contentment.

Tippu waited patiently until Akela finished and let out a loud belch. He belched a second time because he liked the sound.

By this time, Tippu's patience had worn thin. "What news from our master?"

Akela blushed and blurted out, "I need to make water."

Tippu sighed and waved her hand toward the outhouse. "Go and be quick about it."

The little boy dashed off and extracted his package. He stayed long enough to urinate and then rushed back to Tippu. The young woman, squeamish at the thought of touching the damp cloth, had Akela drop it into her shawl and hurried upstairs to the other wives.

Akela followed closely behind.

Pearl, Madric, and Tippa exclaimed when they saw both the package and Akela.

Pearl took the package and placed it on a table while Madric handed her a sharp knife. She carefully cut the string and unfolded the cloth with the tip of the knife blade.

"Do you know what it is, Akela?" asked Madric, holding her breath.

Akela shrugged his shoulders. "Just some stupid feather."

"A FEATHER!!!" exclaimed the women in union.

Akela's dark eyes widened at their excitement. He nodded.

Pearl hurried until the package was open and gingerly pulled out a large white feather with a tip that was partially died purple. "The Dinii," she whispered.

Madric touched the feather. "It is Empress Gitar!"

Tippa and Tippu gathered Pearl's cloak and boots, while Pearl retied the feather.

Madric produced a small pair of boots for Akela.

He looked at them questioningly.

"Put them on," Tippa requested. "You are going to join Pearl and me."

"Where are we going?" questioned Akela, as he sat on the bed, taking off his worn slippers.

"To see a woman about a large bird," Tippa replied. "Now, hush. We must hurry."

Fear crept into Akela's eyes. "We must be traveling outside the city if you are putting on boots," he said to Tippa. He stared at his feet and suddenly stood up realizing the women's true intention. "I won't go with you!" he exclaimed. "She eats children. I've heard about her. She is a demon. I hear women at the well talking."

"Hush. People will hear you." Tippa boxed Akela's ears and instantly regretted it. She knelt down and clasped a stunned Akela to her small breasts. "I'm sorry, but many people's lives depend on us getting this information to the empress. It is not true what the well women say about her. They are Bhuttanian and fear her because she is Hasan Daegian. I swear to you on my life she will not harm you, but I need—we need you to come with Pearl and me to give witness to what you have learned. Please trust me. You will be safe. Please." She kissed his forehead. "Please."

Shamed, Akela bowed. "My mother is only a little memory. I do not know where she is. I will travel with you, because I do not want to go back to the streets, and I have nowhere else to go."

Pearl, touched by the little boy's speech, placed her rough hand on Akela's shoulder. "You will always have a home with us, Akela."

Akela shook his head. "Master KiKu may not want me."

Madric let out a brittle laugh. "Hittal women decide the children in the family. If we want you, there is nothing he can say. Come now. Dry your tears. Pearl and Tippa must go."

Akela started to blow his nose on his tunic hem until Tippu handed him a clean rag.

All four women kissed him and helped Akela put on his little boots with their breasts grazing his legs and arms. He enjoyed being enveloped in their clean, sweet smell. They gave him new clothes and placed a red wig on his head.

Minutes later, Pearl and Tippa carried their food baskets as though they were trekking to the market for the day's food with their travel bundles secured under their skirts. Pearl had the precious feather under her shirt tucked in her waistband.

Akela acted as their servant.

They gamely marched down the streets to the market while holding their headscarves over their noses to keep out the dust.

Stepping through the doorway of an abandoned house, they quickly shut the door. From large baskets they had placed there previously, they threw off their cloaks and put on the white gowns with the colorful belts belonging to the Siva men. Tippa helped Pearl tie down her breasts and then drape the elaborate headdress around her head. When finished, Pearl looked like any Siva man, which was to say a white enigma. Pearl then helped Tippa.

"What about me?" asked Akela, admiring the beautiful girdles. His face fell when he saw Pearl pull out an ugly black tunic with a rip up the side.

"Sivans don't let their male children out of Siva until they are at least sixteen," Pearl replied. "You will have to travel as a servant's child we are escorting to Hittal."

Disappointed, Akela threw the black tunic over his new clothes but kept his boots on. Before he knew it, he was trotting after two "Sivan men" who walked with quiet purpose.

24

The three joined a Sivan caravan.

It passed through the gates after being inspected by the guards.

Akela was surprised the Sivan men said nothing to the Bhuttanian guards after they discovered three stowaways in their midst. It was only after they were out of sight of Bhuttani that the caravan stopped, and the Sivan leader approached Pearl, Tippa, and Akela.

Both women knelt in supplication. Pearl extended her arm, pulling back the white robe.

All Akela could make out was a henna tattoo, which most Siva men drew on their arms for adornment.

The leader inspected Pearl's henna design without comment. He looked at her and then at Tippa. Finally at Akela. Without warning he grabbed Akela and placed him on the back of a borax cow. Saying nothing to anyone, he strode to the front of the caravan and gave the signal to continue.

For two days, they traveled until they came to a small stream. The leader of the caravan approached Pearl and whispered in her ear.

She nodded and gathered food from the cook's wagon before striking out in an easterly direction.

Tippa and Akela reluctantly followed her into the wilderness, sad to give up the protection of the Sivan caravan.

They walked for several hours under the hot sun until Tippa had to give Akela a ride on her shoulders. They continued, even though they tripped over rocks, bruising their feet. The trio trekked across the edge of the Plain of Moab and could see to the west of them for several miles.

There was nothing, not even a tree, except for scattered clumps of wild yellow grass.

Examining her surroundings, Tippa despaired. She wondered if Pearl was lost. After hours of carrying Akela, Tippa's shoulders ached. She called to Pearl. "I must set the boy down and rest."

Pearl helped the younger woman lower the boy onto the hard-packed terrain. She looked for grass to place on Akela's face to shield him from the blazing sun. Seeing a tall clump of bazera grass, she went over to it and began pulling its long stocks until a hand reached out from beneath the grass and clasped her wrist. Startled, Pearl screamed and tried to pull away.

Akela awoke with a jerk and followed Tippa, who was running toward Pearl. They both stopped short upon seeing a Hasan Daegian woman, camouflaged in bazera grass, step out in front of them.

Still holding Pearl in a tight grip, the scout put two fingers in her mouth and made a bird call. Turning her attention to Pearl, she whispered in Anqarian, "Be quiet," and let go of her wrist.

Minutes later, several Hasan Daegian ponies carrying warriors emerged from the plains. They had been hiding behind a small rolling hill blending into the landscape.

The scout jumped on her horse. She gathered Pearl about the waist and hoisted the woman behind her.

The others followed suit with Akela and Tippa.

Never having seen a Hasan Daegian woman before, Akela was dumbstruck. He had never seen women so big and strong, being used to the smaller Bhuttanian and Hittal women. He pinched the woman in front of him to make sure all that flesh was hers. The warrior turned around in her saddle, giving Akela a fierce look.

The boy lowered his eyes and held tightly onto the scout's belt, as he had never been on a horse before. He watched the tiny hooves of the pony race over the dry, windy plain and felt as though he must be flying. He felt strangely happy and simultaneously terrified at the same time.

They rode for almost an hour until they were beyond the foothills abutting the end of the Plain of Moab.

Akela gauged they were riding northeast.

Without warning, the ponies stopped near a crop of trees. The scouts brusquely told Pearl to dismount, which she obeyed without question. From the midst of the trees, other Hasan Daegian women stole forth, leading out Bhuttanian warhorses.

Akela shrank back against Tippa. He was familiar with the sight of the monstrous horses, but the thought of mounting one chilled him to his dusty boots.

The warriors gestured for Pearl and her companions to mount behind them.

Servants carried wooden steps to one of the prancing horses.

Pearl, without comment, strode up the steps and attempted to raise her leg over the saddle.

The horse was still too high for the middle-aged woman to pull her weight up so several of the soldiers pushed on her backside and lifted her upon the animal. Following Pearl's example, Tippa and Akela gamely walked up the steps and were more successful in mounting the giant horses.

Before they could catch their breath, the steps were taken away, and the soldiers kicked the horses with their heels. The horses reared their front hooves in one mighty salute before trampling the ground before them.

Pearl, Tippa, and Akela fearfully held on, sensing the soldiers did not have total control over the galloping animals.

Tippa pulled her headdress over her nose, protecting her face from clods of dirt thrown up by the pounding hooves. Doing so made her momentarily lose her balance, only to have the Hasan Daegian warrior reach back and pull a dangling Tippa up by the collar of her white kiva.

The Hasan Daegians drove the warhorses hard until Pearl's legs went numb from gripping her horse and Akela's mouth ached from the constant jarring of his teeth.

Without warning, the warhorses slowed to a bouncing trot. This caused the Hittal women and the Bhuttanian boy more discomfort, but it awakened their stuporous minds. They looked about them and saw they were heading toward a small rise.

Pearl strained her eyes. Upon the hill, she saw someone waiting for them and sighed with relief. The horses lurched up the hill and stopped.

A small contingent of Hasan Daegian women dressed in hunting apparel, with pheasants hanging from their belts, grabbed hold of the bridles of the head-tossing, snorting horses.

The mounted Hasan Daegians jumped off and helped their passengers down.

Pearl and Tippa felt their legs quiver while Akela just plopped on the ground. Each was given a waterbag filled with cool, clean water. All three of the adventurers drank with relish and poured water over their dusty faces.

A redheaded Hasan Daegian with thick braids waited patiently until the party quenched their thirst before approaching the group. She spoke in Anqarian. "Have you business with the Hasan Daegians?"

Pearl pulled back the sleeve of her kiva and held out her arm.

The Hasan Daegian saw the secret mark of a spy. She nodded. "Wait here," she ordered before rushing off to a small grove on the other side of the hill.

Hasan Daegian warriors in full military dress stepped out of the copse and searched the trio. Pearl and Tippa did not resist, but held their arms up obligingly.

Akela squirmed and called the women several filthy names he had learned in the bazaar, causing the combat-hardened women to blush. They looked at the boy curiously and muttered about his bad upbringing.

A Hasan Daegian lad appeared. He put his fingers to his lips and motioned to them.

They followed him into the thick of the grove.

Pearl did not see anyone, but felt many eyes upon her and her party. She dare not make a false move, fearing twenty arrows might fly toward her chest. Pearl hoped Akela did not try the Hasan Daegians' patience. She knew the Hasan Daegians loved children but would not hesitate to run a sword through the boy's side if he was perceived a threat.

The Hasan Daegians were no longer idealists. They had been hardened by years of war.

The lad stopped and turned to Pearl. "Enter the veil. It will not hurt you."

Pearl was confused. She saw nothing but endless trees. "Forward?" she asked.

The lad nodded.

Summoning up her courage, Pearl strode forward, only to pass through something that felt vaguely wet and silky. The sensation startled her, and she stopped only to have Tippa bump into her. "Goodness!" blurted Pearl, stumbling.

Strong hands reached up and helped stabilize Pearl.

"Thank you," said Pearl, catching a glimpse at the helper's hands. She gasped. The hands were blue. "Goodness, goodness," she gushed. She immediately knelt as did Tippa.

"Forgive me, Great Mother," Pearl said kowtowing.

"Pearl, isn't it?"

"Yes, Great Mother," Pearl replied.

"And you are Lady Tippu."

"Tippa, Great Mother."

They could hear Akela yell, "I'm not going in there. My mothers disappeared. YOU CAN'T MAKE ME!!!" An exasperated Hasan Daegian soldier tried to calm Akela.

"It seems your companion is reluctant," commented Maura.

"Yes, Great Mother," replied both women with their foreheads still touching the ground. They heard Maura move closer to the veil and reach beyond it. There was a rush of air followed by a loud thump. Out of the corner of her eye, Pearl saw an astonished Akela pick himself off the ground and charge the woman in front of him dressed as a hunter. He did not seem to notice or was too frightened to care that the woman's skin was blue.

Pearl closed her eyes, expecting the worst. She saw the woman reach out and pull Akela up into the air by his loose clothing. He tried to kick her, but couldn't reach with his feet.

A soldier rushed in and grabbed the little boy into a headlock.

Akela could not move. His feet dangled uselessly.

Maura cautioned, "Little boy, I do not know who you are, but if you don't show some manners, the good woman who is holding you will take you away and give you a thrashing you will never forget. She has three children of her own and knows what to do with little boys who irritate their queen and empress." Seeing she had Akela's attention, Maura pressed forward. "If you give me your word as a gentleman and promise to do everything Lady Pearl tells you, my guard will put you down. Blink if you agree."

As his throat was held in the iron grip of his captor, Akela had no choice but to blink.

Maura commanded, "Let him go."

The guard gently put Akela down and stifled a laugh as she saw the boy insinuate himself between the kowtowing Pearl and Tippa.

"You stupid boy," Pearl hissed. "Don't you see who this is? Keep still if you value our lives."

Akela shrugged his bony shoulders while lowering his head like his two companions.

"Tell me your news," ordered Maura harshly. Inside her chest, Maura's heart was pounding. She prayed she would not be disappointed with this Hittal woman.

"Great Mother," said Pearl. "I have something I think will interest you."

Maura barked impatiently, "Show me quick then."

Pearl quickly pulled on a string from around her waist, exposing a pouch. She handed it over.

Maura carefully took the pouch and turned away from the spies and her guards. She opened it up and peered inside. Gingerly, her calloused fingers reached into the darkness of the pouch and took hold of a stem. She slowly pulled out the object and stared at it for a moment. She held the feather aloft and observed its sparkling reflection in the sun's rays. "Great Goddess, it is the feather of a Dini! A royal Dini!"

Maura turned toward Pearl, extending the feather before her. "It is from Gitar!"

Pearl breathed with relief, peeking at Tippa.

A broad smile covered Tippa's face.

The empress had identified that the feather was from Gitar, Empress of the Dinii and Overlord of Kaseri.

They were on the road to being saved from Maura's edict and might yet cheat death.

Maura was drunk with joy. "Tell me! Tell me quick! How did you come to find this?"

"Our young friend can tell you better than I," replied Pearl, nudging Akela.

Akela looked up at the beaming empress and ventured a smile.

"Who are you, young squire?"

"My name is Akela, and I am from the household of Timon de Berechial from Qued Zum. I am his manservant," he boasted proudly.

"Really," replied Maura, observing the little boy kneeling before her. "Well, Timon is my servant, so that makes you my servant as well."

Akela's smile disappeared. He did not like that idea at all.

"I can see it gives you pause." She bent over into the little boy's face. "I give Timon and KiKu pause, so your response better be good. Now tell me the truth, boy. How did you get ahold of this feather?"

Akela pulled away from Maura's feral eyes. He did not like this woman towering over him. "Master Timon found it under a priest's prayer mat in the temple of Bhuttu."

"When?"

"Four days ago. KiKu gave it to me and told me to escape through the tunnels underneath the temple grounds. From there I was to find his wives. They have brought me here. That is all I know. Honest."

"Did KiKu have a message for me?"

"He said something strange about a bluebird needing to protect its own." He shook his head. "I don't remember all of it."

"A bluebird that sings all day and does not stay in the nest will die with the rest."

"Yes, that is it." Akela looked happily up at the woman, but she was not smiling.

"Tippa, take your young friend and pass back through the veil. Have the guards give you something to eat."

"Yes, Great Mother." Tippa paused for a moment.

As if reading her thoughts, Maura said, "Pearl will follow later."

Tippa's face relaxed, and she rose, gathering Akela by the hand. They passed through the veil, hesitating only for a moment.

Pearl could see them, but they were muted and indistinct.

"Please speak, wife of KiKu. I haven't much time."

Pearl glanced uneasily at the veil.

"They cannot hear nor see us," offered Maura. "No one can."

Pearl opened her mouth only to shut it quickly again.

Maura took note of her confusion and let out a low chuckle. "I know what you must be thinking. We Hasan Daegians do not practice magic, so how did we get a security veil? You must be tired. Rise and sit."

Pearl hesitated.

"Please, Lady Pearl. We are old friends, are we not? Let's dispense with the formalities."

Maura handed Pearl a wine goblet after helping her onto a stool. Pearl was glad to get off her knees and drank heartily. The wine contained a stimulant, which started to work immediately. She looked questioningly at Maura. It was very similar to one she had given Timon.

"Mingo bark mixed with pemh grass. No side effects," comforted Maura, trying to reign in her impatience. After all, Pearl had traveled a great distance and had put her life at risk to carry a message to her.

Pearl closed her eyelids and enjoyed the delicious effect of renewed energy and well-being. Suddenly, she jerked forward. "OH, THE MESSAGE!" she blurted. "Please forgive me, Great Mother." She leaned toward Maura's ear. "The Dini feather was found in Bhuttu's temple as Akela told you. It was discovered under the mat of a priest by Timon, during worship where the wizard Zedek appeared before the congregation. He was trying to speak, but no one could hear his message. At least, that is what everyone claimed. KiKu believes the Dinii are held captive with Zedek and possibly Dorak as well."

Maura held up her hand in disbelief. "This is impossible. Zedek is dead. I know for I killed him."

Pearl licked her lips and proceeded with caution. "The sighting was confirmed by many. Zedek appeared to the congregation of Bhuttu and tried to speak with them. It was no trick. Even the High Priest became unsettled and fled."

Maura ran her hand through her dark blue-black hair, thinking of all the possibilities. "What do Timon and KiKu propose to do?"

"They are waiting for your instructions, Great Mother."

"What of Jezra?"

"She is biding her time until you strike. All of the storage houses have been filled with grain, and her soldiers exercise battle drills daily."

"And Cappet and Prosperot?"

"Prosperot is neutral. Cappet will side with the victor. My advice, Great Mother, is to get in contact with Cappet. Bribe him whatever the cost. Give him and his band of criminals immunity for all I care, but get him on our side."

"I want all the gates opened upon my signal. Do you think this Cappet could manage it?"

"It will take much gold, but I think he could arrange it. He has many men under his control. Even Jezra dare not confront him."

"Good. I will have our people inside the city contact him."

Pearl asked, "We have more spies inside the city?"

"You didn't think I would let Timon and KiKu go in Bhuttani alone, did you? KiKu never dismantled his spy network. They are still working, but reporting to a different master."

"I didn't realize."

"Take this emerald and gold bracelet," said Maura, pulling off her gold cuff. "It has my royal seal on it. KiKu's people will recognize it."

"Yes, Great Mother. Thank you," said Pearl, hiding the bracelet in her undergarments.

"Tonight, you will rest. Tomorrow, you will return to the city with another Sivan caravan. I will give you a message before you leave on how to use the amulet to free the Dinii. I dared not give it to them before in case they were captured. Do you understand?"

Pearl looked anxiously past the veil.

Maura understood the Hittal's fear. "The boy and Tippa will remain with me. They need not be in Bhuttani during the coming weeks, and you will travel faster without them. Once you have delivered your message, you shall return to me with Madric and Tippu. Timon and KiKu will have to manage on their own the best they can."

"I will need the boy, Great Mother."

Maura thought for a moment. "Alright, but Tippa will remain as my 'guest.'"

"I understand, Great Mother."

Maura stood.

Pearl immediately jumped to her feet and bowed. When Maura did not speak again, Pearl raised her head and found the empress was gone. Pearl shook her head and passed through the humming veil. There she saw Tippa and Akela eating with gusto while the guards raised a water vessel in a tree so they might bathe.

Akela smiled at Pearl and waved her over. "Look at all of the food!" Akela exclaimed with his mouth crammed full of cakes.

A senior officer approached Pearl with a tray heaped with food.

Pearl thanked her while noticing the woman's high rank.

"A Sivan caravan will pass several miles from here tomorrow. You are to join them and pass through to the city again. As soon as you deliver your message, you are to rejoin our empress."

"How will I find her?"

The officer smiled. "An army of fifty thousand people is hard to miss. You will find us. After you have eaten, we have prepared water for bathing."

"Are we not to return with you?" asked Tippa of Pearl.

"You are to be a guest of the empress until your friend returns to us," said the officer.

"Oh, I understand," Tippa whispered.

"I thought you might," replied the guard softly. She turned her attention to Pearl. "After you have eaten and bathed, a clean Sivan robe will be provided for you. A tent is waiting when you wish to retire," she said, pointing.

Pearl turned and looked at the sumptuous tent awaiting.

"A healer will join you later and rub herbs into your feet. They must be sore."

"Thank Her Majesty for such accommodations. We appreciate her thoughtfulness," Pearl stated, weary from all the intrigue.

The senior officer kindly touched Pearl's arm. "The war cannot last forever, and then we will all go back to our lives."

Pearl nodded in concurrence, hoping with all her heart the Hasan Daegian officer was right.

25

Maura pulled her horse to a stop.

There it stood—Bhuttani in all its foreboding glory. Dusty, gloomy, and formidable.

It was nothing like the graceful and beautiful city of O Konya.

Bhuttani stood like a hard knot upon the land. As the first rays of the sun stole across the plain on which the capital stood, Maura could see its massive walls needed repair. The city was decaying from a lack of leadership.

Maura smirked and quickly replaced her expression with a dour expression. She did not want the Bhuttanians to see her gloating at the sight of their beloved capital in such disrepair.

In her heart of hearts, she wanted to put a torch to it and burn it to the ground, but she now would have to rebuild it if her daughter was to become aganess.

The Bhuttanians were leeches upon the rest of the world, and they would have to be contained with a firm hand in order for the land to recover. Maura was determined they would never gain the upper hand again. She glanced at Alexanee.

His face was ashen as he stared at his beloved capital. Always before, Alexanee had wondered if he was doing the correct thing by throwing his effort behind Maura and not Dorak's first wife, but now he saw he had been right in his judgment.

Jezra had let the city deteriorate into such a state that capturing it would not take long.

Disgusted, Alexanee gave the signal for the soldiers to surround the city.

When his fellow Bhuttanians awoke this morning, they would find a massive army of their fellow Bhuttanians and Hasan Daegians standing with a mishmash of Anqarians and mercenaries from every country the Bhuttanians had conquered, waiting to exact a painful retribution upon the city. He prayed Jezra would have the sense to surrender or else much blood would be spilled.

A courier rushed a message to Maura.

She bent down, grabbing the message and dismissing the young woman.

Alexanee looked on as Maura broke open the sealed scroll. "What does it say?"

Maura quickly read that coded message. *The boy and the woman have made it into the city unharmed. The boy is in the temple.* She replied, "It states that Cappet has agreed to our terms."

The general bowed his head. "Everyone is moving into place."

"His men will open the western gate when we give the signal."

"What did we promise him?"

"A percentage of all tax on river trade in the Bhuttanian Empire."

Alexanee chuckled. "He's not a thug. He's a business man."

Maura nodded. "If he survives the attack, Cappet will become a very wealthy man."

"And he will keep the eastern gate open, too?"

"The gate will stay open as ordered. He is letting out as many civilians as possible. We have people stationed intercepting them."

"Yes, I want to make sure Jezra and Mikkotto don't flee the city hiding with the refugees."

"Make sure you search for that boy of Jezra's. She might send him out alone with a trusted servant."

"Your will be done, Great Mother."

Maura studied her army spreading across the great plain surrounding Bhuttani. Win or lose, today would be the day of reckoning. Both she and Bhuttani would be judged.

As Maura and Alexanee considered the city, a swoosh sounded. The horses bucked while whinnying and snorting loudly.

Something soft brushed Alexanee's face. After getting his horse under control, Alexanee regarded the sky. "Don't shoot! Don't shoot!" he cried to his men, watching a contingent of huge birds fly away.

Maura's war steed had run off, but a soldier captured it and brought it back.

The saddle was empty, and Maura was nowhere to be found.

26

Maura controlled her trembling.

Almost in shock, she checked herself for wounds where claws had pinched her.

A hand gave her a skin of water.

"I can't believe it!" she cried, not yet looking into the face of the Dini standing before her.

"Please calm yourself," spoke a familiar voice.

"Is it you, Benzar?" whispered Maura, grabbing his hand and feeling his feathers. "Is it really you? I thought you were with Empress Gitar." Overcome, Maura began to cry.

"Now. Now," comforted Benzar. "Don't cry, little sparrow. I guarded the hallway and was never in the Mother Bogazkoy's chamber." He patted her back.

"Where have you been?" Maura stared at the rest of the Dinii standing in a little knot surrounding them. "Why haven't you helped me? Gitar? Is Gitar here? We thought she might be in Bhuttani. I'm so confused."

Maura grabbed Benzar around his waist and hugged him, taking in his familiar Dinii scent. "I searched everywhere."

Benzar patted Maura's head. "All will be explained to you. We haven't much time. Please stop crying. Compose yourself."

The other Dinii nodded their heads in agreement. It grieved them to see Maura so distressed.

Maura pulled away, wiping her eyes. She reached for a handkerchief inside her vest.

Benzar squatted so he could be on eye level with Maura. "Someone is here to see you, little sparrow. Chaun Maaun."

Maura gave a start. "Oh, he can't kill me now. Not on the eve of victory!"

"He is not here to harm you. He wants to find his mother. We think she is held in Bhuttani." Benzar smiled. "But Chaun Maaun will explain all to you. Will you agree to see him?"

"Do I have a choice?"

Benzar grinned, shaking his head. "Not really. It will be fine. You'll see. Ready?"

Maura nodded.

Benzar offered Maura a comforting smile and gave the signal for his group to fly away.

Maura watched them disappear into the sky.

"Maura?"

The empress swung to see Chaun Maaun standing ten feet from her. She pulled a knife from her leggings. "Stay where you are."

Chaun Maaun stared at Maura with curious detachment. "You look handsome, Maura. Fit and comely. Your skin is noticeably darker. You must have the Bogazkoy with you." He stepped closer.

Brandishing her knife, Maura commanded, "That's far enough. I'm on the verge of capturing Bhuttani. You must not stop me."

Chaun Maaun laughed. "I have no intention of stopping you. In fact, I'm going to help you."

"Help? Why?"

"I think Mother may be in the temple of Bhuttu."

"I think that, also. Why do you?"

"From the reports you have been getting." Chaun Maaun laughed at Maura's confusion. "We have been following you all along. You know how silent we can be. We just fly in and listen to the conversations in your tent."

Maura gave a look of disbelief. "I would have known if a Dini was there. I would have smelled you. Felt you."

"But you didn't. You have been preoccupied with your new baby and all your lovers. We were with you, Maura, and you didn't even know it. We watched in the woods where you had your uultepes dispatch that poor man. We watched KiKu smuggle Prince Bes Amon Ptah away from the scene. We watched you fake your injuries. Yes, we have been witness to many things."

"What do you propose now?"

"A truce. We help you take over Bhuttani, but our main goal is the temple of Bhuttu. I want to search for my mother and kinsmen."

"What if you find Dorak?"

"Dorak. Always Dorak." Chaun Maaun spat out the words as though spitting out something rotten. "If he has helped my kinsmen, then we will spare him. If my mother tells me he has harmed my people, then I shall kill him. I cannot believe you are still concerned with his welfare. Don't you have a daughter to put on a throne regardless of Dorak? Priorities, Maura. Priorities."

"I have your word you will not fight against me and, once the city is taken, you will fly away without exacting revenge?"

"My people and I will go away if Gitar is found. Alive or dead, we will go away. But remember this, Maura, you and your people may go back to Hasan Daeg. We will uphold the treaty between our peoples, but if you or any other of your kind enter the Forbidden Zone, then we will have war, and we will destroy your threat for good."

"Only the Forbidden Zone. What about the City of the Peaks?"

"I hope to never set eyes upon it again. You may have it." Chaun Maaun gave a bitter laugh. "That is all I have to say. I leave you now. After this is over, I hope never to see you again."

Maura fell to her knees, reaching out to him. "I loved you. I truly did and still do. You must believe that. I never stopped loving you. I wish things had been different, but my love for Dorak is something that I can't control. The heart desires what it wants."

"Yes, how well I know."

"Even if war had not come, our people would never have allowed us to marry. Surely you must see that now. We never had a future."

"The Dinii will fly into camp before the battle. Send a flaming arrow into the sky when ready for us. We will come. We will come." Chaun Maaun stretched his mighty wings and flew into the oncoming rays of the sun.

"CHAUN MAAUN, WHY WON'T YOU FORGIVE ME?" screamed Maura, shielding her eyes against the brightness of the rising sun as she watched Chaun Maaun disappear.

Epilogue

Maura stood on a ridge.

She would lead the charge if the city did not surrender.

Beside her sat Alexanee on a horse overlooking Bhuttan.

Everyone was in place—the cavalry, the archers, the infantry, and the catapults to break down the walls.

Alexanee glanced at Maura.

Maura nodded.

Alexanee gave his prancing white horse a small nudge, and it danced to the front of the line. The cavalry fell in behind him as drummers began to beat loudly on their instruments.

A trumpet blew, giving the signal.

The battle had begun.

Bhuttani would fall before nightfall.

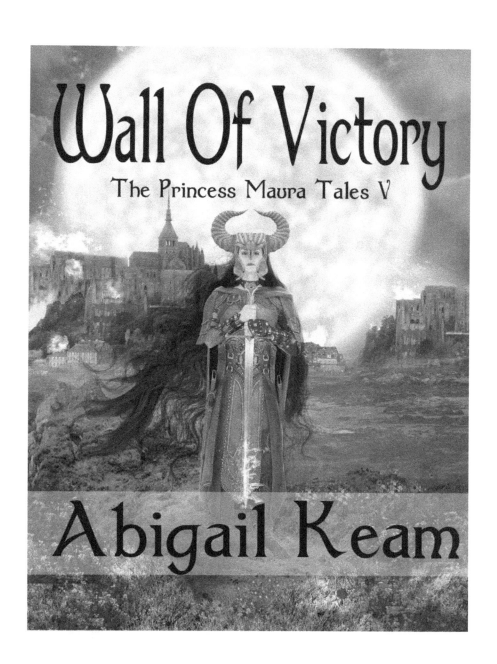

Wall Of Victory

The Princess Maura Tales
Saga of the de Magela Family

Book Five

Abigail Keam

Worker Bee Press

Wall Of Victory
The Princess Maura Tales
Copyright © Abigail Keam 2018

ALL RIGHTS RESERVED

No part of this book may be reproduced or transmitted in any form without written permission from the author. All characters are fictional, and any similarity to any person, place, or thing is just a coincidence unless stated otherwise.

Worker Bee Press
P.O. Box 485
Nicholasville, KY 40340

Acknowledgements

Thanks to my editor, Faith Freewoman

Artwork by Karin Claesson
www.karinclaessonart.com

Book jacket by Peter Keam
Author's photograph by Peter Keam

Preface

Maura gathers the reins of power upon the disappearance of the legitimate aga, her husband Dorak. She begins the long trek to Bhuttan to take the capital city and defeat Dorak's first wife, Jezra, who wants the throne for her son, Dorak's firstborn child.

She sends Timon, a scribe, and Prince KiKu, the spylord, to scout the area and report any sightings of Dorak or the Dinii. She believes they may still be alive.

Now at the gates of Bhuttani, Maura is determined to conquer the last remaining rebel holdout.

War has finally come!

1

War!

War came to Bhuttani.

The city, which had wreaked brutal destruction upon Kaseri, was now facing its own ruin.

The great warrior Maura de Magela was coming to claim the throne of the aga with a coalition of battle-hardened Bhuttanians, Hasan Daegians, Anqarians, Camaroons, and mercenaries from within the Empire.

At first, Bhuttanians refused to believe their kinsmen would take up arms against them, but as terrified refugees fled the countryside and flooded the great city with stories of mighty machines which caused the earth to tremble, soldiers as numerous as the stars in the heavens, and a queen with blue skin and unforgiving eyes who pressed relentlessly toward the capital of Bhutan, citizens began to wonder.

"The Blue Queen wants revenge for the death of her parents," they lamented.

Others speculated that she wanted to place her daughter by Dorak in the Bhuttanian Royal Palace.

Still, many carried on as though nothing would interfere their comfortable lives, believing a Bhuttanian soldier would never fight against his own people. "How can a mere girl harden the hearts of Zoar's men against their kinsmen?"

The refugees babbled, "That she-devil sits upon Zoar's throne of bones atop a great platform dragged across the plains by many beasts. Sitting with her are two great felines which act as bodyguards. She is stronger than any giant and swifter than any bird."

"Nonsense," laughed people in the marketplace as they listened to the wild tales of the frightened newcomers.

"You'll see. You'll see," warned the refugees as they begged for food. "The Hasan Daegian women are tall like our men and as strong too. They have no mercy, obeying their queen without question. Even the noble General Alexanee is at her beck and call. The White Queen is no match for the Blue Queen. We'll all be dead before the seasons change."

Many threw coins at the refugees, shaking their heads in disbelief, but as more exiles flooded the city with similar tales, the people became restless and took to the ramparts to study the horizon.

Could it be true? Could a vast army be coming to exact vengeance? Could the Blue Queen raze Bhuttani as they had leveled Anqara?

They didn't have long to ponder.

One night the lookouts spied pinpoints of distant light. Many said it was the fires of the Blue Queen's camp getting closer and closer. Others remarked it was merely the reflection of a moon upon rocks, but all Bhuttanians went to bed troubled and restless.

The next morning their worries intensified when a cloud of dust and smoke spanning many miles arose along the searing horizon across the plain.

A Sivan caravan entered the city with alarmed traders claiming a vast army was burning every house, every barn, every village across a ten-mile swath, while commandeering everything of value and killing anyone who resisted. "The Great Mother is determined to bring Bhuttan to its knees and the capital Bhuttani along with it. Get out while you can," the Sivans advised the terrified citizens.

While many gathered around for news, no one noticed two "Sivans" leaving the caravan and throwing off their desert robes in an alley.

Now dressed as Bhuttanians in ballooning pants and dark tunics, Pearl and Akela raced toward the temple.

Bedlam had descended into the heart of the city, with merchants closing shops, soldiers marching toward the western gate, and people hoisting children and possessions on their backs, hurrying to escape. Pearl wrestled through the crowd, holding Akela's hand. The escaping throng of citizens grew so unruly, she finally had to pick up the small boy and run with him in her arms. Reaching the portico of an abandoned house, Pearl stopped to rest. She heard looters already at work inside. Putting Akela down, she looked carefully behind her. The last thing she needed was a thug hitting her on the back of the head and stealing Akela for the slave trade.

Pearl squatted down to Akela's level. "Akela, we are only two streets from the temple. You must go and give Empress Maura's message to KiKu. Do you think you can sneak back in?"

Akela glanced at the multitude of people scurrying along the street. He nodded at Pearl with resolve. "I can, Mistress. I know I can."

"Good boy. Repeat the message."

Akela parroted the message that had been drummed into him during the journey back to Bhuttani.

Pearl nodded with relief. "Yes. That's it. Now you must give the message to KiKu and then make your way to the east gate, where the Sivan caravan will be waiting. Can you do that for me?"

Akela nodded, his eyes wide.

"I must go to the inn and collect Madric and Tippu. We will meet at the Sivan caravan. You must be there before the sun vanishes tomorrow or the caravan will leave without you. Do you understand, Akela?"

"I will give the message to KiKu and meet you at the east gate before the sun sets."

"Yes, tomorrow. Do you understand what will happen if you fail to meet us?"

Akela remained silent, thinking of the possibilities.

Pearl grabbed his shoulders. "You will be stuck in this city during the attack. Many people will die if they don't get out. You must be by the east gate by dark tomorrow. Promise me you will be there."

Akela looked into Pearl's worried face and saw the mother he never had, but desired. "I will be there, Mistress. I promise."

Pearl gave a wisp of a smile and kissed the top of Akela's head. "Blessings upon you, child. Be off with you now, and be safe."

Akela judged a space in the crowds where he could push his way through. Within seconds, he was swallowed up by the sea of people scrambling for their lives.

Pearl hoped she would live to see Akela again. Taking a deep breath, she pressed her way into the mob, hoping to find Madric and Tippu safe at the inn. She had to get them out of this city.

Hopefully, KiKu and Timon would be successful in their endeavor. If not, she wondered if the Great Mother would be merciful to KiKu's wives.

One could always wish.

2

Akela pressed through.

He made his way through the city, ducking between legs and squeezing through the crowds until he came to the temple. Hiding behind a refuse bin, he waited until dark. By this time soldiers had established order, and the streets were mostly deserted. Akela stole out from the shadows and scampered into the temple using the route he had taken to escape. Pausing only long enough to allow his eyes adjust to the dim light, he crept along the dark and moldy walls, desperate to make his way to KiKu and deliver the message.

Finding the small oil lamp he had stashed on his way out, Akela fished for the flint he had hidden behind some loose bricks. It took him several minutes to get the damp wick to ignite from striking the flint, but he finally managed. Though the flame from the oil lamp was dim, it illuminated enough to allow Akela to hurry along the damp passageways to KiKu's sleeping room near the wine cellar. KiKu had convinced the priests he could kill more rats if he slept where they kept their nests. They agreed and allowed KiKu to move his pallet into the cellar.

Akela found KiKu resting on his mat near the wine vats. "Master! Wake up!" Akela said while pulling back the ragged blanket, only to find rushes bundled together to resemble a sleeping person.

A hand reached out of the shadows and covered Akela's mouth. "Hush! Do you want to wake the entire complex?"

Akela pulled away from the hand. "Everyone is asleep," he protested, turning to look at KiKu.

"You can never tell who might be listening." KiKu shoved the boy onto his pallet and bit his lip in exasperation. "Akela, tell me the news before I rip out your liver."

Akela gulped. "We met the blue lady with the fancy title. Pearl was afraid of her, I could tell. That made me afraid as well. I didn't like her. Not Pearl, I mean. The blue lady. She didn't have kind eyes."

"Yes, yes, yes," KiKu sighed impatiently. "What did the blue lady say?"

"She kept Tippa, and that made Pearl sad."

"Just tell me what the blue lady *said*, you damned impertinent child!"

Akela sucked in his breath. "Pearl says the empress will strike at the first quarter of the second moon, and you are to get the birds out at all costs. Destroy the temple if you have to, but get them out."

KiKu paced back and forth in his cramped chamber. Stopping suddenly, KiKu grabbed the little boy. "What took you and Pearl so long to get back? Don't you realize our time has all but run out?"

Akela tried to turn his head to escape KiKu's fierce gaze, but KiKu held him so tightly he couldn't. "The caravan had a hard time getting through because of all the people on the roads. There was much thievery and mayhem. With my own eyes, I saw bandits kill an old woman over a bowl of soup. We had to take the long route around."

KiKu exhaled deeply, nodded, and loosened his hold on the boy. "I understand, Akela. I didn't mean to criticize. It's that time is of the essence, but you wouldn't understand, would you? How can a mere boy realize what is at stake?"

"I understand I might get killed."

KiKu chose to ignore Akela's last statement. "Did the blue lady say how we are to use the amulet?"

Akela recited Pearl's message. "As I am blue, press the stone of the same hue and 'will it.'"

"Will it?"

Akela's eyes grew large at KiKu's menacing expression. "Honest. That's all Mistress Pearl told me to say."

KiKu didn't like the way the boy's eyes darted away from him. "You wouldn't be holding back information for some gold coins?"

"I swear on my mother's grave, that is the message." Akela turned away, but KiKu gripped his arm.

"You little liar. Your mother is probably not dead, and Bhuttanians don't have graves."

"Well, if Bhuttanians don't have graves, what is General Prosperot guarding, then?" asked Akela, drawing himself up.

"Shrines, you fool. Don't you know the difference between a grave and a shrine?"

The boy shook his head. He did not understand why KiKu should be so mean to him when he had risked his life to help. Akela believed he had been very brave, so why was KiKu treating him harshly?

This was the way of the Hittals. They were opportunists with little innate sense of loyalty. Yes, Akela recognized who was standing before him. A man so important that the White Queen would pay handsomely to find him. He could turn KiKu in for a neat profit and buy food for many months.

KiKu's grabbed Akela's throat. "Don't even think it, boy."

"I don't know what you mean," Akela wheezed, grasping at KiKu's iron fingers.

"If I go down, so do the women."

Akela pulled away, rubbing his throat. "I still don't know what you're talking about." Akela was astonished that he could have such a thought. He had come to give the message and then escape with KiKu's wives, who were waiting for him even now. KiKu was right. To betray KiKu was to betray the women, and this Akela would never do. He wanted nothing more than to leave this horrid city before it was overrun with grief and bloodshed. "I would never betray you!"

KiKu grimaced. "One rat recognizes another." He released his grip and tousled the boy's hair. "Stay out of trouble, my young friend. We might make something out of you yet."

Gulping, Akela wondered how long it would be before he could sneak out of the temple and rejoin Pearl.

It couldn't be soon enough for him.

3

Timon was incredulous.

"That's all she had to say? Press the blue stone and 'will it?' Why didn't she tell us this before? We had the amulet and could already have summoned them."

"Perhaps Maura didn't trust us with the information and waited until she had proof the Dinii were in the temple."

Timon curled his hands into fists. "She thought we would betray her to Jezra."

"It was safer if we did not know how to make use of the amulet."

"Who else knows?"

"Until now, only she and the Black Cacodemon knew how to summon the powers of the amulet. The various stones on the amulet command different abilities."

"Such as?"

"I wouldn't know. She didn't entrust that information to me."

"Liar!"

KiKu shrugged. Knowing Timon's nerves were raw, he took no offense at the insult. "The Great Mother and her army will be here within hours, and she wants the Dinii freed. I don't think she's prepared for a long siege. She wants to capture the city quickly."

"Well, why doesn't she ask for one of the moons while she's at it!" Timon uncurled his fists and threw up his hands in disgust.

"She must have identified the feather we sent. We know the Dinii are here. We need to release them. The lives of my wives depend upon it."

"Threats. Threats. Always threats. Why don't we leave? Disappear with the fleeing crowd?"

KiKu drew back. "Too many depend upon us. Besides, Maura would search the world to find us. No, we must do this. We must go to the great hall. That's where the Black Cacodemon was sighted, and where you found the feather."

"What if we release him as well as the Dinii?"

"We must try to kill him. He must not be allowed to come to Jezra's aid."

Resigned to his fate, Timon sighed. "Let's go to work then. I want to get out of here as soon as possible. This place gives me the chills." He extended his hand. "Give it here."

KiKu blinked at Timon's hand. "Give what here?"

"The amulet, of course."

"I don't have the amulet. I gave it to you."

Timon's eyes widened. "What do you mean? I don't have it. When I awoke, it was gone. I thought you took it for safekeeping."

Timon searched beneath the frayed blanket and tore open the crude straw pallet on KiKu's bed.

KiKu strode around the room at a frantic pace. "Amulets don't get up and walk away!"

"No, they don't, loyal Bilboa, but they can be summoned."

KiKu and Timon looked up to see Hilkiah standing in the doorway. Their eyes caught a multi-colored glimmer below Hilkiah's collarbone.

Timon let out a loud groan.

Hilkiah was wearing the amulet.

A crooked smile spread across the priest's face. "I see thou both dost recognize the sacred amulet. It belongs to Zedek, my mentor and sponsor into the great society of Bhuttu. All magical objects can be summoned. I have felt its presence since ye both joined our community. It has been calling to me in my dreams. I knew it had to be somewhere in the temple.

"Thou needn't be so aghast, Bilboa. I could have been an apprentice to a cheese guild or a wine merchant or a royal scribe of the Blue Queen, but here I am instead, ready to help my Master."

KiKu murmured to Timon. "That's the extent of Bhuttanian wit for you."

Hilkiah cast a baleful scowl at Timon. "Thou dost not remember me, Prince Bes Amon Ptah, but I remember thee at the court of Zoar. It was just a few occasions when I had to bless something or other at the palace, but thee and thy older brother were present. Just a little thing thou wast, but thee had a peculiar mark on the side of thy neck like this one."

He pointed a finger at a small flower-shaped mole on the back of Timon's neck. "How unfortunate for thee that all novices must shave their hair."

"I don't know what you're talking about, Priest. I am Timon de . . ."

Hilkiah waved his hand. "Save thy breath, young prince. I make no mistake." He slowly inched closer to KiKu. "I am puzzled about thee, though I think thou wast Zoar's man. I never got a good look, as thou wast always lurking in the shadows just out of sight."

KiKu struck his hand out quickly, but Hilkiah jerked his head back. KiKu's hands were met by an angry purple shield, stinging him terribly. He jumped, cradling his singed hand. "Damn you, Priest!"

Hilkiah turned to Timon. "Well, it is clear this man is no Bilboa. It doth not matter. We shall soon have the truth out of thee."

"What do you mean?" Timon asked.

"He means you are going to tell us everything hidden inside your insipid skull," said Mikkotto, stepping into the small sleeping cell.

Timon's eyes narrowed. "Who are you?"

Mikkotto lounged against the doorjamb, slapping her gloves against her thigh. She righted herself and strode over, pressing her lean body against him.

"Stay away. Don't touch me," squeaked Timon.

"Settle down," purred Mikkotto as she stroked the boy's cheek. She leaned into Timon's face until her lips glanced off his. "Very comely in the face. I did not expect you to be so appealing, but you are a tad thin for my taste." Mikkotto's eyes unhurriedly traveled down Timon's body as her hands wandered below his waist.

Timon recoiled from her touch.

Chuckling, Mikkotto reached out and grabbed Timon's tunic, pulling him to her. "I am Baroness Mikkotto from the House of Sumsumitoyo—a royal cousin of the House of de Magela. Surely you have heard of me?"

Timon felt deep fear. "I've heard of you."

"Yes, I can see in your eyes that you have."

"Baroness, we must not keep Aganess Jezra waiting," Hilkiah said nervously.

Ignoring the priest, Mikkotto pulled Timon even closer. "How fares Lady Maura?"

"You mean the pretender? I do not know, Baroness."

Mikkotto smiled. "Come, come now. Make it easy on yourself, Prince Bes. You can tell us what we want to know and dine sumptuously tonight, or you can suffer unspeakable pain and still tell us what we want to know. The choice is yours."

"I don't know what you want of me."

"We have the amulet. We know you work for Maura. We just want to know why."

"Why what?"

Mikkotto asked, "Why did she entrust the amulet to you and permit you to bring it into the temple of Bhuttu? Why would Maura run the risk of the amulet being discovered? Surely she must have realized the priests would sense the presence of the amulet. It doesn't make sense, my young man."

Hilkiah stepped forward. "We needed the amulet to set Zedek free, so why would she allow the amulet to leave her control?"

"You know where Zedek is?" gasped KiKu in a sarcastic tone.

"Silence! No one gave thee permission to speak," hissed Hilkiah. "Lashes across thy back will cure thee of thy insolence."

Mikkotto smiled. "I don't think I would waste my time on the Bilboa. My guess is no torture would be effective on him."

"Why not?" sneered Hilkiah.

"Because while you have been babbling, he has swallowed something. Probably poison."

Timon jerked free from Mikkotto and raced to KiKu. "Don't let it be true!" He peered into KiKu's strained face. "Don't leave me alone with these villains!"

KiKu's eyes rolled up into his head.

Grabbing KiKu's tunic, Timon began shaking him, "You coward! How could you?"

"I . . . was . . . commanded to . . ." gasped KiKu, slipping into unconsciousness and slowly sliding to the floor.

Timon caught the collapsing spylord and held him, weeping against the KiKu's neck. "Don't leave me! You can't abandon me!"

KiKu shook violently several times and went limp. His still-open eyes stared back at Timon as his mouth went slack and a thin trail of blood oozed from his mouth and down his chin.

Timon let out a piercing cry that filled the small chamber and echoed down the long hallway, holding KiKu tightly to his breast.

Mikkotto closed her eyes for a brief instant while she savored

KiKu's death. She learned long ago that death was a useful tool in achieving her goals and vanquishing her enemies, even if it meant using her children as assassins—well, her male children.

Her daughters must survive at all costs. She had left them in hiding with a trusted relative in Hasan Daeg, where they awaited her triumphant return.

She straightened her pose while inserting her gloves into her belt, then beckoned to a sentry standing outside the cell. "When the boy stops weeping, bring him to the aganess. She wants to question him."

The guard returned the Bhuttanian salute and stood in the doorway.

Hilkiah squeezed past the large sentry to follow Mikkotto as she swaggered out of the cellar.

"What shall we do now?" asked the High Priest.

Mikado turned a lazy gaze upon the anxious, pale man. "If I were you, I would be making up a good story."

"What dost thou mean?"

"The boy's servant killed himself with poison. If he truly was Zoar's traitorous hetmaan, the aganess will not be pleased to learn of his death. He would have been a fountain of information."

Hilkiah's face became livid with red streaks rushing up his neck onto his cheeks. His eyebrows arched high while his mouth took on an unpleasant shape. "Thou wast present as well. I wasn't the only one standing by while that creature swallowed poison."

Mikkotto smiled. "Not my temple. Not my responsibility." She pointed to the priest's chest. "I don't think the aganess will appreciate that you revealed the amulet." She whispered into his ear. "I believe it was to remain a secret. Now I'll have to kill the sentry in case he overheard."

"Oh, great Bhuttu!" exclaimed Hilkiah, grabbing Mikkotto's arm.

She scowled disdainfully at his chalky hand.

Hilkiah removed his hand quickly and pleaded, "Canst thou not help me? Of course, I would assist any endeavor thou seest fit in the near future, perhaps?" Hilkiah's voice had taken on a silky quality.

Mikkotto smiled. "I can think of something you can do for me right now. Let us return to your chambers and discuss it."

Hilkiah's smirk faded, since he knew of Mikkotto's reputation for deriving pleasure from engaging in practices that could prove painful to others, but he did not wish to anger the powerful woman. "It would be my honor, Baroness," Hilkiah assured, thinking he would just have to endure whatever Mikkotto had in store for him.

"After you," responded Mikkotto, bowing before the priest. As Hilkiah trudged to his chambers, Mikkotto signaled to her entourage waiting in the hallway.

They nodded.

When the two were out of sight, Mikkotto's Hasan Daegian women stormed the room, garroted the sentry, pulled Timon off KiKu's lifeless body, and spirited him away into the misty gloom.

4

"Where is the boy now?"

"Outside, awaiting your command," Mikkotto replied.

"What could I possibly want with him?" sneered Jezra, popping a sweet wafer into her mouth.

Mikkotto's golden brown eyes narrowed. "I don't know. I thought perhaps you would like to interrogate him, since he came here at Maura's behest, and her forces are practically on our doorstep."

Jezra delicately wiped her mouth with a lace napkin. "I know all I need to know," she answered with smug satisfaction.

"Really?"

"I observed what took place in the temple's cellar."

Mikkotto began to slowly circle Jezra. "How is that, my sweet?"

Jezra dropped the napkin to her lap in exasperation. "I hope you don't think your stalking intimidates me, because it doesn't, so sit down." She reached for another wafer, which Mikkotto swept out of her hand.

Jezra glared at the broken wafer on the floor. "Look what you have done, you stupid Hasan Daegian! You people have no manners. None. You're just like these crude Bhuttanians. Barbarians! The lot of you!"

"I want to know the meaning of your comment. Why do you say that you know all you need to know?"

Jezra smiled sweetly and replied in a voice full of venom. "I know what you think of me. I know what all you barbarians think of me, but I will reign as queen. Oh yes, I will. I will rule, and use Bhuttanians as slaves to rebuild Anqara, and she will rise from the ashes to be greater than ever. I swear I will. I swear it," she said, throwing a wafer at Mikkotto.

"And I will help you," offered Mikkotto. She gently stroked Jezra's hair. "But first things first. What do you know, and how did you learn of it? Demonstrate to me just how dim-witted I am in the presence of an imposing Anqarian."

Jezra spread her diaphanous red skirts out and played with their pleats. "I am able to conjure up sights," she said with some satisfaction.

"Is this something Zedek showed you?"

"Yes," replied Jezra, now smoothing the bodice of her dress.

Mikkotto frowned. She wondered if Jezra's childlike behaviors were more worrisome than simple immaturity. She feared the aganess was losing her mind due to the stress of the civil war.

"Show me," Mikkotto coaxed.

"Really?"

"Yes, really. I am always impressed by magic."

Jezra nodding with delight, sat straight up on the divan, mumbled an unintelligible incantation, and waved her hands in a circular motion. The air thickened and blackened, as if with smoke.

Mikkotto reached out to touch the wavering air, but was repulsed by a thick vibration that singed the hair on her arm. Fearing she had been burned, Mikkotto pulled back in alarm and checked her arm.

"Now watch closely when the circle begins to clear," Jezra advised.

Mikkotto watched in amazement. She had never really gotten over the Hasan Daegians' distrust of magic, but she had to admit to herself its use excited her. Peering closely, she saw the black circle clear to a yellowish, shimmering mist.

"Here it comes now," said Jezra. Giggling, she tucked her legs and feet under her on the divan. Slowly the image of Timon and Mikkotto talking began to emerge as though Jezra had been present in KiKu's small chamber. The image swung around to Hilkiah and then to the Bilboa.

"The vision is fading. Can you brighten it?" asked Mikkotto.

"No. I grow tired. I find it difficult when I am fatigued."

"You were observing us the entire time?"

"Yes." Jezra thought for a moment. "I am surprised, Baroness. I hesitated to share my talent with you because I thought you would be angry."

"Angry? Quite the contrary. I think it is wonderful. With this gift, you can spy into Maura's tent. We can overhear her consulting with her generals and learn of their plans for attacking the city."

Jezra shook her head slowly. "My power has only a very limited distance. I am unable to go beyond the city walls, much less venture into Maura's encampment."

Mikkotto's face fell. "Why can't anything be easy?" she said to no one in particular.

"I am sorry," said Jezra earnestly. "I only studied with Zedek for a short time." Tears welled in her eyes.

Mikkotto eased down onto a stool. "Why did you study with that odious creature, anyway?"

Jezra wiped her tears with her lace napkin. "I wanted the power to bring harm to Dorak."

"Oh, is that all?"

Jezra looked surprised. "It is everything, Mikkotto. I can see you have never been in love. You don't understand how the loss of love can bring utter devastation. It can twist someone's mind. I hardly recognize myself sometimes. I used to be so full of gaiety and happiness. Now I am the lowest of the low." She stared at her hands folded in her lap.

"Why don't you just put Dorak out of your mind and forget him?"

"That's what most people would say, but that is the curse of love. One can't forget. You become consumed with the loss. I've tried. I can't move on, so I want only to hurt him the way he has wounded me."

"Dorak is dead, Jezra. He is gone, and beyond your ability to bring harm to him."

The pale-haired girl shook her head. "I don't feel it. I sense his presence, his life force. He is alive somewhere. I know it."

Mikkotto said nothing, thinking it best not to respond. The pain of others was usually nothing to her, but she felt sad for this young girl who had been so badly used by powerful men.

"Have you never been in love, Mikkotto?"

Mikkotto's mouth turned down, and she wearily rubbed her forehead. "When I was very young, I was in love."

"What happened to him?"

"He died," replied Mikkotto, slowly recalling that long-ago time in her life.

"What happened to your beloved?"

"He committed suicide."

"Oh!"

Mikkotto rose to her feet. "He died by his own hand after my mother arranged my marriage to another man. My husband's family was very wealthy, and my mother wanted his estate. To exact my revenge, I made my husband's life so miserable, he committed suicide, too."

"Was it really suicide?"

"It was ruled as such."

"I see."

"I suppose you do."

"Truly, I am sorry," Jezra said.

Mikkotto shrugged. "I am going to check on our young friend waiting in the hallway." She strode to the door and stopped. Without looking back at Jezra, she said softly, "You are right. Loss of love does change a person, and not for the better, I'm afraid."

She was going to prove it now. The baroness was determined to get the truth out of the young Prince of Moab, even if she had to slowly flay him inch by inch. With the knowledge she gleaned, she would capture the daughter of Queen Abisola de Magela, her cousin and kinswoman, take the usurper's place, and become queen of Hasan Daeg. She then would have Jezra poisoned and establish a subservient puppet to rule Bhuttan.

Secure in her power, Mikkotto ordered for Timon to be taken to the deepest subterranean reaches of the Imperial Palace. She did not want to be disturbed while the young prince was "coaxed" to give up his secrets.

Isolated in the catacombs, Mikkotto never received early reports that Maura was now a mere stone's throw from the city.

She was too busy . . . with Timon.

5

Akela awoke.

Lying on a pile of cloth bags stored in the cellar where the root vegetables were kept, he listened. A half-eaten tuber fell out of his clutched fingers. Sitting up, he shook away the cobwebs of sleep. Where was he? Then he remembered. He had been hungry, so instead of going to his assigned pallet in one of the outer rooms near the kitchen, Akela had stolen into the root cellar and stuffed his tummy with tubers until he fell asleep. Now Akela was awake and listening to a myriad of footfalls running about the temple.

Something had happened!

Had the blue lady entered the city?

Akela strained to listen. There were no screams—just people moving about upstairs quickly and dragging things across the floor. He decided people were moving furniture and boxes.

Why?

Were they looking for him?

Akela jumped up from his pallet of rags and lit his small lamp. Feeling his way along the wall, he found the entrance to the secret passageways and hurried down one of them to uncover the novice's robe and sandals he had stashed in one of the anterooms.

If the temple authorities were searching for him, the disguise should make it hard for them to find him. As soon as Akela slipped into the novice's robe, he would look like hundreds of other little boys serving in the temple complex. And he could always escape into the secret passageways, which he knew like the back of his hand. He had spent many hours exploring them with KiKu.

KiKu!

Perhaps Akela should find KiKu or Timon and ask them what was happening and see if it was time for him to join Pearl and the other wives.

Yes, that is what he would do!

6

Mikkotto wiped away her sweat.

"Tell me what you know, and your pain will stop. Otherwise, this will go on until I get what I want."

Stripped of his clothes, Timon struggled against the chains binding his wrists. He hung from the ceiling, his toes barely touching the floor. He never dreamed a person could be in such agony and still be conscious, much less alive. "I tell you again. I don't know anything. I'm a nobody."

"You are Prince Bess Amon Ptah—a royal. Your people would never have allowed you to abdicate to become a mere priest of Bhuttu, but you might have been sent on a mission by the pretender. Now, I ask you again. Why were you sent here?"

Timon tried to laugh, but his voice could only manage a sound resembling a raspy horn. "I . . . don't . . . know who this Ptah is. My name is Timon Ben Ibin of Moab. I am the son of a wealthy barley farmer."

Mikkotto snorted, "Oh, stop this nonsense. There are no barley farms in Moab. You've changed the story of who you are so many times that even you are confused." Mikkotto plunged an iron rod into a blazing fire. "Maybe a white-hot poker can release the truth from your tongue. You think about that while it warms up."

Timon stared at the metal rod as it began to glow red, then orange, and finally a white-blue flame. In the waves of intense heat, the poker seemed to dance from side to side. He realized he couldn't keep up the pretense much longer. He was going to crack. He knew it, and what was worse still, Timon realized Mikkotto knew it too.

He could only hope he had given Maura enough time to move her soldiers into place around the city walls. Although he had failed to find the Dinii, Timon hoped Maura would have mercy on his people and KiKu's wives. His parched voice could only manage a faint whisper, "Have mercy, Great Mother."

"What was that?" asked Mikkotto, looking up from stirring the poker in the searing embers. "What did you say?"

Timon's head drooped, and his chin rested on his chest. His body twitched uncontrollably. Mikkotto dropped the poker and grabbed Timon's legs, taking the pressure off his swollen wrists. She turned to the sentries standing guard behind her. "Help me, you fools. Can't you see he's trying to swallow his tongue!" she cried to the guards.

The guards rushed over and undid the chains binding Timon's wrists. They let him down with a loud thump while one of them pried open Timon's mouth and pulled on his tongue while another one roughly inserted a round piece of wood between his teeth. Mikkotto stood over Timon in a blind rage. "Get him breathing again. He is not to die until I've finished with him."

She nervously paced the floor around Timon's limp form until a healer rushed into the room. She watched intently as the healer administered a stimulant.

Seconds later, Timon's eyes fluttered open, and he begged for water.

The guards looked at Mikkotto, questioning.

She nodded.

A guard wet a rag from his personal flask of water and squeezed it over Timon's mouth.

Timon coughed at first, but then greedily gulped the water.

"This boy is too weak. Any more torture and he will die," the healer cautioned Mikkotto, barely concealing his distaste. He lowered his eyes, fearing Mikkotto could sense his loathing. He knew of her reputation and did not want to become her next victim.

Mikkotto shot the healer a look of extreme irritation, but did not tarry long with him because a courier rushed into the dungeon. Giving Mikkotto a salute and falling to one of his knees, he bowed his head and extended his arm to hand her a sealed report.

"I said I was not to be disturbed," hissed Mikkotto, striking the courier.

The courier kowtowed. "I beg your forgiveness, Mistress, but I was charged with delivering this bulletin to you upon pain of death should I fail." He pulled a dagger from his belt and offered the hilt to

Mikkotto.

Mikkotto swept the dagger to the floor in irritation, knowing that if her orders had been disobeyed the report had to be of vast importance. Her heart thumped wildly.

Grabbing the report, Mikkotto hurried over to a sconce to examine it in the flickering light. Recognizing the official wax insignia, she quickly broke the seal. "You, there," she called to the healer. "Come here and read this to me."

The surprised healer gingerly took the report from Mikkotto and scanned it quickly.

"It must be bad news from the expression on your face. Mind you, be careful and whisper so only I will hear what is written."

The healer leaned over and, cupping Mikkotto's ear, reported the details of the report in a faint, trembling voice.

If Mikkotto was alarmed, her expression did not betray it. She snatched the report from the man's shaky hand and thrust it into the burning embers that still held the poker. "Stay with your patient, healer. If he dies, you will share his fate."

The healer bowed so low he nearly toppled over. "I'll do my best, Great Lady."

"Pray, my good man, your best will be good enough. I make no idle threats."

A guard standing behind Mikkotto chuckled faintly.

Mikkotto swirled around in a flash of anger. "You guards, go immediately to the west gate." She looked at the courier. "Go with them."

The courier, relieved that he was not going to die at the hands of this foreign woman, jumped up and ran out of the dungeon.

"We are waiting upon your pleasure, Great Lady. We don't want to lock you in," said the senior officer.

Grabbing her gloves from her belt, Mikkotto stormed up the stone staircase and out of the dungeon.

The guards grabbed their weapons. "What was in the message, old man?" one of them asked.

The healer cautioned, "You'd better hurry. How do you know she's not listening from the hall?"

"Let's go," barked the officer. "The old man may be right. Whatever it was, it couldn't have been good."

A subordinate complained, "It doesn't matter one way or another. We're all going to meet our deaths."

"That's what we do. We're soldiers. I'd rather die in battle standing on my feet than be an old man pissing in my pants," his superior replied.

The officer waited until all the others had stomped up the stairs. He slammed the iron door shut and shoved the rusty key into place. Peering down into the chamber through the bars in the door, he made a quick decision.

Watching down the dank corridor until he was confident his brothers-in-arms had rounded the corner, the guard took the key and threw it between the iron bars. It landed on the bare stone floor with a loud clang.

Startled by the sudden noise, the healer looked up, and his eyes fell upon the worn key. Glancing at the door, he saw the guard standing with his arm still between the bars.

Nodding to the old man, the guard gave a ghost of a smile, quickly withdrew his arm, and hurried to join his comrades.

The old man rushed over and grabbed the key, kissing it. Then he snatched up the courier's dagger.

The gods had consented to give him and the young prisoner a reprieve. He wondered who the young man was, to be granted such divine favor. It surely wasn't due to him.

The old man shook his head. It didn't matter. What mattered was getting the youth and himself away from the palace.

The boy looked too heavy for him to carry any great distance. The healer did not want to leave him, but would if he had to. The young man had to get to his feet and be able to move.

He simply had to.

7

Maura sat astride Dorak's black steed.

Beside her was Alexanee, mounted on another massive warhorse. They were on a promontory studying the city.

"Do you think Bhuttani will surrender? I don't want a bloodbath."

Alexanee's horse shifted its weight, which gave him time to evaluate the question. "Great Mother, I hope they do, but knowing the Bhuttanian mindset as I do, I'm sure my brothers will fight to the death."

Maura pondered Alexanee's words. "That is not my wish. They are guided by a weak ruler. Surely Jezra will not challenge me."

"She must resist, Great Mother, for she knows it will mean death for her son and herself if she surrenders. Jezra will fight, for she has no alternative."

"I would consider showing mercy and allowing them to live. We could communicate this to her."

Alexanee scoffed, "Where? What kind of life? An austere existence in some dark prison in a faraway province, where they'd have contact with only their guards?"

"It's better than dying."

"Is it?"

Maura turned in her saddle to face Alexanee. "What troubles you, General? You've never spoken so harshly to me before."

Alexanee glanced momentarily at the city below and then looked back at Maura. "May I be frank, Great Mother?"

"I expect you to be so always."

"The fact that tomorrow I will rain fury down upon the capital of my homeland makes me quiver with such revulsion I can barely stand it."

"Revulsion, yes, but misgivings? Is your loyalty compromised?"

Alexanee looked once more at the city before responding. His forearms flexed as his grip on the horse's reigns tightened. "It must be done, I'm sorry to say."

"Yes, we agree it must be done if the world is to recover. Jezra must not hold the reins of Bhuttanian power any longer. She will bleed the world dry if not deposed."

Alexanee nodded.

"Give the signal, General."

Alexanee closed his eyes for a moment. He knew Maura was watching him. The Blue Queen was right, though. This had to be done, but how he dreaded the thought of killing his people. He raised his hand and gave the signal to set up camp.

Tomorrow, when the two moons had set and dawn broke, the combined forces of Maura's army would conquer Bhuttani, and the world as Alexanee knew it would cease to exist.

Grunting her approval and giving a curt nod, Maura turned her horse around and cantered away.

Alexanee remained behind, staring at Bhuttani and knowing tomorrow the Bhuttanian Empire would be no more.

8

Akela searched everywhere.

He searched Timon's small cell. He searched the alcove where KiKu slept. He searched all the halls where KiKu might be working. He searched the main chambers where the novices prayed. He searched the empty kitchen. Finally he went back to explore the cellar.

It was all the small boy could do to shove panic back down his throat. He wanted to scream with fear, and struggled mightily to appear calm whenever he encountered anyone.

Had the real identities of Timon and KiKu been discovered? Knowing their quest was doomed to fail, and fearing the blue lady, had Timon and KiKu cut and run, deserting him? Were KiKu's wives waiting for him by the east gate, or was that a ruse to get rid of him?

Akela ran from room to room. He searched the entire kitchen and cellar region, all except one room where the cooks stored vinegar and hard cider. Akela tried the door. Locked! That was strange. This room had never been locked before. He would know, since he had fetched buckets of vinegar many a time for KiKu, who used it in hot water to scrub away mold in the dank rooms of the temple.

He shook the doorknob. The door rattled on its rusty hinges, but it would not open. "Master? Are you in there?" whispered the boy.

Silence was his only answer.

Akela studied the door and the lock. The lock was nothing more than more than a flimsy strip of metal which slid into a roughly carved-out niche in the doorjamb. He had heard it referred to as a lover's lock. It should be simple to open.

Determined to get into the room, he looked around for something to pry the door open. In a corner, the boy spotted a small rusty knife that had been used to peel root vegetables, probably left by some careless boy like himself.

Akela smiled. He knew he could open the door with the knife. He hadn't survived on the streets all his life just by begging. Sometimes he had broken into a rich man's house at night, stuffing himself and his pockets with sweetmeats and soft rolls and left before footsteps sounded on the floor above him.

He inserted the knife into the keyhole and deftly turned the blade. Nothing happened. Akela frowned. He tried jimmying the lock again, this time putting more pressure on the knife. The blade broke. Akela took a step back, astonished. Such a thing had never happened to him before. The young boy felt tears burn his eyes and spill down his cheeks. He wiped them away with the hem of his now-dirty yellow robe. Not knowing what else to do, Akela sat upon a sack filled with grain and stared at the knife handle with its broken blade, pondering.

He remembered a gang he used to shadow before the older boys ran him off. He was glad they did, since they were cruel and pinched his share of food, but he remembered how one of the lads inserted a knife between the lock and the doorjamb when they broke into a bakery for some honey cakes.

Akela looked at his broken blade. Maybe there was enough metal that he could use the same technique. He hopped off the sack and went over to the door. This would be his last attempt to find KiKu. If this failed, he would give up his search, sneak out of the temple, and hurry to the east gate where the caravan and safety awaited him.

Gingerly, Akela inserted the broken blade into the niche. He jiggled the knife until the blade caught on something. Hoping it had caught on the lock, Akela pressed the blade to the left, causing it to move right. Slowly he felt the lock give way. He adjusted the knife and pressed some more. The metal of the lock slid back somewhat to the right.

Feeling confident, Akela put more pressure on the knife handle, causing the door to squeak. Grabbing hold of the grimy, wooden handle, he pulled. The door creaked open.

Akela peered inside but saw nothing, as it was pitch black inside. Usually-lit torches in the room were extinguished. Gathering his small lamp, Akela lit a torch by the door.

Blowing the lamp out, he took the torch and placed it in a stand inside the room. Looking about the storage room, Akela's heart sank. There was nothing but wooden barrels of cider and earthenware urns of vinegar stacked floor to ceiling. KiKu was not here, and Akela had no other place to look. He had failed Pearl. Akela's thoughts immediately turned to the city and joining the caravan. There was nothing left to do but save himself. He hoped KiKu's wives would understand and let him stay with them.

Akela's ears perked up, catching a faint sound behind some wooden barrels of cider in a dusty corner. Poised to flee in case he encountered a huge rat, Akela peered over the barrels and discovered a long bundle wrapped in a burial shroud. He shrank from the sight, but then thought better of it.

Why would the Bhuttu priests conceal a dead body in the vinegar cellar with the door locked? Death was a celebration for the adherents of Bhuttu—not something clouded in secrecy and hidden away.

Akela heard a noise again, and it sounded like a weak moan. He inched closer and prodded the bundle with his foot.

The bundle twitched.

Akela poked the heap on the floor again, this time harder. He was greeted with a muffled cry followed by a stream of obscenities.

Akela immediately recognized the voice. "Master!" he cried, taking his rusty, battered knife and carefully cutting away rope from the shroud until KiKu's face emerged.

KiKu sputtered, "Water!"

Akela surveyed the storeroom. "There's no water here."

"Wine, then. Find me something to drink."

Akela frantically sawed the knife back and forth to release KiKu's hands.

"Careful, you little alley boaep. Do you want to slash my wrists? Face the blade away from my hands."

Akela freed KiKu's hands and dropped the knife as he ran to search for something to drink. He hurried to the wine vault and, snatching the sampling cup the kitchen staff used to taste the wine, he rushed back to the vinegar cellar. Yanking the cork from a barrel, he filled the wooden cup with hard cider.

By this time KiKu had managed to free his feet and was on his hands and knees, feebly trying to stand up. "Help me, boy," he muttered.

Akela placed the cider on a small table and rushed to KiKu's side, distressed at seeing the spylord so weak and disoriented. "Put your hands on my shoulders," suggested Akela. "I will help you stand."

Pressing his weight against Akela's small frame, KiKu finally managed to rise. "I'm getting too damned old for this," he grumbled.

Wobbly, but erect at last, KiKu leaned against some shelves. "Just give me a minute while I catch my breath."

Akela handed him the cup filled with cider.

KiKu drank it all in one gulp. "Nice and cool," he said to no one in particular. Turning his attention to Akela, he asked, "Has the city been attacked? Tell me, lad, what is our situation?"

Akela replied, "No, Master, but the blue lady is not far. We see lights from her camp."

KiKu grunted in Bhuttanian fashion. "Good. That means we still have time." He paused in thought. "Master Timon?"

Akela shrugged.

KiKu nodded. "It's up to me." He placed a hand on the boy's shoulder. "You have done well, but it's time for you to leave, Akela. Join my wives and flee the city. Tell them to honor my memory by living full and happy lives. All that was mine is now theirs for the taking."

"Are you not coming? What about Master Timon?"

KiKu assured him, "I will find him, and if fate permits, we will join you outside the city, but you must go now. Find my wives and tell them what I said. You won't forget?"

Akela parroted the message. "Honor you by living happy lives."

KiKu smiled sadly. "Go now, Akela."

Akela looked at the shroud shredded on the floor. "Were you dead, Master?"

"No, my boy. I was playing dead. A trick I learned using a special herb."

"Will you teach me how to play dead, too?"

"Be off with you, Akela." KiKu pushed Akela away.

Akela started for the door, but stopped. "Maybe I should stay with you. You seem weak."

KiKu threw the wooden cup at him. "LEAVE! I HAVE NO NEED OF YOU!"

Akela shot KiKu a wounded look before rushing out the door. It was all he could do not to cry.

KiKu stared at the empty doorway. "Goodbye, my little thief. May the gods bless you and keep you safe." Resigned to his fate, KiKu picked the rusty knife up off the floor "This will do nicely. Very nicely, indeed!"

9

Timon was too weak to go far.

Getting Timon safely out of the dungeon was a slow and arduous process, leaving the healer exhausted. He gently set Timon down on the stone floor against a wall near the palace stables. "I'm sorry, my friend, but I can do no more. We must get help."

Timon clutched the old man's hand. "I must get to the temple of Bhuttu. It is of the utmost importance."

"You're in no condition to travel on your own. We must find a place where you can hide. Then I will take my leave of you to gather my household and escape the city."

Shaking his head and tightening his grip on the healer's arm, Timon insisted, "I must go to the temple. Many lives depend upon it. Can you give me something? A stimulant? I need to get back on my feet."

The healer shook his head. "I know of no herb or medicine that would help you in your condition."

"You must have something in the pouch that you're wearing. Please. If I don't finish my mission, the Blue Queen will tear this city apart looking for Aga Dorak."

"The aga? He is dead. No one has seen him for a very long time. It is believed one of his wives had him assassinated, probably the very queen you speak of." The healer looked troubled. "What has going to the temple got to do with the aga?"

"We think the Black Cacodemon put a spell on Dorak and he is trapped in the temple of Bhuttu."

The healer spat on the ground contemptuously. "Zoar banned that accursed demon, but rumors abound that Dorak brought the pestilence back into the world."

"It's true. With my own eyes, I saw the wizard materialize at Zoar's funeral. Dorak released him to do his bidding, but the wizard, in turn, hexed Dorak. We think he is in the temple, held there by black magic."

"So the Blue Queen did not kill Dorak?"

"No, and neither did the White Queen."

"Who is 'we?'"

"I am in the service of the Blue Queen."

The healer recoiled and spat again. "Traitor! Why should I help a false claimant who wants to destroy my country?"

"The Blue Queen wants to find Dorak, not kill him."

"Foolish knave. How can you be taken in by her deceit? Everyone knows she seeks to install her daughter on the throne."

"The Blue Queen will unite this city and bring an end to all this bloodshed and suffering. All of Dorak's generals support her, even the powerful Alexanee, and they are willing to fight their kith and kin to bring an end to this senseless civil war. The world is dying. The Blue Queen is our last hope of salvation."

Rubbing his eyes, the healer slumped against the wall. "I am near my time of leaving this world. All is in chaos. This city, my home, is on the brink of annihilation. What to do? What to do?"

Timon squeezed the old man's hand. "Help me to bring an end to this carnage, I beg of you."

The healer finally nodded. "I can give you something that will give you strength, but I warn you—it will affect your heart. Once it wears off, your heart will be irreparably damaged."

"Give it to me! I must have it!"

"The dangers."

Timon tried to straighten, but fell back against the wall. "I must be off. I must find my friend and finish my mission."

"You swear to me upon all that is holy that your queen will set things right?"

"You have no idea how powerful she is. She has the strength of ten men and is swift like a bird in flight, yet there is good in her. Wherever her forces have been, law has been established, trade routes connected, and the land has begun to recover from Zoar's policy of slash and burn. The Blue Queen will do more good than harm. But I tell you this—she is determined to capture the throne, and she will do anything to accomplish this. Believe me when I tell you, Jezra is no match for Maura de Magela."

The healer studied Timon's face for what seemed like a long time, looking for deceit. At last, he decided. "I will help you. My name is Siddig. Remember me in your prayers, and make it known to your queen how I aided you, and implore her to have mercy on my family."

Timon said, "Look inside the pocket of this robe."

The healer prodded the pocket of the dirty robe he had found on the dungeon floor and used to clothe Timon. Rummaging through the frayed pocket, he pulled out a child's wooden signet ring with a borax bull carved on it.

"If the Blue Queen does not honor you, take this ring to the nomads on the steppes. Find the mother of Prince Bes Amon Ptah and give her this ring. She will honor any request from you. This is my word."

The old man's eyes widened as he recognized the symbol of royalty from the people who lived on the grasslands. He bowed in respect. "My lord."

"Now give me the stimulant. We've no time to lose."

The old man fished inside his pouch and pulled out several dried leaves. "Take only a little as needed. It will take away any pain and give you immense energy, but each leaf you chew will weaken your heart until nothing, not even this sacred plant, can help you."

Timon's hand trembled as he grabbed the leaves from the healer's hands.

"Only a little bit of the leaf at a time. Chew until pulpy, and then swallow quickly. Remember—a little at a time."

Timon had trouble pulling a leaf apart, so the healer tore a section and put it on Timon's tongue. Immediately Timon felt a surge of energy. He sat up. "This is marvelous. I feel rejuvenated."

"Do not be beguiled, my friend. This plant loves to seduce as she steals life from your heart."

Timon grabbed the old man's hand and shook it. "Thank you. You have saved my life and countless others."

The healer nodded and rising, took his leave with grave misgivings, convinced he had doomed the young man to an early death.

But there would be many deaths in the coming days, and many young men and women would die before their time.

Their fate was written in the stars.

10

P earl paced back and forth.

Madric emerged from the Sivan caravan waiting just inside the mammoth east gate and went over to Pearl. "My dear, you are wearing a hole in the road."

Pearl hissed, "Where is that boy?"

"We must leave now."

"We can't leave the boy in this place. It is soon to go up in flames."

"Regardless, the caravan must leave immediately. You must understand that we are putting the lives of others at risk if we tarry any longer."

Pearl grabbed Madric's hand. "Please. Just a few more minutes."

"No. We must go!"

Madric and Pearl swiveled to the sound of soldiers' leather boots slapping the stone streets. They looked at each other, realizing soldiers were advancing upon the gate.

Others heard the sound too, and rushed the gate, trying to get out and creating a bottleneck. A great wail poured from the people, and the bellowing from frightened pack animals only created more confusion. The throng turned on itself, beating and shoving those in front to the ground. Many people fell and were trampled.

Alarmed, the Sivan leader gave the signal to exit the city. With their beasts laden with goods, they pushed through the crowd, sometimes knocking terrified civilians down under the sharp hooves of their borax.

Pearl and Madric ran to take their place in the caravan, which was now moving forward at a fast pace. Others rushed behind the caravan, as it was moving past the cluster of people fighting among themselves to press through the gate.

Pearl heard her name called and turned around, but was pushed forward by the horde behind her. She could only manage to raise one arm, frantically hoping whoever was calling would see her signaling.

Outside the gate, the caravan pushed onward, the leader determined to leave Bhuttanian territory as fast as possible. He knew the Blue Queen's scouts were stationed out of sight beyond the knolls northeast, watching the mayhem, but he was confident they would not interfere with his people, since Siva was an ally.

Seeing the Sivan leader was determined to leave the city, Pearl dropped out of the caravan and clung to the side of the city's wall.

A platoon of soldiers arrived at the gate and immediately commandeered the gatehouse, which housed the winches and pulleys for the portcullis.

Bhuttanian civilians, frantic to get their families out at all costs, confronted the soldiers by throwing rocks and debris at them.

Angry at the pathetic assault by the ragtag mob, the soldiers made quick work of their attackers with sharp swords.

Fleeing families slipped on the blood from the dead and dying alike. Others stumbled over prone bodies while the soldiers battled to clear the street.

Barely audible above the din, Pearl heard her name again. She scanned the mass of people coming her way and thought she spotted Akela. "HURRY!" she cried, knowing he would never be able to hear over the noisy bedlam. She waved her arms frantically. "Hurry, little one," she mumbled to herself.

The soldiers, now in charge of the gatehouse, began turning the wheel controlling the massive portcullis.

Nearly trampled by the mob spilling forth, Pearl held her ground at the very edge of the gate until the sharpened spikes of the portcullis were almost touching the street.

A small figure shot through, but his robe caught on one of the iron prongs before it clanged shut against the stone pavement.

Akela, thrown to the ground, reached back to pull his robe from the massive iron prong, but it wouldn't tear.

A soldier, angry because he had been hit several times with rubble, approached the boy frantically trying to pull his robe from the gate. "You little whelp. You probably threw a rock at me. I'll show you!" he cried, poking his sword through the lattice grill of the portcullis.

Pearl jumped over Akela with a small knife and stabbed the soldier's forearm as it reached through the grill.

Shocked and wounded, the soldier dropped his sword.

Quickly seeing an opportunity, Pearl picked up his sword and, with one swoop, cut the Akela's robe free from the massive gate. Grabbing the boy, she threw him over her shoulder and ran. They had to make the safety of the caravan, or they would be picked off by soldiers on the ramparts now unleashing a rain of arrows on the fleeing populace, purely for sport.

Dodging arrows, Pearl ran in a zigzag pattern until she reached the caravan and put Akela on the back of the last borax in line. Exhausted, she grabbed the tail of the great beast and let it pull her along.

It wasn't long before Maura's soldiers intercepted the fleeing caravan, offering aid as they did to everyone escaping the city. The soldiers produced flasks of water and patties of fried bread while Hasan Daegian healers treated the wounded before the refugees were sent to a camp where they would be safe from the fighting.

After gratefully accepting the bread and water, Pearl rested against the borax, weeping. Weary from months of anxiety, her mind gave way to blind panic. Not only did she not know if KiKu and Timon had accomplished their mission, but she still had to answer to Maura, regardless of the outcome. It wouldn't be long before the Blue Queen's soldiers realized who she was and came for her, along with the rest of KiKu's wives.

"Mistress Pearl," said a timid voice. "Would you like my bread? It's sweet with honey in it." A small hand patted her head. "Are you crying because I was late? There were so many people coming out of their houses. And there were gangs of rowdy boys attacking people and stealing their things. It took me much time to get past them unnoticed. Please don't cry."

Pearl opened her weeping eyes to see Akela was offering his crumbling morsel of bread to her.

Wiping the tears from her cheeks, she said, "I'm not angry with you, Akela. I'm angry at life. I'm angry at what the world has become. Eat your bread. You must be hungry."

Akela nodded and happily stuffed the bread into his mouth. He had discarded his robe and was clothed only in a filthy loincloth and dusty sandals.

Pearl smiled, watching him eat with such relish. She noticed Akela had grown since he joined their little troop, and wondered if he would live long enough to reach manhood, but at the moment he was still a little boy, greedily eating his fried honey bread and smacking his lips.

Picking up her water and bread ration from the ground where she had dropped it, she took a long drink from the earthenware flask.

"Aren't you going to eat your bread?" asked Akela.

"No, and neither are you. It's been on the ground."

Akela looked at Pearl in dismay. "Waste of food."

Pearl hailed a soldier carrying a basket of bread and plucked three large patties from it. She tossed one to Akela. "There now—another one for you, and two for me. That should fill you up until we get a proper meal."

"What about the one that fell on the ground?"

Pearl laughed. "You are such a greedy little bugger. I'm sure this borax, which has kindly loaned her back and her tail, wouldn't mind if a honey bread has fallen on the ground." She went in front of the borax, which sniffed at the bread and, with a massive tongue, swept it out of her hand.

Akela patted the borax's neck. "He likes it."

"She likes it," corrected Pearl. For a few seconds Pearl forgot about the war, Maura, and even KiKu, but that was dashed when she saw four Hasan Daegian soldiers with a lieutenant approaching.

"And so the last leg of our journey begins," she mumbled.

Akela followed her gaze and, seeing the soldiers, jumped off the borax, melting into the crowd milling around the caravan.

Pearl watched Akela disappear. "If I survive this, I'll find you, little Akela. I swear I will." Bravely, she turned to face the soldiers, who had already collected Madric and Tippu. She fell into step with them. There was no use resisting. The three women clasped hands, wondering what fate awaited them.

11

Maura entered the tent stealthily.

Most of the generals did not even realize she was standing in a corner listening to them discuss tomorrow's campaign. Only when a servant lit the lamps did Alexanee catch a glimpse of blue in the shadows. He immediately gave the Bhuttanian salute.

The other generals followed his gaze and followed suit, each one trying to remember if they had said anything to displease the empress.

Maura was not known for a forgiving disposition. And she was pleased that her generals feared her, which made them easier to control. She knew their hatred of her, since she had placed spies in their tents who repeated every word of treason. As long as they did her bidding, Maura didn't care how they felt about her. Giving them a slight nod, she strolled over to study the map they were perusing. "So, my fine generals, can we take Bhuttani with a minimum of bloodshed?"

"It is doubtful," remarked Alexanee, looking at the other generals to support him.

"Why say you thus?"

No one answered straightaway, and the generals avoided eye contact. A grizzled old general with gray hair braided down his back finally replied, "They will fight to the death. We Bhuttanians are bred for war. It is all we have ever known."

Maura sighed. "Then position our catapults where the city will have an ample view of them."

"Yes, Great Mother," they murmured.

"Any word from Cappet?" Maura asked.

Alexanee shook his head. "We know there have been riots in the streets, which Jezra's soldiers have put down. I hear they are killing civilians for sport."

"All the more reason to convince the populace to support us," responded Maura.

"I do not wish to be disrespectful, but that is not the Bhuttanian way," Alexanee countered. "We expect our soldiers to be brutal at the outset of a battle. The people should not have gone out into the streets."

"I see," Maura said, pondering the cruelty of the people she wished to conquer. Would they ever accept her as ruler, or would she have to utterly crush them for the survivors to obey? She was tired of the war, tired of the killing, tired of the intrigue, but it was almost over. Win or lose, tomorrow it would be over. She would either be the victor or the vanquished, but it would be finished.

Maura turned again to study the map. "What of the Dinii? Have they made contact?" she asked.

The generals looked to Alexanee to answer. Frankly, they disliked speaking to Maura directly. She gave them pause, since many of their comrades' bones had been fused to the Aga's horrid throne. They did not want their bones to be added as well.

Alexanee rubbed his chin with his thumb. "We have not seen them, but have deposited raw meat as well as live animals in the forest east of the city, as you requested, and they were all gone in the morning."

Maura gave a ghost of a smile. "Did you leave ale as well?"

"Yes, Great Mother," several of the generals said together.

"And it was gone as well?"

They nodded.

"Then they are here."

"How can we be sure?" asked Alexanee.

"Because they suspect Empress Gitar might be here," Maura replied.

One general, whose face bore an ugly scar from a sword across his face, asked, "But shouldn't we consult with them about tomorrow?"

Maura shrugged. "There's nothing to discuss. Chaun Maaun has sworn a blood oath to exact revenge for the death of his sisters and the destruction of the City of the Peaks. He will help us if he so chooses—or not.

"Even if there is not a battle, and the Dinii wish to rain retribution upon the city by killing every man, woman, and child they find, we will not interfere. Not a single Dini shall be harmed—upon pain of death."

The generals looked at each other in disbelief.

Stunned, Alexanee blustered, "Surely, Great Mother, you are not going to give carte blanch to these savage animals."

Maura slammed her fist on the table, on top of the battle maps. "YOU DARE TO CALL THE DINII ANIMALS AFTER YOU HAVE NEARLY BROUGHT THE WORLD TO ITS KNEES?"

The generals drew back at Maura's anger. Many put their hands on the hilts of their swords.

Maura confronted them. "The world is changing, my fine generals, and we must change with it. Either Bhuttani surrenders tomorrow, or it will be ground into dust like Anqara."

"But our homes—our families," protested several of the generals.

"For those who still had kith in Bhuttani, you were told to send word advising your families to leave. At this very moment, Hasan Daegian soldiers are meeting those who left by the east gate and taking the refugees to a safe place, away from the fighting. Couriers will bring word of your families as soon as they can. Don't worry. We are providing food, water, and tents for their comfort. If they haven't left as ordered, then they will be considered traitors."

"But the Dinii?"

"As you know the Bhuttanian mindset, I know the Dinii. They will not harm those in the refugee camp."

Several generals gave sighs of relief, though others understood the implications of Maura's rounding up their families and placing them in a camp. She was holding them hostage. No doubt they would be put to death if the generals did not obey her.

Obviously, Maura had doubts about the Bhuttanian generals waging war against their capital city. While they admired her cunning, they were distraught to see their culture, as they had known it, coming to an end. The absolute rule of Bhuttan was broken, and the dream of a world empire given up as sand pouring through one's fingers.

Maura gave a ghost of a smile when she saw it dawn on the generals that by rescuing their families she had made prisoners of them. She had come to despise the Bhuttanian generals for their hypocrisy. They worried about their kinsmen, and wanted Maura to grant mercy to their families, yet it had never occurred to them to show the same pity for the Anqarians, Dinii, and Hasan Daegians they slaughtered. It was all Maura could do to mask her revulsion, for they must never know the depth of her hatred of them.

Alexanee looked at Maura in amazement. He had many spies at court, but they had failed to alert him to the refugee camp with only Hasan Daegian guards. He was glad his wife and child were awaiting him in his tent. However, Maura could have them put to death on a whim, any time she liked.

He hoped no idiot tried to assassinate Maura between now and the morning. Even if an assassin did manage to kill her, the Dinii, along with the Hasan Daegian and Anqarian soldiers, would exact a terrible price from the Bhuttanians.

Alexanee tried to rub away the throbbing in his forehead. The world had turned topsy-turvy. Tomorrow, a Hasan Daegian queen would sit upon the throne of the Great Aga. How had this come to pass?

Maura motioned for a servant to bring a lamp over to the table so she could examine the maps more clearly. She pulled out a detailed map of Bhuttani and pointed at the west gate. "If Cappet does not open the gate at dawn, we can assume he is either dead or has struck a deal with Jezra. Either way, we will batter the city gate down with the catapults. I want to be riding through the streets by midmorning."

"Yes, Great Mother," murmured the generals.

"If any of you stumble upon Mikkotto Sumsumitoyo, bring her to me."

"What of Jezra and her son?" asked Alexanee. "After all, the boy is Aga Dorak's firstborn."

Maura was ready for this question. She understood the implications Alexanee was raising, and pointed a finger at the generals. "Let us remember Aga Dorak never made Jezra his princess royal or his empress. I was crowned empress, and I am his royal wife. My daughter, Princess Dyanna, is his legal heir. Jezra is to be considered his concubine, and any issue from that alliance to be of no consequence. My marriage and offspring take precedence over any other child conceived by Dorak. Also, I am the queen of Hasan Daeg and a royal. Nothing flows through Jezra's veins but that of a banker's brat who sold out his countrymen."

Alexanee broke the silence which followed Maura's declaration. He spoke calmly, trying to avoid a confrontation with Maura. "We do not question your right to rule as regent, but if something should happen to the princess, Jezra's son would be next in line to rule."

Maura leaned forward. "Are you suggesting Princess Dyanna's life may be in peril?"

"I am saying children become ill and die."

"My blood courses through her veins. Rest assured, my generals, she will not expire from illness, nor will she die from an accident. Princess Dyanna will sit upon the throne when she reaches the appropriate age."

"But when will that be? The women of the royal family of Hasan Daeg live a very long time."

"It will happen when it happens."

"But . . ." Alexanee could not finish his sentence because a courier entered the tent. She bowed and knelt before Maura, handing her a scroll.

Maura took the scroll and broke the seal. Leaning near a lamp, she read the names listed. Determined not to gloat, she threw the scroll onto the table. "Your families are safe and under the protection of the royal House de Magela. I must leave you good men now. I have much to prepare before dawn, as do you. Make sure everything is in order. I bid you good night."

The generals saluted her and fell to planning the assault for the morning. They dared not discuss their families or the Dinii, since many unseen ears might be listening to their conversation.

They knew in their hearts that Maura had bested them, and regardless of how they felt, at dawn they would fight their countrymen in order to put a small babe on the Bhuttanian throne lest their families be obliterated. They had no doubt Maura had given such orders to be enacted if they deserted to join the city's fighters.

Alexanee looked at the disgruntled officers surrounding the table. He picked up a piece of charcoal to mark the map. "We must hang together in this endeavor, my brothers, or tomorrow we shall all hang together from the battlements of Bhuttani. Let us begin."

The generals nodded and bent over the table to finalize the plans for the taking of Bhuttani.

12

The priests prayed in the great hall.

"Any change?" asked Empress Gitar, coming up behind Iegani. She stood listening to the resonance of the priests' chants echoing off the vaulted ceiling.

Iegani shook his head. "They drone on and on in the same repetitive verses."

"What can they be about?"

"I don't know. It is some sort of ritual, but what for I do not know."

Empress Gitar looked forlorn as she and Iegani stood among the chanting priests, who were unaware of their presence. "I wish I knew what was going on in the outside world. Once in a while, I hear a priest whisper something about the Blue Queen, but then he is hushed up."

"I guess it is safe to assume he was talking about Maura, so she is still alive."

"How long have we've been here? It seems like hours, but Zedek intimated that we've been here for years."

"I wouldn't trust anything that reptile said, my dear niece."

"People rush by as though they were buzzing insects. Only once in awhile do they slow down enough that we can understand what they're saying."

"As they are now?"

"Yes, as in now. I can understand them perfectly, and they are not blurry. Do you think the chanting is having an effect?"

"I hope so. They may be trying to open a portal."

"In that case, we must gather the others and be ready. Where is Dorak?"

"The last I saw of him, he went to find Zedek."

"He should be with us."

"Not that we don't trust him," both Empress Gitar and Iegani said at the same moment, then looked at each and chuckled.

Empress Gitar declared, "It is good we can find some humor in this situation, but I should find Dorak."

Iegani reached out and grabbed Gitar's arm. "No, my dear. You must stay with me. Let us gather our people, and if there is a chance for freedom, we will make the transition together. Dorak is not our concern."

He sent a telepathic message to all the Dinii trapped in the netherworld.

One by one, they found their way to Gitar and Iegani.

13

KiKu's wives stood trembling in a little knot.

They had been summoned to the antechamber of Maura's tent. Their guard escort stood beside them impassively, never moving or responding to any of their questions.

The women waited nervously while they watched couriers and scribes bustle in and out of the main chamber. At one point the Royal Counsel Rubank was brought out in a palanquin, looking peevish, with a servant trying to mop the counsel's brow while shuffling alongside.

Madric said, "No matter what, we must not show fear."

The other women nodded but had little resolve. They were terrified.

A Hasan Daegian officer parted the thick curtains that divided the room and beckoned to the women. Their guards moved forward, so the women shuffled with them.

Once inside the main chamber of Maura's tent, the women spied the Blue Queen occupying the throne of bones perched upon an elevated dais with the uultepes lounging beside her. Maura was arrayed in the State Robe of the Aga, a stunning red and golden cape with embossed dragons. To signify the dual nature of her rule, she held the Royal Fan of the Hasan Daegians.

The darkened room was illuminated only by a few lamps, which filled the air with smoke.

The women let out a small gasp in unison. In the dark, chilly room, the hostages could see rays of bright light emitting from Maura's fingers and head. They knew Maura radiated an aura, but they had never seen her shimmer so. It only served to heighten their collective apprehension.

The guards about-faced abruptly and left the room.

Finding themselves directly before the Maura, the women spontaneously kowtowed, pressing their foreheads on the carpeted floor.

"Arise," they heard Maura say.

The women quickly stood and glanced about them. Near the empress stood Noabini, the High Priestess from the House of Magi, in her blue and green robes.

Madric felt her legs tremble and feared she was going to faint, but she had to stay strong. As KiKu's first wife, she must speak for the rest of the harem. She bowed and said, "Great Mother, we offer you greetings on this auspicious day."

Maura snapped her fan open and kept her eyes riveted on Madric. "Bring in Tippa."

A curtain to the right opened, and Tippa was escorted into the room.

Maura pointed her fan at Tippa. "Join them."

Tippa lit up with joy at seeing her sister-wives and ran to them.

The women forgot protocol and hugged each other fiercely, kissing each other's cheeks.

"Enough," ordered Maura, closing her fan with a loud clap.

The women instantly obeyed, bowing their heads. Tippu grabbed Tippa's hand, not letting go.

"Madric, will you speak?" asked Maura, looking intently at them.

"Yes, Great Mother, I can, but it would be best if Pearl answers your questions," replied Madric, hoping her voice did not quiver.

"Very well," replied Maura, standing. "Follow me."

The uultepes immediately rose. They passed near the women with their snouts grazing the women's clothing, inhaling deeply.

Madric and Pearl dared not move, fearing any sudden movement might cause the great cats to attack. Tippa and Tippu clutched each other, closing their eyes as the beasts passed.

"Come, come," encouraged Maura. "My darlings won't hurt you."

Pearl gave a reassuring look to her companions and followed Maura into an adjoining chamber. Her natural curiosity overrode her anxiety, and she wondered how many rooms the tent held.

"You are Pearl, are you not?"

Startled, Pearl came to attention. "Yes, Great Mother," she replied, realizing they were in Maura's bedchamber. She watched young Hasan Daegian males remove the official robes and headdress until Maura was clothed in only a simple linen shift.

The room was well lit, so Pearl could no longer see light emanating from Maura, which helped her to relax a bit.

Maura sat in a chair, allowing her attendants to minister to her. They brought hot water for her feet to soak in and trays of food.

She motioned for the servants to bring chairs for the women, ignoring their looks of surprise. Maura rarely let anyone sit in her presence unless it was at a state banquet. Otherwise, her subordinates kowtowed in her presence. Generals and nobility stood. Only her personal favorites were allowed to sit before her.

The servants set up small tables beside the women and placed trays of food on them.

Maura ordered, "Bring my guests some colla tea," while studying the frazzled wives of KiKu.

"Does this mean you are not going to kill us?" asked Tippu, her eyes widening at the courteous treatment.

Pearl looked skeptically at the trays laden with tasty tidbits and wondered if the food was poisoned.

As if reading Pearl's mind, Maura laughed and asked for a plate to be given to the suspicious woman. "Would you be kind enough to select a few morsels for me," she instructed.

Pearl selected food from several trays with a utensil she was given and handed the plate to one of the male servants who served the empress.

He took the plate to Maura, who casually ate from the plate while observing Pearl. She could tell Pearl was still not convinced.

"Mistress Pearl, I assure you the food is not poisoned. I have never used poison to kill anyone. I hang them or kill them personally with my sword. If I were to have you killed, that would be the way."

"Are you going to hang us?" Tippu's voice wobbled.

Madric whispered, "Hush!"

Several of the servants giggled.

"You are a brave little bird," remarked Maura, looking amused. She took a sip of the colla tea. "Not at the moment, but I do have some questions."

Tippu gulped and bowed her head.

Feeling relieved, Pearl partook of food and accepted a cup of colla tea. The other women followed suit.

"Yes, Great Mother," replied Madric. "We shall answer to the best of our ability."

Maura asked, "Where is the little boy, Akela?"

Pearl swallowed before answering. "He ran away when he saw your guards coming for me."

"Do you know where he might be?"

"No, Great Mother, but he would not be far from food, so he is probably near the refugee camp."

Maura beckoned to a guard and whispered in her ear, causing the guard to leave the room quickly. The empress turned her attention back to the women. "Did KiKu and Timon receive my instructions?"

Pearl nodded. "Yes, Great Mother. Akela told me he found KiKu and relayed the message about the amulet."

"So you did not speak to KiKu yourself?"

"No, Great Mother. None of us have seen KiKu since he entered the temple. Akela has been the go-between for us. I can tell you this. Akela told me that before he left the temple to join us, he found KiKu locked in the cellar trussed up in a shroud."

"What about Timon?"

"Akela never saw Timon," Pearl replied, using the informal use of Timon's name since Maura was doing so.

"Did KiKu give Akela any information regarding Timon or their mission?"

Pearl bowed her head, afraid to look at Maura when giving her answer. "No, Great Mother."

The rest of the women paused in their eating and drinking, looking in alarm at Maura, who rose suddenly.

Tippu began to cry.

"Someone quiet that silly girl."

Tippa reached over and pinched Tippu, which only made the exhausted girl cry harder.

For once Pearl saw compassion in Maura's eyes.

Maura spoke kindly to Tippu, "Little one, I am not going to hang you. I can see all of you have lost much weight and have a haunted look about you. Your clothes are rags, and not fit for the wives of Prince KiKu. The mission has been a terrible burden. This is evident to all who look upon you."

Smiling, Maura continued, "You will be given a tent of your own with guards, so you need not fear retribution from anyone. Meals will be provided by my private chef, and you will be attended by the Royal Healer if you so desire. If the battle tomorrow is won, you will be sent home with all honors. Whether Prince KiKu and Prince Bes Amon Ptah have succeeded or not is no longer your concern. You have done your part. You may leave now with my blessing."

A servant motioned for the women to rise.

After giving a deep bow, the women began to back out of the tent. Suddenly Pearl looked up and spoke. "Great Mother?"

The servants gasped at the impropriety of Pearl speaking when not spoken to by the empress.

Maura motioned them to be quiet. "Yes, Lady Pearl."

"When next we meet, I will be bowing to you in the Imperial Court of the Agas. May the gods protect you from all harm tomorrow." Pearl bowed again and backed out of the room, aided by one of the male servants who attended the empress. She wished with all her heart that Maura would succeed in her quest.

The capture of Bhuttani would mean life for them all.

14

Mikkotto reviewed the troops.

She inspected repair work for the walls and food silos, giving orders that any looter was to be killed on sight. All gates to the city had been shut for hours and reinforced. Anyone trying to climb the walls to escape fell to their death with an arrow in their back.

Water was Mikkotto's principal concern, and she stationed guards by wells, including stockpiling the precious liquid in barrels near important buildings and squads of soldiers. The last thing she needed were guards leaving their posts to drink. Water boys made the rounds of each guard post every half hour with fresh water.

For days, all households had been encouraged to store as much water as possible, and the people obeyed by filling every bucket, vase, goblet, and cup at their disposal.

All fires were extinguished, except those of blacksmiths who were still fashioning weapons.

The city residents, including the soldiers, had to eat cold rations. Even torches, lamps, and candles were snuffed out on the streets.

If Maura chose to attack in the darkness of night, Mikkotto didn't want to give her an advantage with flickering pinpoints of light emanating from the city.

Exhausted, Mikkotto returned to the palace, eating a quick meal of fruit and cheese while poring over detailed maps of the city. Her chamber was flooded with candlelight since dark curtains covered all the windows.

A doctor stood by, infusing a mild stimulant into a special drink for her.

Mikkotto quickly drank the concoction. "By the grace of Mekonia, this stuff is evil." She threw the goblet against the wall in disgust, but couldn't deny she was feeling refreshed. "Prepare me another one," she ordered the healer.

"Shouldn't you be out on the parapets?"

Mikkotto swung around with her hand on a dagger hidden in her shirtsleeve. "I just came from there," she answered Jezra.

"Are we ready?" asked Jezra, framed by the door wearing a stunning orange dress with golden silk flowers encircling the bodice and a gold tiara crowning her flaxen hair.

As always, Mikkotto was struck by her beauty. "As ready as we can be. The question is—if Maura attacks, will our soldiers fire arrows at their fathers and brothers?"

"Did you not hear what happened at the east gate? The soldiers fired upon those fleeing the city, killing hundreds."

"Why would they do such a thing?"

Jezra laughed. "For sport. What else?"

Mikkotto frowned. After the war, the city would need to rebuild its population again. She considered killing civilians for fun a wasteful squandering of their workforce. "I hope those idiots recovered all the arrows. They are very valuable."

"I received a report that the soldiers opened the gate one last time, recovering the arrows and stripping the bodies of anything valuable before returning behind the walls."

"Did they dispose of the bodies?"

Jezra shook her head.

"Wonderful. Now we have rotting corpses stinking up the east gate."

"What does it matter? When Maura finally strikes, there will be thousands of putrid corpses decaying in the sun," Jezra replied with a sardonic smile.

"It does matter if the city is sieged for a long period. Those corpses could cause an epidemic among the people."

Jezra shrugged while biting into a fruit.

Mikkotto shook her head. "I guess it never occurred to you that there is a slight possibility we may have to flee on horseback. How can horses gallop on a road strewn with decomposing bodies?"

Jezra maintained her nonchalant air. "Regardless of what happens, my son and I will not be leaving this palace."

"You say that now."

Jezra drifted from the room, the train of her stiff gown raking across the stone floor as she muttered, "I will never flee. Never. Never. Never."

Mikkotto watched her leave, firm in her resolve to kill Jezra at the first opportunity and install her son on the throne, to be overseen by a puppet vizier of Mikkotto's choosing while she went back to Hasan Daeg, triumphant as queen.

Yes, at the first opportunity.

15

Maura shunned heavy metal armor.

Instead, she selected a light suit of borax leather. She did wear a metal brace about her neck, knowing that's where her opponents would strike first, since nothing else had killed her thus far.

Stepping outside her tent, she gazed at the heavens. The night sky was at its darkest, but Maura knew it would be dawn soon.

A groom held the reins of Dorak's ebony warhorse while Maura checked the saddle and bridle.

KiKu had related the story of how he cut the girth on Zoar's saddle, causing a serious injury when Zoar fell off the horse.

Now Maura always checked her saddle before mounting. Not that a fall would really hurt her, but a poisoned blade inserted somewhere in the seams of the saddle might slow her down. Sooner or later, someone would discover a poison to which even she would succumb.

Everything seemed in order. She jumped on the spirited horse and pulled the reins out of the groom's hands. As Maura rode through the camp with the uultepes loping behind, Hasan Daegian and Anqarians cheered. The Bhuttanians remained silent, watching her ride past. Nevertheless, they went about the business of making ready for battle, checking their weapons, donning their armor, and stuffing food rations about their persons. Who knew how long it might be before they had a proper meal again?

All the soldiers looked up as a thin ray of light struggled over a distant mountain. Fighting would begin soon.

Maura rode to a steep slope which gave way to a broad plain leading to the city. There were no trees, no vegetation of any kind to impede her army's progress as they advanced upon to Bhuttani—just a desert-looking plain rutted by wagon wheels, animal hooves, and the myriad of footprints made by travelers over the decades.

To the north flowed a river where Bhuttani got most of its drinking water, but it was not like the clear, sweet, sparkling water of Hasan Daeg. It was brown and sluggish like the land surrounding it.

Coming upon a small knot of generals making final preparations, Maura stopped her warhorse and observed her officers, composed of some Hasan Daegians and Anqarians, but mostly Bhuttanians.

She studied them closely. Their armor and horses were decorated with the insignias of their rank and station, but it was the Bhuttanians who stood out, with colorful plumes in their massive helmets and gleaming armor with scarlet cloth showing through the gaps in their shoulder pauldrons.

They bowed their heads and gave the Bhuttanian salute.

"Is everything in place?"

"Yes, Great Mother," they answered in unison.

"Communication established?"

"We have both runners and riders, plus soldiers planted on the hills with signal flags and fire," answered Alexanee.

Maura grunted.

The Bhuttanians grunted as well.

"Then let us proceed. May your gods protect and favor us with a decisive win, with as little death and destruction as possible. Remember, our goal is to capture the city, not obliterate it." Maura turned her horse around, knowing this was an opportune moment for an assassin to strike.

Alexanee pulled his horse alongside her as the others left for their assigned positions.

Maura looked sideways at him, especially the placement of his hands. They were on the reins of his horse, not clutching a dirk.

Maura relaxed. "So it begins, General Alexanee."

"So it does, Great Mother."

"Let's hope your death god Bhuttu slumbers and is not reveling at the prospect of blood being spilled throughout the city."

"I am hoping Jezra will come to her senses and open the gates, sparing the city, if only for the sake of the people still inside the walls."

"You almost make me laugh, General. Do you remember Jezra as being a compassionate and intelligent woman? Even if she wanted to, Mikkotto would never permit it. There is nothing waiting for Mikkotto except a hangman's noose, so she will fight to the death."

"Then I will make it my goal to find her and kill her."

"Only if you have to. I want her taken alive if possible."

"As you wish, Great Mother." Alexanee paused for a moment, wondering if he should ask the next question. "We still have not established contact with Chaun Maaun. Have you had any word?"

"You must trust me in this, General. They will show themselves at a moment of their choosing. They are no doubt watching us at this very moment."

Alexanee swiveled in his saddle. He did not like the thought of the Dinii behind or above him. He had learned to respect their abilities and greatly admired what they had accomplished at Anqara. They had saved an entire civilization almost single-handedly. He had also learned to fear them.

"They are here, even if soaring above the clouds," Maura commented.

A servant rushed to take the reins of Maura's warhorse, which was pawing the ground in nervous anticipation.

Maura jumped off and strode over to the massive royal wagon upon which the throne of bones had been installed again, but the top had been taken off this time so all could clearly see Maura.

With a quick leap, she was on the wagon and allowing her servants to adorn her in Zoar's magnificent robes—the very ones he wore when ordering the city of Anqara to surrender.

Alexanee's brow furrowed.

"You disapprove, General?" asked Maura, studying his face. "You think it is pouring salt into a wound?"

"It's uncommon for you to make such a symbolic statement."

"Are these not the Official Robes of the Aga? Should the citizens of Bhuttani not see that I occupy the position of the aga? Symbolic—yes. Rubbing the Bhuttanian nose in it—perhaps. Stating my claim to rule—absolutely!"

Not wishing to argue with Maura, Alexanee looked at the sky. "Daylight approaches. We must proceed posthaste."

Maura sat on the throne holding the Royal Fan of Hasan Daeg and the ancient Sword of the Agas. Below the dais was an array of goods from all the lands where Maura had established order—precious metals, beautiful bolts of cloth, medicines, plants, tools, cookware, pottery, bags of seeds, shoes, leather goods, jewelry—anything a heart could desire. And they were all things the Bhuttanians needed, since Maura had cut off much of the trade to the city for years.

Taking a deep breath, Maura composed herself and snapped her fan open, giving the signal for soldiers to coax the borax forward. With each lumbering plod of the borax, Maura was moving closer to the true test of her leadership.

By the time the sun sank behind the distant mountains, Maura would either be the Regent Aga, or she would be dead.

16

Timon gnawed on a leaf.

He felt strength leaving him in the hours it had taken him to make his way to the temple. He constantly had to evade patrols, which were interrogating anyone they found in the street as possible saboteurs. The soldiers' methods of questioning were quite brutal, and after stealing everything of value, they left the poor, battered soul lying in the street. Hiding behind some barrels, Timon leaned against a wall, breathing heavily, but feeling new strength surging through his veins as he chewed the pungent leaf. He looked at the sky. It was getting light. Dawn couldn't be far off. Timon had to hurry to the temple, or he would be caught by soldiers sooner or later.

Renewed by the energizing tonic of the leaf, Timon rose to his feet and crept stealthily from doorway to doorway, as KiKu had shown him, until he realized he could see the massive doors of the temple's entrance. All he had to do was step out of the shadows and cross a courtyard, passing the fountain to enter by way of the cellar door on the far side of the building.

Timon looked both ways and listened intently. He saw no one and heard nothing, but he did not budge, for it was light enough that anyone could spot him. Still, he had to move, and move now. Gathering his courage, he emerged from the darkness of a recessed doorway and began across the square when a trio of soldiers stumbled into the courtyard from a narrow side street.

"Hey, you there. Halt!" cried a soldier.

Timon stopped in a blind panic and stared at them. *What am I doing?* Pulling up his robe, Timon turned and ran as fast as he could, with the soldiers hard behind him. He hurried into the alley where the cellar entrance was and pushed against it, looking behind him.

The door stood fast.

Timon pushed again.

The ancient door didn't yield.

Timon looked to his right.

The soldiers were almost upon him.

With all his might, Timon reared up and gave the door a ferocious kick. The door gave way. Timon fell into the blackness of the entryway and slammed the door shut behind him. Leaning against it, he listened. Above his rapid heartbeat, he heard the soldiers muttering.

"Let's be gone. If that lad wants to enter the temple of Bhuttu, he's welcome to it."

Another soldier with a high-pitched voice concurred. "He's no threat. Probably wants to sacrifice himself to Bhuttu to save his family. Poor bastard. Yes, let's be off."

Expelling a sigh of relief, Timon listened until he was sure the soldiers were gone, and then rolled barrels up against the door in case they had a change of heart.

Now Timon had to finish his mission. He must find the amulet and release the Dinii. Betting that Hilkiah would be in the ceremonial hall, Timon made his way through the secret passageways, his breathing becoming more and more labored. Once he stopped and leaned against a wall made slimy by the constant seeping of water and pressed his hand against his chest. His heart was beating so hard, Timon thought it might explode.

Taking another leaf out of his pocket, he chewed it and immediately felt better, but was becoming aware of the awful toll the stimulant was taking on his body. He realized the healer's warning was true. The herb was giving him immediate strength, but ultimately weakening his heart.

Timon finished chewing and swallowed the awful-tasting leaf before continuing to make his way to the great chamber, where he knew all the priests and the novitiates would be praying for a decisive Bhuttanian victory.

He fervently hoped Maura would tear down the temple stone by stone once she had conquered the city. He hated the god Bhuttu and everything the cult of death stood for.

Hearing faint chanting in the distance, Timon stepped up his pace, still pondering what he would do once he found his way to the great hall.

Hilkiah, though a doughy fop, was a big man, and would not give up the amulet easily, and Timon doubted he had the strength to overcome him. He had to find a weapon. Timon smiled at the thought of killing Hilkiah. It would be one evil deed Timon would be only too glad to perform.

17

Alexanee waved a red flag.

Thousands of soldiers from every corner of the empire, stepped out onto the dry, sandy plain and beat their shields with swords, creating a great sound which thundered across the plain.

Those inside the city walls, Bhuttanian soldiers and citizens alike, rushed to the battlements and rooftops to gaze upon enemy soldiers marching in lockstep as they encircled the city.

Frantic women screamed while gathering their babes. Men gaped in horror at the terrifying sight, clasping their hands over their ears to drown out the sound.

Never before had Bhuttan experienced war within its borders, and the people were horrified. The populace now realized the raw terror others had felt at the hand of Bhuttan's powerful army as it swept across the world, destroying all in its path. Many threw themselves down to pray, fearing the wrath of the many foreign gods they had offended, for now the revengeful hand of those gods was upon them.

Bhuttanian soldiers turned to each other and asked, "Are our brothers really about to storm the city? Has that blue witch sowed hatred in their warriors' hearts?"

Mikkotto stood upon a platform high above the troops with Jezra and her son. "Steady, men!" she called out. "This is all for show. Your real queen stands before you with Dorak's son and heir. Remember your blood oaths. Remember who the real aga is!"

Soldiers murmured amongst themselves. "Yes, Dorak's son is the real aga. Surely our generals serving the witch will realize this. They will turn against the Blue Queen before they reach the gate. It's all a ploy to lure the pretender closer to the city."

"Have the boy wave to the people," muttered Mikkotto to Jezra.

Jezra stood transfixed, watching Maura's army march closer and closer, still beating their shields.

"JEZRA!"

Trembling, Jezra pushed the boy forward, but he cried out and ran under his mother's skirts.

A murmur of disquiet rose from the people.

Mikkotto reached down, grabbing the little boy and shoving him in front of her. She whispered into his ear, "Wave, or I swear I shall bite off one of your ears and swallow it whole."

Eyes closed, the boy did as commanded, prodded by Mikkotto's dagger pressing against his bony spine.

Jezra stepped forward and clasped her son's hand while managing a false smile and waving too.

Heartened by this display of solidarity, the city's soldiers rattled their shields as well, and yelled taunts.

Seeing the people's spirit revitalized, Mikkotto gave the signal for Jezra to depart. She barked at Jezra's guards, "Take the aga and the aganess back to the palace and guard them with your lives. That boy must survive at all costs."

Jezra shot Mikkotto a grateful look. She was glad to get away from the noise and the stench. Safe in the Imperial Palace, she would distract her son until the battle was over and the danger had passed. Since the palace was in the middle of the city, they might not even hear the fighting. The thought gave Jezra comfort. She had never experienced a battle, and she didn't want to experience one now.

When the Bhuttanians seized Anqara, she had already been married to Dorak and far from harm's way. As she was hurrying down the steps to her palanquin, it never occurred to her that Maura might capture the city.

Not once.

18

The refugees heard the clamor.

Throwing down their bowls of gruel, they dashed about in panic, thinking Maura's army was coming to kill them. Many climbed into trees to look across the plain on which Bhuttani sat.

Akela was one of them. He scampered up a tree and climbed to its highest branch. Straining his eyes to see the drama unfold, Akela was grateful the camp was on a knoll at the edge of a small forest, which an ancient aga had planted for his pleasure many miles from the city.

Akela could not make out details, and could only discern a broad outline of what was taking place before him.

Pointing, he cried, "The Blue Queen's army is descending upon the city!"

"How many soldiers does that bitch have?" asked an old fighter, retired due to a bad leg.

Akela did not know the exact number of soldiers in the Blue Queen's army, but knew they were many. "More soldiers than there are stars in the heavens," he replied, upon which the old fighter grunted and hurried to his tent to collect his sword. Maybe the gods would be kind and let him die in battle. He was determined to make his way back to the city to fight, even if he had to crawl.

"What else, boy?" a woman cried, wondering if her son was still alive and marching in the service of that blue devil. If it was true, she doubted that she would be able to withstand the shame.

"I see a huge platform pulled by many borax. It is tall as any mountain. The soldiers are parting to make way for the platform, but it is moving very slowly."

"That must be her," cried a young mother who was suckling her baby.

Another woman replied, "Yes, the Blue Queen will demand that the city surrender. Perhaps those left behind the city's walls should yield. I have never seen such might."

Startled at the woman's defeatist statement, the man standing next to her spat at her feet and turned his back.

Unnerved by the man's contemptuous response, the woman said, "If our defeat was not possible, why are we hiding in the woods like frightened animals and eating morsels of food thrown to us by our enemies?"

Many nodded their heads in agreement.

Fearful of retaliation, many fled deeper into the woods, running past the fierce female Hasan Daegian soldiers who stepped quickly out of their way.

One of the soldiers remarked, "They'll be back when they get hungry."

"Or to slit our throats while we sleep," replied a second in command.

"Then we shan't sleep," murmured her comrade, standing on her tiptoes to see the spectacle unfolding on the plain.

"We shall have to round them up later," complained the Hasan Daeg soldier.

The commander-in-charge agreed. "Yes, we will, but right now we have orders to find this Akela lad. The other guards can round up the refugees and put them back in the camp." She looked up into the trees and pointed. "That small boy up in the very top of the tree. He fits the description. Maybe this is our lucky day, and he's the boy our queen wants."

Another soldier stepped in front of her commander, blocking the way. "Let us wait until the boy tires and comes down of his own accord. Otherwise, we will have to cut the tree down. No one willingly goes to see our queen when summoned."

Her superior nodded, "Wise counsel. We will grab the boy as soon as he comes down, but do it quietly. We don't want the others to see us and possibly attack, trying to save him."

The soldier grunted in reply—a Bhuttanian custom the Hasan Daegians had acquired.

They did not have long to wait.

Akela heard a small rustle and felt a rush of wind behind him and looked over his shoulder. To his great surprise, Akela saw many gigantic beings with faces and torsos like humans, but clothed with feathers and sprouting great wings high in the trees behind him. Crying out in fear, Akela loosened his grip and fell from the tree. He tried unsuccessfully to grab onto branches as he plummeted, only to be snatched from certain death at the last moment by a great, clawed talon.

Akela found himself face-to-face with one of the strange creatures, whose face was grinning at him. He pummeled this strange being with his fists, fearing he was about to be eaten.

The bird-woman swooped down and carefully dropped the boy into the arms of the waiting Hasan Daegian warriors, who did not seem to fear the bizarre beasts.

He heard one soldier speak in Anqara to the other. "The Dinii are here. Nothing will stop us now."

THE DINII!

Akela had always heard vague rumors of the strange race of bird people, but thought them to be the tales old women concocted to frighten their grandchildren. He had also listened to KiKu and Timon whisper about the Dinii. That's what the fuss over the feather found in the temple was about!

One warrior threw Akela over her shoulder like a sack of Anqarian apples and carried him to a comrade waiting on a warhorse.

He was very confused, but then Akela was confused about everything that was happening, and yearned deeply for the comfort of Madric, Pearl, Tippa, and Tippu.

Fearing for his life, Akela squirmed in the warrior's grasp and managed to sink his teeth into her neck. Out of the corner of his eye, he saw another soldier on a nearby warhorse rear back to strike him.

That's when everything went black.

19

Maura sat atop her throne.

A team of lumbering, snorting borax pulled the great wagon that housed the hideous chair. Maura, wearing all the regalia denoting her station, was easily visible from a great distance.

Beside the rolling platform was a retinue of generals in her command, in full uniform noting their rank and country of origin, and riding spirited white warhorses. The Bhuttanian generals rode in front.

Behind walked major dignitaries from every country of the Bhuttanian Empire.

Mikkotto eyed this procession from a protected vantage point in a sentry tower. She had instructed archers not to shoot, as she knew Maura would stay out of range, and she did not want edgy soldiers to waste arrows. Metal was at a premium for the arrowheads, so much so that she had ordered more arrows made without metal tips, instead having their points hardened over a fire.

Watching the platform make its way to the west gate, Mikkotto had to admit Maura cast an imposing visage, sitting upright on a throne that barely swayed as it was pulled across the barren plain.

Mikkotto had to assume Maura's army had smoothed the well-traveled road to the west gate, filling in any dips or ruts to provide the platform with a smooth journey.

The line of soldiers encircling Bhuttani still banged on their shields. Only when the platform reached the circle did the soldiers on the west side open their line, letting the platform through and falling in step behind it.

It took an hour for Maura's regal procession to traverse the wide plain outside the city and come to a halt close enough to the city's wall for her to be heard.

By that time all rooftops, windows of high buildings, and battlements were filled with curious onlookers, many of them furious, some of them resigned, but most of them frightened. Never before had a foreign army breached their borders, much less threatened the capital.

It was not lost on many who had witnessed the fall of Anqara that Maura had donned the very same royal robes that Zoar wore when he demanded the city's surrender.

The platform halted, and a trumpet gave the signal for the others to stop as well. The beating of the shields ceased.

Nothing could be heard across the plain except for a harsh wind whistling through the battlements.

Each general turned his horse to form a single line comprised of twenty generals on each side of the platform.

Dignitaries who had been marching behind Maura now proceeded to the front of the platform. They bowed to Maura before forming a line, standing in front of the platform facing the city, each one brandishing the flag of their country or tribal alliance. There were nineteen flags fluttering in the hot wind. Soldiers closed ranks until there was one continuous line encircling the city.

Maura rose from the throne and stood ramrod straight, holding the Royal Fan of Hasan Daeg, denoting her position as queen of Hasan Daeg, and Zoar's sword for the authority of the aga. She held them both aloft and turned back and forth for everyone to see. "Citizens of Bhuttan, I am Maura de Magela, tenth queen of Hasan Daeg, the royal wife of Aga Dorak, Crowned Empress, and Regent Dowager for Dyanna, Crowned Princess. I have come to install Princess Dyanna, blood daughter of Aga Dorak and granddaughter to Aga Zoar, as the legitimate heir of the Bhuttanian Empire.

"Open your gates and rejoice that the royal line of succession will be reestablished, and that I have led home your brothers, fathers, and sons."

"Your claim is a fraud!" cried Mikkotto. "The real heir, Dorak's firstborn, sits upon the throne."

If Maura was disturbed to hear Mikkotto's voice, she showed no sign up it. "You who presumes to address your empress, identify yourself."

Mikkotto shouted back, "You know well who I am. Where is Dorak, Maura? Where is the aga? It is known that you had him murdered." Ignoring her questions, Maura called out, "Why do you claim to speak for my people? You have no authority over them. You are a traitor and cast out from your own country. Now you bring treachery upon this city. You are an illegitimate pretender."

Mikkotto reared her head back and laughed. "As are you, Blue Witch. I serve Jezra, wife of Dorak and mother to his eldest son. Your bastard bitch cannot rule. Women have never ruled in Bhuttan."

"Then why are you shouting at me like a fishmonger's wife? Is there not a man with more authority over you who should be speaking? For as you just said, no woman has ever ruled in Bhuttan."

Maura pointed her fan at Mikkotto and addressed the anxious observers. "Do not listen to this woman. She will lead you down the path to perdition. We have come with food, provisions of every kind, including metal, medicine, and seeds. Your days of deprivation are over. Bhuttan can begin anew—a fresh start."

"Seeds?" shouted an old man standing in the rampart. "What would we do with seeds? War is all we have ever known. It is all we want."

Maura shouted, "I have brought you a bounty of good things. You can live without fear, and help to rebuild Kaseri!"

The old man answered, "We are warriors. We live without fear now."

"Do you? Look about the city. Soldiers from every country of the known world surround the Bhuttanian Empire. I control everything but this city." She pointed the Sword of the Aga at the Bhuttanian generals. "Even your mighty warriors know Bhuttan cannot go on as before."

"They will not fight us!" exclaimed the people.

"I give you one last chance. Open the gates, or the deaths that follow will be upon your heads."

"Maura, since you speak of heads, I have one for you." Mikkotto reared back and threw a severed head over the wall onto the ground, which gently rolled to a stop.

Four soldiers, using their shields to protect them from zinging arrows, ran and grabbed it.

Alexanee gestured to the soldier holding the head to bring it to him. He looked at it carefully and then signaled the soldier away before speaking to Maura. "It is Cappet. I'm sure of it. Jezra must have learned of our pact with him."

There was no more talking to be done. Bhuttani had sealed its fate.

Maura snapped her fan shut.

The pounding of large drums began.

Maura took off the robes, exposing her in full battle dress. One assistant placed a silver-plated helmet with the horns of a wild borax bull upon her head.

Thrusting her sword in the air, Maura nimbly jumped on the back of Dorak's ebony steed and galloped off.

Servants grabbed the halters of the borax and slowly turned them around to take them to the safety of a pasture several miles away from the fighting that would soon begin.

With the generals following, Maura rode around the city walls with her arm thrust upright, holding the Sword of the Aga so it glimmered in the morning light.

Many a Bhuttanian vainly shot arrows, but the generals and Maura were careful to stay out of range.

Once Maura had made a complete circle around the city, she and the generals separated, each one going to a separate division of warriors. The soldiers retreated as well, except for the teams of fifty arming the catapults with massive boulders.

Alexanee gave the signal to those manning the catapults to release the boulders, which flew high into the sky and slammed against the thick walls of Bhuttani. The sound was deafening as the ground shook.

People screamed, fleeing from the battlements amidst falling rock debris.

The war against Bhuttani had begun in earnest.

20

Akela blinked.

He was slung over a warhorse with his hands tied behind his back.

A blue hand grabbed his hair, lifting his head.

Akela looked up to see the Blue Queen staring down at him.

Maura's long blue-black hair blew in the wind beneath her battle helmet, which was adorned with great horns. The Blue Queen looked like an angry goddess unleashing her wrath upon the people.

Akela shuddered with fear at her imposing countenance. He was not prepared for the kind voice that greeted him.

"Boy, have you anything to report?"

"There . . . there are big monsters in the trees."

Raising an eyebrow, Maura looked questioningly at the warriors who had brought him.

After exchanging anxious looks, one of the women was brave enough to answer. "The Dinii have arrived, Great Mother, and are resting in the trees near the refugee camp."

Maura beckoned to one of the guards. "Go to the edge of the forest at the back of the refugee camp. Tell the Dinii to assemble at the west side of the city, where we are."

The soldier rushed off to carry out Maura's instructions.

Maura turned her attention back to Akela and instructed an aide-de-camp, "Take this boy to KiKu's wives. Perhaps they can get something else out of him. Tell no one about that boy or KiKu's women."

The Hasan Daeg guards gave the Bhuttanian salute and turned their horses to escort the boy, but not before they heard Maura order, "And tell those women to give this child a bath. He stinks to the heavens."

The soldiers grunted in agreement. Being Hasan Daegians themselves, they could not understand how people could let themselves get so filthy, even if there was a war going on.

It was downright barbaric.

21

Mikkotto loved war.

She loved everything about it—the noise, the confusion, and the smells of sweat, fire, and blood. Even the moans of the dying sounded sweet to her.

And Mikkotto was fearless.

The Bhuttanian soldiers in the city were shocked to realize their brethren serving in Maura's army were determined to support the Blue Queen, even if it meant slaying their relatives.

Mikkotto strode upright on the ramparts, rousing the troops as huge boulders flew past her. "Your kinsmen are bewitched by that she-devil. Fight so that you may kill her and release them from her wicked magic." Her lack of fear encouraged the soldiers to remain at their stations. "Do not shoot. Do not waste your arrows!" she cried out. "Pick up those rocks and cast them back." Anticipating the use of catapults, Mikkotto had ordered her men build their own. Her strategy was to reuse the invaders' boulders against them. Mikkotto had engineers concentrate on destroying the catapults sitting exposed on the plain. After twelve attempts, they were able to damage one of Maura's catapults, thus raising the spirits of the soldiers. Within minutes another one was knocked down and turned on its side.

To further demoralize the Bhuttanians on Maura's side, Mikkotto ordered the soldiers to throw bodies of the dead over the wall with parchments tied to their bodies saying things like—YOU KILLED THIS BHUTTANIAN MOTHER or YOU BUTCHERED THIS INNOCENT CHILD.

Alexanee immediately commanded any Bhuttanian on the front line to report to the Hasan Daegians on the north side of the city, while ordering Anqarians to take their place on the catapults and drag the bodies out of sight and bury them.

He rode to the knoll where Maura had gone back to the platform to observe the assault's progress. He jumped off his horse and asked permission to speak with her privately.

Maura told her advisors to leave, and immediately servants carried steps to the platform and helped them down.

Alexanee leapt up three steps at a time and rushed over to Maura, who remained seated on the aga's throne.

The uultepes, lying on the dais, tensed and growled.

Maura cautioned them to be quiet and bade Alexanee forward.

He walked slowly past the lounging cats and did not flinch as one stuck out his claw and scraped his boots. Alexanee could feel the cat's claws rake across the leather. As the general learned long ago, the uultepes liked to play games and assert their authority over people whenever possible. He ignored them. "Great Mother, I have come to report that the city's walls have yet to be breached. The taking of the city is not at hand."

"I commend your ancestors' ability to build such a remarkable barrier. It is most commendable."

Alexanee bowed. "Unfortunately, we will not be able to take the city today."

Maura stood, snapping her fan shut. "We risk rebellion from our Bhuttanian troops if this continues for long."

"I couldn't agree more. And Mikkotto is catapulting bodies with subversive messages designed to undermine our soldiers' will."

Maura's brow furrowed. "Civilian casualties?"

"Yes, Great Mother."

"Shouldn't all the civilians have been evacuated to the center of the city, away from the fighting?"

"Yes, Great Mother."

"Are we responsible?"

"We cannot tell. Once they splatter on the ground, it is difficult to say what killed them."

"What say ye?"

"I think she is killing women and children, and then throwing them over the wall to make it look like we killed them with our catapults."

"This is very serious. How long before word of this spills out into our main troops?"

"I have reassigned all Bhuttanians who saw the bodies to the Hasan Daegian division on the east side. The rest of the troops are behind our main line. They wouldn't have seen anything."

"Alas, rumors are like water. They flow very quickly in an army. Soldiers are worse than old men sipping colla tea in a café for spreading rumors."

"Yes, Great Mother."

Maura sat back down on her throne thinking. "Water," she murmured. "The river to the north?"

"It supplies the drinking water to the city."

Maura gave the command for all who were watching to face away, and then held a fan to her face so no spy could read her lips. She motioned Alexanee to lean closer. "What if we created a great fire against the wall on the north side, a fire hot enough to heat up the wall? Then we divert the river to rush against the fire."

Alexanee cupped the side of his helmet so no one could read his lips either and completed Maura's thought. "Causing the cold of the water to crack the heated stones."

Maura leaned back on her throne and replied with a whisper of a smile. "Exactly."

"Such a project would take most of the day."

"We don't have hours to spare."

"Can you convince the Dinii to help? With them, we can implement your plan today."

"They are in the forest. I've sent a message for the Dinii to redeploy, but they will probably stay where they are. They prefer the cover of trees, and will do nothing until they have verified that Empress Gitar is living or dead. So they will bide their time. They do not care about our petty war."

Alexanee snarled, "If I start cutting down the trees from the forest to stoke the fire, perhaps they will be motivated to help, since their perches will be taken away. Might they attack us, though?"

"Announce the reason you are felling the trees before cutting. They won't like it, but they won't attack. Make sure you don't use our stocks of wood. We need ours to make arrows and repair wheels. Is that stand of trees the only wood near Bhuttani?"

"Yes, it was planted so the agas could hunt."

"How will you start the fire?"

"I will use cooking oil and axle grease."

"Make sure our people have adequate protection when building the fire. I don't want our soldiers exposed to arrows from the city when building it."

Alexanee grunted before asking, "One more thing. There are rumors that you assigned two spies to enter the temple of Bhuttu to report on sightings of the Dinii and the Black Cacodemon."

"Did I?"

"I'm sorry you did not trust me enough to let me shoulder this burden with you."

"I wonder how this rumor reached your ears, General. Perhaps you have spies of your own?"

"As you stated, Great Mother, rumors run like water within a military camp."

"Is there anything else you wish to discuss, General Alexanee?"

Realizing this as a dismissal, Alexanee gave the Bhuttanian salute and jumped upon his warhorse from the platform. The horse reared before galloping off with Alexanee firmly on its back.

Maura bit the inside of her cheek as she realized the image of dominance and virility that Alexanee created. Surely many a maiden's heart in the camp fluttered as he rode past on his white stallion. Maura admitted that Alexanee was an arresting man with a keen mind. Besides Mikkotto, he had the potential to become her most dangerous enemy. The sight of Alexanee mastering his stallion turned Maura's thoughts to Dorak.

As Maura's counselors began to ascend the steps to the platform, she waved them away.

Dorak. Dorak. Dorak.

Was he dead?

Was he alive and with Gitar?

What would she do if he were?

Maura knew she could never see Dorak again or her resolve might vanish. Oh, she loved him still. She burned for him—his lips, his arms. She would give anything to hear his melodious voice, to stroke his silky black hair, to have him in her bed, but that could never be. Dorak must never be allowed to ascend to the Bhuttanian throne again.

As soon as Dorak was sighted, Maura had given orders to detain him. A special contingent of Hasan Daegians had been searching for many years.

If captured, Dorak was to be taken to a secret location and tried for war crimes—including the murder of Queen Abisola and Prince Consort Iasos. Even though he had not given the commands for their deaths, his sheltering of Mikkotto made it possible for their deaths to occur.

At best, Maura could offer Dorak imprisonment at an outlying estate, far away from any large population, and guarded by Hasan Daegian soldiers.

A tear escaped Maura's eye. She dared not wipe it away, lest someone see her.

These were the decisions of queenship that lay heavy upon her shoulders. How could she not make this sacrifice when so many others had done so, including giving their very lives in her service?

Truly, she loved Dorak as no other. Her very flesh called out for his, but she would never touch him again and, Mekonia willing, Maura would never lay eyes upon him either.

Maura was determined to conquer the Bhuttanian people and bend them to her will. After that, she was going to restore order throughout all the empire.

Slowly the rule of law from her courts would supplant the rule of the sword throughout the land, so her citizens might live in peace. But it would never happen with Dorak. Viciousness was bred into him, and moreover, despite Dorak's desire to be a tender ruler, cruelty would win out and consume him, corroding his rule.

Maura thought back to how happy her mother Abisola had been with her father Iasos—a contentment she would never know. She felt dreadfully alone, more alone that she had ever been. Except for her daughter, no one loved her. She knew she would never be loved again, and that was a terrible thing to realize.

Maura straightened her shoulders and thrust out her chin.

What was the matter with her, allowing these maudlin thoughts to overtake her?

She had a war to win.

And she would win it.

22

Dorak followed Zedek.

He was lost in a miasma of a murky and forbidding fog. Putting his hand on the hilt of his dagger gave comfort as Dorak was straining to see the wizard ahead, when out of the corner of his eye he sensed light and movement. He rushed to meet it.

Abruptly, Dorak found himself out of the fog and hovering in the air above a multitude of priests on their knees and chanting. Dorak recognized the chamber. He was in the main hall of the temple of Bhuttu.

On the altar dais, Dorak saw Hilkiah, the high priest of Bhuttu. Hilkiah had officiated at his wedding with Maura and had crowned her as empress. He stood in his official robes, waving his arms and touching something on a gold chain around his neck. Dorak peered harder, trying to discern what Hilkiah was doing, and then inhaled sharply.

The amulet! The very one Dorak had plucked from the body of his father Zoar and used to conjure the Black Cacodemon.

Somehow Hilkiah had gained possession of the amulet!

Dorak realized Hilkiah must be trying to release the wizard from whatever state of suspended animation he had cast.

More important, it seemed to be working!

The air began to shimmer as bands of color formed and buckled. A crescendo of a mournful wail escalated to such a zenith that it culminated in a wave of force which flipped Dorak over and over in the air. He managed to arrest his wild flight by grabbing hold of a column.

Wait! It dawned on Dorak that he had grabbed a physical object.

Dorak could feel the cold stone—something solid in his hands.

The incantations were working!

Giddy with the promise of freedom, Dorak watched excitedly as the priests continued their ritual. He could feel his heart pounding so hard against his rib cage, he thought it might it burst from sheer exuberance.

Fierce bolts of lightning shredded the dank temple air below Dorak, but above the heads of the priests. Heat radiated from the lightning strikes, and the very air in the temple glowed as the fire grew in intensity until brilliant red flames erupted, threatening to engulf the entire chamber. They quickly subsided, and in their wake a shimmering aperture hovered in the air.

Dorak cried out in joy, but his excitement was short-lived.

Out from another column stepped Zedek, murmuring an invocation. As he made his way to the portal, the wizard morphed into a fearsome creature, complete with scales, claws, and fangs.

A dragon!

Realizing Zedek was making his way to escape, Dorak pushed away from the column, rushing toward the monster.

Just as Zedek was stepping through, Dorak grabbed his scaly neck and pulled the wizard back.

Dorak could not allow Zedek to pass into the dimension of the living.

Even if Dorak had to sacrifice his own life!

23

KiKu was asleep.

He had dozed off, slumped against a wall. Hearing the loud peal of a gong, he shook himself awake and quickly took in his surroundings. Had he given himself away?

Realizing he was still hidden and safe, KiKu indulged himself by giving way to emotion. He would have snapped the necks of any of his operatives if they had fallen asleep on a critical mission. Now he had done the same. Shame welled up within him.

KiKu thought back to his wives. They were facing acute danger, and he had almost added to their peril. He thought of Maura, struggling to rescue a world. He might have easily failed them all.

He had to admit he was getting old, and intrigue no longer thrilled him. The notorious spylord would rather be in his tent, sitting by a nice fire, and surrounded by the chatter of his wives.

The hetmaan wanted the war to be over, and the slaughter to stop. KiKu was sick of death and senseless suffering.

When the war was over, KiKu would take his wives to live in Hasan Daeg. He knew Maura would reward him with sanctuary, even a large estate with a grand house—perhaps Mikkotto's estate. KiKu grinned at the irony of that. Yes, he would ask for Mikkotto Sumsumitoyo's land and palace. KiKu knew Maura would delight in that.

The spylord had to put those thoughts aside, because the chanting of the priests was growing in volume and intensity. KiKu peeked from his hiding place.

The very air above the priests was transforming. It began to sparkle and vibrate, supplanted by what looked like a thick liquid one could almost touch.

Astonished, KiKu shot a look at Hilkiah, who was standing on the altar, carefully cradling the amulet and muttering with his eyes closed. All the other priests were kneeling on the floor, ardently chanting incantations with their eyes closed as well.

It was apparent Hilkiah had learned how to manipulate the amulet, and it was working. The hole in the fabric of the temple's dank air was expanding.

KiKu put his hand on his dagger, ready to strike.

The entire temple shuddered violently.

The priests' eyes flew open, and they gaped up in amazement.

An enormous reptilian leg shot forth from the roiling darkness above the priests. Then a second leg punched through the portal, followed by a spiked tail uncoiling and whipping dangerously.

Some of the priests moaned while others screamed joyfully and danced upon their mats.

Bhuttu would be so pleased.

They had called forth a dragon!

24

Timon stumbled.

He used a massive column to steady himself before lurching into the ceremonial chamber, but no one noticed because their attention was riveted on the hole emerging in the smoke-filled air of the temple.

Timon followed their gaze and gasped.

The space above them flashed while pulsating bands of color fluctuated halfway between the ceiling and the floor until a loud noise thundered, sounding like a cracked whip.

The portal was opening!

A hole, devoid of color, undulated and grew larger and larger, until a monstrous leg and tail emerged.

Before Timon could react, KiKu sprang from his hiding place and threw himself at Hilkiah. Timon expected KiKu to be repelled by the protective aura Hilkiah created about his person, but the High Priest, weakened by hours of continuous chanting and ritual, could not sustain the shield as before.

KiKu tussled with Hilkiah, trying to snatch the amulet off his neck, but the High Priest was still stronger. The spylord struggled to subdue Hilkiah, who screamed for help. In the melee, KiKu dropped his dagger.

Several of Hilkiah's attendants sprang to his aid, only to be beaten back by Timon, who rushed behind the High Priest.

A blast of frigid air knocked everyone down as the Dinii, long captives of the netherworld, exploded through the portal with such force that many hit the back wall of the chamber and were knocked unconscious, plummeting to the stone floor. The Dinii, who managed to avoid flying into walls, descended and formed a tight circle around their fallen comrades. Others hovered in confusion looking for a way out.

The priests advanced upon the Dinii.

The powerful Dinii fended off the priests, picking them up and breaking their necks, but the priests, fueled by religious frenzy, threw themselves at KiKu, Timon, and the Dinii.

Losing his grasp on Hilkiah, KiKu made a final move to break Hilkiah's leg. A sickening snap sounded in the din as the High Priest's thighbone cracked, causing the High Priest to howl in pain. More priests ran onto the altar, mauling KiKu and Timon.

A fierce blow to the head knocked Timon down, leaving him defenseless. Three priests leapt on him and bludgeoned him in the kidneys. Overcome by the intense pain, Timon feared he might lose consciousness until he spied KiKu's dagger. Lunging for it, he barely caught it by its blade and pulled it to him. Ignoring the searing pain as the blade sliced his hand, Timon swept his arm upward, slashing the throat of one of the priests holding him down. The other two priests stepped back in alarm, freeing Timon to careen toward Hilkiah, sending the knife blade deep into the priest's back.

Seeing his opportunity, KiKu snatched the amulet off Hilkiah's neck.

Another freezing blast burst forth from the portal, which was pulsating wildly as Empress Gitar and Prince Iegani swept out to join their comrades.

Gitar, having watched events from the other side of the portal before flying through, shouted orders for her warriors to save KiKu and Timon.

The Dinii, led by Yeti, plowed through the priests by bashing their heads against the mighty stone columns holding up the roof. As the Dinii, KiKu, and Timon fought for their lives, the portal groaned and quaked.

The empress moved to reenter the portal to seek Dorak, when Iegani pulled her back. "Gitar, think of your people. Dorak means nothing to us."

Resigned to let Dorak meet his fate, Gitar pushed her uncle away and flapped her powerful wings to hover in the air while giving orders to the Dinii.

A great crash sounded, and the walls trembled as if in an earthquake. Gitar was hurled against a wall, breaking one of her wings, slamming her to the temple floor.

Enraged that their High Priest had been slain, the infuriated priests set upon the wounded Dinii empress, but they were no match for Gitar. Even though weakened, she seized her attackers with her talons and tore their heads off.

Iegani, with several other Dinii, forced their way through the mob surrounding her. Even though there were close to a thousand priests, novices, and attendants, they were no match for the Dinii, who caused the blood of the slain to coat the floor. The Dinii made quick work of them, throwing their dead bodies into a pile in the middle of the floor until they formed a barricade which the surviving priests had to climb over in order to reach the fray.

All the while the temple quivered and moaned as walls crumbled and tall columns toppled over.

Gitar scanned the chamber for an exit. With the help of Iegani and Toppo, Gitar followed other Dinii fleeing the temple. Yeti and Tarsus were the last Dinii to fly out of the temple, carrying Timon and KiKu, who was clutching the severed head of Hilkiah.

They did not see the portal quake one last time and disgorge a battling Zedek and Dorak, locked in fierce combat.

Zedek, now in human form, pulled away from Dorak. "Fool! Don't you see the temple is destroying itself?"

Dorak cried back, "I don't care. You must not be allowed to live!"

Zedek held his arm out straight with his palm flat, pointing toward Dorak, unleashing a white-hot bolt of energy, which slammed Dorak against a falling column, knocking him senseless. Zedek recited an incantation and disappeared.

Dorak, coming to his senses, lurched to his feet to resume the fight, but realized Zedek was gone. Climbing over dead bodies and rubble, Dorak made his way through the maze of debris until he came out onto the city street as the lofty ceiling of the temple twisted and collapsed.

The ground shook, and the grand temple of Bhuttu inclined to one side, seemingly frozen for a moment before collapsing in a ground-shaking rumble of dust and debris.

The aga bowed his head and whispered a Bhuttanian prayer for the dead. He wondered if all the Dinii made it out, but was sure he had glimpsed them fleeing the main chamber when he fell out of the portal.

Hearing the whoosh of arrows piercing the air and the crash of boulders pounding against the walls of the city, Dorak knew Maura must be attacking. He quickly weighed his options. If he tried to contact Maura, Dorak knew he would surely be killed by his enemies in the Hasan Daegian court before he could reach her.

No, it would be better if he could make his way to the Imperial Palace. Dorak hesitated. If he occupied the throne, the fighting might stop. But what if Maura had given orders for him to be killed on sight? Dorak realized the Dinii from the temple would immediately find Maura and inform her that he was alive. She need only to give the order, and every Dinii would hunt him down.

If he were in Maura's place, that's was what he would do. Dorak's heart sank. He knew Maura loved him, but he had placed her in a terrible position. He'd left her with no choice but to kill him or take him prisoner.

Dorak took a deep breath. The only thing he could do now was save his son and flee. Perhaps once Maura took control of the city he could contact her and work out some sort of a treaty. He had no doubt Jezra and their son were in the palace. She would have had to stay to keep the city's soldiers loyal and willing to fight Maura.

A man running in the street stopped in his tracks staring at Dorak. "My lord, are you . . ."

Dorak extended his hand as if offering a greeting, but as the man came within reach, he grabbed the man's tunic and broke his neck, saying softly, "No, I'm not, my friend." He gently lowered the man's body before rushing to the palace.

He had to save his son. Dorak pleaded to any god that would listen, "Let me do one honorable thing before I die. Let me save my son."

But the gods were not listening.

25

Maura heard shouting.

The cries were coming from soldiers pointing at the sky.

Maura bolted from her throne as counselors and foreign dignitaries moved to get a better look. They all looked toward the heavens, watching as a black cloud shot up from the city into the sky with a great cacophony reverberating throughout the land. Even those working the catapults stopped and gaped.

"The Dinii!" shouted the Hasan Daegians, pointing and waving their arms. The rest of the army cheered while the Bhuttanians winced and looked away. They hadn't forgotten the terror they felt when Maura and the Dinii first attacked them at the wall of mist on the border of Hasan Daeg.

"They're on our side now, chum," remarked a Bhuttanian private, nudging his companion, who looked upon the ascending swarm with dread.

"Let's hope they don't have a change of heart and rip our heads off," his friend replied.

Another great cry came from within Bhuttani, probably since the city's residents had never seen a Dini. The city's defense forces began shooting at them immediately.

Alexanee shouted at his men working the catapults to get back to work, hoping to provide covering fire for the Dinii leaving the city.

The cloud flew straight up as Maura knew they would. If confused or in danger, the Dinii always flew straight up. To the right of the city another massive cloud ascended.

Maura knew it was Chaun Maaun and the rest of the Dinii rushing to meet Gitar. They would fly beyond the clouds and hover until a decision was made. Maura hoped they would return to the camp Maura had set up for them and not fly away to the Forbidden Zone, leaving the war and its terrors behind.

Maura called for her palanquin. She urgently desired to run to the Dinii's camp, but knew she had to ceremonially welcome Gitar, who, as the Dinii empress, had higher status. All things had to be done according to protocol, since many eyes watched, eager to find fault. To reassure her forces, she must project serene confidence when entering the Dinii camp.

Alexanee watched while eight Hasan Daegian female soldiers, all equal in height, bore the royal palanquin on their broad shoulders. Although he knew the Dinii were a military necessity, he despised them, and hoped they would fly back to the mountains, once the war was over. Alexanee hated their high-pitched voices and the dreadful clicking noise they made when talking to one another. He was repulsed that they had feathers where there should have been flesh, and feared their retractable claws that could rip a man to shreds.

Let the Hasan Daegians make all the treaties they wanted with those loathsome creatures. He wanted no part of the Dinii. As soon as possible, Alexanee would use his considerable influence over Maura to have them excluded from Bhuttan, because he never wanted to see another Dini as long as he lived.

If Maura would not see fit to send the Dinii away, perhaps he would circulate a rumor his spies had uncovered to undermine her. He rubbed his chin, thinking.

But would anyone believe that Maura and Chaun Maaun had once been lovers? The very idea was ludicrous. He didn't think the rumor had merit, but if one repeated a lie often enough, people believed it, and it would put the reign of Princess Dyanna at risk. After all, who was her real father?

And if one pounded a wall long enough, it would fall. "Put your backs into it, men!" yelled Alexanee as he peered through a field glass.

Was that a tiny crack in the wall? No, he concluded. Alexanee slapped his saddle horn in frustration. Right now he wanted Maura to convince the Dinii to help with the river. He needed their assistance, or the taking of Bhuttani would be delayed.

Alexanee would work with the Black Cacodemon himself if that's what it took to take Bhuttani and install Maura as the aganess.

Then, when the time was right, Alexanee would make his move, but for now he had to bide his time. He spat on the ground at the thought of a foreigner on the ancient throne of the Bhuttanian agas.

And a female foreigner at that!

26

Maura reached the Dinii camp.

By the time she exited her palanquin, all the Dinii had retreated from the sky to the shelter of the tents Maura had provided behind the protection of her vast army.

Servants were serving platters of raw meat and flagons of ale to ravenous Dinii while the wounded were attended by the women from the House of Magi who applied healing salves and bound wounds.

Maura concluded from the number of wounded Dinii that a fierce battle had been fought in the temple. Walking through the camp, she heard her name whispered as the Dinii recognized her. "Maura. Great Mother. It's Maura. Little sparrow."

Whispers turned to shouts as the Dinii stood up from their stools or jumped off perches. Several tried to embrace Maura, but were held back by her guards. Reaching the royal tent, Maura formally requested an audience with Gitar. Standing before Gitar's private quarters, she waited patiently, thinking a private audience could be rejected. After all, Gitar might hold her responsible for her people's suffering.

A Dini sentry opened the flap of the tent and bade Maura to enter.

Empress Gitar sat, being tended by a healer who was setting her broken wing.

Realizing that Gitar was injured, Maura cried out, "Mother!" and ran to her, collapsing at her feet in a heap.

"My little sparrow," cooed Gitar, stroking Maura's windblown hair. "My little sparrow. It has been so long. So long. Let me look at you."

"Get up, child," Maura recognized the unmistakable voice in her mind. Rising and looking about, Maura whispered, "Iegani?" Seeing him standing in a corner and smiling warmly at her, Maura ran and

wrapped him in a hug.

Iegani patted Maura's head with great affection. "Is this anyway for a great warrior to act? Haven't we taught you better?"

Wiping away her tears, Maura pulled away, nodding. "I have looked for you so long, and now to see you again . . . alive. This is a great blessing from Mekonia."

"That hurts," Gitar snapped at the healer, giving the woman a quick peck on the hand.

The healer drew back in astonishment.

Maura exclaimed, "Second mother of my heart! Let me minister to you as only I can."

Gitar gently pushed Maura away. "No! You must conserve all your strength for this war. That is most important. You must not waste your energy. I am in capable hands."

Maura cautioned the healer. "Empress Gitar and the royal court of the Dinii are to be your only patients. You must see to Empress Gitar's every need."

The healer bowed, "Yes, Great Mother."

Gitar scoffed, "It is nothing, little sparrow."

Maura looked questioningly at the healer.

"The empress has sustained a minor break in the wing. She should be whole in a couple of weeks," replied the healer, all the while staring at the floor and trying not to tremble with fear.

Maura asked, "You cannot fly?"

"With help, I can."

"We shall make your stay as comfortable as possible." Maura turned to the healer. "Leave us now. And I warn you not to breathe a word of what you see or hear in this tent. As far as anyone is concerned, Empress Gitar is resting, and that is all that will be said."

"Yes, Great Mother. I understand and will obey."

"Leave us now."

Once the healer removed herself from the tent, Maura picked up a stool from a corner and sat before Gitar. "You must have many questions as I do." She grasped Gitar's hand and held it to her cheek. "I thought I had killed that beast, but Zedek must have uttered a spell with his last breath. When I turned, you were no longer there."

"I understand it has been years, but seemed only hours to those of us bound in the netherworld."

Maura nodded. "Yes, second mother of my heart. I have been searching for three years."

"You are now ruler of all of Kaseri?"

"Except for Bhuttani."

Iegani intercepted, "This is the final battle of the civil war?"

Maura turned toward him. "Yes. Once I capture Bhuttani and imprisoned Jezra and her son, this nightmare will be over."

"It is what we hoped for, little sparrow," chirped Gitar. "All that I and your mother, Queen Abisola, had sought for so many years. Our efforts have now borne fruit." She looked at Iegani. "We can go home to the mountains and begin anew."

Iegani reminded, "My dear niece, you are forgetting our companion in the netherworld?"

"I have not forgotten. We were not alone. Dorak was with us."

Maura gasped, "Dorak!"

"Yes, little sparrow. He helped us in many ways."

"Where is he now?"

Gitar shook her head. "I know not, my child. The priests opened the portal through which we escaped. When I saw Dorak last, he was battling a dragon which I suspect was Zedek. I don't know if he made it through or not."

"If he didn't," said Maura, "Dorak may well be lost forever. The temple of Bhuttu has collapsed. It is a pile of rubble."

"That would solve one of your thorniest problems," commented Iegani.

"Iegani! Dorak was Maura's husband," sputtered Gitar, shocked at his bluntness.

"Yes, and he was the cause of the loss of our home and the death of your daughters."

"And the loss of my eye."

Maura looked up in surprise. "Chaun Maaun, I didn't realize you were present." She quickly stood with her hand on her dagger.

Empress Gitar growled, "Stop it, both of you. If Maura hadn't married Dorak, she never would have been in a position to become empress. We all did what we had to do."

"I must take my leave and let you rest, Empress," said Maura, ignoring Chaun Maaun, who loomed menacingly over her. "Before I do, I wish to present you these tokens of my esteem and gratitude." Maura called for her servants, who quickly entered the tent and carefully placed several boxes before her.

Maura opened one of them. "Diamond dust for your personal adornment."

Gitar clicked happily in the Dinii language at the sight of the glittering powder.

Pleased to see Gitar excited over the crushed diamonds, Maura opened another box and withdrew a stunning tiara with a myriad of colored stones. "A crown fit for an empress."

"Ooh," replied Gitar, reaching for it and placing it on her head.

"I will take my leave now," announced Maura. "But before I go, my forces need your help to take the city. We cannot get past the gate."

"We have sacrificed enough," snarled Chaun Maaun, with a downward twist of his mouth. "As soon as my mother is able, we shall fly to the Forbidden Zone."

Gitar threw up her hand to silence her impetuous son. She was weary of his continuous harping over his wounded pride. "The Forbidden Zone will not protect us if Maura is not the ruler of Bhuttan. We must see this through to the bitter end."

She turned to Maura. "I pledged that I would do everything in my power to make the Lahorians' prophecy come true. They said you would become a great warrior and rule the world. I will complete my promise to them and to your mother. Command the Dinii as you see fit. My people are yours."

Maura bowed deeply to Gitar. Before leaving the tent, she assumed an impassive countenance, once more showing no emotion, even though her heart sang twin songs of joy and trepidation at the same time.

Dorak was alive!

Dorak was alive!

27

Chaun Maaun protested.
"Mother! Let us leave this land of doom."
"My son," Gitar replied despairingly. "You always pluck the same string on your lute. It's time to play a different tune."
"This war has cost us our home and the lives of my sisters!"
"This war has cost Maura the lives of her parents, Abisola and Iasos."
"That's nothing compared to our sorrow."
"You are thinking only of yourself, Chaun Maaun. I was told by the Lahorians many years ago that our world was open to destruction by a force from the east. I have dedicated most of my life to making the sacrifices needed to stop the Bhuttanians.
"Maura is key to our survival. I know you once loved Maura, and now feel bitter hatred for her because you believe she abandoned you, but I tell you this ... your marriage to her was never to be. Your destiny follows a different path. You must marry your own kind. Maura was right to marry Dorak."
"You knew about us?"
"Chaun Maaun, everyone knew about the two of you."
Chaun Maaun looked stricken.
"After the war is won, I intend to sign a new treaty with Maura, recognizing her as rightful sovereign. I also will be relinquishing our guardianship over the Hasan Daegians. They no longer need us to watch over them. We must be concerned with rebuilding our territory in the mountains and reinvigorating our people. Our numbers are too few now. Our people must conceive and bring up new generations."
Iegani added, "Yes, we must revitalize our culture, and you must

not do anything to jeopardize our future, Chaun Maaun. Maura must be convinced to sign this new treaty."

"Does she know of your intentions, Mother?"

"No, but that's why we must stay and render assistance. We will need the help of the Hasan Daegians to recover from the devastation of this war. Once we have accomplished this feat and our people are strong again, we will retreat to our city in the Forbidden Zone forever, and hopefully never see another non-Dini being again unless we desire it."

Chaun Maaun asked, "Will we rebuild City of the Peaks?"

Gitar cast a glance at Iegani. "I think it best we go back to the Forbidden Zone and rebuild Atetelco. I don't think the Lahorians will bother us again, since we have come to Maura's aid. That was their charge to us, and we have complied."

Gitar stood and put her arms around her son. "Enough of this morbid talk. I tell you this, my son. Cherish the time you spent with Maura. Don't ever forget it. It will warm your nights when you are old, but put it behind you for now. Please, son. For all our sakes, move beyond your grief."

Gitar pulled Chaun Maaun closer to her. "Believe me when I say you will be happy again. Not every day will be dark and full of woe. Things change, as does one's heart."

"I have shamed you, Mother."

"I never felt shame." Gitar smiled at Chaun Maaun. "I have felt concern, but you must follow my guidance now. Maura has no one in this world. Everyone she has ever loved is gone, except for her child. She needs our help. She must emerge victorious from this war. Help her, Chaun Maaun. Help the woman you once loved."

"I love her still, but Mother, I must confess I hate her as well. Sometimes I think my hate for her is stronger than my love ever was." Chaun Maaun glanced at his mother's horrified face. He bent down and kissed her hand. "But for you, I will do as you ask."

Iegani stepped forward. "At present, Maura needs help to divert a river."

Chaun Maaun asked, "Why don't we overtake the city by night and kill the soldiers?"

"Because it would cause mutiny within Maura's army. The Bhuttanians on her side would rebel if they saw us perpetrate such a slaughter. The taking of the city must be done with as little bloodshed as possible," replied Gitar.

Chaun Maaun replied dully, "That is unfortunate. We could make the city ours in a matter of hours."

"Yes, 'tis true, but there are other things to consider," replied Iegani. "Take command of those Dinii who are fresh and help the soldiers in the forest. The rest of us will join you once we have rested and eaten."

Chaun Maaun bowed. "I will obey. You have only to command."

28

Dorak ran through the streets.

A small gang of soldiers chased him, obviously planning to beat and rob him, but Dorak outran them, finally hiding in a butcher's shop that had already been looted.

Peering between broken shutters and watching the men search for him, Dorak stifled laughter, realizing the absurdity of his situation. The Aga of Bhuttan was in a butcher's shop hiding from his soldiers. "Oh, Maura, if you could see me now."

After the soldiers gave up and left, Dorak waited a few minutes and then ventured out into the street. He didn't meet anyone beyond a few women darting from their homes to fill their water jars from the few fountains still running. He thought it humane that Maura had not cut off the water supply yet, but he knew that would change if the city did not surrender soon.

The relentless pounding of stones hurled against the west wall strained Dorak's nerves, and he put his hands over his ears. As he traveled deeper into the center of the city, the sound of the catapults diminished, but still reverberated off the buildings' walls. Dorak lengthened his stride. He had to reach Jezra before Maura did.

Once he was within sight of the palace, Dorak climbed onto the roof of the abandoned home of one of his generals. Crawling to the edge of the roof, he saw scattered squads guarding the palace entrances.

Scrutinizing the men's demeanor, Dorak decided they were too unruly and skittish for him to approach. He thought them capable of running a sword through him for the fun of it before he could identify himself. Dorak decided it was best to bide his time until he could approach the palace under cover of darkness. He'd use his great-grandfather's secret tunnel located on the next street.

In the meantime, he went back downstairs to search for a suitable place to hide until nighttime. Finding a larder full of food, he stuffed himself while drinking the general's colla tea and then wine. Finally satiated, Dorak fell asleep exhausted, even amidst the pounding of the west wall and gate, which he was certain would hold. Known to him, but unbeknownst to Maura and even any of the Bhuttanian generals, all gates and walls were bound by magic. No boulder, no matter how large and powerful, would breach the walls of Bhuttani.

Unless a miracle occurred for Maura, the walls would stand.

29

Jezra shrieked.

"Can't you make them stop?" she cried out. "I can't stand that constant pounding."

Zedek replied, "Yes, I can, but I think it's better if I conserve my powers. You can hardly hear the noise, and I think we should let Maura's army use up their arsenal and exhaust themselves. It does very little harm to let them continue."

Jezra threw herself into a chair, pouting. "Where have you been all this time? I could have used your help."

"I am sorry, Jezra. I was inescapably detained." Zedek studied Jezra closely. Something was not right with her. Her eyes appeared vacant, and her entire demeanor seemed strained. It had to be more than the little pounding at the west gate that set her teeth on edge. He wondered if she was drugged . . . or simply losing her mind.

"You will address me by the title aganess."

Zedek bowed. "Forgive me, Aganess."

Jezra nodded. "What do you intend to do about Maura?"

The wizard stifled an urge to yawn. Dealing with people with such limited insight drained him. "At the moment . . . nothing."

"What? Nothing!"

"Calm yourself, my sweet girl. Your general, Mikkotto, seems to have everything under control."

Jezra snarled, "I told you not to be familiar with me."

Zedek took a deep breath to restore his tranquility and bowed slightly. "Forgive me, my lady. My brain is addled after being away for such a long period. May I excuse myself? I must eat and rest."

"But what about the assaults on the walls? Sooner or later they will fall."

"No, Aganess, they won't."

"What do you mean?"

Zedek laughed. "Trust me. The walls will hold . . . and hold . . . and hold," he said, gliding out of the room, leaving Jezra glaring after him.

30

Alexanee was relieved.

The Dinii were no longer in the forest. The last thing Alexanee wanted was to coax huge birdmen with razor-sharp talons from their perches. "Throw your backs into it, men!" he shouted from his majestic warhorse.

He felt even more relieved when his lieutenant related that all the Dinii had gathered in a camp the Great Mother established for them in the rear lines. However, the cutting down of the ancient trees and transporting them to the north wall of Bhuttani was more laborious than he had anticipated.

Pulling off his helmet, he wiped the sweat from his brow. Regardless of how many men they threw at this task, the fire at the wall was not going to happen today. It was too monumental a task.

Alexanee knew his men. Sooner or later the Bhuttanians under his command would rebel. It was only a matter of time before they turned on him and Maura. Only a matter of time.

He turned in his saddle, studying the city. Why were the walls of Bhuttani not falling? It was almost unimaginable that they still stood.

The general sighed and gratefully accepted water from a water boy, careful not to touch the nozzle of the leather bag with his lips while squeezing it to squirt water into his mouth. That was one thing he had learned from the fanatically clean Hasan Daegians, who insisted the communal water dippers and buckets be abolished. He did notice that his men were ill less frequently since they adopted this new custom.

Alexanee also squirted water on his neck and face before handing the bag back to the boy. Why was he thinking such nonsense at a time like this? He didn't understand his own thoughts sometimes.

After watching thirty men descend upon a fallen tree, using axes to section it into manageable pieces before throwing them into a wagon, Alexanee turned his attention to the sun. It was after midday. His stomach lurched.

They would never get the fire at the north wall started before dark, and even that might be unattainable.

Hearing a loud whoosh, the general cupped a hand over his eyes, looking up into the sky. The hot air stirred, and the plumes on his helmet fluttered while his horse whinnied and pawed the ground nervously.

His men shouted and hurriedly back away from the logs they had been working on as thousands of Dinii descended upon the ground and into the tops of standing trees. Immediately, the Dinii picked up the heavy logs with their taloned feet and flew off with them.

Feeling another sudden breeze, Alexanee cast his eyes upward to see Chaun Maaun hovering just above his horse, causing the alarmed beast to rear up. It was all Alexanee could do to keep the horse from bolting while keeping his seat.

He was sure Chaun Maaun meant to unsettle the beast. "Gods," he muttered darkly, looking at the fearsome creature, whose face was marred by one wrecked eye. It took all his will not to shudder at Chaun Maaun's fearsome appearance.

Relishing the shock on Alexanee's face, all Chuan Maaun muttered before flying off was, "We will help."

And help they did.

The Dinii searched for fallen and decayed trees, which would burn better than the green wood the Bhuttanians were cutting. Soon the sky was littered with black dots of flying Dinii carrying colossal logs with as little effort as children carrying a feather.

Alexanee watched while Dinii threw the logs against the north wall and returned for more. Even though the city's men were shooting arrows, the Dinii were too quick, and soon the Bhuttanians fled the parapets when a couple of huge logs were hurled at their heads.

Alexanee chuckled. He had to admit his warriors still might have a chance to end this civil war today, and he hated the thought he had been aided by these birdmen, but Zoar had drilled into him—the enemy of my enemy is my friend. Though it might stick in his craw, the Dinii might be the key to victory.

31

A courier ran with a scroll.

She found Maura departing from the Dinii camp far behind the main army. Kneeling, she raised her arm to hand the scroll to the empress riding in the veiled palanquin.

One of Maura's guards grabbed the scroll, waving the courier away.

"What is it?" asked Maura from inside the palanquin.

"Great Mother, a message."

Maura stuck her hand through the curtains, grabbing the scroll. Expecting a message from Alexanee, Maura drew back in surprise when she saw the seal. The message was from Meagan of Skujpor.

> *Come quick. The Dinii dropped off two bolts of cloth to your tent and they are torn beyond belief.*

Shaking her head at Meagan's lame attempt to hide the message's intent, Maura ordered a horse to ride back to her tent. It would be faster and more expedient.

Her first lieutenant hopped off her pony and surrendered it to Maura, doubling with another rider.

Maura jumped on the little pony and gave the command to gallop. She must reach her tent with all haste.

What awaited her, she did not know, but knew Meagan would not have sent the missive if not of dire importance.

Had her warriors located Dorak?

Was he waiting for her?

Had something happened to Dyanna, her baby?

What did it mean *torn beyond belief*?

As she galloped, her guards rode behind holding aloft the Imperial banners while the uultepes loped beside her pony, excited by Maura's agitated demeanor.

Warriors of all nationalities stood and waved streamers, scarves, and flags as Maura galloped past, hoping she was riding fast because the battle was to begin soon. They were restless with boredom, and the strain of waiting was beginning to wear on them.

Maura brandished her sword in the air as a gesture of encouragement, realizing her troops' morale might be on the wane. Hoping the news waiting at her tent was good news, Maura quickened the pace.

Still, Maura's heart was filled with dread.

She feared whatever waiting for her was not good.

32

Maura jumped off the pony.

Striding into her private chambers, Maura slapped her riding quirt against her knee-high boots.

"Where is Meagan of Skujpor?" she demanded to know.

Several of Maura's young male servants whispered in unison while pointing, "In your chambers."

Why would Meagan take anyone into Maura's private bedchamber unless it was someone or something she was trying to hide? The only people allowed into the inner chamber were Maura's servants, who were very trustworthy.

"My bedroom?" questioned Maura. "Oh Mekonia, it must be my child who in danger!"

Maura ran through the various compartments that made up her tent, throwing open curtains until she came to her private chamber.

Almost all the lamps in her bedroom had been dampened, with Meagan leaning over the bed administering a draft to someone in Maura's bed.

"Is it the princess? Is she ill?"

Meagan looked up from her ministrations and pointed to a dark corner of the chamber.

Maura whirled around.

KiKu, attended by one of her male servants, was sitting at a table calmly eating a roasted boaep.

KiKu nodded, but did not rise or kowtow.

Maura ordered, "Get out, everyone!"

All the servants scurried away except for Meagan.

"You, get out too," barked Maura.

"Great Mother, I can't leave my patient. It is essential that I stay," challenged Meagan.

Maura huffed with frustration.

Didn't Meagan and KiKu know that being familiar and neglecting protocol affected her prestige with the troops and the people? Still, Maura had to push those thoughts away as she hurried to the bed.

Was Meagan treating Dorak?

Would she have to make a terrible decision regarding her husband so soon?

Meagan stood aside as Maura peered down.

"Timon!" Maura gasped, shocked at his wrecked condition. "My poor lad." She turned to Meagan. "What is wrong with him?"

"His heartbeat is faint," saucily replied Meagan of Skujpor, "but he is in surprisingly good condition for someone who's supposed to be dead." She pointed at KiKu drinking ale and wiping his mouth with the tablecloth. "And didn't he and his wives leave in a huff many months ago?"

"I don't know what you're babbling about, healer. Timon Ben Ibin Moab is dead. He died from a borax attack in the mountains, and Prince KiKu from Hittal *was* sent away from court for his unruliness."

"Yet, here lies Royal Scribe Timon, and there sits Prince KiKu." Meagan gave her queen a sharp look. "But I can see where I've made my mistake with these two vagabonds. Just to be on the safe side, you'd better tell your servants not to mention seeing them, or it will be all over the camp within an hour."

"I need not worry there. My servants are bound to secrecy. Besides the uultepes are with them."

"I hope those cats are not using those poor boys as scratching posts." Meagan pushed Maura out of the way to attend Timon who was moaning.

Maura strode over to KiKu. "Good to see you alive, my fine friend. I knew you would not fail me."

KiKu ignored Maura and kept eating.

"Will you not speak to me, friend? Surely, you paid no heed to my chatter with Meagan? I am relieved to see both you and Timon."

KiKu pushed his plate away and picked up a wet clay tablet with a stylus.

"Writing on a tablet? Must we resort to that old spy trick? I can read your mind if you push hard enough," said Maura, irritated at the subterfuge. She needed information immediately.

KiKu shook his head.

"All right then. Have it your way," sighed Maura. "I have seen Empress Gitar and the rest of the freed Dinii."

KiKu shook his head nervously.

Maura was so frustrated that she almost shook her oldest and most trusted counselor. "Hetmaan, I don't have time for this. If information you have, then give it to me freely. I must make haste."

With a shaky hand, KiKu began to write.

Maura glowered at KiKu as he wrote. He had lost a great deal of weight. The little potbelly KiKu had acquired was gone. There were deep creases around his forehead and mouth, and when he looked at her, his dark eyes seemed haunted. KiKu looked old and used up. He must have suffered a great deal to free the Dinii.

Maura instantly regretted her sharp words, but her face remained immobile. Many people had to sacrifice for her and Princess Dyanna, but she showed no regret to KiKu. Regret was a luxury Maura could not afford, but she was not without compassion.

"Oh, KiKu. My brave KiKu," she whispered, putting her hand on his shaking arm.

A tear slipped from KiKu's eye. His hands trembled so, KiKu feared he would not be able to communicate by the written code he had taught Maura, but once he had delivered the information to Maura, he was done. He shot a look at Maura, who smiled warmly at him. Immediately, KiKu felt better.

Pointing at Maura's face, he claimed, "That's the smile of a young girl. I've seen that smile before. It is as though the sun broke through the clouds. I thought I would never see that girl again. I'm glad to see she still exists."

"You are safe now," Maura reassured him.

KiKu whispered, "No, we're not, Maura. The Black Cacodemon was trapped with the Dinii. He lives."

"So, it is true that demon still exists. If only I had been a few seconds earlier with the deathblow, I might have saved us all much suffering. Tell me more."

KiKu hesitated.

Maura coaxed, "Do not fear to tell me what is already known. The enemy has the same information. Speak freely to me."

"It was neither Timon nor I who freed the Dinii. Zedek somehow manipulated the priests into freeing us."

"The amulet was of no help?" asked Maura, astounded.

"Yes, it was, but only at the very end of the priests' incantations. I believe the amulet focused the energy of the incantations to open a portal into another world."

"Why did Empress Gitar not tell me of this?"

"For the same reason, I hesitate to speak out loud now. Ask no more questions. We may be watched and overheard, even here. Magic," warned KiKu before returning to his clay tablet describing the priests opening the portal allowing the Dinii burst through and fight their way out of the temple.

Maura was bursting with a myriad of questions, but fought to remain patient. If KiKu thought they might be overheard by magic, that meant he believed the evil wizard Zedek had escaped and was at large somewhere in the city, but her time with KiKu was limited. She had to get back to the front or questions would be asked.

"Tell me what you witnessed."

KiKu began writing of the last moments in the temple before its collapse.

Maura grabbed KiKu's hand. "This is foolish, my friend. The hardship had addled your brain. We need not fear discussing the past. I can understand caution discussing battle plans and our next move, but the past cannot be undone. Speak to me." Maura threw caution to the wind. "Get to the important stuff, man. Was Dorak with the Dinii?"

KiKu shrugged and spoke only in clipped sentences. "Did not see Dorak. Can't confirm."

"Did the Dinii speak of him?"

"They said nothing, but carried us out of the temple, dropping us off here."

"Empress Gitar said she saw Dorak fighting with a dragon before she flew through the portal."

"I did not see this. I am sorry to report the temple collapsed. Dorak might not have made it out in time."

Maura closed her eyes and felt grateful. Dorak crushed by the rubble of the fallen temple would solve a terrible dilemma. She would not have to make the awful decision to execute him. Yet, Maura felt her heart tighten at the thought of Dorak's death and turned away from KiKu, hiding her emotions.

"Where is the amulet now?" asked Maura, wanting to change the subject.

"Here." KiKu leaned over and picked up the lid of a platter.

Maura's eyes widened.

On the platter lay the head of Hilkiah with the amulet placed upon his forehead.

"A gift for you, Great Mother."

"For the love of the goddess Mekonia! You know I don't relish such gifts."

"You don't want my gifts? I went to a lot of trouble retrieving them."

"You know what I'm talking about."

"Don't scold me, Maura. We are both capable of great mischief, and have engaged in much to get you thus far. If you don't appreciate my gifts, I will take my trophy with me, but there is no need to reproach me . . . or I shall reproach you," huffed KiKu, insulted.

"Great Mother!" called Meagan of Skujpor.

Maura jumped up and ran over to the bed. She peered down at Timon's feverish body. He was covered with nasty cuts and painful-looking bruises. Blood was seeping from wounds on his head. Maura gingerly touched his forehead with her fingers. "He looks gravely ill."

"The boy is slipping away," Meagan said. "He has been severely tortured."

"Is there anything you can do for him?" KiKu asked.

"No, but you can." Maura commanded KiKu, "Bring the amulet and place it around his neck."

KiKu did as bidden, looking expectantly at Maura. "Now what?"

"How is he?" asked Maura, looking to Meagan.

Meagan pressed an ear to Timon's chest and listened. "The beat is stronger, but far from being sound. You must help him."

"I cannot now. I must reserve all my strength," replied Maura, remembering Gitar's warning.

KiKu held out his hand. "He deserves to live."

Maura pulled her bed sheet over Timon. "Yes, he does, but unfortunately, we don't always receive the life we deserve. Isn't that what you taught me, KiKu? Life is not fair?

"Do not despair yet, my old friend. You are to take Timon and the amulet to his people in the steppes. They are north of here, almost at the foothills of the mountains. You will stay with him until I send for you."

"That is too arduous a trip for one as ill as this boy," burst out Meagan. She pointed at KiKu. "And this one is as weak as a newborn borax. No. No. No. I protest, Great Mother. I insist these two stay here and recover."

Meagan had pieced together from their whispers that Maura and KiKu had concocted a secret mission months ago, but now it was time for the subterfuge to stop. Enough was enough. Her patients must have rest.

Maura understood Meagan's concern. "I beg you, listen. Have you not heard the pounding of the catapults all morning, Meagan of Skujpor? Do you not wonder as to why the west wall has not crumbled under such punishment?" Maura put a fresh, wet cloth on Timon's head and wiped his feverish brow. "I have. The wall and the gate should have been pulverized to rubble hours ago, but they stand as if nothing has touched them. That makes me suspect a spell surrounds the walls of the Bhuttani. Perhaps that is why the city has never been captured in a millennium."

"Magic?" Meagan asked.

Maura handed the bloodied cloth to the healer and answered, "We know the Bhuttanians used magic and kept wizards at court. Did not Dorak use magic to capture Hasan Daeg? I think the walls of Bhuttani will stand forever, especially if that amulet stays here. Perhaps, when it has left the vicinity, the spell surrounding the walls will weaken. It must go, and with it shall go our young friend, back to the north steppes of Moab. The amulet will help to keep our young Timon alive."

"Truly?" murmured Meagan, looking pitifully at Timon's struggles to breathe.

"I believe it will." Maura turned to KiKu. "I'm sorry, but you must leave immediately. You and Timon will be secreted in a laundry wagon as it proceeds to a stream, supposedly so my servants may do the wash. There a contingent of my warriors and provisions will meet you. They will take you to Timon's people, and there you shall remain until I summon you."

"My wives?"

"They will stay here under my protection."

Crestfallen, KiKu sputtered, "I want to see them. I have that right. I have done as you asked."

"That cannot happen. A large laundry wagon sent to the tent of your wives will have Mikkotto's spies following it."

"Put me in a cooking vessel and sneak me to them," KiKu begged.

"I forbid it. It's too risky. Every moment the amulet lingers near Bhuttani, it is a threat. It has served its purpose of freeing the Dinii. It must go, and you must take it away."

"Wait. Does it not provide invisibility? Did you not visit me wearing it, but unseen by all until you took it off. Bestow it upon me so that I may see my wives?"

"And what if Timon should die because he no longer wears the amulet while you go traipsing off to see your women? Is this what your stubbornness is about? You think I have killed your wives in a fit of pique because it took so long to free the Dinii?"

"My wives are alive? You swear to me?"

"They have a private tent and are in excellent health. They have the best of everything—food, clothes, servants. I have given them everything to which women of their stature are entitled. You needn't worry."

"May I send them a message?"

"Give me a verbal one, and I will deliver personally, but nothing in writing."

"What if I write something down and you hand deliver it?"

"Should I be captured or killed and the scroll is found before I can deliver it puts their lives in danger. Very few people know they are here. Everyone thinks they have been banished. I take a risk as it is."

Frustrated, KiKu threw a bowl against the felt walls of the tent. "This is untenable. I want proof of life." He looked at Maura and could tell she was not going to relent. "Very well. Tell them I wish them good health, and I shall see them soon."

"You cut me to the quick with your mistrust, my old friend, but I will overlook it because you have been betrayed many times. I understand your suspicion, but I will do you a favor. I will elaborate on that message since you are too shy to relate your feelings about them."

"Feelings? My wives and I are not young people in love." KiKu hesitated. "I have only touched one of them as a man desires a woman."

"Why is that?" asked Meagan, curious.

"Because they were related to my family through either marriage or blood and left without a protector. I married my wives to safeguard them. They are educated and highborn. They represent my house well, and we take mutual care of each other. What else does a man need from a woman?"

Maura grinned. "I will add that you miss them."

"Harrumph," coughed KiKu, obviously embarrassed. It would not do for others to know that a spylord cared about anyone. That Meagan and Maura knew he worried about his wives might put them in more danger. Maura could use his concern as leverage, as she had done with the Bhuttanian generals. It was certainly a tactic Zoar used. Look at KiKu's poor sister, Mamora. Timon and his brother. Even KiKu himself.

Zoar ripped children from families to control opposing royal households. Now Maura was using the same method. The looming question was, would she release her "guests" after the war was over?

KiKu's stomach was queasy. Yes, he must be getting old to slip up so much. "What about Akela?"

"He is with them, safe and sound. Now you must hurry, KiKu. Take Timon to safety. My servants will take care of everything, but I must go now. I can't be too long from the front." Taking one last look at Timon lying prone and helpless in her bed, Maura called for three of the young Hasan Daegian lads who served her.

Taking them to a corner of the room, Maura gave explicit instructions about KiKu and Timon. They nodded, excited to be given such an important assignment, even though they had trained for every contingency.

In case their mission was compromised, they had been given lethal poison hidden behind their gums to use if captured by the enemy. Before they left, they would make sure KiKu and Timon each possessed the poison as well.

And they would use the poison if necessary without hesitation. All had pledged never to fail the Great Mother, daughter of the great Queen Abisola, who had freed them from servitude.

Yes, they would swallow the poison if they failed her.

To a man.

33

The Dinii made quick work.

They accomplished in several hours what would have taken Alexanee's soldiers days.

The forest had been picked clean. Only a few trees were left of what had been the lush royal hunting park for the great kings of Bhuttan. Now the gigantic trees were stacked as a mountain of logs and branches against the north wall of Bhuttani.

Alexanee ordered several catapults over to the north wall, realizing the west wall would never fall. But Alexanee still had the remaining catapults thumping great boulders against the west wall for he knew the noise alone was unsettling to those inside. He had to admit it was wearing on his nerves as well. Regardless of his personal discomfort, Alexanee had a job to do, and he would do it.

The north wall catapults were loaded with bundles of straw, twigs, and dried borax droppings, which the cooks used for fuel.

Alexanee tested the wind. It was in his favor and blowing from northwest to southeast. He was sure the stench of the many borax arse biscuits would waft throughout the city. To cause further distress, he ordered fresh borax droppings loaded into catapult buckets as well.

None of the Hasan Daegians and Anqarians assigned to the north wall complained of pushing wheelbarrows of pungent fresh droppings to the north wall. If this would hasten the end of the siege, they were happy to oblige.

Great ewers of oil were smashed against the mountain of timber, saturating the logs and making them more flammable.

Mikkotto did everything she could to counter Alexanee's maneuvers. She was reluctant to use precious reserves of water since

Alexanee had now cut off the city's supply as predicted, but she could not have foreseen the return of the Dinii, who accelerated the building the dam. Having no other choice, Mikkotto ordered great vats of water to be poured over the great heaps of logs, making it harder to ignite the incendiary material below.

Seeing that Alexanee ordered more containers of oil, Mikkotto rescinded her command to drench the pile of logs. Instead, she directed her troops to hurl sand over the walls to impede the outbreak of fire.

Worried that the sand might inhibit the ignition of the wood, Alexanee ordered the lighting of the logs.

Twenty Hasan Daegian archers targeted the mound of wood and let loose flaming arrows. Every one found its mark.

A great conflagration sprang forth like a wild beast that had been coiled for attack. The fire enveloped its prey—snarling, spitting, and ripping. Flames shot above the ramparts, pushing back the Bhuttanians trying to put the fire out.

Alexanee heard the screams of Bhuttanian soldiers, whose sleeves or tunics had caught on fire and were now engulfed in flames.

Men became flaming torches and fell over the wall into the inferno, their screams striking fear into those working on the catapults and the river dam.

Alexanee wanted to look away but couldn't. He had to remain strong for the soldiers under his command, but he was sickened as they were.

Why didn't Jezra or her commander, Mikkotto, put an end to this carnage and open the west gate?

Would Maura be forced to undertake a full-scale annihilation in order to take the city?

He knew the Bhuttanians under his command would never stand for it. There would likely be open rebellion among his men if they didn't conquer the city before nightfall.

That wall had to give way—and soon!

34

T he battle was in full force.

Maura ordered the catapults from the west wall moved to the north wall.

The Dinii, each one ten times stronger than any man in Maura's army, made quick work of moving the heavy machines.

While the catapults were relocated, she ordered a male contingent of Hasan Daegian archers to continually harass the remaining soldiers on the west wall.

The Bhuttanians fought bravely, but they were not prepared for the sheer number of arrows flying over the battlements.

Many a rebel warrior was struck down by a Hasan Daegian arrow piercing his neck and spurting his life's blood on his comrade.

Confident the north wall would hold, Mikkotto ordered the surviving soldiers to collect the Hasan Daegian arrows, even if it meant pulling them out of a comrade's flesh.

She knew Maura would soon order troops to deploy ladders to the west wall. In anticipation, she prepared a little surprise for her cousin.

Exhausted but determined, Mikkotto wiped the grime of battle off her face. A fresh shower of arrows rained down upon her men. Taking cover, she ducked into a stone guardhouse, cursing Abisola for giving rights to Hasan Daegian males. Who knew the dainty men of her country would be such deadly archers?

When Mikkotto became queen of Hasan Daeg, she would undo this travesty. No rights for the males—back to domestic life where they belonged.

Mikkotto had many things to set right, but she had to win this war to accomplish them. She assessed that the city was holding its own against the invaders, but it was not winning. She had to find something or someone who would help turn the tide against Maura. If Mikkotto could somehow eliminate the Blue Witch, the renegade Bhuttanians would rejoin their brethren within the city walls.

Maura must die—but how? Every assassin she sent to terminate Maura failed. Poisoned darts, poisoned food, poisoned water, or hired mercenaries with sharp blades had all come to naught. She had even enlisted her own child to kill Maura, but nothing came of it but a dead son.

Perhaps she was concentrating too much on paid assassins. She still had many supporters in Maura's camp, especially among the nobility, who disliked Queen Abisola's reforms.

And Mikkotto knew from her spies that a growing number of Bhuttanian generals were disgruntled. Only Alexanee's stern discipline kept them in line—and the fact that the generals' families were secluded in a camp on the east side of the city guarded by Hasan Daegian women.

Perhaps if she sent a contingent of soldiers to release the generals' families, they would not be so inclined to serve the usurper, Maura.

Hmm, that was a thought.

35

The city was on fire.

Winds from the plains carried embers to rooftops, scattering the flames.

Mikkotto and her soldiers fought bravely to contain the inferno, but the fire was too strong, and the heat drove them off. Soon all the buildings near the north wall were alight.

Mikkotto ordered her soldiers away, realizing that even if the wall gave way, the smoldering rubble would be too hot for Maura's forces to cross.

It would take days and even weeks for the debris to cool, and her soldiers would have established a foothold in that section by then.

Mikkotto was positive the fire was a diversion to draw soldiers away from the west side of the city, which was where she convinced the main attack would happen. She ordered her men back to the west wall again. As they hurried across the city, the men collected thousands of Hasan Daegian arrows and threw them into carts to be reissued to other soldiers.

Chuckling, Mikkotto muttered, "Thank you, Maura, for replenishing our munitions. We were low on arrows, and you solved our problem. We will happily send them back to you, hopefully landing in the chest of one of your darling archer boys."

Returning to the task at hand, she yelled from the battlements. "Is this all you've got? The wall stands. Bhuttani is unvanquished. The Aganess Jezra is still queen.

"You puny little Hasan Daegian men. When I'm queen, you will all go back to the kitchens where you belong."

An arrow whizzed past her cheek. Mikkotto felt her face and saw blood on her fingers. "So, you've drawn blood, you creatures of Maura. I will have my revenge on you all," Mikkotto cursed. "I will. I swear I will. Even to my last breath."

36

Maura sat atop Dorak's steed.

Alexanee rode beside her, his mount pawing the ground impatiently. He shouted against the roar of the fire. "Mikkotto has moved her men back to the west gate. The north wall is white hot. We need to strike now."

"She's not fighting the fire?" Maura asked.

"With what? She must preserve what little water she has. And the fire burns too hot for her men to get close enough to throw sand."

Maura agreed. "That leaves this wall wide open. Now is the time to strike. Give the order to break the dam."

Alexander waved a purple flag as his nervous horse pranced to and from the embankment of the water canal.

The trumpeter sounded the signal to open the dam.

Engineers on either side of the river cut ropes holding logs in place. As the logs tumbled into the water, the river surged forward. A tall wave of water littered with debris, including rotting bodies of both people and animals, rushed into the canal bed, overflowing its banks. The wave consumed everything in its path, engulfing the raging fire at the base of the wall.

Maura and Alexanee watched expectantly, knowing this was their one chance to breach the walls of Bhuttani. Would the cold water against the hot stones cause the wall to crack?

Alexanee peered through his field glass as the other Bhuttanian generals rode up from behind Maura and Alexanee, encircling them.

Maura unsheathed her sword, knowing this was where the Bhuttanian Generals planned to make their stand against her. They were furious that Bhuttani was on fire.

Sensing danger, the uultepes by her side turned and growled.

Maura would be hard to kill, but she was still mortal, and surviving against ten battle-hardened men attacking her at once would be difficult, even with the uultepes by her side.

Anticipating that the Bhuttanian generals would strike, Maura had ordered her guards to watch over Dyanna, for the generals surely would send men to kill her daughter at the same time they attacked her. But they didn't know Maura had removed Dyanna from the royal tent and placed her in the care of Empress Gitar. If they received word of Maura's death, Gitar and the Dinii would fly away, taking Dyanna to safety with them.

Taking a deep breath, Maura was readying her sword to strike when Alexanee rose up in his saddle.

"Do you hear it? Do you hear it?" he cried out, handing the field glass to Maura. He pointed toward the wall. "Look. Look!"

Maura looked through the lens, the skin on her neck crawling, since she expected this might be a ploy to get her guard down.

"Don't you hear it, Great Mother?"

"I hear the hissing of the water against the rocks."

"Under that. Don't you hear a rumbling?"

Maura strained to listen. Something significant did seem to be happening. "We need to take a closer look."

She untied the strap of the shield wrapped around her saddle horn and urged her horse forward.

Water roiled against blistering stones and plaster, creating a cloud of steam.

Alexanee reached over and caught her horse's bridle. "You mustn't. It's too dangerous."

"I can't see what's happening, which means Mikkotto can't see either. Believe me when I say she's watching."

"All the more reason for you not to go nearer."

"Let go of my horse, General. I'd rather die by a Bhuttanian arrow to my chest than a Bhuttanian sword to my back."

Realizing Maura's meaning, Alexanee snapped his attention to the generals surrounding them. Acting unconcerned, he ordered a younger general, "You, there. Take a closer look."

The young general glanced at his comrades before urging his horse forward.

In that brief moment, it was obvious that Alexanee was not going to support any attempt to kill Maura, and would stand against them. If they acted, they would have to kill him as well, but the rest of the generals did not make their move, recalculating their strategy. They had not taken into account that Alexanee would stand with the blue witch.

Reluctantly, the young general rode into the blanket of smoke and embers.

Maura held her breath until he emerged again, steam rising off his armor and warhorse.

He paused before the queen and the knot of generals. "There is a continuous crack going from the base to the top, but the wall still stands."

Maura spoke, "General, identify the position of the fracture and direct the catapults against its location."

"No."

"No?" echoed Maura. "We have a chance to break down this wall."

"The wall will never fall. It will not rupture. It will hold fast until we squander every resource at our disposal and exhaust every man and woman in our army."

"Obey your empress!" ordered Alexanee, turning his horse to face the band of generals. He feared the moment of reckoning had finally come. The Bhuttanian generals under his command were making their move.

"Think about your families, men!" Maura cautioned.

"Indeed, we have, my lady," replied the most senior of the generals. "We have sent troops to the refugee camp to rescue them. All your Hasan Daegian guards are dead, and our families have been set free, along with the rest of our people you have held in confinement. Once we receive word our families are unharmed, we will give the signal to our troops to switch their loyalty and begin fighting against you, Blue Witch."

"My good generals. I'm afraid you have overplayed your hand."

Fear and distrust crept into the generals' eyes.

"Your families are not in the refugee camps. They are secured in Hasan Daeg."

"That can't be. Hasan Daeg is thousands of miles away."

"That is correct, and that is where your families are. I knew you would switch loyalties . . . again. I had many of your families rounded up and sent to Hasan Daeg."

"She's bluffing!" came a voice from the group of generals.

"Am I?"

"There's no way you could capture our families."

"You forget. Members of your family travel. They have business in other cities. You all have summer homes on the river where the families congregate during the worst heat. It was nothing to send special units disguised as Bhuttanians and capture a family member here and there, especially sons. According to my reports, we captured most of your sons, since Bhuttanians have such high regard for their male heirs."

"Our sons are in this army fighting beside us."

Maura looked around. "They are? Where? You will not find them because my women rounded them up this morning."

A general rushed Maura, whereupon a uultepe leapt up and knocked the general off his saddle, then crouching over him, his head in her mouth.

"Stand down," Maura cautioned the other generals. "My uultepe's automatic response is to close her jaw. She would crush this man's head like a melon without meaning to."

Maura cooed to her uultepe. "Let the man sit up, my pet." She looked down at the fallen general. "Xizing, isn't it? You have a grown daughter by your first wife and an infant son with your second wife, who I think is the daughter of . . ." Maura hesitated and pointed at another general. "A daughter of yours, General Ju Li. In fact, she is your favorite daughter. They are in my custody and safe. They were on their way to meet you both several months ago when my warriors intercepted them and started them on their journey to Hasan Daeg."

General Ju Li protested, "You lie. They could not join us because illness prevented them, but we both have been receiving missives from them, even recently as several days ago."

"Yes, I know about those letters. My people began intercepting your letters several years ago. In fact, all letters written by you have been decoded by my scribes, who took the liberty of writing back to your families in your name. And letters from your families were written by my scribes as well.

"As for the refugee camp? Well, your men will find an empty camp with only a few smoldering campfires. But you are right, I could be lying. Your families could be hidden nearby, and if I fall to your swords, my guards have been ordered to slaughter them."

The Bhuttanian generals looked dumbfounded.

General Ju Li bowed. "Empress Maura, you have bested us. We underestimated your cunning. We will fight to the death on your behalf, if you promise to honor the safety of our families." Alexanee, bitter at this betrayal, snarled, "Get back to your posts, men, or I swear I'll have you hung for this."

General Xizing argued, "You'll have us hung anyway. Our families are good as dead. Let's kill them both now."

"Kill them. Kill them. Kill them," chanted the other generals.

General Ju Li pulled out his sword and pointed it at the other generals. "What are you doing? She promised our families are safe. Stop, I tell you. Stop!"

Maura looked around. She was on her own, because she had sent her guards to protect Princess Dyanna. She was not sure which side Alexanee would choose at the last moment.

The other generals pushed General Ju Li aside, and were tightening the circle to attack when suddenly a pulsating orange light passed through the group, catching one general in its beam. The general and his horse were burned to a crisp without a single cry from either man or beast.

Confused, the generals pulled their horses back.

What was this!

Alexanee shot a look at Maura. She seemed as surprised as he.

Maura cried, "Look! The beam is aimed against the crack in the wall."

A courier pushed through the circle of neighing and stomping warhorses, dodging under the beam of pulsating light, and ran up to Maura. "Great Mother," she cried, excitedly handing over a scroll. "The river! The river!"

Maura broke the seal and read quickly.

"What is it?" asked Alexanee, noting that Maura's face had drained of color.

Looking at Alexanee, Maura crushed the message, throwing it on the ground. "We have won! We have won! The city is ours!" Spurring her horse, she pushed through the knot of generals and galloped to the river.

Alexanee had the courier retrieve the message and hand it to him. He read it slowly.

"Well?" asked the surviving generals.

"It's in a language I have never seen before. I can't decipher it. Whatever it is, our empress knew what it meant, and that's why she's heading toward the river. That's where this beam is coming from, and where the answer lies."

Alexanee folded the message and secured it in his tunic. "Go back to your posts, generals. You have lost your bid for freedom. You are Maura's creatures yet. Direct these catapults to fire directly where that beam hits the wall.

"And men, I tell you this. If one hair on Princess Dyanna's head is mussed, I will skin each and every one of you alive myself, but not before I do the same to your sons and make you watch."

Furious, but realizing they had been outmaneuvered, the generals headed back to their posts, with one general rushing to call off his men sent to assassinate Princess Dyanna. Two others raced for the river. They wanted to determine the source of the magical orange beam of light.

Everyone was in disarray and confusion. The sky above the river had turned dark with Dinii hovering above, shouting, hooting, hissing, and obviously threatened. The Dinii's distress caused a great deal of concern among the troops congregating near the river. Discipline among the soldiers collapsed as the frightened soldiers argued among themselves.

Some were pushed into the intense beam and were burned while officers struggled to restore order and avert a full-scale riot.

Maura heard Iegani calling to her in her mind, "Maura, hurry. Hurry to the river!"

Maura spurred her horse through the mob of soldiers until heralds ran in front of her, trumpeting the empress's arrival. "Make way! Make way! The Great Mother is coming!"

The trumpets and cries of heralds caused the hordes in front of Maura to bow and clear a pathway. Behind her warhorse, commanders ran with whips and barked threats, ordering their soldiers back to their positions, but no one moved.

Maura's horse, sensing the tension in the air, grew skittish and reared high off the ground until Maura urged him forward.

As Maura neared the riverbank, she saw Empress Gitar in a palanquin with Iegani and Chaun Maaun close behind, all hurrying to the source of the pulsating beam.

"Out of my way!" yelled Maura to her troops as she urged her horse to a fast trot.

She and Gitar reached the river at the same time.

Maura couldn't believe the sight that greeted her.

Over the still-swirling waters of the flooded river were more than a hundred spheres of varied sizes and every color imaginable. The

Lahorians!

"They've come!" cried Maura, stunned. If the Lahorians were here, it meant they had determined she would fail without their intervention.

Fear clutched Maura's heart. She tried to rationalize their abrupt appearance. Perhaps they had planned to intercede all along.

She jumped off the horse and sprinted into the water until waist deep.

Gitar's bearers also splashed into the water, accompanied by Chaun Maaun and Iegani.

Dinii warriors swooped from the sky and formed a barrier between the empresses and the multitude of soldiers, servants, cooks, and farriers who had rushed to the water to watch. Many took to wagons and even climbed upon one another's shoulders to witness what was happening.

Maura walked farther into the river until the water rippled up to her chest.

One of the orbs opened, and a naked man emerged. Maura could see his internal organs pulsing beneath his translucent skin. He flicked his wrist, and the river's murky brown water receded from around Gitar and Maura. "Do not come closer, Great Ladies. I will come to you."

With another flip of his hand, a wave carried him forward until he was only a few feet from the empresses.

Other spheres opened, revealing more Lahorians.

Both Maura and Gitar inclined their heads, for they realized they stood before the real rulers of the planet Kaseri.

"Greeting, Lords of the Water," said Maura. "We welcome you."

"Empress of the Dinii, please tell your people to calm themselves. We are here only to assist."

"They recognize ancient enemies."

"We are enemies no longer, since our treaty regarding Abisola's conception of Maura. Tell them to stand down. They must not breach the orbs with their talons."

Gitar nodded to Iegani, who sent a mental message to all the Dinii hovering in the air above the Lahorians. The Dinii flew off and settled along the riverbanks.

"I only have a few moments to speak with you. You cannot break down Bhuttani's walls without us. Do not interfere. Do not touch us. We are one. We are one."

The man flicked his hand again, and a wave carried him back to his orb, which immediately closed around him. Water rushed forward, surrounding Gitar and Maura, and they made haste to escape the disturbed river now lapping angrily against its banks.

"Get your people ready, Empress," shouted Maura over the din of her troops. "We attack soon." She jumped on her steed and waved her sword high above her head. "Back to your positions. We attack upon my signal," she cried, rallying her forces. "We shall put an end to this war, once and for all!"

37

Mikkotto raced to the north wall.

A beam of pulsating light was searing through the thick stones of the wall.

Maura's foot soldiers, archers, and cavalry stood between the river and the city, waiting for the wall to crumble, and portable bridges, to be placed over the hot debris, were pulled from the river by the Dinii. The waterlogged wood would not catch fire, and thus would provide a way for soldiers to march into Bhuttani once the wall gave way.

Mikkotto marveled at the power of a ray of light that could cut through stone. From whence did it come? Did Maura have wizards now?

A lieutenant rushed up to Mikkotto.

"What news have you?"

"All archers have assembled at the west gate."

"News from Maura's Bhuttanian generals?"

"They are standing firm with the usurper. They have not swayed."

Mikkotto waved the lieutenant away. She did not want him to see the anxiety in her eyes. Once Maura breached the walls, Mikkotto's soldiers would likely falter. The war would be lost. She motioned to one of her warriors and whispered, "Have a swift horse waiting for me at the south gate."

"There are no more horses, Baroness. You commandeered all the horses for the army."

"Then steal the best one you can find."

The guard shook her head. "The army has eaten them. There are no more horses. Besides, you ordered the south gate barricaded. It would take hours, if not days, to remove the debris."

Mikkotto's greatest fear was realized. The north wall would soon give way.

Was there nothing that could save her and the city?

38

Zedek awakened.

Sensing a disturbance in the magic he had cast, Zedek sniffed the smoky air and waved his bony hand in front of his face. The spells throughout the city were in flux. Something was happening to interfere with his enchantments.

Zedek roared. Jumping out of his bed deep in the bowels of the palace, he raced to the rooftop, cursing the fact that he no longer had the amulet. At least it was safe under the piles of rubble that had been the temple of Bhuttu. There it would remain until he could retrieve it.

Zedek forgot about the amulet when he spied a beam of yellowish-orange light pulsating from the direction of the river. Zedek could feel his magic weakening. The wall was going to give way, and much of the city was either on fire or smoldering. How could this be?

Furious at being bested, Zedek drew himself up and, using all his hate and anger, changed into a mighty dragon. Screeching a terrible cry, the dragon leapt from the roof and swooped down upon the very heart of Maura's army. If fire was what that damned bitch Maura wanted, then fire she would have. The dragon took a deep breath and exhaled a blaze of fire so blistering, it turned sand on the ground into bits of glass.

Soldiers scattered, trying to find cover from the dragon's barrage of fire, but entire squads were burned beyond recognition.

Maura rode her horse into the river. "Direct your beam upon the dragon!" she cried out to the Lahorians. "Kill the dragon!"

The Lahorians ignored Maura and continued directing their beam of energy at the wall.

Realizing the Lahorians were disregarding her commands, Maura charged the fearsome dragon, screaming, "Chaun Maaun. Kill the dragon! Kill the dragon!"

Stunned, the Dinii remained on the opposite side of the river. They had never seen a dragon, much less encountered a flying creature that breathed fire. Confused, they glanced around, not knowing what to do.

Seeing the Dinii unfurl their wings, Maura grasped that the Dinii would dart up into the sky and hover above the clouds until they felt safe. If that happened, all would be lost.

Yesemek and Yeti shouted to their Dinii comrades, "Stand your ground. HOLD FAST!"

Maura turned her horse around and found Chaun Maaun close behind her, lounging against a broken-down wagon, watching the dragon, unfazed. She kicked her mount toward him. "Give the order to attack, Chaun Maaun. We must kill that dragon."

"So that's what it is."

"Don't be a fool," Maura screamed.

"Would you be willing to die to kill it, Maura?"

Without hesitation, Maura snapped, "Yes! Hurry, before the dragon destroys both our peoples. Hurry!"

"Beg me."

Astonished, Maura blinked. "Have you gone mad? Your hatred of me runs so deep that you would let our people die simply to thwart me?" She glanced over her shoulder to see the dragon swooping toward her troops, who were rushing to the river. "I'm begging you, Prince Chaun Maaun of the Dinii. Save us. Save my people. Save the Dinii. Save me."

Chaun Maaun unfurled his wings and fluttered, motioning to Maura to climb on his back. She jumped from her nervous warhorse onto Chaun Maaun's back as she had done hundreds of times before, and held on with one hand while brandishing her sword with the other.

The Dinii prince shot into the air and circled his warriors. "Grab a soldier and follow me!" he cried.

One by one, Dinii warriors lowered themselves into the water, allowing drenched and terrified soldiers to climb on their backs before vaulting into the air. A few soldiers fell back into the river. Others, who had the sense to hang on, were flown into the smoke-filled sky screaming cries of the horrified, the determined, and the damned.

39

Soldiers rushed to the north wall.

They helped the dragon annihilate Maura's army, leaving the palace unprotected. Bhuttanian scum saw the opportunity to plunder the Imperial Palace of every last bit of metal, coin, tapestry, utensils, food, drink, oil, and candles they could lay their hands on.

Seizing the opportunity, Dorak found it easy to enter the palace and, ignoring the looters, hurried upstairs. Calling out Jezra's name, he went first to the nursery but found no one. Hastening to Jezra's chambers, he passed his mother's old suite. The door was off its hinges, and inside women were pawing through his mother's clothes. Aghast, Dorak thought about killing the thieves. But no. He needed to find Jezra and his son. Time was running out.

Arriving at Jezra's apartments, he tried the massive wooden door. It was locked. "Jezra. Jezra. Open the door. It's Dorak!"

Dorak heard a faint click and pulled out his dagger, not knowing what awaited him on the other side. The door opened a bit as a servant woman peered out. Upon seeing Dorak, she exclaimed, "Lady, it is your husband. It's Lord Dorak!"

"Lock the door, you idiot."

"But my lady," protested the servant, doubt clouding her eyes.

Upon hearing Jezra speak, Dorak burst through the door and pushed the servant aside, locking the door behind him. "Jezra, it is I, Dorak. Don't you realize the palace is under attack? We must make haste from here."

"Shall I go with you so you can slit my throat? Why aren't you dead? I thought surely Maura had done away with you." Jezra grabbed her frightened son and clutched him tightly while she slowly inched towards the balcony.

Dorak shot a look of disbelief at the servant, who shook her head at him.

Taking a further step into the room, Dorak said, "I will give you my dagger, Jezra. I only want to take you and our son away from here, to somewhere you both will be safe." He placed the dagger on a table.

"So you can hand us over to Maura?" scoffed Jezra.

"No, my wife. I am no longer in league with Maura. You must believe me."

"Why should I, after you abandoned your son and me for that blue witch?"

Dorak put his hands out in supplication. "Jezra, come to me. We can escape through a secret tunnel in the dungeon."

Jezra squeezed the child in her arms more tightly until he burst into tears, squirming to be free.

"You would like us in the dungeon, wouldn't you, so you can enthrone your Hasan Daegian whore in my place. Then her bastard child would inherit the throne."

"No, Jezra. I'm trying to save you and our son. You can't stay here. We will flee together to the land below Siva, where we can hide from Maura."

"You'd leave the throne of your father? You expect me to believe that you will leave Bhuttan?"

"I have lost the throne to Maura. She will never take me back. I either escape with you or face her wrath."

"I saw a dragon circling in the sky. It is Zedek. He will never let her win. He will crush her. Then you will sit upon the throne again, but this time I will be by your side."

"Jezra, it is over. We have gambled and lost. There is no way a single dragon can defeat thousands of Dinii. They will fall upon him as Sivans upon a borax corpse. Bhuttan will be absorbed into Maura's new order. Jezra, Maura has won."

Jezra's cornflower blue eyes grew moist as she stepped out onto the balcony. "Then all truly is lost. All is lost . . . lost," she said, looking over the railing.

"My lady," cautioned the servant. "Please come back into the room. You or your son might be injured by a stray arrow."

"Jezra, back away from the railing," Dorak ordered in his harshest commander's voice. "Come with me. We can start over."

"My son will never sit upon his grandfather's throne. He will never be the Great Aga, Lord of the Bhuttanian Empire. You have seen to that—you and your father!"

Dorak inched closer to Jezra, calculating the distance between them before he rushed the balcony.

Seeing his intention, Jezra turned and hurled her son over the railing.

Dorak froze in terror at the sound of his son's screams as he fell. Then the sound of a thud and silence.

Jezra cast Dorak a sweet smile before leaning over the railing and plunging headfirst to the cobblestones below.

Dorak and the servant rushed to the balustrade and peered over.

Looters swarmed the cobblestone courtyard, surrounding Jezra and tearing jewelry and hair ornaments off her twitching body. Seeing she was still alive, one of the looters viciously stomped on her head. The twitching stopped.

Beside her lay the body of her son, whose unseeing eyes stared at the sky.

Dorak groaned.

"Sire, you must hurry. Time is precious, and you can do no more for those poor, wretched beings."

Dorak stared at the servant in disbelief.

"Sire, her mind was never strong, and at the end was completely gone. Even if you had gotten out of the palace with them, you would have had to kill her eventually."

"But the boy? My son?"

"He was as she. He would never have been capable of ruling. Now you must flee, with utmost haste."

"What of you, good lady?"

"I will follow my mistress. My life was dedicated to her service. It is my choice. Now go, and leave this wicked place."

Dorak retrieved his dagger from the table and hurried into the hallway, where he blended in with the looters and made his way down to the dungeon. Finding several forgotten prisoners, he set them free and, once they left, Dorak collapsed upon a battered stool and wept. He wept for Jezra, his son, his father Zoar, and Maura. But most of all he wept for himself.

40

Chaun Maaun soared high above the cloud cover. The Dinii followed. "Hang on," he shouted.

Maura tightened her legs and strengthened her grip on the sword.

The prince shot down through the clouds like an avenging demon, his talons extended. Hundreds of Dinii followed, flying in formation until the city was in view again.

Hearing a piercing roar, Maura peered upward.

The dragon was high above, making straight for the Dinii. The Dinii scattered like a flock of crows, realizing they had made a serious tactical error.

The dragon streaked after them, opened its mouth and shot out flames, instantly killing scores of Dinii and their passenger soldiers. They fell burning to the ground.

For a brief second, Maura turned away, horrified at the sight of so many falling to their deaths. Others screamed when their feathers were so badly scorched they could not sustain flight, and they too plummeted from the sky.

Chaun Maaun roared, "Take evasive action."

Those who could regrouped.

Maura looked back and saw the dragon veer to the river and unleash fire upon the clustered Lahorians. As the wind blew the smoke and burning embers away, Maura saw scores of Lahorian spheres charred beyond recognition.

Hasan Daegian archers rushed to the river and fired arrows into the sky, many of them finding their mark in the thick, scaly hide of the dragon. Angry at being struck, the dragon bore down on the archers, who had the good sense to rush into the river and duck underwater.

Those who survived the dragon's blast leapt up and fired again, but their arrows were torched mid-flight by another fireball. The archers ducked under the water again, only to re-emerge with their bows loaded and let loose another barrage of arrows.

As the archers distracted the dragon, a new contingent of Dinii, headed by Yesemek, attacked the fearsome beast from behind.

The dragon snapped its head around in anger.

Seeing his chance, Chaun Maaun dove under the dragon's exposed neck and sliced its slimy green skin with his talons while Maura hacked with her sword. Other Dinii followed, flying under the dragon's belly so their human companions could slash at the creature's most vulnerable parts.

Besieged on all sides, the dragon roared and, with a flip of his tail, knocked Yesemek and many of her warriors senseless. As they fell unconscious through the sky, other Dinii flew to their rescue and caught them. Burdened with soldiers on their backs and holding wounded comrades in their arms, these Dinii had no choice but to retreat.

Chaun Maaun came to rest near the catapults, letting Maura jump off.

"Where is he?" she cried, regarding the sky with a livid glare.

"Maura, you're on fire!" muttered Chaun Maaun, slapping the flames out on Maura's back. Indeed, Maura's face was burned on her right side, and her uniform smoldered.

A Hasan Daegian water girl, seeing Maura with Chaun Maaun trying to beat out the fire, ran over and threw a bucket of water on her.

Maura turned to thank her as the lass took an arrow in the back. Grabbing the girl as she fell, Maura lay her motionless on the ground and gently closed her eyes.

Alexanee ran over to Maura. "Look, the wall is starting to crumble."

Maura could barely hear him over the tumult of the catapults. Her gaze followed his outstretched arm to the wall where the Lahorians had concentrated their destructive ray of light. "Hit it!" she bellowed. "Hit it hard!"

A great cry pierced the sky. Everyone ducked as a shadow passed across the ground.

Maura stood up, screaming, "Keep the catapults going! That wall must come down."

The dragon circled the city and landed on the ramparts, launching a stream of fiery retribution at the catapults, which burst into flames like dried-out shocks of fodder after a fall harvest. The dragon then flew to the ground where he tossed petrified soldiers into the air while stomping on others. There was utter chaos among Maura's foot soldiers as they fled for their lives.

Maura grabbed Chaun Maaun's hand. "Take me to him. This must end."

Nodding, Chaun Maaun picked Maura up in his arms and flew to the left of the dragon while the Dinii flanked the dragon on the right.

Chaun Maaun looked questioningly at Maura.

She nodded.

He let go.

Years of training had prepared her to fall skillfully. Somersaulting in midair, Maura pointed her sword downward so she would land feet-first and drive her sword into the dragon's neck.

Crashing into the back of the dragon, Maura's feet went out from under her, and she slid across its oily scales, landing next to its feet. Maura rolled underneath the dragon, which was now beset by the Dinii striking behind its head.

Furious, the dragon bellowed, snapping at the Dinii and belching great waves of fire, but the Dinii were too quick for him now. Like all born predators, they quickly learned the dragon's abilities and weaknesses, adapting their skills to combat it.

Maura recognized many of the Dinii's cries—Chaun Maaun, Yeti, Benzar, and Tarsus were just a few of the Dinii battling the great behemoth, giving Maura the time she needed. She moved to the part of the dragon's chest where scales didn't cover the skin as densely. She plunged her sword into the dragon's breast as far as she could, thrusting through the thick reptilian skin.

The dragon halted, then staggered and lurched forward.

Maura ran until Alexanee caught her. Behind him marched several squads of Hasan Daegian women, ready to pounce upon the beast. "Be still, Empress. You are safe."

Blinded by the smoke and ash, Maura grabbed Alexanee's arm and steadied herself. "Give me your sword. I must finish this."

"The dragon is severely wounded. The Dinii can dispatch it. You must see a healer. Your eyes are damaged."

"I'll heal myself. Give me your sword." Maura seized Alexanee's sword and made her way back to the dragon, which was now stumbling around, desperately trying to pull out the Aga's sword.

Seeing Maura make way for the dragon again, Chaun Maaun flew over and silently whisked her up into his arms.

Maura made not a sound as they landed on the back of the dragon. Chaun Maaun guided Maura's hands upon the hilt of the sword, and together they plunged it into the base of the dragon's skull.

The dragon breathed one last cry and staggered, shuddering, until it came crashing down.

The Dinii descended upon the dragon, rending its flesh and eating it with such a fury that Alexanee turned away in disgust. The Hasan Daegians broke rank and rushed the dragon, stabbing it with their pikes and daggers.

Chaun Maaun flew to the river and bathed Maura's eyes, although the debris floating in the river made it hard to scoop up clean water.

Metal clanging against metal reverberated over the din of soldiers whooping and hollering.

"What's happening? What's that noise?" asked Maura, straining to see.

"The Lahorians are leaving. Iegani is having our people push their spheres into deeper water."

Maura struggled to get up. "Is he mad? They can't leave."

Chaun Maaun grabbed her and spun her around to face Bhuttani. "Maura, can't you see? The wall is crumbling. It's coming down!"

"Chaun Maaun, help me stand. I can't make it on my own."

Alarmed, Chaun Maaun helped Maura stand, noticing that she was holding her side. "What's this? You're bleeding."

"Be still," she commanded. "Help me bind my wound before anyone notices."

Chaun Maaun reached and pulled over a dead soldier floating in the water. Tearing off part of the soldier's tunic, he wrapped the cloth around Maura's midsection and bound her wound.

"Look fast. Alexanee is approaching."

Alexanee rode up to the couple with Maura's warhorse in tow. "Empress, the north wall has crumbled, and the west gate is demolished. We await your word to enter the city."

Maura mounted Dorak's steed.

Alexanee handed the reins to her.

"General Alexanee, give the signal to enter the city and clear my path to the Bhuttanian throne."

Alexanee nodded to a bugler.

Upon hearing the signal, archers let loose a flurry of arrows with red ribbons. Hasan Daegians, Camaroons, Hittals, Anqarians, Bhuttanians, and a multitude of mercenaries from other nations marched into Bhuttani while the Dinii flew overhead and came to rest on rooftops across the city.

Maura's army was met with little resistance. Word had spread throughout the city that Jezra and her son were dead, as was the great dragon. The city was on fire. The people of Bhuttani were resigned to their fate. Once the terror of Kaseri, the Bhuttanians were now the defeated.

The war was over!

41

The empress opened court.

Maura, wearing the State Robes of the Aga, held both the Royal Fan of Hasan Daeg signifying her station as queen and the Sword of the Aga signifying her station as dowager aganess. A step higher on the dais sat the assembled Dinii royalty—Gitar, Iegani, and Chaun Maaun. A step below Maura stood a nurse holding Princess Dyanna.

Yeti, Toppo, and Benzar stood guard in front of the dais, doing their best to hide their grief. Tarsus was no more, burned to death by Zedek's dragon.

Maura studied the people congregating in the great hall of the Imperial Palace, which stank of smoke and blood. Filthy from battle, her generals watched the proceedings, as well as high-ranking Dinii and Hasan Daegian officers, priestesses from the House of Magi, and anyone else who could squeeze in the hall.

Bhuttanian noblemen, quaking with fear, were pushed to the front of the dais and made to kowtow. The scent of fear aroused the uultepes, which prowled around, nipping here and there for good measure.

A squad of soldiers pushed through the crowd, delivering KiKu's wives to a vantage point in the great hall. Saluting to Maura, they left the women and returned to their stations.

Madric, Tippu, Tippa, and Pearl glanced around. Pearl, clutching Akela's hand, grinned at the kowtowing Bhuttanian nobles. She enjoyed their humiliation.

Akela tugged on Pearl's skirt. "There's that blue lady. Is she our new king?"

"Quiet, Akela. Watch and remember. This is an auspicious day.

You will regale your great-grandchildren with tales of it."

Akela frowned. Great-grandchildren? What silly notions Mistress Pearl had at times.

Maura leaned forward and pointed her fan at the quivering nobles. "Were not most of you at my wedding to Aga Dorak, and saw me crowned as Empress of the Bhuttanian Empire?"

The nobles bobbed their heads.

"Why do you shake? Have you committed a crime? Should I be displeased with something you have done?"

The nobles shook their heads.

"Why were the gates of Bhuttani closed to me, your ruling empress?"

One noble lifted his head to explain. "Empress, the first wife of Dorak, Jezra, forbade it. She said you had murdered Aga Dorak and your crown should be forfeited in favor of her son."

"Did she provide you with proof of my supposed heinous deed?"

A strained silence ensued until a lone voice spoke up, "No, Empress."

"Do you even know if Aga Dorak is deceased?"

"No, Empress."

"Where is Aga Dorak, then?" yelled someone from the crowd.

Maura answered without hesitating in a booming voice that filled the hall. "Aga Dorak was caught in a spell brought on by his own wizard Zedek. For years, the cursed wizard Zedek and a band of my Dinii comrades languished with Dorak in the temple of Bhuttu, unable to inform the outside world of their whereabouts. It is believed that Aga Dorak died when the temple fell as a result of more spell-weaving by his wizard. We are looking through the rubble for his remains now."

The couturiers muttered among themselves while Maura's Bhuttanian generals puffed themselves up for being on the winning side, their aborted act of regicide entirely forgotten—by then.

Maura gestured for the court to be quiet. "You took up arms against me without proof. On nothing more than the word of a young woman whose mind was unsettled."

"Forgive us, Empress," they begged in unison. "Forgive us."

Maura stood upright and pointed her fan at them. "I forgive nothing. You had no authority to keep the gates of Bhuttani closed to me. Your treasonous actions have resulted in many deaths. Many deaths!"

"We did as we were bidden."

Maura strode down the steps of the dais. "Did even one of you counsel Lady Jezra to open the city and welcome me as her royal sister?"

Another noble popped his head up. "We were forbidden to see Lady Jezra. The Hasan Daegian Mikkotto refused our every effort to see her."

"So, you admit to failure?"

"We failed, Empress Maura!" they cried.

"Should you be punished for this treachery and failure?"

They stared at the floor, not answering.

Maura turned and went back to her throne. "I am fatigued by war. I wish no more of death." She waved the royal fan wearily. "But there must be punishment for wrongdoing. An example must be set, and a price will be paid. You, the nobles of Bhuttan, acted without prudence, and without any evidence of the charges leveled against me.

"Let this be law. I, Maura de Magela, tenth queen of Hasan Daeg, Empress of the Bhuttanian Empire, Great Mother of Kaseri, declare those kowtowing before me now to be enemies of the state. You are to serve as lowly field workers on the most northern estates of Bhuttan. Your wives, concubines, livestock, property, and wealth shall be transferred to other great houses —the ones who remained loyal to the House of de Magela. Your children shall be hung by the neck until dead in a public place so there will be no revenge wars in the future. Your houses will cease to exist. All this shall be carried out until the pleasure of the Empress is withdrawn."

A great gong sounded, drowning out the wailing of the disloyal courtiers.

Gitar, Iegani, and Chaun Maaun remained expressionless.

Maura snapped her fan shut.

The weeping nobles were led out by Hasan Daegian warriors.

Maura stepped off the dais and faced Gitar, Iegani, and Chaun Maaun. "My Empress, Lord Prince, and Duke Iegani. I bow to you three times to demonstrate the respect and gratitude we owe to you and the Dinii. May our paths always intertwine with peace and fellowship."

Maura bowed, as did the rest of the court.

"Bow," called out a herald. "All bow."

After the third bow, Maura returned to her throne.

Gitar stood and addressed the court. "Empress Maura, daughter of my heart. The Dinii and I have fought the brave fight alongside you.

We have lost many comrades, but we shall begin anew. My advice to those remaining in court is to let go of the past and act for the future. What great things you can accomplish if acting for the common good. It is my greatest hope that *peace* will reign as *queen* in your hearts. As for those Bhuttanians who still feel the need to fight—direct your anger towards injustice, hunger, and poverty.

"I and my kind will fly to the Forbidden Zone. There we will rebuild our civilization. It is our hope that when next we meet, friendship will extend on all sides.

"Empress Maura and I have signed a new treaty between our peoples to express our devotion to peace. May your gods and goddesses protect and guide you thus. We leave Kaseri in good hands."

Empress Maura stood as well and bowed once more.

As Gitar was helped down from the dais, she paused by Maura, who was still bowing. "My sweet little sparrow. May your goddess Mekonia be a comfort to you."

"Goodbye, second mother of my heart."

Gitar stepped off the dais. Helped by Chaun Maaun, she passed through the congregation, who made a path for her as they bowed in respect as well.

Iegani stopped in front of Maura. "*Little sparrow?*" he said telepathically. "*Should be little dragon, no?*"

Maura fought the urge to smile.

Yeti, Toppo, and Benzar followed Iegani.

Out of the corner of her eye, Maura saw them leave little tokens for her at the foot of her throne. As they passed by, their wings brushed Maura's arms. That was their way of saying goodbye.

Maura and the entire court remained bowing until the Dinii left the palace and they heard Empress Gitar call to her warriors. One by one, they joined her in the sky and silently flew away to the Forbidden Zone.

42

Alexanee ventured to the dungeon.

Snarling, he demanded that the door to Mikkotto's cell be opened.

"I have orders that no one is to see her," claimed the guard.

"Surely you realize that doesn't apply to me."

"It doesn't?"

"Ah, hand over the key, you impudent fool."

The guard reluctantly handed the key to Alexanee.

"Now go away, and speak of this to no one."

The guard agreed, not wishing to get into trouble.

Alexanee opened the door and strode into the gloomy cell with his hand on the hilt of his sword. "Couldn't they at least give you a candle?"

Mikkotto emerged from a dark corner. Her clothes were in tatters and bits of straw matted her hair. "They do, but the guards steal them." She shrugged. "Have you come to separate my head from my shoulders? I should have known Maura would prefer such an atrocity to be committed in the dead of night."

Alexanee harrumphed. "As if murdering a wounded queen lying in the arms of her husband was not an atrocity."

"Maura exaggerated my culpability regarding the unfortunate death of her mother. After all, Dorak was there. He should have controlled his men better. I was merely a bystander."

Alexanee laughed. "You are a wonder. Even at the bitter end, you lie through your teeth with such audacity, it is as if you are gathering flowers in a field."

"If you are not here to kill me, why have you come?"

"Don't flatter yourself that my intentions might be of a carnal nature. I have read reports on your pursuits of pleasure. They don't appeal to me at all."

"Then what?" asked Mikkotto, her interest piqued.

Alexanee threw a dagger onto the straw floor. "There is a secret way out. After you kill the guard, take his keys and travel the hallway to the left. You will come to a metal door. It looks like it hasn't opened in a hundred years. Use one of the keys to open the door. Traverse the tunnel. It empties out into an abandoned field. A horse and a satchel of supplies will be waiting for you."

Mikkotto merely glanced at the knife. She was familiar with this old trick. She was supposed to go for the knife, and then Alexanee would kill her, citing self-defense.

"How am I to kill a guard using that tiny dagger?"

"I'm sure you will find a way."

"Why are you helping me to escape?"

"I want Maura preoccupied with searching for you. I have plans of my own, and do not want her poking around in my affairs."

"And what might those be?"

"My plans are of no concern to you. Use the dagger or not. Escape or not. I will waste no more of my time with you." Alexanee turned and left the cell. "Guard, I'm finished with this prisoner. Lock the door."

Alexanee watched as the guard locked the cell door. "Make sure you keep an eye on her. It's true what they say. She's a devil."

"A what, my lord?"

Alexanee shook his head sadly. "Obviously, you've never been to Anqara."

"No one has for many years now, my lord. People say it's haunted."

The general thought back to the razing of Anqara. It had been a miscalculation on Zoar's part, for sure. If Zoar had established a more benign policy, Dorak and not Maura would be ruling in the Imperial Palace.

He had to respect Maura. Still so young, and yet she had outfought and outwitted them all. She deserved to be empress.

At least for the time being.

43

A trumpet sounded.

Bells, flutes, and drums accompanied a caravan of Sivan merchants guiding borax laden with expensive goods and richly-decorated wagons exhibiting many colorful flags. Behind the wagons rode many warriors on Hasan Daegian ponies. They were almost naked, wearing only thin tunics that came to their mid-thighs, metal helmets, and sturdy leather boots with steel toes. Each woman carried a sword, a bow slung over the saddle horn and several daggers secreted in their boots.

The people of the steppes didn't know what to make of this procession. Was this a military expedition coming to rampage through their community? Was this a simple trading caravan, and the women employed by the Sivans?

An elderly woman, moving stiffly due to arthritis, emerged from a mustard-colored yurt. Men gathered around her as she forged ahead to greet the caravan. Recognizing the Bhuttanian royal crest on one of the wagons, the woman bowed, as did the men.

The wagons stopped, and a blue-skinned noble emerged from one, casually fanning herself. She wore simple white robes, and black hair fell unrestrained down her back. On her feet were leather slippers sheathed in gold leaf.

The elderly woman ran over to Maura and kowtowed, pleading, "Do not kill my son. Please spare him, Great Mother."

Maura, not understanding the woman's language, asked, "Does anyone know what she's saying?"

"I do," said a voice, thick with dangerous undertones. The spylord pushed his way through the nomads.

"Lord KiKu, I see you have put on some weight."

"She's pleading for you not to kill her son."

"So, Timon is still clinging to life. I worried that I might not arrive in time. Please tell Prince Bes Amon Ptah's mother that I have come to heal her son—not to kill him."

KiKu pulled the old woman up from her knees and translated Maura's response to her.

"Ah," she said, her head bobbing like berries dancing in boiling in water.

"She doesn't seem overjoyed."

"I told her that you came to pay your respects before Timon dies."

"Why would you tell such a lie?"

"It's better than getting her hopes up in case your efforts fizzle."

"You are too familiar with me, spylord, but I will give you something to be joyful about." Maura beckoned with her fan.

KiKu's eyes brightened as a door to another wagon popped open, and KiKu's four wives tumbled out.

Tippa and Tippu ran to KiKu crying out his name. "Lord KiKu. Lord KiKu!"

Madric and Pearl followed at a discreet distance, smiling broadly. Reaching KiKu, they waited until he acknowledged them. Bowing very low, they declared, "Lord KiKu, blessings upon you. Salutations from your wives."

With Tippa and Tippu still clinging to him, KiKu leaned forward and kissed both the older women on the cheek. "Blessings to you as well, my honored wives."

"Prince KiKu, we have a surprise for you," Pearl informed.

"Ah?"

Pearl turned and pointed.

Following her gaze, KiKu saw a young, beautiful woman walking toward him, holding Akela's hand. He squinted, and then rubbed his eyes. "Can it be she escaped when Dorak murdered his father's concubines? KiKusan?"

The woman dropped the little boy's hand and rushed to KiKu. "It is I, KiKusan, Father."

"But how? Dorak had all Zoar's concubines and their offspring killed."

"I pretended to drink the poison and acted as if I was dead. When the guards were not looking, I rolled under a pile of blankets and made my escape when night fell. The guards lost count of how many women Zoar had, thus they did not come looking for me."

"But how did the empress find you?"

"Madric spied her," declared Tippu. "KiKusan was wandering in the bazaar, begging for food. She came up to Madric, and first wife recognized her."

KiKu grimaced. "You will never have to beg again, my daughter."

"That's because we're rich," Tippa announced.

"We are?" KiKu asked.

Pearl explained, "Yes, husband. You have been granted Mikkotto Sumsumitoyo's estates, with all her servants and assets." She pointed to the caravan's borax munching on grass. "Many of those wagons are loaded with silk cloth, gems, and precious metal for us. The empress says her debt to us is paid."

"I have wronged my queen and insulted her good intentions. I must apologize for my wrongdoing." KiKu turned around in all directions but could not find Maura.

Where was the empress?

44

Maura unclasped the amulet.

Carefully tucking the jeweled pendant in the sleeve of her robe, she said, "You won't be needing the amulet any longer, my good prince." She leaned closer. "Timon, can you hear me? It is your queen, Maura."

"Forgive me if I don't bow," croaked Timon, his voice barely audible.

Maura returned a whisper of a smile. "All is forgiven."

Timon struggled for breath as he spoke. "It is good of you to come to say goodbye, but there was no need. I am a contented ghost. I helped cast the Bhuttanian yoke from the necks of my people. I die a man who has done right in the sight of the nameless god. I have only one regret."

"What is that, royal scribe?"

"I wanted to go back to Bhuttani and find a veiled girl with bright green eyes. I never asked her real name. I'd like to know and maybe kiss her again. Maybe kiss her more than once. She had such lovely eyes."

"Hush, royal scribe," cooed Maura as she clasped Timon's hand tightly. "Hush, while I give you the gift of the Mother Bogazkoy."

45

Dorak had been sighted.

That's what was rumored from time to time. A Sivan saw him riding a magnificent steed on the road to Kaysia. A former Hasan Daegian diplomat swore she saw Dorak trudging on foot to Camaroon. A vagabond stated plainly he had shared stew with Aga Dorak at a campsite north of Bhuttani on the caravan route.

Maura had all sightings investigated and read the reports concerning Dorak carefully. But like dust blowing over a well-traveled road, the reports stirred the imagination, but in the end, there was no substance to any of the tales.

And so Maura would sit on her throne of bones . . . and wonder.

About The Author

Hello, my friend. I hope you enjoyed all five books of the Princess Maura Tales. I had such fun writing about Princess Maura and her adventures. If you like to read other genres, I also write *The Josiah Reynolds Mystery Series* and *The Last Chance For Love Series*, a happily-ever-after sweet romance series. I would love to hear from you.
abigailkeam@windstream.net

If you like my stories, please leave a review
and tell your friends about me.

Visit me at **www.abigailkeam.com**

Also by
ABIGAIL KEAM

Princess Maura Tales

Josiah Reynolds Mysteries

Last Chance For Love Series

CPSIA information can be obtained
at www.ICGtesting.com
Printed in the USA
BVHW030937030221
599199BV00001B/3